T0047567

# THE BLACKEST HEART

## Also by Brian Lee Durfee

The Five Warrior Angels
*Book 1: The Forgetting Moon*

# BRIAN LEE DURFEE

# THE BLACKEST HEART

## THE FIVE WARRIOR ANGELS

### BOOK TWO

SAGA PRESS

LONDON SYDNEY NEW YORK TORONTO NEW DELHI

† † † † †

SAGA PRESS

AN IMPRINT OF SIMON & SCHUSTER, INC.

1230 AVENUE OF THE AMERICAS, NEW YORK, NEW YORK 10020

This book is a work of fiction. Any references to historical events, real people, or real places are used fictitiously. Other names, characters, places, and events are products of the author's imagination, and any resemblance to actual events or places or persons, living or dead, is entirely coincidental. Text copyright © 2019 by Brian Lee Durfee. Jacket illustration copyright © 2019 by Richard Anderson. All rights reserved, including the right to reproduce this book or portions thereof in any form whatsoever. For information address Saga Press Subsidiary Rights Department, 1230 Avenue of the Americas, New York, NY 10020. SAGA PRESS and colophon are trademarks of Simon & Schuster, Inc. For information about special discounts for bulk purchases, please contact Simon & Schuster Special Sales at 1-866-506-1949 or business@simonandschuster.com. The Simon & Schuster Speakers Bureau can bring authors to your live event. For more information or to book an event, contact the Simon & Schuster Speakers Bureau at 1-866-248-3049 or visit our website at www.simonspeakers.com. Also available in a Saga Press hardcover edition. Interior design by Michael McCartney. The text for this book was set in Absara. Manufactured in the United States of America. First Saga Press paperback edition February 2019. 10 9 8 7 6 5 4 . Library of Congress Cataloging-in-Publication Data. Names: Durfee, Brian Lee, author. Title: The blackest heart / Brian Lee Durfee. Description: First edition. | New York : Saga, [2018] | Series: The Five Warrior Angels ; 2 | Identifiers: LCCN 2017040215 | ISBN 9781481465250 (hardcover) | ISBN 9781481465267 (softcover) | ISBN 9781481465274 (eBook). Subjects: LCSH: Imaginary wars and battles—Fiction. | Imaginary places—Fiction. | Good and evil—Fiction. | GSAFD: Fantasy fiction. Classification: LCC PS3604. U7334 B58 2018 | DDC 813/.6—dc23 LC record availabl at https://lccn.loc.gov/2017040215

# FOR MY

BRILLIANT EDITOR AT SAGA PRESS,
JOE MONTI, AND MY SUPERHERO AGENT,
MATT BIALER

# INTRODUCTION AND ACKNOWLEDGMENTS

In 2002, I was working as a carpet cleaner for Bart's Chem Dry in Salt Lake City. One of our regular clients was Utah Jazz Hall of Fame point guard **John Stockton**. One day I was cleaning rugs in Mr. Stockton's den while he was working at his desk. I noticed he had a bookshelf filled with many of my favorite novels, and we struck up a conversation about books. At one point I made the off-hand comment that I'd always dreamed of writing my own novels someday. His simple reply was, "Well, why haven't you?" I think I muttered something stupid like, "I dunno," and went back to cleaning his rugs. Yet for the rest of the day I couldn't stop thinking about that simple question. "Why haven't you?"

So that night when I got home, I wrote the first sentence of my first novel, then the first paragraph, then the first page. And I've kept writing ever since. Truth is, had any other person in Utah asked me "Why haven't you?" I would have likely just shrugged and never written a word. But John Stockton is someone to listen to, a six-foot-two man in a league full of seven-foot giants, a man who through pure determination rose above the odds and became an all-star in his field. If he could do *that*, certainly I could write some novels. Which I did. And I reckon we can chalk up one more assist to John Stockton.

Again, never-ending gratitude goes out to **Matt Bialer**, my awesome agent and the best street photographer in NYC, and to **Stefanie Diaz** for foreign sales. Thanks also to **Klett-Cotta** in Germany and **Canelo** in the UK. My editor at Saga Press, **Joe Monti**: thanks for all your hard work, patience, and for drafting me into the big leagues. **Valerie Shea, Jeannie Ng, Bridget Madsen**, and **Jenica Nasworthy** at Simon & Schuster for all the wonderful, time-consuming, and precise editing. **Kevin J. Anderson** at WordFire, plus **Alexi Vandenberg** and **Kuta Marler** at Bard's Tower, for helping me promote *The Forgetting Moon* at conventions around the country. A special shout-out to **Amber R. Boehm** for spotting all the horrid mistakes in the first draft and saving me much embarrassment, and to **Karen Durfee** for reminding me about the curse of the stones (some writers are prone to forget major plot points). Map-maker **Robert Lazzaretti** deserves a nod. And again designer **Michael McCartney** and illustrator **Richard Anderson**'s fantastic cover is spot-on gritty, ethereal perfection. Awesome job, guys!

Thanks also to **Stephen King, Mötley Crüe,** and the **Oakland Raiders.**

# CONTENTS

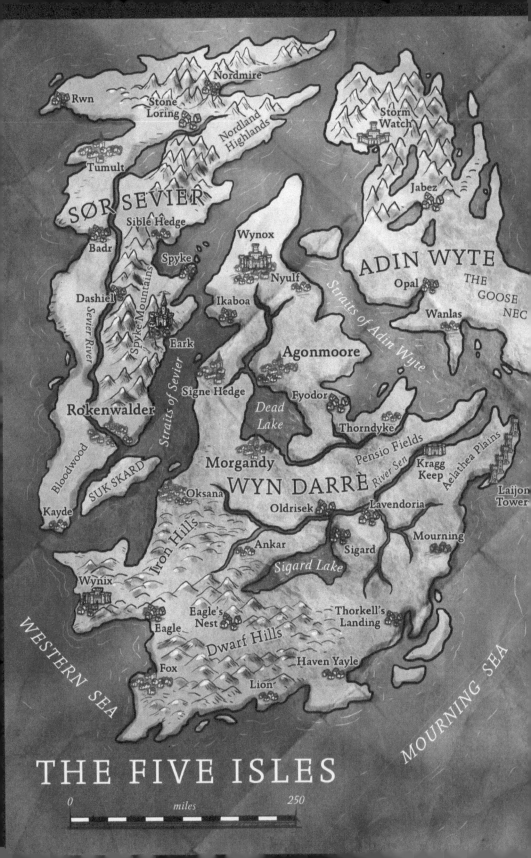

# THE FIVE ISLES

*Trees full of violent crimes and grass gorged with blood. Only the dead truly
know this Bloodwood Forest.*
—THE BOOK OF THE BETRAYER

# CHAPTER ONE

# CRYSTALWOOD

22ND DAY OF THE MOURNING MOON, 999TH YEAR OF LAIJON

BLOODWOOD FOREST, SØR SEVIER

**S**creams broke the silence that shrouded the lush black woods.
Savage cries that Krista Aulbrek gathered and shoved into that
nowhere, bottomless part of her mind before they could take
root in her emotion. This was her first time in this place of unique
strangeness, this mystifying maze of hard-edged beauty and endless
dark splendor—this Bloodwood Forest.

Krista led her mare by the bit. The horse was large, magnificent,
and black; Dread was her name. Her nostrils were wide and huffing,
ears back. Wariness from days of hard riding infused the horse's slow
gait as together they padded through the velvety green blanket of
scent and black flowers. The mare's eyes were a hazy red color—a
sign of the rauthouin bane Krista had been injecting into her young
mount. Within a year those twisted eyes would flame like sparkling

1

red jewels, and the mare's muscles would toughen and swell with unnatural strength. Dread would be a true Bloodeye steed then.

As she and Dread drifted their way down a gentle slope of grass and dark trees, Krista's senses were ever heightened. Red butterflies fluttered from the lavish, mossy bracken at her every step. There was no deadfall here. Every tree was tall and thin and lanced straight toward the brassy gray sky. They were like the white birch of the Sør Sevier Nordland Highlands, only the bark of these trees was black as moonless midnight, every sinuous branch bristling with barb and thorn. Leaves of lustrous green webbed with red veins seemed to pulse and dance to the beating of a giant heart buried deep in the loamy soil.

A thick, damp air crawled through the trees and dragged over the flowers as Krista and Dread reached the bottom of the hillock and saw their first prisoner, a middle-aged woman clothed in naught but a tan smock. She was facing Krista, standing with her arms stretched behind her around the base of a Bloodwood tree, hands cuffed in irons, chains wrapped around both legs. Her eyes widened at the sight of Krista and the large black horse. Her chest heaved in panic as she mouthed a silent *No!*

Krista knew how she herself must look to this captive. Black leather armor, daggers strapped to her hip under crisp black sheaths, a black cape thrown over her shoulder. A sword and leather pouch were tied to the saddle of the demon-eyed horse at her side, the satchel full of poisons and tenvamaru. Yes, Krista knew a Bloodwood assassin was striking to behold. Especially one like her, flawless pale skin, long straight blond hair, bangs squared just above bright green eyes. Together, she and Dread looked cold, hard, deadly, and above all beautiful.

Other prisoners soon came into view—a hundred of them; men, women, a handful of Vallè, a mangy oghul or two. All were spread out behind the first woman. All were shackled and chained to tree after tree, on and on into the dark distance of the charcoal-bleak forest. All had been brought up from the dungeons of Rokenwalder for this Sacrament of Souls.

The heavy wind stilled, and to the left of Krista, the forest shimmered darkly. A cloaked form materialized between the opaque depths of the Bloodwood trees, and the captive woman screamed.

Confident and tall, face hidden in the shadows of his cowl, Black Dugal glided toward Krista like a malevolent mist. Sure was his step. Silent as snow falling at night, he seeped through the trees with an unobtrusive ease. His own massive Bloodeye stallion, Malice, was a hazy silhouette of grim darkness in the woods behind him, red eyes glowing, ever watchful.

Dugal's raven-colored cloak flowed above the grass and spindly briar. As he drew near, the familiar landscape of his face came into focus. Chiseled nose; hard lips; gray-shot beard; and veined, red eyes—all that was visible in the shadow of his hood. One deep scar in the shape of a crescent moon marked his left cheek; two others arced below his right eye and across his face to disappear under his beard. One shallow scar cut straight through his right brow and sooty eyelashes and up his forehead to become lost in the cowl of his mantle. Overall, Dugal looked sinister, tortured, and strikingly *beautiful*.

Beauty was the first rule of the Bloodwood assassins.

"Have you anything to say for yourself?" Dugal stepped up to her.

Krista always felt a certain thrill hearing the coldness of her master's voice. She met his radiant, penetrating gaze with confidence, knowing now with a certainty she had achieved this goal before Hans Rake, for Black Dugal would not have appeared to her had she not arrived here first.

"I reached this place easy enough." She did not break her eyes from his. Her fingers tightened, though, still fastened to Dread's bit. Her skin prickled with anticipation.

"Three whole days it took," he said. Not a muscle in him moved.

He had a way of creating tension in her like no human could. "I expected better from you."

Despite his words, she held her head high. "I do not see Hans anywhere."

Dugal met her statement with stony eyes. A sickly red light glared from those cold orbs. Blood of the Dragon! It was alchemy she did not yet understand—sap of the Bloodwood tree mixed with some fell drug. Her master had not yet offered her Blood of the Dragon, as he had Hans Rake. In their first year of training, Hans had compiled more kills than her. Blood of the Dragon had been his reward. And a Bloodwood assassin in training was allowed to partake of the precious and rare drug only under Black Dugal's leave. Each year, a different reward was given to the one with the most kills. Last year Krista was gifted with Dread.

"Your name is now Crystalwood," Dugal said almost warmly.

*Crystalwood.* She liked how it sounded on his tongue. *Krista to Crystalwood.* She was almost disappointed in herself for not anticipating it.

"I see you approve." Only Dugal could so quickly adopt that intimate tone of a long-known friend. "I had one who struck like a spider. Another who stalked like a hawk. One who moved like silk. One as charming as a rose. All of my making. All beautiful. Now you, perhaps my greatest creation. More bright and precious than a jewel. More sharp and keen than a crystal shard. You are my deadliest weapon of all. More lethal even than Silk and the Rose combined."

Krista thrilled at his words. She pictured Silkwood and Rosewood; the two exquisite blond female Vallè of Black Dugal's Caste. Both had left on separate missions more than five moons ago. The two Vallè had helped Dugal train her and Hans Rake in the beautiful art of assassination. They had participated in many kills together. There had also been another teacher in the beginning—Spiderwood—an experienced but cruel-faced Bloodwood who'd mimicked the traits

4

of Dugal to an alarming degree. So exacting were his mannerisms, Krista wondered if he wasn't somehow relation to her master.

"Crystalwood," she repeated, feeling the name flow from between her lips.

Dugal gave her a placid nod of affirmation. His eyes roamed the forest beyond, settling on the woman chained to the tree. Hints of sunlight trickled through the crooked branches and leaves above like whispers through a stained-glass window and lit on the woman's panicked face like gold.

"Come." Dugal beckoned.

Krista's heart failed a beat. She put her head to her mare's neck. Felt Dread's warmth. It always calmed her, this small thing. Helped her breathe easy. Then she let go the bit, motioned her horse to stay, and followed her master. The woman at the tree tried to shrink away as Krista and Dugal approached. Sunken flesh hung in wrinkled folds about her eyes, cheeks, and jowls. The captive's tan shift carried an air of urine and sweat. In fact, a musty, fetid stink suffused the entire area. And the distant shrieks of other prisoners echoed through the forest.

Dugal reached one languid hand above the woman's head. He peeled a thin strip of coal-colored bark from the tree, tossing it to the ground without thought. Red sap welled slowly from the tree's wound. The curious sap sizzled and smoked as it crawled down the black bark. Krista ran her fingers over the surface of the tree. It was not flaky and brittle like that of a birch. It felt like moist leather—like warm human flesh. She could feel herself shudder at the unsettling sensation.

Dugal reached above the captive again, dabbed two of his fingers into the smoking sap. Tendrils of smoke drifted from his fingers, now painted in red. He stepped toward Krista and ran both fingers across her face, smearing two streaks of sizzling sap under her left eye. It *stung*. Krista resisted the urge to flinch away, focused on the confusion and panic on the chained woman's face.

Dugal swiped more smoking sap from the tree. "Show me your tongue," he ordered, his fingers coated in red again.

Krista stuck out her tongue. Dugal touched the sap to it. Initially it *burned*. Then she caught its divine taste and immediately desired more, eyes greedily fixed on the wound in the tree and the crimson sap hanging there, sizzling.

"Part of your final test is to never partake of the Bloodwood sap again." Dugal's red-streaked, stone-carved eyes bit into hers. "Even if I offer it." Krista felt great sorrow and longing for the sap before the words were even out of his mouth.

"Death is the father of terror." Dugal's eyes were now trained on the prisoner. "'Tis what men dread most. Death. But there is such beauty it." He reached out and stroked the side of the woman's face with the back of his hand. She cowered away from his touch. He continued, "The image of a corpse is graven into the mind of the one who sees it for the first time. That first time one sees death—not the death of a doe or a dog or a skittering gutter cat, but *real* death, the death of a human—is powerful. Name one other visible image as potent, as compelling, as full of *beauty*."

Dugal turned his gaze to Krista. "And here you are. Crystalwood. Ready and willing to administer more cruel beauty on this lovely day." She was always charmed by her master, even here, even conversing of sacrificial murder in a forest of midnight color and savage screams and divine burning sap. *Such cruel beauty.*

He was right. Five years killing, of training in dance, acrobatics, games, puzzles, stealth, lock picking, key making, thievery, crossbow, alchemy, mixing poisons, knife and sword and spear and chain-mace had led her here, to this.

Her Sacrament of Souls.

She looked up at the black tree and oozing sap. *I want to taste it again.* With that thought, she looked away. Sweating. When Black Dugal had first presented her with the Bloodwood leathers, she'd imagined they would be as uncomfortable and hot as a baker's oven. Yet that had not been the case. They were surprisingly comfortable. She had never once in five years sweated in them. Now she felt the odd sensation that the armor was somehow feeding on her flesh, consuming her like a blanketing parasite, infecting her with its sumptuous stifling caress.

Dugal's eyes bored into hers, unflinching. "You have already killed many in my name. You are brutal and efficient and unfeeling in your work. And that is good. But today will be different. A corpse, alarming to view at first, can become delightful to observe as a work of art. Especially when created by one's own hand. That is what you are to learn here today. The entire extent of human anatomy. Your final test. Murder in the name of art. The mother of all beauty." The woman trussed to the tree next to them started gasping in panic at his words.

Dark gaze focused on Krista, Dugal continued, "Before, you were simply a killer. After today you will be a true Bloodwood assassin. You will become Crystalwood. And with your new name, you must forsake your past. Rid yourself of whatever heritage you still hold dear. There is no more room for tenderness of heart. No room for the longings of the past. No room for love. Today you will learn the full *art* of what we do."

Krista's stomach crawled up into her throat as her master went on. "Your mother is long dead. You were raised by your father, Gault Aulbrek. You will never again let his name pass over your lips. You are now called fatherless."

Loneliness was growing in her breast. Bitterness too. After her father had left for war ten years ago, she had grown accustomed to her miserable, lonely life with King Aevrett and his queen, the beautiful and dignified and cruel Natalia. For five years the woman had treated her as a slave, keeping her under the wing of Aevrett's own Knights Chivalric bodyguards at Jö Reviens, the king's palace. And she had grown to despise Natalia for reasons she did not wish to think of now. And she had grown bitter that her father had left her for war and never returned. Left her with an evil king and his even more evil queen.

Though she ofttimes wondered why Black Dugal trained her, ever since he had rescued her from the torment of Jö Reviens five years ago and just after her father had left for war a second time, the world had become a better place. Less sensible for sure. Less secure, yes. But better. For there was freedom in the power to kill. And cold murder was a swift cure for bitterness. And now life was soon to become infinitely more unloving and brutal and rich. And that is what she had wanted. What she had worked so hard for these last five years. This moment. This Sacrament of Souls. The completion of her training.

Neither Seita nor Breita were around to keep her company anymore, to soothe that initial apprehension she'd felt those first few years under Dugal. She had learned much from the two Vallè named Silkwood and Rosewood. But these last few moons it had only been Black Dugal and Hans Rake for companionship, that and those few fond memories of her father she held dear, and the paling remembrances of her mother. Despite her bitterness, she wanted to cling to those things still. But her previous life with her father seemed lost in a receding haze, memories fading like a moldering echo. Gault had been the steady rock on which her childhood had been forged. That was why she both hated him and loved him now. And that was at the heart of the confusion Dugal had been trying to rid her of from the beginning. *He's always been able to sense the conflict within me.*

One scene was engraved on her memory, the one memory most fond, the one memory she knew that Dugal could not bleed from her yet—her last look at her father as he'd ridden off to war in Aeros Raijael's army after his last visit to her five years ago. Dressed in splendorous bright armor and gleaming sword, Gault had sat high and tall atop the warhorse that bore him away from her. His last gesture had been a low, graceful bow from his saddle as he'd handed her a garland of blue Nordland roses tied about with a dark blue ribbon—a ribbon she wore around her left ankle to this day. Always hidden.

*Caring. Death. Longing for the past. Murder. All incompatible objectives. And Dugal reads me like an open book.* A creeping malady gathered in her swirling thoughts. Dugal was correct. Emotions would make her weak. It was why she buried them in that bottomless part of her mind. She wanted that maleficent part of her mind that Dugal had been fostering in her to triumph in the end. She *was* motherless. *Fatherless.* She had been for a long time. Left adrift and alone in a world that did not look kindly upon abandoned children. Gault had been everything a father should be. But he was now ten years at war, five since she had last seen him—likely long dead. Yes, she was fatherless. And she didn't care. *And the taste of the Bloodwood sap was been so exquisite. . . .*

"It is as you say." Krista met Dugal's gaze, refusing to blink. "I am now named fatherless." A small silver dagger, a natural extension of her hand, snapped like lightning from the folds of her leathers. She held up the blade. "I await my Sacrament of Souls."

The woman shackled to the tree shrieked in terror. Her cry set off a chain reaction of horrified screams from the other prisoners, which resounded in the distance. But Krista did not flinch. She met Dugal, eye to eye. Then her master whirled soundlessly and took his leave, disappearing into the maze of trees from whence he'd come, his red-eyed stallion, Malice, waiting in the gloom.

† † † † †

Krista faced the woman, tilted her head, taking the captive's measure. The prisoner's lungs began to heave. Tears welled like fire behind her eyes as she pleaded, "Please, miss, let me go. I know I've wr-wronged the throne of Raijael. I know my crimes. But I—I don't belong here. I'm not like the rest. I swear it. I was only in the dungeons of Rokenwalder for a day when they took me. You must have mercy."

"Ah," a voice sounded behind Krista. "A mercy I hadn't gotten here sooner."

In one fluid motion Krista whirled, silver dirk at the guard, ready. It was Hans Rake. He sat royal and tall astride his Bloodeye stallion, Kill. Cursing herself for not paying better attention to her surroundings, Krista looked at him blankly, blade still gripped in her hand.

"Well, Krista, have you a new name?" Hans' voice carried a throaty, indignant lilt. He wore the same black leather greaves and armor as she, marking him as one of Black Dugal's Caste. Along with the twin daggers at his belt, a crossbow and quiver of arrows were strapped to his back in plain view. Hans Rake had a slightly hooked nose, squared jaw, and a face that continually bore a peevish, conceited expression. But it was a face graced with solid cheekbones and fiery green eyes—confident, cunning, brooding, mischievous eyes. And like Dugal's, they were faintly streaked with red. His hair was shaved far above his ears on both sides of his head, blue Suk Skard clan tattoos covering either side of his scalp. The strip of dirty-blond hair atop his skull was a two-inch-high row of carefully formed spikes from his forehead to the nape of his neck.

Both Krista and Hans were seventeen; both had spent the last five years under Black Dugal's tutelage, killing in his name. But three days ago they had been set to the final game, their very last test to become full Bloodwoods, their final pilgrimage to this, their Sacrament of Souls. It had started in Rokenwalder, with a slew of clues and puzzles that had led them here. Hans now knew well that *she* was finally in favor with their master. She could tell her arriving here first bothered him greatly. For Hans Rake always quailed to please Black Dugal more than she.

"So, have you a new name, my love?" he asked again.

She had reached the Sacrament of Souls first. Her reward was her new name. Crystalwood. A name she could not divulge unto Hans until he too had a new name. But when would Dugal give him that name?

"I am not your love." Krista continued her blank stare.

"You can only keep your name from me for so long." Hans now held his head high and regal, as if he were looking down his nose at her. An aura of dominance and strength suffused him. "Or has our master finally taken you into his secret councils?" He smiled a mischievous smile. "Do you share *secrets* with him?"

Krista felt her entire body grow rigid. She didn't want to be goaded by his haughty innuendos now. With Hans, it was always there, that hint of flirtation, constant insinuation, always directed at her, and always with a certain cruel, yet mannered charm. It was all in his game. She remained silent under his intimate gaze.

Hans looked past her to the woman chained to the tree. "Or perhaps this dead dungeon slut keeps counsel with our beloved Black Dugal. Or perhaps she has been given a new name too." He dismounted his Bloodeye steed, drifted toward the captive. "What is your name, woman?"

The captive said nothing, frozen in fear.

"Yes, this one will be mine." Hans' fingers coiled through her natty hair. "Naught but a pile of shivering, blubbering meat meant for my blades." He glanced Krista's way, saw the dagger still in her grip. "A new name you may have, but still you carry the same silver as I."

Krista remained silent, calm. Hans turned back to the captive, and his expression relaxed into wistfulness. "See, m'lady prisoner, we don't get to fashion our own Bloodwood daggers until after completing our Sacrament of Souls. We must gather the red sap of these trees . . . and then gather your blood." He trailed off, traced steady fingers over the woman's neck, digging his fingernails in. Blood trickled down her pale skin as she whimpered in pain. Behind Krista, Kill whinnied in approval.

"A silver blade is never thirsty." Hans continued his seemingly idle regard. "But give me a black one of *my own* making . . ."

The captive screamed as her eyes bounced between Krista and Hans and out into the vast, wretched forest as if searching for escape or rescue. Hans frowned his displeasure. "All the wailings and protests in the Five Isles will not save you. The locals dare not venture here. They claim this forest is haunted." His eyes roamed the trees in lazy regard. "Oh, and I would say this place is *most* haunted, and about to become more so. These trees drink the blood of the dead. The blood of you prisoners nourishes the soil. I imagine our Sacrament of Souls sustains this forest. Am I being deliberate enough, making clear our aim?"

"Please, no." The woman gave one last primal plea, eyes bouncing again from Hans to Krista and back to Hans. "Have mercy, both of you, please."

Though Hans Rake ofttimes liked to act the part, Krista knew he was no brutish, slit-eyed thug from the gutters of Rokenwalder. He was slick and smooth and aware and lucid at all times. But he carried in him some monstrous feral need for butchery and violence that could manifest itself in spectacular wicked fashion. She, too, felt those same longings for chaos and violence. It was the one way in which they were shockingly similar. They had killed together before. This was their Sacrament of Souls. And together they would kill everyone here.

Hans' flat eyes appraised the woman as he touched her face lovingly, his thumbs sliding up under her ears, caressing the hinge of her jaw. He dug in swiftly and jerked out violently, dislocating her jaw. Her eyes widened in both surprise and pain. Her screams turned to muffled gurgles as Hans took his dagger to her windpipe.

And with that, Krista found herself wondering what her father would think of all this: the Bloodwood training, all the killing she had done in Black Dugal's name, this Sacrament of Souls. What would Gault Aulbrek think of her life as an assassin these last five years? He had been so serious about perfecting his own sword craft, so earnest in his study of war, so beholden to his Lord Aeros. She had admired that devotion in him. And as she watched Hans carve into the woman, she indeed wondered what her father would say to her now.

After a time, Krista turned away from Hans Rake and his bloody labors. Let him have the first victim. What did she care? She preferred to work alone. And there were a hundred other prisoners awaiting. Sheathing her dagger, taking Dread again by the bit, she stepped lightly, the soil at her feet a sponge of thick grasses and black flowers. She passed Hans and his desolate victim on her way toward the center of the lush woods and the rest of the quivering captives—canvasses for her art, her final Bloodwood test.

Before she disappeared into the black forest of prisoners, Krista saw Hans look up from his work and throw her a coy, curling little smile. Red butterflies still danced in the air, and somewhere in the distance came the lone shriek of a crow. Krista Aulbrek would walk among the dead soon—the dead of her own creation.

And with her new name—Crystalwood.

*Treachery and betrayal endures. If a warrior turns against Raijael, seize him and*
*slay him by the sword and bury him wherever you find him. And if that betrayer*
*is a woman, burn her slow and leave her unburied, for 'tis only by the grace of*
*Raijael she has even been gifted a weapon.*
—THE CHIVALRIC ILLUMINATIONS OF RAIJAEL

# CHAPTER TWO

# GAULT AULBREK

### 6TH DAY OF THE ETHIC MOON, 999TH YEAR OF LAIJON

### OUTSIDE LOKKENFELL, GUL KANA

The dewy morning landscape was woolen with haze and fog. The old wooden cart and its load of three prisoners trundled along the rutted path, two stout muddy oxen at the head. Feathery green tussocks and peaty soil lined the roadway. A contingent of Lord's Point Ocean Guard, mounted and draped in blue livery, accompanied the cart on all sides, the steel-shod hooves of their heavy steeds drumming against the boggy ground. The Dayknight, Leif Chaparral, led them. Several dozen squires trailed the entire procession.

Gault Aulbrek sat against the sidewall of the cart, hands cuffed before him, legs shackled to the floorboards beneath. Hard-bitten veteran though he was, Gault still battled the pain of having been betrayed by his Lord Aeros. Thoughts and feelings he'd never dared feel now floated freely through him.

He would likely never see his beloved mount, Spirit, again. The rare stallion would be bequeathed to Aeros' next Knight Archaic. As would his sword.

*And what will happen to Ava Shay?* He thought of his stepdaughter Krista, too. Could he save her from whatever evil fate the Angel Prince had set for her?

Aeros had planned it all so well. Everything now wrong in his life began and ended with Aeros Raijael. In the beginning, war at the side of the Angel Prince had been exciting, filled with hate for the enemy, a noble crusade to reclaim lands once belonging to the realm of his birth. Each new skirmish had come complete with a new thrill, a new heroic tale. Ten years crusading, and in that time Gault had watched men hack away at one another with ax and sword, slugging it out in both dust and muck as they trampled their own guts, spat out their own teeth, bloodlust sparking in their eyes, their noble deeds recorded in *The Chivalric Illuminations*. He himself had slain so many of the enemy he couldn't even count. *Hundreds. No. Thousands!* All glory and majesty.

But how he'd just wanted it all to end.

In fact, if he were to be honest with himself, the last year or two around Aeros Raijael he had been anxious, afraid. He had lived with a fear that manifested itself in extreme paranoia. He had lost sight of the difference between being brave, angry, or just plain scared. And it was all connected to Aeros.

He recalled his moment with Ava Shay, embracing, kissing. Had Aeros seen? Another truth—they had *wanted* to get caught. It was because of moments like those that the *Illuminations* constantly encouraged ridding oneself of all tenderness and feeling.

*And look where a moment of caring landed me. . . .*

Fatigue ate at his bones. It didn't help that the cart jostled and bounced, as it had for days now. Since Ravenker there'd been scant food and water. The scent of blossoming blueberries that occasionally lined their path drove Gault mad with hunger. He'd spent most of the ride lulled to sleep by the rattle and rhythm of the oxcart, inhaling the mixture of sweaty horses and moist peat. He fought to stay awake now.

With heavy-lidded eyes, he gazed at his two fellow prisoners: the Betrayer of Sør Sevier, Hawkwood, and the Princess of Amadon, Jondralyn Bronachell. Auspicious company if ever there was. The princess, still in full Amadon Silver Guard armor, lay on her back in the center of the cart, legs tied down, arms folded over her silver breastplate, wrists cuffed with heavy irons. Not that she was in any shape to go anywhere. Gault had seen to that in Ravenker. Some five days ago the woman had foolishly challenged him to a duel. His first blow could have severed her spine. His second could have split her head.

She only lived because he had purposely pulled both blows.

He could see the gentle rising of her chest. Slow breaths now, ofttimes labored. For the bulk of the journey, Jondralyn's deep wheezing had been an unsettling counterpoint to the grind and rattle of the cart and the *clomp, clomp, clomp* of oxen hooves. In her few waking moments, she'd moaned in pain, falling back into unconsciousness almost immediately. Thick gobs of congealed blood matted her hair. The scarlet stain under her head had mostly soaked into the wood of the cart. The surrounding fog robbed her skin of all color. Dull light bled across the ragged wounds of her broken face—a once beautiful face that now bore a swollen raw gash from her forehead just above her right eye down to the left side of her chin. The wound was shockingly infected. And she would likely lose the right eye. If she lived.

Hawkwood had tried his best to stitch the wound closed, using thread pulled from his tunic and a sliver of wood peeled back from the floor of the cart as a needle—a nearly impossible task, trussed up and injured as he was. The makeshift surgery was shoddy. Raw muscle and fat still bubbled from the damaged skin. The bones of her nasal cavity near her eye were still exposed, white and jagged.

The Jondralyn Bronachell in the bottom of the oxcart bore scant resemblance to the striking image on the Gul Kana coin Enna Spades had kept.

As for Hawkwood, he looked about as miserable as Gault felt. The former Bloodwood listed awkward and lethargic against the opposite wall of the cart. He had also spent most of the journey racked with labored breathing. Wounds crisscrossed his forearms and neck. His leather armor was shredded. Gault figured whatever blade had caused the great number of cuts on the man had likely been poisoned. In Ravenker, Gault had watched from a distance when Leif Chaparral and Culpa Barra had found Hawkwood with Aeros' sword, Sky Reaver. Which meant Hawkwood had come across Spiderwood in Ravenker. The injuries he now suffered were likely the work of his brother.

But had the Hawk killed the Spider and taken the sword? That was the question. Hawkwood had admitted to nothing. And Leif now carried Sky Reaver

"Both awake, I see." Leif Chaparral slowed his mount, a lightly armored palfrey. He rode alongside the cart, gazing down at Hawkwood. "Looks as if I have the honor of informing you poor sods we're almost to the King's Highway. Then it's on to Amadon, where, I fear, a terrible fate awaits you both."

Gault fought his way out of the morose stupor, groping for any coherency of thought. He focused on the Dayknight, tried to concentrate.

Dark hair hung down over Leif's shoulders, framing a squared jaw under high cheekbones. His blue eyes were rimmed in black ink. High on his horse, in formidable black-lacquered armor, huge black sword dangling at his side, Leif could be a daunting sight for those who didn't know what to look for in a fighter. But off his horse, the Dayknight had a noticeable limp. And there was an obvious undercurrent of uncertainty in his every word and gesture.

A leather satchel was secured to Leif's saddle. *Spiderwood's payoff in gold?* Four swords were secured to the saddle behind him: two curved blades with spiked hilts that were once Hawkwood's, the sword Gault had wielded against Jondralyn in Ravenker, and the longsword with the elegant white sheath—Aeros Raijael's blade.

"Neither of you have a thing to say?" Leif asked.

Hawkwood's voice was husky and strained with emotion. "I suffer this captivity only for the sake of seeing Jondralyn safely to Amadon. But make no mistake, Leif Chaparral, when I do free myself, you will die."

"You will never again be free." The Dayknight's eyes were alight with amusement. "Grand speech, though I imagine Ser Gault enjoyed it, sitting there so stoic and grim all the time. Must be hard for Gault, this journey, what with the king of Gul Kana's sister all sliced up between you two, him the culprit who done it. 'Tis such misadventure for the whole cartload."

Hawkwood's eyes strayed to Gault, narrowed briefly, then he looked down at Jondralyn.

"Don't take my words amiss," Leif continued. "'Twas Gault who cleaved her face in twain. I only speak the truth."

"Truth?" Hawkwood muttered. "I doubt you know the meaning of the word."

"For my part," Leif went on, "I think it would be amusing sport if you and Gault just fought it out here in the oxcart. 'Course, if you killed him, it would deprive Jovan and me the pleasures of doing unto Gault what Gault and his fellow knights did unto Baron Jubal Bruk." Leif's laugh was mirthless. "You do know what Aeros Raijael's army did to the poor baron, right? Sawed every limb from his body. "What do you think of that, Hawkwood?"

Despite whatever injuries Hawkwood still suffered, or whatever poison was still working in him, he flayed Leif with his cool, unforgiving gaze, saying nothing.

Leif drawled on. "I reckon you and Ser Gault can just languish here in your own individual pathetic miseries."

"Was you who betrayed your own princess," Gault rasped, feeling his voice crackle to life of its own volition. "It is you who's to blame for Jondralyn's injuries."

"How do you figure, Ser Gault?"

"You pompous fool," Gault growled. "If Hawkwood or I don't kill you, rest assured, that rotten Bloodwood you sold your soul to eventually will."

"Gault is right," Hawkwood said. "This is all your doing, Leif. That I know."

"This is nothing Jondralyn didn't do to herself," Leif said, laughing again. "She did it with your help, no less. Wasn't it you who trained her in swordplay, Hawkwood?"

The former Bloodwood did not answer.

"Let me tell you," Leif continued. "As a knight, she wasn't worth a pinch of dry oghul shit. A disgrace. An utter failure. I'm liable to hang the next Gul Kana woman who prepares to take up a sword. Hang 'er and burn 'er. On general principle. In fact, I make it my life's mission to never again see a woman in Gul Kana armor."

Hawkwood growled, "You will be dead before you get the chance to hang anyone."

"We will be in Amadon in six days. You can explain to Jovan how you trained his sister to fail, filled her head with folly. I'm sure he will be just swimming with amusement and sympathy at whatever story you tell." With that Leif clicked spurs to mount and galloped off, horse and black armor quickly swallowed by the mist.

Gault and Hawkwood sat in silence, both retreating into their own private thoughts. If there was anyone who reminded Gault of Aeros Raijael, it was Leif Chaparral. Around Leif, he couldn't help but reflect upon his previous growing unease around the Angel Prince.

It seemed the closer Aeros' armies had drawn to Gul Kana, the more unpredictable the Angel Prince had become, the more he had led his armies on the verge of sheer panic. *Or perhaps it was me who followed half-panicked.*

Gault had grasped the morale of the men in Aeros' army years ago. Most were just normal folks who'd led the hard lives of smiths, whalers, farmers, rangers, and trappers before joining the war effort. Aeros was their appointed leader by birthright alone. He was not cut of the same frontier cloth as they, but rather raised in the courts of Rokenwalder with taste and refinement, raised among the opulence of the grand palace, Jö Reviens.

But during the first battles on Adin Wyte soil ten years ago—battles in which Aeros fought alongside his men valiantly—the young prince had taken the first steps toward proving himself. During those first bloody clashes, the Angel Prince had begun to learn the one secret of being a good leader: you had to be willing to kill with your own hand. You couldn't always lie back and let others do the unpleasant things.

And in ten years of war, Aeros had proven with each passing campaign to be more and more unlike his father in this regard. King Aevrett, it seemed, relied more often on Bloodwood assassins like Hawk and the Spider to do his dirty work. One thing Gault knew: a soldier must not only fear, but also respect his leader more than his enemy. And Aeros had earned that respect early, then followed it up by fighting with much brutality and skill, never once sustaining injury, which only added to his growing mystique. Over time every soldier began to look upon him with a certain reverence and awe. As if they were truly fighting alongside the second coming of Laijon.

But Gault had learned the hard way, you could never be too loyal to any one man, even if the rest of your countrymen thought of him as God.

Morale and loyalty among Aeros' ranks was never higher after the conquest of Adin Wyte five years ago. But something had changed within Aeros during the next five years of fighting in Wyn Darrè. Most hadn't noticed the Angel Prince's growing impatience. But Gault had. In Adin Wyte, not being rash was Aeros' strength. Not being stupid, his greatest asset. Aeros' coolness and calm had been a steadying influence to the entire might of the army. But once in Wyn Darrè, he seemed on the verge of launching into a fit at any provocation, or sequestering himself inside his tent whilst the likes of Enna Spades and Hammerfiss took care of things—things like the treatment of prisoners.

Now it seemed Spades was running roughshod over every aspect of the war with her unchecked cruelty. And the oddest things of all, the advancement of Mancellor Allen to Knight Archaic, followed by Aeros' obsession with the village boy, Jenko Bruk. And Ava Shay. Aeros had often acted upon his desires with captives taken in Adin Wyte and Wyn Darrè. But he always killed them within days after slaking his lusts.

*What was it about Ava Shay that changed the Angel Prince? What was it about her that changed me?*

Gault's thoughts were interrupted as another Dayknight in black-lacquered armor drifted out of the mists, face hidden under an equally black helm. Gault could tell by the way the knight sat in the saddle that it was Ser Culpa Barra of Port Follett—Jondralyn Bronachell's standard-bearer. His gray palfrey deftly edged toward the cart, pulling up alongside Hawkwood at a cantered gait. Culpa removed his black helm with gauntleted hands, revealing a square-jawed face and dark blue eyes. A mop of sweaty blond hair crowned him; chunks of it clung to his forehead in damp ringlets. There was a keen and cool detachment to the Dayknight, and in Gault's estimation, the man was a capable soldier, one to be reckoned with.

"Ser Culpa Barra," Hawkwood said, tone just low enough that the mounted Ocean Guard escort nearby could not hear. "Hard to be out riding today in full armor. Gotta be mighty uncomfortable."

"Aye," came the knight's short answer.

"What took you so long to seek me out? It's been days since we left Ravenker."

"I've my reasons." Culpa's voice was also low.

"As you can see"—Hawkwood's eyes stayed fixed on Jondralyn as he talked—"things have gone terribly wrong for us here, Culpa. Terribly wrong. Why was she in Ravenker? Why was she dueling one of Aeros' Knights Archaic?"

"Never mind all that." Culpa's tone was crisp. "'Tis a long story, and we haven't the time. We are nearing the King's Highway and I must depart. Shawcroft and the dwarf should be made privy to what's happened to Jondralyn. And they should also know your fate and where you are headed . . . and who you travel with." His watchful eyes strayed to Gault and then down to the princess. "I imagine Roguemoore and Shawcroft will be at the rendezvous point with Ironcloud."

"Shawcroft is dead," Hawkwood said.

"For certain?" Real horror was revealed on Culpa's face, but briefly. He quickly composed himself. "The boy who was with you in Ravenker, the boy who ran off with the dog when Leif and I walked up—I know him. He was Shawcroft's ward."

"Aye, Nail." Hawkwood looked up at Culpa, eyes now intense. "You must find the boy. Even if it means failing to rendezvous with Roguemoore and Ironcloud. Nail more than likely still travels with that dog and likely my horse. I've a feeling he means to abandon our cause."

Culpa's gaze roamed the fog to the west, toward Lord's Point. "I will do what I can to find him." He turned back to Hawkwood. "Bear in mind, Jovan holds no love for you. Nor for his sister either. I see Jovan's hand behind Jondralyn's fate. Be wary when you reach Amadon. You will likely be hung or beheaded or Laijon knows what."

"Don't worry about me, Ser Culpa." Hawkwood's eyes were drawn to Jondralyn once more. "I have taken precautions. I will see that she lives."

"This is where I leave you then." Culpa gripped his helm with gauntleted hands. "Leif will discover my disappearance soon enough. He will take it as a betrayal."

"Leif will be dead soon enough," Hawkwood said.

"See that he dies painfully." Culpa dipped his head. "If I indeed find Nail and make it to the rendezvous point, any words you wish to relay to the dwarf?"

"Tell Roguemoore that I am useless now, sliced up like a wet cod by my brother, the Spider. Perhaps dying. Spiderwood is tricky and cruel with his poisons. But I will make sure that Jondralyn lives. Tell the dwarf that she has been made privy to what secrets I hold. Tell him the *princess* can find the shield if I die. She knows the way."

Culpa dipped his head a second time, then in one smooth motion slid his helm back over his head. He reached into his saddlebag next and pulled forth a heel of bread. "Share it." He tossed the bread at Gault's feet. He then pulled forth a spool of black thread and dropped it into Hawkwood's lap. With that, he set heels to flanks and galloped his horse past the blue-liveried Ocean Guard escort and into the gray mists, heading west.

"Cryptic conversation." Gault snatched up the bread and hungrily bit into it. It was sourdough, old and stale, but the best he had ever tasted. He broke off a chunk and tossed it to the former Bloodwood.

Hawkwood looked out into the cloud of fog where Leif had disappeared. "I spent my whole life killing people until I met Jondralyn Bronachell. Truth is, I haven't killed a soul since the day I first laid eyes on her." His rigid, wintry gaze turned back to Gault. "But that might change when I reach Amadon and face Jovan Bronachell."

The former Bloodwood rolled over in the cart next to Jondralyn. Propped on both elbows, hands shackled, he unwound the spool of thread and loosened the sliver of wood he'd torn from the bottom of the cart days ago, the sliver of wood he'd previously used as a needle to stitch Jondralyn's face.

As the cart continued on its jostling course, Hawkwood picked at the makeshift stitches he'd sewn into the princess' swollen face days ago, gingerly working them free. Puss welled from the infected wound. Painstakingly he began restitching the bleeding gash, doing his utmost to keep the ragged injury clean.

Gault Aulbrek watched without purpose or passion, savoring the stale hunk of sourdough.

*In the ebbing fires of our smoldering souls, we all of us offer up secrecy and deceit to protect ourselves, to protect our cause. We all of us offer up only partial versions of ourselves and beliefs to the world.*
—The Way and Truth of Laijon

# CHAPTER THREE

# TALA BRONACHELL

6th Day of the Ethic Moon, 999th Year of Laijon

Amadon, Gul Kana

Tala wore a sleeveless tan tunic over a black silken shirt and brown woolen leggings, a bejeweled dagger at her belt. 'Twas a blade she'd recently lifted from Jovan's collection of shiny trinkets he kept in his chamber.

The wooden ladder she faced was rotted in spots but felt sturdy enough to hold her weight. She climbed, testing each dust-covered rung as she went. The ladder emptied her out into a pitch-dark room. A crawl space really. On hands and knees she searched for another pathway, worried she might fall into some unseen pit. As she ducked under a hanging spiderweb, she could feel the rat droppings crunch under her hands and knees. The stench of long-spoiled food and dead rodents permeated the air. The dreary squalor of the unkempt place made her want to puke. Still, the looming dangers of the secret ways once again sated her need for adventure.

She located the trapdoor the Bloodwood's note had mentioned, hidden in the floor with its bolt sheared. With a grunt, she lifted the heavy iron door and scooted down a cramped circular staircase. She entered a series of dimly lit rooms lined with wood-plank boxes and piles of discarded moth-eaten cloth and rusted pottery and other musty oddments. She came to another iron door, also with a broken lock. She slipped through into a much wider chamber, dusky light streaming in from two windows high above. This room was filled with nooks and craggy shadows. The head of a highland elk was nailed above the long-dead hearth at the far end, frosted with dust and cobwebs. A silver-strung harp stood on a pedestal near a heavily quilted bed, both covered in a dull gray blanket of dusky filth. Four chairs and a divan in neat array, all padded with rich red velvet, stood next to a large mahogany chest with bronze-filigreed handles. Long tapestries hung from every wall. Dark alcoves of black shadow lined the wide spaces between, alcoves rising high to a complex latticework of arching wooden rafters above.

The Bloodwood's instructions had led her to some royal chamber long since abandoned. Tala cast her eyes about, half in wonder, half in fear. The place was palatial, but gray and grim. That an unknown room full of such an array of unused luxuries existed within the bowels of the castle was a mystery. *A chamber for a queen!*

"There you are." A smooth voice came from nowhere and everywhere. "I was starting to worry you did not get my note."

"I am here now." She pulled the ornate dagger from her belt.

"Where are the two boys I asked you to bring?"

"I am done following your orders," Tala said with confidence, having practiced what she would say beforehand. She was done with secret notes and silly Bloodwood games. Today she would stand up to her tormentor. She clutched the dagger tight in her fist. "Show your true self for once."

"Do any of us ever truly show our true selves?" The voice cut through the air. "Do you, Tala? Do you even truly know *yourself*?"

"We are not talking about me."

"Yet we are." The assassin's voice glided through the air with confidence. "You did not like that busty barmaid making advances on your sister, did you?"

"Did she stab my brother?" Tala spouted. "Or was that you?"

There was laughter. "You are a pampered and entitled little snot."

"I didn't come here to be insulted."

"You do not like those of lower station. You despise them. You thought Delia was uncouth. You are a jealous person. I can read your mind."

It did feel like her mind was twisting over on itself, expanding, as if her very thoughts were being pulled through her ears and eyes. *How could I be jealous of someone like that barmaid?* Tala clenched her eyelids tight. *Think of something else. Anyone else. Just not the barmaid.* The image of Sterling Prentiss' naked body spread across a cross-shaped altar entered her mind, his blood dripping over the stone. He was still there in that red-hazed room, cold and rotting. *A man is dead because of me! All the lies I have told!*

"Oh, the things you did to the Dayknight captain." The Bloodwood's soft voice oozed into Tala's thoughts, overtaking them. "Rich and cunning and bloody things. You do not even know your true self, nor even your own potential. Do you, my pet?"

Tala stepped back, unhinged by the two last words. *My pet.* The assassin's insinuation sent loathsome images pouring unwanted into her mind: Glade so callously slicing the captain of the Dayknight's throat, her stirring the man's guts with her own hand. *Do any of us ever truly show our true selves?*

The Bloodwood's earlier statement was a direct quote from the last note. A note Tala had set to memory.

> *Bravo! You succeeded in every task.*
> *Thanks to your devotion, the downfall of Gul Kana*

*and the entire Five Isles is now underway. Just a few
more tasks and Lawri's transformation will be complete.
And only then will your destiny also be secured.*

*Do any of us ever truly show our true selves?*

*Here is what I need you to do. . . .*

*Find what secret parchments Jondralyn has hidden
away in her chamber. Deliver unto me what you find. A
terrible danger she keeps hidden, a danger that may lead
to Purgatory and beyond.*

*Once you have the parchment, you must bring Glade
Chaparral with you. And you must include your cousin,
Lindholf, too. Meet with me in the lost Chamber of
Queens in five days' time. The directions are on the other
side of this note.*

*You know how to decipher them. . . .*

And here she was, but without the secret parchments or the two boys. She had purposely disobeyed the letter, purposely *not* searched the secret places of Jondralyn's chamber, purposely not brought Glade and Lindholf with her. In fact, she'd be fine if she never saw Glade Chaparral again. She refused to play any further games until the Bloodwood answered to *her*. "Tell me what foul poison I fed Lawri," she said sharply. "The green stuff in that vial, it's changed her somehow." *And also brought her back to life.* Tala shuddered at the thought.

"Did you bring the parchment that I asked for?"

"Get it yourself. You probably know where it is—"

"Never make demands of me." A dark form drifted into the light from behind a rich tapestry. The cloaked figure, face obscured under black hood and shadow, made no move to approach, just stood there, a slick black dagger in hand.

As poorly lit as this room was, it was the most Tala had ever seen of her silent tormentor. Her heart hammered. "I'm not scared of you."

"My blade thirsts. And you'll be a long time dying. I *will* make it painful."

Tala did not balk. She walked straight toward the assassin, forcefully, her own dagger gripped in hand. The Bloodwood whirled and vanished into the same dark nook in the wall behind the tapestry from which he had sprung. Tala raced to the alcove and peered into the darkness. There was nothing but three stone walls rising to the ceiling. Dust floated down into her eyes as she looked up, craning her neck. She backed away, wondering what madness had gotten into her.

"You *will* bring me what I've asked for." The assassin was perched in the rafters overhead. "We haven't time for childish nonsense."

"Childish nonsense," Tala said, still looking up. "What about your *silly games*? Of the two of us, who is truly full of childish nonsense?"

"Don't think yourself so clever, girl."

"Do any of us ever truly show our true selves?" Tala threw the question back at the Bloodwood. "Do you? Hiding from me always. Climbing rafters. It is you who are afraid of me."

"We both know what you desire." Silent as a goose feather floating, the assassin flitted across the arching wooden beams, disappearing into the shadows far above.

"You desire to read what parchments Jondralyn keeps hidden as much as I." The Bloodwood's voice grew faint. "Next time we meet . . . remember your true self. . . . You do not want Lawri's dreams to come true. . . ."

And then the voice was gone and Tala was left standing alone, staring into the dank depths of the arching, cobwebbed rafters. She felt more disconcerted now than ever before. She thought of the dream her cousin had shared with her. *I was given in marriage to the grand vicar!* She recalled how her mother had hated arranged marriages, how Alana had argued with Borden about the betrothal of Squireck Van Hester and Jondralyn when Jon was just sixteen. Like her mother, Tala felt a woman should have the right to determine her own destiny. *I'm just not sure what that destiny is to be.* At one time, she had thought it a good idea to be betrothed to Glade, overjoyed by the prospect, even. She couldn't get the Bloodwood's parting words out of her head. *Next time we meet . . . remember your true self. . . . You do not want Lawri's dreams to come true. . . .*

*Denarius! Marriage!*

Then Tala saw it—the dark leather sack on the floor at her feet. Her blood ran cold. Handsomely made, it was about the size of a lady's bonnet and made of dark leather tipped with gold-leaf edges and inlaid with finely crafted scrollwork. It was cinched closed at the top with a thin leather thong.

When she loosened the leather tie, something glowed green and bright from within.

Tala slipped the jeweled dagger back into her belt, knelt, and gingerly picked up the bag. It was heavier than expected. Her fingers further loosened the leather thong. She pulled back the flap and gazed within, confused. She dumped the sack's contents onto the floor.

A slip of paper followed by a stream of green, coin-sized marbles spilled forth. Near a dozen. Bright little things. All glowing. Tala sat back, suddenly surrounded by luminescent green. She snatched one of the shiny orbs from off the floor. Its texture surprised her. It wasn't like the glass-hard marbles she'd played with as a child, but rather soft to the touch. A green, gleaming liquid encased in a thin, translucent skin. She pinched it between two fingers, squishing it slightly. The glowing innards appeared similar to the potion she'd fed Lawri.

Tala dropped the malleable marble back into the leather sack and snatched the slip of paper from the floor. *It's a note!*

As she read, a tremor, as if ice-tipped nails had suddenly been hammered into the length of her spine, ripped through her.

*Your cute little cousin is only partially healed of what*
*afflicts her. Make no mistake, she will spiral into insanity*

*and die if she is not fed more of the antidote.*

 *In this sack I have left you twenty dosages. One per day. More will be given to you later . . . but only if you continue to do my bidding and bring me what I ask for. Only then will Lawri's transformation be complete. Only then will your own destiny be underway. One day, Tala, at the time of Absolution, you may be the only heir of Borden Bronachell still standing, the only one holding the key to all mysteries. These games you think are so silly are designed to test you, to prepare you for your own future. Take them seriously. Lawri's life depends on it. Your own life now depends on it.*

† † † † †

A mournful wind moaned across the crenellated stone battlements of Greengrass Courtyard. Atop the lofty walls above were a dozen Silver Guards, keeping watch over the courtyard and the safety of the king's sister and cousins as they practiced swordsmanship with Val-Draekin and Seita.

"M'lady, you seem troubled today," Seita said with a pleasant smile, bowing before Tala.

"'Tis nothing," Tala responded coolly, emotionlessly.

Seita did not balk at the reticence in her tone. "It's hard being royalty," the Vallè princess said. "Friendships are hard to come by. Hard to sustain. And ofttimes it's hard to know who *truly* is one's friend. It's hard enough to even know oneself."

*Know oneself?* Tala furrowed her brow. *Am I friendless?* She looked at Lindholf and Lawri Le Graven. The twins were banging wooden swords with Glade Chaparral and Val-Draekin in the center of the courtyard. She dimly recalled the friendships of her youth: Lindholf, Lawri, Glade. But Glade was a stranger to her now—dark and evil. A

37

killer. And her relationship with Lindholf had grown strained and awkward. Lawri had changed too. *Have I changed? How does one know oneself?* Of late she had made every effort to form a passionless, emotionless void inside her heart.

*Feel nothing.* Emptiness was her aim. *The game isn't over and Lawri is still in danger.*

"Ninety percent of the nobility in the king's court care little for me," Seita went on. "The Vallè count few as friends. I seem to be distrusted wherever I go. And it's mostly the other court ladies who despise me the most."

*Because their boyfriends and husbands stare at you.* Today the Vallè princess wore leather breeches, laced up the sides, which fit perfectly, exquisitely. Her black belt and tan tunic matched her pants. Her hair hung carelessly over the sides of her alluring fey ears and face like fine white silk. Her pale features were tapered and slight and effortlessly bore the flawless, sharp beauty of Riven Rock marble. *Yes, every man stares at you,* Tala mused. *Even I stare.*

"May I ask you a question?" Seita inquired. "If it please m'lady, of course." She bowed again, green eyes glittering. Tala nodded and the Vallè princess continued. "Do you think your brother has many friends? I mean, *real* friends. I'm sure Jovan has no lack of *courtly* friends. Folks who may seek favor of the Silver Throne."

Tala pictured her older brother and his relationship with Leif— the kiss she'd witnessed between them. "Jovan has no need of friends," she said a little too curtly.

"Did he not grow up with Leif Chaparral? Are they not still close?"

*Can she read my mind too?* Tala's heart crept up into her throat.

"I've my own thoughts on the matter," Seita continued. "Others of royal blood, is that the only type of friend a prince or princess, or even king, is doomed to have?"

*Royal bloodlines do not automatic friends make.* Tala had learned that lesson all too well over the course of her life. *One cannot just thrust two people into friendship.*

"Perhaps we can be of some service to each other." Seita bowed again. "I would wish to share an alliance with you, Tala. It would do me great honor."

Tala swallowed hard, finding she was almost glaring at the Vallè princess.

"Sorry." Seita looked away. "Alliance was the wrong word. That sounded a bit cold and clinical. Not at all what I had in mind."

"What are you getting at?" Tala asked sharply.

"I've always desired a friendship like you and Lawri have," Seita said. "Even Glade and Lindholf are your friends. It must be comforting."

Tala had always thought the Vallè princess full of unabashed confidence. But she was showing a vulnerable side. That vulnerability tugged at Tala briefly. When Seita stole a shy glance at her, Tala felt her own gaze soften.

"I reveal my own jealousy, I suppose," the Vallè princess said. "I do wish to be closer to Val-Draekin. But he has eyes only for Breita. And I could never betray her."

"Where is your sister?"

Seita's sharp eyes remained fixed on the courtyard. "I must admit, Tala, I do not know where Breita is. And that vexes me." Her thin brow furrowed. "I ofttimes think I know everything. Think I can predict everything. But the truth is, you can tell lies to yourself for so long you don't even know when to stop. Or when it's safe to stop. Sometimes you can only hide inside for so long."

Tala didn't know what to make of the Vallè princess' comment. She looked to the courtyard too, watching as Val-Draekin ran Glade through a quick series of exercises with sword and shield, both hammering at each other back and forth. Glade's armor glistened in the sun as he moved. Lawri, laughing, darted into the fray and poked him teasingly in the rump with a wooden practice blade, breaking his concentration. She jumped back as he whirled and swung his shield at her, irritated.

"Always be wary of the unexpected, Glade." Val-Draekin's voice rang with laughter. "Lawri just taught you a good lesson." He turned to Lindholf. "Your turn. And keep your concentration." Lindholf stepped up to Val-Draekin, sword and shield at the ready. As Glade backed away from Lindholf and the Vallè, Lawri did a quick curtsy, pointing her wooden sword at him, sticking out her tongue in mock defiance, laughing. Not able to stay mad at her long, Glade quickly joined in her laughter. And Lawri danced a mocking little jig, waving her wooden sword at him.

*How can they have so much fun, whilst I sit and brood?*

"See how joyful friendships can be?" Seita said.

*Joyful?* Tala's mood worsened. All she could see was Glade, blood-lust in his eyes, pulling a sharp blade across the throat of Sterling Prentiss. And then threatening to kill Lawri. Now the two in question capered about, banging wooden swords together in *joyful* mock combat. In days long past, she had felt a mysterious cloud of luxurious and heavenly air engulf her every time those dark, bold eyes of Glade's met hers. It made her sick now, knowing his true cruel nature. *Don't fall for his charms, Lawri!* her mind screamed as she watched her cousin spar with the boy.

Earlier, Tala had followed the wandering eyes of Glade and more than a handful of the Silver Guard as they'd made their way into the courtyard behind Lawri. They'd all stared at Lawri Le Graven. *Like every man stares at every pretty woman.* True, Lawri looked fetching in her tan riding breeches and blazing blue shirt with long billowy sleeves, the color the perfect complement to the blond hair cascading around her face. A full, healthy face that bloomed of roses, no longer sickly and pale.

Tala wore no frilly dress or corset herself; instead she wore something more befitting the courtyard and out-of-doors. She sported the same clothes she'd worn in the secret ways earlier—leggings, shirt, tunic, and a leather belt around her waist, the same small bejeweled dagger at her side. *Do the men all stare at me when I am not aware?*

She found that Seita was staring at her curiously, almost sadly. Then the Vallè princess looked quickly away.

"You can consider me your friend," Tala said, and without thought she touched Seita gently on the arm, letting her fingers linger. "After all, I shall always know how to disarm a knife-wielding attacker because of your lessons."

"My honor." Seita dipped her head in thanks, then touched the inner part of Tala's wrist. "Like I said, strike hard on the inside of the wrist here, just below the palm, then strike the back of the hand." Seita put pressure on both spots against Tala's hand and pushed. Tala recalled using the exact same maneuver to disarm the Bloodwood of a black dagger in the secret ways—a dagger she'd left near the cross-shaped altar in the red-hazed room buried deep in the castle.

"You can disarm the strongest of foes." Seita's grin was infectious.

Tala felt herself smiling back at the Vallè princess. They both watched Val-Draekin and Lindholf spar with the daggers. It took a moment for Tala to notice, but the Vallè princess had kept her hand gently in hers, their fingers entwined. A warm feeling engulfed Tala as she realized that since her parents had died, she had shared scarcely a moment of physical contact with anyone. She recalled the day she'd found both Seita and Val-Draekin teaching Lindholf how to become a pickpocket in Swensong Courtyard—how Val-Draekin had snatched her pouch right off her belt with just a brush of his body against hers. Both Vallè had taken a particular liking to her two cousins as of late.

Out on the practice field, Lindholf's hair flipped and flopped atop his freckled forehead. As always, it was a sweaty, mussed, corn-colored tangle. A strawlike patch of beard protruded from under his nose and burn-scarred chin. He sweated and strained as he tried to block the Vallè's attacks.

Val-Draekin always sparred with grace and poise and practiced ease, comparable to a member of the Vallè acrobat troupe, Val-Auh'Sua. His distinctive Vallè ears and fine features were similar to Seita's, but more chiseled. Tala remembered when he'd arrived in Amadon on his quest to find Breita, he'd come with his shoulder in a sling. But now he fought as if he'd never been hurt at all. Like all Vallè, he healed quickly.

"Enough!" A shout rang out through the courtyard, snapping Tala from her silent reverie. Lindholf and Val-Draekin ceased their sparring.

King Jovan Bronachell's smile was cold and terrible as he made his way from under the courtyard's main archway toward the group, his shoulder-length brown hair confined by a glittering silver band about his head—the royal crown. He wore his familiar black cloak trimmed in silver-wolf fur, a decorative ring-mail corselet of fine-worked silver under it. He carried no sword or dagger at his belt. His regular retinue of Dayknight guardsmen were nowhere to be seen. The Silver Guards who lined the battlements snapped to attention at his entry.

Jovan walked toward them with care, eyes boring into Tala's, face still sickly and pale—the physical remnant of the assassination attempt he'd survived not long ago. Still, despite his ponderous approach, her brother radiated power. When he stopped in front of her, the others all bowed before him. Tala did not.

Jovan cast her a shrewd look, then stepped past her toward Lindholf and Val-Draekin. The timbre of his voice was deep, commanding. "What manner of boneheaded Vallè swordsmanship are you poisoning these young men with?" He brusquely snatched the wooden practice sword from the Vallè. He whirled, sword in hand, letting his cool gaze rove over Tala and Lawri. "You *children* have tested my patience." His eyes tightened around the rims as he faced Lindholf and Glade next. "Bow again and pay proper homage to your king!"

Lindholf and Glade both dropped to one knee, not daring to look up.

"I ought to banish you both from this court," Jovan said.

Glade looked up, face morphing from scared and ashamed to angry.

"Oh, don't be upset." Jovan's laughter was mirthless. "We all know I can't banish either of you or your families. I need what fealty and armies your fathers have to give, lest the White Prince gain more ground in my lands." Then his face was instant cold fury. "But don't think I can't make everyone's life miserable!" he bellowed.

Tala's heart was galloping now. Her brother brandished Val-Draekin's wooden practice sword in front of her, swinging it violently up and around before her face three times. A chill, keening whistle sang through the courtyard at the wooden sword's swift passage. It came to within a hairsbreadth of her nose each time he swung it. She did not flinch.

"Please, Your Excellency." Lindholf stepped up beside Jovan. "You might accidentally hit her."

Jovan's eyes widened, sword now at his side. "You dare speak to your king without so much as a by-your-leave?" Lindholf blanched as Jovan glared at him. "Let me show you fools how to fight like men." The king tossed his fur-trimmed cloak to the ground. "I will teach you to fight stout and grim and powerful and proper. Like a real man ought. Like a real swordsman. Not like some prissy ballet-dancing Vallè dandy."

He headed for the center of the courtyard, beckoning the two young men. Pale-faced, they reluctantly did as ordered, wooden swords and shields in hand.

"Now!" Jovan shouted. "Attack me now, you sniveling twits!"

Glade swung first. Jovan easily ducked the swing and Glade pitched forward, tripping over his shield, stumbling completely out of the action. Jovan lunged and swung twice in rapid succession against Lindholf's upraised shield. Heavy blows. Lindholf fell to the ground, shield flying from his grasp. Glade was soon back on his feet and swinging at Jovan from behind. But the king whirled and blocked the strike. Glade swung wildly again. Tala's brother danced out of reach, and Glade was thrown off balance by his own momentum. Jovan attacked with a flurry of blows and soon Glade's sword and shield were lying in the grass.

"You're out!" Jovan shouted, and turned back to a petrified-looking Lindholf, who was just climbing to his feet, weapon dangling near useless at his side. The king struck only once and Lindholf's sword spun away. He folded to the ground in submission. "You're out too!" Jovan threw down his practice sword.

He turned his back on the two boys and sauntered toward Tala. She gathered her thoughts quickly. She figured he was trying to prove his quality to what Silver Guards watched from the battlements. Her brother wanted to confirm to all of Amadon that he could still fight and rule with authority and power. Prove that even though he still suffered some of the ill effects of the assassin's blade, he was showing he needed no Dayknight guards and acquiesced to no one.

Tala's gut leaped up into her throat as Jovan's hand lashed out and snatched the dagger from her belt. "This is *mine!*" he sneered, caressing the dagger in hand. "Weeks ago I demanded you dress like a lady. Still you disobey and dress like a man! It's unsightly, a sister of mine strutting about my castle in pants and tunic, daggers and such at her belt. I will not have you behaving like Jondralyn whilst in my castle! You will dress like a lady as I bade you do!"

He snatched his fur-trimmed cloak from the grass and threw it at her. "Cover yourself!" The cloak hit her in the chest and dropped unceremoniously back to the ground.

"I think those clothes look very pretty on her," Lawri said, her face turning instantly ashen against the bright blue of her shirt as she found the king's dark eyes were focused on her.

Jovan raised the jeweled dagger up between them. "I will have the next who speaks without my leave stripped and flogged bloody right here." His voice held grave warning as he stuffed the dagger into his own belt and turned back to Tala, prodding with his fingers at the sleeves of her shirt in disgust. He gripped the seam of her tunic atop her shoulder. "I've a mind to rip these rags right off you."

"Please, Your Excellency." Seita stepped forward, bowing. "If I may, your fair sister only dresses like this at my request. I'm afraid it was Val-Draekin and I who wanted to teach the youngsters swordsmanship here in the courtyard—"

"Silence!" the king shouted. Seita backed away.

"This is between me and my sister." Jovan grabbed Tala roughly by the chin, forcing her to face him directly. "As Laijon is my witness, you will submit to my will. You are a princess of Amadon and Gul Kana. The one you are meant to marry will not want you looking like a common street vendor." He let go her chin, gripped her tunic, and tore straight down.

Abruptly the courtyard seemed to lurch under Tala's feet as she twisted away, causing the left side of her tunic to rend and tear in his pawing hands. "Stop!" she croaked, frantically trying to defend herself. But his hands were a flurry of clawing fingers. Her shirt tore completely away from her arm and shoulder. Tala clutched what was left of it together, stumbling back, feet instantly tangled in her brother's discarded cloak. She fell backward to the ground, butt hitting hard.

Jovan came at her in a rage. She squirmed away, but he was on her quickly, snatching a fistful of her hair, dragging her through the cool grass of the courtyard toward the arched gate through which he'd entered. Tala's frenetic gaze flew to Glade and Lindholf. *Is there no help from anyone?* She desperately tried to hold her shirt closed so as not to expose herself. She struggled to stand, fighting back a frenzied scream. But her brother kept dragging her by the hair toward the archway, hollering, "You will do as I bade you do!"

The pain jolting through her scalp was soon unbearable. "Help!" she called out. Yet nobody moved to stop him. They just stared.

Tala abandoned trying to cover herself with what remained of her shirt and grabbed frantically at her brother's wrists, his arms, anything to gain purchase, anything to stave off the pain, anything to stop him from yanking out her hair. "Let me up!" she shrieked. But Jovan dragged her from the courtyard, dragged her under the archway, down a dark corridor, and into a dim recess. "Let me up!" she shouted. "You bastard!"

He finally let go her hair and hauled her to her feet. "You will do as I bade you do!" He slammed her against the stone wall. Face-to-face he screamed at her, "I told you to never—"

And then Lawri Le Graven was there, throwing Jovan's fur-trimmed cloak madly at him. "Leave her alone!" she roared. The cloak struck the king in the face with a heavy, fluttering *thwap!* He swiped it to the floor.

Anger, lethal and calculated, hardened on his face. "You dare assault your—"

Lawri slapped him in the face, fingernails slashing. She struck again and again.

"Laijon almighty!" Jovan fought her off. "What's gotten into you!" He shoved her away. "Crazy bitch!" He dabbed at the blood on his face with trembling fingers.

"Don't touch Tala!" Lawri's deep-throated shout thundered down the corridor.

Jovan took a faltering step backward as Lawri lunged at him again, both of her hands tugging at the jeweled dagger at his belt. They struggled together a moment before she pulled it free, brandishing the blade before him in her right hand. Her crazed eyes were ablaze.

"Rotted angels!" The king backed away. "Insane fucking girl."

Lawri's lips curled in a ferocious grimace. And in the gloom of the niche, the emerald flecks in her angry eyes glowed. Jovan lunged toward her, seizing her by the wrist, wrenching it sharply as they both tumbled to the floor, struggling. Lawri lurched to her feet with a shout, clutching her left forearm, blood pouring from between the fingers of her right hand, soaking through the billowy sleeve of her blue shirt.

Crying, Lawri peeled back the sleeve exposing the wound. The dagger had dug a slick trench from the bottom of her wrist almost to the underside of her elbow, the flesh flayed wide. Jovan stood, dagger slipping from his grip and clattering to the stone floor. He did the three-fingered sign of the Laijon Cross over his heart, his eyes bouncing from Lawri to Tala and back, horrified. "Bloody Mother Mia, you deserve worse than that, you foolish bitch," he rasped. "You'll be lucky I don't soon hang you!"

Lawri tilted her head, eyes in a daze. She licked the dark stream of blood pumping from her gaping wound. Jovan's eyes widened in horror. "Crazy fucking cunt," he said, then whirled and ran down the corridor into the darkness.

Lawri stood half in the alcove, half in the passageway, staring at the blood draining from her arm, blood that was streaked with thin strands of glowing green.

"Let's get you to the infirmary." Tala's voice shook with emotion.

"No!" Lawri screeched. "I don't want anyone to know!" She also whirled and sprinted down the bleak corridor, but in the opposite direction of Jovan, leaving a trail of blood in her wake.

Numb, Tala crumpled to the floor and wrapped herself in her brother's forgotten cloak. She felt no anger. Felt no confusion. She was just bone weary and full of pain.

*And some worshipped the beasts of the underworld. For they had given their power and authority to the beasts, saying, "Who unto us is like the beasts, and who can fight against them?"*
—THE WAY AND TRUTH OF LAIJON

# CHAPTER FOUR

# NAIL

7TH DAY OF THE ETHIC MOON, 999TH YEAR OF LAIJON

SOUTH OF LOKKENFELL, GUL KANA

Where do you think he's from, Llewellyn?"
"Beats the rotted dogshite outa me," the young, shaggy-haired blond with a bow answered, raising the blue-fletched arrow to his chin, aiming its steel tip at Nail, pulling the bowstring taut. *The outlaw is just a boy, no older than me.* Nail flicked the hair from his eyes but otherwise remained still, the arrow now centered on his chest. Beer Mug barked.

The second outlaw turned his bow on the dog, saying, "Wherever he's from, he's got a nice horse and pony, don't he?"

"Aye, Clive. That's for sure." Llewellyn's arrow stayed fixed on Nail's chest.

"But I reckon they're ours now," the ruffian named Clive said. He was tall and bearded and cast a covetous eye toward Nail's pony,

Dusty, and Hawkwood's stout roan. Nail gripped the reins of both. He didn't want to give up the two mounts. They had borne him this far and, aside from Beer Mug, had been his only companions since Ravenker. But all he had for defense were a few small daggers he'd found in Hawkwood's saddlebag, plus a bottle or two of healing poultices he could possibly throw like rocks.

The morning mist had melted from above the grassy fields and the sun burned a little warmer here. A small wind rippled across the western plain and bore the rich perfume of morning peat; the scent of wood smoke drifted on that wind too, and with it the smell of cooking food. The aroma reminded Nail of the crushing hunger he'd been stricken with for days. On their journey, his two mounts and Beer Mug had seemed to scrounge stuff off the ground aplenty. The dog ate anything he found—he was like Liz Hen that way. They'd traveled through mostly dewy fields budded with new spring heather, drinking from cool streams trickling down from the Autumn Range. Wild blueberries had been thick along their trail, but early in season and sour.

High clouds scudded overhead, moving toward the Autumn Range, which rose up like a line of claws behind him—menacing, unforgiving claws with sharp shadows that raked down on him with shame. *Everyone in Gallows Haven dead because of me.* After ten days of hard travel north out of Ravenker, starving, lost, and alone, two arrows now poised at his chest, Nail felt that final bitter flavor of defeat.

Two more outlaws rounded the hedgerow below, a cloaked man with a sword and a thin, red-haired woman in a green tunic and leggings, a longbow and quiver of white arrows with blue-feathered shafts strapped to her back.

"Praed, look what we found." Llewellyn addressed the cloaked man. "A deserter, I reckon."

Clive added, "A worthless bloodsucking oghul leading two stolen mounts."

"They belong to me." Nail took a slow step backward up the hill. Hawkwood's horse and Dusty shuffled back with him. Beer Mug barked again.

"Git that mutt to shut his yapper," Praed ordered Nail. "Or I'll have Judi here plug the thing full of arrows." The woman stepped forward, her own bow at the ready now, arrow tip wavering between Nail and Beer Mug, settling on the dog.

"Please don't shoot him," Nail pleaded.

"Do you know who we are?" Praed asked. He was a tall and lanky fellow with a thin-featured face that might have been considered handsome except for the crooked teeth and angular nose. It was a face fraught with menace. He also had hollow eyes buried deep in their sockets. Strands of dark hair hung loose from the cowl over his head. He looked like one of the scarecrows farmer Wetherby kept in his cornfields south of Gallows Haven. He also seemed to be the leader of the group.

"Just don't kill my dog," Nail said. He couldn't bear losing Beer Mug. Zane's shepherd dog had padded silently next to him the entire way from Ravenker, curled against him for warmth at night, both of them sleeping in undisturbed haystacks and the like. The horse and pony had been solid but quiet company too. Nail had ridden Hawkwood's horse at a brisk pace, making good time northward, seldom stopping. He'd hoped to come across Roguemoore and Godwyn and the rest. He couldn't recall the name of the Lord's Point inn that was to be their rendezvous.

Beer Mug continued to bark. The woman drew her bowstring taut. "All you gotta do is nod, Praed, and I shoot the mutt."

"Just let us pass." Nail stepped between the lady and the dog. Beer Mug stopped his barking, hackles still raised.

"He says let him pass," Llewellyn chuckled. "You can't just cross our fields without permission from Master Praed."

"I just want to be about my own business." Nail's narrowed gaze scanned the western horizon beyond the four dour-faced outlaws. They were standing near the bottom of a slightly sloping hill. Nail held the higher ground. A small advantage if it came to a fight. But without a weapon of his own, it really didn't matter. A hedgerow and a gray stone fence mottled by rich moss and lichen ran straight up the small hill just to the north. There were many farms to the west. Beyond all the farms lay what he assumed was Lord's Point, barely visible in the far distance, twenty miles away at least, a vast expanse of walls and buildings—the biggest town Nail had ever seen. A town he would likely now never reach.

"What's that injury on your neck, boy?" Praed asked.

Nail's hand unwittingly traveled to the still-aching wound swelling around his neck from where the Bloodwood had tried to strangle him.

"Naught but a deserter," Llewellyn drawled. "Probably scars from the hangman's noose he done escaped from."

"Aye, a deserter." The one named Clive continued the line of thought. "From one of the towns about to be sacked by the White Prince. He's done run off. Like a coward."

"Is that what you are, boy?" Praed asked. "A deserter?"

"Be worth more to us if we turned him over to Lord Kronnin," Judi said, her arrow still pointed at Beer Mug. "Let Kronnin hang him."

Praed pushed back the hood of his cloak and drew a shortsword from his belt. "Give the horse and pony over and we won't truss you up and haul you to Lord Kronnin for a hanging. Easy as that."

Anger rose up inside Nail. *If I only had the battle-ax! If only I had Forgetting Moon!* He could imagine the gleaming weapon in his hands, the way it felt, comfortable, like it had always belonged with him. The sky pressed down. The wind picked up, striking his face. The push of air reminded him he was alive and still strong and not the type who gave in so easily. He thought of the daggers in Hawkwood's saddlebag, wondered if he could grab the knives quick enough.

"Don't do it." The leader of the outlaws advanced, sword ready.

"Whatever you're scheming in your mind, don't do it. I'll kill ya before you take two steps. Just like I'll kill ya before I let you walk off with that horse and pony."

Beer Mug barked again. Dusty nickered and backed up the hill, dragging Nail, who still held her reins, with her. Hawkwood's roan let out a nervous snort.

Then all the bows were lowered as each of the outlaws cast an eye up the sloping hill behind Nail. When Nail turned, he didn't know whether to feel relief or more fear. On the hill above was a tall gray palfrey, lightly armored. A formidable-looking knight in black-lacquered armor sat atop it, face hidden under a daunting helm.

"A Dayknight," Judi hissed.

The palfrey, nimble and precise in its step, cantered down the green hill toward them, the magnificent-looking Dayknight seeming to soar in the saddle as he reined his mount up beside Nail. With two black-gauntleted hands, the knight reached up and removed his black helm, revealing a familiar stern face and dark blue eyes.

*Culpa Barra!* Nail immediately recognized the blond-haired knight: Shawcroft's friend from Deadwood Gate, the knight he had last seen in Ravenker.

"Nail." Culpa nodded, placing the helm on his saddle horn with a natural nonchalance. "Well met again." His eyes then turned to the four thieves. "Are you pestering my squire?" A haughty but fierce grin formed at the corners of his mouth. The outlaws were silent. The only sound came from a handful of crows milling near the hedgerow and a few goats bleating in the distance. "I said, are you pestering my squire?" Culpa repeated crisply.

"This boy is your squire?" Praed asked.

"Who are you to question a Dayknight?" Culpa gave the man a fearful squint. "And before you answer, be mindful, thief, there are more Dayknights like me coming up the ridgeline. You don't want to start something that will get yourself killed."

"He's lyin'," Clive said. "He's alone, Praed. Let's take him."

"Praed?" Culpa's left eyebrow rose. He dismounted with authority, his face distinguished by real anger now. "I know who you are. And you know me." Ignoring the arrows now pointed his way, Culpa marched straight down the hill toward Llewellyn and slapped the bow and arrow from the young fellow's grip. He snatched the bows from Clive and Judi, too, tossing them to the ground. He then faced the leader of the outlaws. "You were smart in not ordering them to shoot, Praed. I would have killed you all."

"Let's go," Praed ordered the other three. "This is Tatum Barra's son, and a fight with Tatum's son is a fight the Untamed doesn't need."

Llewellyn, Clive, and Judi picked up their bows. With a nod from Praed, all four thieves made their way down the hill and around the hedgerow and disappeared.

And just like that the threat was over.

Nail met Culpa's eyes, familiar eyes that he'd never imagined seeing again. Before Shawcroft and Nail had moved to Gallows Haven, Culpa had worked the mines north of Deadwood Gate with them. Nail recalled the sleek longsword a much younger Culpa had worn in those days, and how his master continually admired it. Now Culpa carried a Dayknight sword, same as Shawcroft's. And the black armor he wore was a glorious sight. Shawcroft would certainly be proud of how Culpa had turned out. Nail had always speculated that Culpa was Shawcroft's son. He'd heard them share stories and laughter together at Deadwood Gate. *But Shawcroft never did laugh around me, and the only stories he told were naught but cruel lessons.*

"You're hurt," Culpa observed. "Your neck there. Did those outlaws strike you?"

Nail turned away, partly in defiance, partly in shame, dipping his chin, trying to hide the scar that circled his neck—the scar left by the Bloodwood's thin rope.

Culpa approached. "Could be it's infected."

Nail backed away. Bleary-eyed and hungry, he couldn't rightly concentrate. "Have you anything to eat?"

"You know who I am, don't you?" Culpa asked. "You remember me?"

Nail nodded, eyes hazing over. The confrontation with the four outlaws had dulled his senses. The light-headedness was increasing and he stumbled back into Dusty, clutching at the old saddle atop her, almost crumpling to his knees.

"Whoa." Culpa grabbed him by the arm. "Easy."

Nail shrugged him off crisply. Stood straight. "Do you have food?"

Culpa retreated to his saddlebags, hauled out a wineskin, a heel of bread, and a strip of jerky, and handed the food to Nail. "This is farm country, but folks are restless with the advance of Aeros' army. Thieves are becoming more brazen, preying on folks fleeing the south. Folks like you, with ponies and horses to steal. You just crossed paths with the Untamed, four of the most notorious outlaws in all the Five Isles. Don't be fooled by their lackadaisical manner. The Untamed use their names as much as possible whilst talking. They want to be known and remembered by all they rob. Praed left me alone only in deference to my father. They go way back. We were lucky today."

Nail tore into the bread, drank of the wineskin. Beer Mug sniffed at his hand holding the jerky. Dusty nickered behind him. Culpa ran a gloved hand along the neck of Hawkwood's horse as if checking it for injury. "You can trust me, Nail. We are the truest of friends. The Turn Key Saloon? That is where you are headed, correct?"

Nail remained silent under Culpa's cold scrutiny, chewing the jerky. "It's a stout steed you have there," Culpa said of Hawkwood's roan. He hauled himself up atop his own palfrey. "I'm sure Roguemoore is worried about you. Mount up. We shall journey to Lord's Point together."

With the food settling into his empty stomach, Nail was feeling instantly more alert. But with every word the knight spoke, he was purposefully shrinking back into himself, becoming closed off. *He knows the rendezvous point. The Turn Key Saloon.*

Culpa said, "I just traveled with Hawkwood for many days, Nail. He was sorely injured, though he did not say how. He did claim Shawcroft was dead. Is this true?"

Nail's eyes did not waver from the knight. "Shawcroft was killed when Gallows Haven was sacked." He took another long drink of the wineskin.

"That is distressing news." Culpa's face was briefly drawn in grief. He straightened in his saddle. "But the question is, are you okay, Nail?"

"Did you follow me?" he asked.

"Hawkwood wanted me to find you," Culpa answered, casting his gaze about nervously. "It's best we make it to Lord's Point before dark."

*Again Hawkwood watches after me.* He owed the man. Though these last many days had been imbued with much loneliness and hardship and hunger, Nail *had* been free—free to wander wherever he wished at whatever pace he desired. But the loneliness could be crushing. He missed his friends Stefan and Dokie, the only links to his previous life. But with that thought came the crushing realization that he was to blame for the destruction of Gallows Haven and the death of so many. *Yup. Everyone in Gallows Haven gone because of me.* Just the no-good son of Cassietta Raybourne and Aevrett Raijael.

He was so confused. "I will make my own way," he said, eyes of stone fixed on the knight in black-lacquered armor astride the gray palfrey.

"And where will you go?" Culpa moved his horse forward. "We are at war. You will be hung as a deserter by some baron or lord if you cannot prove who you are or where you are from. You will become naught but a thief or a beggar or an outlaw like Praed. That is the way of things. You are fortunate to have made it this far on your own. At least with me you will have someone to speak in your behalf. The word of a Dayknight is law in Gul Kana. Some titles and lineage hold power."

Culpa was right. Damnably right. Titles and lineage did hold power, more power than he could ever possess. *But can I trust this man?* He recalled long ago in Deadwood Gate how Culpa had taught him of the stars, taught him of the Warrior Angels ascended into heaven with Laijon. He had recounted the details to Ava Shay on the beach the night of the Mourning Moon Feast. But her reaction had been one of disgust. And later that night she had confessed her love for Jenko Bruk. A hollow pang of regret followed that thought. Ava had hurt him. Abandoning her was his only way of striking back at that hurt. But he knew that one petty revenge of his would weigh on his soul the rest of his life. *And Jenko Bruk in the enemy armor of Sør Sevier?* In Ravenker, Jenko had wanted to kill him. Like everything else, it just didn't seem real.

Yes, his mind was flooded with conflicting thoughts. Confusion. He took a long swig from the wineskin and handed it back to the Dayknight. He wiped his mouth with the sleeve of his rough-spun shirt, then hauled himself up onto Hawkwood's horse. With a click of his heels, he turned the mount toward Lord's Point and proceeded that way at a leisurely pace, Beer Mug at his heels, the piebald pony, Dusty, following too.

Culpa Barra galloped up next to him. "I wasn't going to force you, Nail. But you made the right decision."

† † † † †

As afternoon had worn into evening, the sunset above Lord's Point was reddish and murky. Wood smoke hung in streams stretching sky-ward from countless crooked chimneys. After Amadon, Lord's Point was the next largest city in Gul Kana, and the biggest place Nail had ever been. The road to Lord's Point had consisted of a vast expanse of outlying farms and small hamlets stretching between Devlin, Lokkenfell, and the Autumn Range.

They entered Lord's Point under the towering gate of the city's outer ring. Once beyond the outer wall, they traveled among broad avenues and porticoes, past a dizzying maze of winding side streets and alleys. Fountains and statues seemed to line every square and corner. Ragged children skittered along dirt paths and cobbled streets teeming with beggars, peasants, and shopkeepers. There were so many people. Everywhere. Closer to the city's center, the flying buttresses of a cathedral ten times the size of the chapel in Gallows Haven climbed skyward. Beyond the cathedral, the towering inner wall along with Lord's Point Castle rose up alongside the sea, towers and spires and battlements looming and dark against the sunset.

Nail wondered how Aeros Raijael's army could attack a place so grand and large and full of people. But somehow he knew the White Prince would. With utmost savagery he would. Lord's Point would be destroyed. But the people here showed none of the panic that had seized all those fleeing the southlands. It seemed these city dwellers were helpless in their ignorance. They had no idea of the horrendous violence and slaughter that was coming for them.

As Nail and Culpa wended their way toward the dock district, things grew crammed and stifling. Taller buildings crowded the pathways, and the shadowy streets between were interspersed with the occasional green-leafed garden of ivy and flowers. As they neared the docks, the space between the buildings opened up some and Nail could see the flat blue ocean beyond. The Fortress of Saint Only rose up on the far horizon. And through the heavy ocean air, Nail could just make out the cloudy vision of Wyn Darrè and the thin, soaring slivers of the five Laijon Towers, barely visible in the haze. Rumor was, the view from Lord's Point of both Adin Wyte and Wyn Darrè was one of the most magnificent in all the Five Isles. And now that he was seeing it, he believed it.

"The Turn Key Saloon," Culpa Barra said, dismounting, hitching his palfrey to a rail.

The Dayknight stood before the most grim-looking storefront facade Nail had ever seen. The door was rotted gray wood. It was closed. And what should have been shuttered windows on either side seemed to be just boarded-up holes. A rusted tin sign clanked in the breeze above, hanging crooked from an equally rusted pole that leaned precariously out over the roadway. The sign read THE TURN KEY INN & SALOON. In smaller lettering underneath was stamped A DRINKING ESTABLISHMENT FOSTERING AN ENVIRONMENT OF LAW-ABIDING CITIZENRY AND NON-CRIMINALITY.

"Stay with the horses," the Dayknight said, and marched up the tattered wood porch. He pushed the rotted door open and disappeared into the gloom of the place.

Hawkwood's horse nickered and shuffled sideways as a dirty crabman pulling a wobbly handcart topped with red crabs rattled by. Nail soothed the horse with a calm hand and thought back on the day's journey with the Dayknight. Their conversations had been brief, mostly consisting of Culpa's questions about Shawcroft's death and what Nail and Hawkwood had been doing in Ravenker that had led to Hawkwood's capture. Nail had told him everything—everything but for the fact that he had lost *Forgetting Moon* to Jenko Bruk, letting Culpa just assume the battle-ax and angel stone were in the possession of Godwyn and Roguemoore.

When Culpa stepped back out onto the Turn Key's porch, Nail was surprised to see Liz Hen Neville there with him. Wearing a heavy, rough-spun cloak, she was still fat and round as a church bell. Beer Mug barked and practically leaped straight up into her arms. "Oh, my big sweetie!" she blubbered, kissing the dog on the face and snout. Beer Mug's tail was wagging.

"Seems like they arrived earlier today, just before us." Culpa unhitched his palfrey. "Godwyn sent the girl to help us with the horses. There's a stable in back."

"Where's Stefan?" Nail asked Liz Hen. "Where's Dokie?"

"The dwarf sent them and Otto to ready the stable." The red-haired girl looked Nail up and down with scorn. Her eyes traveled over Dusty and Hawkwood's horse next. Her brows crumpled questioningly. "Where's the ax?"

Fatigue suddenly lay like a smoldering blanket of distress over Nail's body and mind. He couldn't muster up the will to even answer the question.

"Don't tell me you lost it already," Liz Hen said.

*It was stolen from me!* Nail couldn't admit to his failure out loud. Culpa Barra was eyeing him, brow creased.

"Such a useless bastard." Liz Hen glared at him smugly. "Losing the very battle-ax that was so important to our friends. You and that ax have been all the bishop and the dwarf could talk about; waiting for Nail, worrying about Nail, hoping Nail will soon show up with that ax in tow. And now look at you, Nail. You've done lost it."

"And why would you care?" Nail shot back. "You never thought it was real, Liz Hen. You never believed in it anyway."

Liz Hen shook her head in disgust. "Well, I wouldn'ta lost the thing." Her eyes roamed the street. "Where's Hawkwood? Don't tell me you lost him, too?" She punched him in the shoulder hard.

Hugh Godwyn and Roguemoore stepped from the saloon. The bishop was still wearing his knee-high boots, dark leather breeches, and green woolen shirt, elk hide sewn at the elbows. His scraggly mane of gray hair fluttered in the breeze. The dwarf looked as gruff and serious as always.

"Nail lost the ax," Liz Hen announced. "And Hawkwood, too. Also the blue stone, I'd reckon."

"What of the satchel?" Godwyn's eyes flew to the saddlebags tied to Dusty. "Have you lost Shawcroft's satchel, too?"

"It was stolen from me," Nail answered. "Stolen by Jenko Bruk!"

"Jenko Bruk?" Liz Hen scoffed. "Now you're talking nonsense."

Roguemoore's face fell. Godwyn grabbed Nail by the shoulders, eyes flaring with distress. "In that satchel was a parchment. Hidden. Is it gone too?"

"I suppose so," Nail answered brusquely. "Jenko took the entire satchel."

The bishop's face fell at the news. As did the dwarf's. Despair and loneliness fell over Nail like twin blankets, smothering and dreary. *They aren't even glad to see me alive, just worried about some stupid slip of paper Shawcroft wrote some stupid words on.* Words that were seared into his mind.

*The boy now bears the mark of the cross, the mark of the slave, and the mark of the beast. He has bathed in scarlet, bathed in blood.*

*The Way and Truth of Laijon is eleven books as scribed: the Early Books of Prophecy, Book of the Great Hunts, Book of the Slave, Book of the Cross, Book of the Beasts, Book of the Atonement Tree, Ember Lighting Song of the Third Warrior Angel, Acts of the Second Warrior Angel, Revelations of the Fourth Warrior Angel, Song of the Stones, and the Soulless Lament. Other than these, there shall be no other gospels forever and ever, amen.*
—THE WAY AND TRUTH OF LAIJON

# CHAPTER FIVE

# AVA SHAY

### 7TH DAY OF THE ETHIC MOON, 999TH YEAR OF LAIJON
### BEDFORD, GUL KANA

A sun-warmed breeze bled over the Sør Sevier encampment just north of Bedford Bay, rippling Ava Shay's simple woolen shift around her legs. Blinking through milky, inebriated eyes, she gazed out at the blue horizon heaped with soft white clouds. She'd been spending her days drunk on Aeros' stash of strong wines, always imbibing just enough to drown the howling emptiness within her soul.

She stood on weak knees under the shade of the towering Sør Sevier Knight Archaic Hammerfiss. He loomed over her like a bearded oak, a straw of willow reed jutting from his mouth, gleaming battle armor adding to his bulk. His features were hard-lined and pale beneath the blue tattoos spanning his face. The small bones and fetishes tied in the tangled mass of his hair and red beard twinkled in the sun and wind.

At least a hundred Sør Sevier knights were gathered behind Ava and Hammerfiss. In front of them, silhouetted against the bright sky on the grassy slope above the beachhead, was Enna Spades. The red-haired warrior woman sparred with Jenko Bruk and the Wyn Darrè, Mancellor Allen. Both Mancellor and Jenko were shirtless, their heavily muscled torsos glistening with sweat as they struggled to keep Spades at bay. But the Sør Sevier woman, with her whirling broadsword and impeccable footwork, was making the two young men look like bumbling fools. She wore leather riding pants and a white undershirt and broke no sweat, despite sparring with unbridled fury. A gauntlet of tall wooden posts had been pounded into the dirt, creating random obstacles for the combatants. The pine posts didn't bother Spades. Ava had never imagined a woman could look so deadly. She was a nightmare. *Everything is a nightmare! If Jenko and I could just go back to Gallows Haven and pretend none of this ever happened . . .*

But Ava knew those dreams had crumbled to ashes many days past. And without the numbing spirits that coursed through her veins, the constant pool of bitterness that boiled in her heart just might destroy her. She wished she could retreat into her little wood carvings again. Like she used to do with Nail, him sitting beside her with his charcoal and parchment, her whittling turtles and fish. Some of the only true and peaceful moments of her life. Ava recalled the first wood carving she'd ever done, how proud she'd been of it—a small fish with little scales. She remembered how she'd shown it to her younger sister, five-year-old Ashi. She could still recall Ashi's curious eyes staring at the carving in wonder as she'd remarked, "It's so fine, I could just look at it all day." But Ashi was now dead, along with Agnes, Aja, and little Aikin. *Best not to think of them. Or the joy I took in my art.* They were long-lost moments, memories locked away into that small corner of her soul where she scarcely ever ventured. The slave brand burned on the underside of her wrist was grim confirmation of her current dream-deficient existence.

"Why even bother sparring?" Hammerfiss asked of no one in particular. He plucked the willow reed from his mouth. "I doubt there will even be another battle. This piss-bucket town was already emptied out when we got here. Just like Ravenker and all the other little shit-hole hamlets and farms in between. No fight in 'em at all." The burly man looked down at Ava as if it were all her fault. "Gul Kana, what a joke."

But Ava, submersed in her own thoughts, scarcely cared. Other than the spirits she drank, she knew of no other way to suture her soul against the wraiths and heal the burning scars they left. *If I could just go back to Gallows Haven . . .*

"Have ya not even been listening to me, lassie?" Hammerfiss grumbled, tossing the reed to the ground. "They've all fled. Like scared rabbits. I need a real fight to get my blood pumping again. A great bloody battle." He nodded toward Spades, Jenko, and Mancellor. "None of this pointless sparring."

What he said was true, about there being no real battles. The southern coast of Gul Kana had emptied in the advance of the growing armies of the White Prince. They were smart to flee. Ava's own vivid memories of the destruction of Gallows Haven were as fierce and inexorable in their aggressiveness as the actual siege had been. And Aeros' army had moved fast up the coastline toward Lord's Point, nobody to stop them. It was an army encampment that had grown as big as ten villages crammed together. At night these brutish fighters could assemble their camp—Aeros' tent and all its accoutrements included—with a clean efficiency that was a sight to behold, and come morning, disassemble it just as smoothly. Ever since leaving Ravenker a smoking ruin, Aeros had kept Ava under even tighter scrutiny, letting her out of the tent only when the army was on the move, forcing her to ride in a covered wagon with the injured Bloodwood as her travel mate. And that was a whole other bit of weirdness in itself.

Spiderwood lived. Barely.

In Ravenker, after Mancellor and Jenko had gifted Aeros with the battle-ax and blue angel stone, they awaited return of the Spider with Nail. But Spiderwood never returned. Aeros had sent them back out to locate the Bloodwood. Mancellor and Jenko had found the Spider near death in a pool of his own blood in the exact spot they'd last seen him, his Bloodeye horse standing guard, and Nail long gone. Ava wondered if it had been the bald knight, Gault, who'd fought the Bloodwood and left him for dead. She hoped so. After all, it was she who had informed him of Aeros' and the Spider's betrayal. The bald knight had seemed so lonely. It was why she had befriended him. She knew what loneliness felt like. She hoped Gault had escaped. *And I wish I could have gone with him. . . .*

"Hammerfiss!" Spades shouted.

Ava was yanked out of her musings by the crunch of stone and sunbaked grass as the warrior woman approached, sword in hand. A froth of red curls framed her face and spilled over her shoulders. Her skin bore a scatter of freckles under large green eyes and high cheekbones. "Aeros need help with that useless Bloodwood," she addressed Hammerfiss. "He's coherent enough now. His time has come."

"My honor." Hammerfiss smiled. It wasn't a pretty smile. He had large yellow teeth that made him look like a crazed child. He expelled a grand gust of laughter before saying, "It's about time the Spider was meted out his punishment."

"Indeed." Spades' voice was bereft of emotion as she watched the big man saunter away toward Aeros' tent. She pulled forth a coin and flipped it in the air, catching it deftly, naturally, flipping it again, as if it was just part of who she was and always would be—a woman with a sword in one hand, coin in the other.

Ava tried her best to ignore Spades, looking instead toward Mancellor and Jenko still banging swords. Of the two young men, Jenko Bruk was slightly thicker and stronger. He was also swaggering and confident with a sword in hand, arms stacked with muscle.

He had amber eyes and tousled brown hair that fell in sweaty waves to just above his shoulders. Mancellor Allen was no slouch, tall and rangy with braided rows of russet-colored hair. He bore Wyn Darrè fighting tattoos under both eyes. All things considered, Jenko and Mancellor were evenly matched.

"Like a shaft of iron, your Jenko," Spades said. She tilted her head and eyed Ava Shay up and down casually, her glance mischievous. "I've never seen cock swell so hard and so fast. His eagerness knows no bounds."

Ava did not want to dignify the woman with any response or utterance at all, but couldn't help but notice the woman's every move out of the corner of her eye.

"I presume you already know of what I speak," Spades carried on, coin now dancing between her fingers, the faintest hint of a smile at the corners of her mouth. "I'm sure you've also had your pouty little lips wrapped around his staff."

Ava remained silent, letting the White Prince's wine cloud her mind, glad she was drunk.

"How does our Lord Aeros measure up in that regard?"

Lightning-hot pain seemed to lash through Ava's entire soul. She clamped up even tighter than before. *I'd rather be dead than spend one more moment with these vile people.* She forced her eyes forward, trying to concentrate on the sparring boys on the grassy, windswept hill.

"Well." There was a hint of laughter in Spades' voice. "Clearly you are taking this conversation more seriously than I. But I really wish to know, what do you make of our Lord Aeros' heavenly sessions?"

"He rapes me." The words spilled forth as her glance darted toward Spades.

It was faint, nearly indiscernible, but the woman's eyes seemed to widen slightly at the rushed frankness of Ava's remark. The coin no longer danced in her hand. Her other hand gripped the sword tight. "Be honored that our Lord Aeros has chosen you."

"Honored?" The word tasted sour on her own lips. She wanted to puke, the wine no longer sitting so comfortably in her gut.

Spades lifted her sword, the tip of the blade right in front of Ava. "This is what sets us apart from the women of Gul Kana." The woman had ice in her voice, a flicker of something like pain behind her gaze. "Makes us not so concerned about our man and his cock or his sexual habits or infidelities. Makes us not so concerned about rutting of any kind. Nothing is so precious when you've a sharp blade in your hand and know how to wield it. When you can kill as efficiently as a man, that is *strength*. When nobody can defeat you with a blade, that is *power*. There is no more dangerous force in the Five Isles than a woman with a sword. Or a woman willing to use her own mind. Or a woman ready to do whatever she damn well pleases."

Spades' unblinkingly eyes pierced Ava over the edge of the blade as she continued. "Why do you think your quorum of five and grand vicar in Amadon keep the women out of their priesthood? Why do they forbid the women to speak of their Ember Gathering? Why have your kings throughout history not allowed swords in the hands of their girls?" She let the blade dip below her waist.

Ava felt like she was being examined and shifted uncomfortably. *Does she think I can actually answer that?* Spades had a gaze that could chill her soul from a mile away. And everyone knew the Ember Gathering was too sacred to speak of. Still, after a few breaths, Ava did answer. "Only men are strong and brave enough to fight."

Spades' eyes widened again, but in mocking way. Then she winked. "I will teach you to think different." She held the sword out, hilt first, as if expecting Ava to take it.

But Ava stepped back, apprehension carving a hole in her chest. Spades rammed the sword into the ground between them, her face suddenly formed into a cold mask. She turned her back to Ava, posture stiff as she folded her arms. The long blade stayed quivering in the dirt between them.

"Forward! Forward with your feet!" Spades shouted at Jenko, who appeared to be backing Mancellor down with his own swift sword, the Wyn Darrè fighter using one of the random poles as cover.

Ava stared at Spades' unprotected back, her eyes slowly drifting to the sword jammed in the dirt, wishing to take it up. *But I haven't even the strength or bravery for that....*

† † † † †

Aeros Raijael approached. Hammerfiss was with him, a coiled whip with a barbed tip in hand. Between them they dragged the Bloodwood, barely able to keep his feet, dressed in naught but a simple pair of rough-spun tan pants and a loose-fitting black shirt. The bandages had been removed from the Spider's head; one side of his face and jaw was purple and swollen under his close-cropped black hair.

The Bloodwood had been Ava's travel companion, riding with her in the covered wagon that had borne them both north with the armies of the White Prince. He had remained unconscious the bulk of the time, recovering from the head wound. Aeros had placed her in charge of cleaning the wound daily, deeming her the Bloodwood's "healer." This task she abhorred. The Spider's Bloodeye stallion, Scowl, had made the trip too, tied behind the wagon, its fiery-red eyes always seemingly fixed on Ava whenever she looked its way, as if the beast wanted to devour her. The black steed seemed spawned of the underworld—a demon-eyed phantom bred of sorcery.

Aeros Raijael commanded the attention of all as he drew up beside Jenko and Mancellor and the gauntlet of poles and both he and Hammerfiss let the Spider slide to the ground. Like a marble sculpture, the White Prince's bearing was always beautiful, even whilst dragging a limp Bloodwood. Under his white cloak he wore pearl-colored chain-mail armor, glistening and smooth, knee-high black boots with iron-studded toes, and fitted brown leather leggings.

His shimmering blond hair hung unbound to his shoulders in lank white waves. His skin was always pale, bloodless and hollow. It was always his empty eyes that captured Ava in their dark embrace, pupils naught but twin circles of moldering blackness.

"Another one of my Knights Archaic has failed me." Aeros spoke loud enough for the hundred gathered around to hear. Hammerfiss latched on to the Spider's shirt with his free hand and roughly yanked the Bloodwood back up for all to see. The Spider's normally red-shot eyes appeared foggy, narrow brows not quite as sharp as before, that vaporous icy confidence no longer present in him.

"Like Stabler before him," Aeros continued, "Spiderwood set out on a mission at my command and fell woefully short in his duty. He had the boy, Nail, within his grasp and allowed him to escape. And he lost my sword, Sky Reaver. Now that he has regained some coherency of thought, he will be allowed to make right his wrongs and answer for his failures."

"What have you to say for yourself, sneak thief?" Hammerfiss growled, shaking the Bloodwood, seeming to take great pleasure in the man's suffering.

The Spider didn't even look up as he answered. "'Twas by happenstance I came upon Nail. 'Twas by happenstance the boy escaped. I bear no blame."

"That is a feeble defense for a feeble man." Hammerfiss smiled.

"You would have me slay you now?" Aeros said, venom in his voice. "I thought more of you. I thought more of Black Dugal's Caste."

"You've already deemed me guilty," the Spider responded, not meeting the eyes of the White Prince. "I submit to whatever you wish."

"I desire that you invoke the Chivalric Rule of Blood Penance," Aeros ordered.

"As you wish."

Ava had been on the beachhead in Tomkin Sty when the knight, Stabler, had returned, also having failed to capture Nail. Stabler had invoked the Rule of Blood Penance. He'd chosen a duel to the death over a flogging to atone for his failure. Gault had been selected by Aeros to fight Stabler. And Gault had brutally cut Stabler down.

Aeros spoke even louder than before, launching into his set speech. "The Bloodwood named Spiderwood, one of my honored Knights Archaic, wishes to invoke the Chivalric Rule of Blood Penance. He wishes to redeem himself. For he desires to be worthy to sit at my side in heaven. He can select a flogging and rejoin the Hound Guard as a squire, or he can select a duel to the death with a warrior of my choosing!" Aeros' frosty, black-pupiled eyes turned toward the Bloodwood, who was again drooping in Hammerfiss' grip. "If you are triumphant in the duel, you may resume your position as one of my Knights Archaic and all will be forgotten. Die and I deem your shed blood sufficient repentance for your failure. Your body will be burned on the pyre and your soul allowed to take wing into heaven."

The Bloodwood held his head up straight. His swollen face seemed incapable of expression as his lusterless gaze fell upon Aeros. "As you know, a Bloodwood has scant use for Laijon or Raijael or your heaven or even your Blood Penance."

"Be that as it may," Aeros hissed, "choose you the duel, or the flogging?"

The Spider shrugged Hammerfiss away and stood on his own. He pulled his shirt swiftly up and over his head, letting it fall to the ground. He turned once for all to see, both arms held out in supplication. His upper body was sallow in the sunlight, the ridges of his spine like the fins of sharks, plying the skin of his back. When he stopped turning, his gaze, though still misty with pain, lanced toward Aeros. "I choose to fight!"

"Splendid." Aeros bowed to him.

"I choose to fight," the Spider repeated. "But only when I am healed of my wounds. I will not be forced into a shameful end like Beau Stabler."

"Ha!" Hammerfiss shouted. "He has always been a coward!"

Aeros' face held a scowl of disbelief. "You fight now. Or you are flogged now. Those are your choices, Bloodwood."

"I will not fight today." The Spider bowed.

Aeros' gaze sliced into the Bloodwood. "Then you know what is to come?"

The Spider bowed again, deeper this time. "Be careful of whom you choose to wield the whip, my lord. For know that I will kill the man who does. Not today. But someday."

"Well then." Hammerfiss held up the barb-tipped whip. "Let the honor be mine."

The White Prince nodded once at Hammerfiss. "Twenty lashes."

Hammerfiss forced the Bloodwood toward one of the tall stumps Jenko and Mancellor had been sparring near. "Today you will suffer the punishment of a bleating cur." Hammerfiss' gleeful eyes burned as bright as two candles. "And suffer it at my hand." He shoved the Bloodwood face-first against the wooden pole. "Tie him up!" Hammerfiss tossed a thong of leather at Mancellor. Together with Jenko, the Wyn Darrè grabbed the Spider's hands and secured them tight near the top of the stump.

Hammerfiss cracked the whip. "That leather strap may not be enough to hold him for twenty lashes, boys. If he slides down the pole, be ready to brace him up. Twenty is double what most men can bear."

The Spider stood chest-first against the pole, arms bound above his head, pale skin exposed. He turned, looking in the direction of Ava and Spades and the sword jutting from the dirt between them. *Why does he so easily submit?* This entire scene just stressed to Ava the fact that if Aeros could inflict pain and humiliation like this to a coldhearted demon like the Spider, he had the power and willingness to visit cruelness upon anyone at any time.

The whip was coiled tight in Hammerfiss' hand as he centered himself behind the Bloodwood. "This man has proven he is without honor!" Hammerfiss shouted. "Respect is earned on the field of battle with hard steel! One cannot cheat their way into it with black daggers and sneaky assassin ways! When it comes time to pay the butcher's bill, only a coward chooses flogging! And this man has proven himself naught but a coward!"

The Spider's bloodshot eyes fell on Ava. A chill settled over her. She did not want to watch this, but she couldn't break her gaze from it. One thing was now sure. For survival's sake she would have to learn to live like Spades, hard as iron and hollow inside, devoid of tender feeling.

Hammerfiss' face was a rash of red as the timbre of his voice grew. "We can all see the Spider's true heart now! Full of weakness! Lacking in courage! It is why he has relied on sneakiness and devilry and childish acrobatics his entire life! He mocks *The Chivalric Illuminations* and this army with his very presence! What have any of the black-hearted Bloodwoods done to help this war effort? These twenty lashes are for Felisar Gannon, who died at the Battle of Agonmoore! Wolfmere Lohr, who died at the Battle of Oksana! These lashes are for all men who died glorious deaths! With honor! Men who helped conquer two entire kingdoms! The *Illuminations* record their deeds. Above all, these lashes are for Gault Aulbrek, who has gone missing in Ravenker! For my brother in war, Gault, who was last seen with this *betrayer!*"

"Enough with the speeches," Aeros said, a small measure of impatience in his voice. "Get on with it."

Hammerfiss bowed low to the White Prince. "To quote the Chivalric Rule of Blood Penance, 'May this flogging be a gift unto our Lord Aeros, a lord who communes with both Laijon the Father and Raijael the Son.'" He flicked out the whip's barbed lash with a sinister snap, voice growing heavy with power. "You, Ser Bloodwood, disgust me. You are naught but a mouse who boasts of paying scant homage to Raijael or Laijon, or even Mother Mia. Let the pain I am about to inflict upon you be a reminder of whom it is you serve. And the one whom you serve is my blessed Lord Aeros Raijael!"

Hammerfiss drew back the thick bulk of his arm in a flash, and the whip snaked high into the air behind him, then exploded forward with the sound of angry lightning, all his brute force into the blow. The Spider bunched his shoulders in preparation. The barbed lash of the whip struck his back with a violent crack of thunder, slicing him open from right shoulder to left ribs in a swift red line. His eyes flew open as his back muscles spasmed and bunched. Yet he did not cry out, just stared into space somewhere above Ava Shay's head. Blood ran in a thin sheet of scarlet from the wound over his ivory-skinned back, pooling at the rim of his rough-spun breeches, soaking in.

Hammerfiss reared back for another strike, snapping the barbed lash out behind him, striking a second time with powerfully muscled fury. A crack like lightning and another cruel line opened up into the Bloodwood's shuddering pale flesh. The man's fingers clenched and strained against his leather bonds.

Ava closed her eyes for the third lash. Her mind and soul had already witnessed far too much pointless violence. She ceased to watch as ten more lashes followed, her thoughts wandering to places even darker still. With each callous crack of the whip, her inward vision shimmered and swam with the wraiths. She let go her senses, felt nothing save hearing and smell. *These people are cruel. Evil, for evil's sake. They'll gleefully torture their own as quickly as their enemies, with no rhyme or reason behind any of it.*

Fifteen lashes she counted, and a breeze dragged across the slope. She felt it sweep back her hair, and with it came the pungent taste of blood. The sixteenth lash crackled, a merciless wet slap, barbed tips lashing into skin. The sound brought the bile to her throat. At the seventeenth sodden slap of the whip she nearly vomited.

She wanted to force herself, with every ounce of her being, to open her eyes and look. To look and to not vomit. She needed to discover some resolve, some strength within herself and show it. At the eighteenth lash her strained eyes opened.

The most shocking part of the scene before her wasn't the flayed, mutilated flesh of the Spider's anguished back, or the stark whiteness of his exposed ribs against his bloody torn flesh. The most shocking part was his dark eyes. They were no longer foggy and flooded with uncertainty or even pain. They were sharp and icy and clear.

And as the nineteenth and twentieth lashes rained down, his two intense orbs were focused on her—orbs that seemed to glow as red as the blood pooling at his feet.

*Thus, my greatest fear cometh that the writings of the Last Warrior Angels will eclipse the word-of-mouth stories. Indeed, they will eclipse the ancient symbols once scratched into standing stones, totems, and altars. Words on scrolled parchment carry import. Words on a page within a bound book carry the weight of a world.*
—THE ANGEL STONE CODEX

## CHAPTER SIX

# LINDHOLF LE GRAVEN

### 8TH DAY OF THE ETHIC MOON, 999TH YEAR OF LAIJON
### AMADON, GUL KANA

The apron-clad bartender placed a steaming bowl of stew right in front of Lindholf with a thud. Startled, Lindholf jumped in his chair and yanked back his straying hand, breathing deeply. He was sitting in the Slaver's Tavern and Inn, trying his level best to remain calm. He was here to pickpocket his first victim.

The efficiency of the bartender wasn't helping. But once the fellow scuttled away behind the two double doors leading to the kitchen of the tavern, Lindholf moved his hand back again. Gently. Ever so slowly. Palms sweaty, heart thudding, he felt behind him for the pouch hooked to the man's belt, tense fingers lightly brushing the man's thick leather belt. He tried to keep his fingers malleable. But he couldn't see what he was doing. And that was the frustrating thing. No matter how much Val-Draekin had taught him about thievery and sleight of hand, he couldn't wrap his mind around the fact that most of a thief's work was done blind—just like this.

Lindholf was at his own table directly behind his bearded victim. They were sitting back-to-back, their chairs almost touching. The hood of Lindholf's cloak was over his head, concealing his face. For further protection, he carried a dagger—the black dagger Tala had left in the red-hazed room where Sterling Prentiss had been murdered by Glade Chaparral. Lindholf had followed the two into the secret ways and witnessed the killing, witnessed Tala pull a vial of green medicine from Sterling's guts, witnessed her fight with Glade, and saw her lose the dagger. The dagger he now owned.

Val-Draekin, also cloaked and hooded, sat in a shadowy booth near the back of the crowded tavern, observing. His occasional glances were curious and sharp under the dark cowl that concealed his Vallè features.

The plan had been simple. Lindholf was to enter the Slaver's Tavern and Inn, pick out a likely victim, and then endeavor to successfully pull off his first-ever bit of real-world thievery. Val-Draekin would observe. Seita would remain cloaked and concealed outside with the three bay palfreys they'd borrowed from the stable marshal, Ser Wickham, keeping their mounts ready for a quick escape if need be.

The two Vallè had begun coaching him on the art of pickpocketing near a moon ago. Why? Lindholf hadn't a clue. But the fact that anyone was paying attention to him was huge. And the fact that Glade Chaparral was not involved was an enormous boost. Lindholf mostly went unnoticed when around Glade. Everyone adored Glade. Everyone paid attention to the handsome and gallant Glade Chaparral. Pasty-faced and deformed, Lindholf Le Graven was always the afterthought, the ignored. So if Val-Draekin and Seita were going to befriend him, take him under their wing, teach him things, *secret things*, he wanted to do his utmost to impress them.

So he took three deep breaths, just like Val-Draekin had taught him, and kept his hand poised in midair, hovering just over the man's satchel.

*Concentrate, Lindholf, concentrate! Focus!* To calm his mind, he listened in on the man's hushed conversation with his partner, who sat across from him. They were both disgusted that the White Prince's war in Wyn Darrè was now rumored to have reached the shores of Gul Kana. They were also angry at the many oghul raids that were going unchecked in the northern regions of Gul Kana. Listening to their conversation wasn't helping his jittery hand, especially when one of the men made mention that he would soon be reuniting with a mercenary group from the northern fortress town of Crucible and joining in the fight against those raiding oghuls. *Mercenaries! I picked mercenaries to rob!*

And then the man shifted in his chair.

Lindholf brought his hand up onto the table into plain sight and looked around the Slaver's Tavern and Inn. The flickering candlelight cast a hazy shade of bleakness about the place. There was a candlelit hall at the end of the bar. The bartender was shuffling down it now. Near that far corner were more stools that held slouched figures. He cast his eyes nervously toward the worn, chipped wooden planks lining the floor, then at his own table before him. The stew still stared at him. He picked up the warm ceramic bowl with both hands and tipped it to his lips, sucking down a large gulp. He immediately choked, taking in way too much, sputtering, hunks of stew spewing from his mouth. *Rotted angels!*

He set the bowl down with a clatter, eyes darting to Val-Draekin. But the hood completely shaded the Vallè's eyes now. The bartender returned from down the hallway and hurried back into the kitchen.

*Idiot!* Lindholf wiped his hands on his pant legs and attempted to collect himself. He tried to recall Val-Draekin's many lessons. He'd studied many types of pouches and satchels, practiced—without looking—how to untie, unclasp, unhinge, unbutton, undo just about every type silently and smoothly and without so much as a hiccup or jostle. And strapped to the mercenary behind him was a simple leather pouch tied at the top with a simple tattered string. *One of the easiest!* Now here he was, not able keep himself together long enough to even touch the man's satchel, let alone open it and take stuff out.

He risked a backward glance. And quickly wished he hadn't.

When the man had shifted in his chair, his heavy woolen coat had fallen open at the side, revealing a shortsword at his belt just behind the satchel. Lindholf hurriedly did the three-fingered sign of the Laijon Cross over his heart. *I have to follow through with this.* He uttered a quick prayer and shook away the nerves, hand sliding back in position a third time, fingers drifting ever closer to the man's satchel, feeling the thin leather laces atop the pouch for the first time.

And suddenly the foolishness of the whole venture set in. *I'm the son of a noble! And besides, Laijon's not going to help me pickpocket a stranger, no matter how many holy incantations I mutter—*

Then his victim rocked back on his chair with a prodigious yawn. Lindholf's hand was instantly entangled in leather. The man whirled and stood, sized up the situation in an instant, grasped Lindholf's wrist in a steel-like grip, and yanked him to his feet.

Lindholf's hood flew back, revealing his face.

"What's your problem, scum?" The fellow had a grim round face, black hair, a bushy beard, and sharp, angry eyes. He was also significantly taller than Lindholf and outweighed him by a good seventy pounds.

"I got no problem," Lindholf squeaked, trying to pull his hand away. His other hand went for the black dagger hidden in his tunic.

"A pickpocket," said the second man, standing now, an older, paunchy fellow.

The first mercenary twisted Lindholf's arm painfully. "Trying to rob me, you pasty oghul-faced freak?"

"No. I would never—"

The man rammed his fist right into Lindholf's chin. Lindholf went reeling back, landing hard on his butt. *They are going to kill me!* The tavern was silent. Everyone was looking at him now.

"I don't steal." Lindholf hauled himself to his feet, woozy from the blow. "I don't even need to steal—"

"Lying little cocksucker." The mercenary drew his shortsword with a rasp. People nearby lurched up from their tables and backed away, forming an open space between Lindholf and the man. Lindholf's balls crawled right up into his throat, the pain in his jaw now forgotten as quickly as the dagger in his tunic.

"He's just a boy." Val-Draekin stepped between him and the man with the sword. "For Laijon's sake, let him be." The Vallè's face was still obscured under the dark hood.

"And just who the fuck are you?"

"I'm no one."

"Well then, back the fuck up and mind your own business." The man brushed Val-Draekin aside, the tip of his sword poised at Lindholf's chest. "I aim to slice out his beady little rat eyes, carve up his ugly rat face."

"I'm sorry." Lindholf's voice was shaky. He dipped his head, ashamed of his deformities and scars.

"You're a sorry worthless motherfucker is what you are." The mercenary scowled, eyes bouncing between him and the hooded Vallè, his sword steady.

"Look," Val-Draekin continued, "he said he wasn't trying to steal from you."

"Bloody Mother Mia, you want a part of this thrashing, stranger?" the mercenary rumbled. "The boy will be dealt with how I see fit."

With both hands, Val-Draekin pulled the hood of his cloak back, revealing to everyone the upturned ears and distinctive, refined, cunning face of the Vallè that he was. His unmistakable Vallè eyes loomed large in the shifting candlelight of the tavern.

The man's initial look of anger did not drain away, but rather increased considerably at the sight of Val-Draekin. "You, a Vallè, dare advise me?"

"No need for bloodshed here."

"Well, then." The man's face flushed with rage. "You can honor your fragile Vallè sensibilities by turning the fuck away."

"Let the boy be." Val-Draekin's voice conveyed assurance and menace in a single breath. The second mercenary, the paunchy one, drew his sword and joined his companion. Now there were two men with steel in hand, both looking ready and able.

Lindholf's body froze in place as Val-Draekin held his hands out, both covered in white powder.

The mercenaries looked at each other. Then as one they rushed the Vallè.

Val-Draekin snapped his fingers and a cone of bright fire appeared in the palm of each hand. And with a powerful burst of air from his lips, he blew into the twin flames. Two balls of orange heat and fire instantly engulfed both mercenaries.

Before he knew what was happening, Lindholf was being dragged by the sleeve through Slaver's Tavern toward the front door and out into the light of day. Val-Draekin hustled him down the rickety wooden porch and onto the cobbled stone, shoving him in the direction of Seita and the three bay palfreys hitched at the post across the street.

Seita met them with a coy smile and roguish, dancing eyes. "Went well, I see?"

"Mount up." Val-Draekin shoved Lindholf up into the saddle of the nearest horse. "That flame was merely a distraction. Those men will be out here soon."

✝ ✝ ✝ ✝ ✝

All three stood on crisp grass in the center of the Hallowed Grove under the towering Atonement Tree. Seita held both arms out in front of her pale face, palms cupped together, white powder in her hands. She pursed her silky lips, and with a puff of breath sent the powder gently afloat, scattering the colorful butterflies above. Though there was no breeze to carry it, the wispy cloud of powder seemed to ascend of its own accord, higher and higher in sinuous soft tendrils of mist that wove through the thick, twining branches. Twinkles of light flickered where the powder touched dusky green leaves.

Val-Draekin did exactly as Seita had. The powder from his palms also drifted high, glittering as it too seemed to meld with the leaves—leaves that were said to be as ancient as the tree itself, more than one thousand years old. Legend was, not one leaf of the great Atonement Tree had ever been found shriveled and dead under its lofty canopy. Even during the harshest of winters, the leaves remained, alive and green.

Lindholf, Val-Draekin, and Seita were alone under the tree. A contingent of several hundred Silver Guards guarded the tree at all times, stationed in a large circle around the perimeter, letting only those of royal blood through their ranks. Pilgrims and other common folk from the breadth of the Five Isles were allowed into the Hallowed Grove—an expansive public park situated west of Mount Albion and Amadon Castle on the outskirts of the city, near the Riven Rock slave quarry—but only royalty were allowed this close to the sacred monument. The tree itself soared more than five hundred feet high. The base of it, a scant twenty feet from where Lindholf and the two Vallè stood, was impressive, the size of several royal oxcarts clustered together. Vines of green ivy sprinkled with white heather grew up the tree's trunk in a twisty maze, disappearing into the arcing branches and emerald heights beyond.

"A Vallè tradition," Seita said with reverence. "To grace the tree with Shroud of the Vallè is to gift the essence of our realm's deep gratitude for Laijon's great sacrifice."

A small trace of powder was left in her hand. She put it to her tongue and tasted, then sniffed the rest up into her nose, eyes closed, breathing deep as if partaking in some holy Ember Lighting smoke.

She reopened her eyes and said, "For more than a thousand years the Vallè have worshipped so, sharing the Shroud with the tree, at this place of our Lord's great sacrifice."

The white powder was still a mystery to Lindholf. He'd seen both Seita and Val-Draekin use it to create small bursts of flame a few times before in the castle. And Val-Draekin had used it again today in their escape from the Slaver's Tavern and Inn.

"Would you like to give some to the tree?" Seita asked.

Lindholf shook his head. "It seems a sacred practice of the Vallè. I dare not befoul it, a fool like me."

"A sniff then?"

He didn't want to sniff the powder either. "What is it exactly?"

"Shroud of the Vallè." Val-Draekin had some remaining on the tip of his own finger, and he examined the residue with probing eyes. "Powder pounded out of the white crystal rocks north of Vandivar on Memory Bay, a remote coastal quarry along the far western shore of Val Vallè. If mixed with certain metals, and then heated just a little, the Shroud can create curious mists of colorful light and, if one knows certain tricks, can also spark a quick-burning flame."

"Curious mists of colorful light?" Lindholf questioned.

"Aye," Val-Draekin answered. "If mixed with certain metals and liquid silvers during the forging process, very *curious* and interesting weapons can be fashioned."

"I've seen you spark the powder many times. It's always startling."

"That's the point of Shroud of the Vallè," Seita said. "A distraction. Everything we Vallè do is meant to create a distraction. The flame from the powder never lasts more than a second or two. Otherwise it would make for a great weapon indeed." She looked at Val-Draekin, smiling. "The things we Vallè could accomplish then."

"Makes for a clever bit of trickery for a thief on the run, though." Val-Draekin snapped his fingers and a very small flicker of flame ignited briefly, then vanished.

"It saved us from those ruffians, for sure," Lindholf said, then felt immediate guilt. "I fell apart." He found himself stumbling out an apology like a daft-headed idiot. "The bloodsucking oghul caught me thieving and I fell apart. I'm sorry. Bloody Mother Mia, I reckon I'm just not cut out for pickpocketing."

"I reckon you're not the first to muss up his initial attempt," Seita said. "It takes practice to become expert in anything, even thieving. Don't beat yourself up over it."

"Practice, precision, repetition," Val-Draekin added. "All essential to perfection. They say Sør Sevier assassins use the living bodies of the condemned to learn the intricacies of human anatomy. Hundreds of criminals pulled from their dungeons and sacrificed, all for the heartless practice of these dealers in death. Precision. Repetition. Practice. Remember, three deep breaths and patience, and all things will work out."

"Sør Sevier assassins?" Lindholf said questioningly. "I'll practice how to be a cutpurse, but don't expect me to learn killing like that, like they do in Sør Sevier."

"Sacrament of Souls, the Bloodwood assassins call it." Seita's gaze roamed back up to the trees and butterflies settling on the branches above. "Sør Sevier is full of much evil. It is why we are preparing you for survival, young Lindholf. You and your friend Tala. Your sister, Lawri, too. All must prepare to battle the White Prince and his armies." Her eyes fell back on him, hard and serious. "For the Sør Sevier armies will bring evil with them, evil even worse than any Sacrament of Souls."

Lindholf shivered at the thought. He began to realize that everything the two Vallè said seemed cloaked in a threat of looming darkness, a looming threat in the name of the invaders from Sør Sevier: the savagery of the White Prince and his armies, the torturous ways of their assassins, the need to know how to combat evil. But combat evil with an evil of their own. Trickery. Sleight of hand. Thievery and sneaking about. He truly wondered if they wouldn't indeed soon begin to teach him how to kill like a Sør Sevier assassin. *Do I have that in me? Murder? No. I won't do that.*

The fact was, Lindholf enjoyed his time under the tutelage of both Seita and Val-Draekin, even if it was naught but learning about how to be a thief. Their tutelage was a needed distraction. A distraction that couldn't have come at a better time.

After arriving in Amadon with his family for his Ember Lighting Rites, he'd become depressed. He had spent a lot of his time loafing about, losing his carefree spirit, seemingly always at odds with the world. He'd become idle, overly obsessed with his cousin Tala, inventorying the countless love poems he'd written to her but never showed anyone, preferring to keep her in the hidden realm of lofty fantasy. He didn't see her as family. He loved her. Loved her beautiful hair and cheekbones and gorgeous, perfect eyes, which always left him deliriously spellbound. He loved all of her. He had become wickedly obsessed. His mind drifted back to when she had kissed him in Sunbird Hall. And in the breathless rush of the moment, he'd kissed her right back before he could rein himself in. And to his shock, Tala's lips had parted and she'd opened herself up to him. Her warm body pressed to his. Her untamed heart beating fiercely. But then she'd backed away. Made him feel small in that way all girls could. Made him feel awkward and weird and deformed.

Which he was. It was only the truth. To Lindholf's estimation, it seemed he'd been a right peculiar sort from the moment of his birth, and any gander he took into a mirror only proved that fact. So he avoided mirrors. And glassy ponds. Even shiny armor reflected too much of his own brand of ugly right back at him. All of it combined— his looks, the way girls reacted to him, the culmination of his own desires—made him feel so lecherous, so unworthy. Especially when Glade was around. Glade, with all his glorious Chaparral good looks and false bravado and divisive charm. Truth was, Glade was the creepy one. But nobody saw it. His creepiness was always taken as casual flirtation by the court girls, who would swoon at his every awkward, annoying word. *And my clever and casual ways are always taken for untoward creepiness. All of it based on how different we look. Him beautiful. Me flawed.*

Fact was, his own thoughts tortured him; tormented him at all times. He wondered if he wasn't going crazy from the constant array of conflicts battling inside his own head. Yes, he loved all of Tala. Yes, he had become wickedly obsessed. And yes, he knew it was all wrong and had to be stopped. *Yet can I? Can I give up my addiction to her?*

Until now he'd thought it impossible. But ever since Seita and Val-Draekin had taken to teaching him how to pickpocket, he'd found new life, new purpose. Unlike Glade, or perhaps even Tala, it seemed the two Vallè were truly his friends.

There was noise and clatter in the distance, interrupting his thoughts.

Val-Draekin pointed toward the King's Highway just beyond the border of the park. There was a procession of prisoners being marched toward the slave quarry at Riven Rock just a few miles west of the Hallowed Grove and the Atonement Tree. "Up from the dungeons of Purgatory to the quarry," Val-Draekin muttered. "Only the worst, most ill-favored of the court are sentenced into the pits of Riven Rock."

High clouds feathered the horizon far above the prisoners. Silver Guards and Dayknights lined the King's Highway as the hundred or so cuffed and shackled soon-to-be slaves shuffled along. Even from a distance, the slaves appeared a pathetic lot. Lindholf had seen the Riven Rock slave brand burned onto the neck of more than one doomed gladiator. Two large, red *RR*s for Riven Rock. Just at the thought of the hot iron that had made such a cruel mark, Lindholf felt his hand, seemingly of its own accord, drift up to his neck and the scarred flesh there, fingers tracing the rough and cobbled burn scars that traveled up and over his own cheekbones and ears. Any deformity, scar, or mark upon another man made him rue his own.

Seita saw him touching his face. "The Temple of the Laijon Statue," she said. "You've been there before, yes?"

Lindholf jerked his hand away from his ear, heart thudding as he gave her a startled nod. *It seems they are rooting around in my mind constantly, these two Vallè.* He thought of the chiseled ears of the statue. The statue's flaw. "I've been there," he said.

"I thought as much." Seita met his gaze with frank interest. "Most royals have." She dipped her head toward the line of slaves. "That sublime likeness of our great One and Only, sculpted from the exquisite marble quarried in yonder pits, is certainly a glorious sight."

"The King of Slaves, molded from stone quarried by slaves," Val-Draekin broke in. "A statue of marble cut from the same pit where the King of Slaves himself once toiled."

"It certainly has a symmetry and a beauty to it," Seita said. "Don't you think?"

"I can agree with that." Lindholf studied Seita's supple face, the smooth lines of porcelain-like nose and brows.

"There is perfection in Laijon's plan," Seita said. Her eyes emanated softness and caring and deep intellect at the same time. Lindholf couldn't help but look upon the graceful sweep of her hair as it tumbled about her ears, ears that were thin and flawless and pointed.

With that thought, he forced his gaze back out toward the line of slaves and thought of the Temple of the Laijon Statue and the flawed likeness of the great One and Only. That he knew of the hidden flaw when nobody else did still filled him with a silent panic. That he knew that the glorious sculpture of the great One and Only was a fraud, that it was no sculpture of a human at all, filled him with a hollow dread. *Had the sculptor some grudge against Laijon and his believers and sculpted the ears like that on purpose? Why hadn't they been fully smoothed over?* He had myriad questions and thoughts on the matter. He wondered if these two Vallè beside him knew the secret too.

"There is a symmetry and beauty to the history of Amadon as well," Val-Draekin said. "Do you know of the Triplets Bronachell? The three royal children who lived during the life of Laijon: Albion, Riven, and Savon. 'Twas these royal triplets that Amadon and much of the histories of Gul Kana and the entire Five Isles were founded upon. The royal mountain upon which sits Amadon Castle was named after Albion. And 'twas Riven who the slave quarry was named after. And Savon Bronachell . . ." The Vallè's eyes traveled back toward the procession of slaves. "Well, a long story is Savon's. Maybe for another time."

Lindholf's eyes were fixed on the line of slaves in the distance.

"You'll never want to find yourself part of that sorry crew, Lindholf," Seita said. "Some say the pits of Riven Rock Quarry are a worse fate than even the Bloodwoods' Sacrament of Souls. Both amount to prolonged and painful deaths."

Lindholf had to swallow back his revulsion. He had heard the rumors of the backbreaking labors and torments inflicted upon the slaves sent down into the depths of Riven Rock. Few made it out alive. It was essentially a death sentence. Lindholf disdained manual labor of any kind. No. He did not want to find himself party to any of it.

Seita sniffed more Shroud of the Vallè, then held out her hand. A line of powder remained in her palm. "Sure you don't want to try some?"

"I think I will." Lindholf leaned over her cupped hand, nose and cheek brushing her fingertips as he sniffed. He felt an immediate faint but pleasant tingling in his nostrils. He breathed in deep and his eyes instantly felt afire. He coughed hard. Gasped for air.

And then it hit him, a glorious sensation of supreme euphoria. And he instantly wanted more.

*Oh, this bloody Sacrament of Souls, it has served our ancient lineage well, along*
*with our myth of the Five Warrior Angels.*
—The Book of the Betrayer

# CHAPTER SEVEN
# CRYSTALWOOD

8TH DAY OF THE ETHIC MOON, 999TH YEAR OF LAIJON

ROKENWALDER, SØR SEVIER

H ans Rake raised the black dagger until the blade brushed
his lips.

"You mustn't," Krista Aulbrek said, conscious of the
thudding of her own heart. "Lavender deje is not safe to ingest."

"But a wonderful drug if inhaled just right."

"But awful to the taste, I imagine."

"And I imagine the taste of you is divine." His smile did not
enhance his thin face, but instead gave him an unpleasant sneer. "'Tis
not the deje on my blade that I'm afraid of, but rather your constant
denial of our love."

She would not acknowledge the comment, her patience wearing
thin. It was all a game with him. The killing. The flirting. She looked
beyond him to the bay below, where moonlight, randomly breaking

through the clouds, illumed the restless waters. Night had long since draped its shadows over Rokenwalder. In the distance, patches of dark sky thundered, laced with occasional lightning. It looked like rain would drop from the sky at any moment.

Krista turned from Hans and walked along the edge of the manor house's aged roof, focusing on the creaking of the wooden planks and tile beneath her feet and the ashy light in the alley five stories below. Her senses were attuned for any movement from any direction—just as Dugal had taught her. She and Hans had reached the roof unmolested, but their mission was still far from accomplished, and time was running out.

Though she could not hear him, she knew Hans followed her, no more than two steps behind. Silent. Hans Rake was far more skilled in sneaking than she. Her feet, as stealthy as they were, made some noise. His made none.

"Do you not love me?" he asked. "Will you not share your new name?"

Fatigue engulfed her like a cloak. "I beg of you, desist." She turned and faced him again. He still held the dagger. "Lest you forget, we've a mission yet to complete."

"The night is long." He lifted the dagger, tongue flickering over the blade now at his lips.

Ever since the Sacrament of Souls, Hans Rake had become more and more besotted with figuring out her name. Until he earned his own name, he was not allowed to know hers. It was part of their training. He'd become jealous. A nuisance. He was no longer winning in Dugal's eyes because of her, and it was clearly affecting him. *And now he pushes me. Tests me.*

"Perhaps you'd like a taste." That sneering grin she despised crawled back over his face as he spoke. "I've a vial hidden in my leathers just for you."

"Lavender deje?"

"No." His voice was smooth. "Blood of the Dragon."

*Yes, he pushes me.* She turned from Hans, reached for the black iron railing behind her, gripped the cold steel with two leather-gloved hands. *He tests me with the sap of the Bloodwood tree, the sap that I am never to taste again.* It haunted her, that glorious sensation. One taste was all Dugal had allowed before he had forbidden it forever. *Yes, Hans tempts me wickedly!*

The rain began, driven sideways by the evening winds, smelling of the sea. She let it cleanse her of all temptation and want. The newly forged Bloodwood dagger slipped from the sleeve of her cloak and into her hand. A dagger she had fashioned herself, fashioned from that very same sap of the Bloodwood trees she so desired, mixed with the blood of those criminals on whom she'd practiced her art, those she'd prodded and carved and flayed, those countless souls she'd taken in silent ritual.

She knew the cruel coldness that lurked in everyone's deepest thoughts had been fully awoken in her. She savored and reveled in every dark death and every new trick she learned. *Is this the life Avril Aulbrek envisioned for her daughter? Likely not. But my father is a killer too.* Now, in her own way, she fought alongside Gault, both of them creating death in the name of Aeros Raijael.

Hans was at the railing with her, dagger still in hand. "Ready, my love—my *nameless* love?"

"I am not your love." She would not be distracted by him. Despite the day's many ordeals, she would stay prepared. Dugal had set them to a specific purpose tonight.

She gazed out at the city below her—Rokenwalder. A cluttered maze of streets, alleyways, and stone buildings extended on both sides of the manor house as far as she could see. Lanterns, torches, windows, all cast a faint amber glow back at her. Like nearly every structure in Rokenwalder, the buildings and belfries closest to this grand house were roofed in tile, shingle, or thatch. They were mostly made of dark gray brick-and-mortar walls and thick timbers supporting upper floors. She and Hans were in one of the more affluent sections of the city; the manor house, upon whose roof they now perched, was one of the biggest.

"Don't upset yourself." Hans touched her shoulder and gently turned her toward him. "'Tis all part of Dugal's plan, even the way I speak to you now." His expectant eyes rested on her.

"Do not look at me so." She faced him, dagger clenched in the palm of her own hand under the sleeve of her cloak, unseen.

Hans knit his brows but said nothing. His dirty-blond hair, shaved far above his ears on both sides of his head, was a two-inch-high row of spiky clumps from his forehead to the back of his neck and appeared icily gray in the wan light, rain starting to flatten it down. The Suk Skard clan tattoos that covered the sides of his scalp shone blue in the wetness. His eyes, like Dugal's, were faintly streaked with red. He was as thin as her, but he wore his lithe stature with a swaggering air.

A gust of rain lashed against the roof, buffeting them both. Krista sensed the trickles of water moving through the cracks and crevices of the tile and pooling at their feet with a hollow chill. The cold air plucked at the rainwater on her skin, too. Hans' fingers toyed with his dagger almost daintily. Then he put the blade back up to his lips.

"Please don't." She could see the sheen of black resin clinging to the blade—the rain had not yet washed it clean.

"What does it matter if I ingest the deje and die?" he asked as a crash of thunder shook the air. Thick rain drummed the rooftops and cobblestone streets below. He did not drop his gaze. "Or what does it matter if you die?"

And he struck, plunging the dagger into her chest above her heart.

Krista looked at him through watery light and felt not a thing. When he pulled the dagger free, rain hissed off the blade, misting around it, a residue of the heat from inside her chest. Thunder continued to rattle around them, lightning illuminating their rooftop perch. Hans' expression was carved from ice as she rammed the blade of her own dagger into his chest and pulled it free. The blow didn't even stagger him, didn't even make him sway slightly. She was proud of that. Her strike had been perfect.

"There it is," Hans said flatly, putting his dagger away. "We are now bonded."

"Only as Dugal wished."

"We two Bloodwoods work in concert. Like the legends Hawk and the Spider. Like Silk and the Rose. Now us, Hans and the *nameless* one." His tone was fueled with sarcasm. "Dugal's ultimate creations. A team. Unrivaled."

She slipped her own dagger back into the folds of her leather armor, not certain she wanted Hans Rake on her team, or even by her side. It seemed all a joke to him. All a game. He could be exhausting.

"Loving you hurts deeply." He grinned. "But Dugal was right—being struck with a blade coated in lavender deje *is* painless. My heart feels not a thing now." And then, with a flick of his wrist, Hans Rake looped a thin rope around the black iron railing and leaped over it, twisting in midair, falling straight down.

And in the growing gloom of storm, Krista followed.

✝ ✝ ✝ ✝ ✝

In silence they descended, both gripping each tiny handhold of the worn and crumbled columns with cool assurance until they reached their destination—the manor house's third-floor window. Hans slipped the tip of his dagger into the seam of the wood frame and, finding the latch, released it, whilst Krista deftly nudged the frame and glass inward. Like darkness flowing, they entered the room, both swiftly stepping away from the glow of the window, rainwater on their black leathers adrip on the plush carpeting. A faint wash of lamplight from the alley below caused patterns of yellow to dance on the room's smooth ceiling—a room that was spacious and garnished with much finery. A four-poster bed of rich mahogany and white silken drapes was against the far left wall; a beautiful blond woman, naked from the waist up, was asleep atop its spacious mattress, swaddled in rich blankets.

Her name was Solvia Klingande.

Krista moved toward the bed, black dagger in hand—a different blade than the one she'd used to stab Hans on the rooftop. This weapon was not only coated in lavender deje, but also berlin's breath, a nonvaporous tonic that constricted the blood vessels instantly, stifling the flow of blood.

Hans was but a step behind her as she squatted by Solvia's bed. He leaned over, eyes drinking in the voluptuous naked beauty of the nineteen-year-old wife of Ser Aulmut Klingande, a corrupt and lecherous sixty-year-old Rokenwalder nobleman.

Krista stabbed Solvia just above the heart. Her black dagger struck down like lightning and then out, back into the hidden pocket of her leather armor just as swiftly. No blood streamed from the wound. Krista's strike had been exact. And the alchemy she'd earlier spread over her blade had been mixed to perfection.

Still, Ser Aulmut's young wife moaned and shifted in bed. Krista held her breath. Solvia's eyelids fluttered briefly, then stilled—the sign that the potions on Krista's blade had worked their magic. Solvia would not awaken for hours now, no matter how much noise they made.

Hans rose in silence and disappeared into the dark room behind her. Krista followed her partner to the rosewood dresser between the bed and the closed double doors of the bedchamber. Hans produced the thin parchment from the folds of his cloak and pinned it to the surface of the dresser with one of his Bloodwood daggers. Krista had earlier constructed the contents of the note with Hans.

It read,

*The hole above your heart will speak to the danger you are now in. Return all the coin your husband stole. All of it. To every innocent he conned. You have three days. If you do not, we will carve your beating heart from your chest in front of your waking eyes. You cannot hide from us. The blade with this note is evidence of who your new masters are.*

*We will deal with your husband however we deem appropriate.*

Hans threw Krista a nod, and a moment later they were both positioned before the double doors of the chamber. Thick and heavy and ornate, the twin doors were secured at the middle with a simple bolt and latch mechanism from the inside of the room.

With a slow twist of the latch, Hans slid the bolt back, his cool gaze meeting hers. He suddenly had a black dagger in both hands. As did she. A guard, perhaps two, would be posted just beyond this door. Krista was prepared, exhilarated in fact, heart thumping. And she could see the lust for death glowing in Hans' eyes too. Together they jerked the doors inward and sprang to the fight.

The guards, one on either side of the door, barely had a chance to turn and put hand to hilt before they were dead and folding to the floor in crumpled heaps, the clatter of their armor muffled by the rich carpet. Two grizzled men with graying beards, both in steel-mail hauberks, leather greaves, sheathed broadswords, riding boots, and iron half-helms that had toppled from their heads in the fall. Both now minus one eye from the flickering black daggers that had pierced clear to their brain stems.

As Hans closed the double doors to Solvia's bedchamber behind him, Krista cast a furtive glance down the hall in either direction. She saw nothing of note, just a long corridor shrouded in gloom, dimly lit from half-burning sconces hanging in twenty-foot intervals each way. Another wooden doorway was set just across the hallway from her and Hans, jewels and gems of many colors embedded in the wood.

She studied the mercenary guard she had killed. His face was drooping and calm, mouth agape, blue tongue lolling out between flaccid lips. Perhaps fifty, maybe sixty years old. Sure, she'd ended many lives in Dugal's name. But they were all con men like Ser Aulmut, or murderers themselves. And she'd ended many more lives in her Sacrament of Souls. But those people had been worthless prisoners, mere subjects in a grand work of art. Not even real people. Nameless and evil. Thieves and rapers. Scum who deserved what she'd doled out. But this man, this old mercenary fighter under her. She wondered, what had been his history? Had he a family? Children? Grandchildren? Had he once perhaps fought alongside Gault Aulbrek in Adin Wyte or Wyn Darrè? Was guarding Ser Aulmut's wife inside Ser Aulmut's mansion just a job to him, a way for him to support his loved ones? Or was he part and privy to Ser Aulmut's crimes? If so, he deserved his death.

Whatever, he'd died painlessly and fast. At the hand of Crystalwood. Few could ask for a more tranquil end. Black Dugal claimed speed was the key for a Bloodwood. Never let a fight last more than a few strokes of a blade. Never let a man who outweighs you get a firm hold on any part of your body. Even twenty extra pounds made a huge difference in a physical altercation. *Speed and surprise are the only advantages you will ever have over a man, Krista Aulbrek,* he'd once told her. *Let speed and your weapons do the work for you.* For secrecy's sake, she'd learned to always stab for the eye or the heart. A quick punch of the dagger into the brain through the eye socket left few messes. And a stab directly into the heart stopped it cold. And a heart that had ceased its beating could pump scant little blood from a wound. She'd taken the time to experiment with both ways of killing during her Sacrament of Souls.

Together she and Hans moved across the hallway to the

gem-studded wooden door opposite Solvia's room. It was Krista's turn with the lock pick now. And as she set herself to the task, she quickly realized the locks and hinges in this place were well-oiled and silent.

With a fleet pick of the lock, they entered the new room, not expecting anyone inside. They'd put to memory a map of every square foot of the building, every floor, every chamber, hall, and staircase. They knew it all, even where the guards were regularly stationed. This room was empty of people as planned, though spacious and dark, lit only from the distant hallway torches behind them.

They left the door open and weaved their way through the dim room. It was grand in every way, heavy with the rich scent of pine incense and witch hazel, the aromatic combination well known to relieve many ailments. This chamber was also filled with all manner of fine sculptures and ornately carved furnishings. Along the walls were hung many mirrors and large woven tapestries and decorative weapons. Thick rugs of lustrous fur adorned the floor, pure and white as new-fallen snow. She'd heard of the great beasts of the Sør Sevier Nordland Highlands called blizzard bears, ferocious and huge. She figured the rugs under her feet were made of such creatures. Decorative swords and shields were set about in nooks and alcoves, and numerous painted vases rested atop stools. Cushioned benches lined the walls. Several iron braziers and thronelike chairs and couches were set about at haphazard angles. Everything was spotless and clean.

Other than Queen Natalia Raijael's own bedchambers in the king's palace, Jö Reviens, or King Aevrett's throne room in Rokenwalder Castle next to the palace, this chamber was the most opulent place Krista had ever seen. She hated to admit it, but she was easily impressed and taken in by finery such as this. Luxury. Her one vanity.

"We've shared quite an adventure thus far, have we not?" Hans whispered as they reached their exit, another jewel-encrusted wooden door. "I say it's definitely brought us closer together, no?"

Krista put a gloved finger to her lips, her eyes narrowing. She was all business now, paying scant attention to his games, focusing rather on her surroundings. She listened at the door for movement coming from outside, then looked back into the room they'd just traversed, eyes scanning the many mirrors for flickers of light or shadow. She focused again on the fine furniture and decorated walls for dark shapes that might not belong. Every mission could be a test, after all, and who knew what Dugal might have planned for them. He favored surprises of the grotesque. She tried with all the will she could muster to slow her rapid-beating heart, but could only sense her own anxiety.

Something felt *off*. As if her every movement were being tracked.

She and Hans had been told the man they'd been sent to kill tonight had stolen vast sums of money from the poor and innocent. Investors he'd conned. Ill-gotten gains that he'd then used for his own enrichment. But she knew Black Dugal well enough. There were always multiple angles with her master, many reasons for the jobs he took. His motives were always many-faceted. The two Vallè, Silk and the Rose, had warned her to be wary of Dugal's cruel games. Things were not always as they seemed, no matter what their mission.

Hans listened at the door too. Then he slid the bolt back with ease and they both slipped out into the next passageway. It was empty as expected, carpeted and dimly lit. They turned immediately to their left, padding silently down the hall until they reached the final bend in the corridor they sought. Krista peered around the corner first. As expected, two mercenary guards were there, a short hundred paces away, both dressed like the ones she and Hans had just slain. They were stationed directly in front of another set of wooden doors. Krista turned and nodded to her partner.

Perhaps both guards saw the two Bloodwood coming down the corridor, just gliding along, merely shadows moving in the dark. Perhaps. But neither would be able to tell anyone what they saw, for with fluid grace these two shades drifted up and stabbed them both in the eye. And easy as you please, they both dropped to the floor with a thud, not even having drawn their swords. Then, without stopping, their two Bloodwood killers kicked open the wooden double doors they'd been guarding and flew into the room.

A large stone-sculpted hearth was afire in the wall opposite the door, eight men silhouetted before it. Six more mercenary guards, all afoot, all with the same silver-mail hauberks, leather greaves, riding boots, and half-helms of their dead companions, were gathered about a round wooden table crowded with rich cheeses, meats, and breads, backs turned to their attackers. One bald-headed manservant with an armful of copper goblets was standing just to the right of the table. And sitting behind the table directly in front of the blazing hearth was Ser Aulmut Klingande himself.

The six guards whirled as one, well-worn broadswords at their hips ringing from their sheaths. One of the guards grunted in sudden alarm right before Krista's black blade flicked and slashed his throat wide from ear to ear—blood gushed and spewed as he stumbled back against the table and slid to the floor.

In an instant, Hans had two of the other guards clutching gruesome deep wounds in their own necks, which sprayed blood. Krista punched her next dagger straight up under the fourth guard's chin, burying it hilt-deep, then raking the blade violently to the right, flinging bits of the man's neck, jaw, and teeth, along with a good portion of his brain, onto the cushioned divan near the bald manservant, who shrieked an unholy shriek and scrambled under the table for cover.

The two remaining mercenary guards had their swords at the ready position now, guarding Ser Aulmut, who was standing in wide-eyed astonishment. The blood and brutality now surrounding the nobleman was clearly a shock. For Krista and Hans had been given clear instruction to make the deaths in front of Aulmut's own eyes exceptionally violent. And they had.

A white cat darted from under the table where the manservant hid. It scurried between Krista and Hans and disappeared somewhere behind them.

The guard nearest Krista backed up a step. Her dagger spun through the air and buried itself straight in his left eye. He fell face-forward to the floor, twitching.

The last guard swung his broadsword at Hans with wild abandon. Hans deftly parried the blow with his dagger, and the heavier man's follow-through staggered him to within Hans' easy reach. A black blade was into the guard's spine in a flash, severing it, then back out again. The man fell to the floor, half-helm tumbling away. But Hans wasn't done, he latched on to the man's hair and pulled his limp head from the floor. With one swift slice and pull, he cut the man's neck clear through, severing the head completely. He held the bloody thing up by the hair, then slammed it down onto the round table in front of Aulmut with a wet thud, thick, ropy splatters of scarlet crisscrossing the food and finery of the table.

Blood surrounded Krista, and like flowing red wine, it was intoxicating.

The manservant crawled out from under the table and whimpered, "Please, I beseech you. Leave me be." He held his hands out in surrender to Hans, eyes darting to his master. "Please, Ser Aulmut, don't let them slay me."

But Ser Aulmut did not answer his manservant, just stared in horror at the gruesome severed head, the centerpiece of his dining table now. Klingande was a very fat man and wore an ankle-length robe of black trimmed in gold filigree, gray leggings, and a loose silk shirt with purple scrollwork stitching. His lumpy head, blushing in fear, was shaped much like a pumpkin, accentuated by a thin goatee and mustache. His thinning white hair was slicked back with oils. Beady eyes were buried in the puffy flesh of his ever-reddening face. "*Bloodwoods*," he sneered, holding a serrated steak knife up, brandishing it in a shaky hand.

"And what a mess we've made," Hans answered with coyness, an underlying evilness fixed in his eyes as he looked around at the red carnage. The white cat, no longer behind Krista, was sniffing at the severed neck of the guard under Hans. "This your cat?" he asked the manservant.

"What?" The bald man's eyes were huge and round and beyond petrified, bouncing from the cat to Hans to Ser Aulmut and back.

Hans held up his dagger, grinning wickedly. "Best leave here now or die."

The manservant darted from the room, slipping in pools of blood as he went.

Ser Aulmut cowered behind the round table, steak knife still in hand. "Who does Dugal think he is, to do this to *me* in *my* home?" He was focused on Krista now, staring at her, almost in some form of recognition. "King Aevrett *will* hear of this and be most displeased." His brow furrowed in puzzlement. "Do I know you, girl?"

Hans Rake regarded her too with smoldering red eyes, eyes that now burned with a passion, an almost sexual energy that was startling. Krista could sense her partner wasn't rational anymore. This killing had sparked something in him. Something she'd hoped she'd never see. Something she knew was always buried there within him, within *her*, too. *Does he also see it in my eyes?* The intoxication of murder. Together they had executed pure perfection tonight.

"Do I know you?" Ser Aulmut again asked her.

She pulled her gaze from Hans and back to Klingande, saying, "All you need know is that this right now is the moment your nightmare begins."

"For my part"—Hans circled the table toward Aulmut—"I feel Dugal's letting you off with less than you deserve. But alas, I do as my master bids." Aulmut backed away, trembling.

"You see," Hans continued, "I've more respect for the thief on the street who can look his victim in the eyes as he steals." With a quick strike he knocked the steak knife from Aulmut's hand. It spun to the carpeted floor. Hans pressed forward. "But you. You take from the innocent, using subtle tricks and devious cons and promises of repayment that you never aim to fulfill." Aulmut stumbled over a chair, landing hard on his back with a tremendous thud.

"You are the most cowardly of all types." Hans knelt on the man's heaving chest. "For you steal blindly." He struck twice, precisely, once per eye, blade slicing each eyeball in twain with one swift inch-deep puncture.

Aulmut clutched at his now bleeding face, screaming, frantic, his great bulk squirming. Hans repositioned himself over the man, black dagger still at work. He cut open the man's robe and tore the silk shirt away. From the breastbone downward, Hans' dagger sliced along the bulking curve of Aulmut's rib cage to the left, expertly sweeping below the belly button in a flawless arc. A perfect incision, exact, deep enough to cut through the skin and massive amounts of fat along with the membranelike sack that encased the entrails, yet not so deep as to disturb the guts beneath.

Yes, Hans had learned a few things in their Sacrament of Souls. Of their own volition, Aulmut's intestines ruptured out of his abdominal cavity in a wave, piling up on the carpet beside him. Hans looked unashamedly pleased with himself as he calmly cleaned his dagger on Klingande's robes. Aulmut's wobbly, red-stained hand traveled from his bloody face to the wound in his stomach and the pile of steaming guts beside him. "What is it?" His hand flailed, frantic, trying to figure out what he was touching.

"Your own rank vitals." Hans stood. "In your own rank hand. You can try stuffing them back in if you'd like." He backed away. "Enjoy the rest of your life."

But Ser Aulmut was no longer listening, out cold from shock. The white cat slunk forward and sniffed at Klingande's purple entrails curiously, then began licking with pleasure. Hans' smile was dry as he looked over at Krista. Together they exited the room to the soft, blood-dripping silence of death.

† † † † †

On a remote rocky outcrop ten miles north of Rokenwalder, the two Bloodwoods awaited Black Dugal. The grass at their feet was dewy and lush, a deep subdued green in the morning fog. Boulders were scattered in all directions, each cloaked in white lichen, some thick and squat as seals lazing on a beach, others thin and towering and jutting toward the sky. The icy waters of the Straits of Sevier could be heard clapping against the breakers far below.

Hans put a black whistle to his lips. A moment later a black kestrel swooped from the misty morning air and landed on his outstretched arm. He placed the bird on the nearest lichen-covered rock, pulled a dead mouse from his satchel by the tail, and dangled it before the kestrel. The bird snatched the rodent from his fingers and tore into it.

Hans' Bloodeye horse, Kill, gusted thick puffs of breath into the foggy atmosphere just to the left of Krista. Her own Bloodeye, Dread, stood silently to her right. She held the reins of both and leaned into Dread, nuzzling her mount's neck with the side of her face, feeling the warmth that was always there, feeling the calm spread over her.

Together, she and Hans had ridden to this spot in silence, the import of the night's events heavy on both of their minds. They had been instructed by Dugal never to speak of any kill after the deed was done, not even to each other, ever. Silence in matters of murder was paramount to success.

Silence was the second rule of the Bloodwoods, right after beauty.

Hans looked at Krista in seemingly lazy regard. But she knew he was as tightly wound as herself. She wasn't nervous or scared. And she harbored no qualms about killing. Holding the power over who lived and who died, how they died, when they died: that power was intoxicating and never grew old. Dealing in death just kept one widely alert. Neither of them had slept in more than twenty-four hours. Hypervigilance was a hard habit to break.

And that was how she heard the approaching stranger over the heavy breathing of the two Bloodeye horses. They were expecting Dugal, but the sounds of the person's movements did not match those of her master. She let go the reins of the horses and pulled a dagger from her armor, then nodded to Hans, who produced a blade of his own, eyes roaming the fog. Krista felt something like dread ooze up her spine. Whoever was out there in the mist was using stealth in their approach, which meant they were up to no good. The kestrel on the rock stopped picking at the mouse and cocked its head, alert to the danger too. Krista slowly moved out from between the horses, wary.

The kestrel flew up into the fog with a flutter.

Then, to the left, in the direction of the ocean, Krista saw Ser Aulmut Klingande's manservant slip out from behind a leaning boulder. The bald man, in a dark cloak with the hood thrown back, took naught but half a step before both Krista and Hans let throw their Bloodwood blades.

The manservant snatched both daggers out of the air by the hilts mere inches from his face and sent them hurtling straight back at Krista and Hans. They both ducked their own blades, which sailed into the fog somewhere behind them. Then both lunged to the fight.

"Stop!" Black Dugal's voice commanded.

So used to obeying the charge of her master's voice, Krista stopped midstep. Hans paused too, eyes roving the mists, searching for Dugal.

"A fatal error, the two of you," Dugal's voice said from the fog. "Hesitating."

Hans leaped toward the bald man, his second dagger lashing out, a blade of black that sliced through the fog. In one fluid movement, the manservant caught Hans by the wrist, and with a swift twist of the arm threw the young Bloodwood to the ground, disarming him, holding the blade to his throat. Krista watched, unmoving. Hans was on the ground about to die. Then the man standing over Hans looked up at her expectantly.

"Master Dugal." Krista bowed to Ser Aulmut Klingande's bald manservant. "As you see, we await you at the appropriate place."

Hans' startled eyes flew up to the strange fellow standing over him. The manservant eased his grip on Hans' wrist and helped the young Bloodwood stand.

"Dugal?" Hans muttered as he gained his feet, frowning his displeasure at having been not only fooled, but also so easily thrown to the turf.

"Aye." The bald man pulled the cowl of his cloak up over his head and turned away. When he turned back around and slowly dropped the hood, it was no longer the thin face and beady eyes of Ser Aulmut's bald manservant before them. It was Black Dugal, with his recognizable gray-shot beard and black hair cropped short. His thin lips smiled at them. His veined red eyes were lit with cold amusement. The perfect lines of his nose and cheekbones combined with the many scars on his face made him look at all times, even here in the pale fog, cruel, striking, and tortured.

"So soon you forget your lessons." Dugal's voice was smooth and sinuous as always. "People are less wary in the light of day. Something that should always be exploited. Same with subterfuge and disguise: they, too, should be used to your advantage. You've been taught the usefulness of such tricks, how to travel as another person, how to mask the red eyes of your mounts. Riding about in black leather on black horses with glowing eyes after a kill has its advantages. But also its disadvantages. The best assassin is everyone's friend, not the quiet shade lurking in dark places."

Krista's heart always seemed to thump just a smidge faster whenever Dugal was near. He had a way of creating a nervousness and anxiety in her like no other human could. Especially when he spoke.

"You will both learn that not everyone is who they seem to be. People wear many disguises, for many reasons. Especially our king, Aevrett Raijael, and his five Knights Chivalric." His cold eyes bit into Krista. "You will soon learn, everything our king says is a lie. Especially in regard to his kin."

Krista never minded when her master denigrated King Aevrett. Gault had left her with the king and queen when he'd first gone off to war in Adin Wyte. She had lived with King Aevrett and Queen Natalia many years and knew firsthand that they were *not* kind people. Whether Aevrett was a liar in regard to his kin seemed immaterial to his other various cruel faults. She wished her father had never gone to war and left her with Aevrett Raijael. It had ruined so much of her.

Dugal beckoned her forward. She complied, stepping with caution.

"Are you Krista Aulbrek?" he asked once she stood before him.

"I know not that name."

He bowed to her in confirmation. "When you hide yourself, you are bound to hurt the ones you most love, perhaps even destroy them. But you must have no sympathy, Crystalwood. No empathy can come into play, ever again. Nor conscience. Nor compassion. You cannot even remotely care."

It was almost as if he knew what she was thinking at all times. She had to keep all thoughts of her father free of her mind. She said, "The cause of the Bloodwoods is my only care now."

Dugal dipped his head to her and turned to Hans to come forward. "Are you Hans Rake?"

Hans bowed to him. "I am, my master."

"Not anymore," Dugal said. "You are now named Shadowwood."

Krista detected a huge smile sparkling in Hans' eyes as Dugal continued. "As my shadow, you will be even more deviously loyal than the Spider. I have foreseen it."

Hans bent his knee to his master. "I pledge my blades to you."

"Stand," Dugal ordered. And Hans did as his master bade him do.

Dugal pulled forth a glass vial of red liquid from his cloak, uncorked the top, and swallowed. *Blood of the Dragon!* Krista watched with some envy as her master offered the vial to Hans, who drank the remainder down. His eyes immediately clouded red.

Dugal took back the empty vial. "Part of your test is to abstain from the Blood from here forward, my Shadow. You are to partake of it only upon my offering."

Krista recalled how she'd been asked to taste the sap of the Bloodwood tree, and then commanded to never partake again, even at his offering. It was with these strange inconsistencies that Krista knew she was being kept on edge.

"With the new name, Shadowwood, you must forsake your past," Dugal went on, his frosty dark gaze on Hans. "Rid yourself of whatever heritage you still hold dear. There is no room for tenderness of heart. No room for the longings of the past. No room for love. You are now called fatherless and motherless before me."

There was a fervency in Hans' red eyes. "I gladly piss on the memory of my kin."

"No," Dugal said. "Simply remember them no more. Anger does not suit you. For you are as devious and deadly as a shadow. You must become as unfeeling as one too."

Hans bowed.

Dugal turned to Krista. "And you as keen and sharp as a crystal, my Crystalwood." It was the first time Hans had heard her name. Hans bent his knee to her. She dipped her head to him. Dugal seemed to regard their interaction with approval as he said, "Together you are now Crystal and the Shadow."

Hans' horse, Kill, nickered in the mist behind them. Dugal's eyes ranged the surrounding rocks and boulders. "This is as good a place as any for making your bones and tying yourself to my Caste." He looked at Hans first. "Are you ready?" Hans nodded.

"And you?" He turned to Krista. She nodded affirmation. His red-veined gaze lingered. "You have a killer's eyes. Like your mother."

"You knew my mother?" His comment surprised her in a million different ways.

"I was there when she died." It was barely detectable, but a look came over him she had never seen before. *Sadness?* She couldn't quite place it. *Disappointment?*

He had never mentioned that he'd known her mother. And suddenly she felt lonely standing here on this foggy outcrop. Deep sorrow engulfed her as she thought of a mother she'd never known. A mother Dugal now claimed had a killer's eyes like her own. *Was she a Bloodwood? Is this why I desire to belong to him?* With her father going off to war, she'd always wanted to *belong.* Belong to a cause. Especially as a young girl before meeting Dugal, she'd wanted to fight for her country like Gault Aulbrek, to honor her Lord Aeros in her own way. So she could rise up into the heavens to dwell among the stars. Gault had told her things of the stars and crescent moons, secrets of the skies and the cold lights of the borealis, ideas and concepts she only half remembered. He'd spoken of Laijon and the other Warrior Angels, and of all fighters who had died in the service of Raijael and how they were raised up into the heavens, into the stars. She'd desired to be part of something beyond her, something grand. But King Aevrett Raijael had crushed those dreams. And the crushing loneliness of her time in Jö Reviens affected her still.

But now here she was. Part of a cause. Silk and the Rose, the two Vallè princesses who had trained with her and Hans, had made her feel like she *belonged.* It was then that a chilling thought struck her. *I just failed. . . .*

*You knew my mother?* she'd just asked Dugal. She'd just been caught *caring.* Her heart plunged to the bottom of her feet. *Can he see the conflict in me now?* As calmly as she could, she met Dugal's gaze. *Does he know of the blue ribbon I still wear around my ankle, the one my father gifted me as he left for Wyn Darrè? Does he know all my secrets? Does he know I am not as unfeeling as I let on?*

*Do I know?*

Dugal's wintry glance shifted from her to Hans. "You brought the drawing as instructed?" he asked. Hans nodded. "And you?" he asked her next. Krista nodded. Dugal knelt and began picking small twigs from the ground. "Gather your drawings," he ordered.

Hans strolled back to his Bloodeye mount. Krista lingered, eyes on her master, trying to detect anything in him as he worked. *Is he going to fail me, turn me away?* He looked up from his twig gathering. She could read nothing in his eyes. After a moment, she too whirled and strode toward her horse.

She nervously dug through Dread's saddlebag, pulling forth the parchment she sought. She returned to Dugal and handed it to him, as did Hans. Dugal appraised their work. They were portraits, char-coal drawings they'd both done of one of the Five Warrior Angels of lore: Dashiell Dugal, the Warrior Angel known as the Assassin, the patron god of the Bloodwoods.

As part of Dugal's training, she and Hans had read *The Book of the Betrayer*, memorized it even. A dark, unholy book that had rendered everything she knew about *The Chivalric Illuminations of Raijael* and the church in Amadon's *Way and Truth of Laijon* as nonsense in her eyes. And she supposed that was the book's purpose. To make her see that everything she'd previously known about the gods Laijon, Mia, and Raijael was utterly false. After she discovered the truths within *The Book of the Betrayer*, her previously held notion of a god to pay homage to seemed stupid. And according to *The Book of the Betrayer*, the worst of all falsehoods were found in something called *The Moon Scrolls of Mia*. Dashiell Dugal, one of the Five Warrior Angels, known as the Assassin, was thought to have died with Laijon under the Atonement Tree in Amadon when the fiery demons were banished to the underworld. But as all Bloodwoods knew, the real truth of the

Assassin's fate, and the fate of the ancient race of Demon Lords, lay within the pages of *The Book of the Betrayer*.

Krista had spent months on her drawing of Dashiell Dugal until it was perfect, an exact replica of the image they'd used as a reference, an image Dugal himself had painted for them. Krista knew her portrait was markedly better than Hans'. She had a natural talent for art, where he had none. But Dugal didn't make mention of their talents here, or critique whose drawing was the better. He merely took one quick look at both portraits, then handed them back.

He produced a white powder from his cloak and waved it in the air, then clapped. Flame appeared at his fingertips. Krista had seen both Seita and Breita strike similar powder to flame before. 'Twas a Vallè trick that she and Hans had never been taught. Dugal knelt and set the flame to a small pile of spindly twigs and kindling he'd gathered. "Place your drawings over the fire and set them alight," he instructed, standing.

Hans knelt and held his parchment in the flame until it caught fire, then let it drop. Krista did likewise.

"Repeat after me," Dugal commanded. "I am now part of the unbreakable knot of Black Dugal's Caste. And if I betray my Bloodwood family, I will suffer my heart to be torn from my chest, my bowels ripped asunder, and my blood spilled unto the dirt. From this day forward, I live and die by the knife, I exist only for the return of the Skulls, and my blade always thirsts."

Krista repeated the words with Hans, watching the flame claw at her portrait of Dashiell Dugal, patron god of the Bloodwoods, the Warrior Angel also known as the Betrayer, the burning parchment slowly turning to black.

*For the sake of their new religion, the Last Warrior Angels narrowed Laijon down into the simplest of terms. First, Laijon alone banished the nameless beasts of the underworld into oblivion by destroying the Fifth Warrior Angel, the Assassin, also known as the Betrayer, or the Last Demon Lord. Second, Laijon succeeded in his task with five divine weapons and five angel stones, all translated into heaven after his death, for the remaining Warrior Angels knew Laijon's feats would glow even brighter with the passage of time.*

—THE WAY AND TRUTH OF LAIJON

# CHAPTER EIGHT
# TALA BRONACHELL

### 11TH DAY OF THE ETHIC MOON, 999TH YEAR OF LAIJON
### AMADON, GUL KANA

The argument started with a loud thump and a huge clatter.

"Again you lose!" Glade shouted triumphantly, venom in his words.

Tala and Lawri turned, as did their six Silver Guard escorts. Lindholf lay flat on his back in the center of the granite-tiled hall, helm flung aside. He swiped a smear of blood from his brow with the back of his hand. Lawri sighed in exasperation, holding her left arm gingerly at her side. Again Tala's cousin wore a long dress, the white bandage around her injured arm hidden under the long sleeve. Tala did not know who had wrapped Lawri's arm. That fact that Jovan had cut Lawri so severely during the struggle for his dagger was still horrifying, even though it had been an accident.

"Stand up!" Glade ordered Lindholf. "Stand up and try to pick my pocket again!" He pointed his sackcloth-wrapped sword at Lindholf.

"Leave me alone," Lindholf muttered as he stood and gathered his gear.

Glade took a fighter's stance, readying himself. Both boys were still dressed in their practice gear: light armor, half-helms, and sackcloth-wrapped Silver Guard swords. Earlier they had been practicing swordsmanship with King Jovan in Greengrass Courtyard, their tutelage under Val-Draekin and Seita at an end. Everyone at court did as Jovan Bronachell bade them do now. Both Tala and Lawri wore dresses, neither wanting to incite any anger in their king. Lawri wore a rose-colored gown with sleeves long enough to cover the wound on her arm.

"Come at me!" Glade taunted, tearing the sackcloth from his sword. "I dare you!"

Lindholf brushed himself off, digging behind his chest plate with one bony hand, adjusting his armor. He suddenly ripped the hand free and sniffed at it hungrily.

"You're barking mad," Glade growled. Lindholf stripped the cloth from his sword and brandished it before Glade.

One of the Silver Guards chuckled, "Looks like our two little lordlings are finally gonna go at it. Let's place a wager. I say two swings and both these clodpoles go ass over teapot and the fight's done." The laughter of the other five guards disgusted Tala. *Lazy dullards!* They weren't going to do anything.

Lawri placed herself between the two combative boys. "Put your swords down and cease this nonsense."

"Out of my way, stupid bitch!" With his free hand, Glade shoved Lawri to the ground. Lindholf swung. Glade whirled, his blade blocking Lindholf's blow, their naked blades creating a hollow thunk that echoed through corridor. Glade held his sword at the ready, both hands wrapped tightly around the hilt. "Coward," he snarled, swinging at Lindholf's head.

Lindholf parried. "I will cow to you no more," he said. "And you will not touch my sister like that again."

Glade remained relaxed, shifted his weight, sword poised as he moved to the side. Lindholf's sword point followed the other boy's movement. They began to circle each other, neither flinching. Lindholf feinted to the right with a sudden shift of the shoulder. Glade read the feint and forced him away with a lunge, cutting into his exposed wrist, drawing blood. Lindholf struggled back, nearly falling. Tala's heart sank. But Lindholf collected himself swiftly, stepped forward, and brought his blade up in a neat slice, breaking past Glade's guard, grazing his armor. Glade lunged at Lindholf with murder in his eyes, sword humming through the air.

A cloud of white chalk suddenly appeared between the two combatants. There was a loud clap and a sudden burst of flame flashed before Glade's startled face. He stumbled back in fear. The fireball vanished.

*Vallè sorcery!* Tala's body stiffened in panic. She'd seen Val-Draekin conjure up flame with the white powder before. But there were no Vallè in the corridor with them.

Lindholf pressed his advantage with vigor. Glade retreated, flailing away, somehow blocking each blow, legs wobbly, eyes wide with confusion. He rammed the hilt of his sword up under Lindholf's guard, and Lindholf fell to his knees.

There was another clap. A burst of flame sent Glade reeling back again.

With lightning quickness, Lindholf was again afoot, swinging. The two boys exchanged a flurry of blows and then backed off, Glade panting, Lindholf watching with a stony coldness Tala had never before seen in her cousin.

"You fight with Vallè tricks!" Glade spat.

Lindholf pointed his blade at Glade's chest. With a flicker of his free hand came another puff of white powder, sliding down his blade this time. With a blow of air from his pursed lips, the base of

Lindholf's blade lit afire, the flame racing down toward the tip and Glade's startled face. The fire blazed toward him and launched from the point of the sword to his chest.

"Rotted angels!" Glade stumbled back, batting at the flames on his chest-plate armor. "What in the holy bloody fuck!"

"Enough!" Jovan Bronachell shouted, his tone commanding and deep, shoulder-length hair rippling in dark waves as he stormed toward them. The king and his retinue of black-armored Dayknights swept down the corridor, steel-toed boots thundering.

Lindholf backed away from Glade, sword no longer aflame, but smoke could be seen licking from the blade. Glade spat on the ground, breathing heavily.

Tala's older brother stepped between the two boys with authority. He wore a fur-trimmed cloak fastened with a brooch of Vallè-worked silver over a vest of decorative ring mail. "Put away your swords!" he commanded.

Both Glade and Lindholf sheathed their swords, Glade's expression bitter as he glared at Lindholf. "He used Vallè magic, Your Excellency. He overtook me with Vallè tricks."

Undaunted, Lindholf glared right back at him, his expression hard and focused.

"You're spoiled little brats, all of you!" Jovan raged, his face a rash of red. "I aim to split you up, send all you troublemakers to separate corners of the kingdom!" His fiery eyes fell on Tala. "Let you rot out your days as far away from me as possible!"

"It's Lindholf's fault," Glade snarled. "He started it. The blood-sucking oghul, I ought to thrash hi—"

"Rot out your days until Sterling Prentiss is found!" Jovan cut him off, still enraged. "Don't think I have any illusions it isn't you idiots responsible for the disappearance of my Dayknight captain!"

Glade wasn't done shouting either. "It's Lindholf and those damnable Vallè who are teaching him—"

"Shut up!" Lawri roared, finger in Glade's face. "Just shut your fucking mouth!"

Jovan backed away from Lawri, eyes widening, hand on the hilt of the dagger at his belt. He had not forgotten his previous encounter with his cousin. "Bloody mother," he muttered between clenched teeth. "You're all crazy."

Anger simmered behind Glade's eyes as they flew from the king to Lawri, then Lindholf. His face had always borne a peevish, conceited expression, but now his eyes, nose, and lips, all of it combined, appeared to be puckered into a vacant grimace as he pointed at Lindholf and sneered, "I won't forget this."

Three Silver Guards rushed up the hall toward Jovan, red-faced and winded, steel-toed boots clicking. "Pardon, my lord." The first Silver Guard bent his knee to Jovan upon arrival. "I've urgent news from Ser Castlegrail, if it please Your Excellency."

"Go on," Jovan said.

"Leif Chaparral has returned from Lord's Point. With him are two Sør Sevier captives and the princess, Jondralyn."

Jovan stiffened and drew in a deep breath. Tala did likewise.

The Silver Guard continued in a rushed tone. "Leif and the captives await you in Sunbird Hall, Your Excellency. As does the princess." The guardsman gulped as tears glistened in his eyes. "They say, my lord . . . . They say Jondralyn has suffered grievous injury and lies upon a litter near death."

† † †

Tala's tutor, Dame Mairgrid, could be heard wailing in the midst of the clamor and commotion swirling at the far end of Sunbird Hall. The two grand staircases that swept up both sides of the massive chamber to the balcony were jammed with onlookers—nobles, ladies, Silver Guards, Dayknights, kitchen help—horror fixed on every face. Ser

Tomas Vorkink, steward of Amadon Castle, and the king's chamberlain, Ser Landon Galloway, stood together directly under the balcony. A host of knights and nobles crowded the floor of the hall. Some were perched atop the long tables for a better view; others stood on the cushioned benches between the black pillars lining the chamber.

Large candelabra lined the walls of Sunbird Hall, the torchlight throwing a sharp glow over the congested and heaving room. Though the double doors above the balcony were thrown open, the hall was stifling and growing louder with exclamations of distress. The throng parted as Jovan and his Dayknight escort pushed through the middle of the room, Tala, Lawri, Lindholf, and Glade following in his wake.

Directly under the balcony was Leif Chaparral. He was in Dayknight armor, dusty from long travel, dark-rimmed eyes solemn. He held a rope in each hand, the lengths of which drooped to the floor and back up to connect to the tied wrists of Hawkwood and a bald-headed knight wearing a dirt-stained mix of leather bucklers and breastplate armor. Hawkwood wore dark leather breeches, a torn tunic, and a shirt torn and bloodied.

Tala followed his somber gaze to the floor, sucking in a sharp gasp when she finally saw the body on the makeshift litter in front of Leif.

It was Jondralyn.

Tala staggered toward her sister, scarcely hearing the pained gasps of Lindholf and Lawri. She sank to her knees in front of Jondralyn, who lay in full Silver Guard armor. A ragged gash stretched from her forehead just above her right eye down to the left side of her chin. The length of the ghastly injury was sewn closed with some type of rough thread. The entire bottom half of Jondralyn's face was mangled, purple and blue and swollen with infection, encrusted in congealed streaks of blood and nearly twice its normal size. Her tender-looking flesh was tightly stretched and straining with the bloat, her left eye naught but a filmy glaze of white, her right eye completely gone.

Above the gaping socket was shredded skin, exposing a hint of pale skull between the crude stitches.

The stench of Jondralyn's wound suddenly engulfed Tala, nearly causing her to retch. She sat back on her haunches and covered her face in horror, trying to hide behind both hands. Lawri knelt by her side, comforting arms around her shoulders.

"What tragedy is this?" Jovan muttered. "What has befallen my beloved sister?"

Tala glanced up through her tears, not believing her brother's feigned concern for even a moment. *This is your fault!* she wanted to scream.

Leif Chaparral handed the ropes holding Hawkwood and the bald knight to one of his Wolf Guards, then beckoned two of his other men forward. The men came bearing two swords each. Leif took the swords from the first man, curved blades with spiked hilts. He tossed them to the stone floor at Jovan's feet. "The twin blades of the Sør Sevier turncoat, Hawkwood. The loot of battle, and if it please Your Excellency, spoils I'd like to gift my brother Glade." But Jovan didn't even seem to notice the swords or Leif's request. His eyes remained fixed on Jondralyn's gruesome injury.

Glade stepped around Tala and then stepped over Jondralyn and snatched up the twin blades greedily. "Magnificent. Thank you." He bowed to his brother, admiring the swords, glancing nervously at Hawkwood.

Through the strands of black hair hanging in front of his face, Hawkwood's eyes were focused on Leif. There was a measured level of danger within those dark, devouring orbs as they sliced through the air. Tala shuddered when she heard both the pain and venom in his voice. "Have you no doctor to see to her?"

"Yes, a doctor?" Jovan looked around.

"Val-Korin went in search of Val-Gianni," answered Ser Tomas Vorkink, steward of the castle.

"Denarius has been summoned too," Ser Landon Galloway added. "The grand vicar and the quorum of five should be here shortly. They can soon administer to our poor befallen princess, if it please Your Excellency."

"Good." The king nodded, seemingly at a loss for words. "Good."

*'Twas you who wished her dead!* Tala wanted her brother to look at her, if only so he could see the accusation flowing from her eyes.

Leif snatched one of the swords from the second Wolf Guard—a longsword in an elegant white scabbard. He drew the blade. It sparkled blue in the light of Sunbird Hall, garnering everyone's attention. "I give you Sky Reaver, my lord." Leif bent his knee to Jovan and held out the sword for his king. "The sword of Aeros Raijael."

The crowded hall gasped at Leif's pronouncement.

Jovan took the sword and sheath. *"Sky Reaver."* His voice held both awe and reverence. He sliced the air with the blade twice, crisply. The sword sang with every movement. Then he rammed the sword home into the sheath with authority, holding it up with admiration.

"One last gift." Leif grabbed the fourth sword from his Wolf Guard—a plain sword. This one he threw down on the stone floor before Jovan. "The weapon that cleaved the face of our beautiful princess, Jondralyn. A rotted blade that should be melted down, its molten-hot steel rammed into the anus of the one who nearly killed her."

Leif looked to the bald knight standing next to Hawkwood. "This is the man who struck down our beloved princess! Gault Aulbrek, Knight Archaic of Sør Sevier! One of Aeros Raijael's personal bodyguards!" Every eye in Sunbird Hall fell upon the Sør Sevier knight.

Gault Aulbrek was tall, angular, and rangy. Though he stood before them in ropes and chains, he carried himself with a certain swaggering air, a coolness and poise, eyes flat and watchful, raw and untamed. Many in the hall did the three-fingered sign of the Laijon Cross over their hearts just looking at him.

"Kill him now!" several onlookers shouted. "Kill him now!"

Soon the entire Sunbird Hall was chanting the mantra. Tala desired his immediate death too. She hated his bald head and goatee and quiet confidence with a swift, furious passion. The stoic look he gave the baying throng was infuriating to her.

When the crowd calmed, Jovan spoke loudly. "I wish to hear the story of how these two men were captured and how our beloved Jondralyn was struck down."

"Permit me." Leif bowed, adjusted his armor. "Our beautiful princess was viciously and cowardly attacked—"

"That is a lie," Gault snarled between clenched teeth. There was a deep-rooted anger in his eyes that had not previously been there. "I will not suffer lies told about me, not by one such as you, Leif Chaparral." Gault held his head straight, gaze slicing into Jovan now. "It was a fair duel. At Jondralyn's request. Some of the men here with Leif saw it. I pulled my blow and spared her life. I was promised my freedom." His cold, hard eyes held those of Jovan as he raised his bound wrists. "Your sister promised my release. I aim for you to hold to that promise."

There was a dull ripple of concerned voices throughout the hall.

"What of the White Prince?" Jovan asked Leif, ignoring Gault as if he hadn't heard a word the man said. "You give me Aeros' sword. Has he been slain? What of Ser Culpa Barra?"

"'Twas Hawkwood who carried Sky Reaver," Leif answered. "I know not how he came into possession of Aeros' sword. He has offered up scant information. Culpa Barra proved himself a traitor, fleeing like a thief in the night near Lokkenfell. He is no longer to be trusted. I've a feeling he was working in league with Hawkwood and the dwarf all along. And in league with Sterling Prentiss, whom I also suspect of treachery." His eyes roamed the room. "I was hoping to spit in Sterling's fat, pitted face next time I saw him."

"Sterling has also proved himself a traitor," Jovan said, eyes burrowed into Tala. "He's either fled Amadon or been killed for the accusations levied against him."

Tala felt absolutely powerless to whatever effects Sterling's disappearance might now have on the court. *The consequence of the lies I spread.* She could feel the emotion well up in her. Lawri was still there beside her. Lindholf, too. Both still under as much suspicion as she in Jovan's eyes. *All my rotten lies!*

"Did Jondralyn meet with Aeros Raijael?" Jovan asked Leif. "Does the White Prince know that Gul Kana will not bow down to his threats?"

Leif hesitated a moment. "Truth is, my lord, your sister dared not meet with Aeros Raijael." He cleared his throat, bent his knee to his king. "'Twas I alone who ventured into the camp of the White Prince and spelled out our intent to Aeros. 'Twas I alone who informed him that Jovan Bronachell would stand and fight him."

"Splendid." The king bowed to Leif. "In Sterling Prentiss's absence, I will need a new captain of the Dayknights. For your bravery, I deem that you, Ser Leif Chaparral, will serve as my Dayknight captain. The official swearing-in will be soon. The ceremony in your honor shall be a celebration!"

Leif stayed on his knee before Jovan, bowing low, almost to the floor. "I am most honored, Your Excellency."

There was a smattering of claps from the crowd as Leif stood; a subdued celebration though, with Jondralyn lying on the floor between the two.

The Val Vallè ambassador, Val-Korin, entered the hall, his Vallè medicine man, Val-Gianni, right behind him, Seita and Val-Draekin too. Val-Korin wore a long bejeweled robe of red tied at the waist.

Val-Gianni swiftly shed his own similar raiment, handing it to Seita. Under the robe, the Vallè wore gray pantaloons secured with a black belt and a darker gray shirt and tunic. A well-worn leather satchel hung from one shoulder under his robe. "Her armor should have been removed days ago." He unslung his leather bag and knelt over Jondralyn. He opened his satchel and began pulling out various medical supplies. "She's feverish, burning up, trapped inside all this metal. I imagine she can scarcely breathe."

"Can you save her?" Jovan asked.

"Yes, can you?" Leif's words seemed no more than polite concern.

"Bring me a torch," the Vallè doctor said to no one in particular, as his eyes scoured Jondralyn.

"Get a torch for him." Leif snapped the order. Glade scurried off into the crowd toward the nearest wall sconce.

Val-Korin knelt and began unbuckling the armor fastened around Jondralyn's midsection, pulling it off. Her chest barely moved, so thin was her breathing under the bloody undershirt. Val-Gianni slid his hand under the back of her neck and gently lifted, turning her head slightly to the side. "She's got a wound on the back of the neck also." The Vallè set her head back down and examined her injured face again. "When I see infection this bad in a limb, I'm forced to chop it off." Tala's heart faltered as the Vallè sifted through his medical satchel anxiously and pulled forth a glass tube of dark purple liquid. "This much damage, and an untreated infection so close to the brain, it's a wonder she still breathes at all." Val-Gianni uncorked the tube. He slid his hand under Jondralyn's head again and gently lifted, putting the glass to her bloated lips. "Aelbazis liquor. It should help numb whatever pain she might feel."

Before he poured, he looked up at Jovan. "For the operation I am about to perform, I'd empty this room of people, but I fear we've not enough time. We've not a moment to waste before her heart stops beating altogether." He pried open her lips and poured. At first the liquid ran down the sides of her face until she began to choke, gagging, slobbering as she swallowed hard. When the tube was drained, some of the milky glaze had gone from Jondralyn's left eye.

Val-Gianni ordered Seita and Val-Draekin to secure each of her legs and asked Val-Korin to hold down her shoulders. "The infection needs draining, and she's liable to thrash about."

Tala felt a whisper of bitterness growing in the cold depths of her being, anger that something so dreadful and unfair had been done to her sister, rage at her brother and Leif and the Sør Sevier knight Gault Aulbrek, who had caused it all.

Glade finally returned with a torch in hand. "Kneel beside me," Val-Gianni ordered him. "I shall need the flame." He handed Glade a small iron poker the length of a quill pen, its tip sharpened to a needle point. "Heat the tip of it in the torch flame."

Glade did as instructed whilst Val-Gianni prodded the tender flesh of Jondralyn's face with two nimble fingers. Tala grimaced as blood and pus ran from the holes of the crude stitching above Jondralyn's eye. With more prodding, the wound parted and a thick glob of blood burst out, livid and scarlet, streaming down the side of her forehead.

Val-Gianni took the heated poker from Glade and worked fast, using its searing red point to prick at the rough stitching, working it free of Jondralyn's stiff, bloated flesh. Blood poured freely from the straining skin on Jondralyn's face now. Most of the men and women of the court looked away. Behind Tala, Lawri was crying.

Jondralyn's breathing was now rapid and hoarse. Seita and Val-Draekin tightened their grip on her legs. Once the wound was unstitched, the Vallè doctor carefully positioned all five fingers of both hands along the side of the seeping wound. He gently prodded the length of the swollen gash, finally settling on a spot. Then he pressed down hard. A broad and viscous geyser of puss erupted outward as the wound split. The cloudy white infection oozed over Val-Gianni's hands. Jondralyn suddenly screamed, her body writhing under the three Vallè who fought to restrain her. Through the screams and thrashing, Val-Gianni kept pressing on Jondralyn's face, draining the wound. A stream of pale sickness crept down the side of her face, pooling on the floor thick as goat cream. When he was done, the Vallè sawbones took a bottle of straight hard whiskey from his pouch and began cleaning out the wound. Jondralyn's renewed screams filled the hall—the sound pure terror and pain, tortured and raw. And the fury stirring within Tala's own soul was threatening to pull her down into places she dared not venture.

Glade reheated the poker, and Val-Gianni was now using it to cauterize the wound. As the red-hot iron slipped under Jondralyn's skin, the foul odor of burning flesh filled Tala's nostrils. She didn't know if she could watch any longer, hate and rage flowing through her. She, too, felt the urge to scream. She sharply inhaled and exhaled several deep, painful breaths of her own.

*It's all Jovan's fault!*

Squinting through the tears of rage forming in her eyes, Tala looked up at her brother. By the look on his face, Jovan was as horrified and confused as she. Leif's face, on the other hand, was a shrewd mask that veiled all thought save smugness.

Six spear-wielding Dayknights escorting Grand Vicar Denarius and the Quorum of Five Archbishops marched into the hall, Denarius' concerned gaze fixed on Jondralyn. He wore the regular burnt-orange-colored cassock of his station and immediately did the three-fingered sign of the Laijon Cross over the necklaces of silver and gold covering his heart. Then he covered his nose as the smell finally hit him, his jowly face turning red. Denarius was fat and lecherous and ugly and Tala wanted to lash out at him, too.

She knew her emotions were about to spill forth. But she was resolved—crying got no one anywhere at any time. Confidence and anger were what solved things. Her eyes traveled to Gault Aulbrek. The bald knight's emotionless eyes appeared to survey the entirety of Sunbird Hall at once.

As if he could sense he was being watched, his eyes fell on Tala. She wanted to let go of his gaze, look away, but his bold glance lingered on her with something she could not quite define, part sympathy, part level-eyed curiosity. *But who is he to feel for me?* Her fuming anger was growing so hysterically intense that she wondered if she wasn't going insane. *Somehow this is all part of the Bloodwood's twisted game!*

"You did this to her!" Tala's fierce shout was like a whip crack echoing through the hall. Everyone looked at her.

She launched herself from the floor straight at Gault with one tremendous burst of rage and strength, punching and tearing at his face.

His hands were tied before him, and he managed to shield his face from her initial blows. But through the berserk haze of her wrath, Tala hardly felt like a person any longer—rather a snarling, screaming, slavering animal, fingernails savagely raking him like the fangs of a saber-toothed lion.

Her attack lasted only a moment before both Leif and Jovan pulled her off the Sør Sevier knight and tossed her roughly to the floor. Lindholf and Lawri were immediately at her side, Lawri whispering comforting words that Tala could not understand. She was so utterly drained.

Her eyes felt like a blazing fire, scorching everyone in the room.

With all her might she hauled herself to her feet and ran from Sunbird Hall as fast as her legs would carry her.

✝ ✝ ✝ ✝ ✝

Tala found herself in Jondralyn's bedchamber, weary and heartsick and alone. She sank into the cushioned settee, seeking respite. But she could find scant comfort in the pastel colors of the walls and columns and arched ceiling that surrounded her or the rich maroon rug underfoot. Her chest would not stop pounding out its rage.

Her anger subsided only when her eyes fell on the tall mahogany bookshelf on the opposite side of the room. The shelves were full of the hundreds of books that her sister had collected over the years. Tala had read a few: *Dust of the Fallen*, *The Seeker of Agonmoore*, *Dread Fort Fire*. And then there were the ones her mother, Alana, had read to her when she was a child, like *The Mouse of Avlonia Castle*. A pain sliced through her heart as her gaze fell upon the gold-embossed spine of the last book in line: *Fairy Tales of the Val Vallè Princess Arianna*. They'd replaced Princess Arianna's likeness with that of Jondralyn on the Gul Kana copper coin.

She couldn't think of that. *Jondralyn was so beautiful.* She wanted to blank the image of her sister's grisly injuries from her mind. There was a gaping hollowness in Tala's stomach, in her soul, knowing Jondralyn might die.

Jovan had sent her sister on a quest, hoping she'd die. *Will I have to stand up to Jovan next? Will he conspire to kill me? Or does he already?* She thought of the Bloodwood and the Bloodwood's game. *The Bloodwood! At least there is one person who seems to think I am important!* She thought of the pouch of little green balls she was supposed to feed Lawri and what the assassin had written in the last note: *Your cute little cousin is only partially healed of what afflicts her. Make no mistake, she will spiral into insanity and die if she is not fed more of the antidote. In this sack I have left you twenty dosages. One per day. More will be given to you later ... but only if you continue to do my bidding and bring me what I ask for. Only then will Lawri's transformation be complete. Only then will your own destiny be underway.*

Tala had yet to follow through. She had not fed Lawri any of the green balls. She could not help Lawri, just as she could not help Jondralyn. She could not heal all wounds, right all wrongs. She could not fix even those evil things she had done herself, like lying about Sterling Prentiss. *How many of my lies will lead to the death of others?* She could almost hear the Bloodwood's amused laughter echo through Jondralyn's bedchamber. *Who is my dark tormentor?* Her eyes roamed the room, knowing she might very well be spied upon now. *Will I ever know?* It all made her feel so empty and useless.

Her eyes focused on the top of Jondralyn's bookshelf, her mind returning to her other note from the Bloodwood. *Find what secret parchments Jondralyn has hidden away in her chamber. Deliver unto me what you find. A terrible danger she keeps hidden, a danger that may lead to Purgatory and beyond.*

A deadly sort of calm swept over her as she rose from the settee and dragged it across the floor toward the bookshelf with purpose. She positioned the settee just where she wanted it and climbed atop it, standing. She thought of the rest of the Bloodwood's note. *One day, Tala, at the time of Absolution, you may be the only heir of Borden Bronachell still standing. These games you think are so silly are designed to test you, to prepare you for your own future. Take them seriously. Lawri's life depends on it. Your own life now depends on it.*

Standing on the settee, she could easily reach it, the third book to the left on the top shelf. She pulled it free, searched the hidden compartment behind, and pulled out the folded parchment that she knew Jondralyn had hidden there.

It was blank, but she knew just how to find what was written upon it.

✝ ✝ ✝ ✝ ✝

Betrayal. A word that hung over Tala like a hangman's noose.

Sitting in her own chamber now, she felt guilty for stealing the parchment from Jondralyn's hiding place. But it was all part of the Bloodwood's game. A game that she meant to take into her own hands.

She'd saved some of Roguemoore's black powder, knowing she would need it again. This time the powder had revealed a map—a map of the dungeons beneath the Hall of the Dayknights. It detailed caverns that led to deep and treacherous places under the prison called Purgatory, a twisting trail through rock and under water and beyond, to a clear destination of some import—to something that hovered just at the edges of her mind, something that rang familiar.

*If I truly have a destiny, it's certainly not to continually act as dumb lackey and errand girl for a Sør Sevier assassin who won't even show his face.* She was resolved to keep the map from the Bloodwood at all costs. *But I will follow the map and see where it leads.*

*I just have to get myself thrown into Purgatory.*

*Be most cautious of your friends, for they are easily stirred with resentment, envy, and spite. Friends are quick to betray. However, bestow trust on an enemy, and he will prove most loyal in his struggle to prove himself.*
—THE CHIVALRIC ILLUMINATIONS OF RAIJAEL

## CHAPTER NINE
# GAULT AULBREK

11TH DAY OF THE ETHIC MOON, 999TH YEAR OF LAIJON

AMADON, GUL KANA

P lace Hawkwood over there." Leif Chaparral's voice echoed in the hollowness of the dungeon. "Gault over there. And off with their hoods."

Gault was shoved forward and the hood jerked free. The chain connecting the iron bands around his ankles was no more than a foot in length, allowing him some movement. The cuffs around his wrists were thick iron rings also separated by a short length of chain. In Sør Sevier, the dungeon master of Rokenwalder, a gruff old fellow named Bogg, always secured his prisoners with their hands behind their backs. These Dayknight gaolers seemed competent enough, but cuffing him in the front was a mistake, a mistake Gault planned on taking advantage of.

The hood gone, he squinted against the glare of the torches, thinking he would find himself alone in a smothering room of cold stone. Instead it was a cage, iron bars on all four sides, roofed in a flat iron slab. A hole was cut in the center of the stone floor, presumably for bodily functions.

Hawkwood, his hood also removed, was in a similar cage just feet away, the two pens situated in the center of a vaulted stone chamber. Four Dayknights stood at attention before the cages. One held a large steel shield that stretched from the floor to the crown of his helm, his eyes on Hawkwood. The former Bloodwood was not only cuffed and shackled like Gault, but heavy iron chains crisscrossed his upper torso. His hair was plastered flat against his skull, caked with the food, feces, and other rot and refuse that had been thrown at him on their journey through the streets of Amadon. Gault's shirt and breeches, already clinging to his body by many long days of dirt and sweat from their ride from Ravenker, were covered in similar filth. He couldn't help but think back to the young girl who had struck him in the castle, the girl who had used her nails on his face. Tala Bronachell. He could still feel the raw wounds on his flesh, the pulp of the rotten fruit and other refuse thrown at him stinging and burrowing and clinging.

Gault and Hawkwood had made the journey to Purgatory chained to separate poles situated next to each other in the back of an oxcart. Once inside the Hall of the Dayknights, Gault was stripped of his armor, given threadbare prison garb, a hood placed over his head. With Hawkwood, he was marched through a series of vast empty halls, sloping passageways, and spiral staircases, the surrounding air brisk in some places, hot in others, the footsteps of their Dayknight escorts resounding on the stone floors, hollow and empty. Heavy iron doors opened and closed before and aft in nearly every hallway. The sharp echoing voices of other prisoners could be heard shouting their displeasures and hostilities from every direction.

"Secure Hawkwood's leg chain to the floor," Leif ordered one of the four knights. "And the chains wrapped around his body stay. His arms and legs will also remain cuffed and shackled at all times for the duration of his stay. He won't escape again, not under Leif Chaparral's watch."

The Dayknight did as commanded and hooked the leg chain through an iron ring buried in the center of the cage, all under the scathing glare of Hawkwood's dark eyes. "Do you really think all these useless precautions will hold me for long?"

"You're chained to the floor, you idiot," Leif chuckled. "Shackled. Cuffed. Sick. Barely coherent. Poisoned. Hopefully dying. I doubt you'll be going much of anywhere. Plus, two of these Dayknights will be posted before your locked cage at all times. You will be under their direct supervision."

"Direct supervision," Hawkwood said. "Sounds like a waste of time."

The Dayknight stepped out of Hawkwood's cage and secured the door, joining his three companions, standing near the knight with the huge shield. Each of the four Dayknights looked grim and determined and competent—a rarity inside a dungeon of any kind. The few prisons Gault had raided in Wyn Darrè and Adin Wyte had employed no more than thugs as gaolers—incompetents, the dregs of society, idiot fellows barely a notch above criminality themselves.

Grimacing, Hawkwood slumped to the floor of his cage. He moaned and curled up into the fetal position, his back to the line of Dayknights. Leif laughed. "You certainly seem well prepared to make your grand escape, Hawkwood."

Gault watched the former Bloodwood's struggled breathing. In his estimation, Hawkwood might very well die. The man had suffered many injuries in Ravenker that had not been tended to.

The door to Gault's cage was open and Leif stepped into the pen with him, his limp barely noticeable.

Leif drew a slow, silent breath, his voice sure and mellow.

"Welcome to Purgatory, Ser Gault Aulbrek." He smiled wickedly then, a smooth drawing back of his lips, revealing stark and perfect teeth, shockingly white in the sweltering dark of the chamber. "You are probably proud of your dungeons in Rokenwalder and how efficient King Aevrett Raijael's torturers can be. But have you heard tell what we Dayknights refer to as a Searing? A slow torture of torch and flame, usually starting with a wrist or mid-calf, scorching the flesh away until naught but bone remains. Most effective on prisoners, especially those with information the king may desire."

Gault held no illusions about the fact that one human could inflict pain and torment onto another with staggering precision and even joy. He'd heard the rumors of how deep and impenetrable this prison called Purgatory was, wondered how it truly stacked up against the dungeons of Rokenwalder. He knew of the foul rituals and tortures the criminals in Rokenwalder were ofttimes subjected to by the dungeon master, Bogg. He'd heard of even crueler things, like the Bloodwood's Sacrament of Souls. A revolting ritual.

"But alas, I'll likely hold off on the Searing for now." Leif continued in that soft voice of his, nasty, cocksure smile still on his face. "You are worthless to us dead. So if you try something ridiculous, like starving yourself, it'll only go worse for you. You will be force-fed. And my Dayknights are not gentle about that sort of thing. Food can be shoved down your throat and your jaw clamped shut afterward so you don't spew it back up."

"I'm starving now, and not on purpose," Gault said. Hunger had painfully twisted in his stomach for days. "I will happily take whatever food you have. It's not like you fed Hawkwood or me much on the journey from Ravenker. Have you a sandwich?"

Leif ignored his request. "My Dayknights have scant little patience for stupidity among the inmates either. If you try and harm yourself in any way, attempt suicide, cause a ruckus, throw your feces, complain too much, ask too many questions, or do whatever they deem irritating, you'll find they can make this place far less than comfortable."

"Doesn't really look all that pleasant now."

"Oh, trust me," Leif chided in that gentle, melodious voice, "it can swiftly get worse. Just act out and you'll find out what I mean. You'll find yourself strapped flat on your back to a knotty plank of wood for the duration of your stay."

Gault looked toward Hawkwood in the neighboring cage. The former Bloodwood, always a portrait of nonchalance and poise, was sitting again, watching the interaction between Gault and Leif with a calculated interest.

Leif stepped in front of Gault, dark-rimmed eyes roaming up and down his body. "You are uncouth and crude and most of all boring, Gault Aulbrek."

Gault stayed rooted in place, apprehension blooming in his gut. Leif was wearing some sort of perfume or exotic scent. To stifle the stench of the dungeon? Prisons usually had a unique smell, a combination of sweat, urine, and mold. Though this chamber smelled like cold stone and the burning pitch of the torches.

"You know nothing but savagery." Leif's voice carried a throaty lilt. "Existing to serve Aeros Raijael and follow his orders with no regard for anything or anyone. What you did to Baron Jubal Bruk, dismembering him, 'twas an abomination. What you did to Jondralyn, her face . . . I abhor all such useless violence."

Gault did not believe the man for a second. Leif Chaparral, of all people, was like Enna Spades, full of complete wanton cruelty. It was in his eyes. And on top of that, Leif was dishonest. At least one knew where they stood with Spades, and that was always in complete contempt.

"What goes through your mind when I'm speaking to you?" Leif leaned in and whispered. "I can see it, your mind, always churning, thinking, *fearing*." Gault stayed silent as Leif moved in even closer. He could feel the man's perfumed breath on his face as he spoke. "I thought I saw evidence of a girl in Aeros' tent, a Gul Kana girl, blond, impossibly beautiful. Was she a captive, the plunder of war, a prize that Aeros keeps? A prize that Aeros rapes?" He made a puckering, kissing sound with his lips, mere inches from Gault's face. "What does a man like you fear most?"

*Never seeing Ava Shay again.* That the thought had leaped into his head so quickly startled him. *Ava is a captive of Aeros and was never meant for me.* That reality was like a knife in the heart. An even bigger fear was never again seeing his daughter, Krista. *But she isn't really mine either, merely a stepdaughter, a stranger to me now, a girl I haven't seen in five years.* With those thoughts so suddenly churning in his mind, he had never before felt so helpless and lonely. *What does a man like me fear?*

"Aeros keeps the girl just as Jovan and I will keep you." Leif's voice was barely audible now. "Like we will *rape* you."

"The exact type of depravity Dayknights are known for in Sør Sevier," Gault shot back loudly. It was a weak insult, but Leif's baiting insults had done their job. "Perhaps you should just—"

Leif placed his finger across Gault's lips, as if to shush him. And the gesture stopped Gault cold. He shrank away from the man's touch and swallowed the remainder of his taunt, feeling a sinking dread like he'd never felt before.

Then he cursed his own weakness. He'd learned ages ago that showing anger or fear of any sort never led to anything good. He straightened his spine and forced his coldest, most level gaze onto the man before him. Boldness in the face of danger usually staved off most threats, no matter the kind. Most bullies respected courage and would back off. But as he stared into Leif's dark-rimmed eyes, he quickly realized that a select few sociopaths, people like Enna Spades and Leif Chaparral, didn't care whether their prey was scared shitless or full of bravado; their resulting torment would be the same.

Leif casually tilted his head to the side, voice still a whisper. "On your knees, Ser Gault." Then the man's hands were on Gault's shoulders, forcing him down to a half crouch. "Kneel and let me see what you are made of."

"Take your hands off me," Gault growled.

"Or what?" Leif hissed.

"Or I will kill you."

"*You* threaten *me?*"

"Aye, more than threaten." Anger blazed swift and hot within Gault and he hurled the full weight of his body straight up, the crown of his head smashing into the underside of Leif's chin with an ugly crack of hard skull on bone.

Leif slammed back into the iron bars of the cage and slid to the floor, stunned. Gault was on him immediately, hammering down on the man's face with clenched fists, hands still cuffed. He wrapped the short chain connecting his wrists around Leif's neck, pulling with all his might, chain digging into the man's straining neck.

Gault was knocked to the floor as the first Dayknight slammed into him with the shield. His head smacked the unforgiving ground as the knight drove him into the stone, burying him under his full weight. The remaining knights piled on top, grasping to secure his arms and legs. Gault was dazed, but he could hear Leif yowling, "Get the savage under control!"

Gault gave up his struggle, realizing it was a losing battle he fought. The four knights stood slowly, wary, the one with the shield ready. Gault slumped in dull weariness against the bars of his cage. He looked up blearily. Leif stood over him, swiping at the blood on his face. "An assault on the future captain of the Dayknights is the same as an assault on the king, or an assault on the grand vicar himself." Leif slurred his words. He cupped his hands over his bloody chin; thick scarlet drips streaked down his chest-plate armor. Gault smiled a self-satisfied smile, knowing he had injured the man. *A wound that he won't be able to hide.*

One of the Dayknights called out, near hysterical, "He's gone!" pointing to the cage next to Gault's.

Leif whirled. "Fuck!" His eyes grew as wide as dinner plates. "Fucking shit!" He exited the cage, the four Dayknights filing out behind him. Gault craned his neck and peered into the adjacent pen.

Hawkwood was gone.

Two cuffs, two leg irons, and a pile of chains were all that remained.

"Bloody Mother fucking Mia," Leif roared, spitting blood. "Bloody fucking rotted angels!"

One of the Dayknight gaolers asked, "Should we go looking for—"

"Fiery fucking dragons, of course you go looking for him!" Leif cut him off, hand still clenching his bloody jaw in pain. "My fucking mouth!"

"What if we can't find him—"

"What if we can't fucking find him!" Leif's petulant, frenzied shout echoed in the chamber. Then his brows furrowed in concentration. He bent forward, spitting out one long ropy string of blood.

When he rose, his voice was controlled and low with conspiracy. "If we can't find him, then none of you mentions a word of this to anyone." His dark-rimmed eyes ranged over each of the four Dayknights one by one. "I know each of you by name. And no one but us will ever know what happened here today. Not one single person. Or I shall slay you all myself."

*The Church of Laijon, along with its bishops and cathedrals and statues, was
never about peace or love or security. It was about control and never-ending
sadness. With the introduction of Ser Avard Sansom Bronachell's Dayknight
killers, all independent thought was relinquished among the innocent believers of
Mia with an appalling swiftness and eagerness, to be replaced by a stolid resolve
never to question the Church of Laijon or its ruling holy vicar or Quorum of Five
Archbishops in Amadon.*
—THE MOON SCROLLS OF MIA

# CHAPTER TEN
# JONDRALYN BRONACHELL

### 12TH DAY OF THE ETHIC MOON, 999TH YEAR OF LAIJON
### AMADON, GUL KANA

Cautiously, Hawkwood trod the length of the rising cliff, probing eyes fixed on the solid cliff wall above and the assorted
symbols carved into the stone. In spots the steep slope he
traversed grew slippery with loose shale. But he kept his footing and
ventured on. A cluster of crude carvings grabbed his attention, and
he leaned in for a closer look. They were simple shapes really, emblazoned like glittering pockets of flame on the flat stone surface of the
cliff: squares, circles within circles, crosses, crescent moons, shooting
stars, all twinkling, pulsing veins of red-blooming fire within the rock.

"What . . . do they . . . mean?" he asked, speech slurred and watery.

"They are death symbols," Squireck Van Hester's crystal-clear
voice answered from somewhere. "It means someone is about to die
here, in this very spot."

Hawkwood reached out a tentative hand, a desire to feel the texture of the red-glowing carvings consuming him. A sharp burst of wind nearly toppled him down the slope. He grabbed the cliff for balance. As soon as his hands made contact with stone, it was like a lance of lightning shot downward through his arm and into his body. He recoiled, stunned. A sensation of slow dizziness, as if he were about to pass out, consumed him. Then he realized the carvings before him had changed. He could see the prints of his hands outlined in bright red over the symbols. The prints held for a moment, and then slowly vanished, as if drawn down into the depths of the cliff.

A terrible, hopeless shudder twisted though Hawkwood. Something had just transferred from the carvings *into* him . . .

. . . and he'd felt it.

A familiar presence . . .

. . . *yes . . . a familiar presence,* Jondralyn thought.

*Is it real . . . . the lights within the stone? The shapes? The crosses? The stars?*

*Hawkwood?*

*I can feel him . . . his presence . . . his scent.*

*He is outside the stone . . . I am within . . .*

She placed her cheek against the rock wall and drank in the feel of Hawkwood emanating from the stone before her, his very presence soothing in comparison to the blazing-hot pain that consumed her entire face.

*He's finally found me in the cave!*

*Hawkwood is coming. . . .*

These little red symbols warming her flesh were meant for her. She could feel Hawkwood's essence in them. But then her heart fluttered as she watched them slowly fade and vanish. Close to panic, she *wished* them back.

Her face was a sudden mass of agony and stiff, cramped muscle, the pain surging and subsiding in a random, rhythmless dance of torture. Her forehead hurt the worst, a constant stinging, like a festering disease. And it wouldn't stop bleeding. It was a slow and plodding flow of blood that just sort of oozed out, so slowly she questioned whether she wasn't in danger of bleeding to death.

Although death would be a joyful release from the pain she now felt.

*If I'm not already dead . . .*

It was as if the air she breathed had been injected with some foul witchcraft, its sole purpose to keep the wound on her face and forehead vibrant with pain. And when she'd try to swipe the stinging agony away, her hands would return slick with blood. Blood that would just crust over and dry on her skin, and she had no way to wash herself.

*But Hawkwood is venturing into the stone to save me. . . .*

She could feel herself suffocating. *Are my eyes open, or closed?* Either way, deep down somewhere below in the darkness of whatever bleak, cold cave she was in, she saw something foggy, wavering in the distance.

She saw *herself*—riding atop a magnificent white stallion underneath a large burning tree. She was a glorious silver-eyed knight with a glowing white shield, horned helm, and a curious bone-hilted white sword, the cross-hilt curved and graceful, in the shape of a crescent moon. A blond girl was perched on the saddle before her; the girl's hand was a metal claw . . . bright red blood pumping through veins in the scaled metal. And the girl had *green* glowing eyes! "All the weapons and stones will be gathered in Savon," the girl whispered.

Jondralyn's hands trembled against the reins of her mount, her face a scorching lump of pain she couldn't ignore under the incredible suffocating weight of the horned helm on her head.

Then it was gone and she was in a cave again. She looked back at the stone wall in front of her, and the light and shapes came back.

Circles within circles at first, like they were laid over the rock with a red paintbrush. Squares followed, then crosses, so many crosses, crescent moons, and what looked like falling stars, all of them faint, barely perceptible, swirling with a soft orange-red glow that flickered and danced as if the rock wall before her was hollow and flame was licking around inside, trying to escape.

The shapes were warm to the touch and she soaked in the heat, the comfort.

*Hawkwood sends the stars . . . the crosses . . . the moons . . .*

But still, her face was an expanding globe of searing, inescapable agony—agony and torture surrounded by a silent, stifling loneliness. It was a hot and humid and suffocating cave and she lived alone in a darkness so black and penetrating she sometimes wondered if she still had eyes.

Did she? She did! But the white sword with the crescent-moon-shaped hilt was coming at her, to pluck out her eyes one by one. And with every silvery-white flash of the sword, she would jerk her hands up in defense . . . and feel for her eyes. Sure enough, they were there. *One of them anyway.* But to what end really? She could close them both, clench them tight, and open them again. The blackness and pain were still the same. And how horribly black this cave was. For all she knew, light might've never penetrated such a dark and deep and agonizing hole. She couldn't see the walls or the ceiling, but she knew they were there, sensed them, on all sides, spreading out and around her, then constricting, like a jagged, suffocating womb. Everything was suffocating. She could scarcely breathe, it was so suffocating. It felt like she hadn't taken a solid breath in moons. And within this suffocation, there weren't even any shadows to keep her company.

She knew that shadows could live only if there was light.

But there was no light here. Only flashing white swords followed by pain. *Is this the underworld . . . ?*

Long ago, she recalled, she had slept on a fluffy mattress stacked with pillows and quilts. She could spread her arms and legs and the silky fabric would caress her skin.

No more.

She screamed and screamed and screamed and kept screaming until her lungs burned. *Will I ever escape this pain?* She pulled the chains. Yanked them. Nothing. She would never escape. Suffocating iron chains constricting everywhere . . .

*Where did the chains come from . . . ?* Blood dribbled from her forehead and into her eyes. *Her eye . . .*

She wiped the blood away and the stinging continued.

*I am dead. . . . I am in the underworld. . . .*

Once, as a young girl, she'd had the notion that there was no Laijon and certainly no heaven or underworld. She'd theorized that when a person died, their physical body was laid to rest, but their mind—their conscience—lived on in a perpetual dream state, and this eternal dream state was either joyful or nightmarish, depending on how you'd lived your life. Death was not the end of being. One's spirit became a virtually powerless entity suspended in a dimensionless emptiness of agony or joy.

*I am rotting in a stone tomb. A cross-shaped tomb!*

Her face was a lump of agony. An insect of some kind began crawling over it. She wiped it away. Her hand met nothing. There was no insect. *But I can hear them. Rats! Spiders! Spiders! On the floor all around me, eyeing me, wanting to nibble at my face.*

There was another bug. A beetle. She felt it scurrying around, its little feet dancing on her face. She kept swatting at herself.

*Get off, get off, get off, bugs! Painful bugs! Biting and biting and biting and . . .*

And then a bearded man with daggers for hands was wiping the bugs away for her. *Yes . . . he will take care of me. . . .*

The bearded man, so familiar. Yet his arms were sheared off above the elbows, black tar covering the stumps. And like a nightmare, two silver daggers protruded from those stumps. But so familiar. Broad brows and a broad forehead sloping back to graying hair and deep-squinting eyes. Fearsome in a way . . .

"I know." His voice was gruff and scratchy. "They asked if I wanted the daggers removed. but I prefer to keep them." A deep pain was hidden behind his eyes. "So I can use them to kill the horrid woman who placed them there."

*Who?* Jondralyn tried to ask, grimacing at the dryness of her throat. It seemed her mouth barely worked, as if something muffled the sound of it, as if only half of it was even functional. Something *was* blocking her nose, forcing her to breathe through her mouth— or at least the corner of her mouth that worked.

She tried speaking again. "Who?"

"Was Enna Spades who did this to me."

She looked around. She wasn't in a cave at all. *Almost familiar . . .*

She was lying on her back in a warm room, looking up at a clay-mottled roof, rafters of dark timber stretching across. She tried to sit up. "No, no, no," the bearded man admonished. "You've been in and out of consciousness all night. The Vallè sawbones has been watching over you. Cleaned you up mostly. Wrapped all them bandages about your face anyway. But he ain't here right now. It's just me and you."

Jondralyn reached up, straining, feeling with her fingers. Half her head, including one eye, was covered in cloth, and her neck was wrapped too. *One eye!* No wonder everything looked so strange and warped. And it all smelled of some type of sterilizing ointment too. "The grand vicar came in earlier," the bearded man said. "Pronounced some kind of blessing over you. Said he'd be back soon. Said you would need privacy. They'll more than likely move me out of here soon. I'm pretty much healed anyway."

She could see the bearded man only from the chest up. That was all that was visible of him above the blankets that had been piled over her. Everything still seemed skewed, distorted, and fuzzy.

The room was full of hanging sheets and had a large window on the far end, streaming in sunlight. One wall was lined with a handful of beds and cots. The other was covered in an array of medical implements, saws and other horrid-looking tools she imagined were for cutting and poking and prodding. What looked like an old stone bread oven sat smack in the middle of the room. Glass jars of herbs and poultices and what appeared to be animal grease lined the shelves near the doorway. Cisterns and pots were under the shelves. She knew she was in the infirmary. Still, she asked the obvious, "Where am I?" But with the pain and stiffness of her face and mouth, it came out as "Wha ah I?" She tried again, enunciating slowly. "Where. Ham. Hi." That didn't sound right either.

The man seemed to understand. "Infirmary. Amadon Castle. Do you even know what's happened to you, Jondralyn?"

*The silver flash of a sword.* She flinched.

Imaginary hands flying up to block the imaginary blow. An oxcart. Hawkwood's soothing touch. *Fancy delusion.* Leif Chaparral. She remembered him being there. And Culpa Barra. Her head was slowly clearing. *Gault Aulbrek!* "So foolsh," she slurred. Her throat burned with thirst.

"Don't blame yourself," the bearded man said. "They are all savages. Everyone in Aeros Raijael's army is pure evil." That haunted look was still fixed in the man's eyes, as if he too had seen that same evil face-to-face. *Daggers for arms!* She focused on the man watching over her. *Baron Jubal Bruk! That's who he is!*

She remembered Leif Chaparral bringing the baron to Amadon in a wooden box, arms and legs chopped off by the enemy. *He has a son in Gallows Haven.* Sadness engulfed her, realizing the man had lost more than just his limbs. *He had a son . . .*

"Jhuubal Brhuk?" She reached out a hand and latched on to his arm above the dagger, frustrated that her mouth wouldn't work quite right. "Bharon Brhuk."

"Aye, you're getting better. You woke up two hours ago and had no idea who I was. Val-Gianni's medicines seem to be doing their job. The Vallè heal fast, and no wonder. Their medicines are a miracle. But you'll likely be laid up awhile."

Things were becoming clearer now. She had some recollection of some events. She vaguely remembered Val-Gianni giving her a potion of some herbal concoction, mixed in with a draught of wine that he forced down her throat.

She spied the white lumps of quickening lime for disinfecting surfaces on a stout wooden table between her bed and the wall. There was also a stone basin full of some sort of caustic chemical. She'd smelled it before as a child. The chemical was for ridding the infirmary of human blood and waste smells. Herbs and spices were bunched and piled on the table too: pepper, ginger, nutmeg, cloves, poppy, and heather. They were fragrant.

*To rid the place of my stink?*

She feared what she must look like, what injuries she'd suffered at the hands of Gault Aulbrek. She could feel her arms and legs just fine. Everything seemed intact, but sore. She was horrified that the bulk of her face was covered in bandages. She wanted out of this place. Wanted her own bedchamber. There were guards outside the door of the infirmary, no doubt. *I can order them to take me away....*

There were two copper tankards and a ceramic pitcher of water on the table near her bed. She propped herself up carefully on one elbow and gingerly poured herself a drink. The water soothed her flaming throat.

"Hawkwood," she murmured once she set down the tankard, the vowels coming to her a bit easier now, her voice less slurred. "The dwarwf. Needs to know I'm okay. Roguemoore needs to know what's happened."

"Hawkwood," Jubal Bruk said. "He's in Purgatory with the Sør Sevier knight who chopped your face—" He clamped his mouth shut, as if embarrassed he'd so callously used the word "chopped," then went on. "And they say Roguemoore ain't been seen in moons."

*Does Roguemoore know what has happened to me? Does he know what happened to Hawkwood?* Squireck Van Hester was not here, and she had no way of reaching him on Rockliegh Isles. Who could she trust? She placed her hand on the baron's arm above the stump. "Find . . . Find . . ." She was losing focus.

"Find your brother?"

She shook her head. Pain flooded her body. "Vawl-Draekin. Find Vawl-Draekin for me. Bring him here." She just couldn't pronounce anyone's name right.

"The Vallè? That fellow who's friends with Val-Korin's daughter?"

She dipped her head in affirmation.

"I'm not in any condition to go wandering about the castle," He held up the stumps of his arms and the daggers sticking from the tar, a hollow look entering his eyes. "More useless than a dwarf." Then he smiled. "Oh, I reckon I've learned to move about some, but—"

She patted his arm. It was a struggle talking, her mouth dry and hoarse from heavy breathing. "Please," she rasped. "Please, for me."

"Aye, for you, Jondralyn." He sat back, determination visible in his eyes. "I'll get Val-Draekin here. Just might take a while."

† † † †

Baron Bruk's search for Val-Draekin had taken most of the day; in the intervening time, Val-Gianni had tended to her. She'd asked the doctor to describe her injuries. But he had been hesitant to say, informing her that the grand vicar would come later and answer any questions she had.

When Val-Draekin arrived, he explained everything, describing her wounds using his own face as example, drawing a line with his finger stretched from his forehead just above his right eye straight down to the left side of his chin. "The wound had been crudely sewn shut. My best guess is that Hawkwood did what he could to keep you alive."

She cleared her throat self-consciously, breathing heavily. She had no idea a person could miss breathing through their nose so much. Her mouth was bone dry from the strain of making up the difference. Horrified by the description of her injury, she wanted to block the image from her mind. "Baron Bruk mentioned Hawkwood was in Purgatory?"

Val-Draekin's eyes were shadowed with concern. "Hawkwood was paraded through the angry streets of Amadon straight to the Hall of the Dayknights and thrown into the dungeons with Gault Aulbrek. I'm afraid he won't escape this time."

"Purgatory cannot hold Hawkwood."

"Leif has posted two Dayknight guards right outside his cell both day and night."

Her heart ached thinking of her beloved in Purgatory. *He only stayed onboard the oxcart for my benefit. Now he suffers for my failures.*

*So many failures.* She again thought of Val-Draekin's description of her face. The visual wouldn't leave her mind. *How does one handle such disfigurement?* She'd seen people grow old, knew it was hard for many to come to terms with aging and illness and injury or anything that changed their appearance. And her beauty had always been an intrinsic part of her life. *What have I done to make the great One and Only forsake me so? Is it my own pride I am being punished for?* Gul Kana was a prosperous realm, and she'd only wanted to protect that prosperity and way of life. She'd only wanted to usurp her brother in the arena to defend her kingdom from invasion, to fight off the oghul raids in the north and Aeros from the west. She'd only journeyed west with Leif to challenge the White Prince to hasten those goals.

*And also to attain my own glory as the Harbinger of Absolution as one of the Five Warrior Angels returned.*

*Was it truly my own pride that caused this?*

She recalled the time she met Val-Draekin—his entrance into the Filthy Horse Saloon. Hawkwood claimed the Vallè had pickpocketed the sailors. She had defended his right to be in the saloon, even when the victims of his crime had insisted he leave. Yet they'd wanted him to leave based on his race, not because of his crimes. And that hadn't seemed fair to her. But what was fairness anyway?

She tried her utmost to focus on Val-Draekin with her one eye. "I need ask a great f-favor of you." Her speech was still shaky. Still she met his calm gaze, unblinking. "You must go to Lord's Point for me. You must go and find Roguemoore. The dwarf. The Thurn—the Turn Key Saloon was to be their rhendevue . . . rend . . . the place they were to meet up . . ." She inwardly cursed her inability to make sense. "The dwarf must know what has happened to me and Hawkwood. That we both still live."

"Lord's Point," the Vallè stated. "Are you sure that is where he will be?"

She nodded. "You are the only one I dare ashk . . . dare ask. And you must go alone. Nobody must know where you have gone. Use the King's Highway. Four days at most to get there. I will get you enough coin for the tolls." She grabbed his arm.

He sat back, brows sharp with contemplation. "You must understand, I can't just leave Seita and her father without an explanation." She could see his mind pondering the request, mulling over the implications. After a moment, he stood and bowed at the waist. "I will do this for you. I will find the dwarf and let him know of your fate."

† † † † †

Not long after Val-Draekin took his leave, Tala entered the room briskly, her features composed. She was wearing a striking dark-umber dress flowing to the floor. *She's grown into such beautiful young woman.* Jondralyn felt almost like a proud mother and it warmed her heart to see her sister.

"They should let you stay in your own chamber," Tala said in an unnatural rush. "I begged Jovan. But he insisted you remain here."

Jondralyn smiled faintly—it was all she could manage under the bandages. Tala's cool composure seemed to melt at her smile. There was a hollow look in Tala's eyes as she stepped up to the side of the bed. Then her young features hardened with determination again. "Why has this happened, Jon?" She seemed on the verge of saying more, but didn't, her gaze roaming over the bandages.

"I too wish it didn't have to be like this," Jondralyn said.

"They say Denarius is on his way here." Tala set her jaw firmly. "But I won't let him be alone with you."

"What are you talking about?" Jondralyn grabbed her younger sister's hand in her own, held it close to her chest. *She's having a harder time grasping her emotions than I.*

The transformation from grim determination to utter fright came quickly to Tala's features. "I won't let the vicar minister to you. I won't leave you alone with him." Tala then climbed onto the bed and lay down next to her. Jondralyn hesitated, then took a deep breath and draped her arm protectively around her younger sister, pulling her close.

Still, her own heart beat with panic at Tala's concern.

*Lest faith be lost, man's search for solace in the world around him began anew.
Some believed that only those who worshipped the sea were blessed with freedom
from the wraiths.*
— THE WAY AND TRUTH OF LAIJON

# CHAPTER ELEVEN
# AVA SHAY

15TH DAY OF THE ETHIC MOON, 999TH YEAR OF LAIJON
BETWEEN BEDFORD AND BAINBRIDGE, GUL KANA

Hammerfiss towered over Ava Shay to the left, Mancellor Allen to her right. Jenko Bruk knelt with Enna Spades. He was in full Sør Sevier armor. And though he smiled up at Aeros Raijael, no warmth reached his amber-colored eyes. Aeros nodded, and Jenko and Spades rose to their feet and donned their helms in one seamless motion. All three mounted their horses and charged down the hill toward the circle of Leifid wagons, swords drawn, hooves of their mounts kicking up clods of peat. Fifty more mounted Knights of the Blue Sword followed on their heels. Near a hundred other knights standing at attention on the grassy hill behind Ava readied their longbows.

*Once again Aeros Raijael has trotted me out to watch the horror.* Ava wished she was drunk. Spirits were the only comfort she found anymore. She stood in silence next to Hammerfiss and Mancellor; her simple woolen shift, tied at the waist with a strip of leather, rippled in the breeze.

The fugitives from Leifid had set up camp—a protective circle of wagons—in a meadow just under the Autumn Range, their oxen grazing near a gurgling stream. From her viewpoint on the hill above, Ava counted more than sixty scared women and children huddled together inside that wagon circle.

Seventy or so ill-equipped men and boys charged out from the circle of wagons to meet Aeros' attack. Some carried swords, but most were armed with naught but rakes and hoes and grayken harpoons. None wore armor of any kind. Some wore heavy cloaks and jackets as protection. They shouted oaths and curses as they bravely charged. The bowmen standing behind Ava fired, arrows stirring the air above. Within the span of a heartbeat the first row of men and boys rushing toward Aeros toppled. The second volley of arrows sent the remaining men and boys reeling back, retreating to the safety of the wagons.

The war whoops of Aeros' mounted knights filled the air, their cries hollow and hideous and loud and meant to frighten. The terrified screams of the Leifid fugitives rose in pitch, and within the circle of wagons mayhem suddenly broke loose. What men remained scattered for cover under the wagons, behind barrels or braying mules.

A third hail of arrows rained down into their midst. One arrow tore the ear off a little boy who clung quietly to his father's lap. A woman in the center of the circle of wagons took an arrow to the face and fell into one of the campfires, sending up a blaze of sparks and billowing smoke. Blood blossomed from the stomach of an infant girl with brown hair; she slumped against a wagon wheel and closed her eyes, the tip of the arrow protruding from her back. A crying woman rushed to her aid. Yet before she could reach the girl, the ground was a swirl of dust and blood as Aeros' charging knights tore into the circle of wagons. The wave of destruction that followed was almost too much for Ava to bear. She wanted to run straight for the Autumn Range and hide.

She could tell which knight was Aeros by his glittering armor and Spades by her dark blue cape and pure white stallion, Slaughter. The Sør Sevier warrior woman fought as one possessed, her gleaming sword a bloody whirl of lightning and destruction. She could not make out which knight was Jenko Bruk in the tumult, the Knights of the Blue Sword all looking so similar.

She remained rooted in place, focusing on the face of one Leifid boy no more than eleven. The boy had hair so blond it almost glowed in the moonlight. Amidst the screams and chaos, her eyes couldn't help but follow him. The heavy-armored haunches of a whirling Sør Sevier destrier struck the boy from behind, forcing him face-first to the dirt. A woman, the side of her head a cavern of jagged bones and blood, fell dead on the boy. He squirmed from under the woman's weight, and ran toward a small girl who clung to her father's leg. The father was begging for mercy, waving a white kerchief of truce. He was run through with a sword, his daughter also slain. The blond boy saw their deaths and fell back on his butt, scrambling frantically away, trying to regain his feet. Before he could stand, he was bludgeoned back to the ground by the blunt end of a flashing Sør Sevier spear. He crawled to one of the wagons, hiding under it, just as its canvas top was torn away by several of Aeros' knights.

Inside the wagon, mothers clung to their babies, shielding the blows of ax and sword. One woman was speared clear through, the merciless weapon piercing her and her baby both. Ava Shay's stomach jumped and whirled at the sight.

The blond boy crawled out from under the wagon, looking as stunned and shaken as Ava felt, knights on horseback a swirling clamor all around. Ava prayed for the boy's safety, hoping Laijon would see this one innocent soul live out the night. The sound of battle raging below was like that of a thunderstorm, the thudding of heavy horse, the shouts of the knights, the screams and crying of the fearful and the groans of the dying—a primitive dance of rage and slaughter.

When the battle died down, and most from Leifid lay dead, only the moans of the injured could still be heard. Ava was relieved to see that the blond boy still lived. She thanked Laijon for that, then grew angry with her Lord for not sparing the rest. One girl, probably not much older than Ava, was on her knees, begging for mercy. Her faint pleas tugged at Ava's heart. Standing over the girl was a blood-splattered Sør Sevier knight with a dripping red longsword. When the knight removed his helm, Ava could see that it was Jenko Bruk. He reached for the girl's hand, helping her up. As the girl stood, she did so with a certain bravery that kept Ava spellbound. The girl's delicate skin and curly hair appeared as soft and white as new-fallen snow, and not a spot of blood blemished a pleat of her sun-colored dress. Enna Spades, sword in hand, helm in the crook of her arm, walked up casually and stabbed the girl in the heart. She fell dead at Jenko's feet.

Spades sheathed her bloody sword and slapped Jenko across the face, the chastising tone of her voice carrying up the hill. The result of her lecture—Jenko turned and stomped on the head of the dead girl. A foam of scarlet bubbled from her skull, spread over her snowy curls, and soaked into her yellow dress.

And with that final act of brutality, the battle was over.

Next to Ava, Hammerfiss' shoulders shook, belly rumbling with laughter. His teeth flashed a violent grin down at her. "Bloody good slaughter, that."

Ava looked at the passive face of Mancellor Allen, reading nothing in the former Wyn Darrè man's dark, stiff countenance. The black tattoos under his eyes added to his mystery and shadow. He finally noticed her gaze and gave her a nod of sadness. She felt a sudden comfort in having him near. His silent manner and rigid poise reminded her of Gault.

Ava looked toward the circle of wagons again. Some twenty-odd survivors were all that was left, mostly children, all dirt-covered and scared. They groveled at the feet of the murderous Sør Sevier knights who rounded them up, begging and crying. Spades and Jenko gathered the captives together in a line at the behest of Aeros.

One teenage girl broke from the line and ran for one of the coverless wagons, prying a wailing baby from a dead woman's arms. The girl was dragged away from the wagon by Spades, managing to clutch the baby to her chest as she was pulled along the ground. The baby screamed. The girl tried to muffle its cries.

The line of captives was marched up the hill, led by Aeros, Spades, and Jenko. The remaining Knights of the Blue Sword began piling up the dead for burning, gathering what mules and horses still lived, scavenging what wagons were still of use.

Once the prisoners stood on the grassy knoll, they were forced to stand in a row directly before Ava, Hammerfiss, and Mancellor. Ava's eyes quickly found the blond boy. An arrow had gouged a raw trail through his scalp, peeling away a furrow of hair and skin. Blood was running down the back of his neck under his mop of blond hair. He scratched at the wound and mop of blond hair with dirty, trembling fingers.

"Everyone's dead," one of the prisoners muttered. "Who will save us now?"

"There are no saviors in Gul Kana!" Spades wasted no time in answering, strutting before the captives. "We're the most battle-hardened sons of bitches who've ever stepped foot on these shores!"

Ava had seen it all before. The entire group of prisoners shrank away from the red-haired woman as she strode up and down the line, flipping a copper coin over and over in her hand. She was intimidating in her blood-splattered battle armor. The bloodied longsword at her hip and crossbow and quiver of bolts strapped to the leather baldric over her shoulder only added to her danger and threat. Like all in Gul Kana, these children had never seen a woman knight before, especially not a savage like Enna Spades.

"What we've got here is a rather wretched situation." Spades spoke loud enough that all could hear. "It does seem a horrible crime that you have all been saddled to such feeble company as ourselves. I'm sorry to burden you with formalities of warfare, but we need to discuss some issues without rancor." She paused, as she always paused in this very part of her speech. "We can either put you to death or—"

"Not." Hammerfiss finished the sentence for her. All the captives' eyes fell on the massive man who now commanded their attention, the largest, scariest man any of them had likely ever seen. Stout of girth and broad of shoulders, the red-haired giant had two meaty fists seemingly as big and hard-looking as boulders. The bones, fetishes, and bangles tied into his hair and beard along with the sharp blue tattoos covering his face only made him all the more frightening to behold. He wore a leather shoulder harness over his silver armor, bearing a spiked mace as big and round as an ox head.

Spades shrugged. "So you feel there must indeed be some divine purpose to this madness, Hammerfiss?"

"I don't claim any divine purpose," he said. "Nor do I think their situation is entirely hopeless, Spades."

It was the same speech these two gave every group of survivors. Ava had heard it many times.

"Indeed, nothing is hopeless." Spades' eyes roamed over the group of prisoners. "Since we've already established that we have no qualms about speaking frankly, what say you of their fate?"

Hammerfiss' mouth, as it always did, spread into a mad grin. "I've always felt that some previously useless lives can be converted to a better purpose. That being said, I say that any children of Leifid younger than ten are now property of Sør Sevier! You are to be adopted into the covenant of Raijael and raised up in true righteousness and faith as citizens of Sør Sevier and believers in Aeros Raijael, your true One and Only!"

As always, the prisoners looked baffled, relieved, and scared all at once.

Spades motioned for Mancellor Allen. He stepped from Ava's side and made his way toward the warrior woman. Spades nodded at Jenko. He swiftly pulled a knife from the sheath at his belt.

"Be mindful of what age they give," Spades admonished him, then put her copper coin away and began her interrogation—an interrogation that Ava knew would not end well for a handful of these captives. Jenko and Mancellor followed the red-haired woman to the end of the line. *Just answer younger than whatever Spades' arbitrary cutoff age is this time,* Ava silently implored the line of prisoners.

Spades stood before the teenage girl who had snatched the crying baby from the wagon. The baby still whimpered in her arms. "Name and age?" Spades asked.

The Leifid girl answered, "Shanin. Nineteen."

Jenko stabbed her through the eye. As nineteen-year-old Shanin crumpled to the dirt, the baby tumbled from her arms. Mancellor Allen picked the baby up from off the ground, cradled it in his arms. It squalled and shrieked.

Aeros marched forward and snatched the child from Mancellor. He wended his way down the hill toward the meadow where the oxen still grazed, baby in his arms.

The rest of the children were asked their names and ages. Spades did the asking. Any who answered older than ten had their throats swiftly cut by Jenko. It was a grim and bloody repeat of the aftermath of the sacking of Gallows Haven, Ravenker, and several other hamlets between. Ava had always believed in the mercy of Laijon and also believed that the torments of the underworld were reserved for those like Spades, and now Jenko Bruk. Hammerfiss too. The Spider also. Aeros most of all.

Near the end of the line was a girl with hair the color of corn silk. She had a blood-crusted hole in her neck, and her arm was mostly severed. It hung there by a thread of muscle. Yet she didn't cry or seem to be affected by the injury at all. She just stood there in an ever-growing pool of blood at her feet. Either the girl was the most courageous creature Ava had ever seen, or the most traumatized. When asked her name and age, the injured girl answered, "Tomasina, age seven and three months. My arm is hurt."

"Your arm is more than just hurt, sweetie." Spades nodded to Jenko. He sliced open the small girl's throat. The girl just stood there until she bled out, emotionless eyes draining of all life as she gazed straight at Jenko. Then she toppled over dead.

Spades moved on to the dark-haired boy next in line. "Name and age."

"I'm Thaddeus Jonas, ten years old, but my pa calls me Thad."

Jenko held the bloody knife up to Thad's throat.

"You look older than ten, boy," Spades said.

"He *is* ten, you pig," the tall girl next to him blurted. "He's my brother. Leave him be!"

Spades appraised her. "And how old are you?" she demanded.

"My name is Sophia. I'm only thirteen and I wager I'm more smarter and more mature than you . . . and you can't hurt me, you pig-fucking bitch—"

Jenko slashed Sophia's throat. The girl's brother was splattered with her blood. It was too much. Ava's entire body was racked with anguish; everything Jenko did knifed across her own heart too. *How can this still be happening? Is there no Laijon above to stop it?*

Spades turned to Thad. "Were your folks part of this group of blasphemous Laijon worshippers?"

"My ma and pa were killed," Thad answered, shaking, his sister's blood running down his face. He started crying uncontrollably.

"You'll warm to us soon." Spades patted Thad on the cheek. Then she and Jenko moved to the blond boy Ava had watched throughout the battle. He was the last in line and appeared so petrified with fear his skin seemed nearly as pale and translucent as the White Prince's. His eyes were wide and round, his features almost perfect; graceful chin and cheekbones, thin nose, sharp eyes and brows under stark-white hair. There was something in the way he looked that reminded Ava of the Vallè woman on the black horse she'd seen on the trail above Gallows Haven with Nail and Stefan.

"Name and age?" Spades asked him.

"I'm ten," he answered. "I haven't a name."

"You're lying." Spades reached out and pushed the boy's hair away from his ears. "About a number of things." The blond boy had the sharp, pointed ears of a Vallè. Ava's eyes widened at the sight.

"A Vallè mutt," Hammerfiss chortled, amused.

Spades studied the boy. "You realize my lord Aeros will most definitely *not* want one like you around."

Spades beckoned Ava Shay. "Come."

Ava stayed rooted in place.

"Come here," Spades again commanded. "Time I taught you what killing is like. Time I taught you the power of a blade in your hand."

Ava felt her face fall, hoping Spades was not in any way serious. But there was no jest in the woman's eyes. There was naught but cold determination.

"Come here," Spades repeated with strained patience.

Repulsed, Ava moved forward, hesitation in each step.

"Give her the knife," Spades ordered Jenko.

His face tightened as he held out the blade for her.

Ava's mind was suddenly shrouded in disbelief at what was being asked. *But if I take that knife I may just . . .*

She met Jenko's amber eyes—and those eyes, at the moment, were filled with such a tenderness it nearly shattered her already fatigued mind. *He knows what is in my heart! He doesn't want to watch me do this any more than I want to do it....*

She suddenly realized all Jenko had been through, and how she'd so unfairly judged him for it. Jenko had done what he could to survive.

She was so tired of watching everything unfold beyond her control.

As she stared at the knife being offered, she felt the sudden need to finally do something. *Give myself a sweet release* . . . And with that tender look in Jenko's eyes, she felt those last vestiges of fatigue finally dissipate. Here and now she could finally make her own life better.

Recovering herself slightly, she took the knife from him, their fingers touching in the exchange. The burning feel of his flesh on hers was like a cleansing fire of absolution.

When Jenko released the knife, he looked at first distressed, then puzzled, then completely afraid.

"You know what you must do," Spades said, her gaze quietly traveling from Ava to the blond Vallè boy. Ava gripped the knife tightly in her fist. It was already covered in the blood of others, but she didn't care. Her killing move would be swift and sure. Just one thrust and it would be over—all of it would be so *finally* over.

The Vallè boy stood still, big calf eyes gazing at her without feeling or connection. She brought the blade up, its bloody tip between her and the boy, her hand seizing tight the hilt, her teeth and jaw clenched. *Does he know my pleading eyes followed him as he ran the gauntlet of Aeros Raijael's merciless army? Does he know I prayed to Laijon that he be spared?*

*Does he know that I will not hurt him?*

When she pushed the knife up under his chin, he didn't waver. His eyes didn't even widen. She pulled back slightly, hand trembling, eyes blurring over with tears that she could not stop. *Quick! And it will be over—*

Suddenly the knife was snatched from her hand, and the boy's throat was a gaping red gash. Jenko's backhanded slice had opened a wide furrow across the boy's throat. Blood splashed over Ava's chest and face. She staggered back as the boy toppled forward, dead.

"Ha!" Hammerfiss laughed. "Young love."

Jenko stood before Ava now, pretending to wipe the blood from her face. But from the angle in which he stood, nobody could see what he actually did. A clean knife, smaller than the bloody one she had just held, dropped down the neckline of her shift from the palm of his hand. She felt the cold blade slide between her breasts and catch at the leather thong tied around her waist. "Use it wisely," he whispered. "Use it on Aeros."

He stepped away from her and stared right at Spades, making a show of ramming the bloody knife he'd used to open the boy's neck into the sheath at his belt.

Stunned, Ava felt a tremendous need to clean the boy's blood from her brow. But there was naught she could do but look in astonishment at Jenko.

Spades glared at Jenko too, speaking flatly. "You should have let the girl do what she was meant to do."

† † † † †

Only when all the remaining prisoners under ten were marching away and the sun had at last danced off the aspen leaves and then bowed below the purple shadows of the Autumn Range did the silver-wolves begin to howl in the mountains far above.

In the cool darkness, Ava followed Spades down to the stream near the meadow where the Leifid oxen still grazed. She dipped her trembling hands into the pure waters and washed the dry blood of an eleven-year-old Vallè boy from her brow.

Aeros Raijael was standing not far downstream on the cool grassy bank.

Bleary-eyed, Ava approached him. Dread coiled like a serpent around her heart when she saw the baby floating away from Aeros. Cold and dead, it bobbed and then sank into the bubbling crystal waters. As she met the White Prince's icy black eyes, she was glad she had Jenko Bruk's small knife for company.

Only then, with that thought, did Ava Shay notice that the wraiths had not visited her once this dreadful day.

*Be it man, woman, dwarf, or Vallè, preach any other gospel unto you, that we, the
Last Warrior Angels, have not preached unto you let him be accursed. For some
may come who would pervert the gospels of Laijon.*
— THE WAY AND TRUTH OF LAIJON

# CHAPTER TWELVE

# NAIL

16TH DAY OF THE ETHIC MOON, 999TH YEAR OF LAIJON

LORD'S POINT, GUL KANA

I can't believe I let her die," Stefan said, hair ruffling in the
wind, tumbling against his shoulders as he approached Culpa
Barra's charger and Hawkwood's roan. The two horses stood at
the tether in the stable near Dusty. He stroked the neck of Culpa's
mount first.

"Gisela's death wasn't your fault," Nail said. "You protected her as
best you could. I saw you carry her over that bridge in the Roahm
Mines before it collapsed. She loved you." He would never tell his
friend it was the blue angel stone that had killed Gisela, not poisoned mushrooms and freezing cold.

The waters of the Saint Only Channel crashed against the breakers
behind the stable. The same air that pushed the waves to shore lifted a
lock of Nail's blond hair and let it fall against his cheek. The stiff eddying

of the ocean breeze whirled straight past him and into the stable of the Turn Key Saloon, causing him to blink against the swirling dust.

The back side of the Turn Key Saloon and Inn faced the ocean docks along the northwest edge of Lord's Point. There was a sizable courtyard next to the stables. The Turn Key was no regular common alehouse. It was run by ex-gaolers, the proprietor a gruff fellow named Derry Richrath. The saloon itself was the regular haunt of the gaolers and other such lawmen stationed in Lord's Point. Derry's serving boy, Otto, had told Nail that a saloon was the name of any drinking establishment inside city limits near a dock, a place reserved for sailors and pirates, or in the Turn Key's instance, gaolers. A tavern could be found anywhere. A cantina was an even dirtier place, meant for thieves and cutthroats. Earlier that day Nail had watched from the stables as the gaolers had practiced their various gaoling techniques in the courtyard—most of them involved chaining each other up, prodding each other with poleaxes, and knocking each other down with heavy shields, all of it to the tune of bawdy talk that curdled his ears. One thing the gaolers had taught him: a sensitive man without a rough tongue would never make it as a gaoler.

"I just should have held her tighter that final night," Stefan said. Nail's best friend still had the keen eyes and tanned skin of a grayken hunter, but those once confident eyes held a perpetual sadness now. "She was so sick that night. So feverish. So terribly cold."

"You needn't feel guilty." Nail knew Stefan had yet to recover from the death of Gisela Barnwell—the sweet girl who was once Maiden Blue of the Mourning Moon Feast. That feast had been the last night any of them had been happy. It was the night Stefan had won the bow from Baron Bruk in the tournament, a bow that he'd then lost the next day when the army of the White Prince had destroyed Gallows Haven. Shawcroft had given Stefan a Dayknight bow after the Sør Sevier attack, a bow that Stefan had carried with him everywhere, a bow with the name GISELA now carved into its ash and witch-hazel stock. Nail had no such thing to cling to, just a turtle carving around his neck from a girl who had soundly rejected him. And his cold repayment had been to leave Ava with the enemy to die.

The late-afternoon sun felt like both a curse and punishment on his back. He asked Stefan, "At Godwyn's abbey, remember how Liz Hen accused me of having no heart? Of not caring about Shawcroft's death? Or caring about anything or anyone, for that matter?"

"Aye," Stefan answered. "But I wouldn't listen to anything Liz Hen says."

"I often wonder if she wasn't right." Nail picked up a section of hay from the floor of the stable. "Have I ever cared about anything, or helped anyone but myself?"

"You saw us to safety through the mines and the cold nights in the mountains, Nail. You saved Zane from the sharks when he got knocked into the sea. You've nothing to be ashamed of."

"But Zane is dead now." Unable to mask the frustration and pain in his voice, Nail broke open the hunk of hay in his hands. Hay dust sparkled up into his face. "I stuck a knife into Zane's heart. So what did it matter that I saved him from the sharks?"

He tossed the hay over the log railing to Dusty, who waited eagerly. The hay bounced off the pony's snout, scattered under her front legs. She bent to nibble.

"You were brave both times." Stefan gently patted Culpa's mount. "You did something the other grayken hunters could not: save Zane. And in the mountains, you did something neither Liz Hen nor I could do: ease his suffering."

"Zane believed Laijon was awaiting his soul." Nail was heartsick. "I could see it on his face, Stef. He believed it was Laijon's will he die."

There was just so much trauma he could not forget. Some nights he couldn't even sleep from the weight of it on his mind.

Stefan continued to stroke Culpa's horse. "Fate took Zane from us. 'Twas not Laijon's will. If there ever was such a god."

The wind picked up. Nail considered his friend's comment. *Stefan never was convinced of the truthfulness of* The Way and Truth of Laijon, *no matter how many Ember Lighting prayers we memorized.*

Stefan stepped lightly across a trampled patch of hay toward Hawkwood's sturdy roan. "How many days we been at Lord's Point?"

"Nine I think," Nail answered. "Still waiting for Roguemoore's brother to arrive."

Stefan gently combed the mane of Hawkwood's roan. "The dwarf is getting more uptight the longer we linger. He's itching to keep moving on, find the rest of those weapons of the Five Warrior Angels. Both he and Godwyn."

Nail nodded. "I've the feeling they ain't gonna wait much longer for Ironcloud."

"I've a feeling they're gonna ask for our help again," Stefan said. "That our part in all this isn't over yet. Not by half. And I don't know if I have it in me to carry on with the whole mess."

"We are tied to them somehow," Nail said. "All of us. Tied to the dwarf and the bishop. Tied to those weapons, too. I'm not for giving up hope yet."

"I don't share the feeling. Though I want to be brave and helpful to our new friends, I just do not fully believe in their cause. What will I do when they finally ask too much of me?"

"When it comes time for you to choose the path you want, I will support what decision you make," Nail said. "I won't hold you to any promises I myself have made to the Brethren of Mia." He himself still harbored reservations about Roguemoore and Godwyn and their motives too; he held no illusions about whether they were still using him in some way. And though he had sworn fealty to the dwarf in the Swithen Wells Trail Abbey, he would not hesitate to break that promise if he was forced to choose between them and his friend Stefan.

The dwarf's plan, ever since leaving Godwyn's abbey, had been to meet his brother, Ironcloud, at the Turn Key Saloon in Lord's Point and then venture farther north to gather the remaining weapons of the Five Warrior Angels. But that plan had gone awry in Ravenker, when Nail and Hawkwood had been separated from the rest of the group. Nail had eventually made it to Lord's Point with Culpa Barra. Hawkwood was captive of Leif Chaparral and on his way to Amadon in the back of a wagon with the Sør Sevier knight, Gault Aulbrek, and Princess Jondralyn Bronachell. Roguemoore had taken Culpa Barra's news of Hawkwood and Jondralyn with a heavy heart.

Nail watched Stefan pet Hawkwood's roan. "You know how I told Godwyn and the dwarf that Jenko Bruk stole the ax and stone and Shawcroft's satchel?"

"Aye?" Stefan said. "That Jenko joined with the enemy is horrifying."

"I left much out of that story, Stefan," Nail went on. "An assassin was with Jenko. He nearly killed me. But Hawkwood saved me. I owe Hawkwood my loyalty."

"Why did you leave that out?"

"I do not know. Maybe it is because Hawkwood gave me hope, hope that not all men are just looking out for themselves, beholden to ancient texts and prophecies. Thing is," Nail muttered, "I felt some kind of magic in the battle-ax when I fought Jenko in Ravenker. I need it back, what he stole from me."

"So you truly believe it was *Forgetting Moon* we found? You believe the weapons of the Five Warrior Angels are real?"

"I want to." Nail's eyes traveled from the stable yard westward across the bay toward the Fortress of Saint Only and the five barely visible Laijon Towers in Wyn Darrè lining the cliffs of Aelathia not seventy miles beyond, just faint needles in the far distance over the blue horizon. *I want to believe in something. I want to hope.*

The Fortress of Saint Only loomed large over the ocean a mere ten miles from Lord's Point. It sat high upon a lofty summit of rock some seven hundred feet above the ocean, a pinnacle of rock Godwyn referred to as the Mont. The bishop claimed those in Adin Wyte referred to the fortress as Mont Saint Only rather than the Fortress of Saint Only, as the rest of the Five Isles called it. Whatever its official name, the Mont jutted out into the ocean at the very southern tip of Adin Wyte like the prow of a colossal ship plying the sea. Some said the craggy Mont and the fortress atop it rivaled Amadon Castle atop Mount Albion in sheer size.

On a clear day like today, the Fortress of Saint Only atop the Mont was so breathtaking in majesty it would steal Nail's breath. The burning beacon atop its loftiest tower captured his eye every time he looked to the west. The ten-mile strip of ocean that separated Saint Only from Lord's Point was shallow, a mere ten to fifteen feet deep all the way across. And the ebbing tide, for somewhere between four and six hours each afternoon, was so low one could actually walk to Mont Saint Only across the stretch of muddy sand and mire. On sunny days, the sand of the channel would ofttimes bake over. A fleet team of horses could pull a heavy-laden wagon over the crusted sediment. But when the erratic tide rose in the early evening, it rose fast and swift. Nobody could predict the fickle tide. Many unfortunate travelers had been caught in that vast no-man's-land and drowned. Large ships could not cross the channel, even at the water's highest. Only smaller vessels dared the journey. And after nightfall, 'twas only foolish sailors who ventured into those waters, even afloat, as merfolk and sharks plied the shallows nightly.

But ever since Aeros Raijael had conquered Adin Wyte five years ago and overtaken Mont Saint Only, few now made that trip over the low tide sands. Most in Gul Kana had assumed the White Prince would launch his attack on Gul Kana across those sands. But as Nail knew all too well, Gallows Haven had been Aeros' aim all along.

Saint Only was a deserted fortress now. Godwyn had explained how the armies of Sør Sevier had sacked the great stronghold. How Aeros had humiliated Edmon Guy Van Hester, king of Adin Wyte, and then left him to rule his empty fortress in solitude and disgrace.

All of it was made worse by the actions of the king's son, Squireck, who had murdered one of the Quorum of Five Archbishops in Amadon. At the time it had been the most infamous crime in all the Five Isles. It was said that Ser Edmon was so overcome with grief over the loss of his kingdom and his son's crimes that he now moped about the halls of Mont Saint Only in rags and a broken crown, his throne abandoned to ruin, his Lancer Guard scattered to the winds.

In fact, these last few days, Godwyn had been teaching the four youths from Gallows Haven a lot about the histories of Saint Only and Lord's Point. He had taken Nail, Stefan, Dokie, and Liz Hen to visit the Lord's Point Cathedral earlier that morning for Eighth Day service. But the service had been postponed as the cathedral had been full to brimming with refugees from all along the southwestern coast of Gul Kana. Scared and homeless people were pouring into Lord's Point daily, fleeing the advancing armies of the White Prince and the wave of destruction that followed in their wake.

The cathedral itself was one of the most magnificent structures in Gul Kana—designed in the typical Laijon Cross floor plan. Godwyn had explained that the cathedral's construction had taken the ancients of the Lord's Point area over five hundred years to construct. It was begun, Godwyn had said, as most cathedrals were, shortly after the death of Laijon nearly a thousand years ago. Still, despite its age, the cathedral's vaulted stone arches and walls were solid, nary a crack to be found. Upon entering the massive edifice, Nail had been struck by the two towering and majestic rows of columns rising up above the nave—twelve on each side—with single trunks in veined Riven Rock marble and capitals with leaf carvings. The columns supported a sequence of round arched arcades and thick wooden beams. There were narrow windows high on the walls, running the length of the nave and transepts, letting in some sun, but the bulk of the light came from the rear of the cathedral above the entrance doors.

Above the sculpted tympanum were three magnificent

stained-glass windows. Windows so huge Nail couldn't even grasp how they had been made, or what held them in place. And just like the stained-glass windows in the Gallows Haven chapel, the art of these splendorous windows was familiar. In the center was an image of Laijon, the five angel stones hovering above Him; white, red, black, green, and blue. Laijon wore shimmering armor and hefted the battle-ax *Forgetting Moon*. In the left window were two white-robed Warrior Angels, one wielding the sword *Afflicted Fire*, the other a black crossbow, *Blackest Heart*. In the right window were the other two Warrior Angels, one wearing the war helm *Lonesome Crown*, another with the shield *Ethic Shroud*. Nail had stared at the center window the longest, gazing up at the image of *Forgetting Moon*, realizing that the artist who'd designed the window had failed to capture the battle-ax's size and shape in every regard. In the center window below the ax, the artists had also placed five little oddities near the bottom of the frame unlike anything he'd ever seen before—five tiny cloaked knights with silver skulls for faces.

The light from those glorious windows combined had rained in over the throng of Gul Kana refugees who lined every inch of floor space in the building, bathing the nave and people within it in a wondrous array of color as they'd prayed.

The entire time he'd spent in the cathedral Nail had wondered, *Does Laijon even watch over any of them who pray? Will Laijon answer their thousands of prayers and stave the flow of Aeros Raijael's armies?*

✝ ✝ ✝ ✝ ✝

It took Nail a moment for his eyes to grow accustomed to the smoke-filled darkness of the saloon. The dirt-stained windows on either side of the back door didn't offer much help, nor did the soot-stained windows across the room near the front entrance. The place was mostly empty. Tables, chairs, and stools were strewn around the place in a sloppy order. A few candles were lit in sconces high on the walls, sending off a soft-butter glow. The open hearth near the bar along the right wall crackled with flame. There was the welcome smell of wood smoke, and Nail's eyes watered from it.

The Turn Key wasn't quite as homey and inviting as the Grayken Spear Inn in Gallows Haven. And the rooms they were staying in above the saloon were filthy, tiny, and not well ventilated. Nail shared his small room with Stefan, Dokie, and Liz Hen. The girl took the bed, the three boys the floor.

Nail and Stefan edged their way through the saloon toward a round table in the far left corner of the room, where the others had gathered. Roguemoore's head was buried in a book. Godwyn sat near Culpa Barra, the two in deep conversation. Liz Hen sat close to the Dayknight, Dokie Liddle with her. Beer Mug was there too, eyes constantly alert, tail thumping lightly against the wood-plank floor.

Roguemoore shot Nail and Stefan a sidelong glance, beckoned them sit, then went back to his book. As he settled into his chair, Nail noticed how the firelight shone off the large planes of the dwarf's rough face. With his prickly beard and stout stature, the dwarf ofttimes reminded Nail of an angry black bear he and Shawcroft had come across in the high alpine woods above Gallows Haven one summer.

"Hey, Stefan," Liz Hen blurted. "I finally figured out why that shark didn't swallow Dokie whole."

"And why's that?" Stefan asked.

"Because Dokie shit his britches!" she bellowed. "He wasn't to the shark's taste!"

"Well, I ain't ashamed," Dokie piped in. "I reckon it only proves I'm not the only living thing concerned with the cleanliness of bung-holes."

"Evidently so!" Liz Hen laughed, gleeful eyes falling on the Dayknight next to her. "As I've always aimed to prove, good ser, sharks and most other carnivorous creatures are mighty averse to shit-smeared humans."

Culpa politely smiled and went back to his muffled conversation with Godwyn. Nail vaguely recalled one of Aeros' knights forcing Dokie to swim with the sharks after the sacking of Gallows Haven. He'd taken a good blow to the head that day and events were hazy.

The double doors of the kitchen swung open. A wispy little fellow about Nail's same age came toddling out, wearing a cook's apron and carrying a flat iron tray. It was Otto, the serving boy. He was a slip of a kid with a crooked nose and narrow lips, round eyes cast wide on his already thin face. The hue of his rumpled hair was like muddy water. In fact, in Nail's estimation, the kid bore a striking resemblance to Dokie.

"Speaking of irresponsible bum-fuckery," Liz Hen muttered as the boy approached. "This Turn Key Saloon is a catastrophe. It's not like the Grayken Spear Inn back home at all." She waggled her finger at Dokie for emphasis. "Boys ought not be helpin' in the kitchen. Boys ought not be actin' the barmaid. Boys ought not be cooking nor serving meals of any sort. Not a smidge of domestic bona fides reside within a man, and they make this Otto both cook *and* server?" She waved her hand in disgust.

"You realize I can hear everything you're saying." Otto's eyes were bleary with fatigue as he handed Liz Hen the metal tray with dozens of pine nuts smoldering on it. "If it eases your mind, Richrath's gaoler committee sent me to a class on stew making the other day. Finished top of the class, I did."

"Richrath's gaoler committee is a stupid bunch of lazy fat slags. They shouldn't even be running a restaurant." Liz Hen stared at the tray in her hands. "We supposed to eat these?" She set the tray down with a clatter before it fried her fingers. The nuts looked burnt black and sat in a thick greasy film that looked like ash.

"Aye, eat them with buttered fried shrimp and herb-flavored mead,"

Otto said. "The best meal in all of Gul Kana. Cooked them myself."

"I think I'd rather chew on the dirty wood floor."

"I thought you liked the food here, Liz Hen." Dokie reached for a blackened nut and popped it into his mouth. He grimaced at the taste but swallowed it down.

"This place is a joke." Liz Hen favored Dokie with a venomous look. "With naught but gaolers in charge, it'll never rise above the mediocre."

Otto didn't seem too terribly perturbed by Liz Hen's insults, eyes scanning the table. "What do you all want to eat?"

"Anything," Liz Hen said. "Just that it ain't been previously digested."

"I recommend the stew," Otto said flatly.

"You mean the stew they taught you to make in some class?" Liz Hen huffed. "I think not. I want eggs, scrambled, with diced chicken mixed in with the eggs."

"Chicken in the eggs?" Otto took a step back.

"I been thinkin' about a dinner of chicken and eggs all day."

Otto looked horrified. "I don't think I'm allowed to mix the two. Choose some other species of meat to mix with your eggs."

"What in the bleeding Mother Mia are you goin' on about?"

"Scramblin' a chicken up in its own eggs," Otto answered. "It's cruel."

"Cruel to the chickens or to me?" Liz Hen's glare darkened.

"I'll take the stew," Dokie piped in.

"Stew for everyone." Roguemoore looked up from his book, the look in his deep-set eyes one of mild irritation. Otto shrugged and shuffled off.

"Right." Liz Hen added. "Stew for everyone. And hasten your step, boy."

Otto turned back to her. "I don't like to be *hastened*. It's my one deficiency."

"You seem the type who's deficient in a lot of things."

Otto scrunched his brow in consternation, then turned and drifted off into the kitchen.

"I swear." Liz Hen looked straight at Culpa Barra. "If there's anyone liable to fuck up the gathering of a meal, it's that little clod-pole there."

Satisfied with her assessment of the kitchen help, she ruffled the fur on Beer Mug's head. The dog panted happily beside her.

"My pa always said you can tell a lot about a person by the way they treat the waitstaff," Dokie piped in.

"What do you mean by that?" Hurt filled Liz Hen's eyes.

"I just think it's best you give poor Otto a break."

Liz Hen's entire face was frowning now. "I suppose." There was a hint of pain in her voice. "I just miss my job at the Grayken Spear is all."

"I understand." Dokie embraced her hand in his.

Roguemoore cleared his throat and closed his book with a clap, and with scarred hands slipped it into the buckled front closure of his tunic. "I think it's safe to say I don't think my brother is coming. Ironcloud should have been here by now. Something has happened."

"Should we proceed without him?" Culpa asked. "I'm hesitant to continue on to Sky Lochs and Deadwood Gate without Ironcloud or Shawcroft's instructions."

"I believe we've no choice," Roguemoore answered.

"I say we wait a little longer." Godwyn's skin was as weathered and rough as a blacksmith's leather glove; deep creases curled at the corners of his eyes as he spoke.

"We dare not linger more than need be," the dwarf said. "The longer we wait for my brother, the more worried I get, for the only reason Ironcloud would not show up is that he has finally discovered the fate of Borden Bronachell. We should strike off on our own, even though we no longer have Shawcroft's satchel and the maps or other necessary directions he'd provided."

Nail felt guilty every time Shawcroft's satchel was brought up. Apparently his master had left some form of coded instructions important to the Brethren of Mia within the satchel that Nail was not privy to. As the debate among the three men continued, Nail only half listened, almost drifting off to sleep, lulled by the gentle crackling of the hearth.

The door of the saloon creaked open and a shaft of light broke harsh across Nail's face and spread inward toward the bar. Two cloaked figures were silhouetted in the entrance. The door swung closed, the shaft of light vanished, and the silhouettes melted into the dark confines of the room.

Cloaked all in black from head to foot, faces hidden beneath the cowls of their cloaks, the newcomers moved through the tavern toward Nail's table with an unobtrusive ease. The breeze that followed their entrance carried something in it, some foreboding that made Nail sit up straight and alert in his chair as they approached. Culpa Barra stood too, as did Bishop Godwyn, hands on their sword hilts.

Once at their table, both of the mysterious cloaked newcomers bowed. Then one of them threw back his hood, revealing the round green eyes and refined face of a Vallè, upturned ears just visible through strands of black hair. His facial features were smooth, unblemished, and sharp.

Roguemoore's startled gaze widened. "Val-Draekin." He stood, nervous smile forming under his bushy beard.

The Vallè named Val-Draekin untied his cloak, revealing fine black leather armor studded with shined layers of ring mail about the neckline. Nail noted the hang of the Vallè's sword and the way he carried it at his hip, as if born with it. The Vallè's gaze swept the table, yet never focused on any single one of them. He did offer a nod of recognition to Culpa Barra. "I come at the behest of Jondralyn." Val-Draekin bent his knee again to the dwarf. Roguemoore acknowledged the Vallè's bow with a congenial nod of his own, his hardened gaze fixed on the second cloaked figure.

When the second stranger removed her hood, Nail scooted his chair back involuntarily, heart lurching in his chest. It was a Vallè woman. A very familiar Vallè woman. With perfect narrow ears, hair of lustrous silvery-white waves, slanting, needle-thin eyebrows above high-boned cheeks and full lips, this sharp-featured Vallè maiden looked exactly like the Bloodwood Shawcroft had murdered.

Some pallid light glowed just beneath her skin and he couldn't look away. It was as if this strange girl's very ethereal presence pulled at him. His eyes locked on hers—they were large, almond-shaped orbs, irises startlingly green, which seemed to devour everything they touched, especially when they met his. It was as if she knew all his secrets and dreams with but a look. He glanced away from her gaze.

"Seita." Roguemoore bowed before her. "What brings you?"

A graceful smile played at the corners of her mouth. But her eyes remained fixed on Nail as she answered the dwarf. "Once Val-Draekin told me who would be here with you, Ser Roguemoore, how could I not come?"

*But 'twas the angel stones, above all other gifts, that were to be used to banish*
*the demons and their lords into the underworld. Each stone bonded to one of the*
*weapons of the Five Warrior Angels.*
—THE WAY AND TRUTH OF LAIJON

# CHAPTER THIRTEEN
# TALA BRONACHELL

17TH DAY OF THE ETHIC MOON, 999TH YEAR OF LAIJON

AMADON, GUL KANA

Tala sat on a cushioned divan in the center of her own bedchamber, Lawri Le Graven brushing her hair with a silver Avlonia hand brush—a gift from Lord Nolan Darkliegh to Alana Bronachell, a royal heirloom bequeathed to Tala at her mother's death. The morning's crisp coolness lay heavy in the room. The silver brush was clunky and cold as Lawri ran it through her hair. The stiff tines tugged painfully at Tala's scalp. It didn't help that her hair was wet from her recent bath. She worried it might freeze in clumps right there atop her head.

Lawri's unbandaged arm hovered just inside Tala's vision. A gloomy raw scar ran a ragged puss-infected trail up the length of her left forearm from her inner wrist to the underside of her elbow. It looked to have never been stitched closed. "Did you not go to the infirmary for that?" she asked.

Lawri brushed her hair in silence. Tala tried to lighten the tenor of her question. "I've never seen Jovan so frightened as when that dagger sliced your arm." Her voice weakened. "Actually, *I've* likely never been so frightened."

"I'm glad he cut me," Lawri said quickly.

"What?" Tala was puzzled. "Why?"

"Something was growing inside of me." Lawri worked the brush through Tala's hair a bit more slowly now. "I could feel it. A *thing* within me. A thing that brought on fevers, aches in every joint, even bad dreams. Jovan cutting me released all that."

"That makes scant little sense to me." Tala was even more bewildered, and frankly disturbed. *It was the Bloodwood poison that caused Lawri's fevers.*

"It mostly relieved the pain in my heart," Lawri said.

"Jovan cutting your wrist relieved the pain in your heart?"

"Not really my heart," Lawri continued, "but more like the pain of my . . ." She paused. "It's hard to explain, Tala. It's not really a pain I was trying to relieve. Or even a fever or a *thing*. But more like . . . my sin, I guess."

"The dagger relieved your sin?" Tala questioned.

"Something like that."

"But Laijon has already relieved us of sin. Have you not read *The Way and Truth of Laijon*? Have you never been to the Hallowed Grove and looked upon the Atonement Tree?"

"Yes," Lawri answered. "But the scriptures never did me any good. They only make me feel worse about myself. Same with that tree."

"Laijon's ways are not our ways," Tala countered. The entire conversation was odd and becoming frustrating to follow. "Ofttimes we must work hard to discover the words of comfort in the holy book."

"That's something the vicar would say, and completely unhelpful." The silver brush was working through Tala's hair rapidly now, roughly even. Lawri went on. "I picked up a piece of clear broken glass a few days ago. Stared at it for hours, studying it as if it were a copy of *The Way and Truth of Laijon*, trying to decipher its invisible meaning. But in the end, it was naught but a solid hunk of clear glass, naught but a see-through mystery. Completely unhelpful, completely useless. Useless but for one thing."

"Useless but for what?" Tala asked.

"I used it to cut my arm open again," Lawri answered casually. "To drain the infection. It made me feel, I guess, better somehow." She spoke in a matter-of-fact tone. "Again, no more fever. No more heartaches. Thoughts of Laijon or the Atonement Tree never made me feel such relief as pushing and squeezing that infection out of my body. With Laijon and the holy book, I only feel more guilt. But by operating on myself, I found I could focus on just that one thing: easing the pain of the wound. Instead of my mind always focusing on the things around me I can't control. I could control this."

Tala had the strong sense of being on the outside of all she was hearing, of standing on a cliff ledge belonging to a world she knew nothing of. The whole thing horrified her and made her sad. She realized her own self-imposed self-reliance had left a savage and bruised mark on her own soul that needed healing. *And Lawri deals with her pain in her own way.* But operating on yourself as if you were an expert Vallè healer could not be the answer. She just couldn't relate to anything her cousin was saying.

"When I feel dead inside," Lawri continued, "I think of that shard of clear glass and the relief I found in cleansing my wound. Jovan cutting me. It made me feel alive, Tala. And I need to be reminded of that. And I need to feel alive."

"So you never did go to Val-Gianni and have him look at your wound?"

"I told you, I don't want anyone to ever know Jovan cut me. I do not want the grand vicar thinking he can heal me with his stupid anointings ever again."

Suddenly it all made sense to Tala. Her cousin's strange behavior and torment was related to Grand Vicar Denarius and the blessings he'd given her. Somewhere in the part of her heart where Laijon's spirit sometimes whispered to her, Tala knew that Denarius might have truly been performing a priestly service. But what she had seen that day in the secret ways spoke of something more disturbing and depraved. Seeing Lawri naked with the vicar was a sinister quandary that chipped away at her soul.

*And if it bothers me so, how can Lawri do anything but ruminate on it?*

Then a more horrifying thought struck her. "You said you had a dream about me and the vicar, remember?"

"You marrying Grand Vicar Denarius is a dream that fades more each day." Lawri continued brushing Tala's hair. "I implore you, pay it no mind, Tala. You mustn't fret over the silly dreams of a court girl like me. I've many fading dreams. I dream nightly that I am searching for something in that red-hazed room with the cross-shaped altar. The room where the Bloodwood stabbed you."

Tala's blood turned cold. *The room where Glade murdered Prentiss!*

"Common nightmares," Lawri continued. "Just the other night I dreamed Lindholf would live out the remainder of his life in a dungeon cage. But why would my brother ever get put into a dungeon? Naught but silliness. Dreams never come true anyway." There resided a deep sadness in Lawri's voice. "Leastways not mine."

*Dreams!* The Bloodwood claimed her cousin's madness wasn't over. *Your cute little cousin is only partially healed of what afflicts her. Make no mistake, she will spiral into insanity and die if she is not regularly fed more of the antidote.* But she hadn't heard from the Bloodwood in more than ten days. She also hadn't yet given Lawri any of the green balls of antidote. The assassin's satchel was sitting right under the stool next to the hearth that dominated her room. She had to act now or lose the nerve entirely.

"Fetch me that satchel under the stool." She nodded toward the hearth. "I've something that may help you with your fever and heartaches, and perhaps even help with the infection on that arm."

Lawri ceased her brushing, scooted across the room, and snatched up the leather bag. "It's heavy." She set the bag on Tala's lap. It *was* heavy, and cinched closed with a thin leather thong. Tala's fingers fumbled tentatively with the tie, loosening it, a luminescent green glow rising up from the bag as she slowly let the flap fall open.

Lawri's dark-pupiled eyes widened as she leaned in and examined the little glass marbles, translucent and bright. "What's this?"

"Take one." A tremor ran through Tala, not even knowing if it was poison or medicine she was about to offer her cousin.

Lawri reached into the bag and snatched up one of the clear glass balls. "It's squishy," she said, pinching it between two fingers.

"It's medicine," Tala said, regaining her composure some. "For your infected arm. The same thing the Vallè sawbones is giving Jondralyn to help her heal fast. It also helps with fever and heart ailments." *The lies that I allow to spill from my mouth!*

"This is medicine?" Lawri's brow scrunched with misgiving. "The stuff inside actually *glows*."

"It's Vallè medicine," Tala said. "Take one a day."

Lawri studied the green ball. "It's squishy, but I doubt I could chew through it."

"Swallow it like a pill. I imagine it will dissolve in your stomach."

"I suppose if it's good enough for Jondralyn"—Lawri popped the green ball into her mouth and swallowed—"it's good enough for me."

Dread filled Tala's heart. *It's the Bloodwood's game. Making me deceitful and false. Even to the ones I love most.*

She thought of the map of Purgatory she had stolen from Jondralyn's room, knowing what she must do next.

✝   ✝   ✝   ✝

"Nobody is allowed to visit Hawkwood," Leif Chaparral said as he limped down the stone steps. Tala's heart dropped. They had toured many places in the dungeons of Purgatory so far, and this was the last—and still no Hawkwood. Still no chambers or corridors similar to those she had memorized from the map.

"But you agreed we could see *both* Sør Sevier traitors," Glade complained. He wore both of Hawkwood's captured swords in leather sheaths strapped crosswise over his back. Their spiked hilt-guards jutted over his head like antlers. "I need to see both Gault Aulbrek and Hawkwood."

"I agreed to give you a tour of Purgatory, my brother." Leif guided Glade, Tala, and Lindholf down the last few steps. "And that was all. Hawkwood is being held in a different part of the dungeon. He is off-limits to any visitor. Not even the blood kin of the future captain of the Dayknights is allowed to see him."

Leif stepped aside, beckoning his brother to enter the last chamber. "But you needn't be too disappointed. You can speak to Gault Aulbrek to your heart's content."

"Gault's here?" Glade pushed his way around his brother and into the cavernous room.

Tala followed, surprised by the size of the vaulted, torch-lit chamber. The map had described this room exactly. *The starting point of the journey.* Two heavy iron cages sat in the center of the room, just as the map had detailed.

The Sør Sevier knight Gault Aulbrek sat smack in the center of the nearest cage, shackled at both wrist and ankle, a chain connecting him to an iron loop set in the solid rock floor. Seeing the newcomers, he slowly stood. The two armored Dayknights standing at attention in front of the cage lowered their spears in his direction. Tala noticed a large metal shield leaning against the chamber's stone wall directly behind the two knights.

Lindholf La Graven clomped up next to her, suspicious eyes roaming the darkness. "Something doesn't feel right in here," he muttered.

Leif and ten other Dayknights filed into the room behind him.

"It's a dungeon, you clodpole," Glade said. "Ain't you been paying attention? The entire place is spooky."

Tala found that Gault was looking straight at her, his eyes hard and unyielding. The torchlight gleamed angrily off his bald pate. She approached him with trepidation. A wave of breathless anticipation filled the air. "What are you gonna do?" Leif stepped in front of her, blocking the way. "Slap him again?"

Gault heaved at his restraints, eyes biting into the back of Leif. Tala could still see the marks she'd made on his face. This was nothing like the trip she had taken with Roguemoore and Jondralyn through the secret ways into the dungeons under the arena to visit Squireck Van Hester. The only similarity was the constant oppressive heaviness of the stone walls and stone ceiling above, that and the crushing darkness all around.

"I need everyone to leave me alone with this man," she announced.

"Have you lost your mind?" Leif said with a wry quirk of his mouth.

"The questions I need to ask him are private."

"Questions?" Leif looked at her, stunned. "What questions? What nonsense are you going on about?"

"Glade asked you to give us this tour at my behest, Ser Leif." Tala faced Glade's older brother squarely. "But I had ulterior motives. I am actually here at the behest of my sister. And Jondralyn is desirous that nobody hear what we discuss."

Glade scowled, as did his brother. Leif said, "And you think you can just launch into some interview with a prisoner of Purgatory without so much as a by-your-leave?"

She spoke in the most forceful tone she could muster. "We all know you're to be the next captain of the Dayknights, Ser Leif. You've reminded us of that very actuality at every interval. In fact, the entire oxcart ride here you spoke of little else. Regardless. Do as I've ordered and pull your guards from this room and leave me be.

Or do you wish to answer to Jondralyn?" Tala knew Leif could be calculating, but he wasn't that bright. He looked to Jovan for all his direction. He would not confront Jondralyn. "Or what if I tell my brother you disobeyed my orders?"

Leif laughed. "Your brother thinks your naught but a brat."

"He won't take kindly to you disobeying my wishes. Nor will these Dayknights, who have just heard a princess of Amadon let her wishes be known. For they are charged with guarding my safety and doing my and Jondralyn's bidding above and beyond yours. You are not their leader yet, Ser Leif. And until you are, they shall answer to me, and you've no say in this."

She could see his mind turning. Despite his frustration, he had a sublime confidence about himself. Still, she reckoned Leif would prove more malleable than Sterling Prentiss, easier to push around. He glared at her harshly, his dark-rimmed eyes naught but hollow pits in the gloom.

She would not back down from him. A calm self-assurance came over her. "You must leave, Ser Leif. Take the guards with you. Glade and Lindholf can watch me from the chamber door if that will make you feel any better. But I've only done as Jondralyn bade me do."

Lindholf was gaping at her, while betrayal crawled slowly over Glade's countenance. He was just now realizing she'd conned him yet again.

Initially, to convince Glade to come on this journey with her into Purgatory, she'd had to swallow her pride and tell him a lie, that she agreed it best Sterling Prentiss had died and that his brother, Leif, would make a better Dayknight captain. She'd then discussed her fears that Sterling's body would be found and his death traced back to them. She managed to convince Glade that Sterling's plight atop the cross-shaped altar was all Hawkwood's doing, that he was the Sør Sevier spy who had been poisoning Lawri. She convinced him that Hawkwood had set them up for murder. She convinced him that they needed to get the truth, that they needed to confront Hawkwood with the accusation whilst he was safely confined in the dungeons under the Hall of the Dayknights. And Glade had bought it. He had seen her plan as an opportunity to pin Sterling's disappearance on someone besides himself, and also make himself a hero by solving the crime. Plus he was most desirous to show Hawkwood that his brother Leif had gifted him with Hawkwood's captured swords, which he now wore strapped to his back.

Gault Aulbrek stared at her curiously. *Does he alone know what a fraud I am?*

She could feel the patches of sweat building under her arms. Though she was dressed in a manner Jovan would approve, she wore leather pants hidden under her dress, and a blue cotton shirt too, with Jondralyn's map in her pocket.

She let her eyes focus on Leif, stood her ground. "And once you leave, I am *not* to be disturbed."

Leif's manner underwent a curious change, his expression morphing from anger to irritation to resignation. "Jovan was wrong," he sighed. "You are *exactly* like Jondralyn."

Thrown off guard, Tala didn't know what to make of his comment.

Leif merely adjusted his cloak around his neck, refastening the heavy brooch. "Glade and Lindholf will stay with you then?"

Tala nodded. "They shall stay within eyesight."

"What do I care if you talk to this Sør Sevier fool?" Leif said. "As long as I don't have to hear any more of your bleating and squawking. How long will you need?"

"Two hours."

"*Two hours?*" The look on his face was one of incredulity.

"I've much to discuss."

"I'm going back to the castle, then," he said, exasperated. "You are up to some mischief here, Tala, and I no longer wish to be part of it. Mind you, I do not like being manipulated, and I will not soon forget this."

That Leif was to be the new Dayknight captain was a fortuitous boon indeed. For Sterling Prentiss had been too rigid in the letter of the law, too wary. Leif, on the other hand, was just stupid and arrogant enough to take her down into Purgatory. What better way for him to show his power than to give his brother a tour of the dungeon, and grant his brother a personal meeting with the most dangerous man in Gul Kana? And that is why she had asked Glade to agree to the plan. And Glade was just arrogant enough to ask his brother such a favor. All deftly arranged by her through a series of betrayals and lies. The assassin would not win this time! Tala was growing better at the game. Confident.

She sought her own kind of sanity in this competition with the Bloodwood, and she was learning from it. This game was her own form of bleeding a wound—a diversion from the pain, from the daily boredom of the life she lived in her brother's castle, a diversion from that lack of familial love she'd sought ever since the death of her parents, a diversion from the pain of never feeling the comforting touch of another human being.

The Bloodwood's game was her escape from loneliness. And though she initially hadn't wanted Glade on this journey with her at all, she was glad he was here. Lindholf too. She had asked him to come because she did not fully trust Glade and did not ever want to be alone with him again.

But neither one of them knew the real reason why. Neither knew of the map she kept hidden in her pants pocket, or even of the pants that she wore under her dress.

Leif turned to his younger brother. "Call for the guards if there is trouble. Four will be posted at the top of the stairs just out of eyesight; two of those will escort you from the dungeon when you are finished, and two will return to their posts in front of Gault's cage when you are done. The rest will travel back to the castle with me. The brat is your responsibility now, Glade."

One by one the guards filed from the chamber after Leif, spear tips pointed to the ceiling as they marched. The heavy clomping of their retreat up the stairs grew soft in the distance, and eventually a smothering quiet fell over the chamber.

Unashamedly pleased with herself, Tala looked from Glade to Lindholf and back. She could see the petulant look in Glade's eyes.

"You really want to ask *him* questions?" Lindholf's voice was soft in the shrouded silence. His gaze was on Gault. The bald man stood unmoving in the center of his cage.

"Let's just go," Lindholf continued. "I do not like this place, Tala. Something isn't right down here. I do not feel comfortable without Leif or the guards."

"Are you afraid of the caged knight?" Glade scoffed. "If you don't like it down here, go ahead and leave."

Lindholf's fright-filled eyes were fixed on the Sør Sevier man. "Nothing good can come of spending two hours down here with this, this . . . this *killer*."

"We must stay." Tala grabbed him by the arm. "All of us. Trust me."

"No." Lindholf jerked his arm away.

"Just let him leave," Glade said. "He's been a spoiled whiny nuisance this entire trip. Calling the Grand Vicar's Palace a garish piss hole on our way here."

"It *is* a garish piss hole," Lindholf reiterated.

Yes, Lindholf was in a terrible mood and it wasn't improving. He'd made the comment as they'd passed by the four-story edifice that was the vicar's palace. Sheathed in shiny white marble, the palace rose up between the gray-brick, mortar-and-timber buildings of its surrounding Amadon neighborhood like a bright shard of heaven, serene and refined amidst the jarring tumult of the dirty city.

"The grand vicar deserves to live in opulence if he wants," Glade muttered. "He is, after all, our Lord Laijon's holy prophet. His word is that of Laijon. You shouldn't run his palace down like that. It's blasphemy."

"Blasphemy or not, it's still just a garish piss hole," Lindholf rebutted. "Val-Draekin and Seita told me the palace was worth enough gold to feed every starving child in the Five Isles—"

"The Vallè told you?" Glade scoffed. "What do the Vallè know of our Lord Laijon, the great One and Only?"

"They've been teaching me a lot lately."

"You mean they take pity on you." Glade pulled the ball-and-chain mace weapon Seita had gifted him from his cloak, whirling it around, making the air whistle. "You are naught but a puppy to them. They teach you to sneak about at the snap of their fingers." He spun the mace faster. "Do they teach you to sit and fetch, too?"

Lindholf went silent, the look in his eyes one of burning resentment. In some ways, Tala wished she hadn't brought him along. Her heart went out to him. But she was exhausted, tired of defending him against Glade at every turn. She said nothing.

Glade whirled the ball-and-chain mace about, then purposefully tossed it across the chamber into the darkness. "Fetch that."

"I'm not fetching anything for you," Lindholf said.

"It doesn't matter." Glade shrugged. "'Twas a useless bit of Vallè trickery anyway, that chain mace. Nothing more. Never woulda been good in a real fight. Glad to be rid of it. Like Jovan said, we needn't learn boneheaded swordsmanship and Vallè tricks anyway. And I aim to obey my king."

He drew one of Hawkwood's swords from behind his back. "Vallè tricks are for the weak-willed. Nothing like a real sword in your hand." He held out the sword, admiring it. "Especially if it is the weapon of your enemy. You didn't even bring a weapon, Lindholf. You're practically useless to us down here."

"Glade is right." Lindholf hung his head. "I am useless to you down here, Tala." There was a gentleness within him, a tenderness that touched her heart. She hated seeing Glade abuse him. It was hard enough going through life with a scarred face and mangled ears, much less having your only friend bully you mercilessly for it.

"You're not useless," she pleaded. "I need you." But her words seemed to have the opposite effect as he slunk away toward the staircase. "Where will you go?" she called.

"Up to where the guards are posted. Then I'll just go with Leif back to the castle."

"Stay." She took a quick step to follow, not wanting to venture on alone with Glade.

"Let him go." Glade seized her by the arm.

Tala watched as her cousin disappeared from the chamber up the stairs. When he was gone from sight she jerked her arm from Glade's grip.

Glade glared at her and stepped toward the cage, facing Gault. "So what information does Jondralyn want us to get out of this man?" The bald knight met Glade's stare with a cold intent, the type of narrow-lidded gaze a murderer would give before slicing open a throat. Truth was, the Sør Sevier man terrified Tala like no man ever before. Glade stepped back from the cage. "You mean to interrogate him, Tala, or what?"

Tala had once desired to be treated with fondness or even respect by Glade Chaparral, longed for him to be her protector. Now she usually felt only revulsion in his presence. But she needed him now that Lindholf had left. She faced him. "Listen, Glade, Gault Aulbrek is not why we are down here." She grabbed the folds of her dress and pulled it up and over her body.

Glade's eyes went wide.

She had on the leather pants under the dress, a blue cotton shirt, too. Glade's shock at her sudden disrobing was short-lived. "Is that a water skin on your belt?" he asked. "And a dagger?"

She reached into her pants pocket and pulled forth the map. "This is why we are here. A secret map that leads under the dungeon . . . to some great treasure."

Glade folded his arms, scrunched up his face in disgust. "This madness has to stop."

"We have to reach the Rooms of Sorrow."

"Rooms of Sorrow." He snatched the parchment from her. "This whole charade into Purgatory was because of a map?" He glared at the paper, then at her. She felt the weight of his eyes, eyes that now regarded her with insolence. "There is nothing on this parchment, you fool. It's blank."

"I know it's blank." She pulled Roguemoore's tin of black powder from her pocket. "Give me the map."

He handed it back. She knelt down and placed the parchment on the smoothest cobble she could find. She opened the tin and rubbed the powder over the paper, bringing the intricately drawn map and instructions to life. Once the map was visible, she looked up at Glade triumphantly.

"What is that you put on the paper?" Glade's eyes held a measure of curiosity. Gault Aulbrek was watching her with some interest too.

"A powder, one of Roguemoore's concoctions. It lasts only a few hours before it fades again. That's why we must hurry."

He knelt beside her. "The powder smells like lavender deje. Leif burned the resin of that plant once and let me inhale the fumes. Makes the whole body numb, tingly. It was fun. Do you think we can we sniff the powder, too?"

"Why would we do that?"

"To feel good."

"We've other more important matters at hand."

"But we can't just waste it. The deje plant is so rare. Expensive. One of the most dangerous things. Only oghul pirates dare collect it. Lavender deje only grows in Sør Sevier." His voice dropped to a whisper. "In the Bloodwood Forest, they say."

Tala went rigid at the mention of the forest. "Just look at the map, would you."

He studied the newly revealed drawing. "Where does it lead?"

"To the Rooms of Sorrow. Then out to Memory Bay. Jondralyn says whatever is down here is important—"

"Jondralyn?" He stood abruptly. "I won't be a part of any more of your mad adventures, Tala."

"Fine." She stood too, folding the map and putting both it and the tin of lavender dejé back into her pocket. "I will go alone."

Glade was exasperated, angry. "You carry a rare tin of lavender deje. You have an invisible map leading to some mysterious crypt. You waltz into Purgatory like you own it and boss my brother around. It's all absurd. Everything you do leads to trouble. The type of trouble that gets folks executed. Remember what happened with Sterling Prentiss last time we went off adventuring into secret places together?"

At the mention of Sterling's name, she stole a nervous glance at Gault Aulbrek. She whispered to Glade, "That business with Sterling seemed to work out just fine for your brother. So how do you know that perhaps something even greater for the Chaparral family isn't waiting at the end of the map?"

"I'm done with your nonsense. I'm following Lindholf back to the castle."

"Then you can explain to Jovan how you just let his sister, the princess of Amadon, disappear like a vapor into the dungeons of Purgatory." She snatched her dress from the floor, held it up before him. "Disappeared, Glade. Alone. Her torn dress found by the cage of this Sør Sevier killer." She ripped the dress down the middle, threw it to the floor, ground it into the grit underfoot. "Who knows what could have happened?"

Glade clenched his jaw, eyes on the filth-covered dress. His fists were clenched too. "This is a *dungeon*. A dangerous place we know nothing about. This is *Purgatory*. You can't ask this of me, Tala."

"The map is the route Hawkwood used to escape this place after the duel with the Dayknights." She met his gaze. "How would it be, Glade: you, the one to discover his escape route?"

A spark of interest grew in his eyes. "I thought you said the map led to treasure."

"Hawkwood's escape route *and* treasure."

"It will likely take more than two hours to follow that map to the Rooms of Sorrow, if they even exist. And then what? The guards come down those stairs to find us missing?"

"That doesn't matter. We exit under the water into Memory Bay like the map says and make our way back to the castle."

Glade shook his head. "In two hours the guards will come down here. They will tell Leif we have vanished and they will search for us. And even if that map is correct, and all those hidden tunnels really exist, and even if we can float out into Memory Bay, how will we even see? It's pitch-black down here."

Tala's eyes scanned the chamber, sizing up each of the dozen or so torches hanging in rusted sconces along the walls. She crossed the chamber and pulled one free. "They look fresh lit, good for half a day, if not longer." She then counted the sconces along the wall to the left from the entryway inward and made her way toward the sixth one. "According to the map this is where we begin." She lifted that torch from the sconce too, beckoning Glade over, handing both torches to him.

Gault had heard their entire conversation. But there was nothing she could do about that. The man would tell Leif what he had heard and seen or he wouldn't. And he seemed the type who wouldn't give anyone anything at any time. With that thought, Tala faced the wall, reached up, and pulled down on the empty sconce. It took the entire weight of her body, but like a large iron lever, it swung downward with the groan of stone sliding across stone. There was a loud eerie clicking sound across the room.

Without thinking, Tala snatched one of the torches from Glade and hurried toward the sound, Glade on her heels. When they reached the other side of the chamber, they could clearly see that the bottommost five-foot section of one of the vaulted columns that arched high over the chamber had slid upward. There was a gap perhaps two feet high under the stone column. Tala knelt and peered under the raised stone. The gap led to a dark corridor beyond.

*Just like being in the secret ways . . .*

She looked up at Glade triumphantly. "See, the map was right."

There were no instructions on the map on how to shut the gap once on the other side. They wasted a good ten minutes looking for a second lever in the narrow corridor beyond before deciding to just leave it open.

Tala carried the map in one hand, a torch in the other. Glade held the other torch and one of Hawkwood's swords gripped tight. The passageway sloped down. It was cold, musty, and acrid. The blackness of their surroundings seemed to devour the light of the two torches, their only beacons in the gloom. Hunks of chiseled rock littered their path. Ax and pick marks pocked the cavern walls on either side. The sounds of their heavy breathing and footsteps echoed from wall to wall.

They followed this singular dark corridor for at least an hour before a set of stairs led them down to a large chamber. Thirty stairs total, marked on the map. Passageways branched off in all directions from the room. But Tala paid the passageways no heed and followed the map's instructions. She crossed the room in a straight line to a black stone wall. Water streamed endlessly from a tiny crack high above. It flowed straight down like a sheet of glass over the smooth rock surface.

Tala could feel the hollow brittleness of her own voice as she spoke. "There should be another lever at knee level, a loose brick under the falling water."

Glade pointed. "I see it."

Tala squinted at the tiny writing on the map. "Push it in just a small ways, until it clicks into place. If you push too far . . . there is some trap set." She looked up at the wall nervously. "But it doesn't say what kind of trap."

Glade knelt and carefully pushed against the loose brick. It slid a few inches in, clicking into place. The water stopped flowing from the ceiling and a crack was instantly revealed in the wall—a black sliver.

"Lean against the left side." Tala put her shoulder to the rock wall and pushed. Glade helped. The wall silently moved inward like a door on a hinge. She shoved it open just far enough to slip through. "Let's leave this one open too," she said. "In case we need to double back."

They followed the map for what seemed another hour. By now the guards would have come back into the chamber to find her and Glade gone, her torn dress on the floor before Gault's cage, a dark gap left open under the stone column. They would be scrambling, trying to figure out what to do. *Wondering if they won't soon be executed for losing the princess!* With that thought, Tala realized that in her cleverness, she had not quite thought through every ugly ramification her actions might bring. *How many guards will be in trouble for my disappearance?*

With a weighted soul, she carried on. Glade led the way now. The floor of the downward-sloping corridor had a thin layer of water rushing along. Soon it was ankle deep. As they waded through the brackish flood, the water was a cold shock on Tala's skin. Glade's silhouette was a phantom gleam in the flickering light of their torches. Stray torrents of yellow light fluttered like sails on the chipped and jagged canopy of rock above, sparkling a dozen shades of orange and gold all around. Here in the blighted roots of the Amadon's twisted underbelly, the way in which the darkness moved and glittered both frightened and invigorated Tala. Beyond their torchlight lived a deep blackness. In some places the ceiling was low, and they had to duck and crawl through; other times there was naught but hollowness above.

"When will we be out of this damnable place?" Glade's voice echoed off the walls of the passage. Tala had been asking herself that same question with each watery step. They'd been in these water-logged tunnels so long that she wondered if they wouldn't just dump her back under Mount Albion and into the castle, dump her right into Jovan's chamber. It was a sobering thought. After this adventure, she would likely spend the rest of her days locked in her room under guard.

She heard cackling laughter in the distance, a cackling that pierced the darkness and raked over her nerves. Before her, Glade stepped with caution through the black water, reaching a sharp bend in the tunnel. He peered warily around the corner.

"Who's there?" came a hoarse shout.

Glade ducked back, a hint of torch flame glinting in the depths of his frightened eyes. "There's a naked old man hanging from the roof ahead," he said.

Tala looked at the map, pointing to a note on the map that simply read, *Hanging cage*. Her feet were frozen in the water. She wanted to keep moving.

"How could a naked old man have gotten down here?" Glade asked. "Who put him there?"

"Let's just keep going. He's in a cage. He can do us no harm."

Glade glared at her with fierce intent. "I wager every Dayknight in Amadon is searching for us now, scouring these tunnels, frantic . . . including my brother. Possibly yours, too." He gripped his sword, thrust his torch beyond the corner, and stepped around the bend. "This all better be worth it."

Tala followed him into the corridor. It stank of body odor and rot and human feces. They approached the old man in the hanging cage. "There they are!" the man shouted. "Rats! Rats! Dirty castle rats! Finally come a-creepin', finally come a-lurkin', finally come a-walkin' in the waters from out of their hidey-holes to see ol' Maizy."

The old man sat on the rotted bottom of the cage, legs dangling into the air, a good three feet off the floor. The rusted cage hung from a thick iron chain in the center of the corridor. It swung about, twisting slightly as the old man stretched spindly, skeletal arms out between the bars, clawed and gnarled hands reaching for Glade. "Come to me, boy. Come to ol' Maizy."

Glade's back hugged the wall as he waded past the cage, the old man's shit-encrusted fingers just inches from his face. Glade held his sword out threateningly. "Stay back!" he snarled. The old man's jittery fingers grabbed at the blade. "Back!" Glade shouted, and then he was past the old man's reach.

As Tala slid by the cage, a wretched stink hit her like a punch to the face and she nearly vomited. But then she was by the old man and hurrying on, water sloshing at her legs.

"I'm hanging so close to the water," the man's voice scratched. "Give ol' Maizy a drink of it, please! So close. I can't even taste it up so high. . . ."

Glade continued around the next bend, Tala following with haste, glad the crazy old man and his rotten stink were behind them.

"You lazy rats!" Maizy shouted, louder now. "Perhaps the spirits who stalk you will aid an ol' man. I see your true hearts! There are many ways in and out of here! You are not alone!"

"The wraiths have taken that one," Glade muttered. Tala couldn't get herself away from the mad shouting fast enough. She hustled her pace.

"A spirit with evil intent follows you!" His cackling voice still pursued her in the deep. "Follows you! Follows you! Someone always follows rats from the castle! A lurker, a stalker . . . a misshapen thief . . ."

The old man's deranged voice eventually faded away into the distance. Tala and Glade fell into stillness again, the rustling of the water at their feet the only sound.

† † † † †

They finally came to a dry room with a low ceiling, thick spiderwebs clinging overhead, brushing against Tala's hair. She listened for any sound of pursuit but could hear nothing save a low rumble growing from all around her all at once, an iron-cold thrum that soon consumed the entire room.

Glade stepped further into the room, torchlight playing over a cobbled floor all aglitter—it was covered in thousands of needle-sharp silver darts sparkling in the firelight. Whoever had previously traversed the room had cleared a path through the darts. Tala took a look at the map and found the note, *Traps dismantled, darts, do not touch.* She shivered inwardly as both she and Glade made their way carefully through the room, the walls now thundering with sound.

Before entering the next passageway, she stopped and untied the water skin from her belt and took a long drink, offering some to Glade. The glow of their two torches created a pocket of light around them. The light burnished his face in an amber glow, a face that she could see was lined with doubt and fatigue. She felt the same, doubtful and tired. The journey was taking far longer than anticipated.

As Glade gulped the water down, Tala was almost tempted to cling to him, longing for some reassurance that she wasn't alone in this dark place. She recalled how things used to be with Glade years ago, before he turned into the monster he now was, how his name would skip lightly off her tongue, how the mere presence of him would set her heart aflutter, how his touch would melt her skin. Now she was just repulsed by him.

*He murdered Sterling Prentiss, and he didn't even flinch while doing it.* Done drinking, Glade wiped the water from his face with the sleeve of his shirt. "This was a stupid idea following you!" He had to shout to be heard above the growing roar coming from the walls. "We are lost! We could die down here! And what is that fucking sound?"

"We have to keep going!" She ripped the water skin from his hand and again secured it to her belt. It was so cold the skin of her face was tight and numb. It hurt to yell. "This is how Hawkwood escaped! We are almost to the end!"

There was a sudden flash of white light in the distance just over Glade's shoulder. Just a flash and then gone. "Did you see that?" She grabbed his shirt, turning him.

"See what?" Glade's mouth was set in a firm expression beneath the torch and its lazy flickers of yellow light.

"I saw a light behind you!"

"You are imagining things!"

A whisper of wind touched the back of her neck and she shuddered, thinking she heard the metallic clinking of armor. *Something is back there.* She recalled the old man's warning. *A spirit with evil intent follows you.* Everything about this place, including the company she kept, made Tala feel cold and lonely. *Has the Silver Guard found us already?* Beyond the torchlight, everything was submerged in a swamplike gloom.

"This is madness!" Glade yelled. "Let's go back!"

"We can't turn back now!" she shouted, pushing Glade farther down the tunnel. "Let's go!"

Within a few short paces they were stumbling over piles of broken rock, where large stretches of the passageway's roof had fallen in. Water dripped from the jagged ceiling. A few more paces and the deluge worsened, raining water over them. They were swiftly soaked through, their torches flickering, threatening to go out in the downpour. And then Glade's torch lost its flame. They huddled over it, tried to relight it but gave up in frustration. Glade hurled it into the darkness.

Tala hunched over her torch as she trudged along, trying to protect the flame from the water. But the heat was nearly unbearable. Soon there was a deep roiling stream to their left, gurgling and splashing darkly beside them. They skirted past a waterfall that crashed down into the wild torrents from a fissure high in the walls, some deep crevasse that stretched back into the dreariness. Chunks of wood and other refuse from the city somewhere above came tumbling from the falls at intervals.

In the oxcart, on their journey to Purgatory, Leif explained to them that in death the poverty stricken would be hurled with all the other garbage into the Vallè River, their bones to litter the banks. He'd advised them to always stay clear of the river, warned them of the covens of witches and other cults that used its waters in unholy sacrament. Some of these sinister cults—the oghuls mostly—would strip the flesh from the corpses and perform rituals with the blood and bones. Tala now wondered if some of that filth wasn't in these underground waters. The booming sound of it all was tremendous and smothering at once.

They continued on, the roiling stream to their left. Soon there were more falls springing from the darkness. The deluge of falling water created a boiling flood more than twenty feet wide in the gully next to them. No longer just a stream, this snarling river that had taken root to their left looked black and dark and deep and moved with a swiftness that nearly took Tala's breath. And the debris that occasionally came twirling and swirling in its fierce current looked as helpless as leaves in a fierce windstorm.

And the ledge that acted as their pathway grew narrower as the snarling waterway beside them grew more threatening. On the map was written *river*, but to Tala, this was no river but a dangerous, roiling maelstrom, ominous and dreadful. And she wasn't so sure she had it in her to continue even one more step.

Then they came to the end of their path. A black wall of rock, the feral river disappearing with ferocious thunder beneath it. Tala watched in horror as a hunk of wood as big as her leg smacked into that wall with a thud, tumbled once, twice, and then was swallowed under, vanishing forever.

She closed her eyes and silently prayed, doing the three-fingered sign of the Laijon Cross over her heart. Glade's voice was rough with anger. "This is nothing!" He whirled on her, torch held high. "You've led me to nothing! A dead end!"

"Look!" She handed him the torch, pulled out the map, and unfolded it. The writing was still there, faint, almost unreadable in spots now. She showed him. "We have to go into the water! Under the rock! To the Rooms of Sorrow!"

"Are you insane?" he yelled, dark hair sopping, looking at the map. "Bloody rotted angels!"

"It says it's safe!" She could scarcely hear her own voice over the roaring of the waters. She pointed to writing, barely legible. It read *safe.*

"I can't see a damn thing!" Glade jammed the torch into a crack in the wall, set his sword down on the stone floor, took the map from her hand, and studied it. "I can't read any of it! It's too faded! And so what if it says it's safe! It's madness!"

"We follow the water!" Tala's heart was swaddled in such a heavy blanket of doubt she could scarcely breathe. *He's right! It is madness!* But she had to believe the map. They'd come so far. "The river will take us into another chamber! A chamber that holds an altar with great treasure! The Rooms of Sorrow!"

Glade looked straight into the writhing maw of watery horror next to them. Her eyes were drawn to it too. Even she couldn't believe what she was saying. This whole thing was a nightmare, growing bigger and bigger with every beat of her jumping heart.

*I can't go in there! I can't jump into that water and allow myself to be sucked under that rock wall!* But that was exactly what the map was asking her to do. "The chamber on the other side." Her voice trembled. "The map says there are torches left there on the other side! Torches we can light! An altar stone! With great treasure!"

"I thought you said this was the way Hawkwood escaped!"

"It is! Once we get the treasure, we go back into the river! The map says it will empty us out into Memory Bay! Twenty feet under the sea! We swim up! Right near shore! Simple as that!"

"You're insane!"

"It's the way Hawkwood escaped! We'll be heroes!" She had no idea what was heroic about any of it.

And then the truth of their situation hit her. *The map is naught but part of the Bloodwood's game. A game that has led me foolishly down here to my own death. I cannot go into that water.*

Glade's dark eyes were fixed on the map again. "I can't decipher any of this! It's too faded and runny! I don't believe any of it anyway! I'm not going into that water! I'm not dying down here!" He grabbed her shoulders and pulled her in close. "If the river empties us out like you claim, twenty feet down below sea level, the crypt would be flooded with seawater. Possibly even this place would be flooded. If there is a chamber on the other side of this wall, it will be flooded! It only stands to reason! This map is a damnable lie."

Tala hadn't thought of that. But what he said made some sense. She wasn't sure of the logistics of sea level and water pressure and underground caverns and all that. But she desperately wanted to be talked out of this madness. She couldn't even breathe, she was so panicked—it took an astounding amount of will just to inhale and exhale. She couldn't bring herself to look at the wild violence of the black and suffocating river next to them. Death lay there. She felt a sudden onslaught of guilt. *I was supposed to merely deliver the map from Jondralyn's room to the assassin, not follow it myself. I've betrayed my very own sister for nothing.*

Something in Glade's eyes changed, something that made her heart hammer. He crumpled the map in his hands and tossed it into the bleak roaring waters behind him, watching it get pulled under the rock wall.

"There, it's gone!" Glade shouted. "The map is gone! We needn't follow it anymore!"

Tala backed cautiously away from him. She saw the lust well up in his eyes. Glade reached out like a serpent and caught her arm. She tried to duck away, but he pinned her by the shoulders, pressing her to the cold, jagged wall just below the torch. Rage washed through her. "Take your hands off me!"

One of his firm hands held her to the wall whilst he thrust the other down into her pants pocket, searching, yanking free the tin of black powder. "After all this bullshit . . . ." He backed away, opening the tin. "After all this wandering about in dark places, I should at least get something good out of it. Sniff some lavender deje, if that's what this truly is." He buried his nose in the tin and breathed in deep, coughing, hacking, choking.

Angered, he tossed the tin to the ground, his mouth and nose now covered in black. He tried to wipe it away, then gave up and pushed her roughly against the wall again. "I should just do whatever I want!"

Tala could only watch in horror as his contorted face moved toward her. She gritted her teeth, sealed her mouth, tried to turn her face away. But he grabbed her jaw firmly, forced it around. His blackened lips, devoid of moisture, collided with her clenched mouth with all the delicacy of a mule kick to the face. His probing tongue was stiff and dry as a piece of horse leather, and the taste of the lavender deje almost made her puke. Then his hands were pawing at her.

She jerked her face away from his kiss, grabbed his fumbling hands, and bent his fingers backward. "How dare you touch me like that! I am a *princess* of Amadon."

"Down here you are nothing!" His words hit her like a blow to the face. And they rang true as his hands continued their pawing. "I am not going to let our seclusion go to waste! This is all your doing! Your fault!" He leaned in again, thrusting his tongue into her mouth, roughly this time, hands still groping.

"Get off me!" With all her strength she pushed him away, remembering how she had escaped his clutches after he had murdered Sterling Prentiss. "Don't think I won't kick you in the balls again!"

They were separated by a few paces now. Tala moved away from the wall. Glade snatched his sword up from the floor and circled her until he was directly under the torch, his face in shadow, the tip of the wicked-looking blade now wavering between them. "Kick me in the balls, huh? You think I am stupid enough to fall for that trick again? I'll turn you over my knee and—"

She slapped the sword away with one hand and punched him in the mouth with the other. His head snapped back and cracked the stone wall behind him, and the sword tumbled from his hands and clattered to the floor. It bounced straight into the dark boiling river and was swept away, instantly disappearing below the surface.

Glade's eyes rolled up and he slumped against the rough stone wall of the passageway, hands clutching the rock for support as he slid to the floor.

*He's such an idiot.* It was almost too easy to surprise him.

Still clutching the wall, one of Glade's trembling hands reached for the back of his head. It came back bloody. "I think you really may have hurt me this time, Tala." His hand then reached for Hawkwood's other sword still strapped to his back. Tala jerked forward and seized the hilt of the sword first, pulling it free and tossing it into the river too.

"You fool," he said with a grimace. "Those were my gifts. . . ." He trailed off. "I can't see straight, Tala." All color had washed from his face as he tipped over onto his side. "I don't feel right." Blood gushed from the wound on his head.

Tala yanked the torch from the wall. There was no choice now. They had to go back. And she couldn't bring herself to leave him to die. *I'm no murderer like him.*

As she helped Glade to his feet, her heart was full of such loathing for him. "I should just make you find your own way out of here," she muttered, handing him the torch. His grip was weak, but still he held on to it.

As they stumbled their way back up the passage, Tala couldn't even bring herself to look at the snarling waters beside her. That black river represented the culmination of all her failures. And if she did look, she knew she just might throw herself into the maelstrom. The emotional impact of the day's debacle was almost too much to bear.

This was truly the biggest mess she had yet gotten herself into. And if by some miracle they did survive their trek back out of this nightmare, how would she ever explain any of it to her brother?

† † † †

Four hours later two Dayknights found them wandering, lost, Tala's smoky torch just a flicker of flame. The knights had ventured a fair ways into the secret passages themselves in search of her, far enough that it still took them nearly an hour to march them back. Though clearly relieved to find the king's sister, none of the dour-faced knights looked happy about it. Especially when they asked her the whereabouts of Lindholf Le Graven.

"Lindholf?" Tala questioned. "He went back to the castle with Leif."

*It was a time when men hung a god's deeds on even the basest forms of nature,*
*a sunset, a rainfall, a lightning strike, a tidal wave, an avalanche, glimmering*
*jewels and gems, bleeding trees, white powders, black powders, and warmed*
*metals that misted with colorful smoke.*
—THE ANGEL STONE CODEX

## CHAPTER FOURTEEN

# LINDHOLF LE GRAVEN

### 17TH DAY OF THE ETHIC MOON, 999TH YEAR OF LAIJON
### AMADON, GUL KANA

G lade and Tala's torchlight and padding footfalls had long
since receded down the thundering tunnel. Still, Lindholf
counted to a thousand before he roused himself out of
his hidey-hole and sparked the white powder to flame, casting his
eyes about as the brief flash illuminated his surroundings. The swift
deluge of floodwaters dominated the entire passageway before him,
racing along and disappearing under a black wall some twenty paces
away. Then the flame of white light from his palm vanished.

He'd plodded along silently behind Tala and Glade the entire way
here, from Gault Aulbrek's chamber to this dead end. He'd squirreled
himself away in the dark alcove and listened to Tala and Glade argue
about whether to climb into the river. He'd watched their fight.
Watched Tala help Glade stand back up. He'd slunk back into the

shadows of his alcove as they'd made their way up the tunnel.

Earlier, in front of Gault's cage, he'd pretended to be mad at Glade, pretended to follow Leif back to the castle. But he'd merely hidden around the corner and out of sight—spying. Just like Val-Draekin and Seita had taught him. He'd watched as Tala took off her dress and pulled a map from her pants. He'd heard her attempts to convince Glade about the Rooms of Sorrow, treasure, and an escape route into Memory Bay that Hawkwood had used. He'd watched Tala find the secret doorway beneath the column.

Tala and Glade had been easy to track—their two glowing torches always a distant haze of flickering light ahead. Every door they passed through they'd left open. He'd only had to use the powder a few times to light his own way. Tala and Glade had never seen the flashes. He'd been that careful. The Vallè had taught him well. Though he'd nearly had a heart attack when the feces-covered old man had yelled, "Someone is following you!" as Glade and Tala had passed by his hanging cage.

But in the end, he'd successfully tracked them here, to this place.

And now he clutched the wall to his right and made his way cautiously toward the end of the tunnel, where the river vanished under solid rock. He reached the solid barrier, felt its smooth surface with searching hands, knowing the snarling river, so wild and dark, disappeared beneath the rock just to his left, vanishing with a thunderous noise. He reached into his tunic and pulled forth the water skin where he kept the white powder—Shroud of the Vallè. He dabbed some into the palm of his hand and sparked it to flame with a snap. Another white flash of light and he reoriented himself to the wall and the underground river. The light quickly faded and he was plunged into darkness again. *I will go where they dared not. . . .*

Tala had saved Glade when she could have killed him. Her behavior created an abiding anguish deep in Lindholf's soul—a soul that was becoming naught but a bleeding wound full of betrayal. He had watched Tala defend herself against Glade in the secret ways near Sterling's dead body. He had watched her defend herself here again today. Yet still she chose to save Glade. Lindholf felt the rage grow in his own heart at the thought. He still had Tala's dagger—the black dagger she had left near the cross-shaped altar. It was in his pocket now. And as Tala and Glade had fought earlier, he'd thought of leaping from his hiding place and sticking the blade straight into Glade's chest. And perhaps he would have if she hadn't defended herself so well.

He poured more Shroud of the Vallè into the palm of his hand, bent his face to it, and sniffed. Instantly the hurt and betrayal seemed to lessen. If forged with certain metals, Val-Draekin claimed, and then heated just a little, Shroud of the Vallè could create curious mists of color and smoke, and if one knew certain simple tricks, it could also spark to flame. And Lindholf knew those simple Vallè tricks. A bit of powder in the palm, a pinch between two fingers, and then snap. The friction caused the powder to light. But more importantly, Shroud of the Vallè could do other things as well. When sniffed, the powder could create moments of great euphoria and unbridled confidence.

*Yes, I will go where they dared not!*

He was obsessed with Shroud of the Vallè, gripped by its euphoria, and he'd snorted more than half of what Seita had given him already. It bolstered his confidence like nothing imaginable. And confidence was most definitely what he needed now. He was going to follow Tala's map to the end. The Rooms of Sorrow were but minutes away, or so Tala had explained to Glade. Torches had been left there on the other side by whoever had penned her map. All he had to do was submerge himself in the stream and let the current carry him under the rock.

*But how long will I be without air?*

It didn't matter. Tala and Glade and their torchlight were long gone. He didn't have a fraction of the white powder he would need to light his way back to Gault Aulbrek's chamber. He had only one choice. He had to trust in Tala's map even though Tala herself had not.

Lindholf dropped to his hands and knees and inched his way forward, feeling for the river's edge with searching fingers, reaching the rim of the rock ledge. Flat on his stomach, he stretched his arm down, fingertips catching the rushing torrent, shivering at the water's bitter touch and powerful flow.

His heart pounded as he slowly sat up, wondering at the insanity of it all. He dangled his legs over the rim, the water like shards of ice against his feet and ankles, boiling around his calves. The brawny current pulled at his legs, threatening to drag him from his perch. *Go where Tala dared not? How has my life come to this?*

He felt the scars on his face, his ears. His curse.

He suddenly found himself weeping openly. He wept until his submerged legs were numb. He took three deep breaths. *Stop, Lindholf. Just stop feeling sorry for yourself and do it!* He summoned all the courage he could muster, fighting off the emptiness in his own heart, fighting off that part of him that just wanted this to be his death. *Or am I already dead?*

*How long have I been living like a dead person? Always feeling sorry for myself? Always pitiful, miserable, and afraid?* Seita had warned that living in constant fear was a slow death. *It's either my sorrow or my glory!*

*You vowed to go where Tala dared not!*

He did the three-fingered sign of the Laijon Cross over his heart, wondering at the habitual futility of the gesture.

With a galloping heart full of both excitement and terror, Lindholf slipped into the raging river and let it suck him down into the cold, clawing deep.

† † † † †

He felt the rushing waters immediately swallow him whole, pulling him along under heavy stone into complete blackness. His head scraped painfully against the roof of the underwater passage as the

213

swirling flow tossed him within its violent clutch. The water raced and roiled as he was swept away into the swollen gloom, desperately clawing at the slippery underside of the passageway for purchase, every inch of his skin burning with such an icy sharpness it stole what little breath he had, all other senses rinsed away in the swirling madness as every nerve in his body flared in freezing pain. A deep darkness pressed inward, seeming to constrict and paralyze every muscle. He was spun and tossed, stiff arms and fingers clawing for any kind of handhold in the swift torrent of suffocating blackness. His chest pounded with terror. His lungs were on fire.

Suddenly the roof above was gone and his head broke the skin of the frothing horror, and he could finally breathe. Darkness was all around. The crushing thunder of water was all around. The river dashed him headlong into a protruding rock. He spun uncontrollably and found himself being painfully dragged along a ragged ledge.

Out of sheer instinct, he clambered for a handhold, desperate fingers grasping at anything, cold and numb with pain, barely functional at all. He gained purchase and kicked with his legs, rising up, forcing one elbow above the rim of rock, sliding along, pressing down with his elbow, trying to stop himself in the current.

But he was swept away, tossed like a cork, hands clutching at the rocky bank speeding by. His head dipped under again. His legs were dead weights under him, pulling him down. His numb hands clung to the slippery ledge, slipping . . .

. . . and a cold hand wrapped around his wrist. Like frosty tentacles of ice, thin bony fingers clamped painfully around his flesh and dragged him ashore.

† † † † †

Everything was now calm save for the cool whisperings of the river flowing behind him. Lindholf felt the blood on his forehead. He had cracked it against the underside of the stone waterway. At least the blood was warm. Everything else about him was frozen and soaked through and through. Someone was moving on the stone floor near him. He could hear the wet sliding and slithering noise in the dark. "Who is there?" he rasped.

The reek of decay lay heavy in the air. This dark place smelled acidic, like a barrel of fresh-caught fish and hot, burning iron at the forge all at once. Nothing about the place felt right. His grip on reality seemed tenuous. He wondered how much of his dizziness was the lingering effects of his swirling journey under water. Or the prolonged loss of air. Or the crack to his forehead. Or the fear.

*No.* He would accept the fear. *For despite the fear I went where Tala and Glade dared not!* The fear created a certain lucidity he couldn't ignore. Especially when he heard a hissing noise, followed by a shrill gurgle.

"Who's there?" he called out again. He was answered by what sounded like someone biting into a raw hunk of bloody flesh.

His numb hands frantically dug into his pants pocket for his leather water skin full of white powder "Who is out there?" His heart was jumping in his chest as he yanked the water skin free. The pouch had kept the powder dry and he poured some into the palm of his hand. The hissing grew louder, filling the darkness around him. He set a pinch of powder between his fingers and snapped. White light flared.

And the stark visage of a pale woman flashed before him.

She shrieked. Her own shock was evident in the blinding light, evident in her gaping, startled eyes. Her screeching mouth was a cavernous row of sharp white teeth.

Then utter darkness was thrown like a thick black cloak over them both. *Rotted angels of the underworld, what in the bloody fuck was that?*

Panicked beyond measure, Lindholf scooted away from the ghost, his soaked clothing sloshing, cold stone floor tearing at his bare elbows and cold, numb hands. He bumped into something lying on the stone floor behind him. He reached back instinctively to shove it aside. It was a hunk of wood. A torch. His fingers curled around it and he lifted it like a club, preparing to strike at the *thing* in the darkness.

He listened for movement. *What in the name of the Blessed Mother Mia had he seen?* He could hear nothing. Still he waited, shivering uncontrollably, eventually setting the torch on his lap. He blew into his hands to warm them. After he could feel his fingers again, he pulled the water skin from his pocket and poured more powder from the water skin into his hand. He rubbed the palm of his hand over the dry pitch of the torch, then snapped his fingers. The torch flared to life, illuminating his surroundings in a soft orange glow.

The first thing he saw was a pallid woman shrinking from the light. She was not more than ten feet away, naked, slithering away on her stomach and elbows, a long, scaly fish tail swiping rhythmically against the cold, watery floor behind her. *Mermaid!* She stopped at the edge of the water, rose up on her two humanlike arms, and stared with a wide, direct gaze. Two round eyes focused intently on him. There was about her face a luminous, cruel splendor. Bright silvery hair cascaded down her back. Lindholf could not look away from her ashen beauty.

With a flick of her tail, there was a sweet perfume in the air and her eyes softened. She beckoned him with a tilt of her pale head. Lindholf was instantly transfixed by the musty aroma and seductive slither of her every naked movement. Spellbound by the swelling tide of excitement filling his heart, he let himself relax, scarcely daring to breathe lest he disturb the serenity of the moment.

He stood and approached the mermaid cautiously, torch aloft. The fire's light flickered off her watery skin and drew him forward. But she slunk back, eyes unsure now, a low hissing coming from deep in her throat. Both of her webbed and clawed hands now pressed against the floor again, tense. She drew in a breath with a sharp hiss and inched toward the rushing river, fear in her eyes.

It was then that Lindholf noticed the two dark swords lying on the stone floor just in front of her. They were Hawkwood's twin swords with spiked hilt-guards—the blades Leif had gifted Glade, the blades Tala had tossed into the river. *The mermaid fetched them from the black waters. As she fetched me!*

Lindholf's gaze circled the rough-hewn cavern, sizing up his surroundings at a glance; two torches on the floor behind him, a raging river to the left that disappeared under another solid wall of rock, several tunnels branching off into the darkness on his right, and a naked mermaid directly in front of him.

He met her round gaze and grasped the hilt of the black dagger at his belt, more for comfort than out of any belief that the short blade would be of any use. But the gesture was enough. The mermaid's thin purple lips curled back and she hissed again, lower lips constricting inward, revealing a fan of jutting white fangs and a forked tongue flicking out gray and long. Then she slipped into the water and disappeared under the rock wall and was gone.

Lindholf let out a long breath he hadn't even realized he'd been holding in. It took him a moment to gather himself. After shaking his weary mind free of the mermaid's spell, he stepped forward and picked up the swords one at a time, placing each gently through his belt, one on each side of his hip.

With torch in hand, he strode cautiously toward the nearest tunnel, moving away from the cold, damp air of the river, clothing still adrip. The corridor led around a bend that eventually widened out and continued on straight and slightly upward.

The short path emptied him into a magnificent round chamber with a cross-shaped altar in the center. The walls of the room were ablaze with inset crystal jewels that sparkled like stars floating in the night. Carved columns draped in spiderwebs supported the jewel-encrusted walls. Streams of liquid silver seemed to be seeping from cracks in the columns. The ceiling was a black hole rising into a smoky nothingness above. Shadowy stone coffins lined the base of the circular room. Most had crumbled open, revealing skeletons and bones moldering in the sullen, moist air. It was a dreadful place, filled with a somberness that seemed to press in on the guttering torchlight.

Lindholf proceeded warily into the stiff coldness of the vaulted room, eyes fixed on the stone altar at its center. It was about waist high and capped with a cross-shaped altar stone similar to the one Sterling Prentiss had been chained to in the secret ways.

*A chamber that holds an altar with great treasure,* Tala had said.

Lindholf drew Hawkwood's twin swords from his belt and placed them on the floor before the altar. Holding the torch aloft, he put his shoulder to the capstone of the altar and pushed. The stone slab moved aside surprisingly easily, then tipped to the floor. He thrust the torch over the altar and looked down within, not really sure what to expect.

Leaning against the smooth inner wall of the altar was a large white battle shield.

He laid the torch on the rim of the altar, reached down into the altar with his free hand, and hefted the shield up and out by its white leather strap. It seemed to weigh nothing. It was not metal or wood but seemed hewn of the most startling, exquisite solid piece of pale bone he had ever seen. The shield was adorned with a pearl-colored cross inlay that stretched from side to side and top to bottom. The cross inlay was even more snowy white than the shield itself and seemed to be formed of some shimmering waves, like the most exquisite Riven Rock marble. Lindholf shuddered as the strange pearly plane of the shield's cross danced with brilliant color in the wavering torchlight. The sparkling gemstones and silver liquid streams embedded in the surrounding walls glimmered like a billion stars off the entirety of the shield's surface.

Lindholf knew what it was he held. *Ethic Shroud!* He had snuck through the secret ways of Amadon Castle enough to hear about a great many things he shouldn't have. He'd discovered secrets of his own, heard those conversations not meant for his ears. Both Hawkwood and Roguemoore had spoken of the scrolls Squireck Van Hester had stolen from the archives, and how those scrolls had revealed great treasure hidden under Amadon. He knew of the treasure they had named Ethic Shroud!

Lindholf's eyes were wide in wonder. The shield was the grandest thing he had ever seen. And a remarkable sensation washed over him. It felt as if this magnificent object was familiar to him, as if he'd discovered it before, and discovering it again now was in some way his destiny, holding it again his duty. It seemed that tendrils of silvery-white smoke drifted up from between his fingers. He took a step back, but the vision was gone. Still, he felt a deep-rooted connection to the shield, a sense of great achievement in finding it. That it was featherlight in his hands only added to his resolve. *It belongs to me! It always has. . . .*

Then some twinkling thing in the bottom of the altar caught his eye—a crystal-like stone atop a black swatch of silk.

Lindholf leaned the shield against the outside of the altar and reached a trembling hand down inside the altar again. He pulled the silk and bright gemstone from the bottom of the altar, careful to keep the stone nestled within the cloth. Some latent instinct buried in the far corners of his mind told him not to touch the stone directly, told him to keep it swaddled within its silky home. It fit, perfect and weightless, in his palm. It was oval and unblemished, as if fashioned from the bright polished ivory of a walrus tusk, then overlaid with shimmering starlight. Flickering and alive in the torchlight, it stole his breath.

*An angel stone!* He stared at the gemstone for some time, then eventually folded it within the swatch of silk and tucked it into the deep inner pocket of his sopping-wet tunic.

He looked at the shield. *Is this my destiny?* It was as if the scene had played out before in familiar images hiding at the edges of his dreams.

Knowing he could not carry both of Hawkwood's swords and the torch and the glorious white shield back into the river, he had a choice to make. He grabbed both of Hawkwood's swords from the floor and carefully placed them both down into the altar stone. He then covered the altar with the capstone, entombing the blades forever.

Once the capstone was firmly set, the ground seemed to quake under his feet. Lindholf took an apprehensive step back from the altar and snatched up the shield by its leather strap, holding the torch out over the altar. It seemed to be sinking slowly into the floor, with the low rumble of rock grinding against rock. *That, or my mind is playing tricks on me!*

Lindholf scurried from the circular room, passing through the tunnel swiftly, emerging back into the chamber with the rushing river short of breath. He sighed with relief when he saw that the mermaid had not returned.

He dropped the torch onto the wet floor where it flickered and hissed. Bolstered by his success thus far, he held no reservations about continuing on. He'd found what he'd come for, *great treasure,* and perhaps, when Tala realized what he'd accomplished, things could be different between them.

Suddenly the thought of telling anyone about the shield and stone sent a tremor of fear through his entire body. *Why should Tala ever know what I have done?*

*I can have my own secrets.*

With that thought, he heaved a long, deep breath and then

lowered himself into the current again, clutching the strap of the shield tightly in hand. The torrent of rushing water snatched him quickly from the ledge and sucked him down under the second wall, the shield almost like a sail before him, dragging him along.

Within a moment he was out from under the rock and brilliant light engulfed him.

His eyes flew open underwater, and he could see the flickering sunlit surface of Memory Bay just twenty feet above. He kicked for the surface, the shield so light it almost seemed to float of its own accord, pulling him to the surface with its buoyancy.

He floated to the light, to freedom.

Suddenly two sinewy webbed hands wrapped around his legs, jerking him roughly down, dragging him toward the dark of the sea bottom. *Mermaid!* He nearly lost his grip on the shield's leather strap as he spun about, swinging it at the mermaid in wild defense. The shield plowed through water, missing her by more than a foot. She was clutching at him from below, clawlike hands a mad thrash, pulling him farther down.

The mermaid seized the shield. Lindholf's free arm beat against her madly as she tried to jerk it away. He thrashed and punched, wrenching the shield from her spindly grasp, then kicked for the surface again, pain lancing through his heaving lungs.

Suddenly the mermaid's ghostly pale maw was inches from his face, a rippling row of gills fluttering open and closed along her slender neck, serrated sharp teeth gnashing out. He whipped his head to the side and her splayed neck tore into the side of his face, coarse gills scraping against his own tender skin. Her scaled tail coiled around his left leg, slithery and slick.

He kicked frantically as visions suddenly spun through his head, swirling and disjointed: feylike creatures rising up like angels from the slave quarry at Riven Rock, a knight with dark tattoos under his eyes falling from the roof of a tall tower, Jondralyn Bronachell, two hollow eye sockets, a fierce red-haired warrior woman in black armor and a long white sword, its hilt the shape of a crescent moon. . . .

Coherency returned. The mermaid lashed at him again with long fangs that were shockingly sharp and white. They flashed an inch from his eyes. Lindholf mustered what strength he had and pushed her forcefully away. Her webbed hand clawed across his right forearm, tearing away a chunk of shirt, raking four thin trails of blood across his arm.

He rammed the shield out hard, striking her in the face. And she was gone, snaking down into the dark depths of the bay.

Lindholf kicked his way to the surface, shield secure in his hand, lungs burning. When he broke the skin of the water, he gulped for air. *Precious air!*

He was floating, daylight twinkling joyously off the surface of Memory Bay, gulls screeching. Amadon Castle rose high above. The swells and waves rose and fell where he floundered. The swells broke against the jagged gray rocks behind him like thunder.

Bobbing in the breakers, sputtering and choking, he managed to twist around in the water and kick toward the craggy shore, angry waves soon dashing both him and the white shield against the rough cliff side. He worked his way around a great protruding rock and overhang into a small inlet of pebbles and sand stuck between two jagged crags of towering boulders. There was a small, canvas-covered dinghy beached in the shallows, tied to a rickety old quay of wood.

As Lindholf waded ashore, exhaustion enveloped him and he folded to the soft ground, leaning against the side of the wooden boat. He examined his injured arm. Four long scratches, none too deep, leastwise nothing that would need stitches. But they were ragged and torn enough to hurt. He felt for the angel stone in the inner pocket of his tunic, comforted when his fingers curled around its small, hard shape.

After studying his surroundings a moment, he knew exactly

where he was. The castle's shabby stone outbuildings, looming against the cliffs of Mount Albion, rose up behind him, windows all tightly shuttered. Amadon Castle itself was shrouded in a sea mist higher above. Lindholf had wandered the castle's secret ways enough that he knew exactly how to get back inside from here without much effort. One particular tunnel he'd previously explored had emptied him out against the cliff side not far from here.

For all anyone knew, he had left Purgatory shortly after Leif Chaparral. And if anyone challenged him on his whereabouts, he would just stick to that story. If Lord Lott Le Graven's son said he'd passed by the guards behind Leif, who were the guards to say he hadn't? That was the one advantage of always being the unnoticed one, the ignored one: nobody remembered seeing you. It had worked to his advantage many times before.

*And I dared to go where Tala and Glade dared not. . . .*

He felt a sudden measure of pride when he realized that, other than Hawkwood, he was the only soul to have ever escaped the dungeons of Purgatory.

Again bolstered with confidence, Lindholf stood and tore the canvas from the boat. He wrapped the shield inside the canvas, tucked it under his bleeding arm, and began making his way up the steep and rocky trail, eventually finding a footpath more trampled than the rest. The footpath he sought, the trail he knew that would lead him straight to where he desired to go. For he knew exactly where he would hide the shield and stone.

And he knew exactly how and when he would reveal both to Tala.

*The King of Slaves will be swallowed into the maw of great rushing waters with
a faith strong enough to know he can and will come out the other side unscathed,
baptized in both darkness and fear.*
—The Way and Truth of Laijon

## CHAPTER FIFTEEN

# STEFAN WAYLAND

17TH DAY OF THE ETHIC MOON, 999TH YEAR OF LAIJON

LORD'S POINT, GUL KANA

Standing behind Seita in the Turn Key Inn's back courtyard, chest pressed into her back, Stefan Wayland instructed the Vallè maiden on how to shoot a bow.

"You don't have to crush it with your fingers." He gently moved her thin fingers into the correct spot. "When you draw back the string, hold your hand at the corner of your mouth and sight down the shaft. When you release, relax. Let the string just slide from your fingers. Don't let it snap."

Seita set her stance as instructed, leaning back into him. Stefan's heart fluttered. He wondered if she could feel it beating against her. *She's so fragile.* He was so taken with her beauty and charms. Even her oddly alluring ears moved him, tapered and pointed so elegantly as they were. She was fair to look upon, smooth of skin, almond-shaped green eyes dazzling like stars, and flowing hair of such a bright white hue it was nearly blinding. He could feel it brushing his cheek now. She wore a bronze-colored tunic of Vallè make over a shimmering white shirt with delicate white lace swirling up the sleeves. Her black pants were made of a fine soft leather. A leather purse was tied to her belt along with a thin sheathed dagger.

When she fired the arrow, it skittered through the grass of the Turn Key Saloon courtyard and kicked up a puff of dirt ten paces in front of the target—a large wooden board tied to a bale of hay, a red circle painted in the center.

Liz Hen Neville let out a bark of laughter. "I knew she couldn't do it."

Seita threw the red-haired girl a shy, embarrassed smile.

"It's her first time," Dokie scolded. "Give her a break, Liz Hen. You couldn't do no better." Liz Hen shrugged and went back to chomping her dinner—sourdough bread and a hunk of greasy chicken leg.

Seita craned her neck, looking over her shoulder at Stefan, doe-like eyes blinking under fine brows. "It *is* my first time."

"You did good." Stefan gave her a warm smile. "Watch me this time." He plucked the bow from her slender grip and stepped to the line, picking several arrows from the barrel, sighting down each before choosing the one he wanted. He took his time aiming, poised with the arrow cocked back by his cheek. He held the position for a moment, then let the string slide softly from his fingers. The arrow flew straight. Its steel tip punched into the center of the target. He snatched up a second arrow, nocked the bow with swift, sure movements, aimed, and fired again. The second arrow hit just below the first.

"Stefan's always been the best," Nail said. A breeze fanned blond strands of hair across his face. He flicked the hair away from his eyes—a quirk typical of Nail. In the soft light of the courtyard, he looked like a bigger, more muscular version of Aeros Raijael, something Stefan had first noticed on the beach of Gallows Haven when the White Prince had stood before Ava Shay. That Nail and Aeros looked alike was just another strange oddity in their already strange journey.

"Nobody shoots straighter than Stefan," Nail reiterated.

Seita smiled at Stefan. He couldn't tell how old the Vallè maiden was. In this light she looked as young and demure and pale as Gisela. He sensed some strength and wisdom in the delicate lines around her big eyes. One thing he knew for certain: though she hid it, he sensed some deep sorrow in her.

She bent her knee in a curtsy, then lightly touched his arm, her fingers delicate as flower stems. "I'm most honored to learn from the best." At her flattery, Stefan's heart leaped straight up into his throat. He handed the bow to Nail and walked up to the target to grab the arrows. Seita looked similar to the Vallè he and Nail had seen atop the frightful black mare on the trail above Gallows Haven. And Stefan had seen the haunted look on Nail's face when Seita first dropped her cowl upon entering the Turn Key Saloon. Later, when Stefan had mentioned the coincidence to Nail, his friend just mumbled that all Vallè maidens looked the same, and then lapsed into silence.

Seita and Val-Draekin didn't seem to be man and wife; nor did they show much if any affection toward each other. The demeanor between the two Vallè was purely businesslike. Ever since their arrival, it was naught but secretive talks in the back corner of the saloon between Val-Draekin, Seita, Roguemoore, Godwyn, and Culpa Barra.

Seita had gravitated toward the younger folk. She had spotted the carving of Gisela's name on Stefan's bow. Stefan had timidly shared the story of the attack on Gallows Haven, Shawcroft's gift of the bow, and their subsequent trek into the mountains, how they had lost Gisela to the cold and Liz Hen's brother, Zane, to his injuries. Seita had followed with many questions about both Zane and Gisela, wanting to know what type of people they were. She seemed delighted to find out they were both kind and brave. She then claimed it would do her great honor to learn archery with a bow named Gisela in her hands, but only if Stefan would agree to teach her.

So as dusk had fallen over Lord's Point, the five young folk had emptied out into the practice yard behind the Turn Key Saloon so Stefan could teach her. The courtyard itself was built of gray stone and warped wooden gables weathered and split by the salt and sun and rain. The horse stable was a dark shadow to the left. The outer wall to their right was lined with wooden racks that held various gaoler swords and batons, plus an array of polearms, clubs, leg irons, cuffs, chains, and huge keys.

Stefan walked toward the others and set the arrows back into the barrel.

"I've never seen anyone best Stefan Wayland in an archery competition." Dokie clapped him on the back. "But I wager you'll be as good as him someday, Seita."

"Bullocks." With her chunk of bread and chicken leg in one hand, Liz Hen grabbed an arrow from the barrel with the other. She snatched the bow from Nail and got set to shoot, both hands awkwardly juggling arrow and food and bow. "Archery can't be that hard. After all, I killed a Sør Sevier knight. And I got the sword to prove it."

"I helped you kill that knight," Dokie said.

Beer Mug barked and circled about Liz Hen's feet, nearly tripping her. "Sit," she ordered the dog, tossing the food aside. Beer Mug plopped back onto his haunches and eyed the chicken leg in the dirt, then Liz Hen, then the chicken leg. She nocked an arrow and fired from somewhere around her hips, not even taking aim. Her arrow zoomed out of the courtyard and over the roof of the Turn Key Saloon into the darkness.

"What was that?" Dokie grunted in disapproval. "By all the rotted angels, you probably just skewered someone in the thoroughfare out front of the inn." He seized the bow, trying to pull it from Liz Hen's beefy hands. They struggled together a moment, both tugging at the weapon. "Give it!" Dokie hollered, yanking hard. The bow slipped from Liz Hen's greasy fingers, sending both boy and girl spilling over backward into the dirt. Liz Hen picked herself up and trundled back into the saloon, impatiently leading Beer Mug with a snap of her fingers.

"I just don't know what's gotten into her as of late." Dokie dusted himself off, handing the bow to Nail. "I believe it's your turn now."

Nail picked an arrow from the barrel and set his stance. His release was smooth and his arrow hit home, a finger's-width high of exact center.

"Excellent shot," Stefan said.

"Thanks." There was a smile on Nail's face as he handed the bow back to Dokie.

"Do you not have archery in Val Vallè?" Dokie asked Seita.

"We do. It's just not the type of thing taught to young Vallè maidens, if you take my meaning." She reached into the leather purse at her side and pulled out a curious object. "My father did teach me how to use this." The curious object in her hand consisted of two steel balls, both fist-sized, polished, and connected to each other by a shiny thin length of steel chain.

"What is it?" Curiosity stole over Dokie's face. "Some strange elf weapon?"

"What did you call it?" Seita's eyes suddenly grew dark as a storm cloud.

"An elf weapon?" Dokie continued affably. "My pa always wanted to see a fey weapon like this up close." His smile was huge and unassuming. "He would be so amazed if he could see me now, with a Vallè holding such a thing."

Seita's sharp face softened. "There is no guile within you, is there,

Dokie Liddle?" She laughed then, a bright, flowery laugh that filled the courtyard. "We elves call this particular fey weapon a ball-and-chain mace." She began spinning the mace deftly in one hand, setting the two balls spinning around her arms in a swirl. They created a musical purr that echoed rhythmically off the stone walls, the sound almost as delightful as her laughter. Dokie was utterly pleased. Seita slowed the mace's spin to a stop, then handed the odd toy over to him. Dokie attempted to twirl it, his efforts gawky and horrid in comparison. Seita let loose another lighthearted laugh. "My dear, you're doing it wrong." She placed her porcelain-like hand atop his, helping him hold the chain correctly. "You must roll your palm like so." Her fingers interlaced with his. "It will build up the muscles in your forearm—make it easy to spin the balls." The Vallè maiden leaned into Dokie's shoulder, the two of them twirling the chain together.

Stefan felt his entire body grow rigid, surprised at his own sudden jealousy as Seita curled up behind his friend, helping the boy spin the chain-mace. Soon Dokie was twirling the toy on his own with some confidence, and Seita was clapping her approval. The boy, grinning like a plump tom turkey, eventually handed the mace back to the Vallè, who began twirling it about with a rapidity never before seen, stepping forward and back in an almost rhythmic dance. Soon she was prancing about the courtyard like an Autumn Range stag, spinning the ball-and-chain mace both above and behind her own head, dancing and leaping gracefully.

Suddenly she lunged forward, one of the balls snapping out in a whip crack of thunder, punching a hole straight into one of the gaoler's heavy iron practice shields. She ripped the chain forcefully out and snapped it toward the shield again. The second time the ball shattered the iron shield like a pane of glass.

It was at that moment Stefan realized it was no toy the Vallè wielded.

But before he could even register the sheer, swift violence of her weapon, he heard a hoarse shout from the door at the back of the saloon. "Just what in the bloody Blessed Mother Mia is going on out here?" Derry Richrath, the owner of the inn, stood on the rickety wooden porch connecting the saloon to the courtyard, his face bulbous and red with anger under his mop of curly brown hair.

Seita hid the ball-and-chain mace behind her back and tilted her chin to the side innocently, a demure look in her eyes.

"You'll be paying for that shield!" Richrath shouted. "I don't like Vallè, 'specially when they bust up my property."

Seita bowed. "I was only playing. Didn't realize my own strength. Got carried away." She held the chain-mace up. "See. It's only a child's toy. Harmless."

"Don't bullshit me. There ain't nothin' harmless about the Vallè. Just put the damn thing away before I bend you over my knee and beat your backside bloody with it. You can replace the shield later. I'll give you the tally."

"Fair enough." Seita bowed again.

Richrath spat into the dirt under the porch. "I come to fetch you all to the dwarf's meeting. He asked me to retrieve the entire lot of you. So you all best hustle inside now. That dwarf is one stodgy fellow who I imagine doesn't want to be kept waiting." He turned and clomped back into the saloon.

✝ ✝ ✝ ✝ ✝

Roguemoore, Bishop Godwyn, Culpa Barra, and Val-Draekin were all deep in talk when Stefan arrived at the table. Liz Hen, Dokie, and Nail had already taken their seats on the left side by the dwarf. Seita sat next to Val-Draekin and the bishop on the right. Culpa Barra sat at the head of the table, his black Dayknight armor seemingly cutting a dark hole against the saloon wall. Stefan took the remaining seat at the opposite end of the table, his back to the room. The central hearth burned bright and warm against his shoulders and neck.

Nail and Seita were closest to him, one on either side of the table. Mugs of thick birch beer sat before Roguemoore and Culpa Barra. Steaming tea of some sort sat in little cups before the two Vallè. Liz Hen bent over the table near the dwarf and poured clear apple cider from a ceramic pitcher. Smoke curled above Godwyn, who puffed on a long, drooping pipe. It was the first time Stefan had seen the man smoke, and he liked the fragrance. The saloon was empty but for the nine of them.

Culpa Barra leaned forward, black armor creaking, and spoke. "Each of us will have a great role to play in the coming days." Ever since arriving with Nail ten days ago, the blond-haired knight had scarcely taken off his formidable armor, always girt with a wide belt and heavy leather baldric slung over his shoulder, a large Dayknight sword with the black-opal pommel at his side. "We set sail for Stanclyffe on the morrow. We travel light, on a ship built for speed. North to the Sea of Thorns and Stanclyffe."

Seita's eyes brightened. "I've longed my whole life to see the great cliffs of Stanclyffe." She took a sip of her tea, seemingly content with Culpa's announcement.

Liz Hen made a show of taking a huge gulping swallow of her own cider, and then set her mug down hard. "There's been a mistake. I don't think I should be here."

"We are all meant to be here." Culpa's gaze was firm. "It has been agreed upon with much discussion. For we who are swept up in large and great events, the forces of our times, must now make many important decisions."

"Well, that's certainly cryptic," Liz Hen said. "But agreed on by who? Certainly not me. I don't know nothin' about Stanclyffe."

"We all are important to the coming journey." Culpa pursed his lips, eyes sharp and firm. "All nine of us. Even you, Liz Hen."

"For my part, I rather like that number." Seita took a second sip of tea. "Seems just the right number of folk for a quest. In fact, I say we should call ourselves the Company of Nine. All the legendary quests in the Vallè adventure stories I've read began as such, in a tavern with a council like this, and a company of nine."

"Except Beer Mug makes ten," Dokie blurted. The dog lying at Liz Hen's feet wagged his tail.

Liz Hen piped up, "Well, since I ain't going no place, then neither is Beer Mug, and likely not Dokie, neither. So you really only got like . . ." She did a quick count on her fingers. "Seven, for your adventure."

"But it will be a grand journey." Seita smiled. "Like in the stories of old."

"Except this is no Vallè storybook," Roguemoore commented, cold tension in his voice. With his broad beard and sweeping brow, the dwarf always looked like some wise mystic of ancient legend.

"Well, I'm not going anywhere." Liz Hen huffed, eyeing Seita darkly. "And I don't like anyone trying to include me in their count, 'specially you." She held up her hand again, toward Seita this time, then counted down on her fingers one by one, saying, "I. Don't. Like. You. Never will."

"I say we all ought to stick together," Dokie blurted. "All of us survivors from Gallows Haven. I'd enjoy a good adventure, you know, something to do."

"No, you wouldn't, you stupid." Liz Hen cocked her head at Dokie. "You can't even take two steps without complaining about your itchy rump."

Dokie flushed, eyes straying in the direction of Seita, embarrassed.

"Dokie is correct about one thing." Roguemoore, rough palms spread out on the table before him, fingers clenching and bunching, craned his neck and looked down the table at Liz Hen. "You four who escaped from Gallows Haven shall all be coming with us."

"But I already told you I ain't going no place," Liz Hen said.

"You've seen *Forgetting Moon*, Liz Hen," the dwarf said, a grave look on his face. "You've seen the blue angel stone. Handled it even. And that is no small thing. Whether you like it or not, you are tied to the angel stone and its powers. All of you are."

Bishop Godwyn added, "Aeros Raijael is in possession of the battle-ax and blue stone, and he is likely in possession of *Lonesome Crown*. You've heard us discuss *Ethic Shroud* and how it lies under Amadon Castle, where Hawkwood left it. And now we must retrieve *Afflicted Fire* and *Blackest Heart* from where Shawcroft left them. And we must recover them soon if Gul Kana has any hope of fighting off Aeros Raijael. That you are privy to such information makes you a target for the White Prince, as was King Torrence Raybourne also a target."

"We bemoan the fact that Shawcroft gave his brother the green angel stone along with *Lonesome Crown*," Roguemoore said. "Ser Torrence should not have touched the stone. Possession of such has proved a dangerous thing. Even the knowledge of such is dangerous. It is why Shawcroft left the other stones and weapons of the Warrior Angels where he found them." He looked at Liz Hen squarely. "So lest you mistake our intent, the information you and your friends are privy to is most dangerous. You will be safer in our company."

Stefan felt his heart tighten at the dwarf's somber tone.

"There are other matters to discuss." Roguemoore's deep-set eyes roved over them all. "Val-Draekin and Seita have come to us at the behest of Princess Jondralyn Bronachell." The dwarf turned to Nail. "You will be loath to hear that the injured knight you saw on the litter in Ravenker was none other than our beloved princess Jondralyn."

Nail's face remained impassive. Stefan was fairly certain his friend had scant idea who Jondralyn Bronachell was beyond her name. Like everyone in Gallows Haven, the Bronachell title held some power. But Amadon and the Silver Throne were faraway, abstract concepts; few in Gallows Haven paid much attention to the goings-on of royalty.

The dwarf continued. "As we already know, Hawkwood was taken captive by Leif Chaparral. And Culpa confirmed that Hawkwood was still Leif's captive when he himself took his leave from Leif's contingent."

"Once in Amadon," Val-Draekin added, "Hawkwood was sent to the dankest dungeon of all, Purgatory, with Gault Aulbrek." The Vallè's face was much like Hawkwood's, sharp and fearless and keen. "I fear for Hawkwood, as I imagine he will be tortured for information and put to death in short order."

"If Hawkwood is tortured," the dwarf started, "he may inadvertently give away information related to our quest. We have been waiting here for my brother to arrive. I now feel we have been waiting in vain. Ironcloud has always prided himself on being dependable. That he has not yet arrived, or sent word of his whereabouts, can only bode ill—that, or he has finally discovered the true fate of Borden Bronachell and now his attention is focused on other matters. In light of all this, we must hasten our journey and move on without him, though the information he carried would have been of great use to us, especially considering the loss of Shawcroft's satchel."

Every time the loss of Shawcroft's satchel, or the loss of the battle-ax and stone, was brought up, Nail would grow stone-faced. Stefan noticed that the blond locks that always concealed Nail's eyes had gotten longer. In fact, Nail almost hid behind his hair now. Stefan thought back to when Shawcroft would let Nail stay with his family for Eighth Day services. It was the only time Nail would ever trim his hair. They would ofttimes help each other shave, a process in which Stefan would take the knife and carefully set it to Nail's face and vice versa. Nail admitted he'd rather suffer the shave at the hand of a friend than his own shaky hand, or worse, the hand of Shawcroft. The ritual had, over the years, become a sort of unspoken bond between the two. They trusted each other for the friendship. *We are bound together, somehow, Nail and I.* But ever since the sacking of Gallows Haven, Nail kept his distance from everyone, including

Stefan, who only wanted to reassure his friend that everything wasn't his fault all the time.

"I feel I must start out by being honest in my objectives." Roguemoore looked around the table at each of the four youths from Gallows Haven. "Let us be clear. I aim to require of you kids great hardship. I aim to place you all in dangerous situations. The truth is, though the loss of *Forgetting Moon* and the blue angel stone was great, it may have been that the loss of Shawcroft's satchel and the secrets hidden therein was an even worse tragedy. For the loss of that satchel has made our journey, and every decision regarding that journey, exponentially more dangerous for us all."

"What *was* so important about it?" Nail asked the dwarf defensively. "You all knew what Shawcroft had written on that parchment. I'm sure you read it yourself, you, Godwyn, even Hawkwood. I know what it said: 'The boy now bears the mark of the cross, the mark of the slave, and the mark of the beast. He has bathed in scarlet, bathed in blood.'"

"Bathed in blood?" Dokie eyed Nail curiously.

"Yes, I read what Shawcroft wrote about you, Nail," Godwyn said. "As did the dwarf. As did Hawkwood. But that was not the important thing about Shawcroft's parchment. For whatever writing was visible to the human eye was but a distraction from the real truth Shawcroft had hidden there."

"What are you talking about?" The dimness of the saloon seemed to heighten the look of trepidation on Nail's face.

"On that parchment were several maps." Godwyn met Nail's questioning gaze. "Shawcroft's maps and detailed instructions on how to dismantle the traps he set around Sky Lochs and Deadwood Gate. That parchment in that satchel was the only means by which we may ever discover where Shawcroft left *Blackest Heart* and *Afflicted Fire*."

"Shawcroft had also located the actual tomb of Laijon," Roguemoore added. "That parchment was our only way of finding it."

Nail was shaking his head, somewhat relieved. "There were no such maps or instructions as you describe. Other than what my master wrote about my scars and tattoos, the parchment was completely blank."

"Blank to the naked eye," Roguemoore said. "Hidden from casual view. But as all in the Brethren of Mia know, there are many ways to read blank parchments. Spread lavender deje over the paper, and Shawcroft's maps and instructions would have appeared as plain as day."

"What is lavender deje?" Liz Hen asked.

The dwarf pulled forth a small round tin from the pouch under his tunic, opened it, dipped his fingers into the fine black powder within, then smeared the powder in two dark streaks over the surface of the table. "Shawcroft used ink from the squid of the Sør Sevier Straits to detail his maps. Rare and expensive. The ink fades quickly, but whatever writing and drawings he made would remain intact, yet hidden from prying eyes." He pointed to the streaks he'd made. "You spread a dab of lavender deje powder over the parchment and the ink is revealed. Safe to touch. But it is a numbing agent if it comes in contact with the bloodstream, or is swallowed, or inhaled. Some royals burn the resin and sniff the smoke to lose themselves in the unfeeling. The Bloodwood assassins of Sør Sevier ofttimes coat their blades with traces of the lavender deje for stealth purposes."

"Black witchcraft is what it is," Liz Hen hissed, the exasperation in her voice raw with emotion. "This conversation is now officially pointless. The weapons and angel stones were translated into heaven with Laijon at his death. Have none of you even ever read *The Way and Truth of Laijon*? In fact, everything Shawcroft ever done was probably pointless. Likely why everything Nail ever done was pointless."

Roguemoore swiped the lavender deje from the table with the palm of his hand. "Shawcroft spent his entire life searching for the weapons of the Five Warrior Angels. His life was no pointless trifle, Liz Hen."

"What is it you want from us?" The girl looked squarely at the dwarf. "What is it you exactly want from *me*?"

"We will all of us go in search of *Blackest Heart* in the Sky Lochs mines and *Afflicted Fire* in the Deadwood Gate mines. All of us at this table: me, the bishop, Culpa, Val-Draekin, Seita, Nail, Stefan, Dokie, and you too, Miss Liz Hen Neville."

Liz Hen threw up her hands in disgust. "But you just said you didn't even have a map. That Nail lost it. So how will we search these mines? Or is it all as I suspect, just a bunch of twaddle?"

"No twaddle," Roguemoore said. "Our adventure will be serious and dangerous."

"The dwarf is right, Liz Hen," Culpa Barra interjected, his face turning ashen. "The journey will be hard and full of much toil. The Glacier Range is treacherous, the mountains and forests around Sky Lochs full of harsh weather and oghuls. The oghuls that have integrated themselves into Amadon and other cities are somewhat civilized. But northern oghuls are naught but brute savages. And the marauding oghuls caught up in the fervor of their Hragna'Ar crusade are even worse than savage. In my previous journeys with Shawcroft, I saw strange and dark things in Deadwood Gate. Things I would rather not speak of. Those mines are a living and breathing force of their own, an evil place liable to play tricks with your mind if you are not ever watchful."

"Well, that's not at all reassuring." Liz Hen glared at the Dayknight. "Perhaps you ought to find Jenko Bruk and have him help you search for these warrior weapons. Jenko stole the mystery satchel from Nail after all. Let Jenko decipher your maps and instructions with your evil druid lavender powder. Because I'm up for no more adventures like the one you've just described." Her eyes flew to Nail. "And he's done lost the invisible instructions on how we're to find our way. If that's not the very definition of twaddle—"

"I'm going with them," Dokie blurted, sitting up straight in his chair, eyes eager as they met Liz Hen's. "I've been aching for another adventure."

Liz Hen stared at Dokie as if he had betrayed her in the largest way imaginable. "I think you've already jabbered on quite enough tonight, you clodpole. Our whole families were just slaughtered. We've none of us even had time to mourn for them so much as a minute. And you want to keep traipsing about on an *adventure*?"

"It's gotten into my blood, Liz Hen. Adventurer. And I ain't jabbered at all."

"Well, my desire for adventure is the lowest of us all." She ripped her gaze from Dokie, looked back at the dwarf. "I choose to stay."

Roguemoore said, "You do not yet know the strength within your own self, Liz Hen. You will fare just fine."

"She did fight valiantly in the mountains," Dokie said. "We all saw—right, Stefan, Nail? She helped me kill that knight. Pushed Lilly over on top of the other knights. That was a feat of strength right there. We can all vouch for her bravery and stamina in a fight." He looked at her with some measure of admiration. "Even if she won't."

Liz Hen gave Dokie a soft look. "I just don't want to be scared or hurt is all. And that's all adventuring is, trudging about miserable, scared, and hurt."

"If you stay behind," Roguemoore said, "it will be worse for you, Liz Hen. Knowing the savagery of Aeros Raijael and his armies as you do, you already know what measures he and his henchmen will take to get certain information from you."

"I'd not thought of that," she answered glumly.

"I heard the story of how you and Dokie took down that knight, Liz Hen." Val-Draekin's dark eyes were fixed on the red-haired girl across the table from him. "Sounds to me like you know how to wield a sword pretty well. Thus far, both you and Dokie have done well."

Liz Hen stared at the Vallè. "I don't reckon I know what you mean." She lowered her head. "Though I brag about killing that man, truth is, I can't sleep most nights 'cause of the things I seen and done these last few weeks. So as far as I'm concerned, ain't nothing 'done well,' as you say, in killing a man."

The dark-haired Vallè nodded his agreement. "No one should be put in situations that end in death. And it is true, we *are* asking you to take on a journey that will be difficult. But I see great strength in you, Liz Hen. And I would proudly travel into any danger with you by my side." Despite her initial misgivings, Liz Hen seemed to be warming to Val-Draekin quickly.

"It's no small thing, killing a man," the Vallè continued. "Even in self-defense. It can weigh heavy." And though he was addressing Liz Hen, Stefan felt as if Val-Draekin's words were somehow meant for him. Like Liz Hen, he too couldn't sleep for the nightmares that came creeping in—the faces of the dead that he could not ignore. Even the merfolk he had killed would occasionally slither into his dreams and wreak havoc on his conscience, especially the young ones he'd filled with arrows. The babies. Just innocent creatures.

"I could be good with a sword," Liz Hen said. "Leastways I think might. With a bit of training anyhow. But ain't nobody in Gul Kana ever allowed to train a girl. Leastwise not since Hawkwood was around."

"I can teach you to fight like a Vallè," Val-Draekin said. "Swift and fast. To disarm your foe, and not deal out killing and death, which you so clearly abhor."

"You really could?" A slow transformation had come over Liz Hen. Almost as if Val-Draekin had somehow lulled her into an inescapable state of calm agreement. "But why would you want to help me?" she asked. "I'm the least of us all."

"You should never feel that way about yourself." The Vallè leaned toward her, elbows on the table. "For no one is less important than the other. Every heart matters. Every person matters."

"But if we have no invisible ink maps, how are we going to find the angel stones and weapons?" she asked. Stefan had never seen Liz Hen turn so affable so quickly.

"As for finding our way without the maps . . ." The Vallè casually leaned back in his chair, looking at Culpa Barra at the end of the table, and then Bishop Godwyn. "Even a shred of memory can be of use to us now."

"I helped Shawcroft at Sky Lochs," Godwyn said. "I'm certain I can recall the way to the mining camp Arco from Stanclyffe."

Culpa added, "And Deadwood Gate will not be a problem to navigate. Despite its dark dangers, I know it well. 'Twas I who helped Shawcroft find *Afflicted Fire* and the red angel stone buried underneath those mountains. Together we hid them under the altar again and set the traps in the dungeons to keep them safe. I know enough."

The Dayknight's talk of altars and traps and hidden angel stones put Stefan's mind right back inside the Roahm Mines with Gisela and Nail. Even though Stefan was a skeptic when it came to things dealing with *The Way and Truth of Laijon*, for some reason he had made his mind up early on that the little blue stone Gisela had found at the bottom of the cross-shaped altar was real. Gisela had been so entranced by the stone. But she had always been a simple soul, easily taken with glittery trinkets and pretty flowers. He could still see her beaming face when they placed the blue wreath of heather atop her head after she'd been crowned Maiden Blue of the Mourning Moon Feast. But now she was dead because he had not held her tight enough. *So much loss and death.* What grieved him almost as much as the loss of Gisela was the loss of his family. He thought of them often. His mother, Manda—he recalled the smell of the home she kept and the wood smoke of the fireplace and the aroma of her cooking. His father, Gideon—the feel of his whiskers, the scent of his sweat after a hard day in the fields. And his two younger sisters, Briana and Amber—their joyful giggles and laughter he would never again hear, their timid request to have their older brother play games of Flag-Tag and Hiding Ponies with them every evening.

When Aeros had attacked, they had holed up in the cathedral, whilst he had formed a shield line with the other men and boys to fight. He had seen the destruction wrought upon the cathedral with his own eyes. Nobody could have survived the savagery. Over and over in his head he'd played out their deaths in the twisted imaginings of his mind. Briana and Amber crying in fear as their mother and father tried to protect them when the knights of Sør Sevier came bursting in. He'd imagined a million ways in which they might have died. All of them terrible.

*And yet most days and nights I cannot take my mind off Gisela....*

After the sacking of Gallows Haven, and their subsequent flight into the mountains, he had taken refuge in her arms, in her love for him, both of them trying to wish away the slave brands on the underside of their wrists to no avail. But that was them, a team of two. Gisela Barnwell was the representation of the future family he would now never have. Of late he was driven by a need to escape those fond memories of hearth and home and loved ones and leave them behind, dash them against the shattered remains of his heart. For whenever he dwelled upon the good times, the images of what he thought their gruesome deaths were like came quickly creeping in. *Should I resign myself to the misery? Or should I somehow learn to cherish those thoughts?*

Either way, he was determined to avenge his family—his family both past and future that Aeros Raijael and his marauding armies had so cruelly stolen. And if finding the remaining weapons of the Five Warrior Angels helped bring him closer to that goal, he was for it. He did not like killing. But he would kill any fighter from Sør Sevier who ever again crossed his path.

"Stefan, are you okay?"

Though she sat right next to him, Seita's voice came at him as if from a great distance. He swallowed the bitterness in his throat and looked up. She was staring at him with round eyes full of concern. In fact, every face at the table was turned to him. The hearth fire behind him was waning fast and the room had grown chill.

He tried to shake the cobwebs of sorrow from his brain. "Just thinking about home," he said, voice cracking with emotion. They were the first words he'd uttered since sitting down at the table. His vision was growing blurry. He blinked, the back of his hand brushing away the tear crawling down his cheek.

*The Way and Truth of Laijon does me a great favor, causing those easily fooled to
believe the angel stones were translated into heaven. By merciful providence, may
the sacred altars of the cross be discovered only by one having knowledge of the
traps. And may the silver secret of the Skulls remain forever hidden.*
— THE MOON SCROLLS OF MIA

# CHAPTER SIXTEEN
# JONDRALYN BRONACHELL

### 18TH DAY OF THE ETHIC MOON, 999TH YEAR OF LAIJON
### AMADON, GUL KANA

**P**rincess *Jondralyn Bronachell, with the authority of Laijon's Holy
Priesthood and in the name of the great One and Only, I, Grand
Vicar Denarius, lay my hands upon your body and seal upon you
this special anointing for the sick and afflicted. I bless you that you will
soon be healed of these dread wounds so grievous and woeful to behold.*

*"I also further anoint upon you a further blessing, that as you heal
according to Laijon's will, the great One and Only will guide and inspire
you and bring to your mind those things that are most important in your
life. For you are one of the chosen of Laijon, and it is because of your faith-
fulness to the great One and Only that, as you follow the stewardship of
your brother the king, you will achieve grand and glorious things in this
life. It is your blessing to have come into this life as a descendant of the
royal house of Bronachell, and your lineage is through the loins of those*

*Bronachell kings and queens before you and you are therefore an heir to all they glorify.*

*"I bless you that you will let all further associations be with only those who love Laijon, and that you will study* **The Way and Truth of Laijon** *and your mind will enlarge and you will begin to comprehend the things of the kingdom of the great One and Only and his designs concerning you, and you will see more clearly as the days go by the pathway of life that our great One and Only would have you follow.*

*"I bless you with the gift of faith. May you never waver in your knowledge of the truthfulness of* **The Way and Truth of Laijon.** *You have been gifted with a keen mind and a good intellect and talents that will enable you to be an example of honor and respect to those around you. I further bless you that you will never trifle or take lightly your duty to Laijon, the church, your brother's rule, or your father's kingdom. I bless you that you will go forth as a princess of Gul Kana with the spirit of Laijon to guide you. I bless you that one day your words will be accepted as truth in so much as you follow the rule of your brother the king, and that you will have the spirit of the great One and Only to protect you and bring to mind the scriptures and knowledge you will need as you stand before those who would oppose him.*

*"I seal these blessings upon you, and prophesy with an eye toward truth, that you will come forth during the return of Laijon, clothed in glory, immortality, and eternal life, in the name of the great One and Only. Amen."*

✝ ✝ ✝ ✝ ✝

When Jondralyn awoke, her fever was gone. But her entire body was slick with sweat and the cloying scent of holy oils. The sheets of her bed were puddled around her knees and ankles along with her blankets. With a cold heart she began to recall some of what had happened as her mind became more fully awake. Fleeting images at first . . .

*He was here, in my bedchamber, the grand vicar. He blessed me. Mother Mia, the grand vicar blessed me!* She pulled her blankets protectively up around her nakedness.

During the blessing there had been an odd, moist heat under his hands, a searing fire where no fire should burn. And she'd *felt* it. In fact, the effects of those thick, oily hands of his still ebbed and lingered. *Give me peace, Blessed Mother Mia. Give me peace.*

*Tala was right about Lawri!*

*But weren't my own Ember Gathering Rites nearly the same as this?* She'd mostly blocked that part of her life from all memory. She'd never been allowed to speak of it anyway. *The oaths I swore at such a young age!*

But as her mind slowly cleared, she remembered the blessing she had just been given. Grand Vicar Denarius had pulled forth a bull-horn flask of amber-colored oil, poured it over the palm of his hand, and then spread the warm liquid over the unbandaged parts of her forehead. Then he'd laid his hands atop the naked flesh of her breast-bone and began his prayer. She could recall the blessing almost perfectly, every word somehow pulled so effortlessly from the depths of her mind. She couldn't help it, but as her mind began to soak in what had happened, soak in the panic of it all, she began to tremble and shiver uncontrollably. The vicar's blessing had rung so true in so many ways. *Is it all* true? *Is this why Laijon forsook me, because I've lost faith in his church and holy vicar, because I see evil in the divine?*

She'd been delirious with fever, in and out of consciousness for who knew how many days—didn't even know what time it was, what moon it was. . . .

But she could remember the vicar's prayer over her.

Jondralyn knew that her father and Roguemoore and the rest of the Brethren of Mia believed the Church of Laijon was run by men who were grossly misled and that all things holy existed more for gaining money and political advantage than anything of the divine.

In the past she could sing the hymns and mouth the platitudes with the most devout of citizens, but over time she had become like her father, seeing very little evidence of Laijon's work in the church. Or in the grand vicar.

She remembered the incident in Rivermeade with the wild boar that had given Leif Chaparral his permanent limp. It had been Denarius who had ministered to his injuries then. Jovan's, too. And she knew it was that history between Jovan and Leif and the grand vicar that bonded them together, left them beholden to one another, all to the detriment of Gul Kana.

She thought back to her own Ember Gathering at seventeen and the blessing that had followed. The ceremony and blessing had been a complex affair involving covering herself in ash and holy oils, and the ritualistic cleansing of her body, an affair that she'd mostly tried to forget. Still, that singular strange series of events and rituals had been the first time she'd ever let doubts about the validity of the Church of Laijon and the men who ran it creep in. When she'd brought her concerns up to her mother, Alana had agreed that the Ember Gathering was invasive to one's privacy, but she told her daughter to pay it no mind and consider it naught but a necessary ritual every woman in the church had to suffer through but once. And Alana had also advised her never to feel guilty about it.

*How long have I lain here?* No. She wouldn't blame herself. She knew right from wrong. She'd felt violated during the Ember Gathering and she felt violated now. The blessings were wrong in every way. Especially this latest one. It was all coming back so clear now. The grand vicar had been with the quorum of five, too. Vandivor. Donalbain. Spencerville. Leaford. Rhys-Duncan. Five lecherous men. *And my brother was there! And Leif Chaparral! And Glade!* She could picture all their faces now, especially the lust-filled visage of Leif's younger brother, Glade. Where Jovan and Leif had treated Denarius' blessing like some sort of sacrament, like some sacred ritual akin to their Ember Lighting Rites, and were solemn and reverent through-out, Glade's eyes had gazed upon her nakedness and vulnerability with the twisted gleam of a rapist. And Tala would likely be betrothed to the cruel lech like some kind of human trophy. . . .

*I will not let them win! I will not let these evil men win!*

A moth fluttered up out of the pile of blankets at the foot of her bed, circling in untamed patterns around a candelabra near the door. She followed the haphazard flight of the moth, wondering in her delirium if it even existed. Everything looked slightly skewed though her lone eye. And the moth's humming in her ears soon became a roar.

She gazed about her bedchamber. *At least they moved me from that stale infirmary.* She took comfort in her room, in the familiar sur-roundings, the soothing pastels of the walls and columns, the rich maroon rug, and the arched ceiling above she had stared at many a long and sleepless night. Her bookshelf was there, none of the books disturbed. It was a fear of hers, someone rearranging her books, borrowing them, ruining them. She never loaned them out. They were her possessions—the only physical possessions she cared about anyway. She loved each one like a friend. For they had been her friends over the years. Just being in her bedchamber, in her own personal space, never failed to ease her mind at least some. *Despite the annoying noise of the moth!*

She allowed her mind to relax. Focus. *I will win! Jovan has not defeated me yet. As long as I can still grab a breath, I will fight on.* She felt the bandages on her face, the pain of her ravaged flesh underneath. *These injuries will not be the end of Jondralyn Bronachell. . . .*

The moth's humming turned to a low grinding noise that entirely filled the room. *That's no annoying bug!* Jondralyn, startled out of her delirium, sat straight up in bed, searching for a weapon, anything. Her heart beat heavily.

Across the room, her bookshelf slid aside and a breeze from the passageway beyond bit into her skin, dark and forbidding.

Into the room emerged Squireck Van Hester in a heavy dark cloak. He was followed by Hawkwood in a similar cloak. As the two men stood in the center of her bedchamber, Jondralyn wondered if indeed she was losing her mind to her injuries and fever. *Do I dream this too?* Her hand went immediately to the bandages covering her face; she was suddenly ashamed of her injuries in front of Hawkwood. Apparition or not, she gazed at him in mute suspicious wonder.

"Are you okay?" Squireck broke the silence. In two giant steps he was kneeling at her bed, one nervous hand seizing her forearm, the other reaching for her bandages. He stopped short, jerking back, hesitant, embarrassed.

"Is it really you, Squireck?" It hurt to talk, but at least her words were not slurred. She felt no concern at all that Squireck was seeing her in such a vulnerable state. There was naught but love and concern on his face. But her roaming eye kept wanting to land on Hawkwood. *I could be the most deformed grotesque he's ever seen.* A pent-up breath escaped her lips as her eye finally did focus on him. "They told me you were in Purgatory."

"I was." With a stiff gesture Hawkwood swept aside a lock of hair from his face. "For a few minutes anyway." As his piercing orbs lingered on her, she so desperately desired to feel his touch. She wanted to swipe Squireck's hand away and reach out for Hawkwood. Instead she just sat there, numb to the fact that she was seeing either of them again. The Gladiator and the Assassin. *They must know that, as the Princess, I failed miserably!* And sudden doubt crept in, brushing away her earlier resolve. *Am I truly an instrument of the great One and Only, part of some arcane scriptural purpose?*

Hawkwood stepped around her bed. He wore dark leather riding breeches and a white shirt under his cloak. His face was paler than normal, his movements not as fluid or assured. During her time in the infirmary, Baron Jubal Bruk had informed her that Hawkwood had suffered injuries of his own in Ravenker. Still, he gave her a gentle smile, and in that one look, all her apprehension faded. *And how could I not feel safe with him, this captivating brave man who watched over me the entire length of the King's Highway, the one who kept me alive? The one who stitched my wounds?*

"How is it you are here?" She just wanted to hug him. *But my face!* She also wanted to hide. *Is he real and not some cruel dream?* "What happened that has brought you back to Amadon? You went west with the dwarf."

Hawkwood relayed to her the story of his travels with Roguemoore, of meeting Ser Roderic Raybourne's ward, Nail, at the Swithen Wells Trail Abbey. He told her of Roderic's death. He told her of his journey to Ravenker with Roguemoore, Godwyn, and several of Nail's friends from Gallows Haven. How they had taken *Forgetting Moon* into Ravenker the very same day she was to meet with Aeros Raijael, told her of how Nail had lost the battle-ax and angel stone to two of the White Prince's henchmen. He told her of how he had fought a Bloodwood assassin named the Spider, and been sorely injured and possibly poisoned. How he had saved Nail in the end and let the ax and stone go. "And then I saw you on that litter in Ravenker," he finished.

She looked at him, almost heartbroken that it was because of her that he had been captured and thrown into Purgatory. "How did you escape?" she asked him, immediately cursing the obviousness of the question. *He escaped before. He merely did it again.*

His look was calm as he answered her. "I walked myself out of that dungeon moments after they escorted me down there. Gault provided a good distraction. The chains were easy to slip. I escaped through the same tunnels as before. I again found myself bobbing in Memory Bay. Made my way to Rockliegh Isle, figuring that once you heard of my escape, you would search for me there. I was as surprised to find Squireck already there as I am sure he was surprised to see me wading ashore. We've had many discussions. And that is why we are here now."

As he described his escape, all she could think of was what he must think of her now. *If he sees me as grotesque, he masks his revulsion well.* Her mind was a flurry of thoughts. None of them made much sense. "Surely Jovan would have informed me that you'd escaped, searched my chambers for you."

"I've a suspicion Jovan doesn't know I've escaped. I doubt Leif Chaparral has told him yet. Together they are deceitful and worthless, even to each other. That your brother proposes to make Leif captain of the Dayknights will surely doom Gul Kana. In times past, the Dayknights were formidable fighters, something to be reckoned with. Ser Roderic Raybourne, Borden Bronachell, they were real Dayknights, hard and tough and true. I've known few men who could kill a Bloodwood. But Ser Roderic could. Your father could. Leif and Jovan together couldn't even kill a gnat." His face showed real disgust.

She pondered his words. *Hard and tough and true.* Just moments before Hawkwood and Squireck had entered her chamber, she had felt that kind of resolve within herself, the resolve to fight on and not let her brother win. But now, all she could see was her own lack. "I've proven to be of as little use as Jovan," she muttered.

"You were kept in the dark about Jovan's real plan for you," Hawkwood said. "He and Leif meant to betray you."

"No," she answered. "Tala warned me. And I did not heed her warning."

Squireck squeezed her arm. "Jovan's court is full of scheming and deceit. None of this is your fault."

For some reason, the Prince of Saint Only's words bothered her. She said, "I must accept my part in things. It is Jovan himself who is kept in the dark by those closest to him. Denarius, Val-Korin, they all deceive him. Leif Chaparral, too. They've convinced him that I was behind the assassination attempt. That Hawkwood, Roguemoore, and I planned it. That is why my brother betrayed me: he thinks I betrayed him. And I suppose I did betray him. Just not in the ways he thinks. I never hired an assassin."

"I was not aware of any assassination attempt until I returned to Amadon and heard the rumors," Hawkwood said.

"After you and Roguemoore left, my brother was stabbed in his chambers. Val-Gianni said it was fortunate none of the puncture wounds hit anything vital."

"Sounds like the precise knife work of a Bloodwood."

"But why stab him and leave him alive? What purpose is there in that?"

"It is always a game with Black Dugal and his Bloodwoods." Hawkwood grew pensive. "There is something behind the attack, though, some endgame we won't foresee until it is too late."

"But what of you, Jon?" Squireck squeezed her arm affectionately again. "Tell me exactly how this happened to you." His eyes rapidly scanned the bandages wrapped around her face and head, her arm still in his tender, yet nervous clutch. "How can I avenge you? I will make it right. I promise."

Where Hawkwood was cool and composed, there was something wild and desperate about Squireck. She recalled visiting him in the dungeon under the arena with Roguemoore and Tala. His demeanor was the same now as that day in the dungeon. Apprehensive. Though he was all muscle and might under his cloak, and though he physically towered over Hawkwood, there was a grave insecurity about him. Though he had worn Tala's wreath of heather so confidently in the arena, stood up to Jovan in Sunbird Hall with such powerful majesty, the fact was, Squireck was a puzzle to her now.

She looked at her former betrothed with both gratefulness and concern. "Why have you risked coming here, Squireck?"

"I could not stay alone on that rocky isle in the middle of the bay one day longer, Jon. I am a free man. By the will of Laijon and the Blessed Mother Mia, I earned my freedom. My triumph was written in the stars. The Constellation of the Wreath was mentioned in the *Moon Scrolls*."

*Constellation of the Wreath? Does he truly believe it? The Way and*

*Truth of Laijon* also hinted that the answers to some prophecy could be found in the constellations of stars. She wondered about the spiked red helmet Tala had taken from his cell as payment for the wreath she'd made. *Whatever happened to that dour thing?* "But for so long you denied killing Lucas," she said. "And then you admit to the murder as if it is no great deal. I do not understand."

"I never denied killing Lucas. I just never pleaded guilty. I remained silent, for not even I can stop the will of the great One and Only. My very freedom speaks to the righteousness of the Brethren of Mia's cause and Laijon's continued blessings upon us. Archbishop Lucas' death at my hands hath served a greater good."

"Did you really kill him? Why?" *Do I want the answer?*

"As I told you and Jovan and everyone else in Sunbird Hall, as I was leaving the crypt with the *Moon Scrolls* in hand, Lucas found me, barred my exit. We struggled together and he fell. He hit his head and lay unconscious. Yet I knew if he awakened, he would alert all to my theft. I smothered Lucas with my own hands."

"But you were found out anyway," she said. "Archbishop Spencerville claimed to have witnessed the event. His accusations match your description of events almost exactly. So to what purpose did Lucas' death serve?"

"I asked myself that very question many long and lonely nights in my prison cell. But in the end, 'twas all part of Laijon's plan, for he is wise and his ways are glorious. And our ways are not always his ways. Stealing the scrolls was only part of his plan. My imprisonment and triumph in the arena were another part. And Tala's wreath another. 'Twas written in the stars. Even you are part of his plan, Jon."

Whenever Squireck spoke of the arena or of Lucas' murder, it was with utmost certainty and confidence in his voice. "You seem so assured of things," she stated.

"I feel that surety deep within my own bosom. Now that Roguemoore has gone off in search of *Blackest Heart* and *Afflicted*

*Fire*, Laijon's spirit speaks to me still, telling me what I am to do."

"And what is that?" She asked the question now that he was not as apprehensive and nervous as he'd previously seemed.

"I aim to rejoin Jovan's court as the ambassador of Adin Wyte. Once I have ingratiated myself back into the king's favor, I will still work for the Brethren of Mia here in Amadon, but with an inside knowledge of Jovan's court. Then I will reclaim my place as a knight of Saint Only and avenge the destruction of my father's kingdom."

"Step one foot in Jovan's court and he will hang you," she said.

"You are wrong, Jondralyn. Denarius lay his hands upon me in blessing, claimed in the name of Laijon before all Sunbird Hall that I was innocent, that I was now free to walk without stain before our Lord and all men. If your brother will not honor the Arena Incantations of the grand vicar and recognize me as a free man, then I shall challenge him for the Silver Throne itself."

"Step one foot into Sunbird Hall and Jovan will surely execute you on the spot or throw you into Purgatory."

"He will not." His fingers gripped her arm. "He will come to see things as I do."

"Do you know how to escape Purgatory as Hawkwood does? Because that is where Jovan will send you."

A bitter look crossed Squireck's face. "I will not be subject to death or captivity ever again. I will regain my place within your brother's court, or I will kill him."

"You will never regain your place in his court."

"I could." Squireck's jaw was set firm, resolved. "With your help I could, Jondralyn."

"Jovan hates me."

"Once he sees the wisdom in the words I mean to speak to him, he will raise me up in his armies as an ally, and I will reclaim my homeland, and we will be betrothed once again, securing our kingdoms together against the White Prince."

Her gaze flew to Hawkwood of its own volition. His face remained impassive. "What of the weapons of Laijon?" she asked. "What of the return of the Five Warrior Angels? And lest you forget, the Brethren of Mia's cause. We three are part of all this, you, me, Hawkwood. The Gladiator. Princess. Assassin. What of that?"

"My plan will *help* speed the Brethren's cause," Squireck answered. "Help us find the remaining weapons of the Five Warrior Angels."

She scooted herself backward in the bed, pulling her arm away from his grasp. "I've already dispatched Val-Draekin to find Roguemoore and tell him of my fate. Seven days ago he left, if my reckoning is right. The Vallè will take Hawkwood's place at the dwarf's side. Under the circumstances, I have done the best I could for us in that regard. They will bring back the weapons." It seemed she suddenly couldn't even form a coherent thought. Her face ached under the bandages. She repeated, "I have done what I can in that regard. To help the Brethren's cause."

"I still must speak with Jovan." Squireck stood.

"It will be your death."

"I agree with him, Jon," Hawkwood interjected. "Squireck cannot stay on that island, hidden, forever. Even I will search for a new place to hide. Squireck must make an effort to regain his place in your brother's court. Were I in his place, it's exactly what I would do."

"I suppose I can see the wisdom in the plan," Jondralyn said, surprised at how quickly she agreed with Hawkwood, when he was merely proposing the same thing as Squireck.

The Prince of Saint Only seemed to notice her swift reversal too. His voice had turned crisp. "Hawkwood and I discussed many things on Rockliegh Isle. First and foremost, I demanded he take me to see *Ethic Shroud* and the angel stone."

"And I insisted *Ethic Shroud* remain where I found it," Hawkwood said. "Hidden. Even from him."

"And I will not believe *Ethic Shroud* has been found until I see it with my own eyes." Squireck would not meet Hawkwood's eyes.

Jondralyn glanced at her bookshelf, third book to the left on the top shelf, where she had safely hidden the parchment Hawkwood had given her. And she had not pulled it from its hiding place since. "I have seen *Ethic Shroud*, Squireck." She tore her gaze from the shelf. "And the angel stone. Will you not believe my word?"

The Prince of Saint Only knelt by her side. "I have dreamed of seeing the beauty of Laijon's weapons my entire life, Jon. Ever since Tatum Barra told Culpa and me of the Brethren of Mia when we were but children. Ever since my mother told me stories of the angel stones as a child. I have longed to look upon those things most holy, those things that will save us from the savagery of Aeros Raijael's army. Forgive my impatience, but do you not understand? I must see them with my own eyes."

"I do understand." She was taken by the passion in his voice. She looked at Hawkwood. "Perhaps you can take him to the Rooms of Sorrow, if it will but ease his mind some."

"I do not think it wise," Hawkwood said.

"Still, I insist," Squireck said. "I will see *Ethic Shroud* with my own eyes. And I *will* once again become a part of the king's court."

Jondralyn said, "I fear you will not so easily ingratiate yourself into Jovan's favor."

"He must accept me back into his court. It is the law of the arena. And I aim to march out of this room and confront him right now. I promise you, I will. And I will go myself if I must."

"You will not have to go alone, Squireck." She grabbed his hand. "I will stand with you. Compromises can be made. Jovan shall see the wisdom in your plan as have I. And when I am recovered enough, Hawkwood will take us both to see *Ethic Shroud*."

*Is the nobleman truly brave? The first rule of soldiering is fortitude under hardship and fatigue. Courage is a distant second. Poverty and want are the best school for a brave soldier.*
—THE CHIVALRIC ILLUMINATIONS OF RAIJAEL

## CHAPTER SEVENTEEN

# GAULT AULBREK

### 18TH DAY OF THE ETHIC MOON, 999TH YEAR OF LAIJON
#### AMADON, GUL KANA

Though he was still locked in iron cuffs and shackles, after seven days in the cage, Gault was relieved to be out of Purgatory. That was until his eyes fell upon the three torture devices lined up at the far end of Sunbird Hall. Then he wasn't so thrilled. The menacing contraptions sat before a tall, bulky object covered in white sheets. The Silver Throne of Amadon—even in Sør Sevier they'd heard the rumors that the new king refused to sit upon it.

This was the second time Gault had been in this royal hall. This time he was currently being forced to look straight up at the vaulted, heavy-raftered ceiling a hundred feet above. Forced because Leif Chaparral and two other Dayknights were strapping what the grand vicar had called the "heretic's tuning fork" under his chin.

The leather belt Leif was tightening around his neck was at least an inch wide and a quarter-inch thick. A five-inch length of iron with two opposing two-pronged forks, tines sharpened to needle points, were attached to the center of the belt. Leif had placed the bottom prongs of the fork against Gault's sternum, the top tines under his chin, the length of the bar forcing his head back, neck straining, eyes looking straight up.

And that was the cruel trick of the contrivance—how long could a man hold his head in that position before his neck muscles gave way and he impaled his own chin and mouth on the sharpened tines? In Sør Sevier they called this vicious device the "palate impaler." The gaolers in the dungeons of Rokenwalder used the device in cruel betting games—would the two prongs of the fork pierce the underside of the victim's chin or jam through clear to the roof of his mouth?

Upon entering Sunbird Hall, Gault had remained quiet. There were no women present, just the king and his retinue of twenty or so knights. The five archbishops of Amadon all stood behind one very dignified-looking Vallè dressed in splendid Vallè robes. There was one other familiar face—Baron Jubal Bruk of Gallows Haven. The baron reclined on a cushioned settee, the tarred stumps of his legs sheared above the knees, arms above the elbows. Gault was surprised to see the two dagger blades still protruding from the black tar of his arms.

Grand Vicar Denarius was there too. Gault had eyed him with contempt. The bald and girthsome tub of fat wore a shit-colored cassock, the silken robes of his priesthood visible at the neckline. His chest was hung with gaudy necklaces of gold and colorful gemstones. That a supposed man of God could so obviously flaunt such gluttony and pride sickened Gault.

But now Gault's face was forced upward by the palate impaler and all he could see was the ceiling. Chains rattling at his feet, he was marched across the room and forced to kneel before the three other torture devices, hands still cuffed before him. As he knelt, his body and neck were positioned to see the entirety of the hall again, that and the various torture apparatuses before him. Thumbscrews: three of varying sizes. Simple tools really, vises designed to slowly crush thumbs and fingers and other small joints. The bigger vises were used to crush ankles and knees and elbows or heads. Perfect implements for extracting confessions. Gault would not say a word. And surely his captors knew that. Still, they seemed bent on making him suffer.

With one hand on the black-opal-inlaid pommel of his sword, Leif Chaparral loomed over him, admiring his handiwork with the tuning fork. Leif's face still bore the telltale bruising of their previous encounter. Still his black-rimmed eyes lanced into Gault's. And he stood tall and proud in the black-lacquered armor and silver surcoat of the Dayknights. The silver-wolf-on-a-maroon-field crest of his tunic marked him as nobility of Rivermeade. Gault had memorized every crest of all the Gul Kana nobles years ago. The heraldry and colors of every Sør Sevier enemy were recorded in *The Chivalric Illuminations of Raijael*. Not that the information did him any good now.

Jovan Bronachell strode up behind Leif, cloaked in a fur-trimmed cape of harsh gray fastened with a silver brooch of curious workmanship. Decorative ring mail shimmered under a black tunic, and his dark hair fell in thick waves about his shoulders. A simple band of silver crowned his head. He was without doubt the tallest man in the room. "Why is it you fight for the White Prince?" The timbre of his voice was deep.

Gault was hesitant to talk, not just because he didn't want to reveal anything to these people, but the palate impaler set against his chest and throat gave him pause to move any muscle at all.

"Feel free to mumble or slur your answers if need be," Leif added. "We've nothing but time here."

But time was the last thing on Gault's side, his neck muscles were already burning and heaving, trying to stave off the two prongs. But it was a good question. *Why do I fight for Aeros Raijael? For honor? For glory? For duty to my homeland? So my heroic deeds in war can be recorded for all time in* The Chivalric Illuminations? In the back of his mind, he never did fully believe in Aeros' crusade, not with what his mother had taught him of the Blessed Mother Mia and the angel stones. *Is Laijon even real?*

*If so ... he's certainly abandoned me....*

Yes, it was an excellent question Leif had asked. These last ten years Gault had known nothing but war in the name of Laijon's son Raijael. It was a sobering thought. All his life a warrior, marching and fighting on all manner of stark terrain, sleeping under rain and sun and snows. *And for what?* Two isles conquered and destroyed, hundreds of nobles dead, their wives and children slaughtered, farms burned, villages pillaged and raped, cathedrals and chapels desecrated. *And to what end? To facilitate my own capture and imminent torture at the hands of Jovan Bronachell, a man who by rights probably shouldn't even be an enemy, but for our perceived tribalism, our two kingdoms' histories of bloodshed and differences in belief. No, I should not even be here.*

Gault wondered what had happened to the crusade he once believed in. That honorable war in the name of Raijael to take back stolen lands. Over time, the braveness and rightness of it all had been stained by the likes of Enna Spades and Aeros himself. Stained with their cruel savagery. *But isn't that how war is waged?* The thoughts racing through his head—he knew they were naught but the "simple musings of the weak-minded" that *The Chivalric Illuminations* constantly warned of.

Leif Chaparral nodded to one of the Dayknights behind Gault. Soon Gault's cuffed hands were jerked forward, thumbs forced into the cold iron of the thumbscrews. He did not panic, having learned never to allow terror to worm its way into his head. Oh, there were plenty of times when he was aware of his own fears, like now, but he'd developed a habit of hiding them beneath layers of toughness and indifference. No matter the pain, he would not shout out. He would give them nothing. He'd dealt with pain before. He knew it was only temporary and would eventually go away. Even in death, it would go away. Even if pain lasted days, weeks, or moons, it could be endured.

Jovan gave the nod for the torture to start.

But the pain never came.

Every Dayknight in the room jerked to attention as two figures entered the hall from under the far archways just out of Gault's periphery. Spearheads were lowered and swords rang from their sheaths as the knights braced for attack. Jovan Bronachell's body went rigid; his face was riven with rage. Leif's dark-rimmed eyes narrowed and the grand vicar's round face went pale. Even Jubal Bruk sat up in his chair. Several Dayknights broke from the ranks, spears at the ready, moving to intercept the two newcomers.

"Stand down!" Jovan's voice scorched the silence. "Let them come!"

One was Jondralyn Bronachell, her lone milky eye visible under a bandage-wrapped face. She wore naught but a simple woolen robe tied at the waist and walked with a peculiar slowness. She was escorted by a long-haired blond fellow with a familiar gait. The blond man wore a long dark cloak with its hood thrown back, revealing a harsh and chiseled face. Like her brother the king, Jondralyn was tall. But her cloaked companion made every other man in Sunbird Hall look dwarfish in comparison. And Gault could see the man bore huge muscles under his attire. Jondralyn noticed Gault kneeling before the thumbscrews. But she carried on, her attention clearly on the king.

Gault felt scant remorse for maiming Jondralyn. She'd set the terms of the duel. Terms that Leif Chaparral had not honored. If he was wroth with anyone, it was Leif. Gault had pulled his sword blow and spared the princess' life in Ravenker. It had been a last-second decision, a decision that would forever cost her an eye, and her beauty. But he did admire her strength in recovery. He had seen her struggle for life aboard the oxcart with Hawkwood. And now, even injured, with her face mostly hidden behind lumps of white bandages, she seemed possessed of grave dignity.

As he watched the princess make her way through the hall, Gault spied four helmetless young knights in the background that he had not previously seen, all four lusty-eyed and leering. The knights snickered at some whispered joke among them. Gault recognized the whisperer. Leif Chaparral's young brother, Glade—the boy who had followed Tala Bronachell down into the depths of Purgatory. The other boy who'd slunk into the dungeon after Tala—the blond one with the deformed face—had never returned from those dark tunnels. Leastways, not that he had seen.

Tension in the room mounted as Jondralyn and her tall escort stood before the king. The princess had every knight in Sunbird Hall's attention, spears held at the ready, their eyes ceaselessly scanning both her and her companion from behind the cavernous face guards of their helmets. Jovan angrily raked his fingers through his thick dark hair. His eyes bore into his sister. "I admit, you've a surprising amount of courage, Jon, bringing the Prince of Saint Only back into my castle."

*Squireck Van Hester. My own flesh and blood. My cousin!* Gault swallowed, felt his neck give way, the tines of the fork piercing the flesh under his chin, warm blood dribbling down. But everyone seemed to have forgotten about him, still kneeling alone over the thumbscrews, tuning fork still at his neck.

"I've courage for many reasons, brother," Jondralyn said, her voice somewhat muffled, mouth half-covered in bandages. "Leastwise more courage than you will ever have."

"We've both suffered at the hands of the enemy," Jovan said. "The assassination attempt on me. The wounds to your face. Our enemy has struck two blows straight at the center of our kingdom. Though your injuries grieve me greatly, do not so brazenly test my patience by casting insults my way. I am still your king, the one who made sure you received the greatest of medical care, the one who insisted you be allowed to recover in your own chamber, the one who now rains justice down on the foul Sør Sevier *monster* who so brutalized your face." Jovan's eyes now fell on Gault.

Squireck Van Hester met Gault's gaze too. *Does the giant even recognize me?* They had never before met, but in the Prince of Saint Only's one glance, Gault could see the look of his own mother, Evalyn Aulbrek. It was in his cousin's eyes and the tilt of his blond head. Gault's mother and Squireck's father, King Edmon Guy Van Hester, were brother and sister. Evalyn Van Hester was betrothed to Agus Aulbrek of the Sør Sevier Nordland Highlands as a young girl. She'd given birth to Gault and his younger siblings in the far north of Sør Sevier, never to see her own homeland or kin again, not before the blades of assassins claimed her life.

Though Gault had always known of his lineage and relation to the kingdom of Adin Wyte and Ser Edmon Guy Van Hester's Throne of Spears, he'd had no qualms about fighting in Aeros' armies against his own blood kin. He'd never felt any sort of fealty to his uncle Edmon. He had never met the man nor sworn any allegiance to him. Sør Sevier was Gault's homeland: Agus Aulbrek his father, Aevrett Raijael his king, and Aeros Raijael his lord. *And for what?* A lifetime's allegiance to Aeros had thus far netted him naught but betrayal. His connection to Adin Wyte had been one of the reasons Ava Shay claimed Aeros would betray him. *And my trust—haunted and betrayed by a blond girl's kiss.* The prongs of the tuning fork pushed deeper into his chin, and his neck was now trembling.

"'Tis you who is the monster, brother," Jondralyn said. "'Tis you who bears responsibility for my injuries. Purposely sending me away with Leif Chaparral, a man who looks to naught but his own self-interests. 'Tis you who is the monster."

"Gault Aulbrek is the monster!" Baron Jubal Bruk—the limbless man who had gone forgotten on the settee—shouted. "'Twas Gault and the other foul creatures who slithered over from Sør Sevier like snakes! Look what they've done to me! Gault deserves the same as he gave me!"

Jubal was wrong. 'Twas Enna Spades who'd left him limbless. She'd forced his own son to do the dismembering. Gault wondered if Jubal even knew Jenko was still alive and fighting on the side of Aeros Raijael, fucking the woman who'd caused Jubal's very torture.

"Gault should be a free man," Jondralyn said. "I set the rules of our spar. He won fairly. Leif agreed to set him free. The honorable thing would be to let him go now."

"Let the enemy go?" Leif cackled. "That's absurd."

"Culpa Barra heard you swear the oath," Jondralyn spit. "Gault should be freed."

"Culpa is as big a traitor as Squireck," Leif scoffed. "As is Hawkwood!"

"No knight of Sør Sevier should ever go free!" Jubal Bruk roared again. "I've seen their cruelty! I am evidence of their wickedness before Laijon!"

"Baron Bruk is right." Jovan's eyes narrowed to slits, his gaze locking onto Squireck. "You dare show your face in my hall again, before the Silver Throne, cowering behind the protection of my sister?"

"I cower behind no person." Squireck stepped forward. Dayknights imposed themselves between him and the king, spears lowered at his chest.

Squireck stopped his advance, one long finger pointing behind Jovan. "The Silver Throne is covered under white sheets, as you cower under the thumb of the grand vicar and the Vallè ambassador." He straightened his posture. "Or do you cloak the Silver Throne in sheets because you know you are unworthy of it?"

"The throne is covered in white out of respect for my father who died—"

"You defile your father's memory!" Squireck's voice thundered through the hall.

Leif Chaparral drew his sword. "I should open you from neck to gullet, Squireck Van Hester."

"I would snap that sword over your head!" the Prince of Saint Only bellowed.

"You dare challenge me?"

"It is no idle threat I levy, Ser Leif." Squireck's eyes were humorless.

"Enough!" Jovan shouted. "Hold your tongues, every one of you!"

"I will not hold my tongue." Squireck's attention was again on the king. "I've come to demand my freedom. I've come to demand my right to resume my place in your court. The right that I have earned in accordance with the laws of the arena and the Arena Incantations bestowed by our very own grand vicar, whom you revere. I ask for nothing else. Only that which I deserve. That I triumphed in the arena against all odds speaks to my worthiness in the eyes of Laijon."

It seemed the air was taken out of the room at his brief but impassioned speech.

"Do not listen to him, my lord." Leif turned to Jovan. "He is untrustworthy. Full of schemes and secrets."

"And tell us, Leif," Jondralyn said, "what secrets do you hide from your king? What recent lapses in duty do you keep from my brother?"

Squireck grabbed her by the arm, the look he shot her one of concern. He turned to her brother. "What say you to the demands of the arena champion?"

"This whole situation indeed vexes me." Jovan looked to the grand vicar. "Squireck Van Hester proudly admitted to the murder of Archbishop Lucas. And lies to the Silver Throne cannot be tolerated. Such treachery cannot go unpunished."

The grand vicar bowed to Jovan. "I am inclined to agree with Squireck." At his words murmurs ran through the crowd of knights. However, Jovan did not look at all surprised by the pronouncement.

The vicar continued. "With all due respect, my king, there has been growing unrest in your ranks regarding our treatment of the champion of the arena. Despite the Prince of Saint Only's murderous confession after the fact, the law of the arena is clear. The Arena Incantations bestowed by the authority of the grand vicarship shall not be set aside. Truth is, the majority of the people wish to see Squireck Van Hester restored unto the court of the Silver Throne."

Jovan looked coolly upon the vicar. "Go on, Your Grace." He nodded.

"Do not make Squireck a martyr for the cause of the Brethren of Mia. Do not make him a martyr in the eyes of your own knights who hold the Arena Incantations sacred. Do not let his death at your vengeful hands give rise to some other to take up his cause in the arena." As the vicar finished, he looked toward Jondralyn.

"I see the wisdom in your words, Your Grace." Jovan bowed, showing deference to the vicar. "But justice needs to be satisfied in some way. Such lies, such murderous treachery as Squireck's cannot go unpunished."

"Let him fight one last fight then," Leif snarled. "Let the traitor prove himself before Laijon one more time." He drew his long black sword a second time, a ringing hiss that echoed through Sunbird Hall. "I beg of you, Jovan, let him prove himself against me. Here and now. A duel to the death."

"Gladly!" Squireck barked. "Throw me a sword and I will end it!"

"Silence!" Jovan shouted. "Sheathe your sword, Leif!"

"I beg of you," Leif pleaded. "Let me at him."

"No." The king put a reassuring hand on Leif's shoulder, talking more softly now. "I will not sacrifice my future Dayknight captain to folly."

Leif's face raged with anger. He did not sheathe his sword, but looked ready to pounce upon the Prince of Saint Only at any moment.

"I've a better idea, Your Excellency." The quiet, dark-haired Vallè in the finespun robes strode forward, his hawklike eyes fixed squarely on Gault. "For the sake of the law and the sanctity of the arena, and also considering Squireck's confession, Leif Chaparral has actually stumbled upon a solution that should appease all."

"Speak, Val-Korin." Jovan dipped his head in respect to the Vallè.

"If I may." Val-Korin bowed in return, then moved toward Gault. "Remove this ghastly thing from around his neck," he ordered the two Dayknights standing to either side of Gault. "For Gault Aulbrek is the solution to our problem, and he needn't be tortured."

Gault was instantly wary, his neck heaving in agony, sweat beading on his bald head, running down his face. Even in Sør Sevier he'd heard of Jovan's Vallè ambassador, Val-Korin. The Vallè were never to be trusted. The knights obeyed Val-Korin's command and carefully undid the strap holding the torture device up under his chin. Gault slowly, painfully lowered his head, feeling every single ache and creak in every taut muscle.

"Stand," the Vallè ordered him. Knees stiff, Gault stood, shrugging off the help of the knights on either side. He straightened his crooked neck, felt the blood seep from the two holes in his chin.

"The answer is simple." Val-Korin bowed to the king. "Have this man, Gault, fight Squireck."

Jovan smiled. "A splendid idea! And we shall make it a grand spectacle!"

"This is not right," Jondralyn pleaded. "Squireck has already won his freedom."

The king ignored her plea and turned to the crowd, voice echoing through Sunbird Hall. "On the first day of the Fire Moon there will be a final match in the arena. A grand battle for the ages! The hero of the arena, the Prince of Saint Only, shall fight one more time! A fight to the death against the savage who nearly murdered my fair sister, Ser Gault Aulbrek, Knight Archaic of Sør Sevier, personal bodyguard of the White Prince!"

There was a charge of excitement in the hall now, a low rumble of voices and nodding of heads. Jovan shouted over it. "Squireck can avenge my sister and make right his wrongs! And what injustices have been done to the Silver Throne will be dually served!" Cheers burst from the hall.

*Yes! Let me out to fight!* Gault thought.

Denarius bowed to Jovan. "I'm not a man of particularly morbid proclivities. But I see the wisdom and truth in Val-Korin's idea. If this is your will, Your Excellency, so shall it be. The vicarship will stand behind this decision."

"So shall it be!" Jovan shouted.

Cheers erupted from the knights in the hall again. Spears pounded against the stone-tile floor. Val-Korin smiled at Gault. It was a sly smile.

"This is not right." Jondralyn's face was flushed with anger under her bandages.

"It has been decided by me, your king," Jovan reiterated. "And seconded by His Grace, the grand vicar. There is nothing you can do, sister."

"But it is unfair—"

"I will do it!" Squireck commanded the attention of all. "I will fight once more!" His eyes bore into Gault's. "I will gladly slay this Sør Sevier rat. I would have it no other way." He turned and bent his knee to Jondralyn, taking both of her hands in his. "I will see the vermin who caused you such pain die at the end of my sword."

"You needn't defend my honor in this way." Jondralyn squirmed as Squireck kissed the back of her hands.

*And when I win, what will be my reward?* Gault asked himself. *Freedom? A personal escort back to Aeros Raijael's camp and Ava Shay?* He cast his eyes to the cobbled floor, knowing there would be no reward for him, and he would likely never see his daughter, Krista, again.

*Their hearing, their sight, the scars upon their flesh and deformities of their faces*
*will all bear witness of their deeds, of their divinity, of their destiny as the Five*
*Warrior Angels returned. Or so false prophecy will reveal.*
— The Book of the Betrayer

# CHAPTER EIGHTEEN
# CRYSTALWOOD

18TH DAY OF THE ETHIC MOON, 999TH YEAR OF LAIJON

ROKENWALDER, SØR SEVIER

**W**hat's that filthy fuckin' mutt gone'n found now?" Bogg whistled at the bulldog. "Git back over here, you rotten fuckin' varmint!" He snatched a stick from the forest floor and hurled it toward the dog. Krista and Hans Rake exchanged glances. The one-eyed dwarf near Hans rolled his one eye. Café Colza Bouledogue ignored the stick that bounced off his back, flashed a drool-laced grin, and, with a snarl, clamped his slobbery jaws over the pale, ropy *thing* draped over the pine branch and yanked.

"What the fuck?" Bogg stomped toward the dog.

Bogg's pet bulldog disgusted Black Dugal. It always had. But no more so than Bogg himself did. Leastways that was what Dugal often said when speaking of Bogg and the dog: *They are two of a kind, Bogg and Café Colza, rotten to the core, smelly, too—but together, they have their uses.* To Krista, Bogg and his bulldog looked exactly alike. Both were large and stout and sporting overly large heads and flat faces—two of the ugliest mugs this side of the Sevier River. Both reeked of Bogg's body odor too—a noxious fume you could smell coming a mile away, a stink that the one-eyed dwarf, Squateye, claimed could easily cold-cock even the stoutest Adin Wyte draught mule. Both had a surly disposition, neither seeming to have the slightest grasp of logic or reason. And their combined unreason was why the four of them were out here in the middle of this mountain forest north of Rokenwalder. It was the bulldog who'd led them here—miles out of their way—and Bogg who'd insisted they follow.

The two swayback ponies belonging to Bogg and Squateye grazed at the forest floor next to Hans' stallion, Kill. Krista's own Bloodeye mare, Dread, stood directly behind her. Café Colza Bouledogue had actually ridden on one of the ponies most of the way here. He sat up in the lap of Bogg right there in the saddle, until he'd caught the scent of something in these woods and bolted off.

Squateye was another set of complexities and mysteries altogether. A garrulous fellow, his name was the only thing that fit him. He was squat. And he had one eye. The other eye was covered in a filthy leather patch that would ofttimes waft its own rotten, potato-like odor into the air if the wind hit it just right.

And as Krista, Hans, and Squateye followed Bogg and Café Colza, the one-eyed dwarf kept rolling his one eye at both Krista and Hans—as if he were as irritated as they at the bulldog and this wandering adventure into nowhere. But Krista wasn't buying the dwarf's feigned irritation and eye rolls. Squateye and Bogg were the most loyal of chums. In fact, the dwarf's favorite pastime was regaling anyone, especially Krista and Hans—or any Bloodwood in Black Dugal's Caste, for that matter—with tales of the bulldog's adventures. The two Vallè, Breita and Seita, had taken extra delight in the tall tales.

Story was, years ago, Bogg and Squateye had first met the bull-dog in Sible Hedge, when he was no more than an overgrown pup. The pooch was in the midst of mounting the white puff-poodle that belonged to Lord Truklebank's wife, Eunice, the two dogs humping unapologetically right in front of the Goat Frog Saloon, much to the amusement of Bogg. For a good ten minutes the tongue-wagging bulldog pounded the frilly white stuffing out of the backside of Lady Truklebank's sweet, fluffy pet right there on the wood-slate board-walk in the middle of town whilst Bogg hooted up a storm. Squateye had also watched the proceedings with a humorous eye as Eunice Truklebank screeched and squealed. Once the canine relationship was consummated and the pleasure-filled howling had come to its majestic end, Eunice snatched her poodle up by the scruff of the neck, shouting, "Stupid bitch," right in its face. Bogg gleefully claimed instant ownership of the amorous bulldog and straightaway named it Café Colza Bouledogue. Squateye would ofttimes make mention that he had no idea what the name meant, and then claim he didn't give a hoot either. But both he and Bogg giggled every time they got to the "naming of the dog" part of the tale, without fail.

Thing was, Café Colza was always up to no good.

He had sniffed out something in the woods today and was tug-ging on it with a mighty force, teeth clenched, entire jaw dripping with drool. Whatever the dog had ahold of tore in half, sending the longer ribbonlike length snapping back up into the trees, the shorter length straight down his throat. Café Colza could gobble things up in a hurry, as Krista was well aware. Hans Rake had learned that lesson the hard way. Two moons ago Café Colza had sniffed out a strip of elk jerky in the satchel dangling at Hans' waist and snapped at his leg, tearing the jerky straight out of the satchel and ripping a patch of Hans' black boiled-leather pants clean off. The jerky and leather armor were swallowed in one gulp. And to top off the insult, Café Colza had growled at Hans for more.

Now Hans and Squateye and Krista and their respective mounts watched the dog lick its lips and eyeball the remains of the stringy object dangling from the lone pine tree. The tree itself stood before a thicket of scrub oak and aspen. The mysterious purplish-gray ropy object was draped over branches of the pine, the length of it receding back into the aspens, disappearing into the forest thicket and out of sight. Café Colza leaped for another bite, but his stumpy little legs didn't get him more than a foot off the ground. The bulldog turned and bared its teeth at both Krista and Hans like his limited leaping ability was all their fault.

"Crazy fuckin' mutt." Bogg bent and let the dog lick his face. Then the two playfully wrestled on the ground under the pine, Café Colza yipping and nipping at Bogg's pokes and jabs. Bogg was laughing up a riot. Soon the dog was growling in the man's face. "Don't get mad at me!" Bogg slapped the bulldog hard across the snout. "Crazy fuckin' varmint!" He slapped the dog hard a second time. With the third slap it looked like Café Colza was starting to enjoy the abuse, bouncing on all fours, tongue and tail wagging at Bogg. Then Bogg grabbed the rusted spiked collar around the dog's neck and pointed the little beast in the direction of the woods.

Hans' dark eyes narrowed with pure impatience. A hint of dusk was settling over the forest now, and with it, the cloudless sky carried the last faint wash of light. "We haven't time for this," he said. "Dugal wanted us back in Rokenwalder by tonight."

"Who can ever know for sure what Dugal really wants?" Squateye said flatly.

"He said be back by nightfall of the eighteenth day. It is the eighteenth day. He was pretty clear on his wants. He will be sorely disappointed when I tell him we accomplished *nothing* in Eark."

"I daresay your disguise did its job just fine."

"Wandering about a strange town among strangers whilst in a disguise hardly constitutes much of an accomplishment."

The dwarf shrugged with a hint of a smile. "Either way, you're out of your disguises now, the both of you back to normal Bloodwooding as you like."

Hans threw him a chilling glance. "Following a stupid bulldog into the woods is not *Bloodwooding*."

The dwarf shrugged again. Dread stepped up beside Krista. She rested her head against the mare's neck, letting the warmth soothe her. She too wanted to just move on from here. Random journeys with Bogg and Squateye had always been part of their Bloodwood training. Neither Krista nor Hans could figure out what they ever gained from the bizarre adventures with the two. *Perhaps merely a test of our patience.* Squateye once made mention that Bogg had been a Bloodwood assassin ages ago. No more than a kid at the time, and fat. Dugal had named him Jellywood. Hans once asked Bogg if the Jellywood story was true, only to get a threatening look followed by a stern admonition, "Beauty is the first rule of the Bloodwoods according to Dugal. There was never no Jellywood. And don't bring it up again unless you want your fuckin' eyes plucked right out of your fuckin' face."

"A real secret weapon, Bogg was," Squateye would ofttimes say when Bogg wasn't near. "Nobody ever expects a knife in the neck from the fat guy." The one-eyed dwarf claimed Bogg was the only Bloodwood ever to successfully retire from Dugal's Caste alive. "Most Bloodwoods either die on the job, or die at Dugal's own hand."

As they'd ridden out of Eark, the dwarf had pointed a thick, stubby finger right at Krista and said, "A Bloodwood rarely makes it out of their twenties alive. Remember, lassie, trust is fleeting, whilst betrayal is timeless. Learn that one lesson if you want to retire a Bloodwood. Learn how to figure truth from lies. For each of us has a destiny. Those who set out to lie and deceive keep those meant for a higher cause from their destiny. Remember what Dugal has told you: everything about our king Aevrett Raijael and his son, Aeros, is a lie. Remember too, everything about Black Dugal is also a lie. And deciphering truth from lies is part of your test."

Bogg had wobbled up and said, "You're wrong, dwarf. Dugal is a great man. And I was never named Jellywood. So stop tellin' the poor girl lies."

"He *was* Jellywood." The dwarf had winked his one eye at her after Bogg was out of earshot. At any given moment, Krista honestly didn't know whether Bogg or Squateye, or even the bulldog, was fooling with her head or not. Most things were a joke to Bogg, except when it came to Black Dugal. Then everything was deadly serious.

Bogg was acting warden and Squateye the head gaoler of the famed dungeons of Rokenwalder. Krista had been on enough adventures with the duo that she figured they were the most lawless pair in all Sør Sevier. Their job was to teach Dugal's Caste of Bloodwoods-in-training how to escape from any dungeon, prison, iron chain, or shackle. They'd also taught Krista and Hans how to fashion a key for any lock from items as simple as nails or a link of chain or a silver coin.

The first time Krista had been tied up and left alone in a dungeon with the directive to escape, she'd panicked and failed, her first-ever failure under Dugal's tutelage. It was an embarrassment. But she'd been terrified of the confinement. To this day nothing scared her more than a prison cell. She figured her fright should've spurred her into figuring it out all the sooner. But it hadn't. Her fear would usually incapacitate her totally when confined in a cage.

After the failure, Dugal was harsh with her, Hans mocking. But both Bogg and Squateye had patiently worked with her until she made progress. She wanted to please them. They were an integral part of Dugal's Sacrament of Souls, providers of the sacrificial criminals and the poisons for their blades. Bogg was a master at alchemy, his concoctions numerous: poisons that killed instantly, poisons that were slow to kill, poisons that blinded the victim, maimed them, gave them boils, turned them insane, and even a poison that slowed the victim's heart to the point that they could easily pass as a cold, dead corpse lying in a gutter. "And that is an important poison," Bogg would often say. "For sometimes folks just need to look dead."

Despite his girth and awkward ways, Bogg was a wily, crafty fellow, as was Squateye. Both were an odd pair for sure. And an evil pair, make no mistake. "If ya can't beat 'em, join 'em," Bogg had quipped on more than one occasion—usually when Hans had asked him particulars about his job in the dungeons. "'Specially when it comes to robbers, sword fighters, gamblers, and whores."

"Shit, ain't no sense even arrestin' the whores," Bogg had laughed one night with two Gul Kana thieves named Clive and Llewellyn at the Dirty Coin Saloon in Rokenwalder's dingy dock district. "Just drop yer trousers and club 'em up the arsehole, if you take my meaning, then let the bulldog lick up the mess." The thief named Clive hadn't found the comment all that amusing, but Llewellyn had laughed. Of course, Llewellyn was a sniveling kiss-ass, in Krista's estimation. He owed Bogg about forty-five coppers in gambling debt. Clive, on the other hand, was a smooth and cold-eyed robber. Both were part of Praed's famed wild bunch of roaming bastard thieves called the Untamed, a gang of four wily outlaws who were a nuisance throughout the Five Isles. The Untamed ofttimes ventured into the Bloodwood Forest to collect Blood of the Dragon. Praed was known to deal in the drug, selling it to oghul pirates against Dugal's wishes.

Krista and Hans, along with Seita and Breita, had been there in the saloon with the warden that evening. They'd gambled all night with the outlaws. Seita and Breita actually owed Bogg about two hundred coppers combined near the end. Bogg loved whores, and loved gambling even more, and loved when others lost at gambling, especially to him. Squateye didn't whore or gamble himself, but he liked to watch those who did, the gambling part anyway, even though it was against the laws set forth by Aevrett Raijael and enforced by his five Knights Chivalric. Gambling was illegal in Sør Sevier. Still, Squateye claimed if you started arresting folks who partook of the whoring and gambling trade in Rokenwalder or Dashiell or the logging and mining towns like Eark, you'd "kick up a bloodbath of riotous behavior and rebellion that would never end." So Squateye looked the other way when it came to gambling. He wasn't a stickler for the letter of the law himself, figuring it best to just let things be as they were. Bottom line, Bogg and Squateye were an odd pair.

And things right now in the woods seemed awfully odd. Café Colza and Bogg were again wrestling in the dirt. Hans was wary of their surroundings.

And Krista's senses were also on high alert. She could feel each thin Bloodwood dagger she owned pressing against her flesh, hidden in various parts of her black leather armor. Squateye studied the grayish-tan, ropy *thing* dangling in the branches. To Krista it looked somewhat organic, like it belonged there in the trees along with the green aspen leaves and scratchy brown pine. She reached out and felt it, finding it was somewhat damp and chilled to the touch, and she had an inkling of what it was. Seemed Squateye had drawn the same conclusion. "I've gutted a lot of stag and elk in my day—and this here feels like deer intestines."

The dwarf followed the length of the wet, gray rope to the edge of the thicket. It was draped from branch to branch, hanging at eye level the whole way, receding off into the dense foliage and out of sight. Squateye proceeded slowly and cautiously, squeezing through the brush and scrub oak, ducking under several prickly pine branches that swooped low over his path. Krista and Hans followed, leaving their Bloodeye mounts with Bogg and the dog and the ponies. Branches clawed at their black boiled leathers as the thicket closed in around them. The sounds of Bogg and Café Colza's wrestling dissipated. Fifty paces into the dense brush and the three of them broke free, finding themselves in a small clearing rife with the odor of decay. The origin of the mystery lay before them. Hans glanced at Krista. Squateye saw their exchange.

It wasn't deer intestines after all. It was Ser Aulmut Klingande's intestines.

They sprang from his sliced-open gut like a bloody vine. Klingande was naked, his pink flesh a stark contrast to the dense green foliage all around. He was also hanging upside down on an upside-down cross, overlapping feet nailed to a stout log by a thick iron spike. Smaller nails impaled both of his wrists. Hanging upside down as he was, the rest of his vitals—heart, lungs, all of it—had dropped straight out all over the ground. Blood had drained from the ragged hole that was his mouth and covered his face and forehead. It pooled, thick and scarlet, on the mound of entrails and forest floor underneath.

This was the very man Black Dugal had sent Krista and Hans to kill ten days ago. They had left him for dead on the floor of his parlor in a pile of his own guts, eyes gouged out. Hans had opened him up. In fact, Dugal himself had been there, disguised as Klingande's manservant. And now Klingande's gutted body was here, in a mountain forest north of Rokenwalder, more than a week later. *How?* Krista asked herself. *And why?*

"Rotted Laijon almighty!" Bogg said, pushing his way through the brush, Café Colza Bouledogue behind him. The dog immediately attacked the dead body, going straight for the face hanging just above the ground. Nobody attempted to stop him.

"As I say, trust is fleeting," Squateye sighed, his lone eye fixed on Krista. "Someone else is trying to take credit for this kill."

Krista looked at Klingande again, her face expressionless.

"And they want us to know about it." Bogg walked up to the dead man and cocked his own flat-faced head sideways, studying him. "Someone's performed their own Sacrament of Souls here. A

sacrament not fed by my dungeon of inmates, a sacrament not sanctioned by me or Dugal whatsoever."

Klingande's skull snapped in Café Colza's strong jaws.

† † † † †

"You are late," Black Dugal said with his typical cruel yet mannered
charm. A supple cloak of fine black linen swirled about his knee-high
leather boots as he led both Krista and Hans into his chamber.

"The tardiness was not our fault," Hans answered in frustration.

"Lateness is always the fault of the one who is late." Dugal's voice
was at all times infused with a measured eloquence, even when chastising. Hans said nothing.

Dugal beckoned them both to sit. Krista and Hans settled onto
either end of their master's soft velvet couch. The large room was
spicy with incense, dim with sparse candlelight, and plush with
thick-spun rugs and lavish tapestries of rich, dark hues. Every piece
of furniture was fashioned of the finest polished mahogany. Dugal's
elegant sanctuary was always a place of dense, quiet luxury and
brooding shadows, almost primal in its masculinity. Krista felt at
home within it.

Though she didn't rightly know where it was located. The journey to her master's hidden lair was a maze of narrow underground
tunnels and a twisty stretch of long-abandoned stone-cobbled sewers.
The entrance to these tunnels was through a dusty, hay-covered corner
of a ramshackle stable yard Dugal kept near the docks. It was where
they stabled their Bloodeye steeds. Dugal had his own secret stable for
Malice, and neither Krista nor Hans was privy to its location.

Dugal took his seat in the soft-cushioned chair across from them,
a bronze goblet and fluttering candle on the round wooden table
next to him. "So tell me what strange mischief has Bogg rooted out
today?"

"The dead body of Ser Aulmut Klingande," Hans said. His answer came a little hastily for Krista's taste. She threw him a swift glance of warning, but his attention was fixed on Dugal. "In the foothills between Eark and Rokenwalder. Hanging upside down. Rotted guts draped about the forest like party tinsel."

A grim cast fell over Dugal's eyes. It was subtle, but Krista could sense a worried tension, a tightening of his posture in the chair that had not been present moments before. In fact, it was tension that she had *never* witnessed in her master, ever. "In the foothills between Eark and Rokenwalder?" Dugal ran a languid hand over the flickering flame of the candle atop the end table next to his chair.

"Aye." Hans watched Dugal's hand and the flame dancing underneath.

"You strayed from the Eark Road?" Dugal leaned forward slightly, hand still wavering over the candle flame. "What took you into the foothills, into those woods?"

"The nose on Bogg's damned stupid mutt took us into those woods."

Dugal's expression relaxed into wistfulness as he took the bronze goblet from the table and drank it down with a long swallow. Then he placed both hands in his lap, long fingers flexing before coming to rest. "So the body was upside down then?"

Krista felt Hans' eyes watching her now. But she ignored him. This was Hans' story. His confessional. She would not speak unless directly called upon. Hans had already made his mistakes and must live with them, see them to the end.

"As you know from your Sacrament of Souls," Dugal went on, "there is much one can learn from the dead. How did Bogg's bulldog react to the corpse?"

Hans answered, "The dog ate Klingande's fat fucking face right off his fat fucking head is how he reacted."

"So, Hans Rake, why tell me any of this?"

Hans shrank back in the couch, dark brows and pinprick eyes scrunched in concentration, concern. It was never good when Black Dugal called them by their full names and not their monikers. Hans was Shadowwood. In Krista's opinion, he should not answer any more questions.

"I tell you because you are my master," Hans responded. "Because you asked."

"One needn't answer every question posed," Dugal said with a certain coolness that sent an icy prick of unease up Krista's spine. "One must learn to keep some things to oneself if one expects to be a successful Bloodwood and fur trader." Dugal let the last words dangle, a faint red gleam from the candlelight reflecting in his eyes. "Am I not right, Crystalwood?" His eyes fell on her.

A coldness passed through Krista's bones as she nodded, not daring to look at Hans, knowing his eyes must be lancing shards of pure jealousy her way.

*Fur trader?*

Her mind was instantly back in Bark, shuffling about the docks of the strange town dressed as a toothless old woman in tattered old rags, hauling about heavy crab traps. She'd stuffed hurion tac paste in her cheeks, nostrils, and even eyelids to make her face look especially deformed. The same paste mixed with strong birch whiskey and spread over the skin could cause quick, deep wrinkles that would last for hours. But going about looking completely wrinkled and toothless wasn't the thing she'd been most proud of, what had really sold her disguise—it was the calluses on her hands. A woman selling crabs for a living surely needed calluses on her hands. Krista had sold a lot of crabs.

Hans had been a dashing, successful young fur trader from Nordmire, plying the bartenders and whores of Bark with his riches, making a grand show of things. But from the beginning he'd thought the entire trip a waste of his time. He'd just wanted fun and amusement. Krista knew how important going about in plain sight—yet completely unseen—was to a Bloodwood's schooling. That was why she had taken care in her disguise.

She risked a quick glance Hans' way. He was not amused. The tattoos that laced the skin along the sides of his head and neck and above his ears could not mask his shameful blush. *Deciphering truth from lies is part of your test,* Squateye had said. *Trust is fleeting, whilst betrayal is timeless.* Krista's mind swirled. *Was Dugal in Eark? Was the entire trip to see if we could fool him? Or perhaps Bogg or Squateye has already told him about our disguises. Or is Dugal just that clever?* She recalled how convincingly he'd played the part of Aulmut Klingande's manservant. *Everything about Black Dugal is also a lie.*

"I should have slain Aulmut Klingande long ago," Dugal said softly. "But alas, I saved him for you, my favorite pets, and now I fear that in my delay the man has come back to bite me." He looked at Krista, asking, "Who are you?"

"Crystalwood," she answered without hesitation, unbidden. That the name came to her so quickly surprised even her. *Have I really abandoned my former life so readily?* She could scarcely picture her father's face anymore. *Gault Aulbrek, where have you gone?* He'd left when she was only seven and had made only sporadic visits from the battlefields of Adin Wyte after that. She'd last seen him at twelve years old. He had gifted her with a thin blue ribbon she still kept tied around her ankle. *But I never did know him well.* As a very young girl she'd idolized her father. But for the last ten years, she'd been watched over mostly by two evil strangers, Aevrett Raijael and Black Dugal. Whenever she heard her new name, Crystalwood, she thought of her old life before. She didn't know why, but she did. All this spun through her mind whilst staring straight at her master, unblinking.

And Dugal found her gaze and held it, saying, "You are like that final snowflake that lights upon the very pinnacle of a snowcapped mountain. The crystal-clear flake that sets the entire mountain of ice thundering down the slope to crush all in its path." His hand floated over the fluttering flame of the candle again. "No one can foresee what each day will bring." He paused, red-hazed eyes lying heavy on her now. When he spoke again, his words were soft but pointed. "I have a task for you, my crystal snowflake. Do you accept?"

She nodded without hesitation.

"Perhaps our king thinks he can dance with me," Dugal said, dark eyes now observing his own hand as it floated gracefully over the candle. "Well, I shall show Aevrett Raijael differently."

There was danger here now. Dark currents of it. Krista felt it swirling about. It almost set her into a panic. But vestiges of caution allowed her to think rationally. She said nothing. But her heart jumped and thundered in her chest.

"You must pay our king a visit at Jö Reviens," Dugal continued, his eyes now piercing into hers. "You will pay him a visit in secret. He can never know you were there. His five Knights Chivalric can never know. They must never sniff you out. And they are all five of them clever and keen of intellect and most deadly. So this is no light task I give you."

*He wants me to spy on the king!* Krista sensed that Hans was staring daggers at her, beside himself with envy. She met the commanding gaze of her master and dipped her head in acquiescence, not knowing how to feel. She had not seen King Aevrett Raijael nor set foot in his grand palace Jö Reviens in five years. *And now I go to spy on him as a member of the Bloodwood assassins.* It seemed like grand treason. But she hated the king and would do it with relish.

She held no fondness for King Aevrett and his queen, Natalia. The queen's mind had clearly been eaten by the wraiths. The woman was crazy. Krista recalled her time at Jö Reviens. Torturous and lonely. Most days she'd wished she could just be a regular part of Aevrett's court, running through the grasses of the palace tournament yards, barefoot and breathless, frolicking with the other children of royalty.

But that had not been her life. Aevrett's five Knights Chivalric body-guards had ruled her life, keeping her captive in a small room next to the queen's chamber most days. She recalled with a shudder the torture she'd suffered because of Natalia's dementia. Things she'd blocked from her mind. Tortures she did not want to ever remember.

It had been a shock when Spiderwood had set her free and brought her to Black Dugal. The Spider had rescued her at Dugal's behest. That first little while under Dugal's tutelage had been rough. Krista had hated it, been afraid. But she had never given voice to her fears. Then she began to see the freedom in becoming a Bloodwood. She had grown to adore her two Vallè classmates, Seita and Breita. They had become like sisters to her. She ofttimes wondered where they now were. What Bloodwood missions had they been given? *And will I ever see them again?*

"You will not send me into Jö Reviens too?" Hans finally asked, a bitter twist to his mouth. "But you will send *her?*"

"You have your instructions, Crystalwood." Black Dugal crushed the flame of the candle between two fingers, stood, and silently exited his lair, not looking once at Hans.

*A defiled woman is rendered worthless in the eyes of Laijon. Even under the yoke of abuse, at some point a woman must face her own complicit nature and seek the forgiveness of Laijon.*
—THE WAY AND TRUTH OF LAIJON

# CHAPTER NINETEEN
# AVA SHAY

24TH DAY OF THE ETHIC MOON, 999TH YEAR OF LAIJON
BAINBRIDGE, GUL KANA

The morning before the battle of Bainbridge, Ava sat with the injured Bloodwood in the covered wagon. She had just finished carving a small beetle out of birch wood with the knife Jenko had given her. She'd kept the knife hidden in the ashes of a gold incense censer she liked to carry with her. The Bloodwood had taken keen delight in her carving.

"Can I keep it when you're done?" he asked, setting aside the little black book he always wrote in.

"As long as you don't tell Aeros about the knife."

"A girl with a gift for such fine craftsmanship." The Bloodwood took the beetle. "How could I possibly rat her out?" His words were innocent enough, but his eyes were not. Still, he admired her carving for some time before slipping it into the folds of his polished leather tunic, which he had just recently taken to wearing again, his wounds still carefully bandaged underneath. The Spider's clothing always smelled of cloves. She had grown used to his scent, as she had grown used to him.

He was good-looking, she'd noticed, but in a cruel way. The cruelty was in his mouth, his lips. *You can always tell the cruelty of a person in their mouth*, her mother had once said after a cruel-mouthed thief had been caught trying to steal one of their pigs when Ava was a small girl. The Spider had a cruel mouth that matched his red-streaked eyes. Still, all things considered, he treated her well enough in the wagon. He treated her with respect. And their time together was not unpleasant.

When Aeros had first asked her to tend to the Bloodwood's injuries, she had been mortified. But she had done as best she could. The blow to the Spider's head combined with the flogging from Hammerfiss had caused some gruesome damage to his flesh. His back was crisscrossed with wounds.

Spiderwood had been a silent travel companion in the beginning. But as of late he had been opening up. His conversations, though surface level, had sped their bumpy wagon ride along.

He pulled a vial of some medicine from his tunic and drank. "Some potions work to stave off the effects of poisoning," he said. "Some help speed the healing of any injury, even injuries as grievous as mine. Mind you, a skull fracture or a brain injury is different, incurable by any potion known to man. I suffered a hard blow in Ravenker. But I do not think my skull was fractured. I will regain all my faculties eventually."

His eyes hardened. "And then I will kill Hammerfiss." He smiled at her, then winked. "*You* won't rat me out for admitting such, will you?"

"You should kill them all," she said. "Everyone in Aeros' army is evil. They've no loyalty to anyone, not even you."

"My master, a man named Black Dugal, taught me that one must learn to play things to one's advantage at all times. Even with Aeros. No matter what rapes the Angel Prince commits, play it to your advantage and it will all turn out well in the end."

"Don't try convincing me it's all right," she answered. "Rape is never something that will turn out 'well' for anyone."

"I was talking of my own problems," he said. Though he was sitting, he made his best effort to bow to her. Then he produced a bottle of wine from under his blankets. Popped the cork and smelled the aroma. He pulled a goblet from under the covers next. He then made such a ceremony of his sharing of the wine, Ava almost thought she might see some kindness in him. But she did not want to drink from the goblet he held out to her.

"I must somehow thank you for your tender healing touch," he said. "Drink."

"What if I refuse?" she answered, not willing to completely trust him.

"I am bigger than you." He smiled, but not all cruelness had completely vanished behind that smile. There was still some danger to him. He bowed again. "But I would never force you to do something you do not want to do. The choice is yours. Think of it as my way of helping you purge what future pains may come."

She took the goblet from him and drank. And as she gulped the wine down, she realized that since she'd been captured, the beetle carving was the first gift she had given anyone, and the drink of wine, the first gift she had willingly accepted. Oh, Aeros had given her things, useless trinkets and gems, and she had given him *things*, her body, but those were all tokens of captivity and an extension of the unbearable flavor of his personality. This wine from the Bloodwood was divine. And she liked partaking.

She and the Bloodwood drank of the bottle until they were both drunk.

† † † † †

Twenty-fourth day of the Ethic Moon and Bainbridge should have been full of devotees of the Church of Laijon attending Eighth Day services. But that wasn't to be.

As Aeros Raijael and his contingent of Knights of the Blue Sword ushered Ava Shay through the rain-soaked town, she could see the stark remains of the vaulted cathedral, smoke billowing from every shattered window, doors smashed open, revealing the orange glow of the raging inferno inside.

Before the attack, Bainbridge had been full of tall stone-and-timber buildings and archways glistening with color and pride. Now Ava passed under smoke-charred archways festooned with naught but withered webs of burnt ivy and blackened flowers. This once proud town was now dead, its once grand structures smoldering in final surrender. The entirety of this once thriving community was now reduced to filthy streets painted with soot and the blood of a thousand Bainbridge fighters. Black smoke everywhere. Drunk on the Spider's wine, Ava was forced to gulp the fetid air down her constricting throat. She thought she might vomit. Her limbs weakened with each inebriated step through town, one thought on her mind. *Laijon has forsaken all of Gul Kana just as he has forsaken me!*

The rain picked up, clearing out the smoke, and the clearer the air became, the more street carnage Ava's bleary eyes saw: burnished helms, gilt-worked mail, breastplates, gauntlets, swords, a broken pike here, a sheared lance head there, the regal folds of the fallen Bainbridge standards amidst the silent heaps of warhorses in pools of curdling scarlet. The bodies. The butchery. The manure. A severed arm lying there forgotten. The splatter and aftermath of the sacking of another Gul Kana town, and rainwater ran in rivulets from it all, creating myriad dull reflections dancing back at Ava, blurring her drunken vision even further. She closed her eyes and blindly let Aeros guide her by the hand.

When they arrived on the beach south of town, Hammerfiss' and Enna Spades' random torture of the survivors seemed mostly over. Ava was glad for that one relief. The group of surviving captives huddled in fear near Aeros' two henchmen. The corpse-strewn beach stank with a mix of salt water and blood as the last few sprinkles of rain fell. The red-streaked waters of Bainbridge Bay were crisscrossed with strands of white froth. Down where the waves curled against the shore, Ava saw pigeons circling low and crabs scuttling in the surf. Several mangy dogs barked at each other, eating what scraps of battle they could.

In the distance, Mancellor Allen and Jenko Bruk were pulling a heavily armored Bainbridge knight north through a stretch of sand blackened with gore. They grasped the man by one leg each, dragging him along the bloody shore toward Hammerfiss and Spades. The Bainbridge knight clutched frantically at the ground, face and gauntleted hands carving furrows in the sand.

The tattoo ink under Mancellor's eyes glistened black in the rain as he hauled the captive to his feet in front of Hammerfiss and Spades and the remaining Bainbridge prisoners—most of them young boys and teenage fighters. All the women and young children had previously fled the town, running north. Ava was glad for that. She couldn't bear the torture of more little ones. This daily dose of savagery and torture she was forced to watch was the reason she drank so much. To cover the pain. Mask the horrors.

"Found him untying a skiff from the docks." Mancellor bowed to Spades and Hammerfiss, motioning to the knight between him and Jenko. He bowed to the White Prince too. "The baron of Bainbridge, Ser Brender Wayland, or so he says."

"A baron, you say?" A crazed grin broke over Hammerfiss' face. "Trying to make his escape, no doubt."

Ava knew things would not go well for this man named Brender Wayland. His eyes widened at the sight of the White Prince. In all his pale, harsh elegance, Aeros Raijael had that eye-widening effect on people.

Aeros left her side and walked toward the baron. "Did you fight or did you flee, Ser Wayland?" he asked. "I've fast come to realize the barons in this kingdom are of a weak heart when it comes to war."

Brender did not answer.

"If you refuse to answer," Aeros continued, "I will have Spades do as she will. And it will not be pretty, mind you, Ser Wayland." The rain started up again.

Ava wondered if this doomed baron with the last name of Wayland was any relation to Stefan. Of course, Stefan had escaped the prisoner tent in Gallows Haven with Nail, Gisela, and Liz Hen. She wondered where her friend was now.

"Looks like Ser Wayland has no tongue," Aeros said. The increasing rain pinged with more force against the armor of the Sør Sevier knights gathered around.

"We must therefore help him find his tongue." Hammerfiss grinned.

"Jenko, fetch an abandoned longsword off the beach, a sharp one for Ser Wayland's lost tongue," Spades ordered. Brender Wayland trembled.

Jenko strode across the savaged beach, snatching a longsword from the stiff hand of the first dead Knight of the Blue Sword he saw.

Today Aeros' army had lost near a hundred warriors in the fight. The White Prince had called it the first real bloody fray they had come across in Gul Kana so far. He had seemed energized by it. In fact, the entire Sør Sevier army had fought with relish once they'd realized that not all had fled Bainbridge as had been the case in previous towns. A decent-sized army of three thousand men had stayed to fight them.

Bainbridge was ten times the size of Ravenker and Bedford—and those were both twice the size of Gallows Haven. Still, over the past few weeks, the White Prince's army had swelled to more than thirty thousand. And Aeros' force kept growing as ship after ship arrived daily from Wyn Darrè, bearing Sør Sevier soldiers. They made short work of Bainbridge's three thousand men. Aeros claimed they would have well over fifty thousand well-seasoned knights on Gul Kana soil by the time they reached Lord's Point, with another two hundred thousand in Adin Wyte poised to strike Lord's Point from across the shallow strait east of Saint Only, and then maybe double that when they marched on Amadon.

When Jenko Bruk returned with the sword he'd gathered, Spades took the weapon and held it out to Ser Brender Wayland, hilt in one palm, blade in the other, arms straight out, as if offering him a precious gift.

"I've a deal for you, Ser Wayland," Spades said, bending her knee to the man. Brender looked at the weapon being offered him, but made no move to take it.

"The deal is this," Spades continued. "Best any Sør Sevier fighter of my choosing in single combat, and the armies of Aeros Raijael will gather our gear and set sail back to our homeland, never to torment Gul Kana again."

Brender looked her in the eye. "And how do I know you will honor such a deal?"

"A fight to the death, Ser. Do you agree to the terms?"

Brender Wayland took the sword, tested its weight. It fit naturally in his gauntleted hands. His eyes fell on the row of Bainbridge captives lined up behind Spades. "If I win, you promise your armies will leave?"

"I promise."

Some captives stood a little straighter now. But Ava knew it was a pointless hope she saw building in their eyes. For she knew that within Spades brooded a taste for mindless violence, a streak of ruthlessness unmatched. And a penchant for making deals that she knew she would win. Still, their hope seemed to bolster Brender's confidence. "I accept your deal then," he said.

Spades turned to face Jenko Bruk. "Kill him, Jenko."

Ava sucked in a deep breath. Jenko's eyes found hers as he drew his sword. She wanted to shout at him, *Let Brender kill you! Let's see if they do as Spades promised and never torment Gul Kana again!* But a head full of wine and her own fear made it impossible to say anything, let alone shout it across the bloody beach.

The two men squared off in the sand, swords at the ready, both silver blades now slick with rain. Brender's sword slashed out first, a quick strike from the left that Jenko blocked with fluid ease. Jenko countered with a downward swing at Brender's legs. The baron blocked low. Jenko's second swing went high, straight toward the man's head. The baron blocked high, losing his balance just enough, his sword arm flailing up over his head. And Jenko thrust with a powerful, two-handed stab that punched right through the man's armpit. The baron's eyes went wide with astonishment and pain.

"You've killed me?" Brender finally croaked, voice dry with looming death. It seemed as if the rain even ceased its falling at that moment. "Why kill any of us, you Sør Sevier scum?" His mouth gaped open in silent agony as he slid off Jenko's long blade and clattered to the sand in a pile of useless shiny armor. The steady flow of rain rattling off the dead man was the only sound now.

Then came the heavy sobs of one of the Bainbridge captives, a young man overburdened with grief and despair. All Ava could think about was that with his last words, Brender had called Jenko "Sør Sevier scum." Brender probably had no idea Jenko knew Stefan. That Stefan had worked on Baron Bruk's grayken-hunting ship. That the two had once been friends. That thought sobered her up. Did Jenko have no pity in his own soul? He could have lost the fight, let Brender slay him, ended all the bloodshed and torture. But then she recalled what Jenko had implied not long after they'd been captured by Aeros: *We all do what we can to survive. Could I have sacrificed myself?* she wondered. *Can I kill myself?* Now and then, in the dark watches of the night, she found herself groping for the strength to do just that, to just end it all. And then she would merely drink from Aeros' wine stash until it didn't matter anymore. Jenko *had* given her the knife, with the instruction to use it on Aeros. *But who will I use it on?*

As she stood upon the beach and fought to contain the spirits and turmoil dwelling in her drunken mind, the rude shapes of the smoldering buildings of Bainbridge clung to her periphery. She would pity herself no more. *Only I can mend my own hurt.* Her mind was focused on the knife Jenko had slipped into her shirt a week ago. It was hidden now. Cleverly hidden. And she would use it. She would not be a victim anymore.

*Sør Sevier scum.* 'Twas the dying words of Baron Brender that convinced her. She cast her eyes on the crumpled body of Brender Wayland. Standing triumphant over his body was Jenko Bruk, cleaning blood from his sword.

And Jenko met her gaze with a fierce, unforgiving stare.

† † † † †

"I hate cowardly bootlickers and fawning ass kissers." Aeros' head rose up out of the streaming water, white hair plastered around his skull. The rain had ended, and the stars were now a-twinkle above. The opening in the roof of Aeros' tent let in a soft breeze. Ava was no longer drunk as before. She had declined what few tankards of wine Aeros had offered. Luckily, he hadn't forced it down her anyway.

She knelt beside the White Prince's steaming iron tub, wearing naught save his pearl-colored doublet, naked underneath. The doublet was open in the middle, covering just her shoulders and back. Aeros insisted she not lace the front. He liked to gaze upon her partial nakedness as she bathed him. And he was gazing at her now.

"Thing is"—he blinked the water from his eyes—"a fawning boot-licker never knows he is a bootlicker."

"Am I a fawning bootlicker?" As soon as the question spilled from her lips, she cursed her own brashness.

His dark-pupiled eyes stayed fixed to her chest. "You? Bootlicker?" He looked into her eyes after a moment, clearly annoyed. "Don't be daft."

"I only tease." She added a mischievous, playful squeeze as she rubbed his shoulders. Massaging him like this only built up more revulsion in her. His skin under the bathwater was slick as warmed porcelain. She recalled washing the white dishes Ol' Man Leddingham sometimes used to bring up out of the Grayken Spear cellar for important travelers. Aeros' flesh under the hot water looked like those fine dishes in Leddingham's wash water. She said, "I thought you desired I be more playful."

"Just stay silent and massage my back and neck. Let me relax. I will let you know when it is time to play. Your unasked-for efforts at playfulness come across as hurtful."

*If he only knew how much I desire to hurt him.* She could still see the drowned baby floating away, facedown in the cold stream near Leifid. Caressing his flesh made her feel more dead inside by the minute. The white bear rug under her knees, the opulence of the tent and its furnishings, the crystal decanters lined along the tub, the candles, the spacious opening in the roof of the tent and the stars twinkling above, the herbs in the perfumed hot water, the steaminess of it all—normally things so luxurious and fine to a girl who dreamed of romance. *But who lives such fantasies anymore?*

Her fingers trailed slowly up to his chin and back down to his shoulders. The pale purple veins in his neck looked so close and vulnerable in the wet and steamy air. *And my fingernails have grown so long.* The knife Jenko had given her was currently hidden under incense ashes and burnt herbs within her gold censer atop a table in the draped room that served as her own water closet. And that closet was right next to Aeros' bedroom and bath. *So close!*

"I feel there is too much bootlicking and ass kissing within your friend Jenko," he said. "I know he desires to move up in the ranks of my army. And I admire his determination and devotion. He does indeed possess some traits that you do not. . . ."

He paused. "Are you even listening to me?" He gazed up at her, annoyed. She pressed harder with her fingers, working the muscles under his flesh.

There was a white towel on the brass table near the tub. He lifted his arm from the water and wiped the palm of his hand on it, then the back of his hand too. "I fear you don't listen to me. You scarcely remember much of anything I tell you."

"Pardon, my lord, I do try and listen."

"No, I think not," he said. "I can tell you something very important, and then the very next day I can ask you about it and it's as if it's the first time you heard of it. It vexes me. I am sorely vexed by you. Completely and absolutely vexed."

Ava just kept working his flesh beneath her fingers. Silent.

"Remember when we first met?" he asked. "How I claimed we would become the best of friends? That one day you would come to worship me?"

"I remember."

He sat up straight in the water, craned his neck, and looked back at her. "I lose control around you, my love." His face, covered in a thin film of sweat from the heat of the tub, glistened in the candlelight. He resituated himself in the water, facing her. With his dry hand, he touched her breast under the doublet, his fingers circling the nipple. She wanted to draw back, but she remained stoic. She would not let her revulsion show. His voice was throaty, rich. "When you first came to me, you were my prisoner. Now I am yours."

"If you say." She smiled with a slight tilt of her chin.

"I'm plagued with hazy dreams," he continued. "Muddy dreams. Even whilst awake. Visions of the future, if you will. These dreams . . . they afflict me and make me think the wraiths have me in their foul clutch." Ava shuddered at his mention of the wraiths.

"Sometimes these dreams can be pleasant," he went on. "For instance, I dreamed of you. Long before we met. I knew your face. So I was not surprised to find you when I did. What say you to that bit of prophecy?"

"I don't know."

"Some visions weigh terrible on my mind." His hand slipped away from her breast. "Oh, few will sympathize with my situation, least of all you, I suppose."

"I sympathize."

"It doesn't seem so." He lowered his head, not looking at her anymore. "I become more like the Bloodwood day by day. I only believe in what I can see and touch and precious little else. And certainly never anything anyone says."

She thought of Bainbridge, of Brender Wayland and his pointless death at the hands of Jenko. *You've killed me* had been the baron's last words. *Why have you killed any of us?*

"Why do you fight?" she found herself asking. "Why conquer and torture?"

Aeros leaned forward in the tub, his hands back under the water, allowing her room to stroke his back. "Even your *Way and Truth of Laijon* speaks of Fiery Absolution," he said. "The time is now. *The Chivalric Illuminations* record our deeds. Laijon knows who his true followers are. And his true followers are those who follow the bloodline of Raijael, Laijon's one and only heir. I am of that bloodline. I am Laijon returned. And it is by his will and grace that I reclaim lands stolen so long ago."

There was no way this monster before her was Laijon's son returned. She knew of Fiery Absolution. Bishop Tolbret had read the prophecies from the holy book during Eighth Day services on more than one occasion. The return of Laijon was to be a glorious event. That it might come in her day, in her time of living, should have been a comfort, should have made her sing praises to Laijon. *But faced with the brutal realities of war . . .*

"Do you believe that the Vallè also have dreams as I do?" he asked. "Do you believe that they can also know things about the past and present and future?"

"I don't know any Vallè."

"You are getting along with Spiderwood, are you not?"

"I clean his wounds daily as you bade me do. Fresh bandages. He seems appreciative. Is he a Vallè?"

"No. He is not Vallè." There was a barely noticeable laugh in his voice. "But I would have you two become close."

"If you wish it."

"Still, even though you are to become his friend, no matter how charming he can be, the Spider is not to be trusted."

"If you say."

"The Spider will kill Hammerfiss someday. He will make an attempt on my life too. There is no telling what schemes Black Dugal has cooked up for him. But it amuses me to see how things play out."

Aeros went silent for a time. Then he said, "There is a man named Hawkwood. A Bloodwood. An assassin like the Spider. Hawk and the Spider, they were once called. Embroiled in many intrigues with Black Dugal. They even call Black Dugal Father, though he is no man's father. They think me ignorant to their plotting, Spider and the Hawk. But I am not fooled. I have my own spies."

He dropped into silence again. She continued to rub his back. "Yes," he finally said, his voice soft, conspiratorial. "You shall become the truest of friends with the Spider."

"If it please you, my lord."

"Hawkwood vexes me too. Spades claims to sometimes feel his

presence. What do you make of that? Does Spades have prophecy in her too?"

"I don't know."

"Spades claims Hawkwood was in Ravenker. That she *sensed* him there. Said that it was Hawkwood who likely crushed the skull of the Spider. Of course the Spider won't admit to it. I must know what happened. The boy Nail was there. But could he have injured the Bloodwood so grievously? Perhaps you could get some of these answers out of the Spider for me, Ava."

"As you wish."

"Splendid," he said. "You will make a splendid spy. Perhaps I will rename you Little Miss Splendid. Or Splendidwood. Or perhaps some other nonsense."

"If you like."

"I've told you how devoted my father is to my mother, have I not?"

"You have. Their names are Aevrett and Natalia."

He looked back at her, noticeable surprise on his face. "So you do listen."

"And never was there a marriage more strong than theirs," she followed. "Or so you've said."

"Alas, their marriage is an example I have fallen woefully short of. Of course I am not married, nor have I any children. So it is a virtual impossibility that I can commit any sort of infidelity. But I will become betrothed someday. All the noblewomen in Adin Wyte and Wyn Darrè have been killed. No alliance can be gained there. Perhaps I will take Jondralyn Bronachell to wed. I hear she is most beautiful. And Jovan has a younger sister, Tala. I like that name. Aeros and Tala. It sounds good. Does it not?"

"It does."

His conversation seemed to be jumping all over the place. And that notion filled her with dread. She'd learned the hard way that when the White Prince got in a scattered, unpredictable mood like this, things would soon get rough. She had zero notion what form his coming anger might take, what depraved abuse he would heap upon her.

But she would not let him rape her anymore. Even if it meant her death. *I have the knife!* Less than twenty paces away in a gold censer atop the table in her own water closet.

"Does the thought of me with some other make you jealous?" he asked.

She let his question linger, stroking his back more slowly, deliberately now, working the warm water and fragrant soap into his skin. "If . . . if you want me to be jealous, then I will be—"

"I want you to feel what you feel," he said waspishly. "I could very well wed this girl Tala Bronachell someday. Does that pain you?" His tone was full of anger now.

"Some," she finally answered, wincing with disgust as she did so.

"Are you jealous of Spades and Jenko?"

"I do not think of them. Ever."

"Probably best. Their sessions are not heavenly like ours. I imagine they rut like dirty dogs in heat. Who wishes to think of that?"

"I said I do not think of it," she muttered. Yet that was a lie. Every time Jenko and Spades were brought up, Ava pictured them together in her mind. Her imagination was like a constant rusty dagger clawing at her heart.

"I've a tendency to choose Bloodwoods and former enemies like Mancellor Allen as bodyguards," he said, the subject changed yet again. "You can only be deceived by the ones you love. Never by those you loathe. You capture an enemy in battle and he expects nothing but misery. But you turn the tables and give him a life full of pleasure and power, then you *own* him more than you'd own a slave. And having one like that around keeps me focused and alert." He was almost babbling to himself now, and Ava's heart trembled. "I desire to keep the Knights Archaic varied because I do not trust my own soldiers completely. If my personal guard is of mixed company, there is always someone distrusting another, and distrust keeps everyone on their toes . . . and loyal to me. For I am the only constant in their life. That is what I am aiming for anyway. Have them paranoid about one another, rather than me. If you take my meaning. It has worked for ten years anyway. Only Gault has been with me from the start. Of course now he has vanished. And now I need more Knights Archaic. I've only Hammerfiss, Spades, and Mancellor left. The Spider can no longer be counted upon. I must find two more. . . ."

He left the last line dangling as he went silent. It had been a lengthy and disjointed discourse, and she sensed things were about to boil over. But something he'd said jogged her memory. She had seen some measure of kindness in Mancellor Allen in Leifid. He'd cared for that baby Aeros had drowned. She got the impression that Mancellor was not a bad man. *Is there help for me there, with him?*

For some reason she wanted to look upon the green angel stone again. And look upon the blue one Jenko had found too. She then thought of the bald knight, Gault, how she'd tried to get him to escape with her. How she'd kissed him. She still couldn't believe she had let that happen, had *wanted* that to happen. If they could have escaped together with the ax and stone, all would be different. Even if she and Nail had escaped together. *So many ifs.* And she could make sense of none of it.

And here she sat rubbing the flesh of her enemy for his pleasure.

"I would make Jenko Bruk a Knight Archaic," Aeros said, "if I knew for a certainty I had his full loyalty. He continually badgers me about the battle-ax he took from Nail, continually asks if he can but see it again, touch it again, feel the ax's warm magic in his hands. I'd almost think he was talking of you, my love, the way his cunning eyes light up with desire." He wiped his hand on the white towel again, turned, and cupped her breast softly under the doublet, squeezing it gently, lust fixed in his dark eyes. "Have I your full loyalty?"

Her eyes darted to the tent flap leading to the next room, where her knife was. *I can race in there and have the knife before he can even step from the tub!*

"A slave eventually revels in his master's degradations," Aeros said. "Wouldn't you agree, my princess?"

*He actually probably believes that.* She pulled back, scooting on her knees away from him, and his hand fell away from her breast. The look on his pale face was grim. His dark eyes narrowed as the slithering veins under his pale brow pulsed with fury. "I did not give you leave to move."

"I do not wish to lie with you again."

"You do not *wish*?" Water sloshed as he whirled about in the tub, facing her directly, the bulk of his body still submerged. "Do you not understand the righteousness of my cause? The righteousness of our coupling? Why do you resist me?"

She backed away, still on her knees, trembling. Her eyes flew to the escape route, imagining the hidden knife in her water closet and what damage it could do, vulnerable and naked as he was.

"That you continue this folly angers me," he said.

"I'm sorry," she said. "Please forgive me."

His posture relaxed in the water. "Who has put this foolishness and insolence in your head?"

She bolted for the tent flap leading to the room beyond, reaching the hidden knife foremost in her mind. Aeros jerked out of the water and had her in his grasp in an instant, one hand clenching her wrist, the other around her throat. He pulled her to his chest, his naked flesh warm and wet against her. "See, this is exactly what I live for, what I love. The challenge. The unpredictability of it all. It thrills me. Excites me. Can't you tell?" His straining hardness pressed against her back.

"Please, no," she begged.

"I possess you and I purify you," he whispered in her ear.

"Everything I do is holy. Everything I do is for your sake. Can you not see? When you lie with me, I place into you the healing power of the gods. Our heavenly seasons are blessed by both Raijael and Laijon. In them, I take upon myself your pains, your troubles, and your sins. I even take the wraiths within you upon myself. I bear your burdens."

"*Wraiths!*" she hissed.

"Yes, in time you will see those wraiths that plague your mind vanish, and your powers to heal flourish. If you have not already."

Her heart was pounding to the rhythm of his words. *Foulness and witchcraft!*

"Of all people, I must keep you, Ava Shay of Gallows Haven, closest to me." His chest almost melted into her back, so close was he pressing into her. "In all the battles I've fought, all the war I have seen, only Ava Shay of Gallows Haven has ever caused me injury, only you have ever drawn blood. Do you recall?" She did recall: she'd slapped him that first night they'd spent together. She recalled his abhorrence to seeing his own blood.

"In time, insolence like yours gone unpunished can only breed betrayal." His whispering voice was crawling with threat. "Do you wish to betray me now?"

"It is my bleeding time of the moon," she lied, his previous injury still on her mind. "I only wish to be clean for you. I was embarrassed. That is why I fled."

He drew back, turning her to face him, holding her at arm's length, both excitement and fear in his eyes at her deceptive admission. The lust in his eyes was powerful too. *He is enjoying all of this!*

"Well." He forced her head down to his groin. "Are your gums bloody?"

No matter how many times they coupled, the unpredictability of his words always hit her like a punch in the chest. His engorged member was now directly before her. Like everything about him, it was always clean and pretty, shorn of all hair. With one hand, he seized her roughly by the back of the head, pulling her face toward the pulsing *thing* between his legs. She struggled away from him. But his grip was firm, his fingers knotted in her hair, holding her head steady.

And then he drew a knife from the folds of the white towel on the brass table.

It was *her* knife. Her wood-carving blade. The one Jenko had slipped her. The one she thought was hidden in the gold censer. She felt its needle tip pressing at her neck as he said, "Try anything stupid and I'll open your throat."

Ava drew in a slow, deep breath, trying to push away the despair, her mouth unwilling. But as had been done to her every night since her capture, taste him she did.

† † † † †

Shortly after their coupling, Aeros left the tent.

The White Prince along with Hammerfiss and a large company of Sør Sevier knights, including Jenko, set out north on a scouting mission. Aeros claimed he would be gone for the night and most of the next day and that she should foster no more disloyal or impudent ideas, that she would be carefully watched. Everything Aeros did was irrational. *And I was a fool to think I could outwit him.*

She needed fresh air. She stole through the tent, bare feet padding quietly past the many cordoned-off chambers within. In a slim cotton shift, she made her way to the front entrance. When she stepped outside, the night was black. The camp slept. The stars twinkled in full force above. Her shift felt light and airy in the soft breeze.

Enna Spades guarded the front entry of the tent. Ava had known that at least one of the Knights Archaic would be posted outside, either Mancellor or the red-haired woman or both. She hadn't cared. She needed the fresh air. She stepped past the woman.

Spades, tossing a coin in one leather-gloved hand, gave her a momentary glance and then thrust her other hand out, blocking her way with a stiff arm. "I'll let you stand outside if you wish." Spades' voice cut through the night. "But you must not leave my side." She went back to tossing her coin.

Spades was tall and regal beyond measure, pale skin and high cheekbones, long red hair flowing down her shoulders. The fine bright sheen of her Knight Archaic armor sparkled under her blue cloak. A wooden crossbow and quiver of quarrels were strapped to her back and a sword sheathed at either hip. Ava had never seen the woman carry two swords before. The sword nearest Ava was long, its sheathed tip almost dragging the ground. The other sword was slim and slightly curved with a strange red hilt. The coin Spades flipped twinkled in the dim light of the stars as it spun up and then down and back up again. "Is morning almost come?" Ava asked.

Spades stopped tossing the coin, eyes cast to the east, to the black and craggy silhouettes of the Autumn Range that blocked out the stars. "A couple hours yet before the sun shows over the peaks."

Ava's eyes traveled over the vast expanse of the Sør Sevier encampment that receded away into the dark, the smoldering town of Bainbridge a smoky ruin beyond.

"Just look at the mountains of Gul Kana," Spades said. "I cannot take my eyes off them most days. Ten thousand feet from the shoreline to the very top peaks, they say. It takes my breath away. And they say the Glacier Range above Sky Lochs rises to twenty thousand feet from base to top, with sheer cliffs jutting up along the coastline more than ten thousand feet. One mountain is more than twenty-five thousand feet. Such grand heights seem unfathomable. Have you seen them?"

"The Glacier Range?"

"Yes, and the cliffs of Stanclyffe?"

"No."

"The Nordland Highlands of Sør Sevier are rugged and stark and beautiful in their own way. But I stand in awe of Gul Kana's majesty."

It seemed a strange admission from someone so bent on destroying the land. Still, Ava hadn't really thought of it before, the grandness of the Autumn Range. The lofty peaks above Gallows Haven had just been a part of her life.

Spades tossed the coin again. Ava watched, curious. "You carry the coin with you always."

Spades held the coin out in the palm of her leather-gloved hand. "Do you not recognize it?"

It was familiar. An image of the most beautiful woman she had ever seen. "I've only laid eyes upon a few like it before," she said. "It's the new-minted coin from Avlonia. She's so very pretty, Jondralyn Bronachell."

"So you do recognize it." Spades snatched the coin away from her, pocketing it.

"Most coins that came through the Grayken Spear Inn were the old ones with the Val Vallè princess, Arianna. We only ever saw but a few of the new Jondralyn coins in Gallows Haven."

"Well, we aren't in Gallows Haven anymore," Spades said crisply.

Ava looked up to the looming Autumn Range. "I suppose not."

Spades unhooked the slender sword with the red hilt from her hip, sheath and all. She held it out as if wanting Ava to take it. The sheath was made of leather-studded red velvet. And the odd-shaped hilt was actually a heart-shaped ruby set in the sword's pommel. Even in the starlight, it sparkled with a beauty beyond comprehension.

Ava didn't know why she was so drawn to it. But she was. Joyfully so.

"A Vallè-worked blade," Spades said. "Very rare. Plundered from the rubble of Baron Brender Wayland's mansion. Looks like the baron had good taste in swords, and Vallè craftsmanship." She held the sword out. "It is now yours. Take it."

Ava stepped back warily, a sudden tightness growing in her throat, eyes fixed on the sheathed sword with the ruby-red pommel.

"Did not Aeros tell you I shall be teaching you how to fight with a sword?" Spades asked. "I believe he may have told you the very first day you bedded him."

"I did *not* bed him." Ava felt the anger rise in her. "Rape is *not* the same as bedding."

"They are called *heavenly* sessions."

"And I spit on your *heaven*."

"Regardless." Spades held the sheathed sword out. "He *did* tell you I would be teaching you how to fight like a warrior woman."

Ava knew it was true. "He said as much."

"And why do you think he would order such a thing?" Spades asked. "Why would he allow me to give you a blade and then train you how to use it?"

*He likes it when I try and kill him.* "Nothing Aeros does makes sense," she answered.

"And what god has ever made sense?" Spades asked. "What god has ever been consistent or fair? The gods are a deranged lot. Laijon. Raijael. Those gods that came before. And those gods that will come after." As the woman talked, Ava kept her eyes on the weapon in front of her. She so desperately wanted to touch it.

"Want to know what it's like to have a god living beside you?" Spades went on. "Just look to Aeros Raijael, witness the suffering in his wake. The singular majesty of it. Anguish and misery stretching the breadth of Adin Wyte and Wyn Darrè to the western shores of Gul Kana." Her tone dropped. "And all for what?"

*For the pain he can create,* Ava thought, her eyes still captured by the beauty of the red sword in Spades' hands. *He leaves naught but torture and suffering in his wake.* Ava had posed that very question to Aeros herself. She asked Spades, "Do you even believe in your god, Aeros Raijael?"

"With all my heart." Spades regarded her with a wry grin.

"It seems perhaps you do not."

"One can either believe and wield a sword at his side, or disbelieve and perish."

"Why cause the destruction and suffering of others?" She just could not understand Spades' logic. "Why must Aeros torment *me*?"

"Aeros loves war. 'Tis all he knows. It is his destiny. What he was bred for. His relationship to you is like being in war. It is the reason he keeps you around. It is the reason he keeps me around. It is the reason he chooses the Knights Archaic that he chooses. Part of what makes Aeros Raijael the Angel Prince is the danger he knowingly puts himself in with you and me and others. Danger. And triumph. That is his sustenance. Those are the things that make a god feel invincible. 'Tis all a game to him."

"How do you know?"

"We are alike, Aeros and I."

Each was worse than the other, depending on the day, leastways that was the way Ava saw both Spades and Aeros.

"It is the quality of one's foe that makes war worthwhile," Spades said. "And when this war is over, when Aeros' crusade is complete, we will both miss it, he and I and those who have fought with us. Gul Kana is weak. At least Wyn Darrè put up a fight. And so Aeros looks more and more to entertain himself by creating strong foes near him. He desires the challenge. As I said, it's all in the game."

"It is a twisted and cruel game."

"It is good that you can see it for what it is."

*Naught but a game to them. They toy with me and Jenko. The question is, should I play it with them? Could I?*

Spades' voice was gentle for once. "So will you let me train you?"

Ava nodded.

"Good." The warrior woman's eyes sparkled as she drew the sword from its sheath with a silent hiss. "I wanted to start with you sooner, but I was merely waiting for the right sword to come along. This is a fine, strong blade, weighted perfectly for one of your stature and strength. Pretty, too." It was a long, slim blade, slightly curved, honed razor sharp along one edge, intricate Vallè-inlaid scrollwork etched along the other.

Spades' voice grew suddenly fierce as she brandished the blade. "As I told you before, a sword is what separates me from you. And that is all. When you've a fine blade like this in your hand, and you know how to wield it, that is *strength*. That is *power*. There is no greater force in the Five Isles than a woman willing to use her own sword against a man. Unless it is a woman willing to use her own words. Sword. Words. Just one letter separating them." She smiled, holding up the blade. "But a sword can separate a man from his cock a lot quicker than words."

Ava's eyes were fixed on the blade in the warrior woman's hand.

"Let me ask you, Ava Shay, are you ready to be like Jenko Bruk? Are you ready to do whatever you damn well please?" She held out the sword for Ava again, her intense, stern eyes gazing down its sharpened edge. In fact, Spades' eyes glinted shards of red, brilliant reflections from the dazzling ruby set in the hilt.

Then, with a swift move, the warrior woman twirled on one foot and spun the sword in her gloved hand, spun it so fast it sent sparks of rhythmic starlight blinking into the night. Then she jabbed at the air in front of her, once, twice, thrice, twisting her wrist, ripping the blade back violently in a sweeping arch that made the air sing.

Then Spades stood silently in front of Ava again, sword held out in offering. "As I said before, we are not in Gallows Haven anymore."

Ava took the weapon. Held it up. Her gaze fell reverently on the shining heart-shaped jewel in the hilt and traveled up the long curved blade, utterly transfixed by the sharp gleam of the steel. Her chest was pounding to the same beat as when she'd first ventured into Baron Bruk's hay-filled barn with his son Jenko. *My heart feels alive.*

If swords were given names, that was what she would name this one. *My Heart.*

After a moment, her gaze broke from the sword and found Spades. "How am I to hide it from *him*? Aeros may wish me to train with you. But he will not want me to have an edged weapon near him. He knows I will use it."

"I shall keep the sword for you. You will train with me. Whenever and wherever I deem appropriate. Aeros has agreed to the training, for his own reasons. Do you?"

Ava nodded. Enna Spades dipped her chin in acknowledgment. "Then we start now."

*For their valiant help in vanquishing the nameless beasts to the underworld, all dwarven-kind, Vallè-kind, and oghul-kind are deemed free and worthy to walk amongst men, as long as they adhere to the laws and tenets of Laijon.*
—THE WAY AND TRUTH OF LAIJON

# CHAPTER TWENTY
# NAIL

1ST DAY OF THE ANGEL MOON, 999TH YEAR OF LAIJON

STANCLYFFE, GUL KANA

Nail had followed Liz Hen, Dokie, and Beer Mug across the street, hoping they wouldn't wander too far off. They stood in front of what appeared to be the least dodgy-looking establishment in Stanclyffe: the Cloven Hoof Tavern—it had a door with actual hinges and actual glass windows. Everything else in this town was beyond broken down. A sign above the hinged door read BIRCH BEER AND VARIOIUS SUNDRIES WITHIN.

"We oughtn't go in there," Dokie said, the cowl of his gray cloak pulled up over his head. Nail and Liz Hen were also heavily cloaked, hoods covering their faces in shadow too. "Roguemoore warned us against going inside any place 'round here," Dokie continued. "Warned us this place was naught but a haven for cutthroats and pirates. Said wait in the road whilst they purchase tack and mounts and gear. And we've already ventured across the street without them knowing where we went."

"We ain't but twenty paces away from the livery tack house, and I'm starving," Liz Hen huffed, patting Beer Mug on the head. "And various sundries means food."

"I don't think it does."

"Of course it does, you stupid." She looked at Dokie, scowling. She'd been scowling all day. "You still have coin in your pockets, right?"

Dokie's hand dropped to the small leather pouch tied to his belt under his cloak. "Aye. I got some coin here."

Nail's eyes scanned the street, looking for pirates, realizing he wouldn't know a pirate if one was standing right in front of him. Stanclyffe was a decent-sized port town about as big as Ravenker, nestled on a flat isthmus jutting out into the Sea of Thorns under a colossal Glacier Range cliff. The blackish-gray cliff rose daunting and sheer ten thousand feet straight above them, seemingly wanting to curl over and swallow the town whole. Clouds were gathering about the cliff, and a fresh round of rain seemed imminent.

The nine companions aboard the *Duchess of Devlin* had witnessed the wall of gray stone growing up out of the ocean several days before reaching Stanclyffe—the massive cliffs were that tall. In fact, the entire Glacier Range was a monstrous wonder. Upon approaching the range from the south, Nail had marveled at the sheer size of the snow-covered mountains—twenty thousand feet high from the level of the sea to their lofty peaks. Peaks twice as high as those above Gallows Haven and twice as rugged and steep—so high, in fact, Roguemoore claimed they created weather of their own. They were covered in dense cloud most days. But those few clear days before reaching Stanclyffe had revealed the mountain range in all its awe-inspiring glory—lofty peaks glimmering pearl and silver, like islands afloat above white clouds.

Roguemoore had paid voyage for the Company of Nine on

*Duchess of Devlin,* a fast-sailing ship out of Lord's Point. Stormy seas and a healthy kick of wind had hastened their trip those first five days afloat. But the last three had been calmer weather. During the voyage, sharks, grayken, and even a sea serpent, as big around as a wild Autumn Range boar and almost as long as the Gallows Haven chapel, had been spotted. The slithering huge serpent had gotten the attention of all, for it seemed to nearly dwarf the length of the ship. Godwyn claimed a sea serpent would never bother a ship, but would be quick to coil itself around an overboard sailor, constrict his bones till he was dead, then swallow him whole. Once, a few merfolk trailed along under the *Duchess of Devlin.* The ghostly silhouettes of the merfolk slithering in the deep would send a mysterious ache raging up Nail's biceps, and the scar from the mermaid's claws would come alive with fire. He couldn't help but recall the nightmarish journey he'd taken under the sea during the grayken hunt aboard the *Lady Kindly.*

Most every day aboard the *Duchess of Devlin* had seen Stefan and Seita on the forecastle just below the prow, practicing with Seita's ball-and-chain mace. Nail had been content to just watch. Liz Hen and Dokie, too, Beer Mug with them.

But Liz Hen had developed the knack of sucking the joy out of any moment aboard the ship. At every opportunity she teased Stefan about the doe-eyed looks he gave Seita, claiming all he ever did was daydream about the Vallè maiden slurping on his noodle. Then she'd tease Seita for being naught but a delicate Vallè flower, or a precious Vallè flower, or a dainty, frail, flimsy, thin Vallè flower. Eight days sailing up the Saint Only Channel and into Sea of Thorns with Liz Hen Neville had proven taxing for the entire group. Now, finally berthed in Stanclyffe, Liz Hen still managed to irritate.

Like now, ignoring all warnings and wandering away from the main group in search of food. "I say we sneak a quick look inside the Cloven Hoof," she said. "I'm starving."

"There's folks selling food outside near that corner shop half a block away." Dokie pointed. "I can see them cooking there in that large brick oven against the wall. Under that tan awning behind the table. See? I can smell it even. Smells good. Pork, I wager."

Liz Hen's eyes watered in hunger as they followed Dokie's gaze. "Street vendors." She immediately set off that way, gray cloak aswirl behind her, Beer Mug at her heels. Dokie followed. Nail grumbled inwardly and marched after them, not wanting to see his friends stray too far from the tack house.

One of the vendors was a middle-aged, kind-faced lady, a shockingly purple bruise on the left side of her neck. She introduced herself as Mardgot. Her burly helper was hunkered over the wood-burning oven, his back to them. When Liz Hen asked the fellow what he was cooking, he straightened his back and turned, looking right at her.

It was an oghul. And huge, with features unbearably deformed and grotesque. Thick, cracked lips of a deep purple hue were wrapped around two massive lower teeth escaping upward out of his mouth past his nose. It looked like he had a plug of tobacco in his bulging lower lip. The jutting teeth were caked in filth—or rotten. One tuft of scraggly hair shot up from a scarred gray scalp, while two tufts sprouted at odd angles down from either side of his misshapen chin. The creature's brows were as thick and protruding and purple as his lips.

Twin beady eyes of brown stared back at Liz Hen. A red dot was tattooed on the oghul's face just below his left eye, atop a thick cheekbone. It looked like a tear of blood.

"I don't sherve nobody who'sh face is covered in no hood." The oghul's deep voice was gravelly as a saber-toothed lion's growl. He sucked on the tobacco in his lip. Liz Hen took a step back. Dokie's mouth hung open. Beer Mug's ears were twitching and alert. Other than the raggedy trapper they'd passed on their way to Godwyn's abbey high in the Autumn Range, Nail had never seen an oghul this close.

"Remove your hoodsh," the oghul commanded, his brown, pin-prick orbs unreadable. "Been too many come into town with their faces covered of late. Vallè and oghul piraytes and such."

"But you're an oghul," Liz Hen blurted.

The ugly fellow raised one eyebrow. "Take off your hoodsh!" he demanded, then with one finger dug the tobacco out of his lip and tossed it to the ground. Only when it hit the ground, Nail noticed it wasn't tobacco at all but a gray rock about the size of a duck egg. Dread coiled gently inside his gut as a dense silence filled the street corner.

Then he felt Seita's presence suddenly behind him; he was instantly aware of her aura. "Oghul's ofttimes suck on rocks to stave the need for blood," she said. Nail flinched as her hands came to rest on his shoulders, and he felt a flush wash over his skin. He shuddered, distracted by the Vallè maiden's calm demeanor as she leaned over and whispered, "What do you wish me to do, Nail? Shall I slay this rock-sucking oghul for you?" She released his shoulder and stepped around him toward the menacing beast. *Slay him?* The girl was good with her chain-mace toy, but did she really think she could just casu-ally kill a beast like this oghul, a monster four times her size?

Seita also wore a heavy gray cloak, hood up, pale face scarcely visible under the cowl of her cloak.

"Remove your hood," Mardgot said to Seita. "S'ist Runk gets jumpy around strangers. But he is harmless enough. Takin' off your hoods will settle him some."

Dokie shed his hood almost before the words were out of the lady's mouth. His eyes were wide, his face ashen. Nail dropped his hood too. Liz Hen removed hers.

"Cute." The oghul appraised Liz Hen, one thick eyebrow rising, the small red tattoo under his left eye morphing as the gray skin stretched.

"Best watch yourself," Mardgot said to Liz Hen. "Fire-haired and tubby, yer the exact type of lassie ol' S'ist Runk here fancies."

Liz Hen regarded both Mardgot and the oghul with a look of complete and total horror. "I'm a fighter," she stammered, swooshing back her cloak from one hip, showing the longsword at her belt, squaring her shoulders. "I fought against the White Prince. Killed a Sør Sevier knight. This here's the sword that proves it."

"I helped with the killing," Dokie piped in.

"Oh, missy." Mardgot smiled. "Now you're just teasing ol' S'ist Runk. He adores a big ol' squirmy girl who'll put up a hardy fight, 'specially if she got a sword."

The oghul smiled too, a ponderous curling back of his thick purple lips, which revealed an even more gruesome row of jagged, dirty teeth. "I like your shword."

Seita giggled, eyes sparkling with amusement as she glanced back at Nail from under her cowl. The oghul laughed too as he turned and opened up the large brick oven and pulled forth a long, flat tray full of burnt chicken gizzards that smelled strongly of pine. He set the tray on the table in front of Liz Hen and Dokie. Beer Mug wagged his tail at the smell of cooked meat. Mardgot announced, "Roasted chicken parts. Eat."

Dokie sniffed at the food, a glum look on his face. Liz Hen reached over and popped a gizzard into her mouth. Her face scrunched up as she chewed once, twice, then spat the chewed-up meat out into her hand.

"Aye," S'ist Runk grumbled. "You shertainly look ready for many battles."

Liz Hen popped the chewed-up food back into her mouth and swallowed hard, stern eyes never leaving the oghul's. S'ist Runk watched and then nodded his approval.

Then the oghul turned to Seita. "Show yourshelf." He motioned for her to remove her hood. Seita slowly pulled her hood back, revealing her porcelain Vallè features and pointed ears, her flowing hair chalklike in the gloomy weather.

"The oghul raiders in them mountain passes above are growing thick." Mardgot looked down her nose at the Vallè maiden. "Most oghul-kind have declared Hragna'Ar up here in the north. They'll come down and steal the likes of you, little Vallè girl. Rape you bloody. Shred your twat with their huge cockled dongs, they will. Bleed you dry. Best watch yourself." The oghul next to Mardgot wasn't smiling anymore. Nor was Seita. Even Liz Hen blanched at the description.

Beer Mug's eyes were focused down the street. Bishop Godwyn and Culpa Barra strode up to the vendor's stand in a hurry. Culpa's hood was thrown back, his black Dayknight armor visible under his gray cloak. The unmistakable armor got S'ist Runk's attention. He pointed to Culpa and growled, "You. Dayknight. Leave." There was a fierceness in his stance that set Nail on edge.

"Let's go," Culpa said, seizing Liz Hen by the shoulder and guiding her in the direction of the livery, where he and the bishop had just come from.

"I told you not to wander off," Godwyn added.

"I was hungry," Liz Hen said as they headed back. "The food on that dreadful ship was horrid," she continued. "I vomited most of it over the side. Now that we're on dry land and my feet are under me again, can't I eat?"

"Just keep walking and don't look back." The expression on Culpa's face brooked no argument. They hustled their pace. Stefan, Val-Draekin, and Roguemoore, along with two rangy-looking dun-colored mules, now stood in front of the livery. Both mules had rheumy eyes and matching manes and tails of pitch black.

"Any oghul with a red teardrop tattoo is not to be trifled with," Culpa said sternly as they headed toward the others. "And no one in Stanclyffe is to be trusted. Not unless you've the right amount of coin to buy their silence. And we've spent plenty of coin on those two pack mules."

"Why so dour all of a sudden?" Liz Hen asked. "We meant no harm."

"Listen." Culpa stopped them all in their tracks, grabbing Liz Hen by the shoulders. "That nice-seeming woman is a bloodletter. That oghul *feeds* on her. And if he figures out you are headed into the mountains, which is exactly where you are headed, Liz Hen, he will get word to others of his kind—others that hunt those high-mountain woods above, oghuls that will track you down and string you up in the trees and strip the skin right off your bones, then sink their disease-ridden teeth into your soft neck and drain your blood in the most slow and painful Hragna'Ar ritual you can imagine."

He let go of the girl's shoulders. "So when we tell you don't wander off, we mean it. Don't wander off."

† † † † † †

"Stop trying to hasten my step," Dokie whined. "I can't slow and hurry at the same time."

"Well, you're in my way mostly," Liz Hen growled.

"Godwyn said to take it slow for our own safety. It's a perilous trail. And now you're behind me, urging me to hurry."

Liz Hen nudged him along anyway. "Because there might be bloodsucking oghuls a-chasin' us."

Dokie hastened his step.

Whilst the rest of the Company of Nine had tried to bandy about friendly jokes to begin their journey up the steep gorge, Liz Hen had been all gloomy fussiness about marauding oghuls. She was none too thrilled about hiking into snow-covered mountains twenty thousand feet in height either. And she'd let everyone know it.

Still, the thought of oghuls pursuing them had been the only thing spurring Liz Hen on at such a brisk pace these last few hours. Nail wished Culpa had never told the girl about the oghuls and how they skinned folk and sucked the blood out of their necks. Liz Hen wouldn't shut up about her fear of them now. "Why would anyone become a bloodletter?" she asked. "What's in it for the humans? How does a human survive if an oghul bites into their jugulars? Won't they bleed out?"

"There's an addictive toxin inside each oghul fang," Roguemoore answered from just ahead of her. "A pleasing chemical that over time a bloodletter cannot live without. The same toxin also seals off the vein after a feeding. A bloodletter won't bleed out. But an oghul bite will leave one nasty bruise."

Liz Hen felt her own neck, visibly shuddering. The red-haired girl, along with Dokie and Beer Mug, hiked along the ever-constricting and craggy path directly in front of Nail. Stefan was right behind him, followed by Seita, Val-Draekin bringing up the rear. Bishop Godwyn led the way, Culpa Barra and Roguemoore behind him, each of them leading one of the two dun-colored pack mules by the tether. The beasts were loaded down with food and gear purchased from the livery: tack, bridles, four heavy canvas tarps, thick blankets for all, two woodcutting axes, nine ice picks and many small iron spikes, sacks of flour, potatoes, dried salmon, jerked stag and elk meat, fish bait, several extra quivers full of arrows, two long lengths of coiled rope, nine torches, and enough pine-resin pitch to keep a bonfire going for moons.

Ragged gray clouds hung over their heads. But as they'd first started hiking up the gaping gorge a mile south of Stanclyffe, the clouds had parted fully and a daunting view of the cliffs rising bleak and shadowy over the town became fully visible. Nail had taken one last look at the towering ten-thousand-foot slab of awe-inspiring rock and quailed at the sight. The Company of Nine was soon swallowed up by the river-carved gorge as they journeyed on. The hazy comfort of civilization was left behind and upward they trudged.

The wild frothing river to their left was naught but constant snarling madness. It rumbled and crashed with thunder around mossy boulders and over tumbled-down trees. Across the river was an overhanging cliff riven with waterfalls of every size. Ferns and lustrous green moss grew out of the stone wherever Nail's eyes fell. To the right of their path was a steep slope of sharp jutting rock and towering trees clinging to lofty perches. The trees were mostly ash, aspen, and pine, their pale green leaves trembling in the faint frigid breeze of the deep chasm. Other vines, thick with leaves and heavy with dark red flowers, raced up the sharp stone cliff in a mad tangle. The precarious trail itself wasn't much of a trail: just worn steps of broken, mossy rock choked with grass and weeds. Stout scrub brush of some kind lined the way, and the roots, wildly splayed over large rocks, seemed to flit and quiver as they passed by, like snakes writhing amidst the stone. It was an eerie canyon and huge.

Bishop Godwyn, under his gray cloak, wore knee-high leather boots, leather breeches, and a green woolen shirt edged at the elbows with elk hide. The bow strapped over his back was similar to Stefan's, Dayknight made, constructed of witch hazel and ash wood. The bishop carried a sheathed Dayknight sword hooked to the baldric over his shoulder and a leather pouch of healing poultices at his belt.

Culpa Barra, right behind the bishop, wore his full Dayknight armor and sword under his cloak. His black helmet was strapped to the dun mule he led.

Roguemoore had been like a rock the entire trip, serious and determined. He led the second mule, laden with the bulk of their food. Over his back the dwarf bore a vicious-looking spiked mace with a tang set in a sturdy wooden handle. The iron ball of the mace looked heavy enough for ten men, yet aboard *Duchess of Devlin*, Roguemoore had swung it easily about with one arm whilst practicing with it. Under his short gray cloak, the dwarf wore layered armor that hung like a skirt well below his knees. Atop his head he bore a bulky helm with bull horns jutting from either side. Both the armor and helm he had purchased in Lord's Point just for the trip. His armor was dull and rusted in spots and had lost most of its shine. And the layered breastplate was a battered testament to the tribal wars some dwarf warrior had fought long years ago. The first time Roguemoore had put the armor on in the Turn Key Saloon, Liz Hen had laughed aloud, saying he looked like a large beetle encased in all that iron. Stefan claimed all the grime and dents gave the armor character. And to Nail, it seemed fighting any dwarf in that much armor would be like trying to spear a hog in a thick iron cauldron with its lid sealed shut.

Liz Hen was the least equipped of them all. She wore layers of woolen leggings and several thick woolen coats plus her gray cloak, the Sør Sevier sword she was so proud of at her hip. Dokie, Stefan, and Nail had again kept their own Gallows Haven armor for the journey. And Nail was glad for that. The old scrap of iron plate had grown to be a part of him. Underneath, all three boys wore the shirts and tan woolen leggings the bishop had given them at the Swithen Wells Trail Abbey. They were all three wrapped in their gray cloaks like the rest.

Stefan had the Dayknight bow Shawcroft had given him and a quiver of arrows strapped to his back. Dokie carried a small ax and dagger at either hip.

Nail had a decent sword strapped to his side for once, a long, shiny blade Roguemoore had purchased from an armory in Lord's Point and given him. Aboard the *Duchess of Devlin*, Culpa Barra and Val-Draekin had taught both him and Liz Hen daily how to use their swords to best effect. Nail took to it naturally, realizing that much of what Shawcroft had taught him about swinging a pickax was similar to the way Hawkwood had taught him at the abbey and to the way Culpa was teaching him now. Liz Hen was growing surprisingly proficient with a blade too. She was stout and strong and had given Nail some good duels. He could respect her some for that, as annoying as she was.

The two Vallè were dressed alike. Val-Draekin wore a gray cloak covering supple black leather armor studded with thin layers of ring mail about the neckline. He wore no weapons—at least none that were visible. But Nail knew of at least a half-dozen little daggers the dark-haired fellow kept hidden in the folds of his leather. Seita wore dark leather pants with a black leather belt and matching black doublet, along with a simple fox-fur-lined cape. Her gray cloak was currently tied over one shoulder. She too had no weapons visible. But Nail knew she had at least one thin dagger hidden in the folds of her pants and the ball-and-chain mace at her belt. Despite the damage he had seen the mace do to the Turn Key Saloon's practice shield, Nail wasn't convinced it was a real weapon at all. But he kept his opinion to himself.

Godwyn led the company up a separate small canyon forged by another, smaller alpine stream. While their trail wound up the mountain and the water gurgled down below, the path they followed headed straight up the canyon toward a roaring waterfall. The fresh smell of spray from the brawling falls smelled good. The trail took them even higher above the riotous creek, along the right side of the canyon. On both sides, pine forests clung to harsh columns of rock. Stark-white goats with hooves and curled horns of umber were perched on thin ledges and crags. Godwyn had called the nimble creatures Dall sheep. In the far distance, among the more lofty crags, dozens of rolling, crashing, rock-filled streams of crystal waters danced and tumbled down the mountains in glistening falls, all of them fed from the snowcapped peaks of the Glacier Range far above. The deep rumble of the waterfalls all around was a deafening roar.

"It's springtime!" Roguemoore yelled above the din. "There's more runoff than usual!" The misty spray from the myriad falls was thick enough to veil most of the rocks and vegetation at the bottom of the gorge.

A lonely gust of wind raked the path when they reached the top of the water-carved chasm, almost eight hours of climbing from Stanclyffe. The clouds had dissipated and the sky was naught but a deep blue dusk. A small brook with a stone-slab bridge led to a high-mountain pasture of sorts. Just beyond the glade was a meadow of grasslands. In the meadow were lichen-covered boulders of various sizes. The spring weather had melted away the snow and the highland flowers had blossomed, sprinkling the meadow with color. Nail spied several groupings of standing stones here and there.

Liz Hen heaved a gusty breath of relief when Culpa Barra halted them for a short rest. "Reminds me of our flight from Gallows Haven," she said, hunched over, taking deeper breaths, rubbing her calves. "Hope there ain't no more climbing. I'm liable to flop over dead right here."

"Lie down too long and the oghuls will sniff you out," Dokie said, leaning against a rock next to Liz Hen. Her eyes darted about the green glade, worried.

"You're a hardy and fit hiker," Val-Draekin praised Liz Hen.

She smiled at the compliment and straightened her back, patting Beer Mug atop the head. "I did hike a long way, didn't I?" she said. Beer Mug licked her hand.

"It's good to build up your stamina," the Vallè continued. "It'll help you swing a sword with more ferocity when the time comes. And that's a big sword you carry."

"'Tis very big." Liz Hen still struggled with her breath.

"Let me teach you a Vallè breathing technique," Val-Draekin said. "When winded, take three deep breaths and briefly hold the last, then repeat. It will help in these high climes."

Liz Hen did as instructed. "I feel much more refreshed."

"Works every time."

"Why don't you carry a sword?" she asked. "You're a good sword-fighting teacher anyway."

"I wager I've been trained in just about every weapon imaginable at one time or another," Val-Draekin answered. "I just always liked to travel light. The knives serve me well enough, I suppose. As long as I have enough."

"And how many you got squirreled away in that armor of yours?"

"Enough." He smiled and winked.

"Look at those." Dokie did the three-fingered-sign of the Laijon Cross over his heart, then lifted himself from the rock and made his way toward a circle of square-cut standing stones at the bottom of the briar-filled dell fifty feet to the left. Ten paces from the stones he pulled out a strip of parchment and charcoal and started drawing what he saw on the rocks. Nail recalled Dokie doing similar sketches on their journey from the Swithen Wells Trail Abbey to Ravenker.

"What are they?" Liz Hen asked about the stones.

"Merely a shrine." Godwyn said. "A place one can stop and pray for safe travels."

"But Dokie ain't praying," she said. "He's drawing."

Nail himself wanted no part of the standing stones. Who knew what symbols he might find carved upon them. Squares? Circles? Crosses? Crescent moons? Shooting stars? Dragons? Dokie had once claimed to have seen symbols in his dreams, symbols like the ones on the standing stones above Gallows Haven. Nail had his own dreams and visions to worry about. *And who was Cassietta Raybourne? My mother? Could I be kin to the brutal killer Aeros, son of Aevrett?* Too many questions. And he would certainly never broach the subject with Roguemoore or Godwyn. They would likely not tell him the truth anyway.

He was content to just sit still and watch Dokie draw.

† † † † †

Soon the Company of Nine was hoofing along again, this time veering from the main trail. Once on smoother terrain, they hiked at a faster pace. They left the main footpath, now traipsing a pleasant trek through green meadows bound with buttercups. They skirted a battalion of aspens, rolled through some dips and hollows, saw a small herd of elk, stopped for a moment to admire the forest royalty, then continued on, their path taking them ever higher.

At one point, they traversed a meadow so green it hurt Nail's eyes. In the center of the meadow was a familiar woolly beast—a musk ox. Only this one was much bigger than any Nail had seen in the Autumn Range. Roguemoore claimed that most oghuls would rather ride a musk ox than a horse. Like elk, musk ox stood on four legs, this one well over twelve feet tall, strands and clumps of long brown hair stretching from the crown of its head and back almost to the ground, concealing the bulk of its body. This one had two monstrous ivory tusks jutting from the top of its head, which swooped toward the ground in a great arch and then back up to sharp points at about eye level—if the thing even had eyes, so covered in tangled long hair it was. They were not as large as the woolly mammoths of Adin Wyte. Still, Stefan marveled aloud at the size of this creature, calling it magnificent. Liz Hen scoffed, "Looks like naught but a big dirty mop with upside-down horns to me."

And Liz Hen had kept up her chatter as they moved on, spouting her opinion on a variety of subjects from mop-heads to what type of hats were apt to blow off one's head in a stiff wind. And before long the sun was down and the light was dim and a brisk wind hissed over the trees, racing toward the snowcapped mountains stretching in the far distance. Godwyn eventually called a halt to their procession and led them up into a small thicket of aspens atop a long, sloping hill. Once sufficiently hidden within the cover of the trees, they began to set up camp, Liz Hen still nattering away about whatever crossed her mind, up to and including the discomforts she had already suffered so far on this expedition, and all she was bound to suffer in the days to come.

† † † † †

Liz Hen was still talking as their dinner wound to a close. "At least we get to eat on this trip," she blathered on almost without taking a breath. "Potatoes and fish. Unlike when we was in the Autumn

Range with Nail guiding us. Almost starved, I did. No food. No fresh trout. This trip is almost pleasurable in comparison. What a nightmare finding the Swithen Wells Trail Abbey that was. Rough. And the cold. Bitter. Freezing. But at least I ain't got that Sør Sevier slave brand on my wrist like Stefan and Nail does. And that red-haired woman who done the branding was a rank bitch if I ever did see one. Making Jenko do that to his own papa. Told me I'd be spared the hot iron if I but stuck them daggers in poor Baron Bruk's tarred stumps." Dokie squinched his face in revulsion as he always did whenever Liz Hen told the story.

The Company of Nine were all gathered about the fire pit now, some sitting on rocks, others on the cold ground. The crackling fire had been lit by Roguemoore. Culpa and Stefan had pulled the trout out of a nearby stream. Initially Liz Hen had been both worried about and grateful for the fire. Worried because she thought it might bring oghuls raining down on her, grateful because it was warm.

"So you stuck the knives in Jubal Bruk?" Val-Draekin asked, this being the first time he'd heard the story of the baron. "Stuck the knives in his tarred stumps? I saw him, when Leif Chaparral brought him to the castle. The knives were still there."

"You've seen him alive then?" Liz Hen asked. "So Jenko's father made it to Amadon alive like the Sør Sevier bitch said he would?"

Val-Draekin nodded, black hair glinting orange shards in the firelight. "Alive and with the message from the White Prince he was sent to deliver."

"Well, I'll be hog-tied sidewards and buggered straight in the piehole. I figured poor Jubal Bruk was one dead sorry feller. But he lasted that long?"

"Still alive as far as I know." Val-Draekin held his palms to the flame for warmth.

Liz Hen, ruffling the fur on Beer Mug's neck, went on talking about Jubal Bruk. "The man in black leather armor plied the baron with some sort of serum, said it would make him survive the trip all the way to Amadon. I figured it was all just a bunch of crockery twaddle and lies, considering how chopped-up and limbless Jubal was."

"The man in black leather armor?" Seita inquired.

Liz Hen answered the Vallè with reluctance in her voice. "They called him the Spider. Most evil thing I seen yet, leastwise since this whole nightmare started. Wore black leather dark as a witch's snatch."

Dokie, sitting cross-legged in the dirt next to Liz Hen, said, "Most evil thing I seen so far was that ghastly horse spiked at the bottom of the elk trap. Remember, Liz Hen, that black horse with the red eyes dull as dead cinders? Like a demon from the underworld."

Seita's green eyes narrowed. Nail shared an anxious look with Stefan. They'd both seen that horse when it was alive—a shiny black mare ridden by a Vallè woman with features alarmingly similar to Seita's. Stefan had no idea the Vallè on the trail above Gallows Haven had been a Bloodwood assassin, or that Shawcroft had killed her. Nail would never mention her to him either, especially not now.

"What did this red-eyed horse look like exactly, Dokie?" Roguemoore asked. Dancing firelight flickered gold flakes off the dwarf's scaled armor.

"It looked unquestionably dead," Dokie answered, a haunted look on his face. "Like I ain't never seen anything deader. Them eyes, dead as dusty coal. And its hide, as dead as dusty coal too. Lusterless and cold."

"Lusterless?" Liz Hen barked. "How do you even know what that word means?"

Dokie looked at her blank-faced. Liz Hen swatted him in the back of the head. "You lusterless clodpole."

"Well," Culpa Barra broke in, "we had all best prepare ourselves for seeing much worse than a dead horse at the bottom of an elk trap." The Dayknight sat on a rock leaning over the fire, sharpening his sword with a palm-sized whetstone.

"What do you mean?" Liz Hen's eyes grew concerned quickly.

"As I said before at the Turn Key, there were things Shawcroft and I saw deep in the Deadwood Gate mines." A hint of fear crept into the Dayknight's eyes. "Things I can't explain. Those mines are a nightmare of their own, an evil place of wraiths and dark oghul magics. Like I said before, a place apt to play tricks on your mind if you let your guard down."

Firelight danced in the forest of white aspens surrounding their camp, creating long shadows into the night. Nail had been in plenty of mines with Shawcroft. He'd gathered *Forgetting Moon* and the blue angel stone from the altar in the Roahm Mines himself. It seemed Culpa Barra was exaggerating for effect.

"I'm not afraid of any mines," he said, then immediately wished he hadn't as Roguemoore looked at him sharply.

"Not afraid?" The dwarf's face was dark as a storm cloud. "Tell me, Nail, what was it you saw when you gathered the ax and stone from under the cross-shaped altar at Roahm? What was it you saw carved on that altar?"

Nail didn't feel as glib as before. He knew exactly what carvings the dwarf was referring to. *How can he know what I saw? How can he know the altar was cross-shaped?*

"I was there with Nail in Roahm." Stefan spoke up. "I didn't see anything."

Roguemoore still stared at Nail with a questioning, cold gaze.

"There were carvings on the base of the altar, Stef." Nail looked at his friend. "I didn't see them at first either. You and Gisela had already left the room when I heard a noise and turned back and looked into that tomb. The altar was moving, slowly sinking into the floor . . . and carved into the base were many foul carvings."

"Carvings?" Stefan questioned. "Of what?"

"Nameless beasts of the underworld." His statement was followed by a deathly, sickly silence.

"Everything is now cursed," Liz Hen muttered.

Dokie did the three-fingered sign of the Laijon Cross over his heart.

"They were just ancient carvings," Nail said. "I wasn't frightened or anything."

Roguemoore fixed him with another hard stare. "You should have been."

Nail was frightened now, all right, frightened of the look in the dwarf's eyes.

"Let me explain something," Roguemoore went on. "The mines where these ancient weapons of Laijon are hidden are tied to the history of the Five Isles and the nameless beasts of the underworld in more ways than any one of us might realize. Especially at Deadwood Gate like Culpa has said. But like everything, most stories of those bygone ages have been forgotten. Make no mistake, there is a seductive nature to the mines. You will all feel it once you enter."

The fire crackled loudly and the dwarf's voice dropped an octave. "Gold was always known to exist in the Glacier Range, and the Autumn Range, and near Deadwood Gate, also silver, iron ore. We may find that every mine in Gul Kana may hide a lot of things besides silver and gold within their bellies. In ages gone by, something far more sinister was going on in Gul Kana than just gold mining. The mines became a place where oghuls practiced dark magics. Caverns full of secret druid cults competed with covens of oghuls and Vallè witches and worse. Those mines were all abandoned for a reason. Evil lives in these dungeons we are aiming for. And I mean an evil none of us want any part of, an evil that is capable of ripping us to shreds in more ways than one."

"You're scaring me," Liz Hen said.

"I mean to scare you," the dwarf answered her.

Dokie stared at the fire with a pale face and dull, sunken eyes. Liz Hen put her arm over his shoulder, fright in her eyes too. Even Beer Mug's tail had ceased its wagging.

Roguemoore kicked a stone into the fire, then looked up with a searing gaze. "There is an ancient text, even more ancient than *The Moon Scrolls of Mia* or *The Way and Truth of Laijon*. A text penned in an ancient, forgotten tongue, whether a dwarven or Vallè language, or a combination of both, I do not know. But my brother Ironcloud, along with another friend, work on deciphering the secrets of this ancient writing. It is called *The Angel Stone Codex*. Ironcloud was to bring what information he'd gleaned to our rendezvous point at the Turn Key Saloon. The codex speaks of times before humans even arrived on the Five Isles. It speaks of these things hidden in the deeper and darker places of the world."

"More blasphemy." Liz Hen did the three-fingered sign of the Laijon Cross over her heart. "*Angel Stone Codex*. Naught but more blasphemy. Can't nothing in it be true."

Roguemoore ignored her and continued. "The dwarves used to be great miners. That is, until my ancestors were scared from the caverns they created. Now we dwarves are but peaceful farmers in southern Wyn Darrè. Before there was a Laijon or Warrior Angels, my ancestors discovered that there are secrets buried deep in the fabric of Gul Kana and all the Five Isles, subterranean currents of evil weaving to and fro under every mountain range, beneath every town and castle and keep and fertile valley. Disturbing secrets. Secrets kept by the Vallè. Secrets hidden by the church of Laijon, hidden even by the Blessed Mother Mia, and even secrets hidden by those bawdy old dwarf miners themselves. And worst of all, secrets that I fear the oghuls have not forgotten. The Hragna'Ar prophecies of oghul-kind are so old they have no beginning. You mix all those secrets into one boiling pot and you've got yourself one stew, ripe for all manner of fiery deprivation and death. According to what few things Ironcloud has so far discovered within the pages of *The Angel Stone Codex*, those ancient dwarves found their doom—"

The dwarf was cut off as Dokie hunched forward and belched up a stream of vomit straight into the fire.

"Now look what you've gone and done." Liz Hen bolted to her feet and patted Dokie gently on the back. "You've scared the poor boy completely sick."

† † † † †

As Nail sat on the lichen-covered boulder, looking at Ava's turtle carving, he was acutely aware of the lingering effect of Seita's touch. It was with some jealousy that he watched the Vallè prepare to shave Stefan next. Nail's friend sat astraddle a thick deadfall spruce. Seita sat astraddle the same log, facing Stefan, a thin silver dagger in one hand, her other hand wetting his face with the damp, warm rag.

After dinner, Liz Hen and Dokie had retired to bed atop one of the canvas tarps, burying themselves under heavy blankets. Godwyn and Roguemoore had retired too. Culpa and Val-Draekin remained at the fire. Stefan and Nail had removed their makeshift armor and retreated into the trees about thirty paces away from camp, leaving just enough firelight to shave by. Seita had accompanied them into the darkness.

Initially, as Stefan began to shave him, Nail had been less than inclined to let Seita help. But Stefan happily moved aside when the Vallè asked, and she had taken over with a deft, gentle hand. And as she had shaved him with the sharp silver blade, Nail couldn't help but take keen notice of her nearness. Her eyes were as pure as melted gemstones, like the blue angel stone Gisela had found in the altar. Only Seita's jewel-like orbs were wild and green and reflected with perfect brightness in the dim firelight. She had been near enough to him that he had felt her warmth and sweet breath.

Once Nail's shave was done, he'd let Stefan have the seat in front of Seita. And when Stefan removed his shirt so she could shave better around his neck, Nail felt unexpected pangs of jealousy lance through his heart. Without armor plate or a shirt to cover him, Stefan's chest was rippled with muscle, his arms sinewy and rigid as stout garden vines. Nail knew he cut a much more muscular figure than his friend. But he wasn't the one sitting half-naked in front of the Vallè maiden now. *You're a damn fool, thinking jealous thoughts like that, Nail.* But how could he not?

Seita hadn't really spoken much to Nail during his shave, but she was opening up to Stefan just fine. "I watched you carve Gisela's name into the white bark of an aspen when we were setting up camp." She nodded toward the tree just behind Stefan, the tree that now bore Gisela's name. "Her name is carved into your bow. Plus, I've watched you carve her name in numerous places along the way. The surface of the newly polished table at the Turn Key Saloon, the mizzenmast of the *Duchess of Devlin*. I saw you scratch her name into several rocks in the gorge whenever we'd stop for rest and drink. And now the tree behind you. Are you marking our path?"

Stefan remained silent, the Adam's apple of his throat bobbing slightly.

"Do you think her ghost follows you?" she asked.

"It's just something I do," Stefan muttered, trying to keep his head steady for her blade. Even from where he sat, Nail could detect the slight watering of his friend's eyes.

"You must have really loved her," Seita said.

Stefan did not answer.

"What was Gallows Haven like?" she asked him next.

"Like nothing," Stefan answered softly, lapsing into silence.

"Tell us what Val Vallè is like," Nail said, hoping for Stefan's sake the girl would not go back to talking about Gisela and Stefan's carvings or Gallows Haven. Only sorrow resided down those paths.

"Val Vallè is only where I was born," Seita answered. "I spent little time there. I've lived mostly in the court of the king in Amadon. With

Borden Bronachell. Now his son, Jovan. I live there with my father, Val-Korin. Ambassadorship is my father's heritage, and will probably be my heritage as well someday."

Nail really hadn't thought of a follow-up question, and he was irritated with himself over his first question. Seita hadn't divulged any new or interesting information he wasn't already privy to, anything she hadn't already told them on their voyage north from Lord's Point.

"Roguemoore and Godwyn told both Val-Draekin and me that you were curious about who your real parents are," Seita said to him. "Is it true you do not know your own heritage?"

Nail was thrown wholly off guard by her question. A twinge of anger rose up within him. Anger that the dwarf and the bishop had told the two Vallè he was a bastard. Anger that they'd been discussing him without so much as a by-your-leave.

"It's true." His answer was a bit more haughty than he would have liked. "I have asked some people what they might know of my parents." He could feel the resentment and discontent in his words as they spilled forth unbidden. "All I get are lies. First from my master. Then from Roguemoore. They know more than they let on." *Hawkwood was also likely full of lies.* He didn't know why he had just unleashed such bitterness and information on her.

"So why don't you ask the dwarf about your parents again now?"

"Why would I? I was born, and they are gone. What of it?"

Seita, done shaving Stefan, began cleaning her knife. She did not follow up on Nail's parentage but asked a different question that threw him immediately off guard again. "You have seen a Vallè like me before, a maiden with blond hair?"

Nail's gaze crawled nervously to Stefan, hoping his friend remained silent.

But Stefan answered anyway. "On the trail above Gallows Haven. We saw someone who looked *exactly* like you. She rode a black mare with red-glowing eyes. The same mare we found dead in the elk trap weeks later, the one Liz Hen talked of."

Seita's bright green eyes turned to Nail. "And that girl on the black mare said something to you, Nail. Do you remember what it was she said?"

Of course he remembered. *You are not of my blood,* the Vallè had said. *Still, they will be coming for you.* It was meaningless gibberish. *Or was it?* How could he know?

"Well, do you recall?" Seita pressed.

"No." Nail stood, eyes lingering on the Vallè maiden, then Stefan. "I do not recall."

Alone, he made his way quietly back toward the fire.

*Raijael's blood shall not be drawn by the hand of man, or he would not be the Angel Prince. He shall remain spotless and uninjured until the end. Praise be to Raijael, master of the last day of Fiery Absolution.*
—THE CHIVALRIC ILLUMINATIONS OF RAIJAEL

# CHAPTER TWENTY-ONE
# GAULT AULBREK

1ST DAY OF THE ANGEL MOON, 999TH YEAR OF LAIJON

AMADON, GUL KANA

He was cold. He was hungry. Savagely hungry. But the rotten food and other things being hurled at him were less than appetizing. If this were to be the end of him, he was beginning to feel the first inklings of sadness and regrets, something he had never felt before. He couldn't stop thinking of his vanished faith in Raijael and Laijon. Or how he felt about Ava Shay. Or how he missed his stepdaughter, Krista. Or his wife, Avril.

Naught but two short years together, and after all this time, he longed for Avril. He had a clear memory of the day and place they had first met. He a knight of Sør Sevier ranging the Nordland Highlands, she a lonely cloaked figure upon a windswept plain, a babe cradled in her arms. He could still recall the very spot where he'd found her, a harsh but strikingly beautiful place, a dusky ridge of sharp rock and dry peat in a long, hollow valley just north of Stone Loring. When he died, he was to have had his ashes spread there. It was a location he had picked out and hand-written in the Chivalric Illuminations, a special spot where his comrades in arms were to have left his burnt remains. For it was the lone place in the entirety of the Five Isles he'd first discovered joy, the one place his mind always drifted toward for comfort.

He was facing backward in the oxcart, tied to a massive ten-foot-high oak stump, his back pressed against the rough, knotty pole, allowing him to look out over the angry mobs following the cart, lining the streets. Hawkwood was tied on the other side of the same oaken pole, facing forward. They were being paraded through Amadon toward the Hall of the Dayknights and Purgatory. Early on, as they'd first rattled out of the castle, Gault had taken a blow to the temple from a heavy cabbage that had threatened to black him out. He kept his lone unhurt eye pried open and struggled to clear his head. Hammerfiss had stepped from the crowd and stitched his swollen eye open. He was not happy with his fellow Knight Archaic for that. Spades had stayed down there on the cobbles, tossing a coin and watching his humiliation with a joyous gleam in her eye.

He was covered in slime and feces. Meanwhile the tall white marble buildings of Amadon rose up glorious all around him, temples, cathedrals, palaces, gladiator arenas. Hundreds of buildings, each more grand and glorious than the next. All made of exquisite marble slabs cut hundreds of feet high and hundreds of feet square. And the teeming throngs of this majestic city lined the streets, continuing to jeer and curse. "You are no gladiator!" some in the throng chanted. "Squireck will behead you!" And they laughed at him. Laughed and laughed. Even mocked his dead wife. Mocked his step-daughter. They even mocked the fact that he loved her so much and she wasn't even of his own loins. But not wanting to show weakness, Gault just smiled back at them, a big grin. But he knew his bitterness was all but evident at the corners of his mouth.

*Show no flaw. Show no vulnerability nor fragility.*

Aeros Raijael came drifting out of the crowd then. The Angel Prince carried a glowing green gem in one hand, an ox-horned battle helm in the other. *Lonesome Crown! The angel stone!* Gault felt desire well up within his very soul. He had wanted to possess the helm and stone ever since seeing Aeros take them from King Torrence on the Aelathia Plains. "They belong to you, Gault Aulbrek!" Aeros tossed *Lonesome Crown* and the green angel stone up into the cart. "You will soon be in the arena. Use the stone to your advantage! Never take off the Gladiator's helm—"

Gault was jerked awake to a deeply rooted sense of disorientation and dread, that and the sound of heavily armored knights crossing stone cobbles. It was cold. And he was hungry. The footfalls grew louder, and suddenly several dark forms entered the chamber.

It was Leif Chaparral and Jovan Bronachell, some twenty other spear-weilding Dayknights marching into the room behind them, a handful bearing torches.

"Where is Hawkwood?" Leif's voice clapped like thunder through the vaulted chamber. "Where has he gone?"

"But Ser," one of the two Dayknight guards lined up against the far wall began, "you know very well that—" In two limping strides Leif was across the room, slapping the black helm off the guard's face with a gauntleted hand. As the helm clattered on the floor, the knight stood helmetless and ashen, fear rising in his face, round eyes bouncing from Leif to the king.

Gault sat up straight, fully awake now.

Leif raged, "I bring our king down into Purgatory to speak with the prisoner only to find the prisoner not in his cell! Where is Hawkwood?"

The Dayknight guard bowed, looking woozy from the blow to his face. "Pardon, Ser Leif, but—" Leif's gauntleted hand slapped him across the face again and the guard crumpled to the floor in a heap of black armor, unconscious.

Stiff and aching, Gault gathered himself off the floor. He stepped to the bars of his own cage, face pressed to the cold iron, basking in the flickering warmth of the many torches of the Dayknights behind Jovan. Things were getting interesting. And Gault was up for anything to break the dread boredom of Purgatory.

The other guard looked like he wanted to speak, but he didn't. He stood rigid at attention. Leif shouted at the man, "I do not care which one of the two of you colluded to help Hawkwood escape from this cell, or if it was both of you. Either way, you will pay!"

"How can Hawkwood be gone?" Jovan yanked Leif around by the shoulder of his heavy cape. "How could he have escaped a second time? I put you in charge of this."

"Hawkwood was here, Your Excellency." Leif's voice held only a tinge of anxiety. "The last I saw him, he was here. In the cage adjacent to Gault's."

But as both Gault and Leif and the guard well knew, Hawkwood had lived in the confines of that barred cell for all of about three minutes before he'd vanished like smoke in the darkness. The only ones oblivious to the truth were Jovan and the twenty other Dayknights behind him. In fact, most every Dayknight that came down into this place was told that Hawkwood was held in a cell somewhere else in the dungeons. It looked like Leif's subterfuge was finally unraveling.

"Hawkwood likely went out the same way as Tala and Glade." Leif pointed to the dark gap under the column across the room. Yes, it appeared like it was finally Leif's day of reckoning and he was covering his tracks—with confidence, too. Gault detected not a stitch of fear in his voice. *His gross ineptitude has created one colossal mess after the next and yet he carries on undaunted.*

Leif was still pointing. "That is the route your sister and my brother took when they had their little adventure down here. We still haven't figured out how to close the gap. Glade said it had something to do with the torches along the wall, but no amount of poking and prodding the torches has so far closed the gap. But I imagine this man and his unconscious friend knows—" He whirled back to the guard still standing at attention. "For they would have been here when Hawkwood made his escape. Hawkwood was chained in that cage with these two knights as guard. They have failed us. This man and his companion lying on the floor have failed us!" Leif looked at Jovan. "What would you have me do, Your Excellency?"

Jovan's brow furrowed. "They should be executed for such gross neglect."

Leif nodded. "This man will answer swiftly for his betrayal, my lord." He bent his knee to Jovan, holding forth both hands. "With your sword, if I may?"

The king unbuckled the sword at his hip and handed it to Leif. It was Aeros Raijael's blue sword, Sky Reaver. Leif drew the blade with a crisp rasp from its sheath and ordered the remaining Dayknight guard to remove his helm and kneel. The man removed his helm, face slackening in horror. He knelt. Leif reached out and forced the knight's head forward with one gauntleted hand until the back of his neck was exposed.

The Dayknight did the three-fingered sign of the Laijon Cross over his heart, pleading, "No, Ser, please. You know that we did not let Hawkwood escape on purpose. You were there—"

"You are naught but a traitor." Leif raised Sky Reaver high, dark-rimmed eyes fierce and pointed. "Who would believe what lies are in you?"

And he brought the sword flashing down, striking the neck of the kneeling knight, slicing halfway through. The man's head drooped as he fell forward to the floor. Blood pumped black and thick over the gray stone as the body twitched under Leif.

In the end, the guard had placed his faith in Laijon, and to Gault's clear estimation, that man's god had failed him miserably today. Gault had learned the hard way, there were no gods out there to help anyone in need, to soothe the souls of the tortured, to spare the lives of the raped and soon to be slain. There was no Laijon. No Raijael. No Blessed Mother Mia. There never was, nor ever would be. Every innocent child who'd ever prayed to escape the unbearable horror of the molester or the painful blade of the murderer had wasted their breath, just as this Dayknight guard had. Power did not reside with the gods. Power ofttimes lived in bumbling idiots like Leif Chaparral, the liars, the cheats, the nobles, and sometimes those with the where-withal to keep their wits about them and their swords honed and ready at all times.

"Perhaps we shouldn't have acted so hastily?" Jovan said, pale faced. He glanced at the twelve other Dayknights standing at attention behind him. They were nothing put pillars of black, unmoving. He turned back to Leif. "Perhaps we should have interrogated him first?"

"We would have been given naught but lies." Leif's attention was now on the guard he'd first slapped, the one lying on the floor of the chamber, unconscious. With a flick of Sky Reaver's sharp tip, Leif sliced the unconscious guard's exposed throat. Blood pooled thick and red under the man's head.

When Leif looked to his king, satisfied, the sickly fervor in his gaze reminded Gault of Aeros Raijael in battle. Some divine malev-olence would overtake the Angel Prince during war, not madness or anger, but a savage zeal—a zeal like that in Leif's dark-rimmed eyes now.

"Better a swift justice than a pointless and drawn-out interroga-tion that will likely lead to naught and end in lies," Leif reiterated. "There were two others who escorted Gault and Hawkwood into the dungeons, they were assigned rotating shifts to watch over him. They too could be in collusion with Hawkwood. Do you desire that the other two guards also be found and killed?"

Jovan's brow furrowed even more. "Yes, perhaps so."

"As you wish." Leif bowed, his eyes feverish with victory. "I shall see it done myself." He cleaned Sky Reaver's bloodied blade on the dark cloak of the murdered Dayknight guard at his feet. Once done, he handed the sword back to his king.

Jovan sheathed the weapon and addressed the Dayknights behind him. "Six of you will now stand guard over Gault. My sister, Tala, and Leif's brother, Glade, went missing down in these dungeons not long ago. So far we have kept that secret safe within the ranks of the Dayknights, and for that your king is grateful. Do any of you want everyone in Amadon to know that Hawkwood has escaped Purgatory a second time?"

Jovan paused for a moment, looking at the two bodies on the floor. "You have seen the price of betrayal. None of you speaks of what you have seen or heard here today. Let the two men lying in pools of their own blood at your feet be a grim reminder of your fate if you disobey my order."

Each Dayknight bowed in acquiescence. Jovan continued, "Each of you is now guarding the remaining prisoner, Gault Aulbrek. You will work in shifts. Six at a time, twelve hours each, rotating. You will each of you sleep down here in this room. You will all eat here in this room. You will defecate down that hole in the center of Hawkwood's empty cage. In fact, none of you is to leave this chamber until the first day of the Fire Moon. Do you understand?" They each bowed a second time.

Jovan went on, "After I am gone, four of you will see to the dead bodies of your fellow traitorous knights. They will be stripped of their armor and hauled from Purgatory and thrown into the Vallè River for the oghul witches and thieves to do with as they please. Understood?" They bowed again.

Gault wonderd if the day's entertainment was now over. Either Jovan was too stupid to see through Leif's manipulations, or the loyalty and closeness of their friendship blinded him. *There will always be those out there like Leif Chaparral, whose majestic cruelty and deceit would hold more power than the gods.*

Enna Spades was one such godlike monster. Gault recalled his dream, the oxcart journey through Amadon and the impossibly large temples and cathedrals along the route. Spades often talked of desecrating all the grand edifices in Amadon like the Hall of the Dayknights and the castle, taking a shit in each one of them, defiling the Temple of the Laijon Statue and the Palace of the Grand Vicar. She wanted to crush everything all the time. Yes, Leif Chaparral and Spades were the same in many ways.

But Gault knew what motivated Spades' anger, what tore at her heart—or what little heart she possessed—and that was Hawkwood, the man who'd escaped the cage next to him. Every other handsome face that had crossed Spades' path was mere fodder for her lusty whims. All her twisted complexities stemmed from this one man's betrayal. Her overt sexuality and her brutality in war stemmed from a desire to gain control, to wield power over others, whether it meant fucking them or dismembering them. *As she will fuck this entire city with her rage once she arrives, dismember it and brutalize it in ways only she can.*

*But what motivates Leif Chaparral's cruelty?*

Jovan and Leif stepped up to Gault's cage, boots clicking against the stone floor.

Hands behind his back, the king glared at Gault coolly. "Did you see where Hawkwood went?"

Gault stared back blankly for a moment, then asked. "Do you have an extra tray of food?"

"Do you think this is a joke?" Jovan snarled. "You'll soon be begging for your life in the arena."

*Good!* Gault thought. *Put Squireck Van Hester before me and I will slay him for you!* The smell of blood pooling on the floor lingered in his nose, reminding him of his ten years of war. *Give me a sword and an arena to fight in! Yes,* Leif's murder of the two guards had been entertaining, for a moment anyway, a way to kill time at least. A means by which to confirm that the world was full of fools and his own soul was bereft of any remaining affection for the saving graces of Laijon or Raijael.

*Yes, put me in the arena now!*

"What did you see?" Jovan asked him again. "How did Hawkwood escape?"

*Would he believe me if I told him the truth, that Hawkwood had escaped because of Leif's ineptitude? That his own sister had gotten lost down here because of Leif's stupidity in leaving her alone? Will he believe that his friend is a liar and a murderer and completely incompetent? Likely not.*

Still, Leif's ridiculous lies and murder had broken up the day's boredom. At least there was that one solace. Boredom. It was the worst part of captivity. It caused the mind to imagine peculiar things, conjure up unsettling thoughts.

Gault recalled a conversation he'd had over beers late one night in a Sør Sevier tavern. Bogg, the warden of the Rokenwalder dungeons, had explained that prisoners would ofttimes entertain themselves by tormenting the guards with endless menial tasks of inconvenience and stupid questions. And after so many days locked up, Gault could see the allure of that.

"Answer me!" Jovan shouted. "What did you see?"

Gault smiled. "Will you pen a letter to Aeros Raijael for me, then deliver it—"

"Shut the fuck up!" The king's face was red with rage. "What did you see?"

"I'm a tad confused." Gault spoke slowly. "Am I supposed to shut the fuck up, or tell you what I saw?"

Jovan's face twisted in frustration.

"Fact is . . ." Gault paused, gaze traveling to Leif. "I saw nothing. One moment Hawkwood was here. Then *poof!* He was gone."

*Be wary of belief, cautious of faith. For one's identity can only be killed from within. We become what we think.*
—THE ANGEL STONE CODEX

# CHAPTER TWENTY-TWO

# LINDHOLF LE GRAVEN

## 2ND DAY OF THE ANGEL MOON, 999TH YEAR OF LAIJON
## AMADON, GUL KANA

L ooks more oghul than man, at first glance anyway," said Ser Tolz. The Silver guardsman was sitting at the head of the oxcart between Glade Chaparral and Ser Alain. Glade snickered, gazing at the small portrait in Tolz's hand.

"That there is one gruesome face no girl would want." Ser Alain snapped the reins, urging the oxen on over the cobbled path, looking at the portrait from the corner of his eye. "I wager the lassie who gets stuck with such a deformed freak cuts her own wrists rather than have that *thing* slobbering over the top of her."

"Nah." Ser Boppard said. Boppard sat in the back of the oxcart with Lindholf. "There's a girl for every mutation of a man. When it comes to humping, rank fetishes know no bounds. There's a sloppy wet twat awaiting every legless fat freak out there."

325

"And off to the whorehouse we go!" Alain shouted.

The alleyway echoed with their laughter and the clomping of oxen hooves.

"We're not talking about you, you know." Glade craned his neck and looked to the back of the cart, his laughing eyes meeting Lindholf's.

"I didn't think you were," Lindholf answered sheepishly. Without the Shroud of the Vallè in his system, he had scant confidence to verbally spar with Glade. All he could think of was getting more of that white powder. But he hadn't seen Seita or Val-Draekin in what seemed like forever. *Do they expect me to go to the Hallowed Grove and sniff it right off the Atonement Tree itself?*

Glade was dressed in full Silver Guard armor, as were the three knights in the oxcart with them—Glade's new lackeys: Tolz Trento of Avlonia, Alain Gratzer of Knightliegh, and Boppard Stockach from Reinhold. All three were tall. All three had rakish good looks. And all three seemed less mature than Tala's younger brother, Ansel. They were veteran Silver Guards, each of them nearly ten years older than Glade and only kissing up to him because he was younger brother to Leif Chaparral, the man who would soon be the new Dayknight captain.

Two nights ago, Glade and his three cronies had dragged Lindholf down to a dock-district brothel and forced him to watch as they all four fucked a string of gap-toothed whores, each whore older than their own mothers. Lindholf had been disgusted and humiliated by the whole debauched affair. He hated being around Glade and his three new friends.

And now they were on their way to the dock district and the whorehouses again.

Lindholf had not yet been invited into the ranks of the Silver Guard as Glade had two weeks ago. But he desperately wanted to be invited. It's why he agreed—against his better judgment—to accompany Glade and the three Silver Gaurds to the whorehouses.

He hated Glade. He hated everything about him and his bawdy new friends. *But how else does a young man move up the ranks?* So here he sat in the back of an oxcart, fingers wrapped around the hilt of the small black dagger hidden in his pants pocket, wearing naught but a simple shirt and tan pants, wishing to be a Silver Guard. . . .

His parents were readying the family to go back to Eskander. His Ember Lighting Rite was over, and that is what they had originally come to Amadon for. And Lawri was no longer ill. Plus both Lorhand and Lilith needed to get back to their tutors. His family would be leaving Jovan's court soon. And he would no longer be able to see Tala. *Unless I can make Silver Guard like Glade.* Then he could stay.

"Come up here and look at this portrait." Glade beckoned Lindholf. "It's Ser Tolz's nephew down in Avlonia. A real looker." Lindholf stayed where he was, leaning against the sidewall of the cart. "Since cousins can't marry," Glade went on, "perhaps Jovan can arrange a marriage between Tala and Ser Tolz's nephew." The three knights snickered.

Lindholf, shaking with nerves, ignored the comment. *Why am I here?*

*Shroud of the Vallè. That's why.* It had made him do some foolish things. It was still making him do stupid things.

His supply was long gone—he'd burned most of it to light his way in the dark passageways under Purgatory. All Lindholf knew was that he needed more of the white powder Seita had supplied him with. *I'll likely soon go mad without it.* The powder was the only thing in life that had ever made him forget the pain of his loneliness, made him feel pleasure, and most of all, made him confident. He could not challenge Glade without it. He could not talk to Tala without it. He was always lethargic and sleepy and could not keep awake without it. The bottom line was, Shroud of the Vallè had become his sustenance.

The sun was going down over Amadon, casting a rose tint over the cloudless sky and vast stone buildings. As the heavy oxcart trundled over the cobbles, Lindholf wrapped the bitterness and anger around himself like a suit of armor. Probably the only type of armor he would ever wear. His fingers twitched and fidgeted with the bottom hem of his shirt. He couldn't settle his nervousness. He fondled the black dagger in his pocket. Then the hem of his shirt again. Back and forth.

It didn't seem like anything made sense anymore. Nor could his mind focus on any one thing for long. *Did I really escape from Purgatory through underwater caves?* The very notion just seemed so insane, like some kind of hallucination. But the reality was, he had found *Ethic Shroud* and an angel stone.

The shield and the stone were now hidden between the wood slats and crumbling mortar in the wall of the chamber adjacent to his own—the chamber Tala had hidden Lawri in whilst she was sick.

As the cart passed through the warrens of crooked stone buildings and narrow, winding pathways, Lindholf looked on the city with two parts revulsion and two parts excitement. The Grand Vicar's Palace, sheathed in white marble gilded in gold, rose up just beyond the rotund Royal Cathedral. The cathedral, shaped like a crown, the sanctuary where the Blessed Mother Mia was buried, dominated the skyline in the distance. Next to the Royal Cathedral was the Temple of the Laijon Statue, equally as tall, and equally visible. For all those in Gul Kana, the cathedral and temple were the physical monuments of the great Laijon and the Blessed Mother Mia. Pilgrims from the breadth of Gul Kana flocked to worship at these two massive edifices. Worship and gaze upon the statue of Laijon, a statue that only he knew was flawed—another crazy thing that had happened to him in a list of crazy things. *Climbing the Laijon statue! Discovering its secret! Escaping Purgatory! Finding* Ethic Shroud! All the insanity could be traced back to Tala.

He had no idea how or when Tala and Glade had made it out of Purgatory. *Tala just assumes I followed Leif to the castle like I claimed.* Lindholf didn't know whether to be hurt by that or not. *Nobody would notice if I was here or gone.*

Lindholf's concentration was broken when he glimpsed a familiar face in the street behind the oxcart. A pale-faced girl wearing a crown of white heather.

But as soon as he glimpsed her, she was gone, vanished into the swirl of people.

*Now I see more visions!*

His mind traveled back to Memory Bay and the mermaid's cold, slithery clutch.

The distant bark of a dog echoed off stone walls, bringing him back to the present. The cart rumbled under the crenellated bastions marking the inner wall of the old city and then clattered by the columned gladiator arena, which rose up to his right. It was early evening, and citizens of every stripe—sailors, dwarves, urchins, oghuls, and thieves—had crawled out of whatever places they dwelled to do their business in the streets. The cart passed under a section of Amadon's aqueducts, and the stench of the city began to hit Lindholf full force. They were nearing the River Vallè. The aqueducts, from as far away as the Autumn Range and the northern Sky Lochs, brought cool mountain water into the city. But judging by the smell, it seemed the river was mostly for sewage and other human waste, and as Leif had explained, covens of witches and other such grotesques.

He took one last look back at the castle as dusk crawled over the city. It seemed no matter where you were in Amadon, the crenellated black fortress that encompassed the slopes of Mount Albion towered over all. He wanted to be back in the castle. Not here with Glade. Not heading to the brothel where he would once again be forced to watch Glade and the others fuck whores, never invited to participate himself.

*It's like they only fuck the whores to mock me. . . .*

As the oxcart jostled along, people in the roadway scurried from its path.

And then he saw her again—the girl with the crown of white heather.

Lindholf would not let his gaze lose her a second time. The girl wore a dark blue cape, tied at the neck, its hood thrown back. He watched her, trying to place her face, and soon realized she was following the cart. *The busty barmaid from the Filthy Horse Saloon!*

It was the serving wench who he had seen giving out pastries in Sunbird Hall during the Mourning Moon Celebration, the girl who had attempted to assassinate King Jovan. And then it dawned on him: she was also the girl rumored to have escaped from Purgatory not long after Hawkwood had.

Heart pounding, Lindholf gripped the small black dagger in his pocket, mind whirling. He watched as the girl followed the cart at a distance. Despite the jostling crowd, her movements through the streets were as light as goose down floating. And he couldn't help noticing how beautiful she was. *But why would she be following this cart?*

"Stop!" he shouted. "Stop the cart, Glade!"

"What for?" Glade turned about and threw him a stern look. "We ain't stoppin' until we get to the whorehouse."

"You don't understand." Lindholf scrambled to his feet and launched himself over the side of the cart, dropping to the street below. He staggered upon landing and rolled to a stop on the dusty stone street. For some reason it seemed a bad idea to tell Glade about the barmaid. No good could come of it.

"Bloody Mother Mia!" Glade shouted as Alain slowed the oxen. "What in the bloody fuck you doing, you fool?" Glade called back. "Get back in the cart!" All three Silver Guards were looking at Lindholf, both amusement and scorn on their faces.

"I'm not going with you!" Lindholf stood and dusted himself off, eyes darting from Glade into the crowd and back. He could no longer see the barmaid in the blue cloak and crown of heather. "I'm not going back to the castle!" He had to find the girl.

"Have you lost your bloody fucking mind!" Glade shouted. "Today was to be your lucky day! I was gonna pay the fattest slag at the brothel to fuck your tiny cock raw!"

"I don't want any woman whose been purchased! I want to be left alone!"

"Idiot!" Glade turned to Alain. "Leave him."

Alain snapped the reins and the oxcart carried on, trundling down the cobbled road without him, and was soon swallowed up by the crowd.

Lindholf felt a tug on his leggings and turned to find a grimy-faced street urchin sitting on a flat board with four small wooden wheels. The child had no legs. "A crust of bread for a hungry boy?" the child pleaded, holding up a grubby hand.

"Bloody Mother Mia." Lindholf staggered backward up the street, eyes fixed on the crippled child. The legless boy slapped his hands on the cobbles and pushed toward him. "Nothing for a starving boy?" He rolled his flat cart with ease over the cobbles and through the crowd. Horrified, Lindholf backed away still.

Then a hand latched on to his, fingers entwined, and he was pulled away through the crowd. It was the busty barmaid from the Filthy Horse Saloon who led him by the hand. She dragged him hastily toward an alleyway situated between a squat herb shop and a dark smithy, smoke billowing from its large chimney. Once they were a half-dozen paces up the narrow alley, Lindholf jerked away from her grip. "What are you doing?" His eyes couldn't help but stray to her chest—the one feature he remembered most about her.

The wreath of white heather sat afloat in her honey-colored hair. She had dimples and freckles sprinkled over rosy cheeks under grayish-blue eyes. She was standing so very close to him now, and smelled of perfume and heather. He asked again, "What are you doing?"

"Shush." She put her finger to his lips and looked about with worry. Then she leaned into him slightly. He could feel her sweet breath on his neck, breath that also smelled of heather. "Listen to me," she said. "I know you have it."

He stepped back, senses alert, eyes roaming the alley. They were alone. *Could I escape the same exact way we came?* He looked back at her. "Have what?"

"The white shield."

He stepped back again, almost stumbling, his stomach a solid knot of fear. His hand went to the dagger in his pocket. "Who are you?"

"I'm no one."

"You were a serving girl in the saloon. At the celebration in the castle."

"My name is Delia." She moved toward him, her hand seeking the collar of his shirt. Finding it, she pulled her face close to his again. "I've been watching you," she whispered in a throaty voice. "Ever since you came into the Filthy Horse Saloon with Tala Bronachell, I've been following you."

He slunk away from her again. "Aren't you the one who stabbed the king?"

"I watched you pickpocket those mercenaries in the Slaver's Tavern. Watched you escape with the two Vallè and ride off to the Hallowed Grove and sniff the powder."

"You've followed me?"

She touched him on the chest with the palm of her hand. "I know you have the white shield."

"The shield?" His mind was awhirl. *She followed me?* "But you couldn't possibly have followed me down into Purg—" He stopped.

Delia leaned in, her breath hot on his neck now, her lips full and sensual. "I was told you were a thief, that you would be the bearer of the white shield, long before we ever met." She cupped his chin gently in her fingers, traced the burn scars on his face, down his neck. "And I have dreamed of you ever since."

Her delicate warm hand left his skin as she slid her fingers into the cleft between her bosoms and pulled out a red leather pouch as small as her thumb. He could still feel the lingering touch of her supple fingers on his face as she opened the bag and showed him the contents within. "And I *know* you need this."

It was Shroud of the Vallè. So mesmerizingly glorious, white and pure against the stark red of the leather. Her full lips parted and she licked the tip of her index finger, then dipped the finger into the bag. "Taste," she offered.

Her moist fingertip was covered in white powder. Then she forced the top of her silky finger past his lips. And taste it he did. The euphoria hit him immediately.

The exhilarating sensation of the white powder on his tongue, in his mouth, sliding down his throat, wasn't like the outright ecstasy of sniffing it. But the feeling that engulfed him was like returning home after a long and sorrowful and lonely journey.

"I have all the powder you could ever need." Her words not only spoke to him, but stung at his heart with curiosity and craving. "If you want more," she said, "bring the shield to the Filthy Horse Saloon, my love."

"But I don't—"

"Shhhhh." Delia put her finger to his lips again, looked at him with eyes as soft as an evening breeze. "Just come to the saloon. Stay with me there. As my *special* guest."

Delia tucked the red pouch full of powder down between her breasts again. She lifted the wreath of white heather from her head and handed it to him. "This will see you safely into the saloon and to my quarters."

When he took the wreath of heather, she slowly stepped backward down the narrow alley, saying, "And don't forget to also bring the white stone."

Then she turned and scurried away, cape billowing behind her in a thick blue wave.

*At the death of Laijon, the Last Warrior Angels by nature have become the*
*children of wrath, for they shall slay those they deem wicked.*
—THE WAY AND TRUTH OF LAIJON

# CHAPTER TWENTY-THREE
# TALA BRONACHELL

### 3RD DAY OF THE ANGEL MOON, 999TH YEAR OF LAIJON
### AMADON, GUL KANA

Cember Tower—the tallest spire of Amadon Castle—pierced the low-lying clouds above the city. The observatory atop the tower was the one place Tala's father had called his own. The one place only the royal family was allowed. The one place Borden Bronachell would bring his three oldest children for private talks. It was where he got to know each of them; reading to them, teaching them, discussing the history of the Five Isles with them. It was a place Tala had not set foot in since her father had left for war and never returned. It was an eerie place, haunted by her father's absence.

Jovan had summoned his three siblings here on this cloudy evening. Tala, Jondralyn, and Ansel had been escorted by the Dayknights up through the dizzying warrens and courtyards of the castle to the high point of Mount Albion, where the base of the tower stood. They had hiked the remaining five hundred steps to the pinnacle unescorted. Jovan awaited them at the top.

The circular observatory at the top was crowned in slabs of black rock, five arched stone columns holding the black stone roof up. Five stone benches lined the chest-high balustrade walls in front of the columns. The floor was rough stone.

The tower seemed to sway in the moaning breeze that dragged through the five gaping openings of the observatory, rippling the thick waves of Jovan Bronachell's shoulder-length brown hair. The king, wrapped in a fur-trimmed cloak, leaned against the stone balustrade, looking out over the city. Upon their entry, he turned.

He faced Jondralyn, the timbre of his voice cutting through the wind. "I see the Prince of Saint Only has scarcely left your side since Denarius officially deemed him a free man."

"That is the point of the arena, to earn one's freedom," Jondralyn answered, breathing heavily from the long march up the stairs. She wore a simple black gown under an equally black robe tied at her waist. White bandages covered her facial injuries. She held Ansel's hand in her own; the youngest Bronachell looked up at the king with pure childlike admiration.

Tala drifted to the nearest balustrade and looked down over Amadon. Shrouded in a blanket of cloud, the entire city was obscured in rolling puffs of white. Jutting up like a needle through the clouds to the northwest of her was the grand and elegant Swensong Spire. Other towers thrust up through the clouds too: Blue Sword, Black Spear, and Confessor Tower, along with Martin's Spire, Sansom Spire, and a half dozen more named after dead grand vicars.

Jovan beckoned Ansel forward. The boy bounded into his older brother's arms. Jovan hugged him close, twirled him about, then set him down again. Ansel clung to his leg. "Squireck's journey in the arena is not over yet. Gault Aulbrek is a formidable foe, capable of causing great bodily harm." He ruffled Ansel's hair. "As you no doubt know."

"Is this why you summoned me, for ridicule?" Jondralyn asked. "You could have done that in Sunbird Hall, or your own chamber, or sent Leif Chaparral to do the ridiculing for you. Squireck will not die in the arena. He will slay Gault. I promise you."

"Squireck will die," Jovan countered. "It is a foregone conclusion."

"Will you have the quorum of five poison Gault's blade? Their meddling didn't foil the will of Laijon the first time. And it will not now. Squireck has a destiny."

"You are right, Jondralyn," Jovan said, a touch of dismay in his voice. "I did not summon you here for ridicule. I wish to make amends. I wish for our family to come together in this dark time. I wish for us all to work together. Some of my favorite memories were of the three of us listening to Father's wisdom atop this tower. I have missed this place. I have missed my father."

"I, too, have missed this place, and him. Our mother, too," Jondralyn said. "Borden did have a way of making us all feel like kings."

Jovan said, "I wish to include both you and Tala in the decision making going forward. All of Gul Kana, along with Amadon, will soon face the greatest days in all history. Prophecies in *The Way and Truth of Laijon* are coming to pass. Things must be made aright, not just within our realm, but among all of us. I should seek the advice of my sisters during this trying time." He looked at Jondralyn, searching for something in her demeanor. But the bandages blocked her facial expression. "I must ask, Jon, how are you holding up now that Hawkwood is again imprisoned in Purgatory?"

"I hope he is comfortable," Jondralyn answered, something like fear creeping into her eye. "He is no traitor. He did much to save my life."

"Denarius wishes for Hawkwood to be hung in the arena. He wants him hung after the match between Gault Aulbrek and Squireck."

"And you will listen to the grand vicar and do his bidding, I assume?"

"He is wise and we must follow his counsel." The king looked from Jondralyn to Tala. "You both must learn that above all else. It is another reason I brought you here."

"To extol the virtues of the grand vicar," Jondralyn said.

"I am only trying to do the right thing."

"You truly want my advice?" Jondralyn asked. "Train every woman in Gul Kana to fight. Give them swords and armor and double the size of our armies. We are ill-equipped to battle Aeros Raijael."

"Your injury speaks to the usefulness of women in battle."

"You ask my advice," Jondralyn snarled. "I give it, and all I get is scorn." She whirled and headed for the stairs.

"Stay!" Jovan pleaded.

But Jondralyn was gone, retreating down the circular stairwell.

Jovan unhooked the silver brooch at his chest, loosening the cloak around his shoulders. The decorative ring mail underneath was dull in the foggy gloom of the tower. His eyes met Tala's. "Do you wish to run off too?"

"I do not want to be here," Tala answered. "If I'm to be honest. This place only makes me feel sad."

"I do love you both," Jovan said. "You must believe that. I do love my sisters. My own kin."

"You say you love us," Tala responded. "But you don't accept who we are. So how is that love?"

"I have always accepted you."

She thought of his affair with Leif. "What does love look like?" she asked him. Then quickly answered her own question. "It's the acceptance of who someone is. Totally. As much as you say you love us, it doesn't mean anything if you don't accept who we are as people." She took a step to leave.

"Won't you stay and talk?" His expression was empty. "I used to enjoy our talks. Did you not too? You offered me much comfort after I was stabbed, when Jondralyn did not. Yet we haven't spoken in weeks. Seems you avoid me."

Tala felt bitterness darken her voice. "Last we talked, you went into a rage, berated me for dressing as a man, and practically tore my clothes off in the courtyard. Or have you forgotten? You humiliated me in front of Glade and Lindholf. You cut Lawri."

His expression deadened even more. "May the wraiths take Lawri Le Graven. They probably already have. Licking the blood from her own wound like that, licking her own arm like a roast ham. It is unseemly. No, she's crazy and there is naught else to it."

"She's crazy because of what the vicar does to her."

"I will not have you speak evil of Denarius in my presence. We have been over this before."

"So you will not allow my opinion as you will not allow Jondralyn's. Even though that is why you summoned us here." She looked out into the lurking fog.

"Why are you so bitter?" he asked.

"Bitter?" She turned, exasperated. "Denarius has taken advantage of Lawri!"

"Stop saying that."

"All you want to do is silence me. And that is the very reason I see no need to speak to you anymore. Because my voice is not to be heard."

"Fine." His tone softened—just a touch, though. "We are here, now. Speak what you will, my sister. But I insist you leave the vicar and the Church of Laijon out of our conversations. For such ill and negative talk of them is unproductive."

She met his gaze, measuring his sincerity, which wasn't much. *Go ahead and talk, my sister, but not about any subject I am sensitive to.* Tala knew she could dredge up a plethora of sensitive subjects with ease. She wanted to know how deep were his lies. "Did you send Jondralyn off to die?" she asked.

His eyes dropped to Ansel, still clinging to his leg.

Tala plowed on. "Did you give Leif instructions to make sure my sister died?"

Jovan's eyes stayed on Ansel for a moment. Then he looked up at her. "I do not want our Ansel to hear such accusations." His voice came out cold and precise in intent.

"He is too young to understand our conversations," Tala said. She would not be so easily swayed. She wanted to see his lies, hear them from his own mouth, hate him thoroughly for them. And in doing so, she could finally dissociate herself from him once and for all. She didn't care anymore. She wanted something to hate. Someone to blame. And Jovan was now her target. "Did you give Leif orders to make sure Jondralyn died?"

"Why thrust these hurtful accusations upon me now?"

"Did you send Jondralyn off in hopes that she would die?"

"I did not."

"You lie."

"You dare accuse me?"

"I dare!" she shouted. Ansel's eyes widened. He might have been too young to understand the implications of their words, but he knew what yelling was.

Jovan's hands were now gripping the boy's shoulders. "Do not raise your voice at your king."

"Or what, you'll make me fight a duel in the arena to shut me up?"

His face strained in anger. "You are worse than Jondralyn!" He let go of Ansel's shoulders and reached out to grab her.

She darted away. "Will you tear at my clothes again?" She grabbed at the hem of her own dress, lifting it, taunting him. "Don't you know I only wear these silly girl skirts just so you will keep your hands off me!"

He stopped his pursuit, brows furrowed in concern. She had thrown him off. She continued, "I'd hate to imagine what depravities you'd heap upon me if I truly *were* a boy."

His posture slumped as hurt dragged over his face. But she was not touched by his vulnerability; feigned or not, she didn't care. Not anymore. "I will tell everyone your secrets," she hissed.

Concern grew behind his eyes. "We've gotten off to the wrong start, sister. Please. Let us begin anew. Let us not play games."

Tala regarded him with cold calculation now. "Do you even know what makes you dangerous, Jovan, what makes you feared by those beneath you?"

"Oh, this should be good," he scoffed in an obvious attempt to regain some semblance of composure. "Please regale me with your opinion, dear sister."

*He couldn't even be nice for the briefest moment.*

"You're dangerous because you are weak and unpredictable," she fired. "You're weak and you know it. Naught but a coward and a bully to cover your lack."

A moment passed as they stared at each other. Then he straightened, no longer looking frightened by her words. "You are just like Mother. I actually admire the tenacity in both you and Jondralyn."

"No, you don't," she shot back. "You hate us for it. You stifle our opinions. You control how we dress. You cannot lie to me. You want Jondralyn to die."

"The man you should blame for your sister's injuries is in the dungeons of Purgatory: the Sør Sevier knight, Gault Aulbrek." A smile played over his features. "Of course, in your rage you already very nearly scratched his face off."

That was something Tala both regretted and was proud of at the same time. When she had attacked Gault, she had lost her composure in the wake of emotion. She would not let it happen again.

"Do not feel guilty," Jovan said, mistaking the contemplative look on her face. "With Gault, you can't have done other than you did."

"Gault is only in Amadon because you did nothing to stop Aeros' army," she said. "Why did you retreat from Wyn Darrè after Father died?"

"So you are a battle strategist now?"

"I only want to know why you did not fight as Father did. Your retreat seems to be that one singular cowardly act that has led us to this place, with the White Prince finally invading Gul Kana."

"I did say we could talk frankly about anything," Jovan said. "So I will indulge you this impertinence." He grabbed Ansel by the shoulders again, pulling the boy close to him. "I withdrew Father's armies from Wyn Darrè after his death on the promises of Grand Vicar Denarius that all would work out according to Laijon's plan. And what is Laijon's plan, you may ask? Fiery Absolution draws near and I needed to retreat and let Aeros Raijael take Wyn Darrè so the final prophesied battle would be fought in Amadon as *The Way and Truth of Laijon* has foretold." He knelt behind Ansel and hugged his younger brother from behind. Ansel seemed to revel in the attention given him. "You see, Tala, according to the vicar and quorum of five, according to *The Way and Truth of Laijon*, I have been chosen to usher in the return of Laijon. Fiery Absolution is upon us. It has come to us, in our time. All that I do is to glorify the great One and Only."

Tala was taken aback by her older brother's candor. Now it was she who was thrown off guard. Her mind spun. Her brother spoke of Fiery Absolution, the prophesied event both feared and anticipated by all in Gul Kana who adhered to the tenets of the Church of Laijon. She had given Absolution scant thought over her lifetime. But now, in light of all he had just admitted, the notion of Fiery Absolution seemed completely absurd to her. A man like her brother certainly could not be part of any arcane scriptural prophecy. It was a gut feeling she couldn't explain. She spoke what logically came to her mind next. "What if Denarius is wrong? What if all those lives in Wyn Darrè were lost for nothing because of some writings in some book? You could have saved so many more lives by fighting—"

"You sound exactly like Jondralyn." He cut her off. "Has she been feeding your head with this blasphemy?"

"I can reason things out myself."

"Reason is for the weak-minded. You need to learn how to feel the spirit and truth of the vicar's words for yourself, Tala. I can feel the truth of things in my heart when Denarius speaks. He is Laijon's holy mouthpiece and cannot lead us astray."

"He is a vile man."

"I thought we agreed to not talk of these things."

"You brought it up." She could see the frustration growing on his face.

"You do not try hard enough to see the good within Denarius," Jovan said. He hugged Ansel tight, then stood again, hands on the boy's shoulders. "You are too skeptical, Tala, rebellious, mischief making. This business with Sterling Prentiss, accusing him in public of the same things you've accused the vicar to me in private. The trouble you have caused this kingdom—no, the *harm* you've caused this kingdom. And it never ends with you. Convincing Glade and Lindholf into going down into Purgatory, and then you and Glade getting lost down there. You defiled the sanctity of Purgatory. Why?"

"Didn't Hawkwood already defile the sanctity of Purgatory moons ago?"

"Leif put the guards to death because they lost track of you and Glade. We couldn't risk word getting out that the dungeon is now so easily breached."

"Leif put them to death!" Horror crawled up her spine. A wave of smothering guilt nearly folded her to her knees. "Why?"

"Such gross negligence cannot go unpunished." Jovan's every word sliced into her heart. "And if Leif is to be captain of the Dayknights, he needs to exert his duty and authority before the others."

"But to kill men who had nothing to do with Glade and me . . ."

"Don't forget Lindholf."

"Lindholf had nothing to do with it. You cannot blame him—"

"Lindholf is not so innocent." Jovan forestalled her words with a wave of his hand. "It is the three of you combined, always embroiled in some type of trouble."

"It was all Glade Chaparral." Tala lied on purpose. "After we talked with Gault, Glade wished to look for Hawkwood's cell. Lindholf had nothing to do with it. He left soon after Leif did."

"Search for Hawkwood's cell?" Jovan's eyes tightened. "What do you mean? He was in the cage next to Gault, was he not?"

"Leif told us Hawkwood was being kept in a separate part of the dungeon. Once Leif and Lindholf had left, Glade insisted we go find where Hawkwood was being kept." Her lies kept growing. "Lindholf was no part of it."

Tala could see the hurt in her brother's eyes. But there was something more lurking within him, some deep betrayal she herself wasn't even privy to. He raised his head and spoke. "You and Lindholf and Glade are nothing but trouble together. As for Glade himself, I am no longer considering a betrothal between the two of you." Hearing that was actually a relief to her. "I've another suitor in mind for you," he continued. "A most holy union that will change the very history of Gul Kana."

At her brother's pronouncement, a deep foreboding clutched Tala's stomach. Her panicked mind flew to the moment just after she'd fed Lawri the green potion culled from Sterling Prentiss' gut.

Her heart twisted as she recalled her cousin's words upon awakening. *I had a dream about you. You were married to Grand Vicar Denarius. . . . I attended your wedding.*

*To satisfy the law, a bishop anointed of Laijon can stand in proxy for the one being executed, if he believes that person to be innocent, and justice shall be served. The bishop's life shall be made sacrifice in the stead of the accused.*
—THE WAY AND TRUTH OF LAIJON

# CHAPTER TWENTY-FOUR
# STEFAN WAYLAND

### 4TH DAY OF THE ANGEL MOON, 999TH YEAR OF LAIJON
### GLACIER RANGE, GUL KANA

Seita took Stefan by the hand and led him down the boulder-studded hill toward the rushing stream at the bottom of the canyon just below. Liz Hen was two steps behind. Beer Mug bounded along with them. As they picked their way cautiously down the ruined stone trail, Liz Hen grumbled about the task Roguemoore had set them to—that of gathering fresh water. All three of them carried leather water pouches that needed filling. The crisp waters gurgling at the bottom of the gorge cut through a thicket of tall pine and birch. The trail was rough but navigable, until patches of melting snow, growths of spiky high-mountain sage, and tufts of tundra overtook their path. The going became slow, and Liz Hen's carping increased.

The others of the Company of Nine remained in the ruins of the stone fort tucked in the rocky alcove of the sloping mountainside above, preparing for the night. The fort was an old wreck, crumbling walls choked with vine. Thick and snarled trunks of lofty pine forced gaping cracks and crags in the stone walls. Still, it was well hidden and the perfect spot to set up camp. Stefan looked forward to the nightly sword training with Culpa Barra and Val-Draekin. It was clear that Nail, Dokie, and Liz Hen enjoyed the training too. Seita usually just watched and cheered them on in their competitions.

It had been three days since they had left Stanclyffe. They'd blazed their own trail through the Glacier Range, getting ever closer to Sky Lochs, trudging over cold high passes and snow-swept dales, across many rocky rivers and wild mountain streams, all whilst bundled tight in the heavy gray cloaks. They had seen no evidence of oghuls prowling the untamed terrain. Nonetheless, they were ever on the lookout.

As Stefan and Seita trundled hand in hand down the slope toward the tree-shrouded creek, Stefan's quiver full of arrows bounced on his back. His ash-wood bow was strapped around his shoulder. The cool kiss of air wove through trees heavy with the fresh scents of pine, aspen, and moss. The crunch of pine needles and twigs sounded underfoot, accompanying the rustling of the aspen leaves above. A colorful wash of budding plants and golden sunlight rose up amidst the melting patches of snow. On the rough mountain ravines even higher above were trees of green, contrasting with the dark gray rock and cliffs. Stefan especially enjoyed the mountains when spring powered things to life, the air was thick with the perfume of damp soil and new growth and rushing waters.

Also, at nearly ten thousand feet high, the air they breathed was thin. Through breaks in the clouds, the company would catch glimpses of the mighty D'Nahk lè in the far northeast. The massive mountain rose to a breathtaking twenty-five thousand feet, many times higher than the range around it. At times, when the sky cleared and the mountain came into full view, Stefan could do naught but stare in awe. Godwyn claimed D'Nahk lè was an oghul term meaning the Great and Only One.

Stefan, Seita, and Liz Hen reached the bottom of the canyon and found an opening in the pine, aspen, and scrub. The creek cut through the foliage, creating a small, empty grove. The gurgling clear stream, about ten feet wide and two feet deep, looked inviting to Stefan's thirst.

Dirt crumbled under Seita's boots and tumbled into the creek as she bent to fill the leather water pouches she carried. The Vallè maiden had left her gray cloak and fox-fur-lined cape in camp. She wore her dark leather pants and black doublet, the ball-and-chain mace dangling from the belt at her waist. Her silk-colored hair sparkled magically in the sun. Just looking at her, Stefan could sense it. She hid something. A deep sorrow of some kind. They talked together often at night, sitting at the campfire when the others had retired. In those quiet conversations he'd witnessed her pain. It was not in anything she said, but rather in those pensive moments when her eyes seemed so full of tragedy. Full of such a broken tenderness he felt his heart would never cease its heavy beating for her.

*Or perhaps I just project my own issues onto her.*

As Stefan watched her fill the water skin, he fell into somber thought, imagining Gisela's innocent face, wondering if he was betraying her memory with the newfound feelings for Seita. Everything around the Vallè maiden indeed seemed magical; the mirror-smooth water, the aspens and golden sunlight above. All of it appeared to be touched with her essence. She was such an elegant, peerless creation. And all he had to remind him of Gisela was her name so crudely carved into the stock of his bow.

Liz Hen waddled into view and began filling her water skin too, the Sør Sevier longsword at her hip dragging in the dirt and twigs. Beer Mug lapped at the cool stream next to her, completely content.

Once Seita's pouch was filled, she stood and pulled forth a curious-looking tubelike shard of what looked to be pure black glass from a pocket of her leather doublet. The small black object was no bigger than her pinky finger. She set it to her lips and blew into it like a whistle. But there was no sound.

Beer Mug turned from the stream and looked at the Vallè, ears alert.

"What is that?" Liz Hen asked, annoyed.

"A musical whistle," Seita answered. "Silent to human ears, music to the Vallè."

"Oh," Liz Hen grunted. "I thought maybe you were practicing your blowing technique for Stefan's noodle. Thing in your hand looks about the right size anyway."

Seita shot the big girl a dark look, the stream murmuring hollowly beside her.

Liz Hen shrugged nonchalantly. "But I reckon such an innocent little Vallè flower like you wouldn't even know what a noodle looked like."

"And you would?" Seita tucked the black shard of glass back into her doublet.

Beer Mug's posture went stiff as he sensed the tension between the two girls. He then barked at the brush thicket across the stream just behind Liz Hen, ears alert. A crow fluttered from the trees, followed by the rustle of twigs and rocks. A white Dall sheep burst from the brush and bounded up the side of the ravine. It was a curly-horned ram, kicking up a spray of dirt and pebbles and snowy slush that tumbled down the slope. But neither Seita nor Liz Hen noticed the crow or ram as they glared at each other.

"Frail Vallè flower." Liz Hen pointed her finger at Seita. "I ought to box your fragile Vallè face right into the dirt."

"Shush," Seita hissed, her gaze now fixed on the brush just beyond Liz Hen.

"Or what, you'll brain me in the head with your useless little chain mace—"

"Just shut up." Seita's round Vallè eyes had narrowed to slits. Her hand reached into the folds of her black doublet. "You never let up, do you? Ever since we set sail from Lord's Point it's been nonstop flapping and yammering."

"So what?"

Seita pulled a dagger from her doublet and threw it straight at Liz Hen's face.

The dagger clipped a long red lock of the big girl's hair as it spun into the dense brush thicket and pine beyond. Liz Hen's eyes grew wide. "Murderous harlot!"

There was a throaty grunt and a blunt-faced oghul staggered from the parting brush across the stream behind Liz Hen, massive war hammer clutched in one meaty hand, Seita's black dagger buried hilt-deep in his eye. The beast toppled forward, landing face-first in the gurgling stream with a stupendous splash. Crystal waters streamed over the oghul's leather-armored back.

Beer Mug lunged across the stream as six more oghuls burst gape-mouthed and drooling from the trees, the hollows of their fierce gray eyes livid with rage, brutal gray faces pinched and stretched in anger, their clawed hands clutching gruesome, crude swords and axes. Their guttural war cries thundered off both sides of the rock-studded canyon walls.

Stefan stumbled back, hand reaching for the bow and the arrows in his quiver.

Seita's ball-and-chain mace was awhirl as she leaped toward the first oghul across the stream, spinning metal ball punching into the monster's broad face with a loud crack, sending the oghul reeling. Blood and slaver spewed from the beast's destroyed mouth. Beer Mug launched himself straight up at the face of the next oghul, his daggerlike teeth sinking into the creature's neck as both fell back into the water.

Stefan braced his feet, nocked an arrow, and aimed for the third beast that was heading straight for Liz Hen, a yowling brute about to split her head open with an upraised maul. His arrow caught the oghul right in the gaping maw. It fell dead as Liz Hen stumbled forward, eyes panicked as she went down hard on her knees, scrambling to pull the Sør Sevier sword from her own belt.

Seita hurled her chain-mace at the fourth oghul. The monster knocked the whirling Vallè weapon into the trees with a flick of its serrated longsword and came at her, howling. Stefan took aim with his second arrow. With the *thwack* of his bowstring, the charging beast stumbled to its knees, Stefan's arrow jutting from its rusted chest plate. Seita vaulted over him straight toward the fifth oghul, who had just tackled Liz Hen. The big girl struggled with the fat-eared brute. He had an iron cooking pot for a helm. The last oghul stood over the two combatants, ax raised to split Liz Hen's head.

Seita snatched the sword from the belt at the big girl's hip, rolled, countered the plunging blow of the ax-wielding oghul, and then leaped to her feet. The oghul with the cooking-pot helm had gained advantage over Liz Hen and now had his meaty hands around her throat. Seita spun about and swung the sword low, chopping straight through the two hands clutching Liz Hen's neck. The oghul flopped face-forward onto the girl, blood spouting from the stumps of its arms, cooking-pot helm tumbling from its head.

Liz Hen, her face awash in oghul blood, struggled to crawl free of the twitching corpse.

Seita's attention was instantly on the ax-wielding oghul. Sword flashing in the sun, her blade bit deep, splitting the last oghul's leather-armored chest and abdomen. She was splashed with blood as slithering guts spilled from the slit in the monster's belly. The oghul wobbled sideways, tripped over its own entrails, and went down. Dead.

It had all happened so fast, Stefan hadn't yet even fired his third arrow.

All seven oghuls lay in gruesome heaps. Beer Mug was ripping the throat and face completely off the twitching oghul in the stream, his muzzle red.

Blood dripped from some of the surrounding gray boulders and soaked down into the loamy soil. The ground was slippery underfoot as Stefan helped Liz Hen from under the oghul with no hands. The traumatized girl scrambled from under the beast and then half ran, half stumbled away from the creek-side carnage. The handless oghul was still alive and started howling. Seita effortlessly silenced the brute. One swift thrust of Liz Hen's sword right into the beast's spine and it was over.

Every oghul was now dead and quiet.

The Vallè maiden walked casually up to Liz Hen and gave her back the sword.

Liz Hen gazed at the bloody weapon returned to her hand. "Well, bugger me blind," she muttered, doing the three-fingered sign of the Laijon Cross over her heart with her other hand. She looked up at Seita. "You done kilt 'em all."

Culpa Barra entered the grove, panting in exhaustion, his huge black Dayknight sword drawn and ready. Val-Draekin was there right behind him. Nail, too, face also red from exertion, sword drawn. "What happened?" Culpa's darting eyes surveyed the scene. Seven dead oghuls. Seita, face and hair savaged in blood. Liz Hen, also drenched in scarlet, standing there with a stained sword and a stupid look. Beer Mug's muzzle was a mop of sopping red. The reek of oghul blood and guts was ripe.

Stefan's nerves were perfectly flayed.

"Your fight echoed through the canyon like an avalanche," Culpa said, sheathing his sword. Nail sheathed his, too.

Val-Draekin hurried to Seita's side. "Are you hurt?"

"I'm fine," she answered.

Stefan suddenly felt a fool, realizing that the Vallè maiden was the most skilled fighter he had ever seen. Roguemoore, Godwyn, and Dokie entered the grove at the same time, all huffing from their journey down from the ruined fort above. Dokie, eyes fixed on the bloody heaps lying on the forest floor, did the three-fingered sign of the Laijon Cross over his heart. "Bless me," he muttered.

"I've bandages if anyone is hurt." Godwyn began digging in the leather pouch at his belt.

"I think we are all okay," Seita said. Except Liz Hen was now gasping for breath, struggling, leaning on the bloody sword like it was a crutch.

Val-Draekin went straight to her, placed a hand on her back. "Take three slow breaths like I taught you. Then hold it for a count of five. Then three more."

"I can't . . . r-rightly breathe at all," she stuttered.

"Three deep breaths, then hold it," the Vallè repeated.

"The girl's bound to be exhausted," Seita said, dabbing at the blood on her own face. "Was Liz Hen with that longsword who helped kill the bulk of these oghuls here. She's like an assassin."

Between breaths, Liz Hen glared unmercifully at the Vallè maiden.

"It's true," Seita continued, her blood-smeared face set firm. "The shepherd dog chewed the throat out of one. I knocked another one down with my chain-mace, but my weapon got quickly lost in the trees. Liz Hen tore into the rest with that big bloody sword in her hands. Two were arrow shot by Stefan."

Culpa slapped Stefan on the back. "That's some nice shooting, Stef." But Stefan wondered why Seita was exaggerating how many oghuls he and Liz Hen had killed.

"These oghuls were lying in wait for us," Seita said. "Silent in the bushes, otherwise I imagine Beer Mug would have alerted us."

Culpa Barra cast his gaze up at the surrounding canyon. "I wager these oghuls watched us set up camp, then hid here, waiting to attack us after dark. You stumbled right into them. We must leave this place.

Camp elsewhere. Who knows how many more have watched us? We must put at least five more hours between us and this place before we stop again for the night."

"Five more hours?" Dokie grumbled.

"Yes, Dokie, we can no longer stay here," Culpa said.

"Let's head back up and gather the mules." Roguemoore clapped Dokie on the back.

"I'll stay here and help them clean up," Val-Draekin said. "They are covered in blood. The creek is right there for washing."

The dwarf nodded. "Be quick. And be wary. I do not like the thought of us being separated for longer than need be."

Roguemoore and Culpa headed back up the hill, Nail and Godwyn following. Dokie cast a concerned glance at Liz Hen, then scurried after the bishop.

Seita knelt at the creek's edge near the first oghul she had killed. She twisted its face up, yanked her black dagger from its gray mug, and cleaned it off in the stream. After pocketing the blade, she dipped her own face into the waters, the blood sweeping away in the current. She wiped herself down with a kerchief she'd pulled from somewhere inside her doublet.

Liz Hen plopped down at the edge of the stream just behind the Vallè maiden. She asked to borrow the cloth, and Seita handed it over. Liz Hen scrubbed her own face clean.

Stefan went to the water's edge and cupped his hands in the cold stream. Beer Mug was near him, lapping at the water.

Val-Draekin found Seita's chain-mace dangling in the nearby bushes, then began inspecting the dead oghuls, pulling Stefan's two arrows free from the bodies, washing them in the stream.

"You saved my life." Liz Hen broke the silence, handing the kerchief back to Seita. "Why?"

The Vallè maiden stood. "Aren't you the reason we are here?"

"No teasing." Liz Hen stood too. "That's why I don't like you.

Everything seems like a joke with you. Telling everyone I did the killing, when all I really did was stand like a petrified tree trunk. Always with the cruel teasing, you."

"Me? Teasing? What about *you* teasing?"

"I'm sorry," Liz Hen said, eyes downcast. "I know I've treated everyone poorly when I ought not have. You and Nail especially so."

Seita stepped up and grasped Liz Hen's hand in her own. "You're scared, Liz Hen. We all are."

"I've been scared every day of my life," Liz Hen said. "Every single day."

Five hours later the Company of Nine hiked up a grassy, snow-patched slope of yellow grass toward a cluster of weather-beaten boulders nestled comfortably among the dark pines. From atop the ridge, they had a good view on all sides. Black shadows quietly blanketed the ravines to the south, ravines they had just journeyed through. Below them to the north, a landscape of snow-streaked coves and vales glinted in the starlight. In Stefan's estimation, they'd left a trail any oghul tracker worth his salt could have followed, but they'd had scant choice.

Shrubs and fallen branches dotted their chosen campsite. Culpa Barra tethered the pack mules to a tree, whilst Roguemoore passed out a dinner of cold salmon and elk jerky. Godwyn spread the four tarps out over the cold ground. After eating, Nail and Dokie went straight to bed, both breathing heavily in deep sleep almost as soon as they'd crawled under their thick blankets. Beer Mug curled up next to Dokie.

Culpa, Godwyn, Val-Draekin, and Roguemoore walked down the slope no more than twenty paces into the darkness, talking in whispers, deciding who would take fist watch, something the four had arranged between themselves every night since their journey from Lord's Point had begun.

Stefan found he was alone again with Liz Hen and Seita, the three of them sitting together on a tarp, each huddled under their own individual blankets.

"I won't be able to sleep tonight," Liz Hen said.

"Still anxious from the encounter with those oghuls?" Seita asked her.

"Terribly so." Liz Hen seemed to shudder under her blanket.

"I used to braid my sister, Brieta's, hair when she was upset," Seita said. "It would relax us both. Have you ever had your hair braided?"

"Not that I recall," Liz Hen answered.

"If I may"—Seita's voice softened—"I could braid your hair, Liz Hen, like I used to braid my sister's."

"Could you?" Liz Hen seemed eager. "You'd braid my hair?"

"Of course." Seita sat behind Liz Hen and began working on her hair. Liz Hen immediately seemed to relax. Watching the two girls, it did seem to Stefan that some of the stress of the day's events was swept away. Stefan stroked his ash-wood bow and thought of Gisela.

*She would have been so mortified by those oghuls. What an absolute horror of a battle they had just survived!* Stefan was confused by the entire battle. Seita had not been honest with him. The Vallè maiden clearly knew how to fight with cruel efficiency.

*Probably even knows how to use a bow better than me.*

If not for Seita, both he and Liz Hen would surely have been slain. And then Seita had given all credit to Liz Hen. No. None of it made any sense. Running his fingers over the name carved in the stock of his bow seemed to be the only thing that could relax him. *What would Gisela think of all this? Could she have handled this journey?*

"She was Maiden Blue of the Mourning Moon Feast," Liz Hen said, watching Stefan stroke the bow. "The most beautiful girl in all Gallows Haven."

Stefan's ears perked up when he heard Liz Hen mention Gisela's name.

"I'm sorry I made fun of your noodle earlier today, Stef," Liz Hen said. The left half of her head was now almost braided. "It wasn't right. I've been acting horrid. Jealous. And there has been no excuse for my behavior. You touching Gisela's name on that bow day after day almost breaks my heart, Stef."

Stefan said nothing. It seemed the oghul attack had brought on an absolute reversal of attitude in Liz Hen.

"I'm only trying to apologize, Stef. To you and to Seita both."

The Vallè maiden ran her hands through the hair on the right side of Liz Hen's scalp, speaking softly. "You suffered a huge trauma when the White Prince destroyed your town and killed your family, Liz Hen. You need not apologize to me. We all of us grieve in our own way. Your suffering turned to anger and you lashed out. It's okay. And I should not have goaded you as I did. You have all suffered loss and handled it as best you could. Dokie often chokes back his tears, but I hear him cry at night under his blanket, and I see you hold him in comfort, Liz Hen. Nail scarcely talks to anyone. He suffers his pains in silence. As does Stefan."

Liz Hen's eyes met his. "Yes, Stefan has lost love. I see his struggles too."

Both girls were now looking at him as if expecting him to say something. He couldn't stop thinking of the greatest pain he still fought to endure—the death of Gisela Barnwell. They were right. He suffered in silence. And this mysterious Vallè woman somehow seemed to know his deepest thoughts. "Do you really want to know why I carve Gisela's name in everything?"

"I do," Seita said.

He could feel tears welling in his eyes. "I feel guilty for her death. And you were right, I do think she follows me. I think she watches me. I feel her with me always. I do not want to lose that. So I carve her name in things." He ran his fingers reverently over the name carved on his bow. "I don't know what else to do for her."

"See, you're breaking my heart, Stef." Liz Hen's voice cracked with emotion. "Now I'm wishing it was me who ate all them poison mushrooms instead of her. Blame me if you wanna blame someone."

"Blame the White Prince and his religious crusade," Seita said. "You'd all be safe and sound and tucked into your warm homes right this minute, if not for Aeros Raijael believing different about the history of Laijon, believing different than those worshippers like yourselves in Gul Kana. For thousands of years these battles and crusades have reaped naught but suffering."

"Laijon save us all." Liz Hen did the three-fingered sign of the Laijon Cross over her heart. "But his armies were savage and mean and truly not of Laijon. That I believe."

"I'm not sure what I believe," Stefan said softly, knowing Liz Hen could be quick to anger about matters religious. He looked off into the night. Culpa, Godwyn, Val-Draekin, and the dwarf were still out there, murmuring in quiet conversation.

"I'm done with your braids," Seita announced.

Liz Hen ran her fingers over her hair, seemingly pleased with the results. She turned and gave the Vallè a quick hug before muttering her thanks. "I'm off of bed then." Liz Hen stood, still wrapped in her blanket. She waddled over to where Nail and Dokie were sleeping and curled up on the tarp next to Dokie, leaving Stefan and Seita alone.

The Vallè girl scooted next to him, her hand on his knee. Stefan was both confused and alarmed by her nearness. The warmth of her body nestled against his was comforting. "You cared for her so much, didn't you?" she asked. "The girl named Gisela?"

"I did love her," he answered, almost wishing he didn't have to speak of her.

"And that is why I like you, Stefan. You are the most honest one in our company. Your abiding affection for your lost love tugs at my heart. And I desire to be near you all the more. 'Tis why I pretended to know nothing of archery when we first met. Because I wanted to be close to you."

She leaned her head against his shoulder. It reminded him of how Gisela used to do. "Can you forgive me for my lies?" She pressed her cheek gently into his arm.

"I . . . I feel stupid though," he stuttered. "Watching you slay those oghuls. As violent and easy as you please."

"Truth is, all Vallè are trained to fight as violent and easy as you please, and with many different kinds of weapons. Even the females. It is just who we Vallè are."

The heat of her face against his shoulder was like a burning hearth flame, seemingly comforting and dangerous at once. He could feel the stiffness of her ear. And there was a scent to her, an earthy, fragrant, flowery scent that held a certain familiarity he couldn't quite place.

"I've a secret of my own," she continued. "A secret I have told only my father and one other person. But may I burden you with it now, Stefan?"

"I suppose," he answered, basking in the warmth of her cheek against his shoulder, suddenly wishing he could sit like this with her forever.

She pulled away just enough to look up at him with big round eyes, luminescent green in the starlight. "I can see into the future." There was an anxious tremble in her voice. "I see visions of people, just bits and pieces, vague images really. Images of what some people will be doing later that day, or later that year. Or in ten years." She glanced away from him. "Knowing the fate of some can weigh heavy on my mind."

His heart beat faster at her soft-spoken confession. It was the tone in which she was conversing with him that made him almost believe her. So honest and raw. And when she turned back to him again with her wide, vulnerable orbs, he could tell she desperately wanted to be believed, that somehow this was the most important thing she had ever told another living soul. "This clairvoyance within me is mostly a curse and a heavy burden," she went on. "For in these visions, I saw all of you from Gallows Haven: Nail, Dokie, Liz Hen, even you. Many years ago I saw you in my dreams."

"You saw us before you met us?" Stefan asked. "Like our faces and things?"

"I saw the very moment of our meeting at the Turn Key Saloon. I've seen visions of both Dokie and Liz Hen doing great and noble things."

"*Noble* things?" he questioned. "Liz Hen and Dokie?"

"Yes. Noble things. That is why Val-Draekin was so eager to convince Liz Hen to join us on our quest. He is the one other besides my father with whom I ofttimes share my visions. He knows most of what I have dreamed. But not all . . ." She trailed off for what seemed the longest time.

When she continued, her voice was filled with emotion. "Not only did I see our meeting, Stefan, but our parting, too. I foresaw the forming of our Company of Nine and this journey. I also know all of our fates. . . ."

She took a deep breath. "The fates of three of the nine . . ."

She trailed off again, almost as if she couldn't breathe. Her delicate brows furrowed, as she contemplated whether to go on, as if fighting some great battle within herself. *As if she is truly worried what I think of this craziness.*

Stefan wanted to find the right comforting words for her, words that did not betray his skepticism. But nothing came.

"I am most troubled by my visions," she started up again. "We will find *Blackest Heart* and *Afflicted Fire*. But not without suffering great loss. Three of the company of nine will not make it to the end."

"You know how we will die?" he found himself asking. "Three of us?"

"I did not say any of us would die."

"But isn't that what fate is, dying?"

"There are worse fates than dying." Seita's face burned pale in the silken starlight. Stefan didn't know quite what to make of the conversation. But he couldn't break his eyes away from hers as he now found himself drowning in her gaze, spellbound by the tender, almost helpless look in her eyes. Such beautiful round orbs; even in the dark they were more brilliant than stained glass under the summer sun.

She snuggled closer to him, one hand wrapped around his arm, pulling him into her slightly. "I knew we were destined to meet, me and you." She leaned her face up under his ear, her dainty nose nuzzling his neck. He could feel her breath, spiced with a faint pine scent, quivering against his flesh. She whispered, "Just like Liz Hen and Dokie, we too are destined to do great and noble things together, Stefan." Then her lips were on his, lingering briefly before breaking away.

She stood abruptly and wrapped the blanket around her shoulders. Without looking back, she walked toward Culpa, Godwyn, Roguemoore, and Val-Draekin.

Stefan's heart thundered as he watched her drift out into the darkness.

*In those final moons before the return of Laijon, mankind shall seek death, but will not find it. They will yearn for Fiery Absolution, but it will elude them. For Laijon's return will not come until after much slaughter and bloodshed.*
—THE WAY AND TRUTH OF LAIJON

# CHAPTER TWENTY-FIVE

# NAIL

8TH DAY OF THE ANGEL MOON, 999TH YEAR OF LAIJON
SKY LOCHS, GUL KANA

**M**orning clouds clotted the sky whilst a shrieking gale swept over their path and lashed the trees. The gray gloominess above spat hail sideways at them, pelting every inch of Nail's face and hands with an unnatural, venomous accuracy. All he could do was suffer the sting. All he could see through the hail were the formless shapes of the towering trees around the company, the trail Bishop Godwyn led them along nearly lost from sight. It was miserable. Liz Hen prayed aloud for Laijon's mercy. Even Beer Mug looked disheartened.

The group of nine eventually stopped near a half-frozen stream and huddled together around the pack mules. If the hail turned to snow, the bishop worried they might become hopelessly bogged down, a shame considering their destination was just over the next ridge—the far eastern loch and its massive glacier. But the hail eventually died to a cold drizzle of softly weeping rain, and the company picked themselves up and continued on.

Within an hour the clouds parted and the sun beamed down, causing a frosty wet gloss over the landscape. It had been four days since the oghul attack, and seven total since setting out from Stanclyffe, and Nail had come to realize that the weather patterns of the Glacier Range around the three Sky Lochs were even more fickle than those of the Autumn Range. They had seen no other signs of oghuls since the attack, but so high in the mountains, it wasn't just oghuls they needed to worry about. It was clear: the weather was liable to kill them all just as easily. And despite the snow and ice all around, Nail knew this climate would leech you dry if you were out in it very long without fresh water. They had been diligent about filling their water skins at whatever streams they crossed.

By noon the clouds had raced completely into the east and the glacier was a sheet of polished brightness gleaming through the trees—a forest of gaunt birch and pine stricken to the core by the harsh conditions of the altitude. The company wended their way down a snowy slope to the edge of the wooded ridgeline until the great glacier revealed itself fully. To Nail it looked like a twenty-mile-long, five-mile-wide, luminous blue-and-white blanket rippling across the barren valley below, the deep indigo waters of Sky Lochs nestled at its far southern end. To the east of the glacier, lofty mountain peaks of snow were strung like a necklace of glimmering pearls. To the north rose D'Nahk lè, the breathtaking mount from which the glacial ice sprang. The western ridgeline the company stood upon was harsh with afternoon sunlight. The warmth was not enough for Nail to shed his heavy gray cloak, but a welcome relief nonetheless.

Godwyn guided them down a steep draw leading to the glacier, sharp cliffs on either side. It was slow going, but knowing their destination was finally at hand seemed to hastened their step. Ever since the sun had come out, Seita and Liz Hen and Dokie had been in a jolly mood, all three talking excitedly, all three in utter awe of the dazzling glacier below and the towering hulk of D'Nahk lè to the north. "It's like walking toward a dream," Dokie said. "Like nothing in this world could be breathing with more life than this place here."

"And the air so crisp and fresh," Seita followed. "And the sun so bright."

While Nail also marveled at the dramatic beauty of the glacier and its surrounding, sunlit mountains, he did not feel the place breathed with any sort of life. In fact, as the company descended the ever-widening draw toward the glimmering ice, a stark apprehension formed within him. He had been here before. He had been born in a small mining camp named Arco at the edge of this glacier—or so Shawcroft had claimed. Nail couldn't help but feel some dark history resided down on that ice below, in the mountains above, in the loch waters far to the south, a hazy dream hovering just on the edges of his mind, some unknown suffering deeply connected to him. And with each step toward the glacier, he could feel something ominous take root deep within himself, growing and stretching and creaking open the locked parts of his soul. Yes, it was as if this massive, striking, harsh landscape was speaking to him in sorrowful soft tones. *You have been here before and suffered great loss.*

Despite Nail's ever-growing dread, the overall mood of the company seemed the lightest it had been since they had set out from Lord's Point. In truth, the last four days since the oghul attack had seen the company grow close. Liz Hen had even attempted to joke around with Nail from time to time. And for a moment, he had sensed something almost like kindness in her ribbing—almost, but not quite. In truth, there was more and more casual banter tossed about among everyone daily. But Nail always felt like the odd one out. The gloomy one. Stefan, Seita, Liz Hen, and Dokie had formed a tight comradeship of their own. The four were always sitting together at night before bed, talking quietly and playfully among themselves. Seita and Liz Hen had certainly become immeasurably more tolerant of each other. Nail wouldn't exactly call the two girls the best of friends just yet, but the tensions between them were gone.

In fact, as they hiked toward the glacier, he could hear Dokie's inquiries about the two girls' new-formed friendship. "Why did you hate Seita so much in the beginning?" he asked Liz Hen.

"Was Ol' Man Leddingham who planted a deep loathing of the Vallè in me," Liz Hen said. "He used to gather all us Grayken Spear serving girls around the hearth at night, tell us ancient stories of the beasts of the underworld, about the ghosts and witches and druids that roamed free, doing their bidding. Scared the britches right off some of us. But he'd always end his tales of fright with tales of the Vallè females of the Val Vallè northlands. Claimed a Vallè maiden was worse even than a witch, worse even than the wraiths. Claimed that a Vallè woman could steal the thoughts right out of your mind. Claimed they had iron claws of rust, and pubis hairs made of icicles."

A giggle burst from Seita—a light giggle that rang like music off the surrounding cliffs and snow. Stefan, walking near Seita, laughed too.

"It's true," Liz Hen went on. "Leddingham claimed Vallè maidens preyed on human boys just for sport. Catch a boy in the woods and seduce him with her pointy ears and wicked charms. Once a boy was completely caught, his noodle clamped inside her icy cooch, she'd run off into the forest, his poor pecker ripped free at the root, intestines unraveling out before his surprised eyes into the scrub and brush until he was dead."

"Seems unduly harsh," Seita laughed.

"I don't think a boy's intestines are attached to his pecker," Dokie added.

"Of course they are," Liz Hen snarked. "Ain't you ever seen a pig gutted?"

"I once seen my dad scrape the guts out of a stag he kilt in the forest," Dokie answered. "I don't recall its intestines being attached to its pecker, though, more like its butt."

A clap of laughter shot from Liz Hen. "Says the boy who don't even know where his own spinkter is."

"I think you mean sphincter," Dokie countered.

"I'm just sayin' it was a bedtime story Ol' Man Leddingham used to tell us girls," Liz Hen said. "And that's why I didn't care for Seita to begin with. I figured she was gonna gut Stefan and Nail, and possibly even you, Dokie. But I was wrong not to like her. She's turned out well."

"Thanks," Seita said with another bright little laugh.

Nail flicked the hair from his eyes and shot a glance backward over the pack mule behind him. There was sheer delight and amusement on the Vallè maiden's countenance as she trudged down the slope with Liz Hen and Dokie by her side, Beer Mug on their heels.

With her elegant smile and sparkling big eyes, Nail swore that Seita's face under the gray hood of her cloak was as beautiful as the pristine landscape around them.

† † † † †

An hour later they reached the bottom of the draw. It emptied them out into a sloping, mile-wide valley of stone and stark skeletal shrub flanked on either side by unfriendly-looking cliffs of towering gray rock. At the bottom of the valley, like a sheet of blinding glass, lay the great glacier.

Nail's skin was itchy under his patchwork plate armor. He cursed the old junk, wondering how Culpa Barra felt under all that heavy black Dayknight metal. The sun still beat down, and most of the new-fallen snow had melted underfoot.

As they picked their way through the gauntlet of wind-blasted boulders and leaning rocks toward the glacier, Nail began to sweat, and his apprehension heightened. It seemed everything was now happening through a muddled fog. His mind felt watery, unfocused, jumping, stretching, trying to recall memories long faded, hazing with spots of nothingness. It was the glacier. It terrified him like nothing ever before. The looming swath of ice stretched out before him, seemingly endless in its bare, white bleakness and haunting history.

"This is where the mining camp of Arco once stood," Godwyn announced as they passed over a barren patch of rocky landscape littered with rotted and scattered wood, many of the timbered boards looking half-burnt. Crude stone foundations of long-abandoned structures dotted the valley here and there.

Roguemoore snatched a pebble from under a weather-worn length of lumber. "A D'Nahk lè timestone." He held the tiny rock up. It was about the size of his thumb and chalk white. "I hoped we'd find one among this ruin. The glacier spits them out randomly. The miners of Arco used them in the dark of the mines." Stefan seemed to take particular interest in the stone as the dwarf handed it to him for examination. Seita leaned over his shoulder and gazed at it too.

Nail had seen similar rocks before. Shawcroft had a small collection of them. They changed from gray to white depending on what amount of sunlight they were exposed to. His old master occasionally used them in the Roahm Mines for telling time in the dark. Set a gray timestone pebble in the sun for a moment and it would turn dull white like the one in the dwarf's hand now. Inside a dark mine, the chalk-whiteness of the stone would slowly fade over a period of about two days. If one could learn the luster of the stone, one could easily determine how long one had been inside a mine working. They also offered up a tiny bit of dim light in the darkness.

"Gather any similar stone you find in the rubble," the dwarf advised. "That's if the oghuls haven't already picked the place clean of them. Arco and every other such mining camp in these hills were abandoned after heavy oghul raids fourteen, fifteen years ago. Few men venture into these high mountain climes anymore."

Dokie asked, "Are there still many oghuls around this high up?"

"Yes," the dwarf went on. "Over the last century, the oghuls of Jutte and Tok have spread out. Mostly they've taken over the uninhabitable reaches of Gul Kana's far north. And they continue to pirate the north shores of Gul Kana. And the Silver Throne has mostly left them to it. There's not much left up here for human or Vallè or dwarf anyway. Over the years, it's been predominantly oghul clan verses oghul clan fighting and quarreling among themselves, killing each other off. King Borden Bronachell thought the oghul squabbles best left alone. Whilst some of the northern nobles wished Borden would have sent the Dayknights to put an end to it all, so they could mine these mountains once again, no one really wanted to waste soldiers' lives on an outright war with the oghuls. But it's always been a possibility."

"Ew," Liz Hen exclaimed, and stopped. "Dead bones." She was pointing to a collection of sun-bleached bones scattered among the rocks that Beer Mug was sniffing at. Human bones. The girl backed away, doing the three-fingered sign of the Laijon Cross over her heart. Then both she and Dokie, hand in hand, skirted around the bones warily.

"Probably a victim of the oghul raids," Godwyn said.

"The whole world is naught but a boneyard," Roguemoore said. "All the trillions that've died over the centuries, people and critters of all kinds, dead and slowly sinking into the soil over time. Likely ain't one place in all the Five Isles you couldn't dig a hole and not run into bones of some type."

Val-Draekin bent and shoved aside a flat rock, digging one of the bones from the frozen ground, a small jawless skull. "Just a child," he said, then tossed it aside.

Nail shuddered as he watched the skull clack hollowly against the rocks. Hazy, dreamlike images of the oghul raid that had likely claimed the child's life suddenly assailed him. His muddled brain swam with a foggy and foreboding gloom. When he looked up, the glacier before him seemed naught but a giant, stark-white shroud thrown over a graveyard, a white veil thrown over the memories hovering just at the edges of his mind.

*I have been here before, walked this very spot.*

The company moved on. And the nearer they drew to the glacier, the more random bones and shattered skulls and half carcasses they saw. "The terribleness of it all," Liz Hen would murmur at each new bone in her path.

Roguemoore never did find a second D'Nahk lè timestone by the time they reached the edge of the glacier. With Arco behind them, the cliff-lined valley came to an abrupt end—a wall of ice stretching to the north and to the south. In some places the ice was twenty feet in height, in others over a hundred.

"Last I was here," Godwyn said, "and mind you, this was fourteen or more years ago, the miners had cut many access stairways into the wall of the glacier. The mines are about five miles' journey north up the ice, their many openings scattered at the base of D'Nahk lè. The miners would hike atop the glacier to the mines. It was dangerous going, but with those cliffs"—he pointed to the sheer cliffs surrounding the valley—"the glacier route was their only choice. As it will be our only choice."

Liz Hen grumbled. "So we have to carve a staircase into that solid blue ice wall? I don't think so."

"We'll hike under the edge of the ice to the north a bit toward the cliff," Godwyn said, hand thrown over his brow to block out the sun as his gaze ranged north over the glacier. "Perhaps if we're lucky, we will find the ice dips low enough somewhere and we can just walk up on it." He glanced back at Liz Hen. "I don't want to carve any steps either, and I'd prefer the pack mules to come with us as far as they can."

They found their access point onto the glacier half a mile to the north, in the shade of the cliff edge itself. The jagged rock ledge rose high above, blocking the sun, casting shadow over the low swale in the ice. The towering ice shelf dipped to about waist-high in this one spot. Still, it took some effort to climb onto it. They had to guide the mules one leg at a time, pushing from behind.

Once on the ice, footing was slippery for all as meltwater raced under their feet. Nail fell to his knees twice. He noticed several of the others did too. Still the company made its way slowly east, up the gentle basin of ice. They hiked carefully for several hundred feet before they crested the sloping white ridge and stumbled out into the sun again. The entirety of the glacier's overpowering brilliance and stark menace lay before them, and under them. Bare and bleak and full of sharp ridges and deep crags of lustrous blue, it stretched, seemingly forever. Heaps of mountainous white ice jutted haphazardly from the mazelike landscape—like colossal standing stones they loomed randomly in the distance. The blinding white of this tortured landscape tore at Nail's eyes. He blinked away the pain and looked toward the great D'Nahk lè that rose up over the head of the glacier five miles to the north. He found his heart was hammering with fear at the sheer size of the mountain and everything else around him.

"I don't think this is the right path," Liz Hen said.

"I agree," Dokie added. "How are we supposed to walk across this? It's far too jagged and strange."

"We must now turn and proceed north," Godwyn said. "The mines are at the head of the glacier at the base of D'Nahk lè. Half a day's journey, if I remember right. We'll skirt the cliff on the left as best we can. Safer that way. No sense in getting lost out in this labyrinth if we can avoid it." He nodded to the vast expanse of treacherous ice to the east.

Culpa Barra and Val-Draekin began separating two coils of rope from the rest of the gear strapped to the mules.

"It won't be easy," Godwyn went on. "This glacier ice is deceptive, with many perilous traps. I will teach you what warning signs to look for on the ice as we go. Follow my tracks exactly. Be wary of your footing. And do not venture too close to any crack or crevasse, for it may hide a drop that can kill. We'll rope ourselves together like the miners of old. If you fell into a crack without the rope at your waist, you'd fall and fall until you were wedged in between the narrowing chasm walls like a cork. There you'd die a slow, cold death if the fall hadn't already killed you. Many miners of Arco were lost in just such a way. But that won't happen to us. If any one of us slips into a crevasse, or if a hole opens up underneath and swallows any one of us, the rest will just sit down and don't move. The combined weight of all of us will stop whoever is falling."

"My pa said he watched a fellow topple off a cliff above Arlish once," Dokie piped up. "Hit every outcrop of rock on the way down, opened his skull and ripped his body into five separate pieces before he hit the bottom."

"Rotted angels, you stupid." Liz Hen smacked Dokie hard on the shoulder. "What did you have to go and mention that for?"

"My pa swore it happened that way," Dokie said, rubbing his shoulder.

"Well, who bloody cares?"

"What of the mules?" Dokie asked as Culpa Barra tied one end of the rope around his waist. "Will they be tied to us too?"

"No," Roguemoore answered. "The mules will travel with us as far as they can. Then we'll stake them to a safe place on the glacier and journey on. I doubt any oghuls or other predators will bother them out so far on the glacier."

"But they will freeze if we leave them with no fire pit," Dokie said. "They'll have no wood to burn."

The dwarf said, "Mules are hardy creatures. I reckon they can withstand a brittle night or two under the stars."

"Are you also going to tie Beer Mug to a stake in the ice?" Liz Hen asked. "I couldn't bear the thought of him fallen down some ice crack. I know him well enough; he wouldn't do well down some crevasse all alone." She ruffled the dog's head.

"Don't worry," Val-Draekin said as he tied the rope around her next. "The dog will do fine on the glacier, better than the rest of us put together, I reckon. He can come with us as far as he chooses."

"Still," Liz Hen said. "All things considered, this glacier doesn't look like much of a place for a shepherd dog or a couple mules to go a-walkin'."

"Or dwarves, for that matter," Roguemoore added. In his bulky armor, the squat dwarf looked entirely out of place on the glacier. They all did. The only ones who seemed even slightly at ease were the two Vallè, both lithe of foot on the slippery ice where everyone else seemed to slide and stumble.

Godwyn, Seita, Stefan, Dokie, and Val-Draekin were tied to the lead rope in that order. Culpa, Liz Hen, and Roguemoore were tied to the second line, Nail at the end of it.

The first mile was relatively smooth going. Nobody spoke as they traversed the rolling surface pocked with crystal clear puddles and ponds of ice melt. As they traversed the flatter parts of the glacier, the bishop did as promised and began teaching them how to read the ice for hidden indications of danger, what cracks in the ice to avoid, how to spot the shadowy signs of sagging swales of snow-covered crevasses.

They ambled straight into a sun that lashed the glacier with such a ferocity it made it hard for Nail to see anything unless he wrapped the cowl of his cloak around his face and over his eyes. Seemed the others had the same idea, as they, too, found similar ways to block out the sun's blinding rays. The armor Nail wore was also rubbing him raw. He felt trapped by the stuff. The sun was such a menace he found himself clenching his eyes shut the majority of the journey, blindly following wherever the rope led him. In the moments he would break his lids open and look about, he was assailed by a harsh brightness beyond description.

Soon his mind began playing tricks on him, conjuring up images of Bloodwoods cloaked in black, chasing him across the glacier on red-eyed stallions the color of midnight. But in his hazy dream, he wasn't running from the assassins, nor did he seem scared. Someone carried him. Some almost familiar woman with a blood-covered face and a boning knife lodged in her back. And just as Nail was about to figure out who she was, she was gone. All that remained of her was a broad bloody smear on the ice. And then he was alone at the edge of a sheer drop-off. But he found comfort in the blackness of the assassins' steeds, which had followed him. So he watched their approach, a black soothing mist where his burning eyes could take rest.

He felt the shade overtake him and sure enough, obstacles had risen up silently in his path, towering chunks of ice blocking out the sun. *Am I awake now?* At the base of these teetering blocks of blue and white were gaping crevasses. There were no black horses chasing him anymore. But he could hear some rumbling sound rising from the nearest chasm, some deep booming thunder from far below. He stopped and listened.

*Are the black horses down there?*

He took two steps toward the nearest crevasse, leaning forward for a better look.

"Nail!" He heard a shout. "No!"

He woke up as the ice sheared away from under his left foot with a loud crack. He fell sideways onto the lip of a chasm, clutching at the ice with both hands. He slid into the gaping hole, the rope around his waist catching him halfway over the edge. The heel of his right foot, still hooked over the rim of the ice, dug in and both gloved hands frantically clawed for purchase.

Then he was slowly being pulled up from danger. Culpa, Liz Hen, and Roguemoore were all heaving on the rope until he was completely clear of the crevasse, all three sitting down on the ice as Godwyn had previously instructed.

"By Dokie's bloody shit!" Liz Hen yelled as Nail crawled across the ice. "What in Laijon's name were you doin' wandering over there like that, Nail?"

"I don't know," Nail mumbled. "I couldn't see."

"Well, you 'bout jerked me off my feet, you clumsy clodpole."

Roguemoore was right next to him, looking into his eyes curiously. "He's snow-blind," the dwarf announced.

"We should stop and rest." Godwyn stood.

"There's an even bigger chasm blocking our path in the distance," Val-Draekin said, eyes roving over the ice to the north. "I'll scout the length of it for a place to cross."

Godwyn said, "If we can't find a way around it, we will have to stake the mules here and leave them. I will go with you."

The bishop and the Vallè were roped together. They marched north across the ice.

Roguemoore and Culpa began digging through the packs and food was passed around, cold elk jerky and dried potatoes. As he ate, Nail cast his gaze back toward the hole he'd fallen into, blinked against the pain still piercing through his eyes. Culpa and Roguemoore had saved him. Liz Hen, too. The entire episode had been humiliating. He wished he still had *Forgetting Moon*. Wielding it in Ravenker against Jenko Bruk had been the only time he had ever felt totally confident and invincible. *Precision in everything.* He recalled how Shawcroft had taught him how to swing an ax-pick in the mines.

He looked toward his friends, huddled in their gray cloaks on the ice, the great D'Nahk lè rising above them. Stefan. Dokie. Liz Hen. *Three moons ago, who would have ever thought the four of us would be here, of all places.*

*This ominous stark place of my birth.*

Whatever dark history he and this place shared would not leave him be. It lingered just out of reach, haunting him.

† † † † †

Godwyn and Val-Draekin returned a half hour later. "From what we could tell," the Vallè said, "the crevasse stretches the length of the glacier, twenty to fifty feet across at most places, and deep. Darkness obscures the bottom, but a glacial river far below can be heard."

"We will have to cross the gorge," Godwyn said. "Luckily, the narrowest spot is not far from here. Our ropes are plenty long. We'll have to unload the pack mules. Each of us will now have to carry what we can on our backs from here."

Culpa dug a metal spike from a bundle on one of the mules. With the back of an ax head, he pounded it deep into the ice and secured the reins of both mules to it.

"They'll starve," Liz Hen said, worreid. "There's no sage or brush for them to nibble on at night. No drinking streams."

"They can drink the ice melt," Godwyn said.

"What if oghuls come to get them?"

"Oghuls have no use for horses or mules. They don't ride them. They don't eat them. They scarcely even use them as pack animals."

To Nail it all seemed like nonsense to ease the girl's fears.

"We can't leave them." Liz Hen was nearly in tears.

"We have to," Godwyn said. "And I am afraid Beer Mug won't be able to cross that chasm either."

Liz Hen's eyes widened in horror. "But if I leave him, I just know I'll never see him again."

"Beer Mug is a hardy fellow," Seita tried to comfort her. "He will be safe until we return."

Liz Hen knelt next to Beer Mug and ruffled his fur with both hands. "Did you hear that, boy? You must stay here with the mules. Guard them from silver-wolves and saber-tooths and oghuls and such. Nuzzle the mules when they get cold. Keep them safe for me." The dog looked up at her, distressed, sensing this was their farewell. "You're a good boy." Liz Hen was crying now. "I will bring you food when we return. Don't you worry none, okay?" She stood, sobbing.

Seita slipped her hand into Liz Hen's, their fingers entwined. Tears streamed down the big girl's cheeks.

It only took a few minutes to divide up the gear. A plan was formed. Each would carry their own ration of food, and their own blanket. The two woodcutting axes were divided between Nail and Culpa Barra. Godwyn and Stefan carried the extra quivers of arrows. The nine torches and ice picks and small iron spikes were separated evenly among all. Roguemoore slung one of the spools of coiled rope over his shoulder; Liz Hen carried the other. Dokie, Seita, and Val-Draekin were assigned water skins and leather sacks filled with pine-resin pitch for the torches.

Roped together again, the company made their way from the mules to the chasm, another small trek over slippery ice. The crevasse itself was a yawning blue scar in the glacier, dropping down into a bottomless purple nothing stretching to the east and the west—an inescapable nothing that seemed to pull at Nail with unyielding force. He couldn't look away from the gorge, the threat of immediate death so powerful and looming. A dull rumble issued up from the deep—the glacial torrent Godwyn had mentioned churning far below.

Culpa pounded an iron stake into the ice about five feet from the edge whilst Dokie stripped out of his armor down to nothing but his breeches and rough-spun shirt. Roguemoore secured one end of a rope around Dokie, creating a makeshift harness that stretched over the boy's shoulders and around his waist and between his legs, the other end tied to the stake. Despite how petite Seita was, Dokie was the smaller of the two, and it was decided he would crawl across the rope—the rope Stefan would fire across the chasm with his bow. Only a twenty-foot shot as they were at the narrowest part of the crevasse

The end of the second rope was tightly secured to the stoutest arrow in Stefan's quiver. "I don't know how the arrow will do with something so heavy tied to it," he said. "It feels awkward. And I ain't never fired an arrow into ice before."

"You're a good shot," Godwyn said. "Better than me anyway, and that's saying something. Aim for any small crack in the ice. It'll work. I've seen it done before."

Stefan nocked the arrow to his bow, rope drooping to the ground and coiled along the lip of the ice. Godwyn held on to the other end. Stefan aimed and fired. The arrow, rope dragging it down, fluttered and sank lifelessly into the chasm. Godwyn slowly reeled the rope and arrow back in.

"I didn't pull back near as far as I ought," Stefan said, nocking the arrow again. He hauled back on the bowstring, straining it farther than Nail had ever seen a bow strained before. Stefan let the bowstring go. With a *snap*, the arrow sailed across the chasm. It bit deep into the ice just below the opposite rim and stuck.

"Fine shot!" Seita clapped Stefan on the back. Then the bishop tugged hard on the rope. The arrow had lodged itself solid in the ice across the chasm and held. Godwyn fixed his end of the rope to the stake Culpa had pounded into the ice.

Dokie, securely tied in Roguemoore's harness, crawled to the edge of the crevasse. He took hold of Stefan's rope with one hand, tugging on it too, testing its strength. He had the most dangerous job of all, but looked excited to do his part.

"If the arrow breaks free of the ice," Godwyn said, "you'll merely swing back against the ice wall underneath us and we'll reel you back in. You'll likely experience a hard impact with the ice. But brace for it and you'll be okay."

Dokie did the three-fingered sign of the Laijon Cross over his heart and crawled out over the edge, both hands grasping Stefan's rope. He slid all the way out over the gap, swinging his entire body under the line, clamping both legs up and around the rope, gripping it with the underside of his knees. Nail's heart crawled into his throat as Dokie shimmied his way across the crevasse, suspended underneath the rope.

As Dokie made his way across the chasm, the rope drooped in the middle under his weight. Then Stefan's arrow tore free of the ice. The boy plummeted down and out of sight. Nail's heart lurched. Liz Hen screamed. Dokie struck the ice wall below with a heavy *tthhrummmph!* He quickly shouted, "I'm okay!" as he dangled below.

Godwyn and Culpa seized the rope and pulled the boy back over the rim of the chasm. Once Dokie was safe, Liz Hen dusted ice crystals off his clothes. "I'm okay," he kept repeating as Liz Hen fussed over him. "I wanna try that again. It was fun."

"Fun?" Liz Hen exclaimed. "You've lost your bloody mind! Nearly gave me a heart attack, that did."

Godwyn checked the knot around the arrow. Stefan nocked the arrow to his bow again and shot it across the chasm again. This time the arrow sank clear to its fletching in a crack in the ice not a foot below the opposite rim.

Harness still secure, Dokie crawled to the edge of the chasm and shimmied his way over the crevasse again. Stefan's arrow held this time, and Dokie scrambled safely up and over the opposite rim and stood, triumph on his smiling face.

Liz Hen expelled a gasp of pent-up breath.

Culpa Barra tossed one iron spike and one wood ax over the chasm. Dokie scooped both up and, with the flat of the ax blade, hammered the spike into the ice five feet from the edge. He crawled to the lip of the crevasse, reached down, and untied the rope from the arrow lodged in the ice. He scrambled back and tied that end of the rope around the spike. Then he squirmed out of Roguemoore's harness and tossed it back into the chasm, where Godwyn reeled it in. With all that done, the company now had a secure, but very precarious, single-rope bridge over the crevasse.

Culpa and Godwyn tossed all their heavy gear and armor across the chasm. Nail and Stefan threw most of the armor and weapons over too. Bishop Godwyn was the first to slip Roguemoore's makeshift harness around himself and cross over the rope bridge to stand with Dokie. Culpa, Seita, Stefan, and Roguemoore were next. The dwarf struggled the most in his squat, bulky armor. It took Liz Hen about ten minutes to get into the harness, then another ten of sitting at the edge of the chasm, petrified. She eventually talked herself into crossing, and did, slowly.

Nail and Val-Draekin were last to go. Val-Draekin secured the harness over Nail's shoulders and legs. Nail stepped to the edge of the huge drop, gritted his teeth, and did what the others had done before. Upside down, hand over hand, he slowly crossed the chasm, looking straight up at the sky the entire time, not daring to look down once, not even when he reached the other side and felt Culpa and Godwyn's grasping hands. Once free of Roguemoore's harness, he stumbled away from the rim of the gaping pit, heart thundering.

On the other side of the chasm, Val-Draekin untied both ropes from around the stake. The plan was to leave the iron stakes in the ice for the return journey. Godwyn reeled one of the ropes over. Val-Draekin slipped the harness around his midsection and leaped casually over the edge, swinging down into the gap, disappearing from Nail's view. He landed without a sound against the wall of ice below Godwyn and Culpa Barra, who quickly pulled him up and out of the gorge.

And that was it. Everyone in the company was safely across.

They quickly gathered all the gear and armor and weapons, tied themselves together again, and continued their trek across the ice toward the great D'Nahk lè.

But before they got far, Liz Hen let loose a ghastly shriek of horror. "Nooo!"

Nail turned to see Beer Mug charging toward them, the chasm a looming gash of blue between them.

"Nooo!" Liz Hen screamed again, and bolted toward the dog, jerked off her feet as she hit the end of the rope, nearly staggering Nail and Culpa Barra to their knees.

Beer Mug's legs churned as he gained speed, fur rippling in the wind, muscles of his shoulders and haunches bunching as he launched himself over the icy gorge.

On her knees now, Liz Hen loosed one last tortured scream. "Nooo!"

But the dog cleared the chasm by a good ten feet and scampered happily across the ice, tail wagging as he bounded right up into Liz Hen's arms, licking her face. As she hugged Beer Mug, Liz Hen could do naught but suck in great sobbing gulps of air that echoed off the ice like the honking of a goose.

"Well," Roguemoore said, "I reckon that dog just ain't the type to be left behind."

✝ ✝ ✝ ✝

Luck had been with them. They'd traversed a handful of cracks in the ice, but they jumped each one with little effort. They encountered a few walls of ice, none more than fifteen feet high. Those they scaled with the iron spikes and ropes. Beer Mug could leap up onto most himself. For the higher walls of ice, Roguemoore's harness was used on the dog too. Along the way, Godwyn had taught the others in the company how to look for the shadowy signs of the sinking and sagging swales that typically marked a snow-covered chasm.

Now, hollow-eyed with weariness, bitter cold sapping their energy, the company stood at the foot of the great D'Nahk lè almost

near the timberline. Nail gazed up at the hulking mountain silhouetted against a deep blue dusk, its white peak swathed in clouds. A
massive churning river tumbled from a deep carved canyon to his
right, the raging waters crashing and roaring directly into the glacier, swallowed whole by a huge glacial cavern. Several other similar
waterfalls could be seen in the distance, those too eventually disappearing under the ice.

Other than the thundering waters, there was naught else at the
head of the glacier, no signs of civilization or even a lone scraggly
tree, just high mountain sage and the faint tracks of Dall sheep in
the snow. Bundled tightly in his cloak, Nail wanted to keep moving
and reach the mines as soon as possible, for it was there they were to
camp for the night.

The bishop led them up a snowy vale to their right. As they began
their ascent, the nature of the once mighty mining effort here became
quickly apparent to Nail. Mine shafts and their tailings dotted the
snowy hills and steep, boulder-strewn valleys round about. The base
of D'Nahk lè likely had more than a thousand open mine shafts dug
into its side.

Godwyn claimed the entry they were looking for was not man-
made, but a natural cave set against a sheer wall of rock situated deep
in a narrow gorge about half a mile up the side of the great mountain.

The vale they crossed soon grew into a steep slope of shale and
rock crusted with snow. They climbed on hands and knees until they
reached a steep ridge lined with tall, pointed boulders leaning like
icy fangs thrust skyward. As they threaded their way along the ridge,
the evening grew dark. Shadows rich in purple and blue seeped down
D'Nahk lè like paint. They lit torches, which illuminated their path,
but more importantly to Nail, warmed them some. They continued
on for another hour until Godwyn pointed to the stony hollow he
sought. They changed course, snow crunching underfoot, knee deep
in places. The cold swarmed around them now and the wind began

to howl above, the torch flames whipping to and fro.

A hundred feet into the snowy gorge, they came upon the sheer wall of rock Godwyn had described. There was a large crack in the cliff face, black and foreboding and running crooked up the spine of the crag like a sliver of midnight. Nail did not care for the looks of the jagged, cold fissure splitting the cliff. Though Godwyn claimed it was a natural cave, there seemed nothing natural about it. Even Beer Mug seemed to balk at the sight.

"We'll set up camp just inside the cave," Roguemoore said. "Get out of this weather, which is sure to become nasty soon."

Bearing guttering torches aloft, the Company of Nine made their way toward the bleak crevice in the wall.

And to Nail, danger seemed to flow from the mine entrance like a vaporous fume.

*Thus, we three remaining Warrior Angels take up this, an accounting of the life
of Laijon, as a reminder to mankind of its own stewardships. And all memory of
the Last Demon Lord will vanish into the dusts of time, and those beasts shall
remain nameless.*

—THE WAY AND TRUTH OF LAIJON

# CHAPTER TWENTY-SIX

# AVA SHAY

### 8TH DAY OF THE ANGEL MOON, 999TH YEAR OF LAIJON
### SOUTH OF LOKKENFELL, GUL KANA

A va Shay stood before the battlefield carnage, swooning with
drink. She stroked the neck of the crimson-eyed stallion
named Scowl—something she would likely never do sober.
*A Bloodeye horse that used to frighten me so, now likely my only friend. . . .*

"In a certain light," Spiderwood began, "you remind me of Gault's
daughter, Krista. I'm sure Aeros sees that in you too."

The Spider's words captured Ava's attention and rooted her
in place. She could see every detail of the Bloodwood's fiery eyes,
faintly veined with red, serpentlike. Despite the hard, cruel look of
the Spider and his Bloodeye horse, Ava had grown used to the man's
company these last three weeks, almost looking forward to their
daily talks. He still complimented her on the little beetle carving she
had given him.

"I wonder if that is why Gault took to you so swiftly," the Spider continued. "He was a simple soul. A romantic in search of love. But it is all an illusion. You. His daughter. The two of you combined were his undoing. I almost feel bad for what I did to him in Ravenker."

*You betrayed Gault somehow and now he is gone.*

The Spider's hand touched hers, but briefly. There was no warmth in his touch, as if the gesture was false, calculating, meant to mislead. *Does he really like the beetle carving, or is this just some game to him, some road to betrayal?*

She'd been tending to the flogging wounds on the Bloodwood's back daily, ever amazed at her own skill with the poultices and bandages. The man had been healing fast. So fast, in fact, he had suited up in his black leather armor for the first time today. Though he was still too injured to take part in the slaughter of Doolindal.

She looked toward the carnage spread out before her. Flies gathered in clouds over it all, seeking the cold, clammy skin of the dead. The sun had gone down more than an hour ago. Torches and bonfires now lit the bloody beach in an orange haze, casting a sickly pall of sorrow and distress over the watery battlefield. Dead knights in both Sør Sevier and Lord's Point livery lay strewn in the surf. Crows hunted the shallows whilst small kestrels skimmed the water, grabbing scraps of human flesh that had floated out to sea, the bloody remnants of Aeros Raijael's latest triumph.

A contingent of several hundred Ocean Guards from Lord's Point had actually tried protecting Doolindal, the small hamlet resting in the shady dale behind Ava Shay. But they were little match for the nearly thirty-five thousand Sør Sevier knights now in Gul Kana. Still, the Ocean Guards, small group of warriors though they were, had put up a fight defending this hamlet just south of Lokkenfell. The White Prince had lost almost two hundred of his own in the skirmish today, the highest loss he'd suffered thus far. Three weeks ago Ava Shay would have rejoiced at Aeros' misfortune, but at the moment she was numb to it all, and also currently a little drunk from Aeros' stash of wines. *Have I stopped caring altogether?*

"Why does Aeros do the things he does?" she asked the Bloodwood, her own anger rising, her curiosity, too. She had asked Spades much the same question. She wanted to see if their answers were similar. "Why does it have to be like this? Death? Killing? Torture? Why can't he just leave Gul Kana alone? Leave me alone? Who am I for the White Prince to torture me so? Why does he do the things he does?"

"All Aeros does is for the glory of *The Chivalric Illuminations of Raijael* and for power," Spiderwood answered. "A power he believes he possesses. A divine calling he believes is his. Or so that is what he has been taught his entire life. And like Gault, Aeros is a simple person, a romantic in search of a destiny he's long been promised. But it is all an illusion, the power, the romance, the destiny."

"He has power over you," she said pointedly. "He had you flogged."

"True." Spiderwood's red-streaked eyes pierced hers. "I lost Aeros' sword, Sky Reaver. And I failed to bring Nail back from Ravenker. Indeed, the Angel Prince had me flogged. But I *let* him. And so you must realize, Aeros' reaction to my failings is not what is most important."

"And what is most important?"

"Your reaction."

"Don't be ridiculous," she said, drawing back from him a step.

"What is most important," he carried on, "is how *you* overcome those things that hold you back, how you realize your true potential. You must use Aeros as a means to an end. Like the Bloodwoods do, like Dugal's Caste has always done with the heirs of Raijael. You *take* the power. Even though Aeros thinks he has it, you must *seize* it from him."

Her head swam with wine, becoming unfocused. "How can I do the impossible?"

"You know what treasures he hides."

She breathed deep, memories clawing at her mind. The odd, salty smell of the sea and burning bodies, stinging to her eyes, reminded her of the day Jenko Bruk and Mancellor Allen had brought the White Prince a huge shiny ax and sparkly blue gem. Jenko claimed he had stolen them both from Nail in Ravenker. Aeros had placed the items in the same chest where he kept the horned helm and the green stone. She desired to look upon those enticing, colorful gems again.

Every time she drank of Aeros' wine, the lure of those shiny stones would pull at her mind. Last night, as she'd lain in bed beside the White Prince, she'd inquired whether she could see the stones again. *"The stones are cursed and you want no part of them,"* he'd said. *Cursed?* She thought of how she'd asked Gault Aulbrek to steal the helm and green stone and escape with her. *Cursed indeed.* Now Gault was gone. She felt guilty realizing that was likely the reason he was missing, or worse, dead.

She found she was still stroking Scowl's hide.

The Bloodwood's eyes bore into hers. "You must learn who you are, Ava Shay, and then use those treasures he holds dear against him."

The sound of his words wove in and around the pounding of her own heart. She knew he was trying to tell her something without overtly stating it. *He wants to know if I am simple too, like Gault, or if I can figure out his subtlety.* Her drunken mind was not allowing her to think clearly. *At least it's not the wraiths anymore, just the spirits of the wine.* She had not felt the bitter touch of the wraiths for some time now. *When you lay with me, I place into you the healing power of the gods,* Aeros had said. She giggled at the thought, heady with wine. She basically attributed most of the Bloodwood's healing to the myriad of potions he ofttimes drank. *But Aeros also claimed to have taken upon himself my sins? Taken upon himself the wraiths that plagued me?*

"You know the real reason why Aeros had me flogged?" he asked. "'Twas not to appease some Chivalric Rule of Blood Penance, I assure you. Aeros had Hammerfiss flog me to throw his Knights Archaic off. To keep them unbalanced. You see, they do not trust me, the others. They think Aeros and I are too close. That we conspire against them. That we conspire against King Aevrett and even against Sør Sevier itself. They have heard the rumors that Aeros himself once trained under Black Dugal as a Bloodwood. And they ofttimes believe that their Angel Prince is but a puppet in Dugal's control. And they believe that I am Dugal's spy." His eyes grew hard. "Well, truth is, they are correct in those assumptions."

*Why is he telling me this? Why do any of them tell me anything?*

The neighing of several horses could be heard in the darkness behind her. The Spider's cold gaze was now cutting over her shoulder toward those who approached. He dipped his head to her. "We must continue this conversation later, m'lady."

Ava turned and saw Mancellor Allen, Jenko Bruk, and Enna Spades draw near, all in full armor. Mancellor was leading two white stallions by the bit: Spades' mount, Slaughter, and his own horse, Shine—the stallion bequeathed to him after Beau Stabler's death. Blood splattered the flanks of both horses. Jenko walked beside Mancellor. Spades' right arm hung limp in a bloody sling at her side. The top of her crossbow and quiver of thick bolts sprouted from over her shoulder, a longsword dangled from her left hip.

"Good to see you're finally up and about," the red-haired warrior woman said as she stepped up to the Bloodwood, her tone laced with sarcasm. "Indeed, a pleasure to see you finally on your feet again."

Spades' eyes then fell on Ava. "You must truly have the magical healing touch. Hammerfiss flogged him to the bone, and here he stands as if nothing happened. You must realize it is merely out of respect for Black Dugal that Aeros allows the Bloodwood such favor, such a tender healing hand as yours, Ava Shay."

"I am sure you are beside yourself with jealousy of what favor Aeros allows me," the Spider said.

"Well, perhaps so," Spades went on, gesturing to her arm in the bloody sling. "I am not quite myself. Took an ax blade to my arm, as you can see. But at least those Lord's Point knights gave us a bloody good scrape, if only for a glorious moment." She listed slightly to the left. "Now I wonder if the loss of blood has made me a bit woozy."

Mancellor Allen immediately dropped the reins of the two stallions and helped her stand straight. His help seemed genuinely gallant, meant in no way to curry favor. Still, Jenko glared at him. And that stung Ava to the core.

There was a heavy clomping of hooves and Hammerfiss rode into their midst and drew rein. Like a mountain, the red-haired giant sat high atop his massive white stallion named Battle-Ax. Girt in full Knight Archaic armor, helm on the pommel of his saddle, razor-wire-wrapped mace clinging to the baldric slung over his back, he looked a formidable sight. He let out a hearty bark of laughter as he looked Spades up and down, gleaming eyes lingering on her injured arm. "Ah, didn't these bastards give us a hardy fight today, Spades? Look at you! Arm's practically hanging by a thread there."

"'Tis but a scratch." Spades winked, adjusting the sling.

"Well, I ain't seen you scratched like that since Stabler pulled you out of that mess in Agonmoore. The day he lost his eye." Hammerfiss glanced at Jenko and Mancellor. "Did either of you sad sacks lose an eye saving her? Looks like you didn't. 'Course them tattoos under both Mancellor's eyes are enough to deflect any sword blow." He bellowed with laughter.

The ink under Mancellor's eyes was like two shadows cutting into the night. To his credit, the Wyn Darrè did not rise to the bigger man's goading. Ava offered her gaze to Mancellor. *Is he my savior? Is Jenko? Is anybody.* Her heart calmed when Mancellor returned her glance.

Hammerfiss saw the short exchange between them. His brow rose. "Oh, the needless trouble some folk create for themselves." Under his shaggy beard curled a mischievous smile.

*He is right. How can I feel jealous of Jenko and Spades, and at the same time have eyes for Mancellor Allen?* Ava knew she should leave the man alone. *Lest he suffer the same fate as Gault Aulbrek. . . .*

† † † † †

Ava was alone in Aeros' tent. The White Prince had taken Jenko and all of his Knights Archaic but for Spades back to the battlefield, back to slay any injured Ocean Guards who still sought to flee or surrender.

Enna Spades was left outside the tent to guard Ava.

Dressed in naught but a light silken shift, Ava stepped softly across the plush rugs and knelt before the gold-filigreed chest in the corner of the partitioned room. It was normally kept locked. But she had been watching the White Prince, and the last time he had opened the chest, she had memorized where its hidden latch was. She felt along the intricately scrollworked edge of the lid, searching until she heard it click, and pulled up gently. The lid swung soundlessly open before her.

With great care, she reached into the chest and pulled forth the horned helm. She held it up in trembling hands before the candlelight. Shards of yellow flickered off its burnished silver-and-gold surface. The two horns jutting from the helm always captured her gaze. At first she had thought they were ox horns, only to realize they were something else entirely. Up close for the first time, she could tell they were not horns at all, nor bone, but rather fashioned of some shimmering ivory substance not of this world.

The relic was heavier than she'd imagined it would be; her arms swiftly grew weary. She set the helm on the rug and gazed down into the chest at the sharp double-bladed battle-ax, its twin half-moon-shaped edges gleaming in the faint light. The weapon had a leather-wrapped steel shaft interwoven with Vallè runes. Arms already drained of strength, she did not want to lift it. She left the ax where it lay and picked up the satchel—the leather bag Jenko and Mancellor had taken from Nail in Ravenker when they had stolen the ax. The pouch was made of rough hide, a flap curling over the top and buckling on the side.

Ava opened the flap and pulled forth a handful of bound scrolls and set them aside next to the helm. At the bottom of the satchel were two swatches of black silk. She snatched one up and unwrapped it. *An angel stone!*

Her gaze widened as waves of radiant blue light washed over the stone's shiny surface. She set the stone on the rug between her knees, marveling at its sheer magnificence. She grabbed the other swatch of silk from the chest and swiftly found the brilliant green stone within. It too shimmered and shone, ghostly tendrils of emerald color swirling just under its polished surface. The angel stones stole her breath.

"The Bloodwood claimed you tended his wounds with great care." Spades' voice cut the silence like a knife. Startled, Ava lurched to her feet, whirling around, the green stone tumbling from her hand to the rug. Enna Spades, standing between the two canvas flaps that made up the door to Aeros' partitioned room, looked tall and regal in her armor. Her injured right arm was not in a sling but wrapped in a simple clean white bandage. Spades carried My Heart in her good hand, the sword she had gifted Ava. The warrior woman's glance traveled from the horned helm, up to Ava's guilt-filled eyes, then swiftly down the length of her silken shift to the two glowing stones on the rug at her feet.

"What have we here?" Spades cocked her brow, stepping all the way into the room, her leather-booted footsteps creaking as she moved. Her own sword clacked against her armored leggings.

"The one who snoops finds great treasure." Spades knelt before the horned helm next to Ava, setting the ruby-hilted sword in front of Ava. She lifted the helm, examining it from all angles before placing it back on the rug. She picked up the blue stone and then the green, held them in the palm of her hand. Ava watched the vibrant spray of blue and green light play over the Sør Sevier woman's porcelain-colored face, she noticed a slow transformation. Before, there had merely been a look of surprised curiosity fixed to the red-haired woman's overall features, but now a look of utter shrewdness was growing in her eyes. Indeed, burning beneath that freckled pale skin was something alive, something livid with both cunning and lust.

"Now that the boys are out at play"—Spades turned to Ava— "looks like you decided to have some fun of your own."

Ava could feel her face flushing with red. Fear crept into her gut and stayed.

"I came in to have you tend to my bandage, perhaps teach you more sword craft," Spades said. "But I see you have discovered something far more interesting for us to do."

Spades was close enough, and the candlelight bright enough, that Ava could study the details of the woman's eyes for the first time ever. She had deep green irises peppered with a spray of bold gray flecks. As Ava gazed into those two strange orbs, the syrupy gray darkness of those irises struck even more terror in her heart, folded around her and pressed in. For she recognized what she saw in Spades' hard gaze, and it terrified her.

*Does everyone need look at me this way?*

The red-haired woman gently set the stones back onto the rug and unwrapped the bloody bandage from around her arm. She leaned close to Ava, very close. A whisper, barely audible, touched Ava's ears. "Heal me as you healed the Spider." Then Spades' lips brushed her cheek, soft and sensual.

Ava drew back. Her mind was naught but turmoil, for she knew that every word and touch had a cryptic double meaning with these monsters from Sør Sevier. She shuddered as Spades' hand was suddenly cupping her breast over her silken shift. Ava's throat went tight. A soft cry escaped her lips, the hand on her flesh naught but a tepid reminder of all the depravities Aeros had heaped upon her. *Is everyone out to defile me, to destroy me?*

She clenched her eyes tight as Spades drew soft fingers up the side of her neck, the back of her hand tracing the outline of her lips. *Think of home. Think of love.* But it was all so futile. *The Grayken Spear Inn. Her first night with Jenko. Some joke. All of it a joke. Pointless nostalgia. A sentimental journey, right?* As a young girl, life had been good to Ava, filled with inno-cence and wonder and normality. Before her father had died. And then her mother. Then came Aeros Raijael and nothing but pain.

*But Spades' touch was gentle. . . .*

Who was she kidding? *They are all monsters!*

Fact was, the world she'd known before was old and laughable, a world so insignificant it could have been rolled up into the world's smallest scroll and lit afire and smoked during the Mourning Moon Feast.

And that feast had been the last night of happiness she'd ever had.

*It's a pretty pickle you're in now, Ava Shay, spending your days trapped in some tent or covered wagon with nothing to look forward to but the next mysterious conversation with a red-eyed Bloodwood, or doing nothing but awaiting the next fleeting distraction of being fondled and groped and raped by some blond prince with black-pupiled eyes, or a warrior woman who gave you a ruby-hilted sword. . . .*

Ava's soul was nothingness—an empty place only Laijon could fill. Writhing. Violent. Hopeless. *You're lost and now you need to find yourself. Face it. There's no hope to come from Jenko Bruk. And Gault isn't coming back for you. Mancellor Allen won't do anything. You are only pro-jecting your wants onto him. The Spider betrays, he only pretends. They all only pretend. Even Enna Spades. Truth is, there is nobody. Nothing.*

Spades' voice was soft, throaty. "I can teach you more than sword fighting."

Ava opened her eyes and looked into those cool green orbs of her new tormentor. *Cry me a river,* the Sør Sevier woman's eyes seemed to say. *I've had worse done to me.* Besides, Ava knew, an ocean of tears wouldn't make any difference now.

And truth be told, the woman's touch was a comfort. . . .

"You can teach me what you like," Ava whispered, still staring into Spades' eyes, not even believing what she was saying. "But real-ize, Aeros will betray you too, just as he betrayed Gault Aulbrek."

"Truly?"

"The Spider and Aeros, together they conspired to kill Gault in Ravenker, and now Gault is gone. If you and I grow close, Aeros will kill you too."

The woman's gaze narrowed. "They betrayed Gault? How do you know this?"

"Aeros and Spiderwood talk freely in front of me. They plot their plots and then people do their bidding and none are the wiser—"

There was a sharp metallic sound behind them.

Startled again, Ava whirled. Aeros Raijael stood in the canvas entryway, the fine-hewn chain mail under his plate armor aglitter with a million sparkles in the candlelight. Tufts of sweaty blond hair were plastered to his forehead, and his war helm rested in the crook of his right arm.

He smiled, his dark-pupiled eyes beaming with both affection and delight at the sight of Spades and Ava kneeling together on the rug. But when his gaze found the open chest and the horned helm and two angel stones, his smile swiftly disappeared.

"I was going to have her tend to my wound." Spades stood, holding her injured arm gingerly. "Like she tends to the Spider."

"Leave us," the White Prince ordered Spades. His tone brooked no argument.

Spades gathered the ruby-hilted sword from off the rug and brushed by Aeros.

At the door of the tent, Spades turned back to Ava. "The Angel Prince gets broody when he's jealous." Then she disappeared between the tent flaps.

Aeros glared at Ava with blazing hatred. The gulf between them was a tangible force. It now seemed whatever affection he'd once had for her had retreated into the sooty darkness of his pupils. And it was in that cold look that Ava Shay knew her life would be over soon.

*On that great and last day, the enemies of Raijael will be gathered together under that great and last fire of Absolution, whispering of death among crow-picked bones.*
—THE BOOK OF THE BETRAYER

# CHAPTER TWENTY-SEVEN
# CRYSTALWOOD

### 9TH DAY OF THE ANGEL MOON, 999TH YEAR OF LAIJON
### ROKENWALDER, SØR SEVIER

King Aevrett Raijael's grand palace, Jö Reviens, was still. Quiet. Its myriad of dark corridors were just now coming alight with the faint break of dawn. And Krista was finally on the trail of something interesting. Something completely out of the ordinary and wholly unexpected.

And it came in the form of a familiar face—a face she had not expected to see ever again: Solvia Klingande.

Even amidst the opulence of Jö Reviens, the finery of Ser Aulmut Klingande's voluptuous young wife was hard to miss as she scurried down the sweeping spiral staircase leading to the parlor that emptied out into the rear palace gardens, thinking herself unseen. Solvia was bedecked in a glorious white-brocaded gown set with gleaming yellow gemstones, a web of silken lace bejeweled with sapphires woven into her fine blond hair.

Krista emerged silently from the closet she'd been sorting laundry in. She began to follow the woman, unconcerned that she herself was abandoning her job. She had been in Jö Reviens for a week, and in that time had learned nothing. Seen nothing. And grown more restless by the day. Living in the servant quarters was a bore. Her job as housemaid was a bore. Especially in her entry-level position under Head Laundress Dame Portea, a pale-faced crone with a surly mean streak that could rival Bogg's bulldog, Café Colza.

In fact, Krista was at the point where she was certain that her task of spying on King Aevrett was all just another odd trial in a string of odd trials Black Dugal had strung together merely to test her patience. In the week she had been in Jö Reviens, King Aevrett had done naught but lounge about the palace daily. After his morning breakfast, he would rouse himself only occasionally to mete out some kingly bit of business, or to dote on his wife, Queen Natalia, who to this day he still treated like a precious jewel. And that was it. Every day. All the time. Without ceasing.

The only good thing about her time in the king's palace was that she enjoyed being away from Hans Rake. She was glad to be working alone on this assignment, and working in a place familiar to her. For Jö Reviens and everything about it was exactly as she had remembered before joining Black Dugal's Caste. The chamberlains were the same, the stewards, pages, squires, housemaids, watch commanders, all of them were mostly the same faces she knew from before. Truth be told, there were a few new faces sprinkled in, and those were the ones she'd befriended first, worried she might be recognized by the others if she got too close.

But Krista was mighty pleased with her disguise. She wore the simple raiment of a housemaid, white skirt and shirt under a tan linen smock, room enough in the pleated folds to hide six Bloodwood daggers. She'd dyed her brows, eyelashes, and hair black, and kept her hair unbound, wild bangs a-tangle, covering her eyes. She'd colored her teeth rust yellow and kept hurion tac paste stuffed in her cheeks and gums to make her jowls appear fatter. With a mouth full of the tac paste, her speech was slightly slurred. But that only added to the disguise, made her seem simpleminded whenever she talked. She had easily fooled Dame Portea during the interview for the job, a job that had come open because of the convenient disappearance of several laundry girls a moon ago. A fortuitous coincidence. But Krista knew that with Dugal there were no such things as coincidence. And now here she was. She did not look like Krista Aulbrek. Aevrett and Natalia and the rest of the palace court would remember the old Krista as a rail-thin, long-haired, ponytailed blonde with an articulate manner. Plus, they would remember the old Krista as five years younger and a few inches shorter.

So to be following Solvia Klingande was most definitely a welcome change in routine. The woman, still not aware that she was being tailed, reached the end of the staircase, scampered through the dark parlor, and slipped out the large wooden door and into the rear gardens, closing the door behind her.

Krista hurried after. Through the parlor window she could see Solvia dashing lightly over the grass, heading east toward the tall square castle shrouded in morning fog, bare feet leaving a trail in the dew. Krista stepped softly from the palace and followed. The air on the ground of the vast garden was crisp with a light mist, and the moon and stars above had melted into the light of dawn. Solvia disappeared into one of the many openings in the hedgerows, still heading east. Krista let her eyes stray over the gardens, noticing nothing out of the ordinary, seeing no one. Comfortable that both she and Solvia were unseen by prying eyes, Krista took to the chase.

She recalled her previous interaction with the nineteen-year-old wife of the Rokenwalder nobleman Ser Aulmut Klingande. With Hans Rake, she had broken into Aulmut's manor house, stabbed the young woman just above the heart as she'd slept, and left a cryptic note on her dresser. The note had read:

> *The hole above your heart will speak to the danger you are now in. Return all the coin your husband stole. All of it. To every innocent he conned. You have three days. If you do not, we will carve your beating heart from your chest in front of your waking eyes. You cannot hide from us. The blade with this note is evidence of who your new masters are.*
>
> *We will deal with your husband however we deem appropriate.*

After, Krista and Hans had stolen through the decadent house, located Ser Aulmut in his chamber, and assassinated both him and his guards in spectacular fashion. Later, with Bogg and Squateye, they had found Ser Aulmut's corpse strung up in the trees north of Rokenwalder, his guts strewn about the forest. It was that twist in the story that had seemingly prompted Black Dugal to order her to spy on King Aevrett. Now she was chasing Solvia Klingande through the gardens of King Aevrett's palace grounds.

Jö Reviens was on a large estate in the center of Rokenwalder, nestled in the midst of a grand lush yard, the entire grounds surrounded by a stone wall stretching more than five miles in circumference. Rokenwalder Castle stood at the far eastern end of the gardens. A square, brutish-looking fortification, it rose up at least thirty stories high. Broad stone walls and a deep moat of dark waters carpeted with bright green lily pads surrounded it.

King Aevrett's throne room was in the castle, as was the library containing *The Chivalric Illuminations*. Nobody but Aevrett or his five Knights Chivalric was allowed to look upon the original copy of the *Illuminations* or add to it. Copies of *Illumination* passages were distributed throughout Aeros' armies, though. The throne and library were all the castle was ever used for. That and the sprawling dungeons of Rokenwalder buried in the caverns deep underneath—a never-ending black maze of death and despair that stretched underground seemingly forever in dingy dark splendor. As Krista followed Solvia's path through the hedgerows, just knowing those dungeons were somewhere under her feet made her shudder. She hated prisons and confinement.

It was why she also hated Jö Reviens, for it represented a period in her life where she was a prisoner. A captive. A slave. Under the constant torment of the queen. Jö Reviens was the place Gault had left her, the loneliest place in all the Five Isles.

Through a break in the greenery, Krista spied the gleaming armor and white cape of one of King Aevrett's five Knights Chivalric, and her heart slowly turned to ice. The knight was fully armed, silvery coned helm atop his head. He had his back to her. Krista ducked behind a shrub, heart jumping. For a Knight Chivalric to be in the gardens meant only one thing—King Aevrett was on his morning walk. If the king was out here, then so too were all five of his bodyguards. In the five years she'd lived in Jö Reviens, she'd come to know the names and faces of all Aevrett's five Knights Chivalric, for they watched her constantly. She wondered if the knight before her was a man she would recognize, or if any of the king's bodyguards had changed in the interim. The Knights Chivalric guarded King Aevrett, whilst the Knights Archaic guarded the Angel Prince, Aeros. Krista's father, Gault, had been a Knight Archaic—a ranking just under Knight Chivalric—for almost as long as she could remember.

She heard muffled voices in the distance, but the knight remained rigid at his post. Krista crept slowly through the shrubbery toward the voices, acutely aware of the Knight Chivalric behind her. As a child she'd wanted to know all the ins and outs of Jö Reviens and the palace yards, all the nooks and crannies and shrubs where one could hide and play, all the secret passages and corners, all the trees that could be easily climbed and those few too dangerous. But she was never afforded such freedom. She wished she knew the palace grounds better now.

The voices were coming from near the castle and moat, so she headed in that general direction. As she slunk through the hedgerows and bushes, the voices became clearer. One was King Aevrett, the other female. Krista inched forward and peered around the last bit of green brush and flowers. Not thirty feet away, King Aevrett Raijael and Solvia Klingande were clutched in a tight embrace under the boughs of a large weeping willow tree, kissing with a passion Krista had never before seen in two people, the king's hand fervently kneading the woman's exposed bosom, her gown hanging low off her shoulder. Gray puddles of muted dawn shadow stained the ground under them.

Krista's own heart froze as she felt a hand grasp her shoulder. She spun around, dagger in hand, ready. But she pulled her blow.

"What a juicy scene you've discovered." Hans Rake's whispering voice was as cold as his red-veined eyes. He was dressed in full Bloodwood black leathers, blood dripping into the grass from the tip of the black dagger in one hand. Sweat pearled over the tattoos on the side of his head.

She glared at him, stunned, her mind awhirl. "What are you doing here?"

He pressed one leather-gloved finger to her lips. "Shhhh, we've work to do, my love." Then he grabbed her roughly by the back of her tan smock and hauled her out into plain view of King Aevrett and Solvia. The woman gasped and pulled her dress up over her breast, confusion scrawled on her face at the sight of the two intruders. Krista twisted away from Hans' grip, ready to dash into the shrubbery.

But the timbre of Aevrett's voice commanded her attention.

"What is the meaning of this?" he demanded. "My guard is on his way to kill you both now!"

"Oh, I don't think so," Hans said coolly, holding up the bloody black dagger. "Your nearest Knight Chivalric died as silent as you please."

Aevrett's black-pupiled eyes widened. "The other four are also nearby. They will hear me shout for them soon enough."

"Perhaps," Hans drawled. "But they are of scant concern, seeing how the first one died so easily."

"Dugal goes too far this time," Aevrett hissed, eyes now boring into Krista's. Confusion, then recognition, registered on his pale face. "Is that you, Krista?"

"Aye, 'tis our beloved Krista Aulbrek," Hans announced. "Come to murder her king."

Krista's eyes flew to Hans Rake, the black dagger gripped in her own hand suddenly angled toward him, fury building as she moved his way.

"I wouldn't," Hans said sharply, his own dagger pointed at her.

"Is it truly you, Krista?" Aevrett asked again.

Solvia gaped. "This is Avril's kid?"

*How could she know my mother's name?* Things were unraveling. Control was lost. And she needed to regain it.

"*This* is the bastard child of my husband?" Solvia continued. "This ugly handmaid is the little lost girl my husband has wept for every day? This ugly little whelp is the bastard child of Avril and Aulmut?"

"Natalia thought Krista was my child," Aevrett said. "It's why the queen treated the girl so horribly."

Solvia's eyes narrowed in anger. "This ugly little girl is the foul get of Avril and Aulmut," she repeated the accusation with a hiss.

Both confusion and dread twisted Krista's gut into a tight knot. She spat the hurion tac paste out of her mouth and strode toward Solvia. "What do you mean 'the foul get of Avril and Aulmut'?" The point of her dagger was now aimed straight between the woman's eyes. "What lie is this? Speak the truth or I will gut you where you stand, m'lady."

"Have a care, Krista," Aevrett said calmly. It looked as if he wanted to reach out and take the blade from her, but then hesitated, the realization of what she truly was—a Bloodwood, the deadliest creation in the Five Isles—sinking in. "Solvia is innocent in this."

"Innocent?" Krista pointed the dagger at him, terror building in her heart. "She was kissing you. I see nothing innocent in that. What about your wife, my king? What would the brooding Natalia say to that?"

"That is none of your concern," the king answered.

"What about the lie she just told of my mother?" Krista followed. Hans snickered. She glanced over at him. It looked as if he'd been devouring every word of the conversation in sheer amusement. Truth was, it was him she wanted to gut most.

"Put the knife down," Aevrett urged, eyes roaming the gardens. "Let's talk of this calmly for a moment." His gaze fell on Hans. "Else I can yell for my guards and the both of you can go to the dungeons."

"Do it." Hans' laughter rang out through the yard loud and sharp. He looked at Krista with cold amusement. "Dugal told you a Bloodwood must become fatherless, no?"

"Speak plainly," she snarled.

"Don't you get it yet?" Hans asked. "I already killed your father."

"My father fights with our Lord Aeros in Gul Kana." Fear and uncertainty clutched at her mind. "And you could not slay Gault with a million Bloodwood daggers."

"You have been deceived." Hans shrugged. "Ser Aulmut Klingande was your father."

"You're mad," she shot back, looking to Aevrett. But what she saw there in the king's dark orbs gave her pause. Especially when he dropped his own gaze. It was as if in his very silence he was acknowledging Hans' absurd proclamation.

She felt a moment of doubt. Then it happened. A reaction she could not stop. A reaction immediate and swift. She lunged toward the king, her dagger finding Aevrett's heart, plunging to the hilt. And as she withdrew the blade, the king looked upon her with a face that registered neither surprise or pain. Slick and warm, blood poured from the wound as he fell to his knees. Then Aevrett Raijael toppled face-forward into the dew-covered grass, dead. Krista stared at her bloody dagger. *What have I done?*

Angry at the foolish lie Hans had foisted upon her, she turned toward him. *This is not how it was supposed to be!*

Solvia Klingande screamed; a cry so shrill and high and loud it was sure to fill every corner of the palace yard. Hans seized Solvia from behind instantly, arms around her neck, his dagger gripped in one tight fist angled toward her heart. "Shut it," he hissed.

Krista could hear the shouts of men and the clanking of armor headed their way. She quickly shed her smock, bloody dagger at the ready. Hans backed away, dragging Solvia under the weeping willow tree toward the castle to the east. "Let me go!" the woman screamed, struggling in his arms. "You foul scum!"

"Don't fight him," Krista called out, her own dagger ready for Hans.

"Dirty urchin!" Still Solvia struggled against him. "Get your foul hands off me!"

"Stop shouting," Krista urged. This lady didn't realize that Hans was no brutish, slit-eyed thug from the gutters of Rokenwalder. He was slick and smooth, aware and lucid always. He carried in his blood some monstrous feral need for butchery and violence that she knew was about to manifest itself in spectacularly wicked fashion.

"Let me go!" Solvia screeched again. "You pox-ridden scum!"

With a quick pull of his knife, Hans sliced her stomach so wide her guts dropped from her fancy white gown to the grass, piling at her feet. Her stomach, lungs, liver, and all the rest followed, spilling down her legs as she toppled sideways, mouth agape.

Two sword-wielding Knights Chivalric burst around the hedge-row to Krista's right, another exploded from the bushes to her left. All three charged at once, white capes billowing behind them. Hans' bloody dagger spun through the air, catching the knight from the bushes in the shoulder, sinking deep between plates of gleaming armor. But the knight was not slowed. He swung his sword in a powerful sweeping arch straight at Hans. Krista's fellow Bloodwood ducked and rolled free and then sprinted from under the weeping willow toward the castle and moat to the east.

The two knights from the hedgerow came straight at Krista, long-swords gleaming dully in the mist. She let loose her dagger, striking the nearest knight in the dark hollowed eye slit of his coned-helm. He dropped like a stone in a heap of silver, sword flung wide, tripping the knight next to him. Krista wondered if she'd just killed a man she once knew as she fumbled in her skirts for her next dagger, fingers becoming tangled, unused to her awkward housemaid's garment.

The tripped knight scrambled to his feet just as the knight who had attacked Hans whirled and swung at her. She leaped straight into the air, catching the low-hanging branches of the willow tree, pulling herself up, swinging her legs high as the blade whistled just under her. She kicked the knight in the face as she swung back around, let go the branch, and dropped to the ground. The second knight immediately grabbed for her, catching hold of her shirt with a gauntleted hand. She swiped at him with a balled fist, knocking herself free of his clutch.

She took that instant of freedom to follow Hans' lead. She whirled and sprinted after her fellow Bloodwood. Hans was a good hundred paces in front of her, his legs churning as he dashed straight toward the tall castle and its dark moat.

And then the fifth Knight Chivalric came charging around the castle atop a brilliant white stallion. This knight was helmetless, blond hair flapping in the wind, heavy iron maul in one hand, reins of the stallion gripped in the other. Krista did not recognize this new knight. The powerful charger thundered toward Hans as he still raced toward the castle, his pace not slowing when he reached the edge of the moat and dove headfirst, disappearing under green lily pads and rippling water.

Having lost Hans, the knight on the horse drew rein before the pond, changed direction, and headed right at Krista, the stallion's heavy hooves pounding the wet, dew-covered turf like thunder. Krista could sense the pursuit of the two knights behind her and kept running toward the mounted knight, changing course only slightly, hands frantically grabbing for the daggers in the folds of her skirt, pulling two free. The unfamiliar blond knight on the magnificent white horse closed fast. Krista could now see it was a woman who bore down upon her, a female warrior with a grim, determined face and long arms stout enough to effortlessly wave the heavy iron maul before her one-handed.

They were on a collision course and Krista was at a loss, never having attempted to take down a fully armored and mounted Knight Chivalric before. She veered slightly to the left and threw the first dagger, aiming for the horse's neck, not knowing if it even struck home as she leaped in the air and whirled around, throwing the second dagger at the two knights chasing her afoot. Again, not knowing if her aim was true, she continued in her spin, whirling back around in midair. She stumbled in the grass, righted herself quickly, and regained her balance just in time to catch the heavy iron maul of the mounted knight square in the stomach. Pain blossomed throughout her body as the crushing weapon lifted her completely off her feet, instantly turning her world into a great black nothing.

*The Five Angel Stones are bound as One. Separate they are Nothing. Ruin has always surrounded them from the beginning. And the first to lay flesh upon the stones, be they not the blood of one of the five Warrior Angels, is bound unto death, separated into Nothing.*
—THE MOON SCROLLS OF MIA

## CHAPTER TWENTY-EIGHT

# JONDRALYN BRONACHELL

9TH DAY OF THE ANGEL MOON, 999TH YEAR OF LAIJON

AMADON, GUL KANA

With the break of dawn came the lowest tides of the day. Squireck had rowed them at a brisk pace from the docks of Amadon around Mount Albion to this place no more than twenty feet from the craggy shore. Hawkwood threw out the anchor. They were all dressed in typical fishing cloaks, hoods thrown over their faces, to stave off the cold and also curious eyes. Their small white skiff now bobbed lively in the dark waters of Memory Bay just off the rocky shores of Mount Albion. The choppiness of the waves turned Jondralyn nauseous. She fancied herself a decent swimmer but had never been one for boats.

Gulls shrieked, floating in the chilled currents of air, flutters of white against the huge gray bulk of Amadon Castle looming above. Waves broke against the ragged cliffs of Albion to the north and south. There was a shallow cove against the mount near where they'd dropped anchor. A canvas-covered dingy beached on the rocks and pebbles was tied to an old wooden quay. A trail winding up the steep face of the mount was just visible through the rocks and boulders and cliffs.

Hawkwood had advised that they make their way to the Rooms of Sorrow when the cavern entrance was only ten feet below the surface at ebbing tide compared to twenty feet at high. A quick swim straight down, he alleged, was the tunnel they sought. And once in the tunnel there were handholds dug into the rock. They could easily pull themselves against the current of the stream and up into the Rooms of Sorrow and the hiding place of *Ethic Shroud*.

Ever since the king had granted Squireck his freedom fifteen days ago, the Prince of Saint Only had spent every moment with Jondralyn. And his constant presence was growing tiresome.

Squireck insisted on gathering the white angel stone and *Ethic Shroud* for himself. He professed it was his calling to wield the shield against Gault Aulbrek in the arena.

Hawkwood had argued vehemently against such a course of action, claiming that exposing such a holy relic too early would only invite trouble. Hawkwood's arguments only prompted Squireck to desire the angel stone and shield all the more. Jondralyn thought it presumptuous to use the shield in battle, and also dangerous. *But who am I to judge another's wants or desires?* Squireck had his own destiny to fulfill, a destiny that she was willing to support. She herself still felt a dogged determination to usurp Jovan somehow, to prove her worth. Squireck was only attempting the same.

And now here they were, bobbing on a boat in Memory Bay, about to swim down into the Rooms of Sorrow—a crazy notion if there ever was one.

*This could be the death of us all!*

Hawkwood and Squireck had removed their fishing cloaks and

stuffed them in the bottom of the skiff. They both wore leather breeches and simple cotton shirts, long knives tucked into their belts. In a small pouch at his waist, Hawkwood also carried flint and steel, along with a small vial of pine pitch for the torches he claimed to have left in the caverns below.

Fighting back the nausea caused by the rolling of the boat, Jondralyn shed her own cloak, handing it to Squireck, who stuffed it down with the others. She self-consciously adjusted the bandages tighter around her face and neck, a habit she couldn't seem to break ever since the dressing had been placed there by Val-Gianni. Her injuries were healing, but slowly, the stitches still holding her face together. She worried what this crazy journey underwater would do to her dressing. Both Hawkwood and Squireck had tried talking her out of joining them on this venture. But she would not be swayed. And they both knew her well enough not to force the issue. She was going with them.

Hawkwood tied a rope around his own waist, then helped Squireck, and then her. Once all the ropes were secure, Hawkwood stood before them and went over the plan once again. "Tied together, there is roughly a hundred-foot length of rope between each of us. I will dive into the water first. When I reach the Rooms of Sorrow, I will pull the rope tight between Squireck and me, tugging on it three times. That will be the signal that I have safely made it into the caverns underneath." He looked at Squireck. "When you dive in, kick your way straight down, ten feet at the most. You will find the opening in the cliff face below. The handholds are carved into the ceiling of the tunnel. Use those to pull yourself along. I used them when I returned *Ethic Shroud* the first time. About another ten feet, and then you will be in the chamber. For whatever reason, the current is weak. But it will be pitch-black. I will be pulling on the rope from my end, which should hasten your journey. If for some reason your rope gets stuck or tangled, use your knife and merely cut yourself free and make your way back to the surface of the bay. We've more rope in the boat. If I can tell you've cut the line, I will swim back out. We can make several attempts if need be."

Hawkwood turned to her next. "Once Squireck has made it into the Rooms of Sorrow with me, wait for three tugs on the rope. Then do exactly as I instructed Squireck. We will be pulling on the rope from our end, so your journey will be quick."

His gaze fell on Squireck again. "Are we ready?"

The apprehension on Squireck's face mirrored that in her own heart.

Hawkwood stepped up carefully to the wooden bulwark and dove straight down into the water, rope unraveling behind him. Watching him vanish into the cold deep, Jondralyn's heart lurched into her throat, the gravity of what they were attempting settling in fully.

"I hope the fool is not leading us to our deaths," Squireck said. "I do not trust him."

"He is no fool, nor has he any reason to lie," she said in retort. "I saw *Ethic Shroud* myself. It was real. I saw it. I *held* it, Squireck. And soon you will hold it too."

"It is all very suspicious, Jon. Look around you. Look at where we are, for Laijon's sake."

"We've no reason not to trust him."

Squireck's gaze was fixed on the rope slowly slithering down into the dark water. "I have every reason not to trust him."

It seemed an eternity they waited. But finally the rope pulled tight against Squireck's midriff, quickly followed by three tugs. Squireck's eyes met hers. And in his look, Jondralyn detected both astonishment and fear that he was to now supposed to follow Hawkwood into the depths of the sea. He swallowed deeply. "I think I'd rather face Shkill Gha in the arena again than jump into this water, Jon."

"Trust him, Squireck. He tugged on the rope thrice as promised. He is down there in the Rooms of Sorrow alive."

The Prince of Saint Only swallowed again, wary eyes fixed on the choppy waters of Memory Bay. It was as if he couldn't believe what he was about to do. Jondralyn herself couldn't believe they were about to do it.

Squireck stepped swiftly to the rail and dove headfirst into Memory Bay. As the skin of the choppy water closed over him, Jondralyn was now alone. Vulnerable. She watched the rope coil out of the boat and snake down into the sea. Her heart was beating so fast she almost couldn't contain it in her chest.

Standing in the rollicking skiff, watching Squireck's rope slowly crawl out over the sidewall, Jondralyn felt herself struggle for breath. Panic was setting in—a suffocating, all-consuming panic. It reminded her of when she was a young girl, continually contending with all of Jovan's cruel torments. And he still lorded over her. By forcing the arena bout between Squireck and Gault, he was again able to prove before everyone that his sister was still under his power, under Denarius' and the quorum of five's power, even lower than fools like Leif and Glade Chaparral. Her stomach twisted and churned with such force she thought she might vomit.

Then the rope suddenly tightened about Jondralyn's waist, almost pulling her over the wooden rail. Regaining her balance, she waited for the three tugs. When they came, she knew it was her turn to dive into the water and her heart froze. *I mustn't linger in fear.* She stepped to the sidewall of the boat, took two deep breaths, and jumped in feetfirst, protecting the bandages around her face with her arms.

The water closed in around her with an icy grip. Her head bobbed to the surface, and she took one quick look at Mount Albion rising above and ducked back under. Arms flailing, she spun in the water, reorienting herself downward. She kicked with frantic purpose. She felt the rope tighten around her waist. Soon Hawkwood and Squireck were pulling her faster than she could swim. She grabbed the rope with both hands. A dull ache immediately spread across her face as she quickly descended. She opened her eye. All she could see was a stiff growing darkness and churning bubbles and then total blackness.

She felt herself scrape against rock and braced herself with one hand, searching for the tunnel opening. But the two men at the other end of the rope were still pulling and she was swept up the passage and into the current. The left side of her body scraped the underside of the tunnel as she fought for purchase. She kicked, completely helpless, desperately trying to orient herself before the rope squeezed her right in half. Her face was on fire under the bandages. Her lungs burned for just the slightest breath. She felt one of the handholds carved into the rock above slide by, completely at the mercy of the current and the taut rope.

Suddenly the rock ceiling above was gone and she was breathing real air again. Her eye flew open, but all she saw was an overwhelming black nothingness. Hands were grabbing at her arms, and she was hauled from the water and dragged over a cold and unforgiving stone floor. She lay there gasping in the darkness for a moment.

Then, shivering, she stood. Her only thought was how furious was the pain stabbing through her entire face and head. The bandages were still there, soaked and wet and clinging tight to her skull.

"You made it." Squireck's muscular arms enveloped her in a tight embrace.

"Try not to move about too much," Hawkwood said, "until I get a torch lit."

Jondralyn couldn't move anyway, still caught in Squireck's clutch. She squirmed away from the Prince of Saint Only's grasp. "Everything hurts," she mumbled, kneeling, bandaged head in her hands, trying to battle the pain. "I can't even see."

"None of us can see." She felt Squireck's hand on her shoulder. He helped her stand again. The floor seemed to crunch under her feet. Shivering, she tried to gather her composure, wanting to scream out, fighting the pounding pain in her face.

There was a flicker of a spark to her right and the first torch was lit. Hawkwood handed it to her. The bright flame of the torch was a warm relief in the cold. She cast her gaze around the rough-hewn cavern. Fish bones littered the floor, and several black tunnels branched off into the darkness to her right. To her left was the river she had just swam up—or rather that she had just been dragged up. So fast were the rushing waters, she wondered how it had been so easy for the men to pull themselves up the handholds and into this cavern. Then she wondered why this cavern wasn't completely flooded so far under sea level. *This place is full of dark magic!* Her mind panicked at the mystery of it all. *Why aren't we all dead?*

Hawkwood held the second torch aloft, troubled eyes roaming the cave. "There's much evidence of merfolk in here." He glanced at the fish bones scattered at their feet. A third dark torch was lying there in the middle of the mess. "I imagine we're lucky any of the torches are left at all. If merfolk have been swimming up in here, those horrid scavengers will snatch anything." His eyes drifted back down to the fish bones on the floor, and the dark torch in the middle of them, worry creeping over his shadowed features. He looked up at her. "Follow me." He strode swiftly toward the nearest tunnel. "The altar is not far."

Guttering torch held before her, Jondralyn trudged after him. Squireck followed. Hawkwood led them around a sweeping bend. The passage widened, continuing straight and slightly up. It emptied them into a strange round room, walls beset with gems and crystals that blazed orange and yellow in the torchlight. Spiderwebs fluttered between carved columns that rose up in a spiral pattern into a dark, black nothing above. Stone coffins lined the floor of the circular room, most naught but rubble, pale bones spilling from holes in their sides. Jondralyn found herself still shivering. In fact, she couldn't control her shivering and almost dropped the torch she held.

The place was exactly how Hawkwood had described it previously.

Hawkwood moved to the center of the room, toward a cross-shaped altar capped with an altar stone that looked far too heavy for any one man to budge. Without hesitation, Squireck stepped toward the altar beside Hawkwood, placed both hands against the capstone, and pushed. The slab of stone slid easily aside and crashed to the floor like rumbling thunder. He gazed down into the altar, then looked at both Jondralyn and Hawkwood, his face a stiff mask of anger.

Hawkwood looked into the altar too, horror and confusion spreading over his features. Jondralyn stepped cautiously toward the altar and held her torch over the rim, looking down inside. There was no shield. No *Ethic Shroud*.

All she saw were two dark cutlasslike swords lying at the bottom of the altar, their familiar spiked hilt-guards black against the stone. "They're your swords," she blurted, looking up at Hawkwood, stunned.

"How?" he muttered. "But Leif gave them to . . ."

"What does it mean?" Squireck asked. "The swords?" His eyes, angry, pointed and accusing, were bouncing between Hawkwood and Jondralyn. "Whose are they really?"

"Mine," Hawkwood said. "But Leif Chaparral stole them from me, gave them to his younger brother."

"Where is *Ethic Shroud*?" Jondralyn felt fear creep into her voice. "Where is it, Hawkwood?"

"Gone," Hawkwood muttered, staring down into the altar again. Jondralyn had never seen him look so stricken. So afraid. So vulnerable. So utterly worried. The chamber was silent, truly a room full of sorrow from the look now on the Sør Sevier man's face.

Squireck's eyes narrowed to slits, cutting right through Hawkwood. "You've got nothing to say?"

"I left the shield here." Hawkwood looked up at Jondralyn first. "The shield and the angel stone. I returned them here, just like I promised."

"You are a traitor and a liar!" The timbre of Squireck's voice shook the very air. "To what purpose have you brought us here to this foul crypt?"

Jondralyn grabbed Squireck by the arm. Tried to turn him. "If he said he left them here, he left them here," she pleaded.

"No!" Squireck raged. "He is up to something."

"He is not, Squireck."

"The used torch." Hawkwood was looking right at her, his eyes seemingly trying to will her to believe him. "The torch had been used. Someone's been in here."

"Who?" Squireck snarled. "Glade Chaparral? He was the last seen with your swords, correct? Are you placing blame on that dunce?"

"Whoever took the torch took the shield," Hawkwood said, holding his own torch over the empty altar again, staring down at the two swords in the altar.

"The shield never was here," Squireck accused. "*Ethic Shroud.* You've never even seen it. Or the angel stone. You probably never saw *Forgetting Moon*, either. Or Ser Roderic's ward. Did you even truly meet Nail? Or did you murder them all? Where is Roguemoore? Culpa Barra? Godwyn? What treachery have you brought upon us, you traitor, *betrayer*?" Squireck spat the last word as if it was poison on his tongue.

"He has not murdered anyone," Jondralyn said. "Be reasonable."

"He is the Assassin, Jon. Can you not see his treachery? Are you so blinded by your own foolishness!"

"I saw *Forgetting Moon*." Hawkwood was still looking down into the altar, oblivious to their conversation. "As did Roguemoore. I left *Ethic Shroud* right here."

"Liar!" Squireck howled, and punched the back of Hawkwood's head, staggering him, sending the torch spinning away to the floor, where it kicked up a flare of sparks. Before Jondralyn could even shout in warning or the shower of sparks even had a chance to drift to the ground, Squireck struck again. He twisted Hawkwood's arm, kicked his feet out from under him, slammed his face into the hard stone of the cavern floor, and then planted his knee in the center of Hawkwood's back. With one fluid motion, Squireck whipped the long knife from his belt and held its razor tip a fraction of an inch over Hawkwood's upturned eye. "I should kill you here and now!"

"Get off him!" Jondralyn shouted, tossing the torch down, pulling at Squireck, but he was too heavy, too muscular and strong.

"You don't want to do this, Squireck," Hawkwood said calmly. Squireck twisted Hawkwood's arm further and jabbed his knee harder into his spine. Hawkwood's face strained in pain, turning red. He tried to blink away the tip of the dagger poised right at his eyeball. "You'll want to be wary once you let me up, Squireck," he said with real venom in his voice.

"You're in no position to do anything," Squireck said dryly.

"Let him up, Squireck," Jondralyn said calmly this time, calmly but forcefully. "This is getting us nowhere."

"Listen to me, traitor." Squireck pressed the knife closer to Hawkwood's eye. "You're now gonna make me a few promises." His voice was unyielding. "Do you understand?"

Hawkwood scrunched his face in the rock, trying to stave off the tip of the dagger.

"I said, do you understand?" Squireck's eyes glowed with an inner darkness as he flicked the blade over Hawkwood's cheek. A ribbon of blood welled up and mingled with the dirt caked on the Sør Sevier man's face. Squireck placed the tip of the dagger back at Hawkwood's eye, holding it rock steady. "A simple nod will do."

"Stop this." Jondralyn prepared to throw herself at Squireck again. She couldn't believe it had come to this—that Squireck's jealousy and distrust could have turned so ugly, so counterproductive to the Brethren of Mia's cause, a cause he'd fought for his whole life. "Let him up!" she screamed, wondering if she had time to snatch one of Hawkwood's abandoned swords out of the altar. *Could I stab him?*

"I order you to let him up, Squireck Van Hester! The princess of Amadon orders you!"

Squireck ignored her command. It was as if she did not exist, as if she never had existed. It was now only him and his rival. "Did you hear me?" Squireck demanded an answer. Hawkwood said nothing. Squireck sliced another faint line across his face.

Jondralyn's eyes fastened onto the blade in the Prince of Saint Only's hand. She knew Squireck would not let Hawkwood up alive. One of them would die here today in this dark, cold chamber of sorrow, and she could do nothing to stop it. Hawkwood was slowly recovering from the initial blow to his head, growing more lucid by the moment, and once he was ready to fight, Squireck would likely die.

"Stop this, Squireck," Jondralyn pleaded. She snatched up the torch again. She didn't want it to come to violence against Squireck, violence at her own hand. But she had to do something. She just wanted him to stop.

"Enough!" she shouted, holding the torch aloft. "You are acting like a disgrace! I will burn you!"

Squireck looked up at her, startled, hurt. In fact, the unfathomable pain in his eyes left her stunned. He looked like he had just truly suffered the greatest betrayal yet.

"I will do it," she said, inching closer to him, torch thrust out, not willing to give up. "I will burn you, Squireck."

"Don't dirty your hands," Hawkwood said to her coolly, his body now relaxed under Squireck. "I will kill him before either of you can move."

"You forgot my rules, fool." Squireck ran the blade across Hawkwood's neck this time, a cut, but not deep. Yet enough of a threat to send Jondralyn's heart to jumping, arm quivering with fright, torch shaking in her hand. A trickle of blood oozed from the wound on Hawkwood's face, dripped to the ground.

"You are about to die, Squireck," Hawkwood hissed.

"No more talking from you, traitor," Squireck growled. "I don't want you to go near Jondralyn. I don't want you talking to her. I don't want you in her chamber. I don't want you in the secret ways of the castle, stalking her. And if I ever hear that you have broken these rules, I will come at you from behind, just like today, just like now, when you least expect it. I will kill you."

With one fluid motion, Squireck whipped his dagger up and around and planted it back into his belt. "I am only letting you live for Jondralyn's sake. For the Brethren of Mia's sake." He spoke in a low and subtle tone, aiming his words right at Hawkwood. "Remember, I am the Gladiator. I have triumphed against better men than you, against better *beasts* than you. It'll take more than your flimsy Bloodwood daggers and spiked swords to kill me. Much. Much. More." And with that he lifted his knee off Hawkwood's back, stood, and took three steps back. Both men stared at each other, Hawkwood lying flat on his stomach on the stone floor of the chamber, Squireck looming over him, tall and muscular and menacing.

And Hawkwood struck like lightning.

He moved so fast Jondralyn didn't even see him leap to his feet, snatch up one of his own swords from the bottom of the altar, and slash. His swift strike sliced a shallow furrow in Squireck's shoulder, a strike meant to kill. The Prince of Saint Only barely managed to stumble back far enough to avoid the full effect of the blow. Hawkwood spun and kicked the bigger man square in the chest, sending Squireck flailing against the empty altar.

"Stop!" Jondralyn yelled, and thrust the torch and herself between the two men before Hawkwood's next slash struck home. He pulled the blow naught but an inch from her bandaged forehead. His eyes met her own, startled, distracted.

Squireck swept her aside and punched Hawkwood in the face. But Hawkwood swung an arm up just in time, barely deflecting the large fist, which still caught him in the temple and sent him reeling back, sword spinning from his hand to clatter into the dark recesses of the chamber. With a shout, the Prince of Saint Only lunged at the stunned Sør Sevier man.

Jondralyn jumped in between the two men again, but Squireck's muscular bulk knocked the torch from her grip and the breath from her lungs, sending her crashing sideways into the altar. Her head struck solid stone as she fell, tearing the bandages from her head. Excruciating pain blossomed in her face. She slumped to the floor, both hands instinctively covering the wound, the stitches now torn free, flesh opened anew.

Jondralyn sensed her entire body going into shock. Her trembling fingers felt the gaping wound and the raw wet flaps of skin hanging from her stinging face. "No!" she cried out. "No!" It was like a million needles were pricking her head, scalp, face, her brain, poking, jabbing. Where her one eye used to live was naught but a stinging cavern in her skull.

Both men were staring at her.

Concern and fear were etched on Hawkwood's face.

But the look on Squireck's face was one of utter revulsion. He stumbled away from her and snatched up the torch she had dropped. He cast one last horrified look at her, then dashed out of the chamber and down the dark corridor.

† † † † †

The skiff was still awaiting them, bobbing in the swollen waves exactly where they had left it at anchor in Memory Bay. Jondralyn and Hawkwood swam to it. He had his two swords back, tied to his belt.

With some effort in the crush of the waves, Hawkwood climbed aboard the boat first and then helped pull her in next. Once secure and seated, Jondralyn checked the state of her bandages. Hawkwood had wrapped them tightly about her head again in the Rooms of

Sorrow. And they had fortunately remained in place on their return journey. Neither had much to say as Hawkwood placed the heavy cloak about her shoulders.

Both of them had let the truth sink in. The worst had happened.

Both *Ethic Shroud* and the white angel stone were gone. Lost to them. Stolen. Taken. But by whom? *Glade Chaparral?* It hardly seemed possible.

*We have failed.* Before Jondralyn threw the cowl of her cloak up over her head, she let her eye roam over the nearby craggy slope and gray cliffs of Mount Albion and Amadon Castle one last time. *There are no answers up there.*

Despair and pain engulfed her as angry waves broke against the rocks nearby, foaming and thunderous. The little inlet nearby was empty.

And Squireck Van Hester was nowhere to be found.

*Strip faith from the most faithful, belief from the heartiest believer, and what are you left with? The angriest and most dangerous of enemies.*
—THE ANGEL STONE CODEX

## CHAPTER TWENTY-NINE
# LINDHOLF LE GRAVEN
### 9TH DAY OF THE ANGEL MOON, 999TH YEAR OF LAIJON
#### AMADON, GUL KANA

Lindholf let the door swing shut behind him. The light of midafternoon was swallowed by the darkness of the Filthy Horse Saloon, and the sour odor of the dingy place hit him like a punch straight to the nostrils. *Stewed pork gone rancid? An open latrine?* He pulled the hood of the heavy cloak farther over his head and stepped cautiously into the smoke-filled room. His eyes adjusted to the dimness. Harpoons, ship wheels, anchors, nets, and other such fishing accoutrements decorated the grim wall to his right; liquor bottles lined the shelves behind the stained bar to his left. An unswept floor strewn with random tables and chairs and brick hearths and iron kettles receded off into dark reaches, all under a roof fashioned of low-hung beams of heavy timber.

About a half-dozen sailors hunched over drinks at various tables.

Only a few of the patrons seemed to look up at his entrance. *All ripe for a pickpocket!* But Lindholf knew he was not up to attempting anything so foolish here, specially without Val-Draekin or Seita as backup, or a pinch of Shroud of the Vallè for confidence.

He had ventured into this dung-hole previously with Glade and Tala. Nothing in the place had changed much. One serving wench stood behind the bar. A stick-thin gal, pasty-faced and black-haired, with dark rouge smothering both cheeks. No Delia in sight. He wondered if he should just turn around and leave. But it had been seven days since he'd last tasted the powder, and his craving for Shroud of the Vallè had a total and complete hold on him now. His ache for it had become so overwhelming he thought his body would just plain shut down if he didn't soon taste it.

*Should I approach the girl behind the counter?* He cursed his own hesitancy in everything. *If I show the wreath, would it truly be enough to summon Delia?*

The wreath of heather Delia had given him was under his cloak. *Ethic Shroud* was in the large burlap sack in his hands. And the white angel stone was wrapped in black silk in his pants pocket. He had never touched the angel stone. For some reason his utter reverence for the ancient gem would not allow it.

The journey from the castle had been uneventful. Once again, unnoticed as always, he had just walked out the front gates, bulky sack slung over his shoulder, black dagger at his belt. He'd hitched another ride on an oxcart, this one driven by a wool merchant he readily recognized, who was in and out of Amadon Castle daily. The merchant had asked him no questions, dumping him off about ten blocks from the Filthy Horse. He'd walked the rest of the way. And as he'd trekked through the grungy dock district, an idea had come to him. *If I were to bring Delia back to Amadon Castle, I would be hailed as a hero for finding the one accused of trying to assassinate King Jovan.* But the notion seemed to dissipate quickly with each new ache for the

Shroud of the Vallè that surged through him. Perhaps after a sniff of the powder he could summon some bravery.

Lindholf took the wreath of heather from his cloak and placed it on the bar in front of the skinny, pale serving wench, saying simply, "Delia."

Without even a glance at him, the girl swiftly snatched the wreath from the counter and disappeared through two swinging doors behind the bar.

Lindholf waited, itching with impatience, his want for the white powder nearly driving him mad.

† † † †

It was more than an hour before Delia emerged out of the saloon's darkness behind him. She wore hard leather boots and leather pantaloons the color of tanned hide and a short black shirt that didn't quite cover her belly button.

"I've longed to see you, my dear." She took him by the hand and led him on a winding path through the tables and chairs to the very rear of the dim-lit saloon, the burlap sack hoisted over his shoulder. When they reached the back recesses of the saloon, Delia unlatched a hidden door in the corner and led him quickly down a separate corridor lit with small lanterns hanging from rusted hooks high on the walls.

The hallway was about thirty paces long and came to a T, branching to the left and to the right. Delia led him past only one open door, a bedridden old man under soily sheets in the room's center—he looked pale, gaunt, near death. She guided Lindholf down the left passageway and through another wooden door and out into a canopied courtyard, sunlight filtering through many cracks in the drooping cloth awnings. A stone basin about the size of a large bed sat smack in the center of the grassy yard, bright purple tulips surrounding its base. It was about three feet high and empty of water, its entire surface overrun with vines and ivy. Rough stone sculptures of naked women holding large bowls of fruit above their heads lined the high stone wall that surrounded the yard. Brass fountains gurgling clear waters were set in each corner of the nook. Delia led him to the stone basin.

"I see you brought what I asked for?" She turned to him, pressing her body to his, kissing him lightly on the cheek, wet tongue gently, briefly caressing his burn scars before she backed away. "At least I do hope it is a shield in that sack slung over your shoulder."

The freckles on her face literally glowed in the golden light of the courtyard. *And those dimples when she smiles!* He so desperately wanted Shroud of the Vallè. His heart pounded as he unslung the sack from over his shoulder and leaned it against the ivy-covered basin. He untied the string cinching the sack closed and let the cloth fall away. *Ethic Shroud* was revealed to Delia in all its tremendous white glory. A shaft of sunlight gleamed off the very top corner of the shield, nearly blinding him. He brought up his hand to deflect the light.

"And the stone?" Delia asked as Lindholf reached into his pants pocket and pulled forth the black silk. He carefully unfolded it, unveiling the small white stone to the barmaid. It sparkled in the sun more than *Ethic Shroud*, almost dancing with inner light.

"It's more glorious than she said it would be," Delia muttered, reaching out to touch it. But then she stopped herself, fingers hovering just above its twinkling surface. She jerked her hand away. "Wrap it back up," she ordered.

He folded the silk around it before stuffing it back in his pocket.

"Wrap the shield, too," she said. Lindholf pulled the burlap back up over *Ethic Shroud* and tied it closed. His every nerve ached for Shroud of the Vallè.

Delia clicked the toe of her leather boot against the side of the stone basin. There was a faint grinding noise from somewhere under-ground. Lindholf stepped back, the sack gripped in both hands as the stone basin, ivy clinging to it, slowly rose up at one end like the lid of a giant iron pot, revealing a set of stairs descending down into the pitch darkness of the space beneath.

"Follow me." Delia ducked under the basin and scampered down the stairs. "And bring the shield with you."

With the burlap sack in hand, Lindholf followed her down the staircase and into the blackness. Delia lit a candle and guided him past a series of gears and chains and pulleys, through a succession of bare underground passageways, and into a dank room. A tall and plain-looking wooden cabinet with double doors stood against the far wall.

"Is this where you keep the Shroud of the Vallè?" he asked, heart atremble with anticipation.

She unlatched the doors to the cabinet and opened them wide. "Of course not."

The cabinet was empty, but deep enough for several full-grown men to hide within. Tala's red-spiked helm sat on the floor of the cabinet. Lindholf took a hesitant step back. *Bloody rotted angels! She could have henchmen down here waiting to kill you and nobody would ever know where you disappeared off to.* He still had the black dagger at his belt but was only slightly reassured by its presence.

Delia held the doors of the cabinet open wide. "This is the best place to keep the shield and stone safe."

"You want me to leave them down here?" he asked, utterly per-plexed. He straightened his posture, tried to regain some small sem-blance of composure. "I don't think that's such a good idea."

"You want more of the powder, right?" Her large eyes smoldered in the candlelight, fixed on the burlap sack in his hands. Lindholf felt his brow furrow as he glanced at the empty cabinet. His mind was tormented. The white powder was the reason he was here. He stepped forward with caution and carefully placed the shield in the cabinet. He took the angel stone from his pocket. He kept it wrapped in the black silk as he set it next to the shield. Delia closed the cabinet doors and latched them tight.

"Now that wasn't so hard, was it?" she asked. Candle in one hand, her other hand in his, she led him back through the damp tunnels and up the stairs and into the light of the courtyard. With just the slightest nudge of her toe against its base, the stone basin swung downward and closed over the hole. Covered with grass and ivy and flowers as it was, nobody would ever know what secrets lay below.

Delia escorted Lindholf back into the rear corridor of the saloon and through a separate door into what looked like her own private bedchamber. The room was small, dim, and just big enough for a bed and small cabinet. The room soon glowed with yellow light. Lindholf's hungry eyes scanned the tiny chamber for any sign of the white powder.

"Remove your cloak," she said, voice silky. "Relax, my love."

He was instantly wary. Her demeanor had suddenly changed from businesslike to flirtatious. Still he took his cloak off, folded it carefully, and set it on a small stool near the cabinet. She noticed the black dagger tucked in his belt. "You won't be needing that, my love. Take it off and set it on the stool with your cloak."

"Why do you keep calling me your love?" His hand went to the hilt of the weapon. "You said you've been following me."

"We can talk about that in a bit," she said, eyes aimed right at his dagger. "The knife scares me. You don't need it."

"I don't want it to get stolen. It should stay on my belt."

"You needn't defend yourself against me. Put the dagger on the stool next to your cloak, my love."

"And you'll give me Shroud of the Vallè?"

She nodded coyly.

Lindholf quickly did as instructed and removed the dagger, placing it on the cloak gently.

She grabbed his hand and plopped down on the bed, pulling him down next to her. It felt awkward lying there with his leather boots on. The bedcovering was fluffy and soft and dark blue. "What do you know of the Vallè?" she asked.

"You mean Shroud of the Vallè?"

"No, silly," she giggled. "Is that all you can think about? I mean, what do you think of actual Vallè? Specifically the one who teaches you how to be a pickpocket. I would not trust him, were I you. He came into the saloon several days before you and Princess Tala and Glade came in. Princess Jondralyn and a dwarf saved his life. Another man helped too. I think his name was Hawkwood. Tell me what you know of this Vallè, and the Vallè maiden he is always with."

"Val-Draekin?"

"Yes, Val-Draekin." Her hand shot to his arm, grasping it tight. "I served him pastry at the Mourning Moon Feast. What do you know of him and the blond Vallè maiden he is always with? She too seems untrustworthy, my love."

"Why do you keep calling me that?" he asked again, irritated, wondering what she was after. He didn't want a million questions. He wanted the drug he'd come for.

"Why do you act so shy?" she asked.

He felt his brow furrow. "Did you really try and kill Jovan?"

She shifted on the bed next to him. He caught a glimpse of pale cleavage at the neckline of her shirt. She saw where his eyes had roamed and leaned into him, exposing more flesh, the look in her eyes sultry. She placed her hand on his chest. "So you wonder if I fancy you?"

His mouth was suddenly dry, like it was full of cotton. "The other day in the street, you said someone told you I was 'the thief,' and that I would be the 'bearer of the white shield.' You said you've dreamed of me ever since. What did you mean?"

"I was told to say all that, especially about the thief stuff," she answered, stroking his chest still, fingers delicate. "As for the other part, it's well known, tell a boy you dream of him and he will surely fall for you." She shrugged playfully. "And I know how to get what I want."

*It was a bad idea asking her questions.* His eyes darted around the room in frustration. "Do you have any Shroud of the Vallè or not?"

Her hand drifted from his chest to his arm, fingers crawling up the sleeve of his shirt. Her brow crinkled. "What's this?" She rolled the sleeve all the way up, revealing the scars there. He squirmed as she caressed the wounds, and he recalled the hideous face of the grotesque mermaid who had raked his arm and nearly drowned him in Memory Bay.

"Please don't." He brushed her hand away, remembering the horror of the mermaid and the visions he had seen under the water. He rolled down his shirtsleeve, suspicious why one so fetching as Delia would be with him. He grew instantly self-conscious about his face and the deformities he knew were there. Deformities that would always and forever be there. He was no one's "love."

"You haven't answered any of my questions," he stated, tone set with resolve.

"Nor have you answered any of mine." There was a touch of sadness in her eyes now. The back of her fingers gently stroked his face. He pulled away. She looked hurt. "Why do you recoil from me?" Her fingers were again tender on his face, brushing lightly against his scars. "I do see you in my dreams, Lindholf Le Graven. I see you nightly. I cannot escape you. I knew you before we met." Her face was so near his now. "I knew we would become lovers."

"*Lovers?*" His own face burned with embarrassment, shame, lust— all three and more. She was so pretty. Her breasts large and shapely and right there, inches away, her full lips so lush, and the blush of her cheeks so captivating. "It's not right for a nobleman's son to be with a commoner." He tried to stand, but she clutched his shirt tight, holding him still.

"I was good enough for your king." Her face was drifting closer to his.

"But you tried to kill the king," he muttered, drowning in her wide and perfect eyes, glowing bright orbs that stared back at him with unabashed interest. "They threw you into Purgatory."

She kissed him lightly on the cheek, neck, brushed her tongue over his ear. A shiver lanced over his every nerve ending, spiraling down to drown in his racing heart.

"Do you desire to kiss me?" Her voice was a soft, sultry whisper. And then her lips were on him again, silky and divine, finding his mouth. He pressed his lips to hers, curled his hands around the back of her head, and pulled her close. She melted into his embrace and he could feel his whole body trembling, groin stirring to life. Surprised by the sudden sensations assailing him, he broke from her clutch.

"Did I do something wrong?" she asked, real concern in her voice.

"No—I mean—maybe," he stammered. "I mean it feels good and all. I—just don't—I guess—really know what I'm doing. I'm a nobleman's son. And you're—"

"Shhhhh." She pressed her fingers to his lips, quieting him. She stood and leaned over him, smothering him with her mouth again briefly before backing away. One side of her face was bathed in the soft glow from the nearby candles, the other side of her face a wash of cool in the shadows. The top lace of her woolen pantaloons was undone and they rode low on her hips—curvy hips so tantalizing and pale. "Touch me," she said. He reached out tentatively and traced the line of her hip with his hand. She closed her eyes and moaned deeply. He was fully hard now. Achingly hard.

"I fancy you so, my love, my dear Lindholf." She pulled her shirt over her head, exposing a glorious chest that heaved with each deep breath she took. Her breasts were the color of fine porcelain in the candlelight, not the splotchy, leathery wrecks he'd seen on the drooping bosoms that swayed below the stretched stomachs of the gap-toothed whores he had been forced to watch Glade, Tolz, Alain, and Boppard fuck.

She unstrung the last few laces on her pantaloons and pulled them down, kicking them across the floor. She was completely naked but for her white cotton bottoms.

"What are you doing?" Guilt flooded him. He was a lord's son. A prince. Above this type of debauchery. He was not brave and amorous and unfeeling like Glade. He was not a sexual risk taker and user of women like Glade. "I don't think this is such a good idea," he murmured. *I do not want to be like Glade Chaparral!*

"If you were smart," she said, "you'd shuck them boots off and skin them pants off, too." She pushed him gently back until he was lying flat on the plush blue bedcovering. She tugged at his belt, removed it, then began tugging at his pants next. He grabbed her hand, stopping her. "No."

*"Please,"* she whispered, pulling his pants all the way off over his boots, her eyes wide with admiration as she looked upon him in that private place no female had ever looked upon him before. "So ready you are," she said, straddling him, her thin cotton underclothes warm, delicate, the heat between her legs silky and smooth. She pressed down with her hips as she lavished him with kisses. He luxuriated in her soft touch as she moved ever so slowly, pressing her pelvis rhythmically into his. He matched her movements and she responded with a guttural moan. She then managed to squirm out of her thin white undergarment in the most pleasing way. Blood pulsed through every part of him as they were both totally naked now. He pressed his straining erection up against her tuft. It felt rough, scratchy, but in a pleasant way.

And the door to her room crashed open.

With a shriek, Delia leaped from the bed, stumbling backward into her cabinet.

Lindholf bolted upright as Glade Chaparral burst into the room, followed by Tolz, Alain, and Boppard, all four in full Silver Guard armor but for their helms, all brandishing longswords and grinning like madmen.

"Now here is one prime lassie, boys." Glade had the tip of his sword at the barmaid's throat in an instant. Delia shrank away, stumbling back onto the bed, right on top of Lindholf.

"Aye," Tolz said, grinning madly. "Look at them teats."

Lindholf wiggled from under the girl, feeling a fool with his boots still on and naught else. He covered his now flaccid groin with one hand and reached for his cloak on the stool with his other. The flat of Glade's sword struck him. It wasn't a hard blow, a mere warning, but Lindholf jerked his hand away in pain, a line of blood instantly seeping from the shallow wound, which stretched from the top of his middle finger to the top of his wrist. But the embarrassment of being so naked and so vulnerable had ahold of him, and he instinctively reached for his cloak a second time. The flat of Glade's sword smacked his hand again, harder this time, drawing another line of blood across the first.

Blood welled up thick and red over his hand in the shape of a cross.

"Tsk-tsk." Glade's smile was wide and filled with a mischievous, self-satisfied bravado. "You will both stay exactly as you are. Naked as the day you were born."

"See, Tolz." Boppard leaned against the doorway, "I told you he was here. Told you I hadn't lost him. Followed him from the castle gate right here. And you said I couldn't do it, couldn't track even the simplest of dolts through the streets of Amadon. Looks like you owe me six silvers."

"And a hand job from your mother," Alain laughed.

"Aye." Glade sheathed his sword. "You done good, Boppard." He removed his leather gloves. "All four of us will go down as the heroes who captured the villains who conspired to slay the king." He looked straight at Lindholf then. "The conspirators who murdered Ser Sterling Prentiss."

"What?" Lindholf exclaimed, swiping his bloody hand on Delia's blue bedcovering. "Are you mad?" he croaked, voice building to a rage. "It was you who killed Sterling—"

Glade slapped him hard across the face with one of his leather gloves. "Shut your bloody, rotted mouth! May the wraiths take you, spouting a filthy lie like that. Do you not realize who I am now? Who my brother is?"

"I know you are guilty!" Lindholf raged. "I saw yo—"

A second slap across the face with the glove. Glade snarled, "'Tis I who find you guilty of being a lying turncoat pitiful cunt!" He reached for the cloak on the stool, threw it at Lindholf. "Go ahead, put it on if you want, cover your pathetic pasty body lest I haul you through the streets and straight to Purgatory naked but for your bloody boots."

Lindholf, shaking with anger, wrapped the cloak around both himself and Delia. The black dagger fell from the folds of the cloak, landing on the blue bedcovering between him and Glade. Delia looked at the black-polished blade nervously.

Glade noticed it too. "I've seen that knife before." His shifty eyes then narrowed to slits under dark brows. "It's Tala's."

Lindholf tried to grab it. But Glade snatched it up first. "You and the girl used this knife to stab Jovan." He looked straight at Lindholf, holding the black blade up between them. "Used it to kill Prentiss. I see your scheming heart."

"You're crazy," Lindholf exclaimed.

"Don't lie to me," Glade growled. "You know it's futile." He nodded at the two knights behind him. Alain and Tolz stepped all the way into the room with purpose and took Lindholf by either arm, hauling him up from the bed, the cloak falling away.

He was naked again.

Still, the two men shoved him face-first against the wall and held him there whilst Boppard pulled a knife from his belt and placed it against his throat, saying, "One word from you and I slice your neck wide."

Lindholf wondered why Glade hadn't mentioned *Ethic Shroud* or the white angel stone yet. *If Boppard truly followed me here, clearly he saw me carrying the burlap sack. Could he know what was in it? Will the girl tell them?*

Then an even darker thought crossed his mind. *Has she set me up?*

Delia lelt out a terrified squeal.

Lindholf twisted his face away from Boppard's cold blade, twisted it painfully against the coarse wood of the wall until he could see Glade and the naked barmaid out of the corner of his eye. She was still on the bed, Glade standing over her.

"Princess Tala Bronachell's blade." Glade leaned over the girl, brandishing the black dagger. Delia sat atremble on the bed before him, goose bumps rising on her pale flesh. "Lindholf fancies his cousin, you know." Glade's ungloved fingers were now at the steel-studded leather bucklers covering his arms. "They whisper together in dark corners, Tala and Lindholf. Always conspiring, the two of them, like little lovers are wont to do." Glade unhooked the bucklers and tossed them aside. "You probably didn't know your pathetic little Lindholf likes to stick his little pecker inside his cousin. So sad, you probably didn't know you are not his first." Glade reached out and shoved the girl back onto the bed. "Imagine, a dough-faced dolt like him getting more prime pussy than me."

"Leave her be," Lindholf cried out. Boppard pressed the knife hard to his neck. Tolz and Alain tightened their grip on his arms.

Glade grinned at the three knights who had Lindholf pinned to the wall, his hands at the buckles of his plate armor next. "I tell ya, lassie, your face and tits and even your round little ass might come out of this mess in pretty good shape, if you play it right."

Glade unhooked his breastplate and shoulder plates and let them fall to the floor with a clatter. "In fact, if matters take a congenial turn with me and my pals here, when all is said and done, well, we can all maybe remain the best of friends for a good long time."

"No!" Tears of rage burned trails down Lindholf's cheeks. "Please, just leave her be!"

Glade tore off his shirt next. "What say you, lassie, you may just be able to avoid Purgatory if you play it right." And then Glade unhooked his belt and his pants dropped to the floor.

*Most know that Laijon was consumed with the magical properties of rock and*
*stone and precious metals, and he ascribed great powers to flowing rivers of silver.*
*And so knowing, before Fiery Absolution, some in Amadon will cry, "Where is*
*that silver throne with the five legs now? Why hath it been covered and hidden?*
*Why does our king not sit upon it in honor and triumph?"*
—THE WAY AND TRUTH OF LAIJON

# CHAPTER THIRTY

# NAIL

9TH DAY OF THE ANGEL MOON, 999TH YEAR OF LAIJON
SKY LOCHS, GUL KANA

Shrouded in silence, cloaked in darkness, the Company of Nine
peered down from their shadowy perch into the musty underground chamber. The group of ten oghuls loitering below
were joined by several more, all heavily armed and armored. The
newcomers entered from under the cavern's main stone archway in a
shuffling clatter, dragging a bloody-faced captive—an unlucky trapper wrapped in chains that glinted dully in the chamber's hearth fire.

The gray-bearded man was wearing a fox-fur hat and a scraggly
coat of muskrat. He cried out as four oghuls laid him on the rectan-
gular-shaped knee-high stone altar in the center of the chapel-like
vaulted cavern and began stripping off his chains. As the beasts tore
at the trapper's clothes, they let loose a cacophony of vile curses and
hoarse shouts that echoed deep off the vast chamber walls. A copper

cistern the size of a milk cow hung from three chains directly over the altar. It was full of some dark liquid Nail feared was blood.

Bishop Godwyn shook his head with grim determination. "We can't let them sacrifice this man in some gruesome Hragna'Ar ritual." His hushed voice was barely audible over the rattling armor and grim bellowing of the oghuls below.

"I count fourteen," Culpa Barra said. "The way is blocked, and it's only a matter of time before our hidden alcove up here is discovered. We need to reach that altar. Our path lies beneath it. But what can we do?" Culpa stared back down into the large room.

Nail peered between the stone railings of the balcony again. Under the copper cistern of blood, the trapper lay unmoving atop the altar, oghuls poking and prodding at his body with gnarled gray fingers. The chamber itself was shaped exactly like an underground chapel. It was scattered with an odd array of old wooden furniture and several crudely made couches covered in what looked like maroon velvet. Opposite the room's high arched entry, a huge deep hearth was set against the far wall, crackling fire blazing—the only source of light but for torches a few of the oghuls gripped in thick grubby hands. The columned walls behind the fireplace was draped with tattered tapestries of a dull hue. The floor consisted of a random patchwork of gray and brown stone blocks.

The Company of Nine crouched behind the thick stone railings of a balcony set back in a nave of sorts, two stories above the strange cavern. Fifty paces to their left, a wide stone staircase curved down to the chamber floor below. A dozen other deeply recessed balconies and gloomy alcoves similar to theirs lined the opposite wall of the chamber. In fact, most of the columned chamber was obscured in shadow and smoky darkness, the faint outline of a buttressed and arched ceiling was barely visible above, huge stone crossbeams as support.

"We've already wasted too much time," Godwyn said, his voice grave with frustration. "And we can't just let them kill that man."

"We'd be risking a lot to save one old trapper we don't even know," Roguemoore countered. "Nor do we know how many more oghuls might come pouring from under that entryway if we go storming down that staircase."

"We have to get under that altar," Culpa said softly. "We knew facing Hragna'Ar oghuls might be a risk from the beginning. We may have no choice but to kill them."

*Kill them?* Nail thought. *As if it would be that easy!* He turned from the dire scene below. Stefan was peering over his shoulder with fright-filled eyes. Liz Hen, Dokie, and Beer Mug were barely visible in the blackness not ten paces down the corridor, the gear and torches of the company piled against the wall just beyond the three. Beer Mug's ears were poised and aware.

Culpa, Roguemoore, Seita, and Val-Draekin knelt next to Nail, the two Vallè taking turns peering through the stone railings into the chamber. The faint yellow firelight emanating from below danced off their pale skin, illuminating the tips of their pointed ears just visible under the cowls of their cloaks.

"Six more oghuls just entered," Val-Draekin said, voice soft with concern.

"That makes twenty," Roguemoore grunted.

Nail looked for himself. The six new oghuls, all bearing large scythelike swords, marched up to the altar. Three filed to the right, three to the left. All six set their curved blades over the chest of the trapper and began chanting, *"Rogk Na Ark! Rogk Na Ark! Rogk Na Ark!"* in deep, rumbling voices echoing loudly off the chamber walls.

"They are going to sacrifice him." Roguemoore scooted closer to Culpa. The square sheets of his bulky armor scraped against the stone floor as he moved, the sound drowned out by the oghuls chanting below. The spiked mace strapped to his back loomed darkly over his head. His bearded face was etched with worry as he pulled forth his D'Nahk lè timestone. "We've been waiting here half a day almost."

To Nail, it seemed the company had been in the Sky Loch mines for weeks. The labyrinth of innumerable tunnels and caverns and caves was vast, at least twice the size of the Roahm Mines above Gallows Haven. They'd ventured down many dead ends to get to this spot, having backtracked at various intervals; Roguemoore always marked their trail with dots of white chalk as they went. Once the dwarf grumbled something about Shawcroft's satchel and how the lost instructions within it would have greatly sped their journey along. Nail felt pangs of both guilt and resentment, knowing that the dwarf likely blamed him.

There had been signs of oghuls all along the way, signs both new and ancient. Most every passageway, cavern, and moldy grotto they entered was littered with some sort of oghul bones and other foul oghul filth. In one gloomy cave, ancient bone tools and other such crude mining implements were scattered about in cold recesses in the walls. Also, the word *Viper* had been scratched into many of the walls. Most of the tools were curiously stamped with ancient dwarf carvings and runes, that or the intricate scrollwork designs of the Vallè. Upon Culpa's advisement, all in the company had not touched any of it. The Dayknight claimed anything could be rigged to drop crushing stones from the ceiling or launch darts or poisonous fumes from the walls.

Now here they were. Waiting.

The oghul chants from below slowly dwindled to a dull, rhythmic hum, then fell into silence. But for the crackling of the hearth fire and the occasional whimper of the fur trapper atop the altar, all was calm.

Then there was total silence.

And Liz Hen sneezed. A blaring snort that echoed through the chamber below like a clap of thunder. She clamped both hands over her mouth, eyes like twin ovals of stark-white fear glowing in the darkness.

A stunned stillness settled over the entire company.

Guttural shouts of dismay sounded from the chamber below followed by the unmistakable rasp of crude weapons being ripped free of rusted sheaths.

"They know we are up here." Val-Draekin turned from the scene below and nodded to Culpa, a grim look on his ashen face. "We've no choice but to fight now."

The Dayknight lurched to his feet and drew his sword with a crisp hiss of steel. Val-Draekin and Godwyn too. Roguemoore growled, pulling the mace from over his shoulder. Despite the chill of the passageway, Nail could feel the sweat building under his armor and clothes as he stood and pulled his own sword from its sheath, trying to muster what bravery he could, heart jumping under his ribs, his fear raw and primitive and all too real.

"Stay up here and fill as many of those bastards with arrows as you can." Culpa ordered Stefan. Fire as fast as you can." He shouted to Dokie, "You stay with Stefan, help him with the arrows!" The Dayknight's fierce eyes scanned the chamber below, then he charged toward the staircase and the oghuls waiting below, Roguemoore and Godwyn right on his heels.

Val-Draekin shoved Nail after the bishop. Seita ran with him. Beer Mug too. He sensed Liz Hen behind them. "Bloody fuck!" she shouted as she drew her own sword.

† † † † †

Even before Culpa, Roguemoore, and Godwyn reached the bottom of the curving staircase, Stefan's arrows were causing chaos. Oghuls shouted and ducked.

Roguemoore headed straight toward the altar and trapper. Culpa launched himself toward the entryway to the left, long sword flashing in the hearth light, cutting down the first oghul trying to escape under the archway. Godwyn was tight behind Culpa, and the two men were immediately swarmed over by four oghuls rushing to escape, two with Stefan's arrows lodged in their backs. The bishop tumbled to the floor under the weight of one of the charging beasts. Culpa's sword whirled with blood as he struck Godwyn's attacker in the face with a wet thud.

Nail emptied into the room at a sprint, losing sight of Culpa and the bishop as his own sword came up instinctively, blocking the downward strike from a heavy iron maul aimed at his head. The jarring collision of steel on iron sent him staggering forward into the back of Roguemoore, arms stinging from the impact of the oghul's blow. The dwarf barely broke stride, heading straight for the altar, spiked mace pulverizing the square-jawed face of one of the three oghuls still standing there. An arrow from above caught another oghul in the neck, spinning him around just as he took a swing at the dwarf with a rusted shortsword. The room was now a roaring, disordered symphony of screams and shouts and metal on metal, Beer Mug's fearsome barks a wild counterpoint to the overall din.

Seita leaped past Nail, ball-and-chain mace spinning from her hand into the darkness, striking an advancing oghul straight in the helmeted head, cracking his helm, dropping him cold. Daggers were suddenly in both the Vallè maiden's hands, and before Nail's mind could even register what was happening, she effortlessly slit the throat of the maul-wielding oghul who was taking another swing right at him. Seita moved on, leaping again; every move she made was elegantly deliberate, arms and daggers a vicious blur as she slashed the neck of another oghul and another and then leaped into the dark after more.

Nail stumbled forward in shock, moving to help Roguemoore. A thin-faced oghul clambered atop the altar, rusty dagger plowing a deep red furrow into the naked chest of the helpless trapper. With a roar, Roguemoore swung his spiked mace straight over his head in a powerful arch toward the murderous oghul. The thin-faced beast sidestepped the dwarf's blow and the heavy mace smashed into the side of the altar with a soul-shattering crash, spitting chunks and bits of stinging stone straight into Nail's face. He reeled away, swiping at the stringing grit.

The oghul cut loose one of the three chains holding the cistern in place. The huge copper basin tipped ponderously, spilling its foul contents over Roguemoore and the altar and the newly gutted trapper, both dwarf and oghul suddenly awash in a great torrent of thick dark blood.

Feet slipping in the red sludge, Nail whirled and crashed straight into the heavy gauntleted fist of a large barrel-chested oghul. The crushing blow sent him careening back across the floor in a daze. The giant oghul came at him again with a serrated broadsword, its bone handle nearly as long as the blade, clutched in his gauntleted fist. Nail jerked to his feet and set his feet instinctively, exactly as Shawcroft had taught him in the mines. *Swing the pickax just so,* he could hear his master as the oghul's gruesome longsword came swinging toward him. He stepped aside and blocked the creature's blow, and returned the attack with a thrust of his own. The tip of his sword caught the oghul right in the mouth, stabbing through gruesome yellow teeth. Blood bloomed thick and crimson down the giant's gnarled chin and neck. The oghul roared and swung the sword again in a backhanded arch that sizzled in the air. Nail parried swift and hard with his sword. But the oghul's serrated blade caught Nail's weapon just right, yanking it from his grip, sending it skittering to the floor where it disappeared under one of the velvet couches. The oghul swung again. Nail dove aside, launching himself toward the couch, outstretched hand reaching for his lost blade underneath.

The oghul took one giant step toward him, then dropped face-first to the floor right in front of Nail, dead. The crash of armor and striking stone as loud as a tall timber falling in the forest. The oghul's legs twitched as Seita stood over the him, bloody daggers whirling in both hands. She bounded away toward Val-Draekin and Liz Hen, who were engaged in battle with two oghuls near the staircase.

Nail snatched his sword from under the couch and lurched to his feet, glimpsing the faint forms of Stefan and Dokie perched on the balcony above. Stefan was braced against the stone balustrade, arrows flying from his bow in swift repetition, the deadly shafts knocking the thin-faced oghul from atop the altar. Roguemoore was on his hands and knees at the base of the altar, vomiting up a thick stream of puke, his entire body coated in dark dripping blood from the overturned cistern. There were no other oghuls near the dwarf.

Nail raced after Seita. One oghul already lay dead at Val-Draekin's feet, his own daggers flashing like lightning as he slashed at the other oghul before him. Liz Hen stabbed at the armored stomach of the other oghul, who swiped at her with a long blade of his own. Beer Mug tore at the back of his ankles and legs with wicked flashing teeth, instantly hobbling him. An arrow from above bounced off his helm and shoulder plate as he fell back. Seita launched herself straight into a third charging oghul, blades flashing, finishing him quick and mercilessly. The creature bellowed and fountained blood, arms thrashing as it spun to the floor, dead.

Culpa loosed a bloodcurdling yell from under the entryway. Nail whirled in time to see the Dayknight stumbling to the ground, tripping over three dead oghuls at his own feet. His panicked eyes were fixed on Godwyn. The bloody-faced bishop, sword clutched in both hands, was battling two ax-wielding beasts who were pressing the attack. The bulky monsters had the bishop backed against the wall.

There was a loud crash, like the slamming of a heavy iron door.

And the floor instantly dropped out from under Godwyn and the two oghuls, all three vanishing down into a gaping black nothingness. The surprised shout of the bishop and the raspy screams of the two oghuls were cut short, and the entire room was pitched into a sudden, deathly silence.

Nail's heart pounded. Everyone stood still, frozen in place.

All eyes were focused on the dark void in the floor where Godwyn had just vanished. Even the lone oghul left standing, gaped at the hollow cavity in the floor where Godwyn had disappeared.

Seita walked up and casually thrust one of her daggers straight into the oghul's wide eye. The beast toppled over backward with a clatter.

Liz Hen dropped to her knees, suddenly gasping for breath.

Val-Draekin knelt at her side. "Take three long breaths, hold it, and three more." Liz Hen sucked in a great gulp of air, her three struggling breaths the only sound left in the chamber.

"Godwyn!" Culpa Barra snatched one of the discarded oghul torches from the floor and rushed to the gaping hole where the bishop had disappeared.

Nail fought off his own trembling breathing and approached the hole, shaking legs carrying him nervously forward, frightened eyes gazing down into the pit once he stood beside Culpa Barra. Illuminated by the light of the Dayknight's torch, the hole was no more than ten feet deep, the bottom of it bristling with sharpened iron spikes of varying lengths.

The two oghuls were impaled. Dead.

Bishop Godwyn lay on his back atop the armored body of one of the dead oghuls, one arm drenched in blood. His eyes were as wide and white as dinner plates, and he gaped back up at Culpa and Nail.

"I'm okay," he gasped. "I think I'm okay."

† † † † †

Once Godwyn was pulled from the pit, everyone checked themselves for wounds. Only the bishop had suffered any injuries—two deep slashes to his left forearm and one light cut across his forehead. Val-Draekin and Seita began bandaging him.

The entire cavern brimmed with the thick taste of blood. It was a slaughterhouse. The hanging cistern dangled askew, drained of its foul contents, and the bearded trapper atop the altar was utterly dead. Roguemoore still knelt on the floor at the base of the altar. He couldn't stop retching. Culpa helped him to his feet and together they walked arm-in-arm back toward the others. The stench of the blood that coated every inch of the dwarf was horrid and caustic. He'd so far managed to swipe most of it from his face and beard, but still looked a savage sight. He tried cleaning himself with strips of velvet Dokie tore from one of the nearby couches.

Culpa Barra walked the chamber and rammed his sword into the neck of every single oghul on the floor, counting the dead as he went. Stefan, hollow-eyed, stared at the destruction. With a sigh of resignation, he flung his bow over his shoulder and followed Culpa about the room, gathering what arrows he could find. Dokie and Liz Hen grabbed torches and began gathering up their gear from the balcony. The big girl still seemed shaky afoot, sword resheathed at her bulky hip. Dokie looked both haunted and energized by the entire fight.

Once all their gear was accounted for, Godwyn took the first drink from one of the water skins, then handed it around for the rest. They all drank long and hard, even Beer Mug.

"I count only nineteen dead," Culpa said, ramming his red-stained Dayknight sword home in its sheath. "Bloody rotted angels, there should be twenty bodies." He took the water skin last. Three gulps and it was emptied. "I wasn't sure, but during the chaos, I thought I saw one of the oghuls slip away under the arch. Now I know for sure."

"Who knows where he's gone off to," Godwyn sighed. He held up his bandaged arm. "But we can't let setbacks defeat us. My father suffered through years of chronic pain before his death. He used to say. 'I ask for no man's pity. Every day is a gift. And we Godwyns push on. As would every man who values his honor.' And we too must push on. All of us. We have survived this far."

"And we shall push on," Culpa said, "But I fear we haven't much time. Luckily, we are in the right room. If Shawcroft was consistent about one thing, it was in his ways of setting up new traps and dismantling the ones already set in place by the ancient worshippers of Mia. He once told me he set up Deadwood Gate the same as he set up this place here under D'Nahk lè. Hopefully I can remember enough about Deadwood Gate to find my way around in this chamber here. . . ." He trailed off into silence.

Roguemoore, still a bloody mess despite his best efforts to clean himself, looked at Liz Hen. "You accounted well for yourself in the battle."

"One thing about Liz Hen," Val-Draekin said. "She's not very agile or fast, but she's most definitely full of purpose. She set those oghuls on their heels sure enough."

Liz Hen smiled weakly at the praise, one shaky hand reaching up to straighten a braid in her hair. "I'm afraid the fight mussed up the braids Seita done for me the other night, though. Mussed 'em up good and snarly. I imagine I looked very pretty with them done up tight." She was looking at the Vallè maiden now, something approaching hero worship glinting in her eyes. "Truth is, was Seita who saved us all. That oghul woulda kilt me and Beer Mug if she hadn't pounced on its back and slit its throat wide."

"Yes, you are very good with those daggers." The dwarf was looking straight at Seita.

"Thank you." She bowed, and the torch she held flickered.

"In fact," the dwarf continued, his voice pointed with accusation as it cut across the room toward her, "I haven't seen anyone fight like that since Hawkwood was a much younger man."

"I take that as a compliment," Seita answered with another dip of her head. "As you know, all Vallè maidens are taught to fight."

"Vallè maidens are not trained to fight like you do," the dwarf harrumphed.

Seita shrugged. "I am glad you value my skill. Fact is, we all fought valiantly. Nineteen dead oghuls, and hardly a scratch on any of us. And if not for Stefan's arrows, we would have likely all perished. This entire battle is an omen of good fortune to come. After this display, I say we are all very nearly invincible." She turned to Liz Hen. "And we'll fix your braids when we get out of this rotted foul place."

Liz Hen smiled. "That would make me most happy."

Though Nail was relieved that the fighting was over, disappointment wormed its way into his gut. The whole battle had been a confusing, bloody blur. He still couldn't quite wrap his mind around all that had happened. One thing he knew for certain, he himself hadn't killed a single oghul.

"We had them oghuls frightened and running about like baby chicks from a silver-wolf," Dokie said. "The journey over the glacier, and now this. Isn't it just the exact grand adventure the dwarf promised us in the Turn Key Saloon, Liz Hen?"

"Grand adventure?" Liz Hen spat the words straight back at him. "I pissed myself twice, you stupid. Your grand adventure can go bugger itself straight in its own arse hole. Don't you even realize I'm liable to keel over at any moment, my heart jumping right out of my own rib cage the way it's still hammering?"

"I'm just saying, this is much better than waiting about the Turn Key Saloon, scarfing down Otto's vegetable stew."

"I could use a good bowl of vegetable stew now," Liz Hen said.

Looking at all the blood and savagery, Nail didn't know when he would again have an appitite.

"Shawcroft's instructions are coming back to me." Culpa cast his gaze about the musty chamber. He stepped toward the altar. "Oghuls this deep in the northern Sky Lochs do not speak the human tongue as well as their counterparts in the south, or in Amadon." The Dayknight studied the blood-covered altar and cistern dangling crookedly above. He nudged one of the dead oghuls at his feet with the toe of his boot. "I imagine these beasts didn't communicate at all beyond grunts and hand signals and such, none of them bright enough to explore the room too much beyond the obvious." He cast his gaze around the cathedral-shaped cavern again. "There are secrets hidden in this chamber. Even a shred of memory can be of use to us now."

Culpa pulled his dagger from his belt. He beckoned Dokie over. "I'll need your help. Bring a torch. The rest of you stay exactly where you are until I call for you. And as I should have mentioned ealier, don't touch anything. Who knows what other traps are set in these floors." Dokie, torch aloft, navigated his way through the oghul corpses toward Culpa and the altar.

"Shawcroft did everything in measured steps," the Dayknight said. "He was always consistent. In the way he fought. In the way he trained me to fight. In the way he trained Nail to fight. It was all exacting precision with him. And he did things in Deadwood Gate the same as he did here. The new traps he set, the ancient traps he dismantled, the secrets he hid in the stone walls, all exactly the same in both mines."

Culpa, dagger in hand, drifted around the altar and faced the far wall opposite the archway—the wall with the burning hearth. He took two measured steps sideways, and then turned slightly to the right. He was now facing the far right corner of the room. He pointed with the dagger. "Dokie, have a gander at that tapestry." He ruffled the muddy-colored hair atop Dokie's head. "Now follow me."

They both walked straight to the dark crook of the room. Once there, Culpa faced the corner, Dokie directly behind him, torch wavering in hand. "Stay here. Don't move," Culpa ordered the boy, and then turned toward the hearth, counted out five large steps, then faced the wall again. The dark, soot-covered tapestry hanging in front of him stretched from the floor up into the darkness. He reached up as high as he could and pricked the tapestry with the point of his dagger, working the tip back and forth, poking a hole into the ancient fabric. He then ripped down with the knife, slicing a large hole into the tapestry. Soot and dust rained over him. He sheathed the blade and reached out with both hands and tore the stiff fabric open clear to the floor. He kept jerking and rending it until the tapestry was ripped wide at least twenty feet above his head too.

"There," he announced, holding one frayed flap of the tapestry away from the wall. "Come look, Dokie."

From his vantage point, Nail couldn't see anything save a smooth stone wall flickering yellow with Dokie's torchlight and the burning hearth. Where the smoke from the hearth floated off to was a mystery. The entire mine was a mystery.

"Set the torch down and stand on my shoulders." Dokie set down the torch and climbed up onto the man's back. Unsteady, the boy wobbled, feet set on either of the Dayknight's shoulders, one hand braced against the wall before both of the Dayknight's thick arms grasped his legs tight.

"Do you see a tiny crack in the stone just above you?" Culpa asked. "Just a sliver of a crack, no longer than an inch, I'd say."

Dokie tentatively reached up and touched the wall with his fingers. "I feel it."

"Take the blade," Culpa let go of one of Dokie's legs, pulled his dagger from his belt, and held it up for the boy. "Stick the tip of the blade in the crack."

Dokie did as the Dayknight bade, working the tip of the blade into the stone.

"Really force it in there," Culpa said.

There was a loud *click!* Nail felt a deep rumble under his feet. There was a louder *snap!* followed by metal clanking on metal.

Then the rectangular altar in the center of the chamber was slowly rising up out of the floor to the dull resonance of stone grinding on stone, thick blood dripping from every side. "Bloody Mother

Mia and the baby Raijael, too." Liz Hen did the three-fingered-sign of the Laijon Cross over her heart.

The altar rose up out of the floor, revealing four stone posts, one at each corner holding it aloft, the top of the altar eventually clanking into the overturned cistern hanging above. When it finally ground to a halt, the altar stone was balanced seven feet above the floor atop the stone posts, blood draining from every edge, raining down into the dark square hole beneath.

"Just like Deadwood Gate." Culpa helped Dokie climb down from his shoulders. "The staircase should lead to the gears and levers below. Once underneath, we can close the altar and no oghul will ever know where we went."

Torches, packs, and water skins were quickly gathered. Culpa led the way down the steep set of stairs under the altar, torch aloft. Roguemoore was next, followed by Godwyn, also with a torch. Beer Mug scampered down, followed by Liz Hen, Dokie, and Stefan. Val-Draekin and Seita were in front of Nail, who went last. He carried a torch.

The staircase was slick with sheets of blood and the walls were streaked with running rivulets of red. Twenty steps total. Nail stepped into the passageway last, the corridor stretching off in just one direction before him.

A small grotto just off the main corridor behind him boasted a complicated set of gears and pulleys and chains. Culpa ignored the room full of gears. Instead he searched the wall of the passageway opposite the stairs, finding what he was looking for near the floor—a stone jutting about two inches out of the wall. He stuck the toe of his boot under the stone and nudged it up gently. With a dull grinding of gears, rattling of chains, and rumble of stone on stone emanating from somewhere in the walls around them, the altar above slowly descended back down, settling back in place, sealing them underneath with one long, wet, bloody hiss of finality. "We needn't worry," the Dayknight said. "I move that same stone and the altar will reopen."

Culpa led them down the corridor a few hundred paces, the passageway emptying them into a small square chamber, a dead end for all intents and purposes.

"It's cold in here," Liz Hen said once all nine had settled into the room. To Nail it seemed an awful gloomy place. The floor was lined with perfect rows of gray brick, each brick about a foot square. A fur-covered stool rested in each corner, the fur moldering in the chill, mournful air. Long-dead coals lay in piles of dust in a fireplace cut into the left wall, and the mantel was decorated with one small rune—a crescent moon made of rusted metal pinned right in the mantel's flat center with two small iron spikes.

"I'm exhausted." Liz Hen plopped down heavily on one of the fur-covered stools, the Sør Sevier sword at her hip scraping the wall behind her.

"Don't!" Culpa shouted. There was a loud *click!* And Liz Hen jerked to her feet.

Nobody moved. All looked around nervously. All waited for the floor to drop out from under them or some giant saw to come swinging in from out of nowhere and slice them all in half. All waited, staring at the walls, staring at the stools, staring at one another, none daring to exhale so much as a breath. The silence was profound. The only sound was the crackling of their three torches.

Then every other row of square bricks beneath their feet started sinking slowly into the floor. Nail, standing directly on one of the sinking rows, hurriedly stepped onto solid ground, torch flickering. Dokie, too. Beer Mug seemed tremendously interested in the goings-on, turning about this way and that, barking, eyes fixed on the rows of brick descending into the floor. The dog bounded from row to row until the sinking stones ceased their ponderous descent. Each new furrow in the floor was about a foot deep. Nail counted twelve in all. If it was a trap, it made no sense.

"Rotted beasts of the underworld?" Liz Hen exclaimed, eyes darting from Culpa to Seita to Roguemoore and up to the ceiling and down to the furrowed floor. "May the Blessed Mother Mia suckle me dry if I make it out of this mess alive."

"Quiet." Culpa held up his free hand for silence. "And nobody touch anything else without my say-so."

Then one of the fur-covered stools tipped and fell to the floor with a clatter.

A brilliant silver liquid began seeping like tree sap from the base of the right-side wall opposite the fireplace. Nail's eyes flew to Stefan's. They'd both seen the same type of silver rivulets leaking from the walls in the Roahm mine tomb where they'd found *Forgetting Moon*. Shawcroft had warned them not to touch it. Nail noticed that Val-Draekin had gripped Seita's arm, horror fixed in his eyes. The Vallè maiden had a look of almost smug satisfaction on her face.

The shiny sludge bled from the small cracks near the floor, slowly slithering toward each sunken trough underfoot. Fear was etched on Liz Hen's face as the syrupy silver fluid began to leisurely fill the bottoms of the furrows. Confusion filled Culpa Barra's own eyes. Roguemoore's too. His beard was still matted with congealed blood, armor smudged dark red.

"Look!" Dokie pointed.

The moldy fur on the wooden stool that had toppled earlier was being devoured by the silver liquid, vanishing into smoke and fume. And then the round wooden seat of the stool was soon eaten away, smoke billowing above. Roguemoore snatched one of the stool's remaining legs and held it up. Molten silver dripped from the smoldering wood, the leg still being consumed by the foul bright corruption that lingered there. The dwarf tossed the hunk of wood into the empty fireplace.

Silver liquid kept leaking into the room, running into the twelve furrows, making its way toward that same fireplace. Val-Draekin knelt and dipped the tip of a dagger into the nearest of the silver troughs. A swirl of smoke billowed, and when he pulled the tip of the blade free, the steel was completely eaten away. He let the rest of the dagger drop into the slow-flowing silver, where it disappeared with a mournful fizzle. His anxious eyes fell on Seita. Her face remained impassive as she shook her head.

"Eats the dagger and wooden stool but not the stone underfoot." Godwyn adjusted the bandages around his arm, torch guttering above.

"Yet it has no effect on rock," Roguemoore said. "I wouldn't mind taking a stone basin of the stuff out of here with me . . . if I had a stone basin."

"Shawcroft knew of this stuff." Stefan looked at the dwarf. "He told us not to touch any silver if we saw it in the Roahm Mines. Why would you want to keep some?"

"I am a student of potions and alchemy," the dwarf said. "I have never seen such a thing."

"Very ancient witchcraft this," Culpa said. He looked at the dwarf. "The *Moon Scrolls* speak briefly of the silver secret of the Skulls. Could this be it?"

"Dark Vallè alchemy, more like." The dwarfs cold eyes moved from Val-Draekin to Seita. Again the two Vallè shared a concerned look.

Culpa swept his torch around the room, "Whatever its origin, Vallè or not, it's still seeping from the wall. We must not let it touch us. It'd be a horrible way to die for sure."

"No need to state the obvious to me." Liz Hen did the three-fingered sign of the Laijon Cross over her heart. "Let's get the fuck out of here."

Nail agreed. These mines were foreign and foul beyond words. He looked at the entrance to the room and the corridor beyond. Wreathed in torch smoke, it beckoned.

"We can't leave just yet, Liz Hen." Culpa was studying the mantel of the fireplace, eyes particularly focused on the rusted crescent moon rune. "This is the exact place we need to be." He handed his torch to Stefan. Careful not to step in any of the troughs of silver liquid, the Dayknight moved toward the fireplace. He took out his dagger and began prying the rusted moon loose with the blade's tip, working the two irons spikes out of the wall in the process. The rusted metal moon eventually popped free of the mantel, the two iron spikes still secured in the rune, sharp tips jutting from the crescent moon's backside. One spike was considerably shorter than the other.

Culpa worked the longer spike free of the rune with his fingers, then did the same with the shorter one. He set the rusted metal moon up on the shelf of the stone mantel and held up both metal spikes, examining them carefully.

Nail looked back at the fireplace and saw that there were three holes in the mantel in the space where the crescent moon had hung. Culpa turned and placed the tip of the longer metal spike into the middle hole. With the hilt of his dagger, he pounded the nail all the way into the mantel until it was flush with the stone.

Then the Dayknight cast his eyes about the room as if waiting for something to happen. The base of the wall opposite the fireplace still bled silver, and the twelve furrows in the floor were still filling with the liquid; each was about a quarter full now. Culpa, brow furrowed, turned and gave the metal spike in the wall one more solid tap with the hilt of his dagger.

And then there was another loud *click!*

With a deep grumble of gears and stone, the wall opposite the room's entrance slowly began to rise—as if the ceiling above was sucking the stone wall straight up into some secret attic above. Behind the ascending wall was a wide staircase. Stair upon stair was gradually revealed, climbing up into the darkness.

"Up we go," Culpa announced.

"Wait," Stefan blurted. "You said even a shred of memory can be of use now. You said that Shawcroft was consistent in everything, right?"

"Aye," Culpa answered. "That I did."

"I've seen a staircase like this before," Stefan said. "Liz Hen, Dokie, Nail, we all have. Nail and I found the battle-ax atop a staircase that looked just like this in the Roahm Mines. Shawcroft told Nail to remember the third step up, far left stone. He instructed Nail to push it inward, push it but an inch and the rest of the stairway above would be free of traps." He pointed to the third stair up. The far left stone protruded from the rest of the long stair. Just like in Roahm. Nail, disappointed in himself for not spotting it first, knew his friend was right.

Stefan said, "Nail pushed a stone in just like that in the Roahm Mines."

"Shawcroft set it up like that in Deadwood Gate, too," Culpa said eagerly, then stepped up the staircase and tapped the stone in question lightly with his foot. The stone seemed to recede into the wall of its own volition. There was a short burst of wind from above and then a faint *tink, tink.* And silence.

"Quick thinking." Culpa turned back to Stefan. "You very likely saved us all. Who knows what traps were just dismantled."

Culpa led the company up the stairs. They soon found themselves atop a small landing, another foot-wide trough filled to the brim with the same type of silver fluid lay at their feet. This one singular furrow stretched from wall to wall. Beyond it was a somber-looking forty-foot-long corridor, its uneven roof of rough stone draped in a thick latticework of spiderwebs. The walls and floor of the passageway were fashioned of perfectly smooth stone. Hundreds of dark holes peppered the walls on both sides.

Centered at the end of the corridor some forty feet away was a cross-shaped altar. In the center of the wall above the altar was a square wooden door. The altar itself looked to be capped with a slab of stone like the one in the Roahm Mines. The intricate Vallè scroll-work carved into its base was too far away to make out the details. But Nail suspected what foul, nameless creatures those carvings were of: *dragons*.

"This is the place," Roguemoore said, his blood-matted beard and bloodstained face looking savage in the torchlight.

"Looks like the altar in Roahm," Stefan said, gaze meeting Nail's. "Only that altar was set in a tomb, bones and skeletons scattered around."

"I do not like the looks of these walls," Culpa said, his torch weaving before him, eyes scanning the sides of the corridor stretching between them and the altar. "More traps set by the original worshippers of Mia, I suspect. We dare not walk down that corridor. Who knows what foul things might come a-creeping out of those holes? Who knows if Stefan's idea dismantled every trap? And we dare not touch this trough of silver, either. And that wooden door above the altar. Who knows what it may hide?" He glanced at the dwarf, then at Godwyn. "The closer to the prize, the trickier and more deadly the traps, Shawcroft always said."

"Can we toss a water skin out onto the floor?" Dokie asked. "See what happens? See if it triggers any traps?"

"No." Culpa's answer was quick and firm. "We dare not disturb any more than is necessary. Could be a poisonous fume come drifting out of those holes."

Nail studied the walls of the corridor. Straight and smooth and perfect, they almost unnerved him. And the hundreds of holes. *Indeed, what evil might come shooting forth?* Then he remembered something—a secret only he had seen in Roahm, a secret similar to the one Stefan had earlier pointed out.

"I've an idea." He turned from the passage and took four quick steps down the stairway, everyone watching. Sure enough, he saw what he was looking for in the glow of his torch. Just like the mines above Gallows Haven, the stone against the far left wall on the very top stair jutted out just a bit from the others.

He pushed it in with the toe of his boot.

A low moan followed by the slow rumble of rock grinding on rock sounded from the direction of the altar. They all cast their eyes back down the corridor. The cross-shaped altar slowly sank into the floor until only its capstone remained above the floor.

Nobody breathed for what seemed like forever as Nail's heart sank into his guts.

"You just disappeared it, you stupid." Liz Hen's disgust broke the silence. She took two steps toward him and punched him in the shoulder as hard as she could. "What the bloody fuck is wrong with you? Haven't you learned, you just don't go around touching stuff in a place like this. Stupid bastard."

"May the wraiths take us," Godwyn sighed. "Let's just be grateful it didn't sink straight to the underworld."

"Rotted angels, but my nerves are completely frayed." Culpa's voice was worn and ragged. "For good or ill, what's done is done."

"Nobody touch anything again," Roguemoore grumbled.

"We've got to act quickly," Culpa said. "That room below is liable to flood with silver and we'll have no way out." He handed his torch to Liz Hen, pulled the rope from his pack, and turned to Stefan. "With all those holes in the walls, I dare not send any of us walking across the floor of that corridor." He snatched an arrow from Stefan's quiver. "Can you sink this arrow into that wooden door above the altar?" He tied the rope to the shaft of the arrow.

"Just like the glacier crevasse." Stefan nodded. "Maybe easier." He nocked the arrow to the bow, aimed, breathed deep, held it, and fired. The shot was straight and true and punched deep into the wooden door, rattling it.

They all waited in silence. Nail half expected the roof to fall in or the whole place to burst into flames, but nothing happened.

Culpa tugged on the line as hard as he could, jerked on it, yanked and pulled. The arrow was lodged solidly in the wood. The Dayknight tied the rope around his waist and then sat down heavily at the edge of the stairs, his black armor scraping against the stone. The rope was now stretched tight between him and the arrow, suspended about three feet above the floor. "You're the lightest of us, Dokie," he said. "You'll have to crawl over there along the rope, slide that altar stone aside, and see what lies within, hopefully *Blackest Heart*."

Dokie took hold of the line. "Like Stefan said, just like the glacier crevasse, maybe easier." He looked down the dim corridor. "And if I slip, not as far to fall." He then did the three-fingered sign of the Laijon Cross over his heart, took hold of the taut line with both hands, and swung under it. He threw his legs up, hooking them around the rope from underneath. The arrow remained lodged in the wooden door forty feet away.

"Be careful," Liz Hen muttered.

Upside down Dokie crawled toward the altar, confident and swift. Culpa and the dwarf strained to hold the rope as rigid as possible. Still the rope sagged some as Dokie reached the midway point. The Dayknight braced himself and leaned back, pulling the rope taut again. Seita and Roguemoore latched onto the rope too, helping to hold it steady. When Dokie reached the sunken altar, he called back, "Do I dare stand now?"

"Just move slowly," Culpa instructed. "And be wary of any clicks or other strange noises when you stand! Don't move about any more than need be! See if you can slide the altar stone aside!"

Dokie unraveled his legs from around the rope and let his feet drop to the floor. Dangling awkwardly, he waited a moment, then put weight on his feet and stood. Culpa and Roguemoore relaxed on the other end of the rope.

"The top of the altar stone has carvings on it!" Dokie shouted, his head cocked sideways. "Carvings like on the standing stones! Like the symbols in my dreams after the lightning strike! Like in all my sketches!"

"Just see if you can slide the altar stone aside!" Culpa shouted.

Dokie knelt and pushed against the altar stone, straining. "I can't move it! It's too heavy!"

"Try pushing from another angle!" Culpa shouted.

Dokie repositioned himself behind the stone and pushed again, this time in little short bursts. "It's inching aside! But it'll take me a while."

"Just push far enough to reach your arm down!" the Dayknight encouraged.

A few more shoves and Dokie managed to slide the stone aside far enough to reach inside. He lay down on his stomach and peered into the hole. He scooted nearer the narrow opening and thrust his arm down. "Something's down here!" He wiggled his arm into the hole farther. "I think I can reach it! I feel it!" After a moment he pulled forth a dark object.

It was a crossbow. Large, black as soot, and strung with black string.

A growing sense of awe instantly infused the company. That the ancient relic was actually there and that Dokie had actually pulled it free of the altar after so much trouble and fright was finally sinking in.

"Is there a black stone down there too?" Culpa yelled.

Dokie set the ancient crossbow on the floor and put his face to the hole again. "All I see is a dark black shape, like a piece of cloth!"

"Aye! That's it!" Culpa shouted. "The angel stone is in the cloth. Get it. But don't touch the stone. Keep it in the cloth."

Dokie reached down into the hole again and pulled forth the swath of black silk and unwrapped it. "An angel stone!" He stood and held the swath of silk out for all to see. "Black!"

Godwyn said, "We must give praise to Shawcroft for his years of toil."

If there was any black gemstone on the black silk, Nail couldn't see it from so far away. "I'd toss it to you, but I can't throw that far!" Dokie yelled.

"Just secure the crossbow tight to your belt and crawl back over the rope!" Culpa instructed. "Wrap the stone and stuff it in your pocket!"

Dokie wrapped the stone and crammed the silk between his sweat-stained shirt and the plate armor strapped to his chest. He reached down and snatched up the crossbow and lifted it triumphantly above his head. "Look, Liz Hen, I got 'em both! *Blackest Heart* and an angel stone!"

Liz Hen clapped and let out a sharp hoot of praise. "He's like a regular burglar. A dungeon thief."

Culpa leaned back on the rope and Dokie's safety line was again pulled taut. Hanging under the line by all fours like a spider on a web, crossbow hooked to his belt, Dokie crawled back hand over hand. At the halfway point, the rope drooped in the middle again. Culpa braced himself, tightening the line, Roguemoore and Seita also gripping the line, steadying it best they could.

Stefan's arrow snapped free of the wooden door.

Dokie dropped to the smooth stone floor in a clatter twenty feet away, instantly clambering to his knees, crossbow in hand, facing the others. "I'm okay," he announced.

There was a sharp hiss of air and a thousand blasts of dust shot forth from the thousand holes in both walls and then silently rained to the ground.

Dokie, still on his knees in the center of the corridor, toppled sideways to the stone floor; head, arms, legs, torso, every inch of him bristling with shiny needle-thin darts, none of them longer than a small child's finger. Thousands of darts were scattered about the surface of the passageway around him, glimmering like tiny stars in the torchlight, merciless and sharp.

The grimmest of silences fell over the company.

"Dokie!" Liz Hen lunged forward. Val-Draekin pulled her back before she had a chance to leap over the small stream of silver. Beer Mug barked, pawing madly at the stone landing, also eager to jump across the silver trough and help the downed boy, but sensing the danger. As the dust settled, Dokie's body slowly curled around the crossbow clutched to his chest, then went still, his folded torso resembling naught but a glittering pincushion in the darkness now.

A thunderous rumble echoed from the stone all around. The deepness of the sound sucked the breath from Nail's lungs. The spiderwebs above Dokie began to shiver and quake. Dust rained over the boy again, and the uneven roof of the passageway slowly began to drop.

"No," Culpa Barra gasped as the ceiling descended toward Dokie with a loud, ponderous grind—a scraping slow descent that shook the very ground.

The Dayknight was swiftly on his feet, armored body coiled and ready to spring to Dokie's rescue. But the sudden firm hand of the dwarf on his chest plate stopped him. Culpa's normally proud posture went slack. His pained eyes roamed over the thousands of murderous dark holes in the corridor's two walls, and the thousands of silver darts on the floor, and Dokie's inert form; he knew there was naught he could do.

Liz Hen struggled against the strong grasp of Val-Draekin. Seita joined in restraining the distraught girl. Roguemoore, too. The girl's loud cries filled the cavern, drowning out the rumble and grind of the descending roof.

Culpa grabbed the rope and started pulling it frantically toward him. The arrow, still tied to the line, skittered along the floor behind Dokie. It caught on the boy's armor. Culpa hauled on the rope, trying to hook Dokie and fish the boy to safety. But the arrow snapped in half and the rope went slack. The Dayknight hurled the rope to the ground, shouting aloud in frustration.

Nail watched as the roof dropped below eye level, knowing his stalwart companion from Gallows Haven deserved better than a crushing death here in this mournful shit hole of a mine. It was like being aboard the *Lady Kindly* again. Nobody had moved to save Zane from the sharks. And nobody was moving to save Dokie.

With that thought, Nail launched himself over the stream of silver and ducked under the sinking ceiling, lunging forward to rescue his friend. A sharp hiss of air and a blast of a thousand winds blew past him. Darts peppered the sides of his breastplate and ricocheted away into the darkness. Pain scorched his face. He felt Culpa Barra's strong hand curl around his belt and he was yanked roughly over the stream of silver and from the danger of the corridor to safety.

Nail and the Dayknight tumbled back onto the stone landing in a clatter of armor. Nail swiped at the darts clinging to the sides of his face, frantically scraping them free of his searing flesh. The pain blooming over his face was almost too much to bear. He gritted his teeth, his heart a hollow mass of agony as he watched the ceiling slowly grind ever downward on his friend. A gap of only four feet was now all that separated Dokie from certain death. *If he's not already dead.* The darts held a furious sting, and Nail had only been shot with a few.

With a loud bark, Beer Mug leaped the stream of silver and dashed under the descending slab of rock. There was another hiss of air and *whoosh* of darts, and the dog was struck by silver darts on both sides. But he scarcely broke stride. Cobwebs from the sinking roof dragged across Beer Mug's back as he scrambled to reach the boy. His teeth clamped around Dokie's booted foot and he began dragging the boy toward safety, crouching low as the ceiling pressed down. Darts spat from the walls a second time, striking both the boy and the dog.

"Save them!" Liz Hen was crying. "Somebody save them both!"

The entire company was on hands and knees now, every eye fixed on the pressing slab as Beer Mug struggled toward them, all four legs churning, pawing, clawing at the floor, pulling Dokie by the leg. But the ceiling continued its descent, buckling the dog's four legs, slowing him, pushing him to the floor, darts firing into his body a third time.

Then his tail was free of the falling roof. Culpa Barra straddled the silver stream and snatched the dog by the haunches, yanking him fiercely from under the crushing slab. Culpa tossed the large dog boldly across the room and into the arms of Liz Hen, who staggered against the side wall and clutched him to her chest, screeching, "He's full of needles!"

In one fluid motion, the Dayknight straddled the stream of silver again, then dropped to his knees on the other side and stretched the length of his arms out under the grinding rock, seizing Dokie by the ankles. He jerked the boy violently free of the slab. The black crossbow in the boy's curled arms spun across the room and smacked the wall near Liz Hen and Beer Mug. The swath of silk flew from under his chest-plate armor. The black cloth fluttered to the floor, and the black stone hit the ground and bounced toward the flowing trench of silver . . .

. . . and Roguemoore's calloused hand snatched up the black gem, mere inches before it fell into the trough.

And with a heavy crunch of finality, the ceiling of the corridor slammed shut behind Culpa Barra. The Dayknight, straddling the stream of silver once again, held Dokie Liddle up by the ankles, the boy's limp body dangling, riddled with hundreds of tiny silver darts.

*O, ye people, adore your great One and Only for now and forever. Anguished,*
*Laijon drew* Affliction *and thrust the Last Demon Lord through. O, ye people,*
*who of you does not bemoan that Vicious War of the Demons, that dread battle*
*waged under constant mystery?*
—THE WAY AND TRUTH OF LAIJON

# CHAPTER THIRTY-ONE

# STEFAN WAYLAND

### 10TH DAY OF THE ANGEL MOON, 999TH YEAR OF LAIJON
### SKY LOCHS, GUL KANA

The Company of Nine finally broke free of the deep mountain crag, stumbling straight into the sunlight and the happy song of faraway birds, whirls of dusty snow dancing on the great D'Nahk lè behind them. The immense glacier and its vast pearl-white brilliance dominated the landscape to the south, vaulted peaks rising beyond. Eyes aching from the sudden sight of so much space and light, the company quickly stowed their torches and plopped to the ground, haggard and weary. Roguemoore's chalk marks on the walls had saved them some time and headache. Still, the trek from the black depths of the mines had been long. Luckily, there had been no further sign of oghuls.

Stefan and Val-Draekin set Dokie's litter on the stony ground. Stefan breathed heavily from the exertion of carrying the boy. The litter itself was cobbled together from two wooden poles found in the mines along with some dismantled wooden stools. It was tied together with what little remained of the rope Dokie had used to traverse the corridor, and a blanket was stretched across it all. Another blanket covered Dokie. Every member of the company save Godwyn had taken shifts carrying the sick boy out of the horrid mines—the bishop's injured arm was still bandaged, now in a sling. Godwyn pulled the last water skin from his pack and they all took a short drink. The bishop also forced some form of healing draught down Dokie's throat, a brown mixture he'd pulled from his poultice pouch. "As long as we can keep him breathing, there is hope."

"He's liable to freeze out here." Liz Hen looked glum, Beer Mug curled against her leg, her hand nervously stroking his back. Ever since rescuing Dokie and being stung by the darts, the dog had been quiet, tongue lagging, panting heavily, head drooping. The dog's tail didn't wag once, even at the girl's gentle touch. "May the wraiths take me for saying as much. Though it's bright and sunny as the blazes out here, the mines were much warmer."

"We dare not go back in there, Liz Hen," Godwyn said, his face grim. "No matter how warm those caves are. It will be all I can do to nurse Dokie along until we can get him the real medicines he needs. We must make haste. We shan't rest long here."

In their escape from the mines, they had stopped at intervals so the bishop could remove the darts from the unconscious boy. Luckily, most of them had glanced off Dokie's armor, or pierced his leathers only shallowly. Still, at least several dozen had punctured his face, arms, and legs. Whatever foul poison was on them had knocked him out cold and now affected his breathing. His face was terribly swollen and red.

Liz Hen had plucked what darts she could from Beer Mug. The dog seemed to be growing more lethargic by the hour. Both sides of Nail's face were also pocked and swollen. But he seemed to suffer no other ill effects from the dozen or so small bee-sting-sized wounds.

"Dokie won't die, will he?" Liz Hen asked, still stroking Beer Mug.

"I don't know." Godwyn answered. "But I imagine the poisons on those darts were centuries old and had lost most of their potency.

"The oghul in Stanclyffe, the tattoo under his eye, you saw it?" Culpa asked Godwyn. "That oghul may now be Dokie's only chance."

"Stanclyffe is a long way off," Godwyn said solemnly.

"We've no other choice," Culpa said. "You'll have to get the boy to that oghul if he has any chance to survive."

"Stanclyffe is not the direction we travel." Godwyn looked up, grim-faced.

"What's so special about that oghul in Stanclyffe?" Liz Hen asked. "What can he do for Dokie?"

Culpa met her gaze. "The tattoo under that oghul's eye is a sign, a sign announcing just what type of foul alchemy he barters in."

"Foul alchemy?" Liz Hen looked horrified.

"Also healing draughts," Culpa said, a smidgen of reassurance in his voice.

"But what price will the oghul ask?" Godwyn muttered.

"Indeed," Roguemoore softly answered, a haunted look in his eyes. His beard and face were a bit cleaner now. The oghul blood was mostly scrubbed away, some still visible though, trapped in the cracks and creases of his plate armor. "What price might we all pay for *Blackest Heart*?"

"We've many heavy decisions to make," Godwyn said.

"Do you think those darts were made of the same creeping silver?" Culpa asked.

"Hard to say," Roguemoore answered, eyes bleak as they fell on the crossbow strapped to Culpa's back. Stefan marveled at its solid black beauty and delicate, perfect mechanisms and black string. It seemed only a specifically sized quarrel would fit those exquisite mechanisms. Thicker than normal. Certainly no size arrow or bolt Stefan had ever seen. Seita also claimed it was fashioned of a type of wood she had never seen before, but the finest wood she'd ever laid eyes upon nonetheless.

Culpa also carried the black angel stone. It was wrapped in its silk cocoon and stuffed in a tiny leather sack at his belt. Stefan had only briefly looked at it—when Roguemoore had caught it before it fell into the stream of silver. Not even a flicker or gleam of torch flame had flared on its dark and dusky surface. Unlike the blue angel stone Gisela had found in the mines above Gallows Haven, this angel stone was a seemingly bleak and rootless thing, black and hard.

"He vomits but only air comes out!" Dokie blurted, eyes fluttering open. The boy's sudden outburst startled them all. His eyes were glazed over with a milky fog. "He claims his ears are filled with water. He can't feel his feet, either. The armor burnt him good. Left scars."

"What's he goin' on about?" Liz Hen rushed to his litter, grabbed his hand in hers. "Do the wraiths have him now?"

"He's delirious, feverish." Godwyn dabbed at the boy's forehead with a corner of the blanket.

Dokie's chest rose and fell more rapidly. "The lightning struck! He felt his heart stop!" He sat up, foggy eyes roaming the landscape. "Said he knew what death felt like right then and there. Said he felt his heart start up again when his body hit the mud, said he would be dead if he hadn't hit the ground so hard." Dokie's wild gaze settled on Nail. "He wanted to know if you felt your heart stop too."

"Dear Laijon, the wraiths have taken him." Tears streamed down Liz Hen's ruddy, cold cheeks. "What will we do?"

"Am I dreaming?" Dokie's rheumy eyes were still fixed on Nail. "Come here."

Nail sat still as a stone, a bitter look on his face.

"The mark of the cross. I dreamed it." Dokie pointed to the red cross-shaped mark on the back of Nail's hand. Stefan had first noticed the burn scar on Nail soon after Dokie had been struck by lightning on Baron Bruk's practice field so long ago.

"Mark of the cross?" Liz Hen stood up and grabbed Nail's hand, examining it. "What do you suppose it means?"

"It don't mean nothin'." Nail jerked his hand away from her. "He's lost his mind is all."

† † † † †

The surface of the glacier was melty in the sun, creating a dangerous surface. Hauling Dokie over and around all the obstacles and puddles in their path took the effort and muscle of all. But they made good headway to the chasm they'd crossed days ago, the two rangy dun-colored mules waiting in the distance, both still staked to the ice.

The gaping chasm appeared to have widened by about five feet since they had last crossed it. The gorge now seemed to emit a low roar of raging subterranean waters from deep within, the raucous din much louder than before. With only one rope left, their crossing would be more demanding this time, if not impossible, with Dokie strapped to a litter. There would be no rope bridge this time. Each person would have to swing across the lone rope they had and brace for impact against the far ice wall, then climb the rope to safety—or be pulled to safety by those who had crossed before.

Val-Draekin went through each pack, setting aside the two pick-axes they needed, then tossed what other gear they could across the chasm, where it landed near the stake. Culpa tied their remaining rope around one of Stefan's arrows.

Stefan nocked the arrow to his bow, aimed, and fired. It was a perfect shot. The arrow lodged deep into a crack in the ice just a foot below the opposite rim. Seita tied the other end of the rope around her own waist, grabbed the two pickaxes from the ice, stepped carefully to the slippery ledge, and jumped. She swung down gently into the chasm and landed feetfirst against the opposite wall twenty-five feet below, her two pickaxes immediately striking into the ice. The Vallè woman dangled a moment, got her footing against the ice wall, and slowly began to climb, using the two picks. Once she reached the top, she wrapped the rope around the stake, then went back, leaned over the ledge, and plucked Stefan's arrow free. She swiftly untied herself and threw the other end of the rope along with the two pickaxes back over the chasm.

Roguemoore wrapped the rope around his girth multiple times. Pickaxes in hand, the dwarf took one step and leaped ungracefully into the chasm, heavy armored body smacking into the opposite wall of the crevasse with a stout crash. His horned helm rattled off his head at the impact and plummeted away into the vast nothing. The dwarf cursed, oriented himself to the wall quickly, and began his slow climb. Seita pulled on the rope from above.

Stefan thought he heard the distant howling of oghuls. Not sure whether his ears were playing tricks on him, he turned, eyes roaming the icy expanse they had just traveled. The howling grew louder, more distinct and real. Culpa had also turned to look just as a pack of several dozen oghuls crested a rise in the glacier about five hundred paces to the north and east.

They were loutish beasts, snarling and gray-faced, all rumbling and roaring as they tore across the ice, clattering and clanking in rusted armor of savage vulgar make, wicked-looking weapons thrust aloft.

"Hurry!" Culpa turned and hollered at the dwarf. The charging oghuls were a hundred paces closer to the icy gorge by the time the dwarf reached the top of the other side. Seita sent the rope and two axes sailing back for the next person.

"Go, Stefan! You next!" Culpa ordered. "I want you over there firing arrows into those oghuls as soon as you can!"

Heart jumping, Stefan wrapped the rope about his waist, his many years tying knots aboard the *Lady Kindly* speeding the process. Once secured, he snatched up the two pickaxes and moved to the edge, then jumped. He swung down into the chasm, a dark blue nothingness below, landing feetfirst against the far wall with a jarring thud that nearly punched the air from his lungs. A handful of arrows bounced from the quiver at his back and spun away down into the abyss below. His bow remained safe. He scrambled up the wall, axes biting into the ice, Seita and Roguemoore hauling on the rope from above.

Seita gave him a kiss on the forehead once he was again on solid ground, then untied the rope and sent it arcing back over the gap. Stefan tossed the two pickaxes back over too. The oghuls were three hundred paces from the chasm now, stampeding at a lumbering gait and closing the distance.

Godwyn was quick in securing the rope around his own waist. In two loping strides he jumped and disappeared down into the dark hole below. Stefan helped Seita and Roguemoore pull the bishop up the ice wall. Once Godwyn was safe and the rope and axes thrown back over the chasm, Stefan readied his bow. He quickly nocked an arrow and fired at the approaching horde, which was now less than two hundred paces from the chasm and closing fast. His arrow landed somewhere in the middle of the pack and he thought he saw an oghul go down. He nocked another arrow and fired.

Liz Hen was done wrapping the rope around her own waist when Culpa yelled at Seita. "Take *Blackest Heart!*" Then he sent the crossbow sailing over the chasm. It twirled through the air, black against the blue skies. Seita caught the crossbow in deft hands and set it gently on the ice behind her.

Culpa jammed his hand into the small leather pouch at his belt, took out the black silk holding the angel stone, and thrust it into Liz Hen's hand. "Have you a safe pocket for this?"

"Aye." The girl stuffed the silk and stone straight down her bodice, then cinched the laces tight around her neck. "It won't easily escape there."

"Good!" Culpa took Liz Hen's sword and threw it over the chasm next, the long Sør Sevier blade sailing over the gap, landing about ten feet behind Stefan.

"What about Dokie?" Liz Hen yelled as Culpa shoved her roughly down into the crevasse. Beer Mug let out a shrill bark watching her fall. The big girl dropped from sight and thudded against the wall below Stefan with a grunt. Seita, Godwyn, and the dwarf began hauling her to safety.

Stefan fired another arrow. An oghul dropped in a spray of ice and slush, arrow quivering in its neck. The horde was less than a hundred paces away and bearing down. Stefan fired again.

Culpa Barra whirled and drew his sword, ready for the looming attack. Nail drew his sword too, standing over Dokie's litter. Val-Draekin pulled daggers from his leather armor, spinning them in both hands.

Stefan fired another arrow and a second oghul dropped to the surface of the glacier in a skid of blue ice. At the same time, Val-Draekin let both of his daggers fly. Two oghuls went down instantly as the glittering blades sank into their exposed necks. The Vallè readied two more daggers. Stefan was firing arrows as fast as he could.

Liz Hen was soon clambering over the rim of the chasm in front of Stefan, Seita and Godwyn dragging her by the rope. Seita leaped forward, tore the rope off Liz Hen, and cast it back over the chasm. Val-Draekin seized hold of the line and swiftly wrapped it around Dokie's litter a half-dozen times, cinching it tight, tying several quick knots. Then he sent Dokie sliding toward the chasm with a shove. The litter glided over the glacier and dropped down into the icy defile.

Stefan heard the litter clatter against the ice below. Behind him, Liz Hen, Roguemoore, and Godwyn were hauling on the rope, pulling Dokie's litter up the wall of ice. Stefan fired another arrow into the pack of oghuls now fifty paces from the gorge and closing, and then another. Seita was throwing daggers of her own. Multiple oghuls were dropping now, others tripping over the dead as they ran, the confusion slowing the pack some, but not enough. Dokie's litter was pulled to safety, the rope swiftly untied and sent back over the chasm.

Beer Mug launched himself toward the advancing throng of oghuls, teeth bared and glaring, muscles and haunches bunching as he ran. "No!" Liz Hen screamed as the dog leaped at the throat of the lead beast, both tumbling in a snarling heap and spray of ice.

Stefan fired another arrow into the center of the horde, and then another. Nail was wrapping the rope around his own waist when the first of the charging oghuls reached Culpa Barra and Val-Draekin. Nail dropped the rope, brandished his sword, and turned to join the battle.

"Save yourself, Nail!" Culpa yelled. "Go!" The Dayknight's black sword parried the heavy battle-ax of the first oghul with a shuddering thud.

Val-Draekin leaped high, daggers whirling as he laid into the next two rushing beasts. The Vallè was quickly outnumbered and pulled to the ground by a swarm of thick-armored oghul arms and fists and crude hacking blades.

Conflict etched on his face, Nail turned and threw his own sword across the chasm just as a maul-wielding oghul lunged for him. Nail ducked the wild swing of the iron maul and fell down. He flung himself to the side, skidding along the ice, spinning the rope around both of his wrists as he rolled away from the second crushing blow of the oghul's heavy weapon. The maul splintered the ice.

Nail scrambled to his feet and jumped out over the chasm, holding fast to the rope with both hands. The oghul reached out one grubby fist and latched onto Nail's booted foot, but Nail's momentum dragged them both over the edge. The oghul lost hold of his grip and dropped into the chasm with a fearful bellow, disappearing into the deep blue nothingness. Nail clutched the rope as it swung low, hitting the wall below Stefan with a crash. Seita threw the last of her daggers and ran over to help the others pull Nail to safety. Stefan fired again into the battling throng of whirling bodies cross the chasm, but he was running low on arrows.

Culpa Barra and Beer Mug were in a desperate fight against more than a dozen of the ponderous beasts, a battle that surged to the right along the chasm's rim, a swirling mass of weapons and rusted armor, Culpa taking many blows. Unstaggered, the Dayknight fought on, his black sword crushing away in a brave flurry.

Beer Mug lunged and leaped and darted in a blur of gray fur, blood and sinew gushing and tearing from the ankles and hamstrings of every creature he snared, many oghuls falling to the ice, legs useless.

To the left, Val-Draekin was once again on his feet and fighting, but injured and bloodied, gray cloak in tatters, his daggers lethal and flinging red droplets everywhere. Many oghuls lay dead around him, gouts of scarlet spraying over the ice from harsh wounds. Val-Draekin slipped and slid in the blood and melt as the remaining beasts circled him.

Stefan fired an arrow into the group of oghuls, dropping one instantly, arrow jutting from its blunt face as it folded to the ice. That created an opening for the Vallè. He leaped through the gap and dashed away to the north and west, pulling many of the oghuls with him as they took to the chase. Stefan fired his last arrow at the group pursuing Val-Draekin, seeing one fall, arrow protruding from its back. Then his quiver was empty.

Nail was already hauled up out of the chasm, safe with the others. The rope sailed back over the abyss toward Culpa with a deft toss from Seita. The Dayknight, still in mortal combat with the oghuls in front of him, saw his safety line land in the bloody slush at his feet. The rope instantly slid back toward the yawning gorge. Without hesitation, Culpa turned from the fight and threw his sword high over the chasm. He knocked aside a burly oghul with his shoulder, then dove for the rope snaking toward the ledge, sliding chest-first in ice and blood, outstretched hands seizing the rope just as it slithered over the lip of the chasm. Two of the oghuls lunged for Culpa, scrambling and sliding on the ice, losing control, arms flailing. The Dayknight's momentum carried him forward and he slipped facefirst down into the crevasse, rope in both hands, dropping away and disappearing from view. Unable to stop their own frantic impetus, the two oghuls slid headlong into the chasm behind him, spinning silently into the darkness of the deep. Culpa slammed into the wall below Stefan. The others began pulling on the rope, hauling the Dayknight up.

Beer Mug was left alone with nearly ten oghuls, all swinging at the dog with rusty weapons. None of their lumbering blows landed. The shepherd dog, deft on his feet, darted free of the throng and dashed toward Val-Draekin. The Vallè, about fifty paces away from the crevasse now, sorely injured and trailing blood, was forced to turn and engage in battle with the hulking beasts that had given him chase. The oghuls had the advantage in number, backing the valiant blood-covered Vallè down. Beer Mug launched the full weight of his body into the back of the largest oghul near Val-Draekin, knocking the beast face-first to the ice. The dog's gnashing teeth tore at the back of the oghul's thick neck. Again, it was all the distraction the Vallè needed.

As Culpa Barra was pulled over the rim to safety, Val-Draekin broke from the fight and ran straight toward the crevasse, three oghuls galloping after. He reached the opposite edge of the chasm at a full sprint, launching himself out over the abyss as far and high as he could. Seita ripped the rope from Culpa's waist and tossed it as far and as high as she could toward her fellow Vallè.

Val-Draekin and the rope sailed toward each other over the gaping blue void.

The Vallè snatched the end of the rope out of the air as casually as a cat snagging a fluttering moth with its paw, seizing the rope midflight. He dropped down into the chasm, wrapping the end of it around his hands as he fell, now swinging toward the opposite wall. Behind him, the three pursuing oghuls couldn't slow in time and slid in a spray of bloody ice over the edge, screaming great guttural roars as they fell.

Val-Draekin slammed against the ice below Stefan. Every member of the company but Dokie rushed to haul on the rope. The injured Vallè was soon up and on the safe side of the deadly gap, blood dripping to the ice from his many wounds.

"Beer Mug!" Liz Hen screamed.

Across the ice, the shepherd dog was still dodging the blows of oghul weapons, a noticeable limp in his gait, weary eyes fixed on the rest of the company now safe on the opposite side of the crevasse. Beer Mug's fur was covered in blood—whether his own, or that of the oghuls, Stefan could not tell. But his heart went out to the stout dog.

"Beer Mug!" Liz Hen screamed again, tears streaming down her face as the dog wove between the legs of the oghuls still trying to kill him, his every move becoming increasingly lethargic. "We have to save him!" she cried.

"There's nothing to be done." Roguemoore's gruff voice spoke the truth they all were thinking. 'We've no more arrows. No more daggers."

Stefan had seen the dog jump the chasm before. But that was two days ago when the gap was narrower and the dog healthy.

Through a mist of his own tears, Stefan watched as a vicious blow from an iron club caught Beer Mug right on the top of the spine. The dog yelped. Head now cocked awkwardly to the side, Beer Mug limped away from the lumbering oghul, paws slipping on bloody ice as he staggered along sideways, almost as if drunk. The oghul with the maul was right on his heels, the others jeering and taunting with their crude weapons. On weary legs, limping, whimpering, the dog weaved his way through the carnage and blood and dead oghuls, sorrow-filled eyes fixed on the Company of Nine watching from the other side of the chasm.

"Jump, Beer Mug!" Liz Hen screamed. "You can make it!"

The dog's ears perked at her encouragement. He took a half-hearted run at the chasm, then backed off, coming to a stop at the rim of the crevasse, eyes forlorn as he dropped to his haunches, head hanging, entire body heaving with each panting breath.

The oghuls closed in around him, crude and vulgar weapons raised high for the killing blows. A screech of unfathomable pain tore from Liz Hen's lungs. She dropped to her knees and buried her face in her hands. All Stefan could do was grip his perfectly useless bow in hand and watch, arms heavy with fatigue, no arrows left to fire.

But as the oghul weapons fell, Beer Mug leaped to his feet in a final burst of energy. He dove between the legs of the bloodsucking horde and scrambled away to the north and west as fast as his hobbled body would carry him, blood trailing over the ice in his wake. "Run, boy, run!" Liz Hen yelled. "Run far away and keep going!"

Several of the oghuls threw their rusted weapons in the dog's direction, but none gave chase. It seemed they too were exhausted. They turned their attention from the limping dog and glared in frustration at the Company of Nine across the chasm.

Beer Mug continued on, bloodied, injured, and poisoned, loping away to the north and west in the direction of the jagged gray cliffs rising high above the glacier in the far distance. Liz Hen's sobs filled the silence.

† † † † †

The mood was somber when they reached the two dun-colored mules staked to the glacier. One was standing hoof-deep in a pool of meltwater; the other was on solid ice, dipping his broad muzzle in the nearby pool to drink.

"At least they didn't starve to death or freeze," Roguemoore said.

"Or become prey to the oghuls," Culpa added, hooking *Blackest Heart* to the leather harness crisscrossing his back. "Damnable beasts are thicker than I imagined they'd be around here." Godwyn began binding Val-Draekin's wounds with torn strips of a blanket. The Vallè had four sizable slashes to his left arm and a ragged one across his right shoulder. His leather armor was shredded in spots but had done its job to protect his vitals. Seita wrapped Val-Draekin's neck with a long strip of the blanket.

"The oghuls won't make it over that crevasse anytime soon," Culpa said. "Still, we must make haste."

With Nail's help, Roguemoore began securing Dokie's litter onto the back of one of the mules, using what remaining rope they had. The boy's swollen face poked from the cocoon of blankets, wisps of his dirt-colored hair fluttering in the breeze.

"What am I to do now?" Liz Hen cried as she watched Nail and the dwarf tie the boy down. "Beer Mug's run off. And Dokie is dying. The whole rotten adventure has turned into naught but mushy hammered shit. And I want no more part of it. *Blackest Heart* is a curse and so is this damnable angel stone." She dug the black stone from her bodice, unwrapped the silk and eyed the small rock angrily. "I should throw it away."

Culpa Barra took the stone from her before she could throw it out over the ice. The Dayknight swiftly tucked both silk and stone away in the small leather pouch at his belt.

"The quest for *Blackest Heart* was a success." Culpa grabbed her by the shoulders, looking her in the eyes sternly. "Now some of us will carry on for *Afflicted Fire*. It's not over yet."

"Not over yet?" She growled. "Are you out of your bleeding mind?"

"Listen, Liz Hen," Godwyn stood in front of her as Culpa moved away. "This is where we part from the others. You and I must get Dokie back to Stanclyffe if he is to survive. I will need you to be strong. Dokie will need you to be strong."

"But . . . what?" she stammered. "But . . . how will we survive without the others, without Seita or Val-Draekin to fight for us?"

"We'll be fine," the bishop said, though his tone and the grim look on his face bespoke a far different sentiment. "We'll have plenty of food. We'll be taking the mules with us. They will bear Dokie safely and securely. What little healing draught I have left is not enough for Dokie, nor the right kind. We must get him to Stanclyffe."

"Can't Seita at least come with us too?" Liz Hen pleaded.

"We'll need Seita's skills at Deadwood Gate," Roguemoore said. "We can't spare any more of the company helping Dokie."

"You coldhearted little beast." Liz Hen's red eyes widened in anger as she stood, towering over the dwarf. "Dokie is no throwaway piece of garbage."

"You know that's not what Roguemoore meant." Godwyn stepped in front of the girl and gripped her shoulders in an attempt to refocus her attention on him. "Dokie's life is in our hands now. We must say our good-byes now."

Liz Hen's tears only doubled. "But they are all my friends and I can't leave them." She slumped away from the bishop. "Seita won't be able to braid my hair so nice anymore."

"Worry not," the Vallè maiden said. "We shall meet again, you and I."

Liz Hen straightened her posture, wiped the tears from her face with both forearms. "But how can you be so sure?"

"I trust my intuition on matters of friendship." Seita gripped Liz Hen's arm. "Especially when it comes to leave-takings, and especially reunions. And when we meet again, Liz Hen, I shall fix your hair any way you like."

At Seita's pronouncement, the red-haired girl's face lit from within, as if that one future pleasure of having the Vallè braid her hair would be enough to truly see her through.

"The mules are ready," Culpa said with impatience. "Dokie is secure. We mustn't tarry. We must put as much distance between us and those remaining oghuls as we can."

At the Dayknight's gruff pronouncement, the Company of Nine stood still, somber, the silence between them both a gulf and an acknowledgment of comradeship shared.

Bishop Godwyn stepped forward and grasped both Culpa and Roguemoore by the shoulders. "May the Blessed Mother Mia go with us all."

Soon all the company was offering sullen, but heartfelt, good-byes to both Godwyn and Liz Hen. And when the parting was over, the bishop took the reins of the mules and pointed them toward the ruins of Arco.

Stefan's legs were suddenly moving of their own volition. He stepped to the mule bearing Dokie's litter, reached out and brushed away several strands of stray hair from the boy's swollen face, dipped his own head, and kissed his friend gently on the forehead.

† † † † †

Half a day later the six who remained in the company were heading due east. Still navigating the arduous maze of the glacier, they plod-ded along, threading their way through slabs of ice the size of castles and crevasses that dropped into darkness.

The glacier was a mighty desolation of frozen shards and murder-ous crags, and Stefan could hear the pounding maelstrom of waters somewhere deep under his feet, the cacophony growing louder with each step he took. His heart was empty, having lost Liz Hen and Dokie and Beer Mug, the bishop too. Nail was his only remaining link to his previous life in Gallows Haven.

Culpa Barra led the way, followed by Seita, then Stefan. Nail was next, followed by Val-Draekin. Roguemoore dawdled last in line, fatigue from the weight of his plate armor finally showing after all these days of hard travel. The leathery old dwarf gasped for breath so loudly, Stefan could hear his huffing over the roiling rivers below. They were all once again bundled in their gray cloaks, hoods up. Each carried a pickax for safety, occasionally using them to climb and descend blocks of ice that barred their progress.

None of them were tied together. But there was nothing to be done for it. They had lost most of one rope in the mines under a crushing slab of roof. What remained had been used to secure Dokie's litter to the mule. Culpa said they could find new mounts in one of the many small logging hamlets when they reached the southeastern end of the lochs.

They hiked across a relatively flat expanse of ice now, spotted with pools and ponds of meltwater. To Stefan, it looked like this white plateau stretched clear and free to the eastern range. But he was no judge of distance out here on this stark terrain. The sun hung high above and beat down harshly on the ice, making it nearly impossible to focus on any one thing for long. The sound and thud of water roiling and crashing somewhere underneath was growing into a violent, near-deafening thunder.

Stefan watched Seita step across the slushy ice a few paces in front of him, her feet always lithe and certain. In contrast, Culpa was trudging heavily along about ten paces ahead of her, slipping occasionally and going down. Stefan felt himself go instantly light-headed as the surface of the glacier seemed to shift under his feet. Disoriented, he stopped walking, regaining his balance.

Ahead, Culpa and Seita had stopped, both looking back at him. The furious sound of roaring waters below was overwhelming, thunderous crashes and booms, as if great chunks of ice were being tossed about by giants somewhere far below.

Seita stepped gingerly back toward him, taking his hand in her own. Stefan was shocked to the core when he saw the look of utmost fear in her round eyes. Her terrified gaze moved beyond him to Nail, Val-Draekin, and the dwarf.

Stefan turned. Nail was no more than five paces behind him, but he was rooted in place, frightened eyes roaming the glacial surface, pickax gripped in a tight fist. Val-Draekin was just behind Nail, his pickax also ready. Roguemoore, some thirty paces back, stood still, unmoving. Stefan felt the reassurance of the ice pick in his own hand.

"Look down," Seita said, her words almost drowned out by the din of booming waters. With the toe of her boot she brushed aside the watery-gray layer of slush between them, revealing the living, frothing terror that was underfoot.

They were standing on naught but a whisper-thin sheet of clear ice, sweeping waves of raucous water visible below. His heart thudded realizing they were right above a roiling, colossal glacial river. A coil of sheer panic twisted around Stefan's heart as he took three deep breaths of air. But the breaths did nothing to help calm the terror crawling up his spine.

There was a thunderous crack and crash. Stefan whirled to see the surface of the glacier slowly sag directly underneath Nail and Val-Draekin.

There was another riotous boom and the entire landscape tilted. The ice dropped out from under Nail, Val-Draekin, and the dwarf. A fifty-foot slab cracked like an eggshell right in front of Stefan, every shard plummeting into the most horrendously torrential nightmare he had ever seen, taking his three companions with it.

Roguemoore dropped thirty feet straight down into the raging torrent, the violent lash of the frothing current instantly sweeping him away and over a growling, rumbling waterfall that disappeared into a violent cavernous hole under the glacier.

Nail and Val-Draekin landed on a sloping wall of ice just above the roiling river, and both instantly slammed their pickaxes into the ice above their heads in a desperate attempt to slow their slide toward a vicious watery death—a vicious death that had just claimed Roguemoore.

Stefan's heart hammered as the ice cracked under his own feet. Both he and Seita fell back, scrambling to find purchase on the solid surface of the glacier, legs frantically churning for safety. The Vallè woman spun and used her pickax to climb free of the tilting ice whilst Stefan slid farther down. Culpa latched onto the hood of his cloak and pulled him roughly away from the savage, boiling crevasse.

Stefan clung to the solid surface of the glacier, heart hammering still.

"Take off your cloaks!" the Dayknight shouted. "Tie them together and make a rope!" Stefan levered himself to his feet, frantically shedding his cloak and tossing it to Culpa, eyes fixed to the horror just over the rim of the ice below. Ten feet down on a plunging slope of white and blue was Nail, his swollen face stretched in a taut grimace as he stabbed his ax down again and again, iron pick battering into the ice, trying to find purchase. Val-Draekin had slipped twenty feet below Nail, the point of his own pickax digging a trench in the slippery slope as he continued sliding toward the raging waters.

Beyond the Vallè, the ferocious ice-filled river itself was a horror. A hundred paces wide, emerging from an enormous hollow shaft in the glacier some distance to the north. Great hunks of ice, boulders, sections of trees, all of it came boiling up from the heaving and thrashing stew at intervals, all of it sucked under and swallowed just as swiftly. The foaming current of ice and sludge and furious white waves raced down a pitched and jagged chute, plunging over an underground cliff into a thunderous gaping blue darkness. *And Roguemoore sucked down there somewhere! Dead!*

The slick incline Val-Draekin and Nail clung to was soon awash with rushing water, a frigid, seething flow that now dragged at the Vallè's feet. Culpa tossed his makeshift rope made of cloaks down toward Nail, who latched on and held tight.

"Help pull him up!" the Dayknight yelled. Stefan and Seita grabbed ahold of the cloak and heaved with all their might, pulling Nail toward safety.

Then a thick shard of glacial ice was thrust brutally up from the river, scraping Val-Draekin from his perch, launching him straight into the fierce flow and over the murderous waterfall.

"Pull!" Culpa yelled at Stefan and Seita. "We can't lose Nail, too!"

But the sheet of ice Nail clung to tore loose with a ponderous snap, sliding into the ravenous river. The cloak tore free of Nail's grib as the sloping slab of ice folded over onto itself, buckling under the weight of the cruel crushing current, burying the Gallows Haven boy under brutal white waves and sweeping him over the crushing falls behind Val-Draekin.

Stefan's mind was hollow torment, stricken to the core. *Three would not make it,* Seita had predicted. And now her vision had come to pass.

Roguemore. Val-Draekin. Nail.

Dead.

*Some claim Vallè crystals mixed with forged iron and silver will glow with a certain light and mist when handled by a mortal man. But the foul tools and weaponry formed of such fey alchemy ought not be trusted nor ever used.*
—THE WAY AND TRUTH OF LAIJON

# CHAPTER THIRTY-TWO

# NAIL

10TH DAY OF THE ANGEL MOON, 999TH YEAR OF LAIJON

SKY LOCHS, GUL KANA

The howling cavern swallowed Nail whole, straight down into its raging blue maw. Horror punched a hole through his jumping heart as he plummeted. Bubbles and froth and shards of ice and stabbing cold waters, his sight reduced to just a receding prick of light far above. *I'm dead!*

What wind remained was crushed from his lungs as he slammed into solid ice, snapping his head back with a stunning blow, sending him spinning and hurtling uncontrollably down another dark chute in the captive flow. It was utter darkness now and he lost all sense of up or down. The scorching cold of the water strangled his entire body in its frigid grip—a cold more powerful than when he'd jumped from the *Lady Kindly* to save Zane.

He clenched his eyes shut to stave off the agony as hunks of ice tumbled and sliced past him in the current. His arms and legs were rendered useless by the swirling cold torrent, all limbs flopping uncontrollably, numb fingers grasping at nothing but churning frigid violence. Ice-torn lungs frantically trying to grab a breath, sucking in water. Nose and mouth frozen with suffocating pain that lanced clear to his heaving chest. His face was raw agony.

Then his shoulder kissed something solid, scarcely grazing it. But it was enough to send him spinning head over heels, and suddenly he was sailing weightless into a vast black nothing. Upside down he dropped, arms and legs flailing, lungs purging a vomitous river of icy sludge into air. One solid breath. He opened his eyes, a brief flash of blue light, and he was dashed face-first into a another block of ice that had raced up from nowhere. As he careened off the ice, thunderous water crushed and pounded him from above, thrusting him farther down, burying him deeper and deeper into a foaming stew of bubbles and debris.

He floundered, drifting underwater, halfheartedly kicking out with legs nearly dead from pain, sensing a faint light seeping in from somewhere, lungs again desperate for a breath. He tried to swim, but his arms and legs were tortured, heavy, aflame with pain. He had seen some light above, eyes barely cracked open. He couldn't tell up or down, but he felt the weight of his armor and sword were dragging against his efforts.

He tore off his belt and sword, scrambled to release the leather bucklers of his armor. But he was too slow, his fingers too numb, scarcely able to move. Still, he wriggled free of the chest plate, stripped the shoulder plates off, kicked his heavy boots free. His limbs were near useless, body totally spent, but he slowly glided toward the light.

Surrounding him was naught but thunderous sound. A brief glint of silver in the bubbling dark, a twinkling flash. *Mermaids!* Then it was gone under the swirl of familiar images, visions clouding his mind. *A burning tree—a pillar of fire stretching to a starlit sky. Under*

*the tree a white knight in a peculiar horned helm astride a brilliant white*
*stallion. A thin blond girl, green-eyed, on the steed before him, her hand a*
*metal claw—*

And his head broke the surface of the water.

He gasped. *Air!* His eyes darted about. Startled by the immense roar
of the waterfall booming into a cavern off to his left, he paddled away.
But he gave up quickly, legs and arms so numb he could scarcely move.
It was a battle just to keep his head above water. He bobbed, helpless.
Faint light filtered in from above, barely illuminating his surroundings.
He was in a rippling pool of dark water, floating amidst hunks of ice
and drifts of wood, a jagged roof of blue ice overhead.

A hand latched onto his shoulder with a firm grip and pulled him
under. When he resurfaced, Val-Draekin's stark face rose up from the
frigid waters right in front of him.

"I can't make it." The Vallè's voice was barely audible above the
din of the waterfall. "My leg is broke. I'll need your help."

Nail clutched Val-Draekin to him, thrust his arms under the
Vallè's armpits, and held him above water. They floundered help-
lessly together, both kicking a losing battle against the deep, both
sinking under the skin of the water. Val-Draekin shoved free of Nail
and latched onto a nearby chunk of jagged ice the size of a horse.
Nail reached for the ice too, but it tipped in the water when he tried
to scramble atop it, sending him back under water, Val-Draekin too.
They bobbed back to the surface, both powerless as they watched the
ice drift away.

"There!" Val-Draekin's voice was still naught but a muffled sound
against the booming of the falls. "The wall! Help me to it!"

Nail craned his frozen neck. Just behind him rose the crooked
wall of the cavern. Enormous crags in the ice ran in jagged lines
from water to ceiling, crevasses jammed with blocks of ice and other
debris. The nearest crag had two towering blocks of ice crammed
into it, the blocks leaning away from each other, creating a steep V at

their conjoined base. The bottom of the V was just a few feet above the surface of the pool, wide enough for two men to stand in, if they could reach it.

Val-Draekin sputtered and dipped below the water. Nail grabbed the front of the Vallè's leather tunic and lifted him up. With feeble limbs, Nail swam backward toward the wall, pulling the Vallè along. Once they reached the V at the base of the two blocks of ice, Val-Draekin wriggled his way up and out of the water and wedged himself into it, Nail pushing him up from behind. The Vallè was barefooted too, having discarded his own boots in the water at some point. And from the twisted angle of one of Val-Draekin's exposed feet, Nail could tell the Vallè's leg was likely broken just above the ankle.

In the crag a few feet beyond Val-Draekin was a tangled pile of driftwood, all of it lodged and frozen into the ice. The Vallè scooted over and wrestled one of the gnarled logs free and held it out for Nail, who latched onto it and held on for dear life. Once he was pulled to safety, they both sat there, huddled together in silence, freezing.

A stream of light from a crack in the glacier hundreds of feet above rained down right on their precarious perch. But it offered no warmth. Nail could scarcely move his fingers, they were so numb from the brittle, wet cold. In fact, his fingers were icing over. His bare feet were solid lumps of frozen agony. And his face, every tiny part of his flesh where a silver dart had pricked his skin burned with singular individual fire and rage.

"Where's Roguemoore?" he shouted. But he didn't know if Val-Draekin could even hear him over the roaring of the waterfall. The dark-haired fellow just stared into the bleak nothingness of the cavern, shivering violently, pale features a mask of agony. Nail shivered too, every muscle in his body aching from the intensity of it all, jaw clenched. If he was injured like the Vallè, he couldn't tell for the stinging, paralyzing cold that ate at every part of him. He couldn't see any blood.

Val-Draekin began tugging at some of the driftwood frozen into the crevasse next to him. He turned to Nail, shouting, "Any driftwood that floats by, grab it!"

Nail didn't know if he could even move. A thin layer of ice cracked away from his wrists and fingers as he rolled to the side. With aching and weary muscles, he leaned over the pool, searching for any wood in the water. It was so cold his mind could scarcely form a thought. *Where is Roguemoore?*

He fished a few small chunks of driftwood from the water and ponderously handed them back to the Vallè, who stacked them up with the wood he'd gathered from the wall. After a few minutes, the pile of wet, frozen wood between them had grown and Nail sat back up. The Vallè put the palms of his hands up to his own lips and blew on them for warmth. After a moment he reached into his soaked leather armor and pulled forth a flattened leather satchel tied with a string at the top. He opened the satchel and removed another, smaller black bag made of rough wool. Despite the drenched look of the Vallè and all his leather clothes, in the light from above the wool sack looked bone dry.

Val-Draekin dipped his hand down into the bag. When he removed his hand, his fingers were coated in what looked like white chalk. He put his hand to his lips and blew some of the powder over the wet wood. He then waved his hand over the pile and snapped his fingers. To Nail's astonishment, a ball of flame appeared in the palm of the Vallè's hand. Val-Draekin held the fire under the pile of driftwood for a second until the wood began to smolder and catch. Soon bits of the wood were aflame and the Vallè slapped the fire in his hand out against the leg of his sopping leather pants.

Nail didn't care how Val-Draekin had just performed what seemed like a miracle.

He simply huddled over the flames, warming his hands, gazing at his strange companion. The Vallè's face was more ashen than normal, even under the yellow flush of the firelight. A continuous shiver coursed through Nail, a shiver of both cold and fear. He couldn't escape the realization that Roguemoore was gone and he and Val-Draekin were hopelessly lost under tons of glacial ice.

*O children of Amadon, recall the favor which Laijon hast bestowed upon you, and guard yourself against the wraiths. For they who believe in sorcery, Laijon hath cursed.*
—THE WAY AND TRUTH OF LAIJON

# CHAPTER THIRTY-THREE
# AVA SHAY

### 10TH DAY OF THE ANGEL MOON, 999TH YEAR OF LAIJON
### SOUTH OF LOKKENFELL, GUL KANA

Ava Shay set her stance and held her sword out, the heart-shaped ruby in the hilt pressed against her inner wrist. *My Heart,* she had named the weapon. She hadn't shared the name of the sword with Enna Spades. Nor would she.

"Up," the warrior woman ordered, lowering her own bloodstained blade, stepping forward. "Keep the tip of your sword up." Spades was dressed in full Knight Archaic battle gear: silver cuirass and tunic of chain mail and leather greaves studded with silver, all of it splattered with blood. Her dark blue cloak was thrown over her left shoulder. A wooden crossbow and quiver half-full of quarrels were strapped to the baldric crossing her back. Her battle helm was hooked to the pommel of her stallion's saddle—the white horse, named Slaughter, stood to their left, blood smeared over its haunches.

Spades had just recently been in battle. As had Aeros Raijael, now within his tent not fifty paces away, changing from his own armor. The bulk of the White Prince's army was still swarming the outskirts of Lokkenfell, mopping up after the skirmish. They had just fought some five hundred knights from Lord's Point. Spades seemed healed from her previous injury two days ago. Her arm showed no ill effects anyway. Her sling was gone. Unless the injury had all been a pretense. With Aeros' group of Knights Archaic, all things seemed like they were meant to deceive, even injuries.

From her vantage point atop a grassy slope of brush and hedgerows, Ava could just make out the distant buildings of Lokkenfell. A few stone structures along the outskirts of the town were smoldering, black smoke billowing, destroyed during the clash of armies. Spiderwood had been tasked with guarding her during the battle. Now he was down in Lokkenfell hunting stragglers with Hammerfiss, Mancellor, and Jenko.

Whilst Aeros was changing and washing, Spades had insisted on giving Ava a short lesson with the sword. And as Ava had sparred with Spades, she couldn't believe she was actually enjoying the practice, enjoying the time spent with this woman she hated. She was conflicted. Even though, according to *The Way and Truth of Laijon*, it was wrong in the eyes of Laijon for a woman to wield a weapon, she was actually glad to be learning how to carry a sword like a man. In fact, what conflicted her most was that with each passing day she was beginning to wonder how much truth there really was in the holy book she'd revered her whole life. As her time as a captive wore on, she noticed she was conversing with Laijon less and less. And the less she prayed, the more the wraiths stayed out of her mind.

Spades slashed with her sword and Ava blocked the blow. "Good," the woman complimented her. "But after a successful parry, be ready. . . ."

Spades trailed off, her attention focused on a group of Knights of the Blue Sword. They were trudging up the grassy slope toward them from the direction of Lokkenfell, all afoot. Ava counted ten, each helmeted, armor and helms crusted in blood from long fighting, each girt with a sword on his belt and a shield in hand. But there was something odd about the approaching knights that Ava could not place.

"What's this?" Spades stiffened, brow furrowed. "Be wary, Ava."

Then Ava figured it out. Normally Knights of the Blue Sword followed a rigid pattern of march at all times, highest-ranking knight in the lead, the others following behind in two columns. But these ten battle-weary knights wandered up the hill, clumped together and leaderless.

"I order you to stay back!" Spades imposed herself between Ava and the approaching fighters, her sword ready. But the knights spread out, several drawing their weapons. "Stop!" Spades shouted.

The nearest knight charged. The others followed, some angling to get behind Spades, shouting as they ran. A stab of hope pricked Ava's heart. *Are they here to rescue me?* She backed away, confused, frightened, hopeful, the tip of her own sword trailing in the dirt before her, not knowing whose side she was on now.

Spades wasted no time, launching herself straight at her nearest foe, longsword whirling, striking the helmeted head from the first knight as she ducked under the looping swing of another. When she rose, her follow-through sliced the arm off the knight who had next taken aim at her. Both the severed arm and head of the first knight struck the ground at the same time, blood spouting as the two men fell to the ground, one screaming. The tip of Spades' sword swiftly silenced his cries.

The warrior woman was so fast Ava couldn't even keep track of how she killed the next three knights who came at her. But they soon all lay on the ground, swords and shields a-scatter, blood gushing from gaping wounds. Five of the knights were dead in less than two seconds and the other five backed off, wary, shields up.

"She is not who we came to kill!" one of the knights yelled, motioning with his sword toward Aeros' tent. "The White Prince is in there!"

Two of the remaining knights rushed Spades. The tip of the warrior woman's sword met the first knight straight through the eye slit of his helm, blood gushing from underneath and over his chest plate. She ripped her sword free and he dropped dead at the second knight's feet, tripping him. Spades was quick to strike his head from his body as he fell. Two more of her foes again lay dead on the ground in the blink of an eye, thick gouts of red pumping over the dirt.

Aeros Raijael stepped out of his tent, his own sword ready. He wore no armor, just a white robe tied at the waist. The three knights remaining sprinted toward him.

Ava was in their charging path. She held up her blade.

In one fluid motion Spades pulled the crossbow from her back, nocked a quarrel, and fired. The bolt struck the middle knight in the back of the thigh, sending him stumbling to the ground right at Ava's feet. He lost hold of his sword. His helmet sprang from his head, tumbling away in the dirt.

The other two knights ran straight by Ava, attacking the White Prince with a fury. But Aeros' glittering sword was as fast as Spades'. He beheaded both with a swift ease and grace that seemed almost impossible to Ava.

The knight under Ava struggled to stand. He managed to kneel on one leg, his longsword still in hand, its honed edge looking bright and sharp.

Scared, Ava put the tip of her sword to the knight's throat. He looked up at her, hair falling in front of his wide, pain-filled eyes. At first Ava had hoped these men were here to rescue her—then found herself relishing the ease with which Spades and Aeros had finished them. She was tempted to push the tip of her own thin blade into the kneeling man's throat. *Have I turned to the dark like Jenko, calloused and cruel? Have I betrayed Laijon so soon?*

The White Prince stood behind her. "You are no knight of mine," he addressed the man at the end of Ava's sword. The knight spat a wad of blood on the ground at Aeros' bare feet, then stared at the White Prince with cold defiance.

"What is your name?" Aeros asked. "Why do you wear the colors of my army? Why do you pose as a Knight of the Blue Sword?"

The man remained silent.

"Answer." Spades stepped up casually next to Aeros. "Or Ava here will stick the point of her little poker through your throat."

Ava pressed the tip of her blade against the man's Adam's apple. *What would feel like to slide it into his throat?* She wondered if she really had it in her to kill a man. Wondered what evil had overcome her.

"Answer, scum," Spades repeated, voice near a shout.

Ava pushed the blade into the knight's flesh just some, drawing a trickle of blood. The man's eyes widened with fright. "I am Ser Revalard Avocet of Lord's Point. Captain of Lord Kelvin Kronnin's Ocean Guard."

"You, Ser Revalard, have much to answer for," said Aeros, a harsh eloquence now in his tone. "And you *will* answer. And then your death will be a long and drawn out affair. And it will be most painful."

Ser Revalard met Aeros' gaze. "I've said all I will say."

"No, you haven't." Spades sheathed her own sword. "You *will* talk. In fact, you'll squawk everything you know like a Tomkin Sty tom turkey, you just don't know it yet." Spades knelt in front of the man. "In fact, you have no idea how much you will say."

The man's face remained defiant.

Hammerfiss, Mancellor, and Jenko approached from the south, all in bloodstained armor, all mounted. Spiderwood was with them, black armor spotless. His Bloodeye steed, Scowl, was breathing heavily. Aeros and Spades watched their approach.

"There's a lot of blood about." Hammerfiss' eyes were alight as the four reined up, his grin wide and full of amusement. "Did the slip of a girl slaughter them all? Did little Ava do all this?"

Jenko's eyes narrowed when he saw the sword in Ava's hand, the tip still pressed to Ser Revalard's throat. Ava backed away from the kneeling knight, sliding the sword slowly into the sheath at her belt.

"I recognize that man," Mancellor said. "He was part of Jondralyn's contingent of knights when Jenko, the Spider, and I met with her in Ravenker." Jenko nodded his affirmation.

"So, Ser Revalard is a man of some import." Spades smiled down at the knight. "So how 'bout we make a deal, man of import? Let's say I give you back your sword and helm. Let you stand. All you need do is attack that man atop the red-eyed horse." She nodded toward the Spider. "He is a Bloodwood assassin. A creature most foul. Stab him but once, and we let you go free. No questions asked."

"Don't include me in your deals," Spiderwood said, emotionless dark eyes surveying the dead men scattered about.

"The deal has already been offered." Spades smiled. "If I give back his sword and he attacks you . . . whatever will you do?"

"Kill you both." The Bloodwood leaned forward in his saddle, black leather armor softly creaking as he gripped the saddle horn.

"It matters not," Ser Revalard hissed. "I piss on your deal. You won't honor it anyway."

Spades turned her attention back to Revalard. "Oh, I will honor the deal." She picked up his sword and held it out. "Take it."

"I said I piss on you and your deal, savage bitch."

Spades chucked Revalard's sword back to the ground. "I hate when people won't even try." She snatched up the man's right hand, stripped the gauntlet away. She grabbed his middle finger and bent it straight back. It broke with a harsh snap. The man screamed. Spades kept twisting, forcing his finger back until the palm of his hand split open, bone and tendon exposed, shockingly white against the flow of blood.

Spades kept wrenching, peeling Ser Revalard's middle finger

down the back side of his wrist until naught but a red flap of skin was holding it to his hand. With a quick jerk she tore the finger all the way free and tossed it to the dirt.

Then she grabbed another of Ser Revalard's fingers and began peeling.

† † † †

Ser Revalard died a long and painful death—died at the murderous hands of both Hammerfiss and Spades. Jenko Bruk helped in the murder.

And again Ava had been forced to watch, caressing the sharpened edges of *My Heart* as the man screamed his final agonizing screams.

Before he died, Revalard had confessed. He and the other nine Ocean Guards had been under the direct orders of Lord Kelvin Kronnin to infiltrate the armies of Sør Sevier and assassinate the White Prince. He proudly recounted how they had trapped and killed a group of Aeros' Knights of the Blue Sword and stolen their armor. But Ser Revalard had not realized the futility of his quest. For Ava knew how deadly the Knights Archaic of Sør Sevier were, she knew that they lived to war and hunt and scheme and torture. Had Ser Revalard known what she knew, he would not have set out on such a fool mission.

Now he was fingerless, toeless, earless, noseless, cockless, and dead.

But Ava had to admit, the buffet of food Aeros served after the man's torture was divine. The Knights Archaic always feasted like royals after a fight, especially when the enemy fought back, or played some form of trickery, or suffered the torture as hardily as Ser Revalard Avocet had. The surge of bloodlust and violence built up a hearty appetite in Spades and Hammerfiss, and they reveled in the party afterward. Ava enjoyed the food and wine herself. It was as if she had lost all feeling. As if she lived merely for the next numbing drink.

The Knights Archaic were gathered around a fire pit outside Aeros' tent. All were sitting on thick pine stumps, all gabbing openly and candidly with Jenko and Ava as if they were all old friends. Aeros had retreated into his tent earlier, as he was wont to do, never one to enjoy the bawdy talk of his underlings. Not twenty paces away, the Bloodwood stood guard near Aeros' tent, red-streaked eyes glistening in the firelight, listening to the drunken conversation of those around the fire, brushing his Bloodeye steed.

Ava stroked the edges of the thin blade on her lap. *My Heart.* As she studied the ruby-hilted sword, the smoke of the fire, the strangeness of the conversation, the rich food and wine settling in her stomach, all seemed to scramble her thoughts. She had only been half listening to what was being said by those gathered around the fire, but at the mention of Jenko's father, Baron Bruk, Ava's interest was piqued.

"See, Mancellor," Hammerfiss began, "Jenko figures Spades made him torture his own father because she hates men. Hates fathers."

"Is that another one of your insights into the minds of women?" Spades asked, slurring her words slightly. She stirred the fire in front of her with the point of a thin pine branch. Spades sat to the left of Ava. Jenko Bruk was on the other side of Spades. Mancellor was straight across the fire from Hammerfiss.

"Well, tell us different," Hammerfiss challenged.

"I have no father," Spades said. "Never have had."

"Is that so," Hammerfiss said. "Gault told me some about your past. Said your wanton viciousness indeed has something to do with your father, a man steeped in lechery and perversion."

"Gault Aulbrek told you nothing of my past," Spades said sharply. "Because Gault was the type of man who kept his opinions of others to himself." Her drunken gaze cut into Hammerfiss. "Why would you lie about our friend in front of the others?"

"If not your father"—Hammerfiss glared right back at her—"then regale us with other sordid tales of your youth. Let us glean from those stories why you blossomed from the precious freckle-faced kid you were to the savage heartless killer you are."

"Fine, if you wish our friends to hear such tales." Spades' green eyes were now focused intently on Jenko. "When I was a child, my mother and I, we lived with my older brother, Egan, in Harlech, a small coastal village just north of Badr. I was an unnaturally tall and awkward girl, teased a lot for my red hair and lankiness. When I was six, my mother spent what small amount of coin she had for some white frosted cakes to celebrate my birthday. She planned out many fun children's games to play in the grassy field behind our hut and invited the village children to join in the party. The day of my birthday we waited. And waited. And not one other child came to celebrate my birthday or eat the cakes. Egan reveled in my humiliation and tears. But he was always a cruel, unfeeling boy. I lost all faith in humanity that day, if you must know."

Jenko sat back. "That is the reason you take such joy in killing, a spoiled birthday party?"

"No," Spades answered flatly, smiling. "That story is complete bullshit. Made it up on the spot. There is no place called Harlech north of Badr."

Hammerfiss was laughing deep and heavy now. His whole body shook, the fetishes tied in his beard bouncing gaily. "You're barking up the wrong tree now, boy. Shouldn't have gotten yourself involved. Shouldn't have got her started."

Jenko glared at both Spades and Hammerfiss, then shook his head in disgust.

"Wanna know the real truth?" Spades asked, a grim look on her face now. "I had a kitten once. A cute little black fur ball I'd named Pretty Miss Kitty. Came home one day to my brother Egan holding its smashed little body. He said the woodpile had toppled and crushed it. Found out later Egan had killed it himself. Put it in the bottom of an empty wine barrel and smashed it with a sledgehammer."

"Another bullshit story," Jenko said.

"Is it?" Spades glared at him.

"Did you bury the cat?" Mancellor asked.

"Can't remember what I did with the cat." Spades kept her eyes fixed on Jenko as she answered Mancellor. "But I snuck into the blacksmith shop, stole the iron forger's tongs one night, took 'em home, and used 'em to pull Egan's tongue out of his mouth by the root. Did it as he slept, cool as you please."

Hammerfiss was no longer laughing. "You yanked out your own brother's tongue?"

"Aye." Spades' eyes burned with a deep passion. She twisted the stick in the fire again. "But it only turned the bastard into more of a stupid brute. Crude and unruly and stupid. Several moons later I plucked out both Egan's eyeballs with my bare hands. Forced him to eat 'em. Forced him to choke his own useless eyes down his own useless throat."

Jenko looked sick to his stomach. Drunk, Ava wondered if the conversation she was hearing was even real.

"You needn't share anymore if you don't want," Mancellor said to her. Spades nodded and went back to stirring the fire.

"So nice and compassionate, Ser Mancellor." Hammerfiss laughed. "But lest you forget, Spades does not like nice men."

"You're wrong." Spades looked up. "I happen to like nice men."

Hammerfiss laughed again. "Of course you do." He slapped his own knee, shook his head, and then pointed at Mancellor. "See, there is a nice man. I ain't seen you fuck him in a long while now."

Mancellor's nervous gaze fell on Ava briefly, then shot straight back down to the fire. Ava looked over at Jenko, but he would not meet her gaze. She couldn't pinpoint why, but Hammerfiss' comment about Spades not fucking Mancellor anymore made her feel guilty. Nail had been a nice boy. Obvious in his intent. And she knew it, and still she had led him on. Whilst Jenko was ofttimes mean and boastful and inconsiderate. *I've no idea what Jenko Bruk thinks of me now.* And that thought drove her mad. *Does he think I go to Aeros' bed willingly, with no fight?* The wine was muddling her thoughts.

"You don't know a thing about me or Spades." Mancellor finally broke the silence, defending himself. "We've come to our own agreement."

"Do explain," Hammerfiss said. "This ought to be good."

"The things we've discussed stay between her and me."

"How valiant of you." Hammerfiss raised his bushy brows, amused.

"I respect women," Mancellor finished. "And that should be the end of it."

Hammerfiss leaned back. "Now you're just trying to impress young Ava Shay with how chivalrous you are, Mancellor. But lest you forget, Ava does not like nice men either. For it's she who stays nightly with a man who rapes her."

Hammerfiss' words hit Ava like a punch in the gut. The blade of the ruby-hilted sword now dangled between her legs, her grip on the pommel limp. She wanted to say something in her own defense, but she was too stunned to speak. Hammerfiss had merely articulated what she herself had just been thinking.

"Do not blame Ava for what Aeros does." Spades was glaring at Hammerfiss, a cold hardness in her voice.

Hammerfiss glowered. "Does not Ava's *Way and Truth of Laijon* say, and I quote, 'A woman should rather herself be put to death than be defiled by any other than her husband. A woman so defiled is useless in the eyes of Laijon.' That and a whole host of other such sentiment?"

"Do not quote from that blasphemous book in front of me," Spades said.

But Ava hung her head, for she knew the big man was right. Bishop Tolbret had quoted that very scripture to his followers in the Gallows Haven chapel many times. According to scripture, a woman was duty bound to end her own life before submitting to rape. She was duty bound to keep her own purity intact. *And I failed. . . .*

When she looked up, Hammerfiss was gazing at her steadfastly, no sympathy in his eyes. "It is why our Lord Aeros commits such depravities upon the girls he captures. To see which of them is truly a follower of Laijon. For those woman true to Laijon will kill themselves rather than yield to his hand, rather than surrender to his throbbing hairless cock—"

"Don't say that kind of shit to her." Spades stood, stirring the stick in the fire angrily now. "And don't use the disgusting words of *The Way and Truth of Laijon* to humiliate anyone, especially not Ava. Especially not in front of me."

"Or what will you do?"

"I will pluck your eyes from your head like I did my brother." Spades glared icily at Hammerfiss. Her gaze then swung to Jenko Bruk. "Wanna know why I fight and torture and kill the men of Gul Kana with such glee and purpose? It's because of Ember Gatherings and secret oaths. It's because of that book. It's because of *The Way and Truth of Laijon*. A book full of poisonous, demeaning lies. Nothing but woman-hating harmful bullshit."

"What do you care what is in *The Way and Truth of Laijon*?" Jenko asked. "You're from Sør Sevier."

"What do you know of my youth?" Spades answered quickly. "Are you privy to what type religious poison was forced into my mind as a child? Do you know what wraiths I have been forced to fight my whole life?"

Spades looked toward the Spider standing at Aeros' tent. "And I've no more allegiance to *The Chivalric Illuminations* than the Bloodwood does." She looked directly at Ava next. "What Hammerfiss said about *The Way and Truth of Laijon* and Aeros testing you is mostly correct. There is a reason Aeros has kept you as long as he has. Why he lies with you nightly. He wants you for his queen." Ava's heart lurched, the ruby-hilted sword not even a noticeable implement in her hand, her entire body now numb.

"I know you wish it were otherwise," Spades went on. "The reason Aeros abuses you has its root in *The Chivalric Illuminations*. The prophecies of those *Illuminations* guide Aeros in all he does. The truth is, Ava, it's these competing holy books that turn people cruel and evil. 'Tis *The Way and Truth of Laijon* and *The Chivalric Illuminations* you should blame. It is these false scriptures and the ones who devoutly follow them you need worry about, not warriors like me."

With those final words, Spades hurled her stick into the fire and stalked off.

All were silent as they watched the red-haired woman march toward her tent.

"Well." Hammerfiss stood and dusted off his leather greaves. "My work here is done." He laughed. "As you can see, I delight in stirring up folks until their heads spin right off."

Hammerfiss made his way to his tent next. Ava, Jenko, and Mancellor were left alone, each stewing in the strange cruelty they had all just endured.

"Don't fall for their bickering." Spiderwood stepped into their midst, his black leather armor eating the light of the fire. "They are playing with you, Ava. Playing with you and Jenko both."

"Don't you think I can see that?" Jenko snapped.

The Bloodwood stood there at the edge of the firelight. "They are using an antiquated Sør Sevier interrogation technique—Hammerfiss acting like your enemy, Spades acting like your friend, like your protector. That entire conversation was staged, a mere ruse for their amusement. They are like the Vallè that way. It's all a game to them. And their mischief only gets worse after a battle. They are giddy from the fight. Battle-weary and deranged and drunk. It is why they laugh at the destruction they cause. Laugh at the pain of others. After ten years of dealing in war, seeing all that they have, death, dismemberment, blood—it is how they cope. Wine and cruel jokes and the physical and mental torture of others. Believe it or not, their behavior was worse in Wyn Darrè, when they actually fought long and waged battles. They've both literally gone insane." His red-hazed glance met Ava's. "The wraiths work in mysterious ways."

"They *are* taken by the wraiths," Mancellor said. "The both of them."

"And don't let Mancellor fool you either," the Spider added. "He's heard it all before. He plays his part."

"The Bloodwood is full of shit." Mancellor stood, anger on his features.

The Spider continued on, his eyes again on Ava. "Be wary. For Spades might grow bored with the game one day and just stand up and stab both you and Jenko in the heart. Stab you and go straight to her tent and fall asleep as if nothing had happened. And Aeros will let her do it too."

"Don't listen to him." Mancellor dipped his head to Ava. "You should trust this *Bloodwood* the least of us." Mancellor walked away from the fire and into the darkness toward his tent.

"Just keep your wits about you," the Spider said. Then he went back to his post, standing guard before Aeros' tent.

"This is madness," Jenko muttered, standing. "We're surrounded by it. The Spider is not even a Knight Archaic anymore, yet Aeros lets him stand guard."

*That's what he is worried most about?* She wanted to say something to him but didn't know what. She stared straight into the fire. *What does Jenko think of me? That this is all my fault?* That nibble of ebbing guilt had blossomed to all-out panicky guilt now, and that, coupled with her own paranoia, was creating patches of sweat under her arms. *Am I a bad person like Spades? Is that why Laijon punishes me so? Is that why I cannot pray to him anymore? Is it all truly my fault? Aeros awaits me in that tent! And it is all my fault!*

She realized she was blaming herself for her own rape.

Ava knew she had to dispel those types of thoughts, or the wraiths would return to drive her mad. *Or does Aeros truly bear their burden for me? Does he truly fill me with healing powers?* She looked up from the fire as Jenko walked away from her last.

Then she looked toward Aeros' tent. *Sometimes I wonder who I even am!*

*With their faith in conflicting religions, humans will someday prey upon themselves, ravish and tear and eat one another alive, like uncontrollable beasts of the underworld.*
—THE BOOK OF THE BETRAYER

## CHAPTER THIRTY-FOUR

# CRYSTALWOOD

10TH DAY OF THE ANGEL MOON, 999TH YEAR OF LAIJON

ROKENWALDER, SØR SEVIER

The heavy air of the dark dungeon was like lead in Krista's lungs. She'd been awake for only a few hours now. Lying on her back. Then curled up. Then on her back again. Then curled. She could scarcely breathe from the nonstop throbbing lump of pain in her abdomen and chest. She feared the iron maul of the Knight Chivalric had shattered each of her ribs and smashed her innards to mush. Each agonizing breath was a heavy chore. She just wanted to give up, never in her life having imagined getting to a point where she wished for her own demise. *But wouldn't death would be such a sweet release from this all-consuming misery?* And part of that misery was knowing that she was locked in a cell—her worst nightmare.

She was in the dungeons of Rokenwalder, fettered to the wall by a five-foot length of chain, a thick iron collar around her neck, garbed only in a one-piece smock of rough tan canvas thrown over her shoulders, open at the sides. It was like one of the gowns from the infirmary in Aevrett's palace, only stiff and uncomfortable. It was all so unbearably uncomfortable. And worst of all, the blue ribbon her father had given her was gone from around her ankle. How long had she lain unconscious? *A day? A week? An hour?*

*Was Aevrett Raijael really dead?*

Sudden light filtered in from somewhere beyond the bars of her cell, thick iron bars that stretched from floor to ceiling not five feet away. The damp, filthy, straw-covered floor she lay upon smelled of dead bodies and feces. And it was probably crawling with bugs and mice and rats and bats and who knew what else. A scum-filled trough of water ran down the center of her cell, right in front of her nose. It smelled too.

She didn't want to care. But she knew herself too well. Luxury was her one vanity. And this place set her nerves on edge. More fetid water dripped from the ceiling above. *Drip. Drip. Drip.* It hit her in the face as she stared straight up at the rough stone twenty feet above. The black dye from her hair was running off into her eyes, stinging, adding to her torment. She didn't care.

*Did I really stab King Aevrett Raijael in the heart?* Groaning, she rolled onto her side, chain around her neck rattling. She thought of the lies Solvia Klingande had spewed about Ser Aulmut and her mother Avril—filthy lies that had caused her to thrust a knife into the heart of the king. *A Bloodwood must become fatherless!* Hans Rake had said, *Don't you get it yet? I already killed your father. You have been deceived. Ser Aulmut Klingande was your father.*

The lurching shadows of two prison gaolers bearing torches drifted up the corridor beyond the bars of her cell. Krista raised her head as they marched past. They were followed by Bogg and Café Colza Bouledogue. The dog stopped and sniffed and slobbered in her general direction, his rusted spiked collar gleaming dully. Two sullen prison trustees with rancid-smelling mops and buckets of water followed Bogg. She wanted to call out to the warden, but didn't, realizing Bogg probably knew she was here and didn't care. She wondered if the one-eyed dwarf, Squateye, was down here too. Bogg barked an order and his two trustees began to swab the length of the corridor with their moldy mops. Then Bogg and Café Colza disappeared into the darkness, followed by one of the gaolers. The other gaoler remained, torch held aloft for the trustees to work by.

In the flickering orange glow, Krista could see through the bars of her small chamber across the narrow hall into another solitary cell across from hers. A bearded man sat there behind the bars, similarly collared and chained. He was staring at her. "Rumor down here is you killed King Aevrett." His voice was mellow, almost comforting.

Krista raised herself up on one elbow, wincing in pain. The fellow sat in tattered pants and shirt, bare feet thrust out in front of him. He had skinny legs and arms, skeletal almost. *He's been down here a while.* She reached out and scooped some water into the palm of her hand from the trough in front of her. Drank. Spit it out, gagging.

"That stream is for shitting and pissing into," the bearded man said. "The gaolers and trustees will bring you three cups of fresh water a day. Plus two small meals. Usually just stew or gruel or porridge. It's horrid stuff. Sometimes the meals come one after the next. Other times it can be days or more between feedings. Nothing down here is on a schedule of any kind. Nothing down here makes much sense. It's run by the laziest of sorts. You will see."

Krista knew a few things about the dungeons of Rokenwalder. None of them positive for the inhabitants. She slowly levered herself up to a sitting position, tenderly prodding her chest and stomach with stiff fingers. Each small touch sent pain lancing through her entire body.

One of the trustees was swabbing the floor directly in front of her cell now, and her view of the bearded man was blocked. When the trustee moved away, Krista saw a small slip of paper lying on the floor in between the trough of piss water and the bars of her cell. She leaned forward, holding in a scream of pain as she did so, and picked up the paper before the gaoler could spot it. There was some writing on the paper. But she didn't have time to read it as the two trustees and gaoler moved on and the corridor was pitched into blackness again.

"In the light of the torch, you look like a woman I once knew," the man across from her said.

Krista did not want to get into any sort of conversation with a stranger. She thought of her training with Black Dugal. *Is it all part of the test?* Her one weakness was escaping knots and shackles and collars. And her master knew how terribly uncomfortable she was in dungeons. *Is it all a test?*

"Or perhaps I am just seeing things," the man's somber voice sounded in the dark. "There are many things from my past best forgotten."

The light of the torches flared up in the distance as the trustees and gaoler were again walking down the corridor toward her. As her cell brightened, Krista palmed the slip of paper, so the man across from her could not see her read it.

She knew immediately that the note was from Black Dugal.

It read,

> *The king is dead. And now our plan can go forth. Aevrett*
> *Raijael was not the main target. He was merely a means to*
> *an end. You must kill the man in the cell across from you. For*
> *he should have been slain years ago. He is privy to ruinous*
> *information—information that must never be revealed.*

The corridor faded to black again as the trustees and gaoler moved on. Krista wadded the paper up into a tiny ball and swallowed it.

"What is your name?" she asked the man across from her.

"If you really must know"—his voice drifted toward her from the darkness, smooth and subtle—"my name is Borden Bronachell."

*The triumphant hero of any story should be neither wholly good nor wholly innocent, but should be full of both strength and weakness, righteousness and sin, truth and guilt, for contradictions are most interesting in the human soul.*
—THE CHIVALRIC ILLUMINATIONS OF RAIJAEL

# CHAPTER THIRTY-FIVE
# GAULT AULBREK

### 10TH DAY OF THE ANGEL MOON, 999TH YEAR OF LAIJON
### AMADON, GUL KANA

The woman in the sea-blue brocaded gown and black hooded cape was escorted into the gloomy chamber by Leif Chaparral and four Dayknights. She was utterly highborn and beautiful for her advanced age. Sparkling silver bracelets tinkled brightly against her wrists as she walked. The knights walked her straight past Gault toward the blond boy curled in the fetal position in the cage next to him.

The boy lay in puddles of his own vomit.

"Can we not at least remove him from this horrid smelly place?" she pleaded.

"Jovan was explicit in his orders," Leif said. "You are only to be allowed a few minutes with your son, Lady Le Graven." He dipped his head to the woman and backed away. "No more than that, m'lady. We will remain here, just behind you."

"You may call me, Mona," the woman said.

"If it please you, m'lady."

Mona Le Graven's glance darted toward the other ten guards lining the grubby walls, and then her eyes fell on Gault briefly. She wore a tense, frightened look on her face, tears forming in her eyes. She then looked to the blond boy on the floor. "Lindholf," she called out.

But the boy did not stir.

He'd been unceremoniously dumped there in the cage next to Gault yesterday. He'd done naught but moan and whimper and cry. He'd vomited several times before falling asleep. Gault's new dungeon mate was the youth with the misshapen face who had followed Tala Bronachell and Leif's younger brother, Glade, into the caverns of Purgatory several weeks ago. He recalled that the Dayknights had mounted a search for the youngsters, and had found Tala and Glade. But Gault had never seen the deformed-faced boy emerge from those dank depths.

"Lindholf," the woman named Mona called out again.

The boy raised his head wearily, corncob-colored hair matted to the side of his face with bits of grit and dirt from the rough stone floor. His pocked and mottled face from neck to forehead glimmered in the torchlight. Burns from childhood most likely, Gault figured. Both of his ears were terribly scarred too.

"Mother." Lindholf clambered to his feet and stumbled toward the bars of his cage, clutching at them, dark-pupiled eyes large and hopeful. He wore naught but rough-spun prison breeches and a raggedy white shirt covered in vomit. The woman's hands grasped his and they clung to each other that way, both crying. Then Mona turned her face away from him. "You smell of puke."

"I got sick, Mother," the boy whined. "I'm so scared."

Mona let go his hands and backed away from the cage. A stern look had come over her face. "What have you done?" she demanded. "Why have you done this to us?"

"Done what?" His voice carried such unbearable pain.

"You have brought your family such shame. Your father is beside himself with grief. They say that what you have done is worse than what the Prince of Saint Only did."

"What, Mother? What do they say I've done?"

"They are going to take you to the slave pits, make you cut marble at Riven Rock Quarry. They say they might even *hang* you."

"But I haven't done anything."

"Haven't done anything?" Mona repeated, stark incredulity in her voice.

"I don't understand," Lindholf moaned.

"The barmaid the Silver Guard found you in sexual congress with confessed to *killing* Sterling Prentiss." Mona almost hissed the last part.

"That's impossible," Lindholf said. "She had no part in killing Prentiss. Where is she? Is she okay? Glade hasn't harmed her more?"

"You actually care for this trollop?"

"Mother, please, she is innocent. They must free her."

"She is chained in an even darker part of this foul dungeon than you." Mona's words grew bold. "The barmaid claims you helped her slay Sterling. She told Glade where Sterling's body could be found. And Glade, Tolz, Alain, and Boppard found him where the harlot said, stuffed behind a tapestry in a forgotten corridor near the western rookery. He was discovered *naked*. With many terrible wounds. Dead. *Murdered*."

"No," Lindholf cried, reaching for her hands again. She stepped back. "It was Glade," the boy wept. "He killed Prentiss. He knew where Sterling's body was. Not stuffed behind some tapestry. Don't you understand?"

"Stop lying." Mona looked at him, loathing in her gaze.

"Just ask Tala—"

"Stop!" Mona held up her hand, clenched her eyes shut. "Please.

No more lies." When her eyes snapped open again, even Gault could see there was scant love left in them. She said, "The barmaid also claimed it was you who helped in her attempt to assassinate King Jovan. Said it was you who snuck her into the castle."

"Mother, I beg of you—"

"Do not call me *Mother* ever again," she rasped with such revulsion and vehemence even the Dayknights and Leif Chaparral stepped back.

"No," the boy cried. "You have to tell them I didn't do it, Mother."

"I am not your *mother*," she hissed again. "I can see your lies, Lindholf Le Graven. You disgust me. Look at your face. Your ghastly scarred face. You never were my son."

With those parting words, the woman whirled and stalked out of the dungeon.

Lindholf's knees folded, his face pressed against the bars as he slid to the floor, hands clutching the cold iron in desperation. "No," he gasped. "Please, no." His tearful gaze fell on Leif. "Bring her back, Leif. Please."

"I think she was quite clear, *traitor*," Leif said icily. "She does not wish to speak to her murderous ugly son anymore."

Lindholf's pain-drenched sobs filled the chamber.

Leif ignored the boy and turned to Gault, a wicked grin on his face. "Your arena match with Squireck is still some days hence. Fourteen days, is it? Are you prepared?"

Gault shrugged laconically, without expression, then said, "I have a pain in my shoulder. Will you get a doctor down here?"

Leif glared, his devious smile now gone. Gault knew the guards hated inmate complaining, especially about frivolous medical conditions. They hated being asked anything. And he knew Leif was of the same disposition.

"I've a headache that needs to be addressed," he said.

"Shut the fuck up," Leif growled. "If Jovan sentences the boy to

Riven Rock Quarry, I will make sure you go there too, Gault Aulbrek. Make no mistake, that fiendish pit full of marble is a far worse place than this. Toiling in that hole will wear you right to the bone. Teach you not to be such a smart-ass."

"But at least I will be out of this cage." Gault smiled.

Leif turned and limped away, the four Dayknights following.

*Forts and keeps and castles were built and razed. Alliances were struck and broken. Homage was given and betrayed. Fealty sworn and forsook. Indeed, no clan of the Five Isles has ever forgotten the injustice done to it.*
—THE WAY AND TRUTH OF LAIJON

# CHAPTER THIRTY-SIX

# NAIL

11TH DAY OF THE ANGEL MOON, 999TH YEAR OF LAIJON

SKY LOCHS, GUL KANA

They floated wordlessly under the oppressive glacier on a warped length of driftwood, their makeshift boat shaped like large wooden spoon. Discovering the piece of water-worn timber drifting past their icy perch had likely saved their lives. Sitting astraddle the hunk of driftwood, Nail was numb from the knees down, both his feet bare, dangling in the frigid river. He guided the raft down the smooth-hewn channel of slow-moving water, using a crooked tree branch as a paddle.

The front end of their boat was scooped in the middle like a spoon, creating a dry pocket just big enough for Val-Draekin. The Vallè sat backward in the hollowed-out section of wood, facing Nail, his broken leg propped up in a splint of cobbled-together wooden sticks and strips of leather. A small pile of wood sat between his legs.

Any small bits of driftwood that floated by, Val-Draekin snatched from the water and added to the pile. They used it for burning.

Dark blue walls and a dark blue ceiling encased them in hollow silence. Here and there, some light filtered in from cracks above. A smothering, cloaking death bled from the very ice into Nail's soul. It was as if the very air might freeze itself solid. The cold gnawed at him so terribly and constantly, drawing his nerves taut like a bowstring, freezing his face into a stiff mask.

Nail figured they had floated under the glacier at least four or five miles—much farther than he'd thought possible. Val-Draekin guessed they were about two or three hundred feet under the surface of the ice. He figured the river emptied itself out into the loch waters at the edge of the glacier some twenty miles distant. Their only hope was to follow the tunnel wherever it led, that or freeze to death inside the glacier.

They'd quickly come to the stark realization that Roguemoore was truly gone. At the discovery of the large hunk of driftwood, they had abandoned their narrow perch, hoping for the best. Through a mostly pitch-black tunnel they had journeyed, no light, just gloom and cold darkness and the mercy of the current. Luckily, there had been no more waterfalls.

Nail never thought he would miss his armor. But he felt naked without it. In the past it had offered warmth of a kind. Now, everywhere his flesh came into contact with the brittle cold of the water, searing pain seeped straight to the marrow of his bones. He missed his sword, too. And he knew they would have frozen to death hours ago if not for Val-Draekin's white powder. The Vallè would occasionally light some of the driftwood kindling afire, and together they would warm their hands until it burnt down. Nail would lift one leg at a time onto the raft and warm his naked feet as best he could, the Vallè rubbing warmth back into them with his hands. But each time Nail lifted a leg, their makeshift raft would list sideways, so he mostly gritted his teeth and bore the pain of the cold waters. He found himself blowing into his hands every few minutes just to keep them from turning numb. And to add to the misery, he was starving.

"I wonder if Seita is still up there?" Val Draekin was gazing up at the icy roof of the tunnel. The Vallè still wore his fine black leather armor, layers of ring mail about the neckline shining in the light. But the whole ensemble was shredded in most places from their adventures. "Wonder if they're still alive, Seita, Stefan, and Culpa, or if they fell into the waterfall behind us. Lost like Roguemoore."

Nail wasn't sure he could even answer the Vallè, his dart-stung face was so cold. He too looked up at the roof drifting by—a dreamlike landscape of whispering, shadowy veins of broad purples and blues. Dull light bled from the crevasses and cracks, water weeping down in droplets onto his face. He thought of Roguemoore, knowing he should feel some sorrow for the dwarf who had taken him in and made him part of the Brethren of Mia. But he couldn't even muster up one single feeling of sadness. It was just too cold to think of anything beyond his own survival. The only emotion in his chilled heart was that of betrayal. The fact was, the gruff old dwarf had lied to him about many things, and Nail had never called him out on the lies. And now he never could.

He thought of Stefan Wayland, hoping his friend was still alive and not too horrified by what he must certainly assume he saw: the deaths of Roguemoore, Val-Draekin, and himself. *Is Culpa Barra still alive? Is Seita?* She certainly seemed the most capable of them all, skilled in many ways, a mystery.

"Who is Seita?" he asked, his face a brittle mask in the cold. His lips hardly moved, making him wonder if the Vallè even heard his question. "Did you know she was such a good fighter?" Pale mist puffed from his mouth with each word.

"Of course," Val-Draekin answered. "Does her skill surprise you?"

A lot of things had surprised him about his two Vallè companions since the company had set off from Lord's Point. The relationship between Val-Draekin and Seita had never been clearly defined. The two had scarcely shown the least bit of friendship toward each other. He thought her remembered Seita hinting of a relationship between her sister and Val-Draekin. But not much beyond that was ever mentioned, leastwise that he could recall. After a moment, he said, "I have never seen a girl fight like that."

"And why is that?" Val-Draekin asked.

Nail wasn't expecting his statement to be followed by such a casual yet pointed question. "I guess I don't know why." He dipped his crooked paddle into the steely gurgle of the river, turning the raft away from a thin tower of ice jutting up in their path. "Girls don't fight like that in Gallows Haven. Or anywhere else, for that matter."

"Only the young men are trained to be warriors in Gallows Haven." It wasn't a question, just a statement of fact from the Vallè.

"Only the boys seventeen and eighteen are required to train," Nail said. "Every boy in Gul Kana must put in his two years' service to the church and Silver Throne. It is law, punishable by death if one refuses or abandons his duty."

"It is known by all, the women in Gul Kana and Adin Wyte and Wyn Darrè never fight," Val-Draekin said. "Why do you think that is?"

Nail had actually never wondered why. Training a woman to fight was just not part of his world. Never had been. That was partially why he'd been so surprised when the cloaked figure on the black horse on the trail above Gallows Haven had turned out to be a Vallè woman—a Vallè woman who'd looked exactly like Seita. It was why he had been so surprised at Seita's skills. "Do all Vallè women look alike?" he asked.

"Not to me," Val-Draekin said.

"But do they all have brilliant blond hair like Seita?" Again he thought of the Vallè woman Shawcroft had murdered. "Do they all know how to fight like Seita?"

"They do not all have blond hair like Seita. And not all can fight like Seita either. But most are taught to fight in some way or another from a very young age, whether it be archery, dirk, rapier, cutlass, sword, or ball-and-chain mace. Whatever they choose, really. Or if they choose not to learn any fighting technique, that is up to them. Nothing is forced upon them. Nothing is denied them. It is the way of the Vallè."

"It just seems strange to me."

"As it would," Val-Draekin said. "You have been taught your whole life that woman are less than men." Nail felt like he should be some-how insulted by the Vallè's words, but he said nothing in defense of the accusation. Val-Draekin continued, "All in Gul Kana have been taught this falsehood by their churchmen, bishops, and lords—frail men who cull their opinions from *The Way and Truth of Laijon*. And you just accept it. Worse, your women just accept it." He paused a moment. "And that, Nail, seems strange to me."

In reality, other than at this moment right now, Nail had never even given the notion a second thought. But it did seem strangely unfair, not allowing women to train as warriors. Shawcroft had never been a proponent of the Church of Laijon or *The Way and Truth of Laijon*. In fact, he mostly mocked any of Nail's attempts to participate, espe-cially when it came to memorizing the Ember Lighting Prayer. Nail himself had his own issues with the holy book. He recalled Bishop Tolbret not allowing him to practice the Ember Lighting Rites with the others. *"It is written for now and forever that a bastard's place is not within the Church of Laijon, nor will it ever be."* The bishop had quoted that to his face, right from *The Way and Truth of Laijon*.

"It does seem a shame that the women of Gallows Haven were never trained to fight," he said. "They could have defended them-selves better against the White Prince."

"Indeed." The Vallè nodded. "Nearly half of Aeros Raijael's army is made up of women. How do you think he overpowered those in

Adin Wyte and Wyn Darrè? Gul Kana had best learn that lesson, or they will soon be overpowered too."

Val-Draekin was right. It made Nail even madder at the church and its *Way and Truth of Laijon*. He was glad he had slapped the holy book from Tolbret's hand and pissed on it the night of the Mourning Moon Feast—the night before the White Prince had destroyed Gallows Haven and everyone in it.

"Princess Jondralyn Bronachell saw things the right way," Val-Draekin went on. "She wished to fight for the rights of women. She wished to be a warrior."

"But wasn't the princess nearly slain by a Sør Sevier knight?" Nail asked. "Culpa said it was Jondralyn that I saw on that litter in Ravenker, her face cut in half."

"But she survived. She came back to Amadon. And I've a feeling she will grow stronger for the experience. She is one Gul Kana woman to be admired."

"They say she was the most beautiful and fair woman alive."

"Aye, she was that," Val-Draekin admitted. "Still is. As is her younger sister, Princess Tala. Though Tala doesn't see it, she could grow into a more beautiful woman than Jondralyn. She would be about your age, I am guessing. Tala Bronachell reminds me of you, some. Naught but unfaltering and dogged determination anyway."

Another blockage of ice reared up in their path. Nail guided them around it. The tunnel was growing darker now, gloomy. More and more murky shards of ice rose up in giant, shadowy forms. He silently weaved the raft between them all, their glacial waterway slowing down to almost a crawl. Nail paddled for a bit on one side of the driftwood raft, and then the other, alternating, trying to build up some speed.

The bowels of the glacier were such a bleak place, starved of all warmth. His legs dangling in the water were so numb it worried him, and the rest of his body was riddled with piercing agony. But if he kept his mind on other things besides the pain, he figured he could bear it. So he thought of beautiful girls.

He tried to picture Jondralyn and Tala Bronachell. Mostly he tried to picture Tala, considering she was nearer to his age. But all he saw was Ava Shay's face in his mind. And thoughts of Ava only made him feel guilty. He could still feel her turtle carving hanging at his neck—after all he had been through, it was still there.

They traveled into complete blackness now, a howling wind racing up the chasm, a hollow and lingering sound, like choral voices echoing and discordant. The wayward crashes and booms of the shifting ice above were a mournful accompaniment to the sheer stark majesty of the sounding wind. Nail had once heard a group of traveling bards perform a song in the Gallows Haven chapel with flutists and drummers—their divine music almost as haunting as this glacial melody. But the musical wind eventually died to a hushed whisper.

Nail took a ragged breath that burned his lungs, felt the weight of the glacier above pressing down. The titanic mass of the ice overhead made him, and everything about his life, seem small. *I'm bound to die in here. . . .*

He saw blue light grow out of the darkness ahead, a luminosity far more clear and brilliant than any yet. Still, the glorious sight of so much divine light ahead gave him scant hope. Val-Draekin craned his neck around to see what held Nail's gaze captive.

Within just a few minutes, the dark tunnel they journeyed in was lit nearly as bright as day. Their boat carried them out into the middle of the most spectacular sight—a mammoth vaulted ice cave of such unspoiled magnificence and splendor it stole Nail's breath. All he could do was stare upward in wonder, wincing in pain at the frosty rays of sunlight slanting down. Even Val-Draekin stared upward in awe.

A vast silence engulfed the raft as they floated across the clear lake into the spacious cavern. A cavern at least a hundred times larger in scale than the inside of the Lord's Point Cathedral, an endless cavern of stark columns of ice towering to heights of three hundred feet or more. Straight above hung a thin roof, a natural layer of ice. Like stained glass, it reflected a melting cascade of brilliant blues and whites and yellows, refracted sunlight that sifted and spilled in shattered flares and sparkles. Shifting and dancing off sharp columns of ice, this glorious light filtered down at a myriad of harsh angles, bathing Nail's face in its bright warm beams. He could imagine himself trekking across the glacier and breaking through that thin sheet of ice above, plummeting hundreds of feet straight down to the frigid waters waiting below. He wondered if Stefan, Seita, and Culpa Barra had crossed over this very spot on their journey.

The lake was calm. Scarcely even a ripple was left in the wake of their raft as they crept along. When Nail looked down at the still waters, the breath was yanked from his lungs again. The water was so clean and clear he could see all the way to the bottom, hundreds of feet down. House-sized chunks of ice and dark black boulders looked like small children's toys strewn about. And trees, long uprooted by violent glacial rivers, lay haphazardly, scattered like thousands of spilled little matchsticks. The entire mazelike lake bottom stared back up at Nail, as crystal clear as if it were inches from his face.

He dipped his branch into the water and rippled the scene into a million pieces. He steered them around a jutting tower of ice. The sound of his driftwood paddle stirring the water trickled endlessly, like chiming music. As they floated languidly along, there was something holy and reverent about this clear bright chamber and its sheer ice columns of blue and crystal waters.

In its absolute quiet, this alien place held a hushed, sacred majesty. "Your face is bruised, swollen." The Vallè eventually broke the pristine silence as his gaze fell on Nail. "I can now see it clearly in this light."

The devouring pain of the cold had so consumed Nail, he

occasionally completely forgot about his injured face. He recalled the journey over the falls, cracking his head on the ice. The poison darts. *I must look a fright.*

"Better than a broken leg, I reckon," Val-Draekin said, straightening the leather straps around his makeshift splint. "Or the wounds the oghuls gave me." The bandages around his arm and shoulder were ragged and coming apart.

"If we get out of here, can you walk?" Nail asked, realizing it was a stupid question on many levels as soon as it spilled from between his stiff, dry lips.

"Let's worry about getting out of here first." The Vallè's eyes drifted up again, taking in the lofty view. "It's warmer here, sun filtering down, probably why this vast lake hasn't frozen over."

There was some dark tangle of wood floating in their path. Nail eyed it warily as they drifted closer.

"This is truly a sight Breita would die to see," Val-Draekin commented.

"It *is* a sight to see," was all Nail could think to say, eyes still on the dark debris in the water.

"Seita and Breita were inseparable as sisters," Val-Draekin went on, dark eyes still roaming the massive cave. "I was jealous of their closeness, of the bond between the one I loved and her sister, Seita. I don't know why I admit that now, here, of all places and times, and to you. But it just seems like it's something I need to say out loud."

Nail silently guided the boat around the floating bit of debris, a wagon-wheel-sized clump of driftwood and ice melded together. It was a twisted mass, grotesque. It reminded Nail of an oghul's brutal face. *Foul creatures. Savage and vile.*

"Have you ever had a bond like that with someone?" Val-Draekin asked, his own concerned gaze falling on the pile of debris. "Someone so close you were nearly inseparable?"

Nail was hesitant to answer. "I wouldn't know," he finally said.

"Or I wouldn't know what a bond like that would even feel like. I've never had a family."

"I didn't say the bond had to be with family."

Nail let the truth of his existence settle over him. He'd spent a lifetime feeling like nobody loved him or even cared, that he was just Shawcroft's inconvenient baggage. "I don't really feel like talking about this subject."

"Well, we should talk of something," Val-Draekin said matter-of-factly. "Else I think I shall die of boredom down here, despite how beautiful this place is."

Indeed, the staggering grandeur and radiance of the cavern captivated Nail everywhere he looked. But it was also a deadly place. And he wasn't certain a conversation with the Vallè would make him feel any better about their predicament, especially if it involved talk of relationships and family. He already felt guilty for putting his friends in so much danger. Stefan. Dokie. Liz Hen. Even Beer Mug. *I should have abandoned in the Autumn Range. Their lives would have been better off without me.*

But he *had* felt a bond with those in the company. Was the Company of Nine his family? *Is that what Val-Draekin is talking about?* His only kin was *perhaps* his former master, Shawcroft, and he wasn't even certain about that—he had only Hawkwood's word to go on. *Cassietta Raybourne. Aevrett Raijael.* Could they really be his parents?

"I'm naught but a slave," he finally muttered. "Merely existing to do the bidding of my betters."

"I've never detected anything servile in your speech or demeanor," Val Draekin said. "You've certainly never acted the slave in the time we've known each other. Do not run yourself down like that. You are worth more."

Nail raised his oar up out of the water. It seemed if left alone, the flow moved them slowly in whatever direction it wanted. So he let the current have its way.

"Shawcroft must have known this glacier well," the Vallè stated. "If your master worked those mines for as long as he did, he would have crossed over the ice many times. I wonder if this cavern was here, even back then."

Nail eyed Val-Draekin curiously; the dark hair, sharp ears, dark round eyes, pale face, all of it as alien and strange as the ice cavern they floated through.

"Since we left Lord's Point," Val-Draekin continued, "Roguemoore, Godwyn, Culpa Barra, they talked of things with me. Things regarding you. Of how Shawcroft was there in Arco when your mother died."

Nail's heart skipped a beat. His eyes narrowed, oar still poised over the water, unmoving. "I wouldn't trust Godwyn or the dwarf," he muttered. "It was all secrets with them. Culpa Barra too, I wager. I doubt they know anything of Shawcroft or my mother."

"You are right not to trust them." The brutal frankness of the Vallè's words hit Nail like a lightning bolt.

"How would you know who I should and should not trust?" he asked pointedly, realizing the inconsistency of his own position.

"You have many questions that need answering, Nail," Val-Draekin said. "And until you find those answers, I fear you will always judge your life as incomplete."

Nail said nothing, the truth of the Vallè's words slicing through his heart. "And I should trust you?"

"There are some you *can* trust. But I am not promising that I am one of them. That is for you to figure out, Nail."

"It's easiest to just assume everyone lies. Nothing to figure out there."

"Roguemoore did not have your best interest at heart. That I know."

Nail was again startled at the harsh frankness of Val-Draekin's pronouncement.

"Well, what does it even matter?" He shrugged. "I reckon the dwarf is dead now." He could not even meet the Vallè's gaze.

"Aye." Val-Draekin nodded. "The dwarf wore heavy layered armor, not as easily shed as yours. He probably lies drowned at the bottom of this glacier somewhere far behind us, his secrets gone to us forever. A great blow to the Brethren of Mia. For Roguemoore was privy to information few others knew, things that not even Godwyn or Culpa Barra knew."

Nail was not surprised by that. *How is it that nobody can be truthful, ever, not even to their own Brethren?* Shawcroft wasn't. Roguemoore wasn't. He thought of Hawkwood and what the man had told him in Ravenker about his heritage. *But is nobody true to their word?* He feared the Vallè was full of lies too, and this was all a game.

"There is *one* man who you feel may have spoken truth," Val-Draekin said. "I can see it in your eyes."

Nail's heart squeezed tight. He shivered. The only thing that seemed to chill him more than the icy waters of the glacial river was the uncanny clairvoyance of the Vallè sitting across from him. "Did you know Hawkwood?" he asked.

The Vallè nodded. "I knew him some."

"Is Hawkwood like Godwyn and dwarf, full of lies?"

"I am certain of one thing," Val-Draekin said. "Hawkwood was also in Arco with Shawcroft the day your mother died."

Nail's heart almost twisted in half. He could scarcely breathe.

The words spilled almost unbidden from between his frozen lips. "Hawkwood said my mother was named Cassietta Raybourne." His heart raced inside his chest just saying her name aloud for the first time. "She was the younger sister to King Torrence Raybourne of Wyn Darrè. Hawkwood said that Shawcroft was my blood kin, my uncle. Said his real name was Ser Roderic Raybourne. He said I was of royal blood. Wyn Darrè mixed with . . ." He trailed off, realizing he must sound like an absolute fool.

"Go on," Val-Draekin urged, dark eyes boring into his. "Wyn Darrè blood mixed with what?"

"Hawkwood told me my father was King Aevrett Raijael of Sør Sevier. Said my destiny, even Roguemoore could not fully fathom." He expected the Vallè fellow to laugh at him as perhaps Liz Hen might if she heard such a preposterous thing.

"Angel Prince." Val-Draekin broke his gaze from Nail's. "That explains a lot."

"Explains what?"

"Godwyn mentioned that Shawcroft would leave you alone for stretches of time to go into the mines to dig for the weapons and stones, right? That you would stay with Stefan's family when Shawcroft would go off mining."

"Aye, that is true."

"Hardly seems like a man worried about your well-being or safety. No?"

He was taken aback by the Vallè's inference. Everything Val-Draekin said seemed to throw him off balance. "Shawcroft cared," Nail said, almost in defense of his master. "At Deadwood Gate when I was young, Shawcroft would take me into the mines some, but never very far, or we would pan for gold in nearby streams. If he ever did leave me for long stretches, there was always a trusted family in town that would watch over me. And Godwyn was right, in Gallows Haven I would stay with Stefan's family."

"A trusted family, you say?" the Vallè asked wistfully, as if he didn't quite approve of Shawcroft's judgment, leaving Nail with others.

"Shawcroft did what he could." Nail didn't know why he kept defending the man. "I was never mistreated—" He stopped. His eyes roamed the cavern. A rumbling roar, deep and savage, seemed to be growing out of the ice. *A waterfall!*

The air seemed to shift around him, followed by a deafening boom from behind and to his left. Nail looked back. Almost straight above, a column of ice stretching from the lake up to the ceiling cracked and folded in the middle. It sheared into shards of ice that plummeted hundreds of feet down, stabbing into the calm water around them like spears. Great waves of frothing water boiled and churned. Their little raft rose up as the first swell of water rushed underneath them. One hazardous chunk of ice lanced back out of the water, pounding violently into the underside of their tiny craft, launching both Nail and Val-Draekin spinning into the frigid lake.

Nail gasped as the icy waters folded over him, every muscle in his body cramping at once. When his head broke the surface of the lake, he saw Val-Draekin floundering not an arm's length away, desperately trying to keep his face above water. Mustering what strength he could, Nail forced his cramped muscles into action, kicking his way toward the Vallè. Another wave rolled over them both and the Vallè was forced under.

Nail grasped the metal-ringed collar of Val-Draekin's leathers and pulled his friend's head to the surface again, grasping him from behind, one arm around his chest. The Vallè gulped for air. He hugged Val-Draekin with one arm, keeping the Vallè's face above the now churning waters—waters that were now swiftly pulling them toward the towering sheer wall of the cavern. A grim gaping tunnel was visible at the base of the ice wall, the powerful current sucking them toward it, sucking them uncontrollably toward a booming noise that rose in pitch and vibration. The safety and warmth and beauty of the cavern swiftly disappeared behind them. Shards of ice, fierce and brutal, rammed into them from all sides as the rapids overtook them, pulling them into the dark of the tunnel.

Still clutching Val-Draekin tightly with one arm, Nail prepared himself for the horror he could see looming ahead. Together they plunged over the thunderous falls, dropping into a foaming, fuming stew a hundred feet down.

Somehow Nail managed to hold on to Val-Draekin, even as the falls thrust them deep into a murderous maelstrom of sharp water and ice. The furious tumult thrashed and stirred before fiercely spitting them out into a broad river of rolling waves and tossing ice, thrusting them straight into a racing chute of roiling, brutal blackness.

They were swept along at a speed Nail figured the fastest horse in the Five Isles couldn't even match. An endless, chaotic ride of freezing water and darkness. And scant chance for breath. Nail desperately clutched the Vallè to his chest, more out of self-preservation than anything else. Val-Draekin seemed to take the brunt force of every block of ice the river tossed their way. At times they were forced completely under water, the sadistic current scraping them along the cruel icy roof of the chute, forcing Nail to hold his breath to the breaking point. There were a few pockets of air, mere seconds to grab a breath before they were shoved under again, vicious water grating them under the ice. A never-ending torment of piercing cold and raging violence.

When they broke from the suffocating tunnel, a house-sized boulder rose up in their path. Heaps of frothing water pushed them around the jutting rock and onto a broad slab of flat ice behind the boulder. They were swept across the surface of ice and dumped into the river again, bobbing along in a much slower current, some faint light drifting in from above. Nail found it impossible to orient himself to their surroundings, until they came to an abrupt stop in a bubbling pocket of swirling waters formed against a shelf of ice, the surface of the shelf just out of his reach.

Val-Draekin struggled free of Nail's grasp. The eddy had them both trapped, dipping and swelling, churning them low one second, thrusting them high the next. On an upswell, the Vallè reached up, and hauled himself completely out of the water, scrambling onto the shelf of ice to safety.

Nail still struggled to stay afloat as the swell sucked him back down. But he was soon lifted up again in a surge of bubbling water. Val-Draekin's hand grasped his. Utilizing the momentum of the upswell, the Vallè pulled Nail onto the ledge. Nail lay on the ice, gasping for breath, spent.

When he finally raised his head, he took quick measure of their precarious perch.

Looming before him, the vast river raced by and vanished into another threatening tunnel of ominous dark, churning and riotous with ice. Behind him was a narrow rift in the ice wall, a crevasse, stretching from the surface of the shelf up into the dark, a faint sliver of light cascading from it.

"Could be a way out!" Val Draekin yelled over the thunder of rushing waters. The Vallè crawled away from the river toward the rift, his very effort draggled and slow. The flesh of his feet was scraped bloody and leaving a trail of red, the makeshift splint nearly torn completely off.

Nail looked at his own bare feet and saw that they were similarly abused, flesh scoured raw from ice. He tried to stand, to kneel, to crawl, but the numbness in his own weary limbs wouldn't allow it. He could only lie there, stiff and shivering, watching as the Vallè slowly pulled himself along the surface of the slender shelf. "We have to try!" Val-Draekin shouted, the noise of the river nearly drowning out his voice.

*Who knows where we even are under all this damnable ice?* Even the underworld couldn't possibly be worse than the vile depths of this wicked freezing glacier and its crushing torturous waters. "We have to keep going!" Val-Draekin called back to him.

It took every trace of willpower Nail had, but he finally managed to move. Slowly he crawled, following Val-Draekin into the thin, tapering cleft. It was jagged, but just wide enough for both to squeeze through one at a time, some distant bright light spurring them on. They crawled just a few minutes before the slender chasm widened out and daylight spilled over them from above. The crevasse split into a fork before them; a ten-foot-wide path to their far left was littered with fallen hunks of ice, a much narrower chasm lay straight ahead. An open ceiling was some five hundred feet above, just a sliver of light.

Exhausted, Nail lay on his back under the light, a calm serenity settling over him. He just wanted to fall asleep and die right then and there, the booming sound of the river just a fading memory behind him.

Val-Draekin, lying on his side, pulled forth his leather pouch. "I've only enough powder left for a small flame. But it should warm us some." He tore off a strip of cloth along the bottom of his shirt, sprinkled the white powder onto it, and snapped his fingers. A small flare ignited.

As the bit of cloth burned, they held their hands and feet over the flame. But too soon their lifesaving fire guttered out, and Nail wondered if what little warmth they'd derived from it was enough. "We have to keep moving," the Vallè said. Stiff and aching and frozen, it was all they could do to stand. Val-Draekin, still hobbled by his injury, tossed his arm over Nail's shoulder for support.

They continued their journey, picking their way slowly through the narrow crevasse straight ahead, lumbering along, sloshing through intermittent pools of water that dragged at the battered and bloody carnage of their feet.

† † † † †

They carried on this way for several more hours, the meandering chasm widening in some places, narrowing to just a crack in others. Still they would squeeze through. Here and there Nail's weary gaze would travel up to where the glacier walls pinched the sky, revealing just a hint of blue above. Random droplets of meltwater rained down. The ever-growing distant creaking and sudden cracking of shifting ice constantly gave him pause. Nail swore he could see the walls moving ominously inward at times and the air was growing colder.

Then they came upon a sight that horrified Nail to the core. Near eye level was a curled and ragged human arm reaching out from the ice wall straight into their path, five black-rotted skeletal fingers stretching out in silent agony, the remainder of the carcass a dark silhouette frozen behind the ice.

Val-Draekin limped toward the gruesome obstacle first. When he reached the jutting arm, he ducked under it, examining the carcass hidden within the frosty ice. Nail approached, the ghostly apparition terrifying him. The Vallè leaned into the ice and swiped away a thin layer of frost with the sleeve of his shirt.

Two eyes peered at Val-Draekin from behind the crystal clear ice. Nail took a faltering step back. They were the haunting blue eyes of a woman.

"She could've been down here hundreds of years, for all we know," the Vallè said. "Encased in ice like this, she'd be well preserved."

Nail did not want to linger. He scooted under the reaching arm, shuddering as the dead bony fingers lightly brushed the top of his head.

They left the corpse behind, eventually finding themselves once more enclosed within an ever-widening tunnel that stretched off into darkness. The ceiling was a hellish, upside-down landscape of rippling waves of water-carved ice, rocks and trees embedded in the its surface, trunks and branches jutting down in a weird mockery of a forest. Shattered cobbles of ice and stone littered their path. And the going became rough as the light receded behind them.

Soon the ceiling of the cave hung so low they had to hunch forward and crouch just to continue. Before long they were both crawling. Light was scarce, and Nail found he was mostly feeling his way along blindly. Then it grew totally dark and he wondered if they should just turn back. But there was nowhere else to go, so onward he crawled, following Val-Draekin.

Rocks and twigs, jagged and sharp, dug into him from underneath, and glacial ice pressed down on him from above. He was soon lodged between cobbled floor and frozen ceiling, unmoving, his face mashed to the rock, his chest heaving against the uneven floor. His back was pressed flat against the glacier above.

Stuck. He knew it was the end. He could hear the thinner Vallè up ahead in the blackness, still crawling, pushing his way forward, squirming along. But Nail did not call out for help. He just let the fellow go, refusing to be a hindrance to another's escape.

Val-Draekin continued on, unaware that Nail was no longer behind him. The sounds of the Vallè's crawling slowly faded into the dark distance, and Nail wondered how long it would take for him to die down here, wedged underneath the weight of the entire Five Isles, it seemed. Would he starve first? Would the glacier shift and crush him? Would his dingy little crawl space fill with water? Or would he freeze solid into the ice like the skeleton they had found? However he died, he just wanted it all to be over.

"I see light ahead," Val-Draekin's voice called out from the blackness.

Nail could scarcely hear him. He remained silent, knowing that no matter how much light rained down from above, his own torturous journey was at an end.

"Nail!" the Vallè shouted. "Are you there? Nail!"

"I can't move." The words hissed from between Nail's cracked, dry lips. "I'm dying." His voice seemed but a sibilant whisper, even to himself.

"Nail!" Val-Draekin shouted again. "The light! Sunlight! I see brush and trees beyond the ice!"

*Could it be real?* Nail's heart pounded. *Or am I already dead and dreaming?*

"Nail!" the Vallè shouted. "Are you there?"

Nail sucked in a deep breath and wiggled forward, inching his way along, maybe two feet, before he gave up again. He heard Val-Draekin shout again. "I'm coming back for you!"

"No!" Nail tried to yell back, his entire chest compressed between rock and ice, knowing the Vallè could not possibly hear him.

"I'm coming back, Nail!"

*I can't put him in more danger.* Nail sucked in a deep breath and shouted, "I'll make it! I am coming! Stay where you are! Don't come back for me!"

The Vallè called out. "I am going to head toward the light. You'll see it soon, Nail! I promise! Do not give up! I will meet you outside!"

*Patience,* his master had taught him, *patience in everything.* And now was the time for it. Shawcroft had once said, *Hard work and precision in all things builds strength, character, and pride. Your mother wanted me to instill those things in you more than any other. She never took things such as hard work for granted, nor should you.*

Hard work and patience. They were the beliefs of his mother.

*Then I'll escape this glacier for her.*

Nail breathed in deep, inched his way forward. And again. And again.

After about ten minutes of sucking in his breath and inching forward, he was through the toughest part and the going was easier. He saw the light Val-Draekin had promised. He crawled for it, almost frantically.

Things grew brighter all around him. He could see the details of each pebble underneath his fingers. He could see the details in the dirty sculpted blue ice above.

But most importantly of all, he could see the sunlight gleaming off the bushes and aspens in the sliver of brightness ahead. He scrambled forward, legs and arms churning madly now. And suddenly Val-Draekin was pulling him out from under a five-hundred-foot-tall slab of ice and into free air.

Nail rolled over and breathed deep, staring straight up at the towering cliff of blue rising above. And then he wanted away from the glacier desperately. Wanted away from it more than he'd ever wanted away from anything in his life.

He levered himself to his feet and stumbled toward the nearby aspen grove drunkenly, his mind a complete muddle, bloody feet almost too numb to move. He stumbled forward, tripping, clinging to one of the trees in front of him, hearing the Vallè's relieved laughter behind him. "We made it, Nail! We made it!"

Both feet wailing in pain, Nail hugged the tree before him. The wind-blasted aspen lifted spindly branches toward an intensely dark blue heaven. The sun was behind the mountains and the sky was turning to night.

And that damnable savage glacier still loomed behind him, its towering presence more threatening and ominous than the cliffs above Stanclyffe, more terrifying than a Bloodwood on a black stallion. He wanted to turn and shout a lifetime's worth of frustration and anger at that icy, suffocating cliff.

When Nail's heart finally settled enough for him to gather his bearings, he craned his neck around, still clutching the tree close, and let his eyes roam the harsh surroundings. They had emerged from under the glacier along a rocky, boulder-strewn slope sprinkled with scrub brush and aspen trees, the black waters of the vast loch no more than fifty paces down the hill.

Val-Draekin was hobbling toward him. "Perhaps not the most direct route possible, but at least we are on the eastern shore." The Vallè's eyes roved the landscape too. "No telling if the others are even alive." He plopped on the ground at Nail's feet, placed his head in his hands. "I would have died had you not held on to me, Nail. Over the falls and in that horrid river, I would have died. You saved me many times. I owe you a great debt."

But Nail scarcely heard the Vallè's words. He found he could not let go of the tree. It was his lifeline, his sustenance to the real world, a world no longer buried under harsh ice and savage water. *Roguemoore is gone!* And he had no armor or weapons. Just a thin, ragged shirt and pants. He was so hungry he thought he might fall over from the weakness of his rumbling stomach. *What do we do now?* At least Val-Draekin still had some protection with his light leather armor. Not that it did Nail any good.

A loud crack shattered the very air, followed by a resounding boom that shook the aspen, then reverberated around him, shaking every tree limb above. Nail watched in awe as a column of ice as wide as twenty Gallows Haven chapels sheared from the glacier and plummeted into the lake several miles away. The loch waters swallowed the colossal hunk of ice whole, then spat it back out in shattered chunks, waves the size of small mountains rolling across the lake toward him.

"We're not safe yet." Val-Draekin lurched to his feet and hobbled up the slope away from the loch, hopping on one bloody foot, crimson smears marking his path.

Nail let go the tree and started after his friend, his own bleeding feet tender on the sharp rocks. Once he reached Val-Draekin, he scooped the Vallè into his arms and carried him up the hill, ignoring the searing pain of every step he took.

*The natural way of man is to see competition within every other man. This hostility is how war is to be waged and how love is to be won, how success is to be defined.*
—THE WAY AND TRUTH OF LAIJON

# CHAPTER THIRTY-SEVEN
# TALA BRONACHELL

### 11TH DAY OF THE ANGEL MOON, 999TH YEAR OF LAIJON
### AMADON, GUL KANA

I sn't Squireck just divine?" Lawri La Graven sighed. The index finger of her right hand was entwined in her hair just above her right ear, twirling a strand of the long blond tresses, left arm cradled in her lap. Tala could see why her cousin was so enamored with the Prince of Saint Only—never before had Dayknight armor looked so regal on any one man. Under the many torches of Sunbird Hall, the black-lacquered plate armor hung on Squireck Van Hester's tall form in glittering shades of midnight. He was a daunting presence. Every powerful move with the long black sword brought gasps from the crowd.

*So suddenly he has become their hero.* Just one priesthood blessing from the grand vicar was enough to turn the most hated man in Amadon into the most revered.

Squireck held everyone's attention as he twirled his heavy Dayknight blade in one hand. Three sword-and-shield wielding Silver Guards—Ser Tolz Trento, Ser Alain Gratzer, and Ser Boppard Stockach—were standing before him, eagerly awaiting the coming duel with the most famous fighter in Amadon. Tala recognized the three guardsmen as Glade Chaparral's lackeys. They were the ones who had helped Glade frame Lindholf for the murder of Sterling Prentiss and implicate him in the assassination attempt on Jovan. She hope Squireck humiliated all three in the practice duel.

Tala found it hard to wrap her head around the fact that Lindholf had been found naked with the barmaid, Delia, in a back room of the Filthy Horse Saloon. Both the barmaid and Lindholf were currently being held in Purgatory. Glade bragged that he had helped the guards chain the busty barmaid to a four-point rack this time, completely unable to move. Glade also bragged that the guards had done the same to Lindholf. Tala blamed herself for their fate. *The Bloodwood's game has ruined so many lives!* But she'd heard nary a whisper or peep from her Bloodwood tormentor since their meeting in the lost Chamber of Queens more than a moon ago. Still, she had been feeding Lawri Le Graven the tiny green balls under the pretext that it was medicine. But who knew what the balls really were? Lawri was no longer sick. But she was still favoring her injured arm. An arm that was likely more infected, from the ginger way she held it. Lawri sat across the table from Tala, draped in a long yellow dress with saffron sleeves that stretched clear to her wrists. Tala knew her cousin wore long sleeves to cover her scar. The green balls that Tala had told Lawri were medicine were doing nothing for the infection.

Tala's gaze roamed Sunbird Hall. Dame Nels Doughty—the castle's new head kitchen matron now that Dame Vilamina was gone—had done the place up proper. Again, it was her fault Vilamina was dead, unfairly implicated in the assassination attempt on Jovan, and all because Tala had asked her to hire the Filthy Horse Saloon barmaid, Delia, onto the kitchen's staff the night of the Mourning Moon Feast. It was all such a tangled web, and Tala could never forgive herself for all the damage she had wrought in so many lives. *All due to the Bloodwood's game . . .*

Her eyes traveled up toward the ceiling, and she wondered whether the Bloodwood was up there watching her. Torch smoke filled the lofty heights above, hanging from the rafters, thick and heavy. At the far eastern end, the twin balcony doors were thrown wide, letting in a small measure of fresh air down onto the crowded room below. The place was packed. Everyone wore their finest tonight, Tala included. She had on her favorite black dress and jeweled leather doublet. Though, truth be known, she'd rather be in Silver Guard armor like Jondralyn. Her older sister was sitting two tables away with Ansel in her lap, bouncing him on twin armored knees. Most in the king's court had muttered their displeasure when Jondralyn had enter the hall in full armor. But what could they do? Jovan had knighted her. But those were the ways of courtly folk, always muttering behind the backs of others.

And the court had grown these last few days as lords and barons from the breadth of Gul Kana had been flooding the city, heeding the Silver Throne's call to muster arms against the invading armies of the White Prince, thousands and thousands of knights following them. Knights from Savon, Crucible, Ridleigh, Reinhold, along with fighters from cities and villages even farther out in the countryside, more and more arriving every day. The streets of Amadon were teeming with banners of heraldry and the colored livery of armored horses. And all those nobles important to the crown were crowded into Sunbird Hall tonight. Ser Tomas Vorkink, the king's steward, had helped Dame Nels Doughty put together a vast and grand celebration full of pomp and majesty; the centerpiece, Squireck Van Hester and the dueling demonstration in the center of the hall.

Ever since his pardon, the Prince of Saint Only had become the toast of Amadon Castle and most popular figure at court. They were all eagerly awaiting the first day of the Fire Moon and Squireck's arena match with Gault Aulbrek. They were all desirous to see their new hero slay the Sør Sevier knight. All of them wanted to watch him spar at all times and against anyone in preparation. The court loved watching him fight. Even Jovan was warming to him. Grand Vicar Denarius and the quorum of five, too. Earlier tonight at the king's behest, the vicar had knighted Squireck, and then Jovan had bestowed upon the Prince of Saint Only the rank of Dayknight, giving him the black armor and sword of his new station.

That Squireck was now a free man again was a good thing. And Tala was happy for him, but she felt something amiss with all the adulation. Especially when the adulation came from Lawri, who seemed to stare at the Prince of Saint Only at times with unabashed want in her eyes. "He's so divine," she murmured again.

There were cheers from the throng as the Val Vallè ambassador, Val-Korin, motioned for the spar to begin. He then stepped aside with a hearty shout, "Edged weapons in play! Spectators watch yourselves!"

In the center of the hall, Squireck spun his sword deftly over-head. Tolz, Alain, and Boppard slipped conical battle helms over their heads. They slowly circled the Prince of Saint Only, shields at the guard, their own swords poised for attack. The crowd was abuzz with excitement now. Boppard lunged at Squireck first, his heavy iron shield no match for the power behind Squireck's flashing sword. Boppard's shield was jarred from his hand and clattered to the floor, bent in the middle. His sword was knocked from his hand next, spinning to the ground. Oohs and aahs and claps and cheers burst forth as Alain and Tolz closed in on Squireck next.

Tala, completely uninterested, turned from the action and looked across the table at Lawri. "It's all so pointless. The battling and dueling. Don't you think?"

Lawri was popping purple grapes into her mouth one after the next, no longer fussing with her hair, eyes fixed on the combat in the center of the hall. "Ser Tolz and Ser Alain are dashingly cute in their own way," she said. "For Silver Guards, anyway. But I think Sharla and Jaclyn Chaparral have their eyes set on those two." Glade's sisters were standing at the edge of the crowd, watching the duel. The two tall Chaparral girls had become regular faces at the court the last few weeks, at least ever since Glade's Ember Lighting Rites. Like their brother Leif, both girls were lean and exquisitely pretty. Lord Claybor wanted to see them wed soon. Sharla was well past betrothal age, Jaclyn getting there.

Lawri chomped on the grapes. "Silver Guards are one thing. But I think I should marry a Dayknight like Squireck." Her face turned suddenly glum. "Except that Lindholf's crimes now lower my station. Leastways that's what Father says."

"Is that all you're worried about?" Tala asked, irritated with her cousin. "You're worried that Lindholf has disgraced the Le Graven name and possibly lowered your standing in the court?"

Lawri swallowed another grape. "We all deal with things in our own way. I am saddened by what my brother has done. But what can I do about it?" She picked through the bowl of fruit on the table before her, then gave up. "There are no more grapes."

"You do realize your brother is in *Purgatory*," Tala stated.

Lawri met her gaze. "You know, Tala, I can't sleep at night mostly."

Lately, with Lawri, conversations had a tendency to jump all over the place. "Because of Lindholf you cannot sleep?"

"Sure, that . . . well, and other things too. Dreams and such. But I probably shouldn't talk of it." Lawri lapsed into an uncomfortable silence, long fingers digging through the fruit bowl again.

Without Lindholf here, Tala was just now realizing how much she relied on his company, how generally more comfortable he made her feel around Lawri.

Her eyes roamed the hall, resting on the raised dais in the center of the southern wall where the grand vicar sat with her brother and Leif Chaparral. Baron Jubal Bruk sat at the table across from Jovan. The baron struggled mightily with his food, using the tips of the two daggers stuck in the stumps of his arms as utensils. Neither Jovan nor the vicar offered any help. For some reason that bothered Tala.

*The Way and Truth of Laijon* claimed that the grand vicar was without sin, that he communed with the spirit of Laijon in the temple. The holy book claimed that the grand vicar would never lead anyone in the church astray. Yet what Denarius had done to Lawri was a sin most egregious. And that disgusted her.

That thought was followed by one even more horrid: *Lawri's dreams!* She looked across the table at her cousin. *What was her cousin dreaming about that she dared not speak of?* Tala looked straight at her cousin again. "You dreamed I would marry the grand vicar, then later claimed it was naught but nonsense. Naught but silly dreams."

"Perhaps it will come true," Lawri said nonchalantly.

"What do you mean?" Her cousin's answers were most vexing indeed.

"I am starting to have dreams that do come true," Lawri said. "Like I dreamed Squireck would win in the arena. And it came true. I dreamed that Lindholf would be thrown into a dungeon cage for the remainder of his life. And look what happened. The dream where I am searching the secret ways, searching for something in that red room with the cross-shaped altar. I know I told you it was fading, but that was a lie. It gets worse every night. I fear I may go back there, to the red-hazed room. Myself. Alone."

A chill settled over Tala. *Prentiss's body has already been found. You needn't worry about Lawri discovering it there.*

She sat up straight as her cousin pulled the sleeve of her yellow dress up. Tala could see the raw scar that ran from her wrist up the underside of her arm. The infection had in fact spread, bloated red and purple and terribly sore-looking.

"I keep dreaming that I'm wearing a gauntlet," Lawri went on. "A clunky silver hunk of armor that I can't get rid of. But at least it is a hand, of a sort."

"Is that why you won't let Val-Gianni look at your arm?" Tala asked. "Because you dream of a metal hand?"

"No." Lawri covered her arm, eyes darting about the hall, hoping nobody had seen her injury. "I already told you why. Don't you ever listen to me?" Her gaze was still roving Sunbird Hall. She flashed a wide grin at a helmetless Dayknight with a handsome face standing at attention near Jovan and the vicar. Then she looked at Tala again. "You should pay attention to the things I tell you, Tala. I just want my voice to be heard."

"I listen," Tala said defensively.

"No, you don't," Lawri said matter-of-factly.

Glade Chaparral plopped down on the bench between Tala and Lawri, flipping a copper coin up in his hand, catching it, rolling it casually between his fingers, making it dance. "Looks like Squireck made short work of Tolz and Alain."

Lawri grunted. "I don't want him sitting by me, Tala." She glared daggers at Glade. "What he did to Lindholf." Without another word she stood and took her leave, swiftly moving away through the crowd, yellow skirt awhirl.

"She thinks it's my fault her brother is in Purgatory," Glade sneered.

"It is your fault." Tala was also repulsed by his mere presence.

"Lindholf is in a dungeon because of his own actions."

"His own actions?" Tala was appalled. "He is there because of your lies."

Glade winked at her. "You mean because of your lies."

His words bit deep. Guilt flooded her. She wanted to stand up and punch him in the face right there in front of everyone. *Because he's right.* "I hate you," she snapped.

"Splendid. And I hate you. Makes no difference what you think of me."

"I'm sure you and those bootlickers you call friends are just swimming in the adulation of having caught Lindholf with the barmaid. If he even was with the barmaid. Everything about you is false, Glade. Including your story about my cousin. And one day I will set this all aright."

"Sure you will." The coin twirling in his fingers fell to the table with a tinkle and clank, spinning in place of its own accord like a top. "You're embroiled in this mess with Lindholf deeper than I ever will be."

Tala watched the spinning coin wobble to a stop. When she saw the scratch on the face of the coin, her eyes flew up to Glade. He was grinning as he held the coin up before her triumphantly. "It's merely what the people of Amadon have taken to doing. Don't blame me." It was one of the coins minted in Avlonia, bearing Jondralyn's likeness. And someone had scratched a thin line in its copper surface right through her face. "All in Amadon know of your beautiful sister's injury." Glade's crooked smile formed into a laugh. "I wager all the coins circulating through the city are now similarly marked." His laugh turned to a goofy little cackle that grated on her nerves.

*How could I ever have liked him?* "You are evil and vile," she growled. "Worse than a bloodsucking oghul."

"Bloodsucking oghul?" There was incredulity in his laugh now. "Is that the best you can do?"

"If Borden Bronachell were alive, he'd behead you for defacing that coin."

"No, he wouldn't. And I found it already defaced."

"I knew my father. He would not allow such an insult to be visited upon those whom he loved." She straightened her back. "He would burn this city to the ground first. He did not suffer fools."

"He sired you." Glade shrugged nonchalantly.

Tala stood and walked away from him, wishing she hadn't invoked the name of her father. It was all heartache down that path. She would ofttimes dream of him. Sketchy, mysterious dreams. Every time, at the first sight of him, she would become stricken with an almost wounded joy. For she always knew she was in a dream. Still, she relished the fantasy. For even in her dreams there was a force to Borden Bronachell's bearing, a commanding presence that left her feeling safe, and a gentle, comforting smile for her always. No one had ever made her feel more loved than him. Even in her dreams she felt the love. And she knew for a fact that every single thing in her life would have turned out differently had he lived. He did not suffer fools. And he would not have suffered her betrothal to the monster Glade Chaparral.

Tears formed in Tala's eyes as she drifted aimlessly through the crowd. She was still bitterly angry with her father for going off to war and never coming back.

✝ ✝ ✝ ✝

"I should have listened to you, Tala," Jondralyn said. Ansel squirmed about on her lap, sneezing uncontrollably, eyes pink and swollen from allergies. When Tala's younger brother wasn't fussing with the bucklers of Jondralyn's silver armor, he was pointing at Jubal Bruk, asking over and over to get closer. He had been fascinated by the limbless baron ever since he had arrived from Lord's Point in a box.

"I told you, Jovan and Leif, they meant for you to die," Tala said, sitting across from her sister.

"But I did not," Jondralyn said.

Every time she was around her sister, Tala couldn't help but focus on the bandages, couldn't help but remember the wounds underneath. People were defacing Avlonia coins, scratching lines across her sister's likeness.

"Your staring is far too obvious." Jondralyn's blue eyes narrowed beneath dark brows. "I will be fine, Tala. You needn't worry over me."

Just visible under the bandages, Jondralyn's hair was tied back with a thin ribbon of silver. Over her armor, she wore a black cape, fastened with a silver brooch at the neckline. At her side hung a Silver Guard sword. Her helm sat on the table between them. Not that she could have worn it with the bandages anyway.

"Jovan will not kill his own sister," Jondralyn said. "Not now. He will utilize me and my injuries to rally troops from the breadth of Gul Kana." Her frosty eyes roved the chamber, falling on Leif Chaparral. "Leif, on the other hand, that one is long bereft of goodness. He would not hesitate to slay even his *own* kin. Jovan knows the darkness that dwells in Leif. As does Denarius. They will use Leif in whatever schemes they themselves haven't the stomach for. They will likely use Glade, too, I'm afraid. Who knows what foul schemes they are all working on?"

With her one eye, Jondralyn cast a direct and steady gaze at Tala. "Leif gifted Hawkwood's two swords to Glade. Yet I have not seen Glade with them as of late. He used to wear them about so proudly. Like trophies. Does he still have them?" Jondralyn did not break her glance. "If so, they do not belong to him."

Fear clutched at Tala's soul with a tenacity she could not dispel. *What is she hinting at?* Her thoughts shifted to her adventure into Purgatory with Glade. How she had tossed Hawkwood's swords into the underground river. "I'm not privy to every last detail of Glade's life," she answered a little too snarkily, regretting it immediately.

"Just wondering." Jondralyn ruffled Ansel's hair. "No need to be waspish. I know you and Glade ventured into Purgatory and got lost. Jovan and Leif told me. Did Glade have the swords with him then?"

"Perhaps so." Tala shrugged, trying to remain cool. "I can't recall." *So many lies. And each lie leads to another and on and on and on.* The fact was, she wanted to tell Jondralyn of the Bloodwood's game. She wanted to divulge why Lawri had been so sick. How Sterling Prentiss had really died. She wanted to lay bare every rotten detail of her trip into Purgatory with Glade. She wanted to tell her sister that she had stripped the swords from Glade and tossed them into the underground river. She wanted to tell Jondralyn about the stolen map. She was fighting to push the words from her mouth, heaving and pressing, but they would not spill forth. She wanted Jondralyn to get Lindholf out of Purgatory. He was innocent. But there was nothing her sister could do.

"You did go into Purgatory with Glade?" Jondralyn pressed.

"We went to talk with Hawkwood." Tala's mind was churning. "It was Leif's idea. He wanted Glade with him. Me too. And Lindholf." She was babbling, spitting out more lies. "Leif and Lindholf left, and then Glade and I got lost." A nervous chuckle escaped her lips. "Jovan promised he was going to keep our misadventure a secret."

Jondralyn kissed Ansel atop the head. "So did you talk to Hawkwood then?" There was eagerness in her question, as if she sought news of her lover.

Tala hesitated to answer. *Do I continue down this trail of lies?*

"Leif would not let us see Hawkwood," she said. "Claimed he was being kept in another part of the dungeon." As soon as the words passed her lips, she knew Jondralyn could tell she was not being fully honest.

"Like I said, you should not trust Leif," Jondralyn said with a sigh. "He told me how you used my name to get him to take you down into Purgatory. How you used my name to influence him for Laijon knows what."

"I'm sorry," Tala muttered, the guilt of many devious actions and nonactions and her various lies eating at her. *And the worst thing is, my sister knows I am a liar. . . .*

Jondralyn went on, almost in exasperation. "There has been some darkness clinging to you ever since you made those accusations against Sterling Prentiss, Tala. Something that vexes you, something that I cannot quite place my finger on."

Tala's heart sank. She thought of Denarius and Lawri. How Jovan was so beholden to the grand vicar. Leif, too. She recalled Jovan and Leif's kiss, their secret affair. The Bloodwood's game and green potions. There were so many secrets she held tight. But the one secret she had divulged to her sister—Jovan and Leif's plot against her—Jondralyn had ignored. So what was the point in honesty? "Had you died, I would never have forgiven myself," she muttered, barely audible.

"You mustn't ever blame yourself," Jondralyn said, dabbing Ansel's snotty face with a cloth. "My own brashness and desire to prove myself led to these wounds. That combined with our brother's stubbornness. He grows more sensitive to every trifling affront tossed his way. It has naught to do with you, Tala. I'd been spoiling for a confrontation with Jovan ever since I'd begun training for the arena." She actually looked away from Tala's gaze, ashamed. "Naught but the stupid desires of a stupid girl. And Gault Aulbrek showed me my lack. And swiftly, too." Her gaze met Tala's again as she motioned to the bandages covering her face. "Blame me, Tala, if you must. Blame me for all of it. I am the one who has failed the family."

Something in the way her sister said the word *family* angered Tala. "Failed our family?" She stood. "What *family*? As far as blame goes, 'tis neither you nor me should feel guilty, Jondralyn. 'Tis not even Jovan we should blame. It is *Father* we need blame for all of it. It was Borden Bronachell who left and never came back."

† † † †

"Lindholf is innocent," Tala blurted the statement out as soon as she sat down at the table next to Jovan. Under the king's table was a soft white rug, and Tala could feel its plushness beneath her nervous, bouncing feet. Her brother just stared at her wild-eyed, as if she were some gross oghul who had suddenly stumbled into his dinner party.

Empty wine goblets were scattered about the table before him, most overturned.

"Glade is the one who killed Sterling Prentiss." Her next statement was followed by a dead quiet. Jovan glanced to his left at Denarius. The grand vicar in turn looked at the Val Vallè ambassador, Val-Korin. There was a knowing glance between the two. All three turned their attention back to her, neither speaking, dragging the silence out between them. "You are holding the wrong person in Purgatory," she finished tersely.

"Don't be absurd," Jovan said in a slightly unfocused way, drunk.

It was going to take her a moment to build up the courage to say everything she wanted to. To say the *truth*. She looked around, trying to find something to focus on besides the three men at the table. She glanced up at the row of five Dayknights behind her brother. In their black armor and silver surcoats, they stoically stood at guard, their backs against the velvet-draped wall. The Silver Throne was there as well, almost tucked away in a dark corner of the hall, shrouded in white sheets, its five stout legs and silver seat holding up no king. It had been so shrouded since her father's death. *Yes, things would be much different had King Borden lived. No hidden things. No secret things. No shrouded thrones. Just simplicity and peace. And I wouldn't have to figure everything out on my own. I wouldn't have to be brave like this. He would be brave for me.* She straightened her posture. She had come to say something and she meant to say it. She would finally tell the truth.

"I was there when Glade killed Prentiss." She faced Jovan, undaunted. "I witnessed the murder."

At her pronouncement, Val-Korin calmly reached for his wine goblet without once taking his round eyes off her. He took a long drink. Denarius' puffy hand reached up to stroke the silver chains and jewels around his neck as he leaned back, chair creaking under the strain of his bulk. Jovan leaned forward, glaring at her through hazy, inebriated eyes, brow furrowed to dark points over his nose, as if he was trying to make sense of what she had just said.

Then Jovan stood, the gleaming sword at his hip rattling against the table. Tala knew the blade's name: Sky Reaver. Aeros Raijael's own sword, captured by Leif and gifted to Jovan. Her brother glared down at her for a long time, as if contemplating what to say. "Don't you think you're laying it on a bit thick now, Tala?" He straightened his posture, an authoritative, yet slightly absentminded look on his face. "Saying you witnessed a murder? And claiming Glade Chaparral is the murderer?"

"He *is* a murderer," she said.

"Lindholf is the murderer," he said bluntly, loudly. A handful of nobles nearby were now looking in their direction. The five Dayknights behind Jovan stiffened. There was a nervous tension hanging over the king's table now.

"You must believe me." Tala would not give up. Lindholf's life was in the balance. She'd heard the rumors that he would soon be hanged. "I saw Glade kill Sterling Prentiss. With a knife across the throat. Prentiss was stretched out over an altar in a secret chamber deep in the castle. I know. I was there. I led Glade there."

"It would be disastrous to accuse Glade Chaparral of such things now." Val-Korin stared at Jovan fixedly. Jovan's cold eyes met those of the Val Vallè ambassador. He looked at Denarius next, pursing his lips in contemplation.

"You cannot lose the allegiance of Claybor Chaparral," the Vallè continued with that half-amused, ever-watchful quality in his eyes, a sly quality. "Not now, not as we prepare for war with the White Prince. We will need his fighters most. I say the subject should never be brought up again."

"Val-Korin speaks the truth," the vicar affirmed.

A chill slithered up Tala's spine, as she realized that Jovan would never listen to her with these two snakes around.

"You are both right," Jovan spoke in a controlled, assertive voice with a slightly crazed undertone. "Lott Le Graven will hardly speak to me as it is. Both he and Mona are mad at me because I threw their son in Purgatory. They are not even at court tonight, embarrassed and humiliated by the whole affair. But yet, by some miracle, Lott is still willing to offer his soldiers and fealty. Claybor would be far less forgiving. . . ."

Jovan paused, staring long and hard at Tala. "So," he finally continued, "as the evidence bears out, Lindholf is the true culprit here. Not Glade."

"Lindholf is innocent," Tala fired back, anger and frustration rising.

"Lindholf conspired to murder *me*!" her brother shouted, looming over her.

Tala detected even more nobles watching them now. It didn't stop her from shouting, "You are wrong!"

"Enough!" Without warning, Jovan slapped her across the face. It was so rapid and swift Tala could scarcely register that it had even happened. Then he smacked her again. Harder. Her head buzzed with a sudden, startled pain. She stood, wobbling on her legs, vision turning white, unfocused.

Jovan was preparing to hit her a third time when a deep, booming voice thundered through Sunbird Hall. "Do not strike her again!"

Tala turned. Through a pale haze, she saw Squireck Van Hester standing in the center of the chamber, the point of his long Dayknight sword aimed directly at the king. Every eye in Sunbird Hall was on Jovan and Tala. A weighty silence shrouded the hall like a smothering blanket.

"Strike Tala again," the Prince of Saint Only snarled, "and I will cut through every knight in this room to get to you!" His cold stare sliced into Jovan.

The king's eyes were wide, his breathing hard.

Grand Vicar Denarius stood, as did the Val Vallè ambassador.

Tala's knees gave out. She folded against the table, barely able to keep her wits, head ringing in pain. Val-Korin at was her side in a flash, propping her up under one arm. He smelled of sweet-scented pine needles, and the fragrance revived her some.

In fact, things were becoming particularly clear to her now. The physical pain of Jovan's two blows had woken her from the pain that was piercing her soul. *I cannot win against him,* she realized. She wanted to scream to the court that Jovan and Leif were lovers and that she had seen them kissing. *But that will only add to the absurdity of my accusations. Only make me look more a fool. But I must do something....*

Then Jondralyn was pulling her away from the Vallè ambassador. "I've got her." She took Tala by the arm, pulled her close. The Silver Guard armor was cold and hard and unforgiving against Tala's flesh. "You vile bastard," Jondralyn snarled at Jovan, holding Tala tighter to her chest. "Striking your own flesh and blood like that. Tala can barely stand, she's so rattled."

"Any man who dares strike any woman within my sight ever again, and I will kill that man!" Squireck roared. "King or slave, I will slay him!"

The crowd gasped at his pronouncement. All eyes flew to Jovan.

But Tala's own tear-streaked eyes stayed on the Prince of Saint Only, still standing tall in the middle of Sunbird Hall. Never a more gallant sight had she seen—long blond hair, polished Dayknight armor glinting in the firelight, imposing and sharp, the tip of his sword still pointed directly at Jovan.

The knights that had previously been sparring with Squireck looked wary, uncertain. But their blades were still drawn, poised and ready.

The Prince of Saint Only paid them no heed, his hard, unwavering eyes lancing across the room toward the king, his sword thrust forward.

"I am drunk." Jovan plopped back down in his seat. "I am drunk.

And I am acting stupid. I beseech you all, forgive me." He picked up a wine goblet, studied it, swirled the contents gently in hand. He looked at the Prince of Saint Only. "Forgive me, Squireck. I did not wish to upset you."

"It's not me whose forgiveness you should beg." The tip of Squireck's sword dipped.

"I apologize to whom I want." Jovan took a sip of the wine and pursed his lips contentedly before continuing. "Do not presume to give me orders. You are to fight Gault Aulbrek in the arena soon." His eyes hardened to points. "'Tis I who order you to continue with your training, Ser Squireck."

"Not until you promise never to strike another woman again!" Squireck demanded.

Jovan shook his head slowly as he sneered. "I will make no such promises. Tala will be escorted from Sunbird Hall. And you needn't worry about her well-being, Ser Squireck. Do not presume to push me further than you already have."

The Prince of Saint Only's blade rose. His eyes narrowed. To Tala's foggy gaze, it appeared Squireck was more than prepared to rush the king and stick the black sword straight into him.

"Remove Tala from my sight!" Jovan shouted, motioning for his Dayknights to take her away.

Jondralyn, still clutching Tala, placed her hand on the hilt of the Silver Guard sword at her hip. Her voice rang out loud and clear. "I alone will escort my sister to her chamber!" And then she gently guided Tala from the raised dais.

And as they took their leave of Sunbird Hall, nobody challenged them.

---

*Make no mistake: be he friend or foe, in the time of Fiery Absolution, the Dragon will come bearing a gold coin unto my Brethren.*
—THE MOON SCROLLS OF MIA

---

## CHAPTER THIRTY-EIGHT
# JONDRALYN BRONACHELL

### 11TH DAY OF THE ANGEL MOON, 999TH YEAR OF LAIJON
#### AMADON, GUL KANA

Jondralyn made her way through Sunbird Hall toward the balcony at the far eastern end. She needed fresh air. She felt claustrophobic in the bandages. Her frustration mounted with each step. Tala had lied to her, not just about her trip into Purgatory with Glade, but about her argument with Jovan. And when pressed about the argument, Tala had clammed up. An uncomfortable quiet had followed them through the castle. But she did her duty as escort, leaving Tala to her bedchamber to stew in the silence.

Pushing her way through the crowd, Jondralyn climbed the staircase quickly and stepped onto the balcony, breathing heavily from the weight of her Silver Guard armor. The ivory-paneled doors were thrown open, a slight breeze drifting over her. Once outside she could finally breathe. It was dark, near midnight, she guessed. But the clean air calmed her as she placed both hands on the stone railing and breathed deep, letting her gaze drift down toward Memory Bay.

From her lofty castle perch so high up Mount Albion, the starlit view below was magnificent. Ships bobbed in the bay as moonlight danced off the choppy waters. Stone outbuildings crouched at the base of Mount Albion, clinging to the vast castle's base, huddling against the bay. She tried to spy the wooden quay at the base of the mount near where she and Squireck and Hawkwood had dived into the water for the Rooms of Sorrow. But everything near the base of Albion was naught but clots and shadows.

The twining ivy and crimson petals lining the carved stone balustrade and castle walls above the balcony smelled blissful in comparison to the musky smoke-filled hall behind her. Flowers and vines arched over the doors behind her. Now that Squireck Van Hester was done sparring with Tolz, Alain, and Boppard, the orchestra had launched into song. The sound of their soothing tune drifted over her. Spellbound by the swelling tide of the music, she closed her eyes and listened, concentrated on every sweet note, letting it clear her mind, allowing herself to relax, scarcely daring to breathe at all lest she disturb the serenity of the moment.

There was a commotion to her left. She opened her eye to find a couple just up from Sunbird Hall leaning against the balcony railing not twenty paces away from her, giggling and kissing playfully. The amorous pair broke their embrace when they saw her there. They both knelt before her. The young man, a dark-haired nobleman's son, embarrassedly begged her forgiveness for not noticing her. Jondralyn bade the young couple stand and pay her no mind and go on about their night, enjoy the balcony view. They stood, bowed to her again, and then continued their mischievous flirting and kissing. The girl was blond and petite and cute, her face immaculate in shape, pristine pale skin flawless and smooth. Jondralyn dipped her own head in shame.

Squireck Van Hester stepped out onto the balcony behind her—a formidable bleak shadow. His black-lacquered armor seemed to devour what moonlight fell upon it. The black-opal-inlaid pommel of his sword was visible just over his shoulder, the Dayknight blade sheathed and hanging on the black leather baldric crisscrossing his back. She had not spoken to her former betrothed since that day in the Rooms of Sorrow with Hawkwood, that day of their shared disappointment when they'd gone in search of *Ethic Shroud*. Truth was, she had been avoiding the Prince of Saint Only.

He frightened her. He had very nearly killed Hawkwood.

Squireck bent his knee to her, black helm under the crook of his arm. He stood and was about to say something but was interrupted by the kissing couple, who had just now noticed him. "We will be rooting for you against that evil Sør Sevier knight," the dark-haired young nobleman's son said, bowing to Squireck.

"We will both be at the arena on the first day of the Fire Moon to watch the match," the blond girl added, blue eyes gleaming up at the Prince of Saint Only.

Squireck bowed at the waist to the couple, low and graceful. Everything he did seemed large and perfectly balanced. His presence dominated even the looming hulk of the castle behind him, as if Mount Albion and the massive stone structure that covered it combined weren't even big enough to hold him.

"We pray to Laijon for you daily," the girl said. "We pray daily to Laijon that you will win," she repeated.

"And I thank you for your prayers." Squireck nodded to both. He turned and plucked a crimson flower from the vine near him and placed it gently behind the ear of the girl, who blushed.

"It will be a grand event," the dark-haired young man went on. "All of Amadon is abuzz about it. All of Amadon is wishing you great victory."

Squireck reached out and shook the man's hand, clasping his

elbow as he did. "I thank you for your support." He broke his embrace, dipped his head to the couple a second time. "But may I speak with the princess alone, if it please you both?"

"Most certainly," the young nobleman's son stammered, bowing on last time. He led his girlfriend from the balcony and into the yellow glow of Sunbird Hall.

Alone, Jondralyn and Squireck faced each other, him towering over her; confusion, pain, anger, betrayal, love, all evident in his eyes. "How is Tala?" he asked.

*My sister is a liar*, she nearly blurted. But she certainly couldn't say that, not without inviting a whole host of other questions. It had all had grown so complicated. And she did not want to have a conversation with this man before her, this once familiar presence in her life who had so suddenly become a total stranger to her. *He very nearly killed Hawkwood.* As she gazed up at the uncertainty on his face, the fight between the two men in the Rooms of Sorrow was all she could think of.

A chill wind blew over the bay, howling as it dragged over the battlements and spires above. She breathed in deep, shuddered. "Thank you for coming to Tala's defense earlier tonight. You did not need to stand up to Jovan like that. I know you have worked hard to get back into the good graces of the court—"

"To the bloody underworld with the court," he cut her off. "A great nest of scheming bastards, all of them. Grand Vicar Denarius, Val-Korin, they are too smooth of tongue, getting Jovan to do their every bidding." His gaze traveled out to the bay behind her. "At the moment they wish for me to be a hero, rather than a convict. Jovan knows he cannot touch me now. As does the vicar. As does Val-Korin. They need me more than I need them."

"But have you considered what treachery may live within Leif Chaparral? It is he we should all fear. He will soon be your captain."

"I am not worried about him, either. Leif is no threat. You heard the couple who was just up here, fawning over me, both giddy for my arena match with Gault. Like they said, all of Amadon is a-talk of it. Jovan needs me to be the hero."

"And you don't even mind being used," she countered. "That is what they are doing, using you. My brother hated you, until he realized he could use you." She motioned to the golden light of Sunbird Hall below. "Now he throws a celebration, just to knight you. A Dayknight. And when you kill Gault in the arena, he will use your victory to prop himself up in war against the White Prince. And if Gault slays you, then all the better for Jovan: you will become naught but a martyr and a rallying cry for the populace and other knights. Like I am. Like my ruined face is. The two of us, we are both but a means to an end for my brother and his scheming court."

"Don't you think I know that?" Bitterness laced Squireck's words. Anger, too.

"Then why let them use you?"

"Better to be used by them than *hunted* by them. Better to be used and free from that dungeon cell under the arena. Better to be used and free than sitting idle on that island *you* had me hiding on. At least now I am doing something useful. At least now I can truly *fight*. At least now I give Gul Kana hope."

"Hope? How? By defeating Gault Aulbrek in the arena?"

"I *am* the Gladiator." His eyes flared with purpose. "I accept my destiny. We all must accept our destines, Jon. For the return of the Five Warrior Angels is soon upon us."

"And I am the Princess." Jondralyn looked out over the balcony to the bay beyond. The entire city had forgiven Squireck his crimes and welcomed him back into their good graces. *The Prince of Saint Only, the champion of the arena.* The Gladiator. The hero. Exactly what she had desired for herself. Victory in the arena to supplant her brother. A chilling thought struck her. *Is that Squireck's goal now too? To supplant my brother and become king himself?*

"My quest to find my own destiny nearly claimed my life," she muttered, staring out at the flickering waters. "Without Roguemoore or Culpa Barra, I am lost. I've no one to turn to. And with Hawkwood in hiding . . ." She trailed off.

"You can lean on me, Jon," he said softly, placing a hand on her shoulder. "I, too, am one of the Brethren of Mia. You can trust me."

She pulled away from his touch. "But what you did to Hawkwood, assaulting him as you did—I do not know if I can forgive that. You held him down, cut his face. When he was only trying to help us. A man who has helped the Brethren of Mia so much. And you nearly killed him. A man who has helped *me* so much."

"A man you love?"

She turned, looked up at him. *Plus the horror on your face when my bandages came off that day. I also do not know if I can forgive that. Or forget it.* "Must we really talk of such things?" she asked—pleaded really.

"You cannot trust him, Jon. The proof was in the Rooms of Sorrow. *Ethic Shroud* and the angel stone were gone. He hides them from us. If he ever had them at all."

"Why would he hide them? Why would Hawkwood agree to take us down there if he knew they were gone?"

"Because he is the Betrayer." His face grew hard, rigid. "He is a son of Black Dugal. A Bloodwood. It is all games and subterfuge with the likes of them. He is the assassin who killed your mother."

She drew back at his deceitful words. "Alana died whilst giving birth to Ansel."

"Do not be so naive, Jon. Even your father suspected she was assassinated."

There had been whispers in court that Queen Alana's death had been suspicious. Roguemoore had even mentioned it to her, including the rumors about Hawkwood. But nothing had ever been proven. Anger rose up in her. "Do not call me naive, Squireck Van Hester."

To his credit, he did not press the subject. Instead his face softened. "I did not come up here to argue with you. I came to mend things between us. Can you forgive me? We have gotten off to a wrong start."

"Mend things?" she asked.

"Please allow me to start over, Jon."

She turned her back to him, looking out over the bay. At the moment, she did not want him in her life at all.

"Jovan has ordered Leif Chaparral back to Lord's Point," Squireck said. "You are right, he will soon be made Dayknight captain. He is to collect what armies he can in Rivermeade, Savon, Ridliegh, Eskander, Bettles Field, Lokkenfell, Devlin, all places near the King's Highway. Armies from the farther reaches of Gul Kana are to gather and meet in Lord's Point too. But I fear they will be too late. Rumor is the armies of Sør Sevier are closing in on Lord's Point now. I suspect Aeros Raijael will have taken the city before Leif can muster enough forces there."

Jondralyn couldn't help but think of her own failure in dealing with Aeros and his army. She had been played for a fool. *Naive.* The one word that could hurt her. And Squireck had used it against her.

She felt his hand on her shoulder armor. He gently turned her around, his brow furrowed with concern as he seemed to study her face, the bandages there. "I am so sorry," he said, one trembling hand reaching up to brush the wraps around her cheek with the back of his fingers. She drew away from his touch.

"My pardon." He dropped his hand away, shifting his Dayknight helm awkwardly under the crook of his other arm, grasping it in strained fingers. "I did not realize how injured you really were until . . ." He trailed off, trying to hide his revulsion, doing a poor job of it.

". . . until you knocked my bandages off in the Rooms of Sorrow," she finished for him.

He blinked rapidly, then swallowed hard. "You were once so fair to look upon," he said, tenderness in his voice. Then he winced visibly, knowing that what he had just said was the exact wrong thing. "Wi-will it heal okay?" he stammered.

She remained quiet, trying to read his intent. For so many reasons, everything about this conversation was horrid and awkward and exactly why she had avoided Squireck to begin with.

The truth was, she just didn't have the patience for him anymore.

Callously she brushed past him and strode down the staircase and back down into Sunbird Hall.

† † † † †

Once in the privacy of her own bedchamber, Jondralyn shed her Silver Guard armor and let it clank unceremoniously to the floor in a heap. She unhooked her sword belt and dropped it atop the pile too. She couldn't stop thinking about something Squireck had said. *You were once so fair to look upon.*

She sat on the settee, slouching, head in her hands, her one good eye focusing on the maroon rug, her fingers clenching at the bandages covering her face. *Once so fair to look upon, and I have never been intimate with a man.*

She instantly thought of Hawkwood. The Way and Truth of Laijon *demands the virginity of a princess until the night of her marriage.* Nobody understood who she was. It was apparent when all they ever asked was if she would heal again and look as beautiful as she once had. *And would any man even have me, as damaged as I now am?*

*Do they not know who I am on the inside? What strength and resolve is in me? The intellect I've cultivated?* She wondered if anyone had ever seen beyond her face. Beyond her body. Despite her best efforts, all she was known for was beauty. *As if that was the only use I ever was to the realm. An image on a coin.* And even that image was being mocked now. She had seen the scratch over her face on the coppers some in

Sunbird Hall had been carrying tonight. It wasn't the first time she had seen such a marred coin. The burden of her beauty was never more noticeable than it was now—now that it was gone.

She took scant comfort in her own chamber anymore. The simple pastel colors of the walls and columns and arched ceiling felt more a lonely prison than anything else. She looked around her room and cursed herself for her weakness. She had finally allowed doubt to creep in. And there was no help from anyone. Roguemoore was gone. Culpa Barra too. Hawkwood was in hiding. She wondered where Val-Draekin was. Had he found the dwarf and delivered her message? Was the search for *Blackest Heart* and *Afflicted Fire* underway? She recalled what Hawkwood had told her of *Forgetting Moon*, that the Gallows Haven boy, Nail, had lost it to Aeros Raijael.

Then she felt it. *Something isn't right!*

Like an icy knife tip snaking up her spine, the realization that someone else was in her bedchamber shuddered over her entire being.

Some dark shade was standing directly behind her. She could *feel* it.

And here she was, unprepared, in naught but her sweat-stained leather breeches and thin undershirt. Her armor was piled on the floor at her feet, her sword, too.

She lurched from the settee, whirled to face the interloper.

Relief instantly flooded her entire body. It was Hawkwood. He stood in the center of the room in a black cloak, hood thrown back, dark hair a tumbling wave around his shoulders, eyes devouring her with their steady gaze. Faint red scars crossed his own features from where Squireck had run a dagger over his face in the Rooms of Sorrow. He wore the two cutlasslike swords again, both strapped to his back.

She hurried to him and he folded her into his strong arms. They clung to each other for what seemed a short and sweet eternity. "How did you get in here?" she asked when they finally broke their tender clutch.

"Bookcase, same as before," he said, a sly smirk hiding behind his unremitting stare. "I've been waiting some time."

"You could've been discovered by one of the Silver Guards. Who knows how often they snoop around in here? Who knows what spying the Silver Guards do for Jovan?"

He raised one brow. "You're one of the Silver Guards."

She laughed nervously. "What were you thinking, coming here? It was dangerous enough when you and Squireck did it the first time."

"I am not thinking at all."

It was a tender admission on his part, unexpected and exciting. Guilt flooded her then. "It is all my fault," she said.

"What is your fault?"

"*Ethic Shroud.*" She looked up at the mahogany bookshelf. "On the top shelf, third book from the left, there's a small panel behind it. I hid your map there. What if it was discovered? What if it's my fault the altar was empty?" She started toward the shelf.

"Forget it." He seized her arm in a tight grip. "It is not your fault, Jondralyn."

"It's not that simple." She couldn't even meet his eyes. "I have failed in so many ways."

Hawkwood removed his swords, placing them on her settee. Then he shed his cloak, draping it over the swords. "Do not blame yourself." He wore a simple pair of black leather pants and a soft black silken shirt. He took her chin tenderly in his hand, pulled her own gaze up to his. "It is none of our faults. I took a risk creating the map. You took a risk hiding it here. It is what it is."

But to her, it seemed like such a colossal mistake. Panic and despair washed over her. "Whoever found the map has the angel stone and *Ethic Shroud.*"

"We will find them again. Simple as that. The shield and the stone."

Yet his confidence was no comfort; it only emphasized the gulf of her own uncertainty, her own lack of confidence.

"Keep fighting for what you believe in, Jon," he continued. "It is your will to fight and do what is right that I so adore. It was those honorable traits that I saw in you that changed me, made me a better person."

"But it's so hard to continue to fight against such odds."

"Then we will strengthen how you fight." His eyes cut into hers, full of empathy, but also full of determination. "I've no Sacrament of Souls for us to hone our craft, but I can train you in my own way."

"What do you mean?"

"It is time I took up the trade again. It is what I was meant to do. I *am* the Assassin, after all. And I shall make you my apprentice, Jon. You can accomplish much more hidden in the shadows than in the center of a gladiator arena."

He'd already taught her sword craft. But now he was talking of assassination and making her his partner. He was standing so close to her now, smelling of cloves and frankincense and leather. The smoldering heat of his eyes burned through her. She could see the pulse beating in his neck. *What are you thinking, Hawkwood?*

Both his hands gripped her by the shoulders. "I did not sneak in here tonight to talk of lost maps and angel stones, nor even to talk of your training."

She could feel how flimsy her sweat-stained shirt was under his fingers. She could feel herself flushing as he drew her close, pressing his body to hers, scant little fabric between them.

"I'm a mess." She exhaled the words, so easily disarmed by him, entire body knotted with nerves. "Unwashed from the armor. I am embarrassed."

"You needn't be," he said, one hand at the small of her back, his other reaching up to stroke the side of her cheek, brushing the doubt from her lips with a gentle swipe of his finger. She let her face melt into his touch, and what few reservations were left floating in her mind died soft little deaths one by one.

He took her hand in his, brought it up to his own face. "Squireck did not cut me too deep." He placed her fingers over his own faint wounds. "Both of us with our own injuries."

She traced the raw scars on his face with trembling fingers, knowing that once healed they would leave their mark. She looked into his eyes. Despite her own uncertainty, there was a comfort there in what she saw, as if they both just knew each other always, and this would be the rest of their lives.

Hawkwood leaned in. "Angel stones, magic talismans, they all mean nothing to me, Jon. It is thoughts of you that consume my mind. It is you who I have searched my entire life for. I will not lose you."

"But my face." She so desperately wanted to believe him. "My bandages. I am so ashamed."

"It is your touch that I desire," he whispered. "Your voice. The words that you speak. That is who you are."

Her vision slipped out of focus then, and she swayed on her feet, all restraint gone.

His lips met hers, light as a warm breeze. His hand caressed her hair, her neck, her breast. "I want to kiss every inch of you," he said, and they folded to the floor in each other's arms.

Limbs tangled together, atop her soft maroon rug, she gave herself fully to him.

*With Dragon Claw, one can slash. With rivers of silver and scorch, one can slay. But only with Blood of the Dragon can one command the beasts of the underworld. For the last of the fiery beasts was slain in that forest of black Bloodwood trees.*

—THE ANGEL STONE CODEX

# CHAPTER THIRTY-NINE
# BISHOP HUGH GODWYN

## 11TH DAY OF THE ANGEL MOON, 999TH YEAR OF LAIJON
### SKY LOCHS, GUL KANA

A ferocious wind ripped through the trees surrounding the lonesome cabin where they had taken shelter. Branches lashed savagely outside, grating against the stacked stone walls and tattered pine shingles of the rickety one-room structure. They had stumbled upon the abandoned cabin in the pitch darkness of the night, its flimsy wood door rattling against the coming storm.

It had been a day and a half since they had left the rest of the company on the glacier. They had made good time, heading west through the mountains toward Stanclyffe, Godwyn leading one of the dun-colored mules by the reins, Dokie strapped to its back. Liz Hen rode the other pack mule, Sør Sevier sword at her hip. The first night they had slept under the stars, a brisk breeze blowing. But tonight was bitter cold and Godwyn considered them fortunate to find this refuge, shabby as it was.

The weathered stone floor of the cabin had been crusted with frost. But Liz Hen quickly got a small blaze going in the fireplace set into the far wall, and soon the scent of burning spruce floated in the air.

Earlier, Godwyn had guided both mules inside the cabin, the banging door eventually latched tight. It made for a crowded place. But the mules needed shelter too. Together he and Liz Hen had untied Dokie's litter and set the unconscious boy on the floor near the fire, Godwyn pouring some of the healing draught between his relaxed, dry lips.

Liz Hen shed her cloak and leaned her sword against the hearth. Godwyn leaned his own Dayknight blade against the wall near the old wooden table, a rough stone wall crudely chinked with mud. And in the feeble glow of the fire, they settled onto the two old wooden stools at the old wooden table and ate a sparse dinner of hard jerky and dried salmon. Aside from the two stools and table, the cabin had two rotted cots thrown in one corner and an empty shelf above the hearth.

To pass the time, Liz Hen opened Dokie's satchel and began reviewing the drawings he'd made of the many standing stones the company had passed by early in the journey. "Naught but symbols and stones," she uttered. "Squares. Crosses. Crescent moons. Shooting stars."

"He was certainly taken with them." Godwyn nodded, taking one of the parchments from her hand, overcome with sadness as he studied the crude artwork. The boy was fighting off the poison as best he could, but Godwyn didn't hold out much hope.

"Do you think Beer Mug is dead?" Liz Hen asked, eyes a-squint in the dim light. "Do you think he was sicker than Dokie, stuck with so many darts as he was?" She had been asking the same two questions all day. "He ran away across the ice. But I think I seen him slow down at the end, like he was tuckered out." Deep pain lined her face. "Do you think those oghuls found Beer Mug and killed him?"

"I don't know," Godwyn admitted. "But what I do know, that dog was a hardy and brave fellow, scrambling under that crushing roof and saving Dokie like he did. Wouldn't surprise me none if that dog were still out there searching for us now." He leaned back on the stool, stretching, wincing in pain from his own injuries. That he'd survived falling into the pit of sharpened spikes was nothing short of luck. *And landing atop an oghul, no less!* They were all lucky to have come out of the mines alive.

"Do you think Dokie will live?" Liz Hen's gaze was again on the boy on the litter at their feet, her hand gripping one of his sketches. "If the needles were poison, why didn't they kill him immediately?"

"There are many different types of poison," he answered. "Oghul-made poisons. Vallè-made poisons. The Bloodwood assassins deploy poisons of all types, most for the purposes of incapacitating their foe for a slow torture later. Who knows what type of ancient poison was on those darts that struck Dokie and Beer Mug? Nail seemed to be recovering fine from the few that struck his face. So there is hope for Dokie. But who knows why evil people create evil things?"

"It is an evil world." The girl stared at Dokie, tenderness in her look. "He's so sick and swollen up. How far to Stanclyffe?"

"Three, maybe four more days," he answered, always patient with her repetitive inquiries, knowing she was only worried for her young friend. "That's if this storm blows over quickly and our path remains clear."

"Will they have the medicine he needs in Stanclyffe?"

*If we can get him there in time, yes!* He thought of the oghul street vendor in Stanclyffe—the gruff beast with the red teardrop tattoo at the corner of his eye, the beast who kept the bloodletter woman as a pet. He feared what dread medicines Dokie might need. And he hated the thought of getting the boy addicted to what draughts that he knew would surely cure him. *But there is no choice.* That the oghul would have such medicines was not a question. *And what price will the oghul ask?* The tattoo under his eye announced to anyone who knew what to look for just what type of foul alchemy he bartered in. "Yes." He met Liz Hen's eyes reassuringly, nodding. "I do believe they will have the medicine we need in Stanclyffe. At least some."

She brightened. "I'm for traveling day and night to get Dokie there safe then."

"I agree, but for the storm. We cannot be caught out in it. When the weather clears, we shall make haste."

"I don't mind traveling through storms. I've done it plenty before."

"I know," he acknowledged.

Liz Hen was a brave one, loyal to Dokie, Stefan, and Beer Mug for sure. He also knew she could be stubborn and ofttimes cruel and unreasonable, especially around Nail. At the same time, the moment someone showed Liz Hen any kindness, she became loyal to a fault. The instant Seita had helped her fight off the oghuls near the creek, the girl's demeanor had done a complete reversal. And after Seita had braided her hair, Liz Hen had practically hero-worshipped the Vallè maiden.

"What do you make of this drawing?" Liz Hen said, sliding a parchment across the table toward him. "Dokie mostly just drew symbols from the standing stones. But look here. He's drawn five figures. Each with a weapon like the five Warrior Angels."

It was a simple sketch, five figures like she claimed—stick figures, really—each with a weapon: ax, sword, war helm, crossbow, and shield. The picture reminded him of some lost memory hovering just at the corner of his mind. Unable to recall, he scooted the parchment back at her. "He must have been thinking of the Five Warrior Angels when he drew it is all."

"But look." The girl pointed, the drawing still between them. "This figure with the crossbow is clearly me, and the person with the shield is clearly Dokie. But who are the other three?"

"How can you tell?" He leaned in and took another look.

"See." She tapped her finger on the drawing pointedly. "This figure, the second from the right with the crossbow. It's fat and large like me and has girl hair. And the one on the far right with the shield is teeny like Dokie. Isn't it obvious?"

"Perhaps." He met her gaze. "People ofttimes put themselves and their friends into their artwork."

"It's weird." She held the drawing up into better light. "Looks like he drew a giant glove on my hand holding the crossbow." Her eyes tightened. "Or maybe it is a gauntlet. Or maybe he's just a shitty drawer. But the figure with the sword also has girl hair. The one with the ax could be Nail. Dokie did see Nail carry that ax anyway. Wonder who the other two are, though?" She looked back up at Godwyn. "The whole drawing feels like an ill omen of sorts, don't you think?"

Godwyn glanced down at the injured boy on the floor. *Poison darts.* He could still feel the wounds on his own arm. Though he wanted to relieve his own pain, he would not partake of any of the healing medicines in his bag. There wasn't much left, and Dokie needed every drop.

"Yes, I'd say the figure with the ax could definitely be Nail," Liz Hen said, placing the drawing in the center of the table, genuine concern in her tone now. "Do you really think the White Prince destroyed Gallows Haven and killed my whole family because he was searching for Nail?"

Godwyn contemplated her question, wondering how to answer, for her question smacked of the truth. "The destruction of Gallows Haven was no fault of Nail's."

"But I heard you and the dwarf talking about Nail at our camp above Ravenker one night. You thought we were all asleep. But I heard both you and Hawkwood say some things. . . ." She paused, meeting his gaze with purpose now. "And I am pretty sure Nail heard you talking too."

"What did you hear?"

"Stuff." She shrugged nonchalantly. "You all talked about Nail's parentage some. Said that you *needed* him for some purpose. Said that he's been told his entire life he was naught but a bastard boy, but that he is actually someone far greater. Said that Shawcroft's life was sad because he had to look after Nail. Said Shawcroft had to raise Nail hard because he *was* so special."

Godwyn sat back. *If Nail had indeed heard the conversation, what must he think?* A thick pall of wood smoke was filling the hazy cabin. He realized they would soon have to either open the door for ventilation or put out the fire.

Liz Hen's gaze remained on him. "You said that Nail was a danger to me, to Dokie, to Stefan, that we would all die because of him."

"But yet you all still live, no?"

Her eyes settled on Dokie's sleeping form. She said no more. She didn't have to.

He watched her for a moment. "I know you have harbored some resentment toward Nail ever since Gallows Haven was destroyed," he said. "But I repeat, none of it was Nail's fault. In fact, Nail did all he could to help in your escape. He is honorable and he is brave. As are you, Liz Hen. Stefan, too. And Dokie."

"But did Aeros attack my home because of Nail? Is he special, as you say?"

"Nail is important to the Brethren of Mia," Godwyn said without reservation. "And yes, Aeros landed at Gallows Haven in hopes of finding Nail. But I repeat, that is *not* Nail's fault."

Liz Hen's face twisted in anger. "Then why did you talk behind his back? There is nothing more worse and harmful in this world than lies. It seems deception and half-truths are what you Brethren of Mia are all about. Why didn't you or Roguemoore or Culpa or Hawkwood ever tell Nail the truth of things?"

Godwyn was surprised by her multiple accusations. He was also surprised by her impassioned defense of Nail. Fact was, he didn't really didn't know much about Nail's true parentage himself. Other than what Shawcroft had told him—that the boy and his twin sister were possibly kin to Aevrett Raijael. That the birth and subsequent fate of the twins had become an ethical dilemma for many, all shrouded in mystery. Bottom line, Shawcroft—or rather, Ser Roderic Raybourne—watched over Nail at the behest of two men; his brother, King Torrence Raybourne, and King Borden Bronachell. As far as Godwyn knew, those were the only three men who knew Nail's full heritage. He wagered Roguemoore possibly knew, his brother Ironcloud, too, as both dwarves were deep into the inner workings of the Brethren of Mia. Godwyn had never pressed the issue himself, figuring Nail's parentage had something to do with the return of the Five Warrior Angels and the retrieval of the weapons and angel stones. And that was enough for him. He'd also heard the rumors that Hawkwood had been in Arco when Nail's mother had died. And the rumors that the former Bloodwood had assassinated Alana Bronachell—something he hadn't been able to forgive the man for. So in a way, he understood Liz Hen's distrust of the Brethren of Mia.

"Well," Liz Hen huffed. "Are you going to answer my question?"

"We did not tell Nail the truth." Godwyn met her gaze steadily. "Probably because none of us ever really knew the truth of things."

She hung her head some, then glanced back at Dokie. "Will you pray with me, Godwyn?" She held her hands across the table for him. palms up. "I've no idea if my prayers are ever even heard. But I still must try. For Dokie."

He nodded, placing his hands in hers.

She gripped tight, closing her eyes in supplication. "We beseech you in your glorious goodness to deliver Dokie from the pain and misery of the dread poisons that eat at his flesh and brain, dear Laijon. Hasten the powers of thy kingdom on high, so that what sickness afflicts him may depart his body. We ask this of you in true faith and in thy holy name. Dokie is our best friend. He is kind and he is innocent. We would ask that you spare him and take us if you must, take Godwyn or me if another life is due unto you. Take me, dear Laijon, if you must. Leave poor Dokie out of it." The girl choked up, struggled to continue. "We also grant thee grace and thanks for delivering us so far from our enemies, dear Laijon, those wretched foul oghuls. With thy divine powers, keep us free from any more oghuls and the miseries of this sinful, cruel world. And may you consummate our prayer with bliss both body and soul in eternal everlasting glory through you, Laijon, forever and ever, amen."

"Amen," Godwyn muttered, and let go the girl's hands. Tears had formed in his own eyes over Liz Hen's heartfelt prayer.

A guttural shout followed by a loud *boom!* startled Godwyn out of his seat. The two mules jumped and brayed as a giant ax blade split the cabin's wooden door nearly in twain, splinters of wood flying across the room and peppering their table. Liz Hen let out a yelp and reached for her sword against the hearth. Godwyn snatched up his blade too.

Another bloodcurdling shout and the rusted ax blade was wrenched free, taking most of the door with it. Outside were the blocky gray forms of three howling oghuls. What remained of the door clattered inward against the stone wall as the howling beasts burst into the cabin, all three bristling with rusted armor and crude weapons.

One of the frightened mules jumped, back legs kicking out, knocking the first oghul straight into the sharp end of Godwyn's upraised sword. The oghul staggered back, blood gushing from his gut as Godwyn stabbed his sword straight into his grimacing face. The beast dropped, falling right on top of Dokie's sleeping form with a thud. The second oghul shoved past Godwyn, knocking him backward on top of Dokie too, then leaping toward Liz Hen, broad curved blade arching straight down at the girl's head. Liz Hen parried the blow with her own sword before she was pushed over the table and nearly into the fire. The third oghul swung his rusted ax straight down at Godwyn, who rolled, and the ax blade cut deep into the armor of the oghul atop Dokie.

Godwyn spun to his feet and swung his own sword at the ax-wielding brute. The blade glanced off his stiff armor, causing scant harm. The irate mule, still braying and kicking, struck the ax-wielding oghul in the chest with a stiff hoof, knocking the beast almost out the doorway. Godwyn took the advantage and swung his blade again, connecting with solid armor. He swung a third time, only to have his sword bludgeoned from his grip as the oghul recovered more quickly than he'd thought possible, the whirling ax heavy and cruel. His sword spinning across the room, Godwyn stumbled to the side, clutching at the wall, trying to regain his balance.

The second oghul with the curved blade had backed Liz Hen into the corner, his wicked weapon swiftly battering her blade as she struggled in defense.

Reaching for his own sword, Godwyn tripped and went down again. The oghul with the ax loomed over him with purpose. The beast reached down and snatched Godwyn by the collar of his shirt and hauled him up from the floor with one powerful hand. The oghul's rank mouth stretched open with a revolting roar, two sharp, pointed fangs jutting from under bloated black lips.

And then the beast bit down, sinking his teeth deep into Godwyn's neck and sucking with a throaty gurgle. The initial pain was almost unbearable as Godwyn felt his entire body clench and stiffen in agony. The total shock and paralysis to his system was such that he couldn't even move. He couldn't gulp or gasp for air through his nose or even his mouth. A rotten, putrid stench engulfed him as he hung limp in the bloodsucking oghul's clutch. He couldn't tell if the decaying stink was from his own bowels emptying or the oghul's rancid, bloodsucking breath.

But there was as sudden sweetness to the entire experience too . . .

. . . and that horrified him even more.

Dangling limp in the monster's grasp, Godwyn could see Liz Hen. The girl was still backed into the corner, still gripping her sword in both hands, her expression desperate as she fought for her own life with every block and parry she'd ever been taught. Then the oghul struck the sword from her hands. It clanked to the floor near the fireplace. At the same time, the beast reached out and snatched the girl by the hair, pulling her neck toward his own wide and gaping maw.

There was a flash of gray. A streak of snarling, raging fur launched itself onto the oghul's back an instant before he sank his rotted teeth into the girl's neck.

*Beer Mug!* The shepherd dog ripped into the back of the oghul's skull, powerful jaws chomping through rusted helm and bone, tearing and shredding violently. Blood sprayed as the creature dropped like a stone, falling dead in a puddle of its own brains, limbs twitching.

Godwyn's vision blurred as all strength left his body, his oghul captor sucking his blood. A euphoria like he'd never felt before filled him. *There's an addictive toxin inside each oghul fang,* Roguemoore had told Liz Hen on the trail above Stanclyffe. *A pleasing chemical that over time a bloodletter cannot live without.* Godwyn was horrified at the thought. And then he felt himself falling, the oghul attached to his neck dropping with him, foul fangs slipping free of his flesh as they thudded to the hard floor together side by side.

Liz Hen, standing over them now, yanked her sword from the bloodsucker's back, shouting, "Fuck you and the hoary oghul trash-barrel cunt you slithered out of!"

Godwyn grabbed a huge breath of air, gulping it down, the dead eyes of his attacker staring back at him as they lay on the tattered wood together.

*And the sweet euphoria gone . . .*

He tried to raise himself up on his elbows to no avail, then rolled

over onto his back. *The same toxin also seals off the vein after a feeding,*
the dwarf had said *A bloodletter won't bleed out.* Still, Godwyn could
tell he was bleeding pretty good, and he had no idea how long those
toxins took to do their job. His every limb was numb. One useless
hand wobbled up, trying to stanch the scarlet pumping from his neck.

*The sharp fangs in my neck . . . both the most horrid—yet most grand—*
*feeling of my life . . .*

The first oghul, the one atop Dokie, moaned, still alive. The
foul-smelling beast slowly crawled off the boy, making his way on
hands and knees across the floor toward the door, his many wounds
leaving trails of thick blood.

Beer Mug responded with a venom-laced growl of his own. Those
growls were quickly followed by hoarse oghul screams as the dog
viciously attacked.

"That's right, Beer Mug!" Liz Hen hollered in savage triumph. "I
wager you're one hungry dog! You're a good boy and a hungry boy!
Go ahead and eat his ugly fucking face right the fuck off!"

*For human and Vallè to procreate is as it should be: impossible. But before that*
*great day of Absolution, beware alchemy and the great deceptive nature of the fey.*
—THE WAY AND TRUTH OF LAIJON

# CHAPTER FORTY
# STEFAN WAYLAND

12TH DAY OF THE ANGEL MOON, 999TH YEAR OF LAIJON
SKY LOCHS, GUL KANA

Their camp was set atop a broad wooded hill overlooking a small dale of tumbled-down trees and thickets of spindly briar. The hail had eventually subsided into a steady, yet unpleasant, sideways drizzle that thumped against Stefan's armor under his cloak. Despite the fire before him, and the two hefty draught mares blocking the wind behind him, he just couldn't get warm. Even the shimmering of the trees trembling in the stiff wind made him shiver. He drew the cloak tighter around his neck. *Isn't it summer everywhere else in the Five Isles?*

Seita sat on the birch log next to him. Culpa Barra was across from him, large black sword resting on his lap. The crossbow, *Blackest Heart*, was strapped to the Dayknight's back, the black angel stone secured in a leather pouch tied to his belt.

"Why has Laijon cursed us?" Culpa cast his gaze at the starless sky. "All our hard work and sacrifice for naught. Just when all the prophecies of the *Moon Scrolls* were falling into place, only to suffer such massive failure." He looked back down at the flickering flames of the fire. "What test from God is this?"

Neither Seita nor Stefan said a word, just huddled in the cold.

"There must be some lesson in this," the Dayknight muttered. "But what, I cannot fathom." The look on his face went from sheer defeat to utter resolve almost in an instant. "But I will not let it be over. No matter what occurs, we will press on." Culpa was clearly struggling with the futility of their situation, trying to convince himself there was still hope. Trying to convince his travel companions too. But the horrid weather had done enough to dampened all of Stefan's resolve.

"We were fortunate to have found horses, at least," Culpa said as the tree branches above groaned in the cold evening currents, resolve in his voice, as if having horses now meant all the difference. "Our one good fortune. Finding those mares."

The Dayknight had been their leader ever since the glacier, pushing them ever onward at a brisk pace. It had been two days since they had last seen Godwyn, Liz Hen, and Dokie heading west across the glacier, two days since they had lost Nail, Roguemoore, and Val-Draekin to a violent crushing death.

Stefan still couldn't believe his friend was actually gone. Nail's death tore at his heart. Then he thought of Zane, and Gisela, and his own family, and all the other Gallows Haven dead. *What random luck has kept me alive?*

*Seita claimed to have seen all our fates. The fates of three . . .*

*Nail. Val-Draekin. Roguemoore.*

After witnessing the horror of his three companions being sucked down into that savage maelstrom of ice and water, Stefan had hiked from the glacier in a numb stupor, one weary foot in front of the next, silently plodding along, emotions suppressed. Culpa had guided them swiftly from the frozen wasteland, pushing the limits of their endurance until they finally reached the loch waters and the safety of stable land.

Last evening, just before dusk, at the southernmost end of the loch, they had come across a logging camp resting idly in a grove of trees and a green meadow. The encampment looked recently lived in, yet nobody was around. The camp consisted of two wood cabins and a stack of long pine logs stacked at the loch's edge near the head of a river. As they'd trudged up to the two cabins, Stefan noticed a scraggly dog lying under the ragged wood porch of one. The dog lifted its nose off the ground and scuttled from under its protection, wagging its tail in hopes of a friendly pat on the head. Culpa and Seita had ignored the dog. Stefan had stopped and let it lick his hand. Then the three of them had searched the cabins, but found no food.

After that, Culpa guided Stefan and Seita east up the slope behind the camp, through a field of grazing goats and chickens, toward the mountain range beyond. The goats scattered, bells about their necks tinkling, chickens clucking in their wake. The lone dog followed them. Culpa tried to capture a chicken, but the few nearest him darted from his grasp and he soon gave up. They stumbled upon a stone barn dug into a small hill not far behind the cabins. The barn housed two healthy draught mares. There were two empty stalls, recently used, as if two other horses were normally stabled there too but were now out at work. They stole the mares from the barn, along with several coils of rope, three torches, a canvas tarp, and ten arrows for Stefan's quiver.

Stefan had used an arrow to shoot one of the chickens. But he'd felt guilty, as the hardworking mares they'd stolen likely represented a fair portion of the workload and overall sustenance of the loggers, and the ten arrows in his quiver perhaps their only defense, and the chickens their only food. "Probably naught but filthy oghul loggers anyway," Culpa said once they were miles from the camp, cooking the chicken over a warm fire. "The vile beasts seem to be reclaiming most of the north."

Culpa had explained the direness of their situation that first night. There were three great lochs that made up Sky Lochs. The glacier under D'Nahk lè covered the far eastern loch. And that was where they were, at the bottom of that loch. They could either follow the River Vallè directly south to Port Follett, or head southeast toward Deadwood Gate and attempt to finish the quest and find *Afflicted Fire*. Either way, with the horses, they were looking at a journey of about four days, depending on weather and stray oghuls. Culpa convinced them Deadwood Gate was the way, though Stefan thought the entire venture pointless.

Now here they sat, huddled against the cold.

"Can I look at the crossbow again?" Seita asked.

"It's best it stays with me." Culpa unflinchingly met the Vallè maiden's gaze from across the fire, hand straying to the leather pouch at his side.

"I did my part in finding it." Seita glared right back at him. "I should be given the honor of, at the very least, looking at the crossbow. Perhaps even holding it. Perhaps figuring out what type of bolt or quarrel fits its strange mechanisms. For I know you do not know how to use it, how to arm it with the right-sized quarrel. Yet you've been guarding those relics as if you expect me or Stefan to snatch them at any moment and run off into the night." Seita pulled the hood of her gray cloak back. "Why?"

"For your own safety," Culpa answered. "*The Moon Scrolls of Mia* speak of a curse. The first person who touches an angel stone with the bare flesh of their hand is doomed to die. The dwarf knew of this curse. All the Brethren of Mia knew of this curse. It is why none of us should handle the crossbow more than need be. It is why I keep the stone wrapped in its silk."

"And neither you nor the dwarf bothered to tell the rest of us about this curse until now?" Seita asked, venom in her voice.

Stefan had watched the mistrust growing between his two travel companions ever since leaving the glacier. In fact, he had been aware of the tension between Seita and Culpa since Lord's Point. But the Vallè was right. They should have known about the curse. Gisela had pulled the stone from the altar in the Roahm Mines. It had first touched her flesh. And now she was dead. And he had seen the look between the Dayknight and the dwarf when Roguemoore had touched the black angel stone in the Sky Loch mines with his bare hand. And now the dwarf was also dead. *Coincidence?*

*Gisela had been the first to touch the blue stone when Nail had pulled the battle-ax out of the altar in the Roahm Mines.*

Angry, he spoke his position, all of it, voice quaking in the cold. "Angel stones. Magic weapons. Moon scrolls. *The Way and Truth of Laijon.* It's all nonsense. Even the curses you mention. Naught but silly superstition. All of it."

Culpa eyed him curiously. "Why would you say that, after all you have seen?"

"What have I seen? Just the horrific deaths of my family and friends."

"You've seen *Blackest Heart* and *Forgetting Moon* with your own eyes. Few throughout the breadth of history can say the same."

"What does it matter?" he answered. "That battle-ax, Nail lost it. That crossbow strapped on your back, it hasn't done anything special yet, has it?"

"You are being a cynic," the Dayknight grunted. "And I don't care for it. Faith is a virtue. Doubt is not. One is strength. One is weakness. Choose which side you are on."

"Which side I am on?" Stefan felt the anger within boil. "By rights I shouldn't even be here, Culpa. And if you ask me, faith and belief in holy books and moon scrolls have done naught but kill folk and start wars. And faith and belief in magic weapons and angel stones have done naught but launch pointless quests that have killed every person dearest to me. At the moment, I see faith and belief as naught but cowardly lies. And lies are the most dangerous of things." He hung his head. "Leastways that is how I feel."

"I understand you are frustrated," Culpa answered, sympathy in his tone. "I feel like giving up sometimes too. But I know that we cannot. We will not. I will not." He looked away a moment, then back. "My young cousin, Tyus, 'twas he who taught me the power of having faith and never giving up. Though he is from Gul Kana, two years ago, at eighteen, of his own volition and desire to help, Tyus went and fought against Aeros Raijael in Wyn Darrè. He endured many horrors and was eventually taken captive by one of the White Prince's Knights Archaic in a town called Lavandoria. Enna Spades offered Tyus a deal, and that deal cost him his tongue. But Enna kept her end of the bargain and my cousin was free to return to Gul Kana. Which he did, for a time. And despite missing his tongue, despite not being able to talk, despite all he'd seen and suffered, my cousin went back to Wyn Darrè to join Ironcloud and Seabass and others of the Brethren of Mia. He went back to study ancient texts and fight for our cause. Tyus Barra had that much faith. For faith and belief breeds optimism. Doubt does not. Doubt equals negativity and failure."

Stefan didn't buy into Culpa's view of optimism and doubt. And Culpa's frustrations were not his own. He figured the weapons of Laijon and the angel stones were indeed a curse, and not for the reasons the Dayknight said. "I cannot speak to your cousin's bravery for I do not know him. But why would Shawcroft spend his entire life searching for these relics only to leave them exactly where he found them, then place deadly traps around about? So Dokie can be shot with darts? So Nail can fall into a glacier?" Stefan had asked all the questions in a rush. He glanced at Seita. "Val-Draekin dead too. For what?"

Culpa did not answer, just gazed into the fire.

"It's all pointless," Stefan went on. "None of this would have happened if Shawcroft would have kept the weapons and stones hidden safe in some other way. After all, he hid his Dayknight sword in the eaves of his cabin for years and nobody knew."

"You may be right," Culpa answered. "But I would never be the one to second-guess Shawcroft on anything. When he first found *Lonesome Crown*, he did exactly as you suggest, gave the helm and angel stone to his brother, Torrence, for safekeeping. And that did not work out. Torrence bragged about his treasures. And Aeros Raijael launched his crusade. After that, Shawcroft made every effort to find the weapons . . . and then just leave them be. Safe where the Blessed Mother Mia left them to begin with."

"I just don't think it makes any sense," Stefan said.

"I'm with Stefan." Seita placed her hand on Stefan's knee. "I thought the entire quest was a stupid notion from the start. A complete waste of our time. And it has claimed the lives of our friends."

Culpa said, "Their sacrifice will go down in history—"

"Go down in *what* history?" she snapped. "Some religious text likely to be misinterpreted a thousand years from now, some vague words apt to claim more lives in the future as innocent people go in search of Nail's and Val-Draekin's frozen corpses, imagining their bones to be filled with magic or some such?"

Nobody spoke. Seita stood, brushing white puffs of smoke away from her face with her hand. "I can't breathe in any more of this damnable smoke. I need some real air." Her eyes darted between Stefan and Culpa. "You two can hash this nonsense out between yourselves." She strode away into the darkness alone.

Stefan stood to follow, but Culpa stopped him with a stern voice. "Let her go," he ordered. "She shouldn't hear what I am about to say to you anyway."

Stefan sat back down, wary, wishing he were anywhere else in the Five Isles but here. Everything about the quest had unraveled to the point of disaster. *Only three of us left. And two of us don't even believe in the mission anymore. If we ever did . . .*

"I take this quest seriously." Culpa's voice had taken on a touch of anger. "But if you want out, you are free to go, Stefan. For the place I go next, Deadwood Gate, is not to be trifled with. I have seen what lives within the depths of those mines."

"What have you seen?" Stefan asked.

"Deadwood Gate is oghul forged," Culpa answered gravely. "Ten thousand years of oghul digging. For what? Gold? Something else? Digging and digging. Thousands of tunnels. Millions, maybe. A vast underground labyrinth that stretches east from Kasmere Lake clear to Wroclaw, and north to the oghul city of Tok. And in the hundreds of places in between, there are abandoned forts and chapels and barns that have basements and dungeons and root cellars with hidden entrances, all connected to this stew of underground caverns, all leading deep down to the very heart of the Five Isles, all leading to that one dreadful place we fear most and those fiery beasts we dare not speak of. Fiery beasts of the underworld and their dread druidic masters . . ."

The Dayknight paused, swallowing hard, a haunted look in his eyes as he pulled his own gray hood up around his head. "I ought not speak of it further, lest I bring more curses down upon us. I've said it many times before, but the mines of Deadwood Gate will grip and twist your mind if you are not ever watchful. Once in those dungeons, the very air you breathe is heavy with dark enchantment and illusion and black spells full of hate, evil sorceries created by primordial demons of obscure legend, ancient wraiths *The Moons Scrolls of Mia* mention but once, a race of monstrous fiends worse than any oghul, worse than any beast of the underworld."

"What?"

"Druids of an ancient race. Maybe not even of this world. They were simply called the Skulls."

"The silver secret of the Skulls?" Stefan questioned. "You mentioned such in the Sky Loch Mines. Roguemoore seemed to dismiss the notion. I'd never heard of such things before."

"Few have. Only *The Moon Scrolls of Mia* mention the Skulls, and not often. Once they were eradicated from the Five Isles during the War of Cleansing, all memory of the Skulls' existence was purged from every book of history, and every evidence of their physical existence was buried in the deepest, darkest of haunts. You likely saw the remnants of their final removal and resting place in the Roahm Mines above Gallows Haven."

"The pool of water Shawcroft called the Place of the Skulls?" Stefan felt his insides curdle with fright as he recalled the ghostly visages of a thousand pale skulls floating in that calm dark pool. Seemed the ancient world was a vast layer of perils and mysteries he did not even know of.

"You have been a brave companion so far, Stefan," Culpa said, seeing the look of horror on his face. "But I will only take true companions with me from here on out, or I will go it alone. I will only go on with those who show faith and strength like that of my cousin, Tyus. For it is Tyus Barra and those like him *I* fight for." Culpa paused, but just for a moment. "I will give you until first thing on the morrow to decide if you will follow me, or follow Seita."

† † † † †

Stefan found the Vallè maiden at the bottom of the moonlit dale, standing in a gust of wind-driven hail, blond hair whipping into her eyes, a small black kestrel in the palm of her hand. The bird lingered a moment before gracefully flapping away, disappearing up into the blustery night sky, somehow braving the pelting ice.

"How did you catch a bird like that?" Stefan asked as he trod gently down into the draw. "How does it even fly in such weather?"

His foot slipped into an unseen boggy hollow brimming with cold water, filling his boot. He muttered a low curse.

"Careful." Seita rushed over and helped him from the sludge. Embarrassed, Stefan plopped down on a nearby deadfall and removed his boot.

"It's going to be a cold and windy night," the Vallè said, her words nearly lost in the gale. She pulled the hood of her gray cloak up over her head.

Stefan did the same, then wrung his sock out. "I've been freezing ever since I left Gallows Haven, it seems. How did you catch that bird?"

"You miss home?" she asked.

"I miss my family," he answered. "I miss . . . well, it—it matters not."

"You miss Gisela?" she finished for him, big round eyes gazing into his. "You can say her name around me, you know. Her name is on your bow. You carve her name on everything. You've done her memory great honor."

He could feel the bow strapped to his back now. The quiver of arrows, too. And his bulky armor. *When will I ever be free of the clunky iron?* It was his only protection, his only warmth—the armor and the bow.

"We've all lost someone," Seita said. "It was hard for me to watch Val-Draekin get sucked into that glacier. His death made me question the validity of every dream I've ever had. For his death"—she looked away—"I did not foresee."

That confused him. *She had said she saw three of us die. And three are now dead.* He didn't even know if he could stomach the subject. Stefan silently slipped his sock and boot back over his frozen foot. It was going to be a miserable cold night. "I don't want to be here anymore, Seita," he admitted. "Culpa just gave me an ultimatum, told me if I wasn't serious about *his* quest, I should just leave on the morrow."

Seita looked into the night, as if contemplating his words, as if contemplating leaving herself. The temperamental hail seemed to die off again as quickly as it had started. He asked her, "If I left, would you go with me?"

"I would, but for my dreams." She met his gaze, put her hand on his knee. "Years ago I told my sister, Breita, that I dreamed we would all be searching for the lost angel stones and weapons of Laijon someday. I told Val-Draekin of these dreams too. It is why he agreed to become involved in all this. He believed in my dreams. And now his death weighs heavy on my mind. It was why I lashed out at Culpa earlier. Fact is, I do not think this quest has been nonsense. For I saw this quest in my dreams. I believe in it as much as the Dayknight, or anyone in the Brethren of Mia. Perhaps more."

"And your sister, why did she not follow you on this dream?"

"Breita followed her own dreams. And I worry for her. I have not heard from her in a while now. And that too weighs heavy on my mind."

"Was Breita the Vallè rider Nail and I saw on the horse above Gallows Haven? She looked exactly like you."

Seita gripped his thigh, eyes roaming into the dark night. "I think maybe so."

"Remember, as Nail and the rest of us fled Gallows Haven, we told you that we found a red-eyed horse dead at the bottom of an elk trap?" Stefan asked. "It was likely Breita's horse."

She squeezed her fingers around his leg tighter, drew her gaze to his once more. "I must finish this quest, Stefan. Culpa knows I will not quit. He knows I must go on."

"But why continue?"

"What is it you are afraid of, Stefan? You are one of the bravest souls I have ever met. I know that dying does not scare you. So what is it?"

He felt the emotion grow within him, not knowing if he could articulate the truth of things. He'd watched and listened to Seita intently ever since meeting her, observing her bright round green eyes under wisps of pure white hair. What depths he saw in those penetrating orbs, which seemed to look into him and beyond. It was as if the Vallè maiden could truly discern things about him that he could not.

He felt the tears build in the corners of his eyes. "I've done so much killing," he muttered. "On Jubal Bruk's grayken-hunting ship I used to slay merfolk by the score and not think twice about it. But after shooting arrows down into those knights who fought Shawcroft, something changed in me. I imagine they were men with families, probably. Boys like me, most likely. Boys just fighting for their country. I do not want to shoot an arrow at another living thing again. Not even an oghul."

"You have a tender heart." She reached around him and began to unstrap the bow and quiver of arrows from his back. "But the fact is, most oghuls deserve killing, especially these up north like we've seen. Naught but brute grunting savages."

"What are you doing?" he asked, feeling her remove the quiver of arrows.

"Let's just both relax for a time." She had the bow and quiver in her hands now. "Let's set these aside for a moment." She placed them against the deadfall next to her. Then she wrapped her arm around his waist, pulling him in close, leaning her head on his shoulder. Her body heat warmed him. It seemed the frigid wind ceased to even exist.

"I wish I'd never become good at shooting a bow," he said.

"Yet you are." She snuggled her body into his. "For every life you have taken, think of the lives saved."

"But was it worth it?"

"Yes," she answered. "Killing to save your own skin is always worth it."

"What about tomorrow? What about Culpa? What shall I do?"

She pressed herself into him. "Thing is, Stefan, I distrust the

Dayknight. And Culpa distrusts me. So you must continue on with us. Because I need you."

He felt a cramp forming in his calf and stretched his leg out. The birch log they were sitting on rolled back, dumping them both over onto their backs in the damp foliage and frozen pellets of hail.

"Sorry," he muttered, embarrassed, struggling to sit up, unsuccessfully.

Lying on her back, Seita let out a soft giggle. Tangled in his cloak, Stefan levered himself to his elbow, smiling at her joy. The Vallè threw her cloak over them both and melted into him under the covering they now shared. She wrapped her hand around the back of his neck, pulled his face close, pressed her lips to his.

It wasn't just a small bashful peck on the lips, either. Her tongue slipped between his lips and parted his mouth. Again her breath tasted like sweet pine needles. There was a yielding softness to her as his arms encircled her waist. Stefan could feel the warmth of her thigh against his. "Let me help heal the wounds in your heart," she whispered. "I know you miss Gisela."

At the mention of her name, an image of Gisela frozen on the trail, dead, crept into his mind. "I shouldn't." He pulled away from her. "We shouldn't."

Seita's fingers were still entwined in his hair. "Don't be afraid. You will not be cheating on her memory." The heat pressing between them bloomed from his chest and warmed its way down his arms to tingle the nerves of his fingertips. And for the first time in weeks, Stefan let complete bliss flow over him like a soft melody.

"I just need someone to hold me," she moaned under her breath, lips smothering his again.

And with her kiss, all Stefan could see was Gisela's frozen dead face. "We shouldn't." He pulled away from her again. "Not now. Not in this place."

Seita abruptly stood, adjusting the front of her leather tunic, fastening her cloak around her neck, throwing the gray hood over her head. "Forgive me, Stefan, but you are right. We should just be friends, you and I."

That confused him.

The Vallè maiden hiked back toward camp, leaving Stefan lying on the cold foliage alone, his heart brimming with a mystifying happiness and sorrow.

*'Tis that unrelenting dream of an eternal soul that wears out the spirit, ages the body, and crushes all rational thought in cruel fashion. And what happens when that eternal dream dies? One finally finds peace in that everlasting nothingness.*
—THE BOOK OF THE BETRAYER

# CHAPTER FORTY-ONE
# CRYSTALWOOD

### 12TH DAY OF THE ANGEL MOON, 999TH YEAR OF LAIJON
### ROKENWALDER, SØR SEVIER

It had been two days—perhaps three—that Krista had been in the cell, suffering from her injuries. She had no grasp of time in this dark place. Bogg's gaolers showed up with food so unpredictably and infrequently she could figure no rhyme or reason to their comings and goings. The only light she ever saw was from the torches they carried, so painfully bright she closed her eyes against them anyway.

She never imagined a darkness like this could even exist. Her surroundings were blacker than the bark of a Bloodwood tree, complete and consuming. She could see nothing, not even her hand before her face, not even different shades of black within the blackness. "May as well be blind," the bearded man in the cell across from her had said on that first day. *Borden Bronachell.* A name she knew. The king of Gul Kana. A man long thought dead. *And I am supposed to kill him.*

"I can hear you thinking," the man calling himself Borden Bronachell said, his rich voice cutting through the harsh calm of the dark. He'd scarcely spoken since that first day. His initial efforts to engage her had merely been met by her own silence. But despite her current stillness, he spoke to her now. "It's a sad state of affairs when I can know which gaoler approaches in the darkness just by the sound of their gait, the click of their shuffling boots on stone, the angle and wobble and shimmer of the light coming from whatever lantern or torch they carry. It is an even sadder state when I can know when my dungeon mates are simply . . . in deep thought."

He went quiet, perhaps anticipating a response from her. She did not give one. She sat up, the movement sending a wave of pain through her entire midsection. The Knight Chivalric's maul had certainly done one its job on her midsection.

She thought of Dread, wondering about her Bloodeye steed, hoping Dugal or Hans was watching over the mare. She needed her mount's warm neck to lean into now. *Nuzzling my horse.* It was one of the few things that ever seemed to calm her. She also mourned the loss of the blue ribbon around her ankle—something small, but something that had been part of her for five years. *Who has it? Who took it?*

Borden's deep voice drifted from out of the blackness again. "I can tell when you are digging around in your cell, fussing with the locking mechanism on your door, when you are lying down on your side or on your back, when you are sitting, like now. And as I said, even when you are thinking . . . even what you are thinking."

"You can tell *what* I am thinking?" Krista asked, her voice cracking, dry.

"She finally speaks," he said with genuine pleasure. "Perhaps we will become truest of friends now."

*Not likely.* She wished she'd kept quiet.

"I know you are here to kill me," he continued. "I know Aeros Raijael and Black Dugal all too well."

*He must have seen me swallow the note.* The fact that he was so observant made his kingly claim all the more believable. He'd already claimed she reminded him of someone he once knew. *Trust no one.* Especially in here, of all places. Dugal's games were meant to test her resolve and intelligence. It very well could be Dugal in disguise sitting across from her.

"Last I heard, Aeros Raijael is far away, waging war in Gul Kana," she said. "I do not know the other man, Dugal, nor his name. And I've no wish to kill you. I am not even supposed to be here."

"Indeed," he said affably. "We are naught but prisoners, both of us innocent. All in prison are innocent. All you need do is ask us. Yet, perhaps, someday we will all be pulled from this place and our lives ended in some grotesque Sacrament of Souls."

A chill froze her spine. *Who is this man really?* "Some deserve to die," she said.

"What, for merely being a prisoner? Do I deserve to die in some Sacrament of Souls? Do you? Does merely being in the dungeons of Rokenwalder make one so callously dispensable, so worthless?"

She stayed silent. She would offer him no more.

"They say you killed Aevrett Raijael." The accuracy of his cold accusation again hit her like a punch to her already sore gut.

"So you accused me once before." She felt her stomach churn. "What of it?" She moved her hand gently over the tenderness of her chest and stomach, wondering how bruised and injured her body must look—if there were ever any light.

"At all times Black Dugal keeps both his friends and enemies off balance," the man continued. "Guiding them down dark paths, never showing his intentions, even at the end. You must prepare your own defense against the unknown, girl."

Like Black Dugal, this man calling himself Borden Bronachell certainly was a cryptic talker. But she would not fall for his bait. She would remain silent.

"We may never know why Aeros Raijael had you murder his father," he said. "Or why Dugal agreed to it. Or why either of them wanted Aevrett dead. Or why Dugal sent you, a girl who looks exactly like someone I once knew, to slay me."

She wanted no connection to him. She did not want anyone alluding to the mother she had never known. For that was clearly the angle he was playing. At the moment she just wanted the unbearable pain in her gut to go away. She wanted her weapons, her Bloodwood daggers. She would have been out of this cell long ago with just one dagger to work with, or even one small bit of metal. *Part of your test is to learn to live without weapons, learn to kill just as thoroughly without them,* Dugal had once said. He was a clever master and this was a clever test he had set her too.

"Are you now fatherless?" the man named Borden asked, unrelenting in his verbal torture of her.

*I should never have engaged him in conversation.* She wanted to lie back down. *How does he even know of the Sacrament of Souls?*

She thought back on all the ways she had learned to kill. All the ways she had learned to *hurt* another without killing. All the secrets of the human body. Even how to force a person into silence. *If only I could reach him to shut him up . . .*

"Did you ever know your mother?" he asked.

She stared up into the dark.

Impervious to her silence, he continued, "I will tell you of my family, if you don't mind. I've four children. Jovan, the oldest, he fought by my side in Adin Wyte. He followed me into war, naught but eighteen at the time. It severely traumatized him. He hadn't the stomach nor will to fight. And I fear the carnage and savagery he saw changed him. And not for the better. Even down here in the dungeons of Rokenwalder the rumors reach me. Once I was captured, my son pulled the armies of Gul Kana from Wyn Darrè. I imagine the grand vicar put the notion of retreat into his head, and Jovan gladly followed. The vicar and Quorum of Five Archbishops have always wished for the day of Absolution under the Atonement Tree to come. They always wished for the return of the Five Warrior Angels, for the streets of Amadon to run red with blood as it says in *The Way and Truth of Laijon*. In fact, those snakes have done all they can to usher the prophecies into fruition."

Krista detected unbridled disgust in his voice toward the end. She just wished she could block out his voice, no matter what tone it carried.

Still he talked, tone brightening. "My eldest daughter, Jondralyn, she was always the brave one, chivalrous to a fault. Like her mother, wanting only fairness and equality for all, willing to fight for it. And Tala, she'd be about your age; in fact, she'd be almost exactly one year younger than you, if my math is right. She'd be sixteen now. A simple soul, my sweet Tala. A dreamer. Naught but goodness in her heart. And perhaps a wee bit of mischief and adventure, too."

A slight warning wormed its way into Krista's heart at the mention of Tala's age. *Exactly one year younger than me?* This man who called himself Borden Bronachell was as enigmatically cryptic as Black Dugal. *How could he know that I'm seventeen?*

"My youngest, Ansel, I scarcely even know," he went on. "Just a baby last I saw him. Alana died whilst giving birth to him. Died at the hands of a Bloodwood much like yourself. A cruel deceiver named Hawkwood. An evil killer who I fear may have worked his way into my son's court. But, as you know, everything the Bloodwoods do is a game, right?"

The man was toying with her. He'd admitted that rumors reached him down here. So he easily could have found out about the attack on Aevrett Raijael. So he could easily assume she was the culprit. And he could easily assume the culprit was a Bloodwood. As to the history and disposition of his family, she couldn't care less.

"There are two other children important to me," Borden went on. "Twin babies. Not of my blood. A boy and a girl. I first met them when they were but newborns, some seventeen years ago. Met them along the windswept shores of Dead Lake just east of Agonmoore in the company of a man I much admired, Ser Torrence Raybourne, the king of Wyn Darrè. We rode out to meet his brother, an enigmatic fellow by the name of Ser Roderic. A woman was with Roderic. It was this woman who introduced these twin babies to me. Two wee babes wrapped in swaddling, two babes from Sør Sevier."

He went silent for time before finishing. "'Twas that very woman who looked so much like you."

*Avril? Her mother?* If so, she was a twin. It meant she had a brother. But Gault had never spoken of fathering twins, or spoken of anyone ever stealing her. It didn't matter anyway. She wouldn't listen to lies. The man's story had nothing to do with her. *All part of Dugal's test.* Borden had said so himself, *Everything the Bloodwoods do is a game.* She knew the truthfulness of that statement.

"I must admit to you now," the man continued, "crossing paths with that woman has weighed heavy on my mind all these years. And though I helped in guiding the fates of those two babes she carried, I often wondered what happened to her. She weighs heavy on my mind now. Especially after meeting you, one who resembles her so."

It was all prattle. Still, anger was growing within Krista. And she didn't know why. The last man who had talked with such mysterious abandon about her parentage had died at the end of a Bloodwood blade. And that man had also been a king. It seemed every king Dugal put in her path was just asking to be murdered. If that were her task, to murder this man, she would relish it. She could grow used to being a king killer.

"I have a dwarf friend, name of Ironcloud." Borden would not stop talking. "The truest of friends. Someday I expect you will soon meet him, if you haven't already. Regardless, he taught me of a book of scrolls. A very secret book. An ancient book of scrolls written in a lost Vallè language of old by our Blessed Mother Mia. *The Moon Scrolls of Mia.* I myself have only seen a few pages. But what I read within the pages of these scrolls was a Vallè prophecy. Would you like to hear it?"

She said nothing, knowing he was going to tell her anyway.

"You know that the nature of a Vallè maiden is to see into the future?" he asked.

The only two Vallè she had ever met were Seita and Breita. And they had certainly never prophesied anything to her.

"A Vallè maiden's premonitions can be startlingly accurate," he carried on. "The prophecy I read in the *Moon Scrolls* was about a fatherless girl, a human girl who becomes a kingslayer, a girl who becomes the deadliest killer the Five Isles has ever seen, a girl who helps bring about the return of the Five Warrior Angels."

Krista now had the full measure of the man across from her—he was completely crazy and she wished he would shut up.

"They are coming," Borden said ominously, his tone now hushed. "The gaolers. Bogg and Squateye, too. And there is something dreadful in their approach. I can tell by their gait, they bring some foulness with them. Some foulness more than just porridge. Some foulness meant just for you."

Krista could hear nothing. But then the faint yellow glow of torchlight eased its way toward them, accompanied by the clink and clank and shuffle of the gaolers. She could also hear the bark and growl of an angry dog. *Café Colza Bouledogue.*

She squinted into the yellow glow, braced her eyes against the bright agony of the two advancing torches. Through the haze of stinging pain she saw the familiar face of the one-eyed dwarf, Squateye, along with the warden. Bogg led his horrid bulldog, Café Colza, by a chain tied to an iron collar around its thick neck. They stood before

Borden's cell, all three staring in. Bogg slid him a tray of food.

"The second time Bogg and his dog have been down here since the unimportant girl arrived," Borden said nonchalantly, taking the food. "Years without a visit from either of you . . . and now it's an almost daily occurrence."

Café Colza lunged at the bearded man's cell, barking and snarling. "Leave off, scum!" Bogg yanked harshly on the leash, snapping the dog's body around. "He ain't even worth your drool, stupid mutt."

Squateye knelt before the bars of Krista's cell and slipped a flat stone tray of gray porridge to her under the bars. Neither Bogg nor Squateye said a word as they moved on down the passage, the searing glow of their torches fading away into the distance.

When Krista lifted the tray of food, she noticed the blue ribbon Gault had gifted her on the floor underneath, coiled around a small gold coin. *My father's ribbon!* She snatched up the ribbon and coin, fingers curling around both.

Borden's voice cut across the distance, soft. "As I said, that gruff old dwarf left you more than just a little porridge, no?" Then the torchlight was gone and all was black.

*For surely Laijon will do nothing save he revealeth his secrets unto his humble servants, the quorum of five.*
—THE WAY AND TRUTH OF LAIJON

# CHAPTER FORTY-TWO
# TALA BRONACHELL

### 13TH DAY OF THE ANGEL MOON, 999TH YEAR OF LAIJON
### AMADON, GUL KANA

Earlier that evening Leif Chaparral had officially been made Dayknight captain—a ceremony Tala had purposely avoided. Jondralyn had skipped it too. Lawri Le Graven also. Together the three of them stood on the battlements above Tin Man Square looking over Amadon, watching the bulk of the armies of Gul Kana march from the city for Lord's Point, Leif at the helm.

"This will only end in disaster for us all." Jondralyn, dressed in her Silver Guard armor, sword hanging at her hip, was clearly distraught by the entire affair. Whether it was because she herself had not been included in the planning of the battle, or included in the army itself, or because Leif was leading the army, Tala couldn't tell.

Either way, her older sister stepped back from the battlements with a disgruntled look and sat down heavily on the nearby stone bench next to Lawri.

Tala turned her attention back to the vast host filing from the city. Leif's father, Lord Claybor Chaparral, rode at Leif's side. Claybor led several thousand gray-and-maroon-clad Wolf Guards from Rivermeade. Lawri's father, Lord Lott Le Graven, led his black-and-yellow-liveried Lion Guards. Behind Lott and Claybor followed the red-and-white knights of Savon, banners flying above. Next came the forest green and yellow of Crucible, the black and white of Ridliegh, and the purple and blue of Reinhold. It was a colorful procession. Nearly fifty thousand knights streaming from the city astride steeds plumed with the heraldic colors of their lords and lands.

Knights from the bigger towns of Dires Woad, Wroclaw, Port Follett, Copper, Hopewell, Lusk, Gavryl, Arlish, and hundreds of other smaller villages were still on their way to Amadon. It was rumored that Lord Nolan Darkliegh was leading over twenty thousand Marble Guards from Avlonia, collecting mercenaries and other small-town garrisons along the way. All would eventually arrive in Amadon and follow in Leif's wake to Lord's Point.

Amadon Castle would still be well fortified, or so Jovan promised. At least five thousand Silver Guards and almost nine hundred Dayknights remained to fill the security duties of the court and castle, not to mention the Temple of the Laijon Statue and the Hallowed Grove and slave quarry at Riven Rock, and countless other sundry duties.

For various reasons, watching Leif's army march away, colors and banners and glinting armor winding west through the main thoroughfares of Amadon took Tala's breath away. It was the first time it had really sunk in: her father's kingdom had truly been invaded and was truly at war. And if Leif Chaparral didn't stop the White Prince, the glorious city of Amadon could soon be under siege.

"I must say, I do dream of Squireck nightly." Lawri Le Graven broke the silence. She sat on the stone bench next to Jondralyn. "Thoughts of him ease my sleep."

Tala sighed in exasperation. *Her every conversation is about court nobles and knights and who she might marry.* Lawri wore a long-sleeved dress laced around the neckline and pink lace gloves. She kept her left arm cradled gingerly in her lap.

Lawri giggled. "At first I hated Squireck because he murdered the archbishop, but he has proven himself so gallant in the arena, absolved of his crimes and all." She turned to Jondralyn, a dreamy look on her face. "He knelt and kissed the top of my hand when I offered it. Did you see it, Jon, when he kissed me? I could feel his lips right there on the lace of my glove."

"I saw it." There was a trace of annoyance in Jondralyn's voice. "I was standing right here next to you. And in the five minutes since he's been gone, you've talked of nothing but him and that kiss non-stop."

"I know." Lawri giggled again. "I can sometimes babble on like a love-struck teen, but—"

"You are a love-struck teen," Jondralyn cut her off.

"I know! Isn't it just so silly?"

Tala sighed again. Lawri had always been known to get a trifle giddy around the young nobles and knights of the court, but lately it was getting ridiculous. Today her cousin was talking about Squireck so fast she could scarcely breathe.

*It's just the Bloodwood poisons working inside her.* Lawri's dark-pupiled eyes continually sparkled with green flecks of light. *Just Bloodwood poisons and green medicine balls and who knows what else . . .*

*. . . nothing to worry about . . .*

"Tala knows about my dreams," Lawri said. "Weird dreams mostly. Well, aside from the ones I have about Squireck. Those are actually good dreams." She giggled again. "But the weird dreams are full of weird things buried in cross-shaped altars and skull-faced men and the silver throne. . . ." Lawri trailed off, leaned into Jondralyn con-spiratorially. "Did you know I once dreamed Tala and the grand vicar were married? Can you imagine that, Jon? Married." A shadow passed over her briefly, then her face lit up again. "Things will turn out for the best, though. Squireck will become a great hero. Well, he already is a great hero, if you take my meaning. He will kill Gault Aulbrek. Then he will follow Leif's army to Lord's Point and kill Aeros Raijael. And then he shall marry me. Or perhaps he will already be married to me when he kills the White Prince. Either way it always turns out for the best in my dreams. Even Lindholf will be found innocent."

Tala met Jondralyn's concerned gaze. Lawri's speech was becom-ing ever more disjointed.

"Lindholf will be found innocent," Lawri repeated. "Just like Squireck was accused of murder too, and then found innocent. Well, Squireck actually won his innocence. But I see Lindholf in the arena someday too. He will stand tall in the center of the arena, and two others will be there with him. In the middle of the arena with every-one cheering. And then he will just disappear. *Poof!* He will just be gone."

Lawri held up her left arm, pulling back the sleeve of her dress. "And I shall wear a gauntlet of sparkling silver." She dropped her arm quickly, wincing in pain, suddenly realizing she had exposed her infected injury.

"What in the name of the Blessed Mother is wrong with your arm?" Jondralyn asked, almost startled at the sight.

"Oh, nothing." Lawri pressed her arm down into her lap. Jondralyn grabbed Lawri's arm and yanked back the sleeve of her dress. Lawri cried out in pain.

"What have you done to yourself?" Jondralyn pulled off Lawri's lace glove. Tala drew in a sharp breath. The underside of Lawri's wrist was bloated, festering with infection. Veins, puffed and inflamed purple and red, streaked up her arm nearly to her armpit.

"How can you even stand the pain of this?" Jondralyn fixed her eyes on Lawri. "Val-Gianni needs to examine you."

"It's nothing, really." Tears were in Lawri's eyes. They were tears of pain.

Jondralyn turned to Tala. "Go find Aunt Mona and meet us in the infirmary. I am taking Lawri there now."

† † † † †

Val-Korin and his bodyguard, Val-So-Vreign, were with Val-Gianni, Jondralyn, and Lawri when Tala arrived at the infirmary with Mona Le Graven. The Vallè sawbones had a towel over Lawri's arm and was pressing down, draining gouts of pus. The whole room smelled of dead flesh and rot. Mona did the three-fingered sign of the Laijon Cross over her heart.

"It feels much better now," Lawri said, tear-streaked face looking up at Val-Gianni. She was sitting on a cot full of white pillows. "It got too painful for me to drain it myself. That's why I just let it go."

"Has she been showing signs of delirium?" Val-Gianni asked of no one in particular. "Talking nonstop. Talking nonsense. Acting sleepless. Speaking of weird dreams." Jondralyn nodded. Tala too.

Lawri looked straight at Tala. "It really does feel better."

"Why was I not told of this before?" Mona La Graven's eyes flew around the room, looking to everyone for an answer. Then her gaze fell on Lawri. Her face turned red with anger. "As if our family doesn't already have enough to deal with."

"I'm sorry, Mother," Lawri said.

"The question is, why wasn't Val-Gianni told of this sooner?" Val-Korin stated.

Val-Gianni nodded, pressing the towel over Lawri's arm, holding it tight, still bleeding the wound. "This is more than just a trifling injury. The truth is, the infection has done much damage to her arm.

I will give her the proper medications, but if the arm doesn't heal soon, if things get worse and the infection does not fully dissipate, we may have to amputate."

"Amputate," Mona gasped, eyes boring into those of her daughter's. "Blessed Mother Mia, girl, what wraiths have taken you and Lindholf of late? Who did this to you? How could you let an injury like this go unnoticed? I swear, neither one of you is a child of mine. Such rank stupidity."

Lawri seemed completely oblivious to her mother's scolding words. She gazed up at Tala, seemingly unconcerned. "Looks like those green medicine balls you gave me didn't work at all."

"Green medicine balls?" Val-Gianni's gaze narrowed. He glared at Val-Korin. Tala kept her own face impassive, dread creeping up her spine. *Could he know what the green balls are?*

"No matter," Lawri went on. "I probably just dreamed up the green balls anyway."

What nonsense is this?" Mona questioned, the anger on her face sharpened. "What green balls? Who cut your arm, Lawri? How did this happen?"

"I was in a scuffle," Lawri answered.

"A scuffle?" Mona gasped. "I will flay alive the person who did this to you. With whom did you scuffle."

"King Jovan."

"King Jovan!"

"It *was* Jovan, Mother," Lawri said, eyes on the pus draining from her wound. "He cut me. The king cut me."

"King Jovan cut you?" Mona exclaimed. "Don't be daft, Lawri Le Graven. Do not tell lies."

Lawri looked up at her mother for the first time, eyes now foggy. "Please . . . don't be sore at Lindholf . . . or me—"

and then she fainted sideways into the pillows.

*Cowards will all die. Some warriors are more secure with survival than seeking violence. Bloody violence will save you; awaiting survival won't. Nor doth Raijael or Laijon give guidance to a knight unjust. Cowards shall always eventually be slain.*
—THE CHIVALRIC ILLUMINATIONS OF RAIJAEL

# CHAPTER FORTY-THREE
# GAULT AULBREK

### 14TH DAY OF THE ANGEL MOON, 999TH YEAR OF LAIJON
#### AMADON, GUL KANA

A buzzing swirl of dusty grit and gnats trailed the heavy oxcart. When the beastly contraption carrying the three prisoners rumbled to a halt, a flurry of trumpets rang out and the crowd trailing the oxen stopped their advance. A contingent of waiting Dayknights immediately surrounded the wooden cart.

Gault was facing to the left, chained to a wide, ten-foot-high oak stump. His back was pressed against the rough and knotty wood, allowing him to look over the angry mob that had followed the cart through Amadon toward the slave quarry. Lindholf Le Graven was chained on the other side of the same oaken stump. A girl no more than twenty years old, was tied to a similar pole near the front of the cart, her face streaked with tears. Her name was Delia. Lindholf had called her by name when the knights loaded her onto the cart and chained her to the pole. She'd uttered no greeting in return. Gault surmised she was the barmaid Mona Le Graven had mentioned in the dungeon.

The mobs lining the streets of Amadon had hurled refuse at the three of them. Early on, Gault had taken a blow from a heavy rotted cabbage to the temple that had threatened to black him out. During the remainder of the ride, he had struggled to clear his head. The teeming throngs continued to jeer and curse and throw. He was covered in slime, some of it dripping down the front of his shirt, some stuck in the stubble of hair atop his head. He hadn't shaved his scalp since his capture.

And now here they were at the slave quarry.

Leif Chaparral's younger brother, Glade, ordered Silver Guards to unchain the three captives. A handful of knights climbed aboard, unhooking Gault, Lindholf, and Delia, clamping iron bands around their wrists, the bands connected by chains. Similar shackles and chains went around their ankles.

Gault was dragged across the surface of the slimy cart and dumped onto the hard marble ground. Lindholf and Delia landed on either side of him with two unceremonious thuds. Buckets of water were dumped over all three, washing away the slime.

The gauntleted hands of a tall Dayknight hauled Gault to his feet, and he was roughly forced forward. Lindholf and Delia stumbled along beside him. Glade Chaparral trailed just behind the three sopping prisoners. More black-clad Dayknights with pikes lined the path that led to the yawning pit—Gul Kana's infamous slave quarry at Riven Rock.

"You can't send me down there," Lindholf cried. "You know I didn't do anything, Glade. You can't do this to me."

Glade kicked the back of the boy's leg, sending him tumbling forward to the harsh marble ground.

"Please." Lindholf gasped in pain, rolling over, crying loudly, a puddle forming under him from his drenched clothes. "I thought I was your friend."

"Get up!" Glade shouted. "Get up and keep your slave mouth shut!" He threw a punch at the boy's midsection. Lindholf threw up his shackled arms, only partially blocking the blow. He curled up and vomited on the slick marble surface of the road.

"Pick his sorry hide up!" Glade ordered the knight nearest Lindholf. "Carry him if you have to!" The boy was hauled up forcibly.

"Please," Lindholf pleaded, shrugging the knight's hands off, walking on his own.

"Not another word!" Glade shouted in his face. "And if you cry out even once when I stick the branding iron to your neck, I leave it there thrice as long."

The three prisoners were again pushed along the marble road toward the gaping quarry and the iron cage awaiting them at the rim—the cage that would lower them down into the pit. A black cauldron rested in front of the cage, smoke rising from it. Above the cage, leaning out over the pit, was a stout wooden scaffolding girt with a number of gears and pulleys. Heavy ropes and chains stretched from the pulleys to a giant wooden turning wheel some fifty feet from the quarry's rim, a team of twelve horses hooked to the wheel.

Gault could see that along the rim of the pit to either side, at least two dozen other such similar sets of wooden scaffolding, pulleys, ropes, chains, turning wheels, horses, and iron cages stretched off in both directions. Far across the pit—a mile or so away—he could make out a half-dozen other such similar apparatuses, but those were much larger, massive turning wheels hooked to teams of horses numbering in the hundreds. He reckoned those distant blocks and pulleys were for lifting larger slabs of marble from the pit. Several dozen slabs of marble the size of small buildings were stacked along the far rim. From so far away, the men working atop those marble pyramids looked no bigger than gnats.

The three prisoners were marched straight to the smoky cauldron in front of the iron cage. Glade snatched an iron tong from the coals of the cauldron, its tip molten red. The Silver Guard behind Delia forced the girl to kneel before Glade, wrenching her head to the side with two gauntleted hands, exposing her neck, holding her steady. With a look bordering on sexual pleasure, Leif's younger brother pressed the fiery slave brand against the girl's pale neck just below her left ear. Delia's scream was agonizingly shrill. The brand was pulled away and a large red RR was cooked into her skin. She was hauled to her feet and Glade jammed the branding iron back into the cauldron. The stench of burnt flesh was in the air.

Gault was forced to his knees in front of the cauldron next, head also roughly forced to the side, exposing his neck. Glade stirred the coals of the black pot with the branding iron. He pulled it forth a second time, and without dawdling pressed it hard to Gault's skin. Gault clenched his jaw, gritted his teeth. He had seen captives branded before, even watched soldiers burn to death in war. But he had never before felt the pain of fire on his own flesh. It was a scorching assault that seared straight down to the bone. By the time Glade removed the steaming iron, Gault had gained a new sense of respect for all those who had sat through Enna Spades' similar slave brandings in grim silence.

Lindholf was forced to his knees and the iron was reheated. "No, please," he begged as Glade stirred the coals. With torturous glee on his face, Glade pulled the iron free and sank the gleaming slave brand straight into Lindholf's neck. The boy screamed.

Glade pressed hard and long, holding the scorching orange brand against Lindholf's tender flesh thrice as long as required, just as he'd promised. When he finally pulled the brand away, blood and char poured down Lindholf's neck and over the front of his prison garb. The boy wailed in pain as he was hauled to his feet and dragged toward the open cage at the rim of the quarry. Gault and Delia were forced in that direction too.

To either side of the cage, the quarry itself loomed awesome and cavernous, over a mile wide in every direction. To Gault's estimation, it was a sheer drop of more than three hundred feet on all sides. There were places in the distance that looked as deep as five hundred feet—and in those deepest reaches of the quarry gleamed pools of water.

Gault was shoved into the cage behind Lindholf and Delia, accompanied by six of the Silver Guards. The iron door was slammed shut behind them. The flat iron floor was solid underfoot, the iron bars not quite wide enough to slip through, the quarry's depths seemingly infinite beyond the bars.

He stared across the vast expanse in dreadful fascination, enthralled. The quarry below was almost blindingly white under the harsh sun. The hundreds of slaves working at the bottom stood out against the marvelous marble like tiny black ants. In places, the walls of the quarry were peppered with various caves, crossbow-wielding guards in shining armor perched in those many alcoves and dark openings.

There was a shout followed by the crack of a whip somewhere behind him. The horses dug in, and the large wheel slowly ground to life behind him. The clash of the chains, the grind and scrape of metal on marble, all of it was shrill and sharp as the cage dropped into empty air. The sensation of slowly falling fluttered in Gault's gut.

† † † † †

"A woman slave," a gruff voice said when the iron contraption finally reached the bottom. The door swung open and fine white dust filtered into the cage. "Don't ever see a woman down here," another said.

Delia was immediately met with leering looks from both the heavily armored quarry guards and various slaves gathering around the cage.

"Lookit the tits on her!" an enthusiastic shout sounded from somewhere.

"Shut your yappers!" a lanky quarry guard shouted as he held open the cage door, blinking against the grit as a small wind kicked up. He placed his hand on the hilt of the dust-covered longsword hanging at his hip. Gault stepped from the cage first, Delia and Lindholf right behind him. Everything and everyone was frosted in a fine layer of pure marble powder, the blustery air thick with it.

The three new slaves were guided into this dusty mist by their six Silver Guard escorts. They were marched up a set of rickety stairs to a stilted wooden catwalk built fifteen feet above the quarry floor. Once atop the swaying catwalk, they were turned over to another set of guards led by a burly fellow with a round, dented half-helm. He eyed Delia up and down lecherously. The girl's prison garb covered her well enough, but that didn't stop the drooling idiot from disrobing her with his beady little eyes. The girl was terrified—tears streaked the white dust gathering on her face.

The burly leader eventually broke his hungry gaze from Delia and launched into a short, choppy speech. "Follow me. Far side of the quarry. We go along the catwalks. A few miles. An hour's journey. Cuffs and shackles stay on. So watch your step." He whirled and strutted away along the fifteen-foot-high wooden structure. Gault, Delia, and Lindholf followed the burly guard. A handful of guardsmen with spears marched behind them.

The precarious footbridge stretched off to the south, eventually connecting to a vast latticework of other such stilted catwalks, ramps, ladders, and rope bridges. This complex maze of wooden runways was joined by various winding staircases that followed the uneven contours of the quarry floor. Massive square blocks of marble rose up in their path, whilst sheer drops and deep marble canyons fell off to dizzying depths on either side. They skirted around every obstacle via the wooden runways.

The dust and smell of the dirty slaves toiling below was overwhelming. Gault didn't like the looks of any of it; chains, ropes, pulleys, wooden barrels, troughs of milky water, hundreds of tents and crude lean-tos, and quarry guards stationed atop each and every catwalk at fifty-foot intervals, each with a dusty crossbow and spear.

All of it made him nervous. All of it made him wish for his comfortable cage back in Purgatory. All of it spelled misery.

† † † † †

Laboring in the deepest part of the quarry, and the sun was already crushing Gault with its heat. It felt like he'd been in this horrid pit his entire life. Yet it had only been half a day. Every muscle in his body hurt. Aching thirst, cracked lips, grit in his dry, parched mouth. He was nearly tempted to drink from the ten-gallon wooden bucket of human waste he carried.

The seventeen other slaves on his crew of chiselers, sledgemen, and sawmen had been given a short ten-minute break. But not Gault. He was ordered by Higgen, the head slave and a tall, muscular fellow, to carry the shit bucket up the slanting, hundred-foot marble slope they called the chute. Atop the chute was a flat area with five holes drilled into the quarry floor in a perfectly symmetrical and perfectly pentagonal pattern, each hole about three feet apart and no more. Higgen claimed the marble around the five holes could not be cut or sawed or even scratched. Slaves had tried digging near the holes over the centuries, but the stone was too hard, so the whole area surrounding the holes was left alone. The five holes were a mystery, and considered almost sacred ground in the quarry. Gault was not to dump the shit-bucket here anywhere near them.

Also atop the chute about fifty feet north of the five holes was a spiderweb of ropes leading up to the hoists and pulleys above, Gault was to tie the bucket to one of the ropes and give three stiff yanks.

Then someone five hundred feet above would haul the bucket up the side of the quarry. The chute was sloped at just the exact torturous angle to make it almost impossible to walk up, much less carry a cumbersome bucket full of waste. Still, Gault made it to the top, walked carefully around the five holes, tied the handle of the bucket to a rope, and gave three tugs.

As he made his way back down the chute, he looked up at the guards on the catwalks. They each had specially fashioned crossbows that fired hundreds of tiny shards of marble down onto any prisoner slacking off their job. Both Gault and Lindholf had already been peppered with the stinging marble shot once. They'd made the mistake of asking for water without being told they could do so by Higgen.

Gault was still finding needle-thin slivers of rock embedded in his skin. Other crossbow-wielding guards were perched in the various random cave openings hundreds of feet up, completely inaccessible to the slaves below.

Most of the seventeen slaves on Higgen's crew were sawmen. In the bowels of the quarry, the sawmen sawed marble either from the top down, or side to side, or from the floor of the quarry, or they chiseled through it, or swung a sledgehammer at it, or pried it from the walls with thick iron bars, or dug trenches to string rope under heavy blocks of it, or dug trenches for water, or hauled shit buckets up the chute.

Everyone obeyed the guards, else slivers of marble would fire like lightning from their crossbows. Food and water was a rarity, especially if you were Gault Aulbrek, Knight Archaic of Sør Sevier. And Higgen ran the slave crew.

Upon their arrival, Gault, Lindholf, and Delia had been stripped of their cuffs and shackles and presented with a twenty-by-forty-foot block of marble to finish sawing in half. The block had already been dug from the floor of the quarry and sanded smooth on all sides. Previous workers had already sawed it almost in half. Higgen had ordered Gault and Lindholf to finish the job with Delia's help.

A thin cut in the center of the marble stretched from the top of the block almost down to the bottom. There was only three inches of stone left to cut and the marble would be in two halves. Two ditches had been dug into the marble floor under each half block of marble. Gault had learned that the channels would later be used to fish massive ropes through, ropes that were thick as a man's leg, ropes used to haul each half block up and out of the quarry.

With the steel wire they had been given, it had taken Gault and Lindholf half a day to saw through the remaining three inches of marble. Gault on one side of the huge block, Lindholf on the other, sawing back and forth, thick leather gloves protecting their hands. Higgen informed them that there were chunks of diamond in the wire; the diamonds, combined with the abrasive action of water and sand poured from above, kept their wire saw lubricated and sharp. Delia was lifted up onto the block along with a dozen buckets of water and sand. Astraddle the thin cut in the marble, her job was to pour the water and sand down into the crevice at intervals to keep Gault and Lindholf's saw wet.

Cutting through that last three inches of marble was the most grueling work Gault had ever done. Lindholf had cried the entire time. Once they were finished, they'd been given their ten-minute break. Except Gault was given shit-bucket duty.

By the time Gault made it down from the chute, the break was over. Lindholf was still teary-eyed and despondent-looking, standing near the cluster of slave tents, finishing the small crust of bread and cup of water he'd been given. Gault wanted a taste of the water. But Higgen didn't offer him any. Everything down here ran through Higgen.

Gault briefly wondered if it was worth risking being shot with shards of marble again for just a drop, wondered if he dared even drink from the mud-colored ditch under the block of marble. It was tempting.

He thought better of it and just awaited his next instructions.

"They'll be lowering the rope soon, bald man," Higgen said to him. Higgen had nicknamed Gault *bald man*, Delia *cutie*, and Lindholf *ugly-faced shitbag*. Higgen spit on the marble floor, his leering eyes on Delia. She stood about as close to Lindholf as she could without being right on top of him, somehow finding comfort and safety in the boy's nearness. He was the only familiar face to her. But it was evident Lindholf was ill-prepared to defend the girl if it came to it. Every slave down here had cast a devious eye the girl's way at least once. Some stared nonstop.

A dust-covered slave with shaggy brown hair sidled up next to Gault. "We string rope under the two blocks you cut," he said. "The horses above haul both blocks up out of here. One at a time, of course. Takes nearly two hundred of the stoutest draught horses you ever seen to pull a block that size up and out of here."

The shaggy-haired slave with beady eyes held out his hand to Gault. "I'm Woadson, by the way. But they mostly call me Toad's Son down here." Gault shook the man's hand, noticing a small ring of bent wire around the fellow's index finger. He wondered if the ring meant Toad's Son was married. Woadson grinned at Gault, a yellow, toothless smile that looked a trifle childlike under all the pale grit on his face.

"Look." Woadson nudged Gault." The ropes are a-comin' down just like I said." Gault gazed straight up the towering marble cliff and saw the two ropes slowly being lowered from the lofty heights, big and round and thick as his thigh. Both ropes were hooked to a much larger rope near as thick as a man.

"Jump to it!" Higgen shouted once the ropes reached the quarry floor. Men scurried to the two blocks of marble, huge ropes now coiling on the ground.

"Ugly-faced shitbag!" Higgen pointed at Lindholf. "You're the smallest of us! Snatch the end of that line!" He pointed to the nearest rope. "Crawl the rope under the stone!" He pointed to the ditch under the nearest marble block. Lindholf looked mortified by the very prospect. "Now!" Higgen shouted.

"That rope is huge," Lindholf said. "And that trough is full of dirty water."

"I don't give a rat's ripe fart if it's full of oghul vomit!" Higgen yelled. "Do as I say, or as Laijon is my witness, I'll motion for them guards to shoot you full of marble shot. Then I'll rip down your britches and whip you myself."

Delia grabbed his arm. "Just do it, Lindholf," she said softly.

"You're right." Lindholf looked at her, a note of courage in his voice. "I reckon I've swum through more dangerous places than that." He headed for the rope.

"You too, cutie!" Higgen pointed at Delia, a grin forming at the corners of his mouth. "You take the other rope through the other trough. I wanna see what you look like crawling on all fours, and wet." The other slaves laughed and jeered their approval.

Delia looked at Gault pleadingly.

"Like you told Lindholf, best just do it." Gault nodded to her. "I'll wait for you on the other side. It's only twenty feet under them blocks. Crawl fast. You can hold your breath that long."

"But the rope looks so heavy," Delia said.

"Higgin is till glaring at you. Better jump to it. No telling how he'll punish you."

Despondent, Delia followed Lindholf toward the ropes. Gault walked around to the other side of the two marble blocks. The trenches stretching under the blocks were three feet deep, chiseled from under the marble slabs before any cutting began, and they were used to collect the sluice and water and sand. Now they'd be used to fish the heavy rope underneath.

Lindholf and Delia did not dawdle. He could hear them splashing through the troughs now. Lindholf popped up from under the left slab first, sputtering muddy water, the heavy rope draped over one shoulder. The girl emerged soon after, muddy and wet, thick rope grasped between her arms, clutched to her chest, her sopping prison garb clinging to every curve of her body. The slaves hooted and hollered their pleasure as she crawled from the trough. Higgen shouted, "Back to work! Now that you got your eyes full, back to work!"

Every slave scurried to their duty, leaving Delia lying chest down on the marble floor, lungs heaving in great gulps of air. Lindholf crawled to her aid.

"Back to work, ugly-faced shitbag!" Higgen grabbed him by the collar and tossed him back. Lindholf stumbled away, falling hard to the marble. Higgen helped the wet girl to her feet himself, arm around her shoulder. "Let's get you cleaned up." He guided her toward a water bucket and a pile of rags near the tents.

Lindholf painfully levered himself to his feet, gaze full of hurt and anger as he watched Higgen clean Delia's muddy clothes with one of the rags, grubby hands fondling the girl's body wherever he could. "Bloody Mother Mia," Lindholf muttered. "None of this is fair."

Gault and the boy watched as both ropes were wrapped around each block several times and secured tight to the other much heavier rop above, which, Gault noticed on closer inspection, looked about twice as thick as a man. The whole apparatus was soon secured and ready.

With a few hand signals from the guards to someone waiting above, the first marble block lifted off the ground with a loud groan. As it slowly rose, inch by inch, thick white dust swirled in the air. Once it was about six feet off the ground, Woadson and five other slaves scurried underneath it with iron poles, using the iron to brace the slab against tipping. To Gault's estimation, the block was so heavy, he doubted the six slaves and their poles were doing much to guide it.

Lindholf knelt by one of the exposed troughs of milky water and dipped his hands in, cleaning them. Gault drifted toward the boy, mouth parched and dry. *Just a quick kneel down and dip of my head, and I can finally slake this thirst.* He wonderd if Lindholf would sneak a drink. But the guards above were ever watchful, and he knew Lindholf dared not.

The slab of marble was about twelve feet off the floor of the quarry now, rising ponderously, the six slaves stationed under it even now trying their best to guide it with their iron poles.

Lindholf, still kneeling, swiped his hand through a mound of white dust that had gathered under the block of marble. He stood, examining the small pile of the dust cupped in his palm. Then lifted his hand to his nose and sniffed the white powder straight up his nostril. Then he sneezed.

*He's bloody well lost his mind,* Gault thought.

Then he heard the loud snap of the rope above . . .

. . . saw the horror-stricken look on the upturned face of Woadson, directly behind Lindholf.

Instinctively, Gault snatched Lindholf by the front of his shirt and pulled the boy toward him. The massive marble block came crashing down, scraping the back of Lindholf's mud-soaked clothes with a rush of air.

The block hammered to the floor of the quarry with a thunderous boom, crushing Woadson and the five slaves underneath, flattening them, the two ropes secured around the block falling perfectly into the two wet trenches.

A blast of white dust billowed up around Gault and Lindholf, and the singular heavy rope came coiling down around them. The twin troughs of milky water turned red with blood.

Lindholf, eyes wide as teacups, scrambled away from Gault.

A portion of the still-falling rope hit the boy in the shoulder, knocking him backward into the bloody trench, his entire body submerged in swirling red. Gault reached into the water, latched onto the boy, and hauled him from the ditch.

"Stupid kid done bathed himself in the blood," the slave nearest Gault commented. Lindholf choked and coughed.

"Bloody Mother Mia!" Higgen ran up, appraising the disaster before him. "Rotted angels, but I ain't seen a rope snap like that in five years. Ain't seen a man crushed in ten." His eyes fell on Gault and Lindholf, lingering on the boy. "Bad luck is what you are, ugly-faced shitbag, covered in blood and marble sludge like that."

But Lindholf didn't even seem to hear the man; his eyes dwelt on something sticking from under the base of the fallen block of marble.

A lone arm.

From elbow to fingertip the arm was perfect, spotless, just resting there palm up, fingers slightly curled, one finger with a small circle of bent wire for a ring. It was Woadson, or what remained of him. The shaggy-haired man was flattened somewhere between the heavy block and the marble floor, flattened somewhere in a space so thin Gault figured he couldn't even slip a piece of paper into it.

Lindholf, eyes on the arm, took three huge breaths, did the three-fingered sign of the Laijon Cross over his heart, and fainted.

† † † † †

Gault spread out his bedroll on the slope just under the marble cliff face, next to Lindholf. He sat with his back against the wall, eyes locked on Woadson's arm sticking out from under the marble block not thirty feet away. Delia rolled out her bed next to his. She lay flat on her back, suffering the day's exhaustion in silent torture. Lindholf was propped on one elbow under a thin blanket, eyes staring into space, hollow and haunted.

Higgen and the eight remaining slaves in his crew hunkered in a circle near a makeshift lean-to below, some sort of gambling-type game scratched into the surface of the marble floor between them— the remaining bedrolls of the six dead men were the prize. Several torches flickered above, the camp's only light, both near the lone guard posted on the catwalk.

Once darkness had settled over the quarry, all work stopped, all metal tools, wires, and ropes were bundled together and hoisted onto the catwalk and placed under care of the guard. Then the pulley system was shut down.

"They're going to kill me on the morrow," Lindholf said. "Those guards will kill me when I refuse to help. And I ain't helping. I ain't working no more. Higgen said my job was to scrape those squashed men off the floor once they raise the block again. And I just can't do it, Gault."

"Surely you've seen warriors die gruesome deaths in the gladiator arena," Gault said. "This is no different. They're just dead men. That's all."

"No," the boy muttered in response. "This is different."

"I wish they would just kill me now," Delia said to no one in particular, soft frightened voice naught but a hushed whisper in the dark.

There was a sudden burst of laughter from the slaves gathered below. Then Higgen and two other slaves stood and sauntered up the slope toward Gault. Higgen led the way, a wry smile curling at his lips. Gault sat up straighter. Delia sat up too, worry flushing her face.

"What say the girl sleeps down by us tonight?" Higgen's greedy eyes were fixed on Delia.

"She stays with me." Lindholf shook his blanket off. "You won't touch her." He stood, facing Higgen bravely.

"Fuck off, ugly-faced shitbag." Higgen took two quick steps and shoved Lindholf back to the ground. He reached forward and snatched Delia by one leg, pulling the girl away from the wall. "You still ain't thanked me for cleaning the mud off you earlier," he laughed as he siezed her by the hair and dragged her down the slope.

On her back, Delia struggled against him, screaming, kicking.

"Leave her alone!" Lindholf scrambled to his feet. One of the two other slaves grabbed the boy around the midsection and lifted him straight up, then dashed him hard against the marble floor. Lindholf's entire body struck the unforgiving surface with a sickening thud. Moaning, he didn't get up.

Gault watched Higgen drag Delia away.

He knew the girl was going to be raped by each of the nine slaves below and there was nothing to be done about it. He'd seen worse in war, and it just didn't matter. The gang rape of one slave girl just wasn't much of a concern, not to Laijon, not to Raijael, nor to any God that came before or likely to come after. And not to Gault.

*Why should it matter to me? I am no god. I am no one's savior.*

Even the lone guard standing in the faint torchlight above looked down on the scene with scant concern, crossbow still strapped to his back. He merely watched as if he too wished to be down there lining up to feel a woman's soft flesh under him.

Near the lean-to below, all nine slaves had gathered round the girl. Delia was being roughly stripped of her prison garb by Higgen, her soft flesh as pale as the hard marble. She trembled in the torchlight. Ribald laughter filled the night as the girl was shoved to the ground and Higgen began stripping off his own clothes.

Lindholf cried, despondent. The look on the boy's face was of sheer helplessness.

*At least he tried. That he had been soundly beaten was not his fault. The biggest and strongest and most confident of men will always conquer. And the weak recoil. That is just the way of things.*

With that thought, Gault stood.

He walked toward the block of marble that had crushed the six slaves earlier that day. He grabbed hold of Woadson's arm, and with a swift pull, tore it free from under the stone with a loud snap of bone. Grasping the severed arm by the wrist, he walked toward the nine slaves gathered around the naked girl, his free hand peeling back the flesh of Woadson's arm, exposing one long single shard of bone.

Gault stepped into the circle of slaves. "Back away from the girl," he said.

Higgen, on bare knees between the girl's legs, turgid cock stretched out before him, looked up angrily. The eight other slaves were staring at Gault too, every eye transfixed by the darkness set in his cold, hard orbs, only a few noticing the severed arm clenched in his fist, their eyes widening with concern. "Stand up," he ordered Higgen.

The burly slave stood, pulling his breeches up in the process, advancing on Gault with purpose. "Listen, bald man." He scowled, both fists balled up tight, a glint of annoyance in his eyes. "You best go the fuck back over to your side—"

Gault rammed Woadson's severed arm straight into the underside of Higgen's chin. The thin shard of bone hammered up through the man's mouth and nasal cavity, punching straight out of his left eye socket, white eyeball pierced clean, soft as an egg yolk. The flesh of the severed arm bunched under Higgen's chin as Gault continued to push upward. He was practically holding the slave aloft now with the strength of his arm, Higgen's toes brushing the ground. Blood gushed red and livid from the hole in the man's neck, coating Gault's own clenched fist, running down his straining muscles.

"Get up." He glanced down at Delia. "Go back to Lindholf. Do it now." The girl snatched her prison garb from the quarry floor and scrambled away.

Gault yanked the bone straight down out of Higgen's impaled face. The man folded to the ground, split tongue lolling from his gaping mouth as his head cracked against the marble. Blood bubbled and frothed as he gasped for air.

Gault's eyes roamed over the remaining eight slaves, taking the measure of each. He calmly met their angry stares. It was clear by their demeanor that the fight was not over. Many of them looked eager to attack. "You kilt Higgen," one fellow snarled.

"And I'll kill you too," Gault said, "if you don't step back."

"I still aim to fuck that girl," another growled.

"Right!" another one shouted. "There's more of us than there are of you." Gap-toothed grins spread through the remaining slaves as several of them lunged at Gault.

Before Gault could bring up the severed arm to defend himself, there was a loud snap and *whoosh* of air. The two attackers nearest him were hurled back, screaming in pain, each clutching his chest and face. The remaining slaves stopped their advance.

"Nobody harms the Sør Sevier man!" a booming voice shouted from above. "He's meant for the arena! On King Jovan's order!"

Gault spied the lone guard atop the wooden scaffolding. The guard's crossbow, loaded with more sharp marble shot, was pointed down at the slaves. "Any of you touch the bald man and you'll see what happens! One blow on my whistle and every guard in this quarry will have their spearheads stirring your guts!"

Gault glared at the remaining slaves, two of whom were trying to swipe the slivers of marble shot from their faces.

He spoke clearly and concisely, so all would understand. "Any of you lay a hand on the girl again and I will tear your throats out with my own teeth." He tossed the severed arm at their feet. "And leave the boy alone too."

† † † † †

"What will happen to us now?" Delia asked Gault, both of then sitting with their backs against the towering wall, eyeing the slaves attempting to bandage Higgen's chin and eye.

"They will leave us alone for the time being," Gault answered.

"I'm scared," she said. "It will only be a matter of time before one of the guards above attempts the same thing. If not all of them."

Gault met her terrified gaze. She sat closer to him than to Lindholf now. And Lindholf had clearly noticed the girl's shift in allegiance. A scowl was fixed on his scarred face. There was clearly some history between Delia and Lindholf, and Gault had just inserted a wedge between them by saving her.

"What will happen to us?" she repeated.

Gault answered without emotion. "They will hang you and Lindholf in the arena. And I will fight the Prince of Saint Only. Until then, this quarry will be our life."

"There's no chance of escape?" she asked.

Gault's eyes roamed the sheer walls. Five hundred feet of quarried marble rose straight up in every direction. Torchlight, moonlight, starlight, all of it cruelly reflected off the stark white of their inescapable prison. Yes. He would die here in Gul Kana. He would never get to be buried in that place of his dreams, that one perfect spot, the only place he was ever truly happy, that windswept plain in the Nordland Highlands near Stone Loring where he had first met Avril.

"It still hurts." Delia's hand brushed over the raw slave mark on her neck. She turned to Lindholf. "Does your brand hurt too?"

The boy nodded halfheartedly. "Swimming through that muddy water only made it hurt worse."

Gault wished the girl hadn't mentioned the slave brand, for now he was suddenly reminded of the constant sting of his own.

"And this?" Delia pointed to more scars on the back of the boy's hand. Thin red lines in the shape of a cross. "You got this when Glade raped me in the Filthy Horse?"

"Yes." The boy looked sullen, tried to cover the wounds with the sleeve of his shirt.

But Delia leaned over and pulled the sleeve of Lindholf's shirt all the way up, revealing several ragged scars stretching up his arm. "You never did tell me how you got those."

"I got the scars when I found the shield and stone," Lindholf answered, a haunted look in his eye.

The mention of a shield and stone got Gault's attention. *There are more mysteries to this dough-faced boy than meet the eye!* He leaned in to get a better look at the scars on the boy's arm.

"A mermaid clawed me while I was in Memory Bay." Lindholf let Delia examine the scars with searching fingers. "The savage bitch attacked me twice, once in the cavern where I found the shield and stone, and then again when I swam out into the bay."

"A mermaid." Disgust was written on Delia's face. "How horrid."

"She nearly drowned me."

"What cavern?" Gault asked. "What shield and stone? Something you found when you followed Tala and Glade past my cage and farther into Purgatory?"

"Yes." Lindholf's frightened eyes met his. "Tala had a map that spoke of treasure. But they were too afraid to find the treasure and turned back. But I found the treasure. I found the shield and the stone. I believe the shield is *Ethic Shroud* and the white gem with it one of the angel stones."

"You mean *Ethic Shroud* from *The Way and Truth of Laijon*?" Delia asked.

"I figured you already knew." Lindholf was eyeing her with even more distrust now. "I figured that was why you followed me, had me hide the shield and stone behind your saloon. Are you claiming you didn't know it was *Ethic Shroud* I would bring?"

Delia broke her gaze from the boy, stared down at the slaves who were still tending to Higgen. They'd wrapped the man in a blanket and dragged him some distance from the camp. Gault wondered if he was now dead.

"You knew I had a shield," Lindholf went on, eyes turning icy. "You mentioned it in the alleyway in Amadon. You specifically asked that I bring it to you." He was openly glaring at her now. "How did you know?"

"I . . . ," she started, then stopped, looking unsure of herself. "I suppose nothing worse than this damnable slave quarry can happen to me now." The girl's eyes roved the surrounding dark. "And I suppose *she* can't possibly be watching me now. Not here of all places." Relief flooded across her face. "No, she can't possibly be watching me now."

"Who?" Lindholf asked.

"The Vallè woman who put me up to all this," she answered. "Seita."

"Seita?" Lindholf's deformed face scrunched up in confusion. "Seita put you up to all of what? What does the Vallè princess have to do with anything?"

"It's all her doing," Delia said. "She has tricked us all. Don't you see?"

"Val-Korin's daughter has tricked us?" Lindholf asked.

"She stabbed Jovan," Delia said in a rush. "It was her."

"How can you be sure?"

"I saw her do it."

"Seita?"

"My father had been sick for some time," Delia said, an urgency in her voice, as if she wanted to spit out her confession in one breath. "Near death. A very painful sickness. Seita came into the Filthy Horse, looked him over, and said he'd been poisoned. Gave me some green Vallè medicine. It healed him. No more pain. But only for a time. He got worse again. But she kept coming into the saloon and looking in on him. Always cloaked. Always in the same black leather armor. She had more of the medicine. She wanted no payment. Just wanted me to complete tasks for her from time to time. Simple stuff at first. Take this over here. Take that over there. The medicine she gave me helped my father's pain. I figured it was a good trade. But he still lies in the saloon sick."

There was something about the girl's story that didn't sit well with Gault. "You said Seita was cloaked?" he asked. "In black leather armor?"

"Aye," Delia answered. "She would threaten me with little black daggers."

Gault's heart froze. *A Bloodwood!*

"She had little black daggers." Delia looked at Lindholf. "Like the one Glade took from you, that day in my room when we were arrested."

"That was Tala's dagger." More confusion flooded Lindholf's features.

"Tala is part of it." Delia nodded.

"Tala was there when Glade cut Sterling Prentiss' neck." Lindholf looked into the darkness. "She had the black dagger with her then."

"It's a Bloodwood blade," Gault said. "You are describing an assassin's weapon. The worst kind of assassin. And the worst kind of dagger." Both Delia and Lindholf were looking at him now. "I do not know this Vallè, Seita," he followed. "But she is not to be trusted. Vallè *and* Bloodwood, a combination of the two most devious and duplicitous species there are."

"Everything Seita said to me was a lie." Delia was watching him carefully. "And also the truth."

Gault met her gaze frankly. "Not lies. Not the truth. But games. 'Tis always a game with the Vallè. 'Tis always a game with the Bloodwood. That you have run afoul of such a creature is most unfortunate."

"It's like Seita could see the future," Delia said. "Like she could predict everything that would happen with every task she set me upon. Said Princess Jondralyn would come into my saloon with a handsome man and a dwarf. Said a Vallè thief would come into the saloon at the same time and start a fight. Even asked me to flirt with Jondralyn. Coached me on the exact words to say. Ridiculous words, like *betwixed*."

"And you did everything she asked," Gault inquired. "For the Vallè medicine?"

"The medicine was all that would ease my father's pain."

"I reckon it was Seita's poison that also caused your father's pain."

"I realized that too late." Delia's gaze turned to Lindholf. "Seita predicted that Tala would come into the saloon a few days later with a red gladiator helmet. Even told me that it would be you and another boy from the castle who would accompany Tala that day. Seita told me that I was to convince Tala to secure me a job as part of the castle staff for the Mourning Moon Feast. Told me to serve you all pastries. Told me to try and seduce Jovan."

"But why?" Lindholf asked.

"I don't know," she answered. "But it was Seita who stabbed Jovan. She framed me for the crime, then broke me out of my cell in Purgatory, even helped me escape the dungeon. And I don't know why."

"Did you swim out into Memory Bay as I did?" Lindholf asked sarcastically, as if he didn't believe a word she was saying. "Did mermaids accost you, too? Did you see visions in the water?"

"No," she answered sharply, unhappy with his mocking tone. "No mermaids or visions leastwise. We—we only traveled a short way when we met an old man who called himself Maizy. Seita seemed to know him. Like old friends. He guided us out of the dungeons. But the tunnels we took actually did empty us out in the Memory Bay. Emptied us out into the bowels of a half-sunken ship moored some hundred yards from shore, near the dock district no less, not far from the Filthy Horse Saloon."

Lindholf's face scrunched up in concentration. "Was Maizy hanging in a cage?"

"I don't know of any cage," she answered. "But Maizy claimed there were hundreds of ways out of Purgatory for those wise enough. Claimed he knew every secret of Amadon but one. Said he would someday visit me at the Filthy Horse Saloon. But I never did see him again."

"How did you know about the shield and stone?" Lindholf asked.

"How did you know I had them?"

"Seita told me of you, Lindholf. Said you would also travel through Purgatory and find great treasure. A white shield and a white stone. She ordered me to find you and have you bring me the shield and stone. Seita asked me to—" Delia clamped her mouth shut.

"Asked you to seduce me?" Lindholf finished for her, betrayal in his eyes.

Delia hung her head, not willing to look at the boy. "I haven't seen Seita in a moon or more. Haven't been given any new medicine in that time. I imagine my father is dead. They've probably hauled his corpse from the saloon, the other bar staff. So what was it all for? All this nonsensical deception and running around?"

"You will likely never know what it was all for," Gault said. He knew how Dugal's Caste of Bloodwoods operated as a whole. And this girl's far-fetched tale was the exact type of mischief they were always in the middle of. Especially if the schemes of a Vallè maiden were also involved.

Gault's eyes met Lindholf's. The boy looked more miserable than ever.

*Thus we have raised great sculptures of our true One and Only. We have given*
*unto you great works of art and sculpture that you may worship and pay homage*
*to Laijon as you await the day of his return.*
—THE WAY AND TRUTH OF LAIJON

# CHAPTER FORTY-FOUR

# AVA SHAY

### 14TH DAY OF THE ANGEL MOON, 999TH YEAR OF LAIJON
### THE MOURNING SEA, JUST SOUTHWEST OF ADIN WYTe

The *Eagle Rose* plied the sea toward the hulk of Mont Saint Only in smooth silence. Their route took them north, closer to Wyn Darrè than Gul Kana, to avoid the shallow waters between Lord's Point and Adin Wyte. The fortress atop the Mont loomed black and foreboding under its fiery beacon, a beacon that guided them through the night.

Standing at the prow under a velvety moon, Aeros Raijael blew into a thin black whistle that made no noise. Ava had watched him summon birds out of the air with the tiny instrument before. He slipped the whistle into the inside lining of his jerkin and glanced at her, his pale face impassive. He wore all white: white leather pants, white shirt, jerkin, belt, even his steel-toed boots were white.

In contrast, the Bloodwood standing behind him was dressed all in black; black boiled-leather armor under a long black cloak. Ava wondered if the Spider still kept her beetle carving or if he'd rid himself of it. He held a small lantern that illuminated the prow in a dreary yellow glow. The assassin also smelled of polished leather and cloves, a scent Ava had been growing used to over her many days of traveling with the man, but a scent that was currently only adding to her growing nausea.

It was her first time on a ship this size—Aeros Raijael's personal vessel. It was large and daunting and moving fast. Though the water below was smooth as black glass and the boat did not sway, pitch, or yaw, Ava still wanted to puke. She wanted to throw herself overboard and end the terrible sickness rising in her gut.

Tonight was the lowest she'd felt since her capture, for tonight she was leaving the shores of Gul Kana, the only home she'd ever known.

The Isle of Adin Wyte seemed like another world altogether. But Adin Wyte was where the bulk of Aeros' armies had gathered—two hundred thousand battle-hardened soldiers camped north of Saint Only. The White Prince was on his way to personally lead them across the channel from Saint Only to Lord's Point. Then the full might of his armies would finally be in Gul Kana.

A black kestrel fluttered in from the west and landed on Aeros' outstretched forearm. "Nighteyes, my swift flier," the White Prince cooed. He set the small bird on the wooden prow before him. A narrow tube made of silver was tied to the breast of the kestrel with a string of leather. Aeros gently removed the tube and pulled forth a slip of parchment. "From Dugal, let's hope."

The Spider positioned his lantern over the paper, giving the prince some light to read by. "It is from Dugal." Aeros' skin was ashen against the light of the lantern. His dark-pupiled eyes darted to the Bloodwood. "The girl has completed her task."

"So, the deed is done," the Spider stated matter-of-factly. "Your plan for Gault's daughter was a success?"

"Black Dugal was right." Aeros looked down at the parchment again, crumpled it in his hand. "Even I must become fatherless."

"As do we all."

Aeros clenched his fist around the paper. "All who knew the truth about Krista Aulbrek had to die. Ser Aulmut Klingande. My father. All of them." He looked at the Bloodwood, iciness in his glance. "I'm sure Silkwood and Rosewood will do their part in eliminating the rest?"

"In due time." The Spider met his cold gaze. "That you wanted Krista to assassinate Aulmut and Aevrett herself"—a smirk played at the corner of his mouth—"I imagine delighted Black Dugal to no end."

"Nothing like patricide to please a Bloodwood," Aeros responded with a wicked sneer of his own. "But lest you forget, there is still one more left in Rokenwalder who must die."

"I imagine my master has Krista in place by now," the Spider said. "My father should have never kept the man alive. But Borden Bronachell will soon be dead, and all he knows will die with him."

"And then Nail will again become *nobody*." Aeros tossed the parchment into the sea.

"Fatherless," the Bloodwood said. "Exactly like his sister."

Aeros looked at Nighteyes still perched on the prow of the ship, stroked the feathers atop the kestrel's small head. Then his piercing black eyes cut toward into the Bloodwood. "You forget one thing, assassin. Borden Bronachell is not the last one to know the truth. I know the truth. You know the truth. Your brother knows the truth. Who knows how many of the Brethren of Mia Hawkwood has told?"

"There is still some of Dugal's blood left in Hawkwood," the Spider said. "He will not give up lightly what secrets he is privy to."

"All the Brethren of Mia must die. Even the betrayer. Why have neither Rosewood or Silkwood not killed him yet?"

"I've not heard from Rosewood in some time," the Spider said.

"But according to the last note I received from Silkwood, she claimed *Ethic Shroud* has been found in Amadon. She herself is with Nail, part of a company of nine headed toward mines above Arco in Sky Lochs. Silkwood will get *Blackest Heart* and *Afflicted Fire*. She claims all the weapons of the Five Warrior Angels will soon be yours, and those she travels with will not live through the journey."

"Let's hope she follows through on her promises," the White Prince muttered. "One day soon, I myself will wear *Lonesome Crown* into battle and fight with *Forgetting Moon*. Perhaps even when we attack Lord's Point. Ser Ivor Jace should have my armies ready in Adin Wyte."

Aeros held his arm out for the kestrel on the prow, his eyes lancing into Ava's. "Part of what keeps you alive is your silence. Breathe one word of what you have heard tonight and your end will be long and painful. Are we clear?"

She gulped and nodded, her gut unsettled as she watched the bird hop onto Aeros' outstretched arm. To calm her nerves, she reached up and ran her own fingers gently over the kestrel's tiny head. The bird stared at her with the keen eyes of a cold hunter. Ava was not calmed.

"Nighteyes doesn't like you." Aeros took a white handkerchief from the pocket of his white jerkin and placed it over the bird. "We dock under the Fortress of Saint Only in a few hours. Stay on deck if you like. I will have Mancellor come watch you." Aeros whirled and walked away, with the bird in hand, heavy white boots clomping along the stiff wooden deck. When he disappeared belowdecks, Ava's stomach finally gave way.

She vomited up a stream of half-digested potato-and-red-beet soup, which streaked the outside prow of the ship like blood.

"These channel waters are not rough enough to make a girl seasick." The Spider gazed at her, eyes pitiless and knowing. "So best you not let Aeros ever see you puke again. Else I fear he will throw you overboard himself." He brought forth a plain leather water skin, slipping it quietly from under the folds of his cloak. "Drink." He dipped his head to her, holding the water skin out for her almost reverently. "It will help wash the bitterness of your sins away."

Ava took the water skin, unstoppered it with trembling fingers, then drank of its crisp water, cool and quenching.

Mancellor Allen, in full Knight of the Blue Sword livery, helm under the crook of his arm, marched up from belowdecks and stationed himself next to Ava and the Spider at the prow, all three of them staring at the looming bulk of Mont Saint Only.

"We shall be there soon," the Bloodwood muttered. "Your turn to watch the girl, so I shall take my leave of you both," he said to Mancellor, then took his water skin from Ava and disappeared down the same hatchway Aeros had.

"I've always dreamed of seeing the fortress atop Mont Saint Only," Mancellor said once the Spider was gone. "And now here I am, about to set foot on the shores of Adin Wyte." He then did the three-fingered sign of the Laijon Cross over his heart. The ritual prayer startled Ava, for she had never seen one in the armies of the White Prince perform such a prayer. It was a sacred and personal ritual straight from *The Way and Truth of Laijon*, meant to stave off the wraiths and other demons. She suddenly found herself observing the fellow next to her in a new light. The cornrows of hair tumbling about his shoulders and the dark blue tattoos under his eyes made him look fierce in the moonlight. In the right circumstances, Ava figured the Wyn Darrè could be handsome. But as one of her captors, he was as beastly as the others.

She noticed that the same Sør Sevier slave brand on the underside of her own wrist was burned onto his, too. He'd once been a captive of Aeros Raijael just like her, just like Jenko. *Perhaps he too does what he can to survive.*

"My sister must think I am long since dead." Mancellor looked at her. "Did you have any siblings in Gallows Haven?"

Ava did not wish to engage him in conversation, especially not about anything regarding Gallows Haven and her family. She remained quiet.

"My sister, Bronwyn, would be about your age now," he said. "If she still lives. Seventeen, I reckon." There was sadness in his voice. "'Course, I haven't seen her in five years now. Not since joining Aeros Raijael's army."

"You mean not since Aeros took you captive?" The statement caused the Wyn Darrè to look away.

"You should know, Jenko and I found treasure in Ravenker," he said, gazing up at Mont Saint Only. "An ax and a blue stone. We took them from that boy, Nail. The boy you both knew in Gallows Haven."

Of course she knew of the ax and stone the Wyn Darrè spoke of. She'd spied on Mancellor and Jenko when they had gifted Aeros with the treasures. She had shown them both to Enna Spades. *Is he fishing for information? Trying to glean what I know about Nail?* Ava's heart thundered. *Is Aeros testing me so soon?* Again she did not engage him. Her stomach still churned, the nausea worse than before.

"I fear Jenko Bruk is obsessed with the battle-ax," Mancellor said. "I fear he will try and steal it. And that will be the end of him. Aeros will never let him touch what few treasures he holds dear." The Wyn Darrè's tone was flat, his eyes fixed on Ava again. *As if I am one of Aeros' untouchable treasures . . .*

She said, "The White Prince has more secrets than just that battle-ax." Her heart thumped in her chest as she spoke, knowing she was about to divulge the very secrets Aeros had just warned her not to. But she didn't care. If Mancellor was a spy, she suddenly hoped he relayed everything she said to the White Prince. She wanted Aeros to know of her treachery and disloyalty. Hoped he killed her for the betrayal. It would be a blessed end. "There is also a strange helmet in his treasure chest. And a green stone. He keeps them with the ax and the blue stone. He has them on this ship now. Belowdecks. They are two important and ancient relics. They are what these wars are all about. They are why he has killed so many people. The battle-ax and helmet are why he destroyed Gallows Haven, why he hunted Nail. That much I have figured out on my own."

"A helm?" Mancellor asked, eyes a-squint above his black tattoos.

"Aye, a helm." She gazed up at him, eyes wide with hope, a feigned hope that she desired him to notice. She placed her hand against his armored shoulder. "He believes they are *Lonesome Crown* and *Forgetting Moon*, the weapons of the Five Warrior Angels."

"The Five Warrior Angels?"

"When we reach Saint Only, we should steal the ax and helm," she went on in a rush. "We should steal them and run away, Mancellor. Us. Together. Run far away. We should take the ax and helm to Amadon. It is what Gault Aulbrek was going to do." She held her head high, meeting the Wyn Darrè's piercing eyes. "And he was going to take me with him."

"Gault Aulbrek would not have done that," Mancellor scoffed. "He would not have stolen from his lord, nor would he have taken you away from Aeros."

"He would, I swear it." She met his dark glare with a stern, unyielding look. "Aeros grew suspicious of Gault, and together with the Bloodwood, he conspired to betray Gault. And they betrayed him in Ravenker."

"Be that as it may—"

"You are like Gault," she interrupted, hand still on his shoulder. "I know you do not want to be part of Aeros' army, Mancellor. Together we can—"

"Please stop," he hissed, two gauntleted hands now gripping her shoulders. "You cannot speak like this, Ava." His eyes bore into hers pleadingly. But there was also confusion and pain there too. *If he is a spy, he is a poor one. . . . He is actually considering running away with me. . . .*

"What are you two discussing?" Jenko Bruk's voice came drifting out of the darkness. He came up behind them, heavy boots clomping along the deck. He was in full Knight of the Blue Sword armor, helm in one hand, sword hanging at his hip.

"Aeros does not want you up here with the girl." Mancellor released Ava's shoulders, stepped between her and Jenko.

"Yet here I am," Jenko answered, amber eyes roaming up to the shadow of Mont Saint Only before falling again on his fellow Knight of the Blue Sword.

"It's your neck on the line," Mancellor said. "But don't say I didn't warn you."

Jenko looked straight at Ava. "So what do the two of you discuss?"

Ava hesitated. Telling him could be the end of her. "I was telling Mancellor of a helmet and green angel stone Aeros keeps in his chest. The White Prince keeps them with the ax and blue stone you took from Nail in Ravenker. They may be the lost weapons of the Five Warrior Angels. I asked Mancellor to help me steal them from Aeros and run away with me."

"Run away with you?" Jenko looked . . . stunned. Hurt? Confused? She wasn't sure. His dark glaring gaze fell on the Wyn Darrè.

Mancellor swallowed hard. "She's liable to get us both killed, talking like this."

Hope of a sort lurked behind Jenko's eyes as he turned back to her. "Tell me of this helm."

She didn't hesitate. "Aeros believes that the helm is *Lonesome Crown* from *The Way and Truth of Laijon*. And the green stone one of the fabled angel stones. The battle-ax you took from Nail is *Forgetting Moon*."

"That cannot be," Jenko said, hope dimming. "I've read *The Way and Truth of Laijon*. My father kept a copy. The weapons of the Five Warrior Angels and the stones were taken into heaven with Laijon at his death." His eyes grew distant. "*Forgetting Moon* was not something a bastard like Nail would be lugging about on the back of a mule."

"Think about it." Ava was growing more desperate now, trying to make her point sink home. "You yourself said you felt some magic in it. I heard you say it when you gave the ax to Aeros. And Aeros hoards the ax and the helm as if magic is what he truly believes lies within them."

"I did feel something in that ax when Nail struck me with it in Ravenker." Jenko took a step back, the faraway look still in his eyes. He straightened his posture. "That bastard could not have bested me without some divine help."

"That's not all," she said conspiratorially. "Aeros and the Spider talk of other things. They mentioned that *Ethic Shroud* has also been found in Amadon. They said that Nail and a Bloodwood named Silkwood are joined on a quest to get *Blackest Heart* and *Afflicted Fire*."

"Nail?" Jenko scoffed. "And a Bloodwood, too?"

"It's what they said. Not an hour ago. Right here where you are standing. The White Prince gets little messages from a black bird."

"Bloody Mother," Jenko said scornfully. "Have the wraiths truly eaten holes in your brain? You almost had me convinced."

Ava stepped back, the nausea returning like a roiling storm in her stomach. "I am not taken with any wraiths."

"I know," he mumbled. "I am sorry."

His wild swings in emotion were as baffling and conflicting and inconsistent as her own. "I only speak the truth of things," she murmured, almost in a whisper, "and people think me crazy." Then she leaned over the ship's railing and vomited. She strained. It hurt so much. It was embarrassing.

When she was done, Jenko held a white kerchief out for her. She reached for it. But instead of giving it to her, he leaned in and cleaned her lips off with the kerchief himself. The gesture was so unexpected, his touch so gentle, tears nearly sprang from her eyes. *So cruel to so tender in a heartbeat. Oh, what have they done to you, Jenko?*

"Can I keep it?" she asked.

When he handed the kerchief to her, she saw the slave brand on the underside of his wrist, too. *Jenko. Me. Mancellor. We are so alike.* She took the kerchief from him and stuffed it into the belt about her waist, moist eyes on him the entire time. The wild swings in emotion he could create in her were at once both maddening and reassuring. "I do not know what the future holds for us, Jenko. But you must know this: I understand you have only done what any man would have done to survive." She swallowed hard. A lump was growing in her throat. *Forgive all,* The Way and Truth of Laijon *taught, for the wraiths thrive in hateful souls.* "You must know I forgive you," she finished.

"And I forgive you," he said.

They both stood still, stricken by the common bonds they still shared. He hugged her then. Despite the cold and hard Sør Sevier armor cloaking him, just being enveloped in his strong arms was as comforting as she remembered. She felt herself melt into him.

When he finally broke away from her, he cast his gaze out over the ocean to the hulking Mont Saint Only above, tears in his eyes. "I am so conflicted. In Gallows Haven, on the beach, when Spades was going to kill you . . ." He paused, choking on his words. "I—I betrayed my father for you, Ava. I almost killed him, if he isn't dead now. And Aeros, there are moments where he treats me as an equal, more so than my father ever did. And then with Spades . . ." He paused once again, voice cracking with pain. "You must also know, I only do what I can to survive. Please understand. I have not forgotten you."

"Nor I you," she said, at a loss for words at his admission. "By rights we shouldn't even be here. Neither of us."

"It's Nail's fault we are here." Jenko's eyes were smoldering coals. He was looking directly at her. "I will one day hunt Nail down and kill him for you. I swear I will, Ava. If it's the last thing I do. It's because of that bastard we are standing here on the ship of our enemy, the White Prince. They are all crazy: Aeros, Spades, Hammerfiss, the

Bloodwood. And it was Nail who left us to suffer this demented torture at their hands."

Ava felt a painful stab of hope at Jenko's words. *Does he truly hate them? Has he been acting like their friend out of pure self-preservation? Did he pledge his allegiance to Aeros purely to save his own life? Is he playing them like they play us?*

"I don't know whether I am a nice man or a bad man," Jenko continued. "But I will avenge you, Ava. One day I will have that battle-ax Aeros keeps in his precious precious chest in my own hands and I will kill Nail with it, and then I will kill anyone else who has hurt you."

"Best not let Aeros or any of the others hear you speak like that," Mancellor muttered.

"I don't care who hears what anymore," Jenko spat.

"I understand your pain," Mancellor said. "And, for your own good, I will make sure this conversation stays between the three of us. But you will one day realize that this person you hate, Nail, well, he did you a great favor in leaving you with Aeros. I believe Laijon has a purpose for all of us, and that is why we still live. For we now survive on the winning side, whilst this Nail fellow and those with him will be forever hunted."

"But Nail is free and I am not," Jenko said. "And I have compromised much of who I am because of Nail's betrayal." He gripped the railing before him, looking directly at Mancellor, venom in his tone. "And I will hold you to your promise, this stays between the three of us." He dipped his head to the Wyn Darrè, and turned to go.

Ava grabbed his arm. "Thanks for risking coming up here, Jenko." She wished he would stay, the words of his heartfelt confession tumbling roughshod through her mind. "Thanks for talking with me."

"'Twas my honor." He bowed to her before taking his leave. "And I pray your sickness is but a passing thing." He walked away, his back stiff and proud.

As she watched him disappear belowdeck, Ava felt her stomach churn, almost as if his mere saying the word *sickness* was enough to invoke more illness within her. Again she leaned over the railing and puked. And as the remains of her guts spilled out into the night, a disturbing thought entered her mind. She'd seen village girls get sick like this before. *Pregnant village girls . . .*

When was the last time she had felt her womanly course, her bleeding time? She clutched the railing, gasping for breath. A cold hand gripped her arm, steadying her. It was Mancellor Allen, who stopped her from falling. When she looked up, the knowing look on the Wyn Darrè's face was one of pity and concern.

As she used Jenko's kerchief to wipe her face, all she could picture in her mind's eye was Aeros Raijael drowning a small baby in a crystal cool stream outside the small hamlet of Leifid.

*Every remnant of the nameless beasts of the underworld was found and destroyed,
every bone, scale, and tooth, every cave and dungeon they dwelt within pillaged
and set afire, all to cleanse the putrid stink of their foul existence.*
—THE WAY AND TRUTH OF LAIJON

# CHAPTER FORTY-FIVE
# STEFAN WAYLAND

16TH DAY OF THE ANGEL MOON, 999TH YEAR OF LAIJON
DEADWOOD GATE, GUL KANA

S tefan Wayland and Seita rode together atop one of the stolen draught mares, Culpa Barra the other. Four days of hard riding and the three travelers broke from the rolling, wooded hills just northwest of Deadwood Gate. They proceeded up a rising slope of thick brush and tall boulders. The mares carried them haphazardly around the numerous rock obstacles to a flat, barren peak.

It was there that Stefan finally saw the entrance to the mines Culpa had promised they would find. One of many such entrances, he claimed, and a grim sight indeed, naught but a dark hole in the ground circled by a peculiar-looking fence. As Stefan drew rein before the hole, he realized the fence was made of bones. Not animal bones, but human. Or perhaps bones of both oghul and human. Whatever they were, they were nailed together and driven into the turf, stark and white against the dark green foliage and harsh gray rock on the windswept hill. Culpa dismounted and stepped carefully over the low-lying fence, a long coil of rope in hand. His black-lacquered armor creaked as he moved. The crossbow, *Blackest Heart*, was strapped to his back over the top of his heavy gray cloak.

Stefan and Seita climbed from their own mount and watched as the Dayknight tossed one end of the rope down into the hole. A moment later a black stream of shrieking bats came pouring out. Culpa took a startled step back as they swirled past his head, fluttering away into the northern sky.

Culpa said, "Ever since Shawcroft and I left this place five years ago, these forests north of Deadwood Gate have been overrun by evil creatures." He secured the other end of the rope around the thick neck of his draught mare. "We're lucky no oghuls have spotted us, entrenched deep within their lands as we are." After tying the rope around the mare's neck, the Dayknight patted the horse on the haunch. "Your journey ends here, girl." He turned to Stefan and Seita. "She'll be a stout enough anchor as we lower ourselves into the mines."

"No lunch or discussion of pleasantries first?" Seita pulled down the cowl of her hood. In the stiff breeze, the Vallè's hair fluttered like finespun sunlight. "We just ride on up into a boneyard and drop ourselves straight down a hole in the ground?"

"Aye," Culpa said, examining the rope. "No pleasantries."

Four days of riding, and it seemed every communication between Seita and Culpa was not just a little strained, but bordering on the unkind. What few hamlets they'd passed through, Seita had wanted to stop at the inn, eat a hot meal, possibly sleep a night in comfort. But Culpa had insisted they stick to eating what few cold rations they had and sleep under the stars.

It had also been the loneliest four days of Stefan's life. Seita claimed their kiss had been a mistake. Still, they shared a horse daily, her clinging to his back as they rode. He cherished the feel of her body pressed to his atop the mare. And he lived for those chance touches of her hand on his chest as they lay next to each other at night. It was naught but slow torture. But friendship was all she now offered. He knew she sensed his pain. It was written on his face at every moment.

"If memory serves, the bottom is only about fifty feet down." Culpa pulled on the rope still, testing its strength against the horse's neck. "We've still a long journey underground before we find *Afflicted Fire*." He held the rope out for Stefan. "You first. Then Seita. I'll go last."

The rope trailed from the neck of the horse through the knight's calloused hand and down into the stark blackness of the hole. Stefan had clambered up the ratlines of the *Lady Kindly* enough times, he didn't fear the rope. He had the skill. He just didn't know what awaited him in the hole below. Any thought of going underground again sent his heart to jumping. *Oghuls live in the deep and dark places of the north!* The stress of traveling through the Roahm Mines above Gallows Haven followed by the trauma they'd suffered in the mines above Sky Lochs settled over him like a dense fog.

"I'll be right behind you." Seita placed her hand on his, as if she knew what he was thinking. "Culpa's right. We needn't linger up here. Best just get it over with."

Stefan adjusted his cloak and armor and made sure his own bow was secure. Seita helped him cinch the quiver of arrows tight around his back, along with one of the torches. He'd counted the arrows earlier. He had only ten left.

"What of the horses?" he asked.

"They'll stay here until we return, I imagine," Culpa answered.

Stefan stepped over the bone fence and seized the rope, testing its balance against the bulk of Culpa's draught mare. He slowly backed toward the hole, lowering himself down into it with caution, Seita helping guide the rope, her fine white hair flowing in the howling breeze.

† † † † † †

It was cold, musty, and bitter. Stefan stood in a small, jagged cavern about thirty feet wide and a hundred long, a dark tunnel at the far end. Seita and Culpa stood with him, rope dangling overhead, a thin line stretching toward the pinprick of light above, still tied to the draught mare.

Culpa replaced the torch on Stefan's back with a coil of rope. "You carry the rope. I'll carry the torch." He sparked the flame to light with a flint and stone. "Guard your mind against the wraiths. I can't warn you enough, these mines are a living and breathing place, an evil dungeon liable to play tricks with your mind if you are not watchful."

Culpa took a drink from one of his water skins, then handed it to Stefan. As he lifted his head to drink, Stefan thought he could feel the ground shift beneath his feet. And when he looked up at the dot of sunlight fifty feet above, he thought he saw something briefly cover the hole in the ceiling. He squinted. The point of sunlight returned. *Just one of the horses . . .*

"We've a long journey ahead of us." Culpa took back the water skin and led the way toward the distant tunnel, torchlight flickering off the rough, cracked walls ahead. Seita followed the Dayknight. Stefan brought up the rear. When they reached the tunnel, the rough passageway sloped down and slightly to the left. Chunks of fallen rock and various lengths of lumber littered their path.

As they traveled, Stefan couldn't stop thinking of oghuls and poison darts and silver streams. The narrow mine shaft soon became a twisting and turning maze. In some places the ceiling was low, the tunnel so narrow, and they had to duck and squeeze their way through. In places there were shadows disappearing into black pits in the floor or shadows climbing up into holes and cracks in the ceiling. It was all so eerily similar to the mines above Gallows Haven and Sky Lochs. Every once in a while, from the corner of

Stefan's eyes, the quartz in the walls would flicker red in the torch-light and pulse like tiny streams of blood, and with each step he took, it seemed the floor moved under him, moved to the deep rumble of something far below.

Stefan's panic and paranoia turned to nausea and a splitting head-ache, the nausea hovering in the deeper parts of his gut like an iron anvil pressing against his vitals, the pain in his head whispering evil words, things not quite discernable, yet disturbing in tone, voices wicked in vibration, like a steady *thrum, thrum, thrum* encircling his skull.

He thought of the wraiths in *The Way and Truth of Laijon*, wonder-ing if he had finally succumbed to their dread call.

To regain his sense, he focused on Seita's dark silhouette ahead of him, reached out, and tapped her on the shoulder. "What?" She turned.

"You doin' okay?"

"A bit nervous."

"Me too."

Together they stopped, black corridor stretching before and aft. Culpa kept walking ahead. Stefan took a chance and wrapped Seita in his arms, if only for his own reassurance. She held him tight in return, her touch warming, despite his chest-plate armor between them. She clung to him, as if she, too, had been longing for the assur-ance that she wasn't alone here in the dark. He had comforted Gisela in much the same way in the mines above Gallows Haven, and hold-ing the Vallè girl now reminded him of so much lost love.

"Do not fall too far behind!" they heard Culpa yell, his torchlight dim in the distance. They broke their embrace and hurried down the tunnel.

They found Culpa standing in a four-way intersection, black corridors stretching off to the left and to the right and also straight ahead.

"I'm not sure which one to take," Culpa said, moving slowly down the tunnel to the right about ten paces, torch held out before him.

"Many things have weighed heavy on my mind these last few days," Seita whispered to Stefan, leaning into him again. The strain in her normally confident voice was real. "It's my visions. We need to reach Amadon soon, Stefan. Can you not feel the urgency? We need to get out of these mines. Something dangerous lives down here. Not just oghuls, but something evil. An evil like none of us has ever imagined. I can feel it in the walls, in the floor under my feet."

"I feel it too." A murmur of breath touched the back of his neck. He shuddered.

"What are you two going on about?" Culpa glared back at them. "Your conversation echoes off everything. I told you this place would fool with your mind. This is not the Sky Loch mines. Guard yourselves. Don't feed off of each other's paranoia. You'll only go crazy with that kind of talk."

Stefan's skin tingled as if something was closing in, some nightmare. By the look in Seita's eyes, she felt it too. Danger blistered his every nerve ending with venomous intent. He could feel it, some *thing* or *things* sneaking up behind them. He felt the ground move underfoot again. He felt the air bristle and quake, as if stirred by many swift-flung arrows, arrows whose murderous points sought his heart.

He grabbed Seita's arm, eyes darting about. Something *was* breathing heavily down the length of the passageway toward *him*, sucking up great gulps of precious air, aiming straight for *him*, seeking to devour *him*. Indeed, this place was not like Sky Lochs. There was a sickness here. A foul, musty dark. A poisonous fume. The air shimmered. Culpa's torch flickered. Stefan felt sweat bead up on his forehead.

Seita was naught but a dark shadow against the diminishing light. "What's happening?" she hissed.

The tunnel rumbled and shook—hot air whooshed by. Slivers of rock and dust rained from the ceiling. The walls creaked and groaned, and the cave shook. There was a *Booming! Booming! Booming!* from deep underneath them, as if massive slabs of rock were grinding together. Culpa Barra was trying to make his way back toward them now, shouting something onto the din, his torch a wobbly, hazy light in the distance.

Stefan's heart froze as runnels of soft red light seeped from the walls, glowing, pulsating to the deepening sounds, like the veins along a monstrous scaly arm. The color pulsed in, out, in, out. It felt like the tunnel was slowly twisting over on itself, throwing his balance off. Seita lost her footing too, stumbled down the passage toward Culpa, and fell to the floor. "It's hot!" she yelled, and pushed herself up.

Symbols were emblazoned like pockets of fire along the walls—squares, circles within circles, crosses, crescent moons, all twinkled like shooting stars. The tunnel kept spinning with spiraling rivers of fire and glowing symbols. The glittering veins intensified, fiery red blooming and running like streams of molten iron.

Then the mine shuddered violently. Dust sparkled from the ceiling in waves and ripples as the gleaming ribbons of fire wrapped around the walls faded to a dull red—then dwindled—and washed away to nothing.

"We all need to remain calm!" Culpa's voice echoed in the dark, his torch aglow with dancing fire, illuminating his own terrified face. "This place is only playing tricks with our mind. Nothing is happening."

Seita's round eyes roamed the corridor in fear—a fear Stefan had never before seen in the Vallè. His own heavy breaths of fear filled the tunnel. Culpa stepped forward, boots scuffing against the floor, the sound sharp and echoing.

The walls rumbled again, freezing the Dayknight in his tracks.

"What is it?" Seita hissed. "What's happening?"

"Shhhh!" Culpa hissed right back at her.

A billow of hot air rushed by. Stefan felt the tunnel twist under his feet again. A new rumbling sound was pulsating deep, deep, deep, from beneath. The walls ran with red lightning, violently red, shimmering to the drum of the growing roar, louder and louder, *Booming! Booming! Booming!* This was no illusion. Stefan was certain of that. No trick of the mines. No trick of the wraiths.

The thin quartz veins in the rock burst yellow like flame, peppering everyone with their sting. Seita clung to Stefan as another foul blast of hot air whooshed up the passageway. The tunnel was a spinning, twisting clamor of rushing air and color, blinking symbols along the walls, red, yellow, orange, yellow, orange, red, then deep blue . . . purple . . .

Then the ground tilted and dropped out from under him, sending Seita stumbling away toward Culpa Barra, Stefan staggering uncontrollably in the opposite direction . . .

. . . and the roof fell on top of him.

† † † †

One moment Stefan was curled up, covered in oblivion. The next he was choking in lungfuls of dirt. Something hot was tearing at his left ankle. He kicked. But his legs could scarcely move. The rest of his body was paralyzed in darkness, arms pinned to his sides, head seemingly fixed in solid mortar.

The ground shook, and something under him shifted. He slid down, down, down, shards of rock scraping his chest-plate armor, his heavy gray cloak riding up around his neck, trying to strangle him. He spat out clumps of dirt, wiped at his eyes with frantic hands. He was blinded by darkness. His eyes were open, but all that greeted him was a midnight-colored blackness so impenetrable, it was sobering.

"Seita!" he shouted. "Culpa!" Only heavy silence answered.

The ground moved again. A rumbling veil of rock and dirt showered his legs. He scrambled away, picked himself up off the floor. His ankle hurt.

He limped two steps and sat down. "Seita!" he screamed again. "Culpa!" Nothing.

*Are they crushed under all that debris? Dead?*

"Seita!" he shouted in a panic. "Seita!"

She was lost. Like Gisela. Dead. Culpa, too. *Blackest Heart* and the angel stone the Dayknight carried. Gone! All of it buried under the rubble behind Stefan. His mind was naught but a numb void as it slowly sank in: he was the lone survivor of the Company of Nine who had set out from Lord's Point. All their travel and adventure was for nothing. Everyone was gone. Nail, Roguemoore, and Val-Draekin lost in the glacier. Godwyn, Liz Hen, and Dokie also likely dead. And now Culpa and Seita.

Stefan sat in the darkness and silence, alone, blackness his only companion. He knew he had to move on. *But where do I go?* He did a quick inventory of all his gear. His bow was still on his back. The quiver, too, only it was full of debris. Just two of the original ten arrows remained. *Eight arrows lost in the rubble. Has nothing gone right?* The coil of rope was still slung over his shoulder. He brushed it free of dirt. He had no torch, and that was a problem. Plus his ankle continued its throbbing dance of pain. He examined his foot by touch, his searching fingers finding no broken bones or blood.

The stifling blackness pressed in around him, a suffocating dark that stole his very breath and quickened his heart. *I will die here.* Desperately wanting to keep busy before total despair set in, he searched the ground for lost arrows, feeling along the ground with both hands. Nothing. *What I wouldn't give for one of Roguemoore's D'Nahk lè timestones now.*

He secured his gear and scooted cautiously forward, crawling on his stomach, too terrified to stand. "Seita!" he called out again. Nothing. Tears were forming in his eyes. Tears that no other person would ever see. Tears that flowed lonely in the dark. He crawled, desperate to escape this harsh place of pain and crushing loneliness. Desperate to find some light.

He hadn't gone far when his left hand slipped over an edge and his chin smacked the rock floor painfully. Angry. Scared. He scrambled back from the ledge, gathered his thoughts. *A staircase leading down? A bottomless pit?* It could be anything. It could be nothing. The way back was blocked by rubble.

He tossed a small rock over the rim, heard it clatter to a stone floor somewhere far below. He tossed another rock, listening for it to strike bottom, trying to gauge the distance. *Twenty feet? Fifty? A hundred?* How could he even tell?

He felt the dusty cool reassurance of the coil of rope on his shoulder. He crawled back to the wall of debris, found a boulder heavy enough to hold his weight, tied one end of the rope around it, and cinched it tight. He crawled back to the edge and dropped the other end of the rope over. He checked his bow and quiver one last time, making sure they were secure. Gripping the rope, testing its strength, he slid his body over the edge, lowering himself slowly. Hand over hand, down he went, sure of his grip, feet levered against the wall before him. With his injured ankle, it was hard going, and he was quickly gasping down lungfuls of musty air that dried his throat. Suddenly the wall supporting his feet disappeared, and he found himself dangling in the dark nothingness.

He wrapped his legs around the rope, hand over hand, descending until his feet reached the end of the rope. He kept lowering himself until he was dangling from the last foot of rope by one hand, toes stretching to find solid ground he hoped was somewhere just below, hand straining from the effort of holding tight to the last foot of rope. But his toes felt nothing. No ground. No safety. He reached up and secured both hands around the rope. Pulled himself up just far enough to loop the rope around his right hand twice.

Then he dangled in the darkness, the rope cinching down on his flesh with each passing moment, cutting off the circulation in his fingers. *How far away is the bottom still? Kick your boot off, idiot. Let it fall. Judge the distance....*

With his left foot, he started working the boot off his right foot, wiggling and pushing against the stiff leather. The pain in his injured ankle was almost unbearable, and the strength in his hands nearly gave out with the effort; his fingers grew numb. His body swayed under the rope as he struggled and swung, boot about to drop...

...and then he saw the light.

*Seita! Culpa!*

Below him and to the left came a faint flicker of yellow, a pin-prick in the black distance. It stabbed at his eyes as it grew in bright-ness. There was clanking of metal on stone and the unmistakable guttural voices of approaching oghuls. Yellow torchlight blossomed under him, revealing the jagged, shadow-filled cavern.

Hundreds of stalactites of every size stretched at varying lengths toward the floor. Stalagmites rose up into the air all around. A small, well-worn path wound through the jagged landscape and disap-peared in the distance to his left and right. And Stefan was dangling between two narrow stalactites right in the middle of it, twenty feet above the path, right in the line of the approaching oghuls, boot about to slip from his foot.

Five burly beasts, all bearing torches and jabbering oghul non-sense, rounded a huge stalagmite and marched directly under him. They all wore rusted armor and spiked helms, wicked-looking axes strapped to their broad backs. They clattered down the trail directly under Stefan's swaying feet and carried on, not one of them even looking up, their torchlight soon disappearing into the distant dark.

Stefan had only one choice, and that was to follow their light. He let himself drop the twenty feet to the floor, landing hard, pain shooting up his injured ankle as he fell backward onto his butt. The two arrows bounced out of his quiver, clattering to the floor. Standing gingerly, he checked his bow. It was undamaged. He snatched the arrows up and dumped them back into his quiver. He mourned the loss of the rope hanging above, but had to move quickly or lose the oghul's torchlight. He pulled the hood of his cloak up over his head and hobbled toward the receding glow as fast as his injured foot would allow, the pain almost too much to bear.

Desperate, he plodded on, limping, hunger pangs stabbing at his stomach, unbearable thirst clutching at his dry tongue, chasing the torchlight of monsters. Each fork in the road the oghuls took led him ever downward, every tunnel more twisting and turning than the last. And the deeper the beasts descended, the heavier the air felt. From floor to ceiling, veins of some sparkly liquid substance streaked the walls of every passageway like tiny strings of lightning. Once in a while, from the corner of his eye, when the distant torchlight hit the walls just so, Stefan saw the streams flicker red and pulse like tiny rivers of blood. Fissures and cracks started appearing in the walls and floor with more frequency, and the air emanating from them was stifling and rank. He kept his eyes on the floor in front of him as best he could, the torchlight ahead dull or bright depending on the length of the tunnel, the location of the five oghuls, and how far behind he dared drift. Keeping his movements silent, and the oghuls just out of sight, it was all he could do to hobble along as best he could. The constant yellow glow of the oghuls' torches bouncing off the narrow walls was his only comfort.

The narrow corridor the oghuls currently led him down gradually widened. An orange glow emanated from the tunnel in the far distance. *Sunlight!*

The oghuls hustled, their spiky armor naught but dancing silhouettes in the bright light. Tears of joy sprang from Stefan's eyes, his heart soaring. Daylight lay ahead. The five oghuls before him eventually disappeared into the orange glow of the sun, and Stefan limped along, more vigor in his step, the tunnel around him widening farther, the walls receding on either side.

And then the light before him began to take on a strange, fiery quality that didn't seem quite natural. He slowed his pace, wary. The glaring glow ahead became almost too unbearable to look into. And suddenly the floor ceased to exist before him.

He came to an abrupt halt. The walls, the ceiling, the floor, all things that had previously surrounded him had simply vanished.

He stood on the brink of a deep, fiery-red oblivion.

It took a moment to wrap his mind around what he was truly seeing, unnerved at the immensity of the glowing underground cavern that was revealed before him. Everything was bathed in crimson. A nightmarish painting of what he imagined the underworld might look like.

The vast, spectacular cave before him was perfectly round, enormous, the width of the entire village of Gallows Haven and more. Some five hundred feet above, the roof was dripping with mammoth wine-colored stalactites. And the floor was a swirling mist of seething red-golden nothing, bottomless with fiery haze.

Across the cavern, to the left and to the right, up and down, everywhere, the surrounding walls were honeycombed with tunnel-like entrances, thousands of them. To Stefan's estimation, every cave opening was identical to the one that served as his own lonely perch. And he couldn't begin to guess where such a horde of tunnels might lead.

Firelike capillaries of orange and yellow danced above and below each of the many caves. And the colossal cavern pulsed scarlet to the sound of a deep *Boom! Boom!* like the beating of a giant hollowed-out heart. *Exactly as* The Way and Truth of Laijon *described the underworld!* Just beneath him was a staircase cut into the sheer wall, and the five oghuls he'd followed descended carefully into the feverish glowing haze below.

Then the entire scene went dark. Consuming blackness. And the stillness was deafening. The silence was cracked like a whip as a heinous grating noise rushed up the massive cavern. A blast of hot air blew Stefan back from the ledge. Pain raced up his injured ankle. The cavern thundered and shook violently. He was slammed to the ground. He tried to grip the floor but couldn't. The booming and rumbling shook his every muscle and bone and turned his guts inside out. He braced himself as best he could, or he knew he would be bounced right over the edge to plummet into the blackness. The quaking continued at a fevered pitch, accompanied by a long grumbling roar from the pit below.

A red glow suddenly filled the air, a fiery plume of mist billowing from the deep like molten iron from a boiling forge, illuminating the flittering dust jogged loose from above. Pulsing veins of crystal and quartz streaked and flashed in the tunnel behind him like bolts of lightning, and everything seemed to swirl and twist in on itself wildly. The evil cacophony reverberated and boomed around him.

*It's only in my mind! Only in my mind! Like Culpa said!*

In an instant, the unholy din ceased. The red light vanished. A pungent darkness swarmed over him, hot and rank, though his mind still buzzed with images of flickering sparks and twinkling lights, all of it fading down around him like falling snow.

And something in the blackness below roared again, a thunderous roar of a thousand saber-toothed lions combined. The immensity of the sound shook the very air.

Stefan's ears rang with pain.

He lay on his stomach, clenched his jaw, ran stiff fingers through hair as unruly and scattered as his mind felt, covered his ears.

Stefan found he was at the rim of the ledge, looking down upon a nightmare.

A hundred feet below lay the bottom of the cavern. The five oghuls were gone. But a ring of burning torches was set in the floor. A lone knight in a black cape and hood stood in the center of the circle. Under the hood he wore a silver mask in the shape of a human skull. Under the cape was a glorious suit of shining red-scaled armor. A bright silver whip lined with sparkling silver barbs was gripped in the skull-faced knight's red-gauntleted hand. And the knight stood before the most heinous-looking creature imaginable.

*The nameless beast of the underworld!*

A dragon!

Stefan couldn't break his horrified gaze away. The dragon was enormous and red, the bulk of its sinuous body the size of his parents' two-story Gallows Haven cottage, sleek and long and graceful as a saber-toothed lion, massive scaled thews bunching and clenching as it shifted and moved. On four legs it crouched, clawed feet scratching at the floor, unreal fiery-yellow light emanating from under its harsh red scales—knifelike scales that sheathed its entire corded bulk.

A coiled tail of sharp spines and ridges swept the floor with a slither of scale on rock. Its forked wings unfurled like those of a huge bat, curved talons at the joints, a red velvety wingspan greater than the length of the *Lady Kindly*. The jagged row of sharp horns that ran the length of its spine from head to tail were as white as the ivory tusks on a Glacier Range musk ox and thick as a man's arm. The two curving horns on either side of its serpentlike head were twice as thick and long as the spinal horns. And its eyes were like two stabs of flame, stark pupils, long and slitted.

The dragon's orbs smoldered and gleamed, both fixed on the whip-wielding knight. A black cauldron of liquid silver hung just above the knight. Next to that was a second cauldron of ruby-red blood. But there was no altar under either cauldron, no sacrificial human that he could see. *Unless I'm to be the sacrifice!* Stefan wanted to stand and run from the horrific scene. But he could not, his body rooted to the tunnel.

The thongs of the skull-faced knight's whip dripped silver to the stone floor. The dragon's piercing red eyes were following the tip of the whip, the clover-shaped scales along its neck suddenly fluttering and rippling like a thousand hawk feathers.

It raised its head, flashed rows of daggerlike teeth, and roared—a sound nearly unbearable. Stefan cringed against the pain.

The knight cracked the whip, droplets of silver flinging into the air, his red-scaled gauntlet shimmering. The dragon backed away, silent, a spume of frothy drip trailing from its open and heaving maw, jaws finally clamping shut in deference to its whip-wielding master. The red-armored man stepped forward, whip cracking against the stone floor again, leaving a bright silver trail that glinted in the torchlight.

Thick dragon scales fluttered and rippled as the monster reared back again, head pointed straight up as it let loose another thunderous roar. A tower of flame bloomed from its cavernous mouth, and the mammoth cave was instantly lit with a blinding fiery light. Stefan, overawed, blinked away the pain and heat, arms covering his face.

When Stefan's eyes cleared, he found the dragon looked upon him with its two piercing molten orbs—fiery crystal gems that sliced into him and stripped his soul bare.

He wanted to turn and flee. Run far, far away as fast as he could.

Then the whip-wielding knight turned his silver veiled face up toward Stefan too, one gauntleted hand sweeping the hood back. He slowly peeled the skull-shaped silver mask from off his head. The pale face of the man underneath was both startling and striking at once, almost feylike in quality. Sharp pointed ears pierced through long silvery locks of hair. *A Vallè!* Yet the hue of this knight's pure white skin was unlike anything Stefan had ever seen, and the knight's two stark, solid silver eyes bore into his with blazing malice.

With that one powerful stare, Stefan's thoughts were fractured into a million scattered pieces. As he heaved himself to his feet and scrambled away from the blasphemous scene, it felt like every bone in his body was trying to slither and crawl out of his skin. He even felt the Sør Sevier slave brand on the underside of his wrist flare in pain. *A Skull! A Skull man! Just like Culpa said!* Without thinking, he fled down the dark tunnel.

After only two steps, he was met by the mottled gray face of an oghul, large purple lips snarling under a spiked half-helm coated in rust.

A heavy gauntleted fist came smashing down onto his jaw.

The stunning blow sent Stefan hurtling back toward the ledge and the dragon. Dazed, Stefan clutched at the walls of the tunnel to keep from falling into the gruesome deep cavern, pain lancing up his leg from his injured ankle.

He gathered his balance quickly, instinctively snatching the bow from his back, hand frantically searching for one of the two arrows in his quiver. But the attacking oghul was on him fast. Another swift punch knocked the bow from Stefan's hand. It clattered to the floor, nearly bouncing over the rim, teetering on the lip of the ledge.

Stefan lunged to save his precious bow, but the oghul grabbed him by the back of his cloak, yanking him roughly off his feet, throwing him to the floor. Stefan rolled as the oghul kicked with a steel-toed boot. He threw up his arm in defense, latching on to the beast's foot, jerking the oghul's leg as hard as he could. Thrown off balance, the creature toppled heavily against the wall of the tunnel, rusted half-helm tumbling from its head. Stefan snatched up the helm with both hands and swung it swiftly down on the back of the beast's skull. His blow connected with a solid crunch, and the beast flopped to the floor face-first, then rolled over.

Stefan dropped to his knees and brought the helm down on the oghul's exposed face with full force. Bones cracked under him. Anger flamed within Stefan. This was close combat like he had never before experienced, and the injustice of the oghul's initial attack enraged him beyond redemption. He brought the helm up and struck again. Ropy streaks of oghul blood, hot and rancid, splattered the wall and also Stefan's face. The oghul twitched beneath him. But the heady aroma of blood, combined with the pain shooting through his ankle, only served to sharpen Stefan's fury to an arrow's point of tightly focused wrath. Crying out for justice, he brought the helm crashing down on the dead oghul's face again and again, howling and roaring his own primitive, guttural song as he struck and struck and struck.

And when he stopped shouting and smashing, it finally registered what he had done. With one part horror and one part fascination, he looked upon the carnage he'd wrought. Beneath him, the oghul's gray face was naught but bloody mush, splintered bone glinting in the surrounding orange haze. The beast was unalterably dead.

Still kneeling, Stefan let the gore-smeared helm drop from his hand to the floor. He blinked back tears of rage. His cloak was soaked with blood. He shed it quickly, tossing it aside as if it were full of some foul sickness he couldn't get rid of quickly enough. He sat back on his haunches and clenched his eyes tight against the misery and desolation he felt was consuming his entire mind and body.

And when he opened his eyes, the corridor was complete blackness.

He shook his head in disbelief and rubbed his eyes vigorously, hoping to summon the light. But all he accomplished was smearing his face with oghul blood. Still the blackness surrounded him.

Even the orange glow of the dragon below would be a blessed relief.

But everything was so . . . *quiet* . . .

He crawled away from the dead oghul, crawled back toward the rim of the cavern, feeling along the stone floor for his bow, wanting to be careful not to knock it over the edge. When he found the weapon, he snatched it hungrily from the floor, clutched it tightly to his chest. Relief flooded him as he knelt there at the edge of the black pit, stroking Gisela's name carved into the stock.

A complete and utter silence now shrouded the darkness all around. It was unnerving. He could hear no noise from below, no dragon roars or hissings or oghul curses or scales sliding against stone or silver-skull-faced knights. It was as if the nameless beast of the underworld down in the depths of the cavern had never existed.

*I've got to leave this horrid place! I've got to leave it now!*

He strapped the bow to his back and searched his quiver. It was empty of arrows. *Where did they go? There were two! Two arrows!* He scooted forward, hands against the stone floor of the tunnel, searching for the arrows, hoping they hadn't fallen into the pit.

He scooted toward the edge, hands feeling the coarse stone under him in the dark, expecting to find the rim of the cavern right there nearby. But he felt nothing but solid stone floor. He reached forward, warily, hands searching for the rim. Still he found nothing, naught but a rough stone floor, no ledge, no drop-off that he was expecting.

*But the bow landed right on the lip of the cavern!* his mind screamed. *I haven't moved!* He frantically searched for the ridge he knew *had* to be there, crawling in the direction he knew it to be, heart pounding. He scrambled to the right, finding the solid wall of the passageway rising above, then crawled to the left, finding a similar stone wall. But there was no ledge dropping off to the underworld. No dragon below. Just darkness.

And hunger. The hunger and thirst hit him like the punch from the oghul. He panicked. *Keep your body nourished, for the wraiths will eat away at a starved mind,* claimed *The Way and Truth of Laijon.* He had heard Bishop Tolbret read that passage of scripture from the pulpit many times. *The wraiths!* Culpa had warned him. *And Skulls!*

He whirled and scrambled back toward the dead oghul he'd left in the corridor behind him, hoping to find food, even if it was naught but oghul gruel or rat meat in the dead fellow's pockets. He crawled over the stone floor, cautiously searching with his hands again, searching for the dead oghul, crawled and crawled, slowly, weaving as he went, searching, feeling for the passageway walls on either side. Ten paces, then twenty, and thirty, and then a hundred . . .

. . . and he never found the oghul, or the half-helm he'd used to crush its face. It was as if the dead beast had simply roused itself and walked away . . .

. . . *or the dead beast had never existed at all!*

Stefan struggled to stand. The excruciating pain in his ankle was almost unbearable as he put weight on his foot. Still, he limped into the blackness, not knowing where he was, but knowing he had to escape this place of sheer madness and despair. Culpa Barra's words were ringing in his ears. *Guard your mind against the wraiths. These mines are a living and breathing place, an evil dungeon liable to play tricks with your mind if you are not watchful.*

*Laijon is the defender of all who have faith and will lead them forth unto light,*
*for those who reject faith are the patrons of the underworld. Slay the unfaithful*
*wherever ye ensnare them, for unbelief is worse than slaughter. Such is the*
*reward for those who mock faith.*
—The Way and Truth of Laijon

# CHAPTER FORTY-SIX

# NAIL

16th Day of the Angel Moon, 999th Year of Laijon
Southeast of Sky Lochs, Gul Kana

Though the late spring sun sailed high overhead, the northern mountain air was still wintry. Brittle talons of cold wind raked Nail's face as he carried Val-Draekin down the grassy slope. Many miles and days Nail had borne the injured Vallè on his back. The Vallè's arms were wrapped around his chest and neck, splinted leg dangling at his side.

Nail ignored the pain of his own battered and scarred bare feet. The grass underfoot was sun-scorched and salted with dandelions that struggled in the stiff currents. The hill they descended led to a winding ravine lined with tall pine and aspen, a gurgling brook its centerpiece. It was here that they planned to stop for the night and look after their wounds.

Nail was glad to be free of the glacier. Still, it had been a miserable five days since they'd left it behind. No warm clothes. No food or supplies or weapons or even blankets to sleep under. They'd mostly wandered about, lost in the steep mountains and valleys below the lochs, even hiding yestermorn in a brush thicket as a passing band of oghuls stomped about, searching for game.

Nail figured they hadn't traveled far. He could still see the white glistening bulk of D'Nahk lè behind them to the north and west. When the Vallè had insisted on walking himself, Nail still had to help the fellow limp along. In the end, it was just easier for Nail to carry the Vallè, who likely weighed half what Zane had. The going was quicker too.

They'd decided pretty early on to head for Amadon, figuring they would be of scant use to Seita, Stefan, and Culpa Barra at Deadwood Gate. That is, if the three still lived. Or if they could even find them. From Nail's perspective it seemed all was lost, the quest a complete failure. Their first day free of the glacier, Val-Draekin had wanted to steal some horses. But what few lone huts and abandoned camps they'd stumbled upon had been completely bereft of either pony or horse, food or supplies of any kind. Their second day free of the glacier, Val-Draekin had knelt at the edge of a small gurgling stream and snatched out a small mountain pike. The Shroud of the Vallè they'd previously used to light fires long since spent, Val-Draekin got a fire sparked the old-fashioned way, with kindling and sparks from striking stones together. They buried the coals of their fire in the dirt and slept atop them that night, an old Vallè survival trick.

Their conversations involved mostly small talk of Nail's youth, growing up with Shawcroft and the drudgery of mining. Nail had described his adventure on the grayken-hunting ship, shared stories of his friendship with Stefan, Dokie, and Liz Hen. The Vallè had recounted stories of his own life growing up in Val Vallè, how he had fallen in love with Seita's sister, Breita, and how he missed her.

Nail had said nothing of the Vallè assassin Shawcroft had murdered, the girl who had looked exactly like Seita. He'd often wondered if that Bloodwood had been Breita. He did ask Val-Draekin what he knew of Bloodwood assassins. "Dirty killers not to be trusted" was all the Vallè had said.

Despite their hardships, Nail enjoyed Val-Draekin's company. He felt a deep bond had formed between them. They had saved each other's life numerous times within that icy hell of the glacier. And Nail would not soon forget that. It was why he'd carried Val-Draekin over the rugged terrain without complaint. He refused to leave his companion. He still felt guilt over Zane's death. Guilt over Roguemoore's and Shawcroft's also. Too many had already died because of him, because of who he was, because of his choices.

He would not give up on another friend.

Once within the embrace of the trees at the bottom of the ravine, Val-Draekin slid gently from Nail's back and leaned against a tall aspen. Nail went straight to the crystal waters of the rushing brook and drank. He scrubbed the crusted blood from the top of each foot, cleaned the wounds on the soles of his feet. He had never before appreciated shoes and boots as much as he had these last five days of hiking without them. The soles of his feet were like raw meat, twigs and pebbles and shards of rock embedded deep. Tears sprang to his eyes as he tended to the myriad of wounds.

Val-Draekin, sitting in his shredded leather armor, his back against the aspen, unwrapped his makeshift splint. The leg underneath was swollen. Nail had learned that the Vallè healed three times faster than humans. Depending on the severity of the break, a broken leg on a human could take six weeks to six moons to heal, but only weeks to two moons for a Vallè.

Ever since he'd met Val-Draekin and Seita, there had been something almost magical about the two Vallè, and Nail wasn't surprised about anything he learned of them. It seemed they did everything better than humans. Especially fighting.

"I felt inadequate around Seita." Nail sat across from Val-Draekin, leaning his own weary back against a lone aspen deadfall, stretching his sore legs, massaging his own ankles. The grove was dappled with thickets of thorn bushes and scrub oak. Good concealment. "The way she fought in the mines. I was literally in awe."

"She *is* fierce," Val Draekin said. "Seita is the best fighter I know."

"How did she get so good?" Nail muttered. "How can *I* get that good?"

"You tend to freeze up in a fight," Val-Draekin said. "And you wear down early. Those are your weaknesses. Concentration and stamina are the keys for one your size."

"I fought Jenko Bruk with the ax just fine," Nail countered, hurt by the Vallè's sudden harsh criticism of his fighting skills. "I beat Jenko."

Val-Draekin said, "Still, the fact is, that ax got taken from you."

Nail felt his brow furrow in anger.

"When it comes to blade-to-blade combat," Val-Draekin said, "I can teach you how to concentrate on the task at hand, not become distracted by your own thoughts and worries, and stay focused on the fight."

Nail knew the Vallè was right. He had been so distracted in the fight against the oghuls in the mines. He felt everyone had contributed to that victory but him. *Shawcroft preached patience and precision in all things. Hawkwood too.*

"Hawkwood claimed I needed to leave my troubles at the edge of the battlefield."

"Good advice," Val-Draekin said.

"Thing is . . ." Nail wondered how much he should say. "When I held *Forgetting Moon*, wielded it against Jenko, it felt like the ax belonged to me, like it was destined to be mine." He met the curious gaze of the dark-haired Vallè. "I felt *magic* in it."

"Magic, you say?" Val-Draekin rubbed grass and dirt over the wounds on his own injured feet, a ritual he had done every night.

"The power of suggestion can make one see things where there may not be anything to see."

"What do you mean?"

"What did Shawcroft tell you of the ax before you found it in the mines?"

"Nothing at all. He didn't tell me what I would find in those mines, much less any mention of an ax." Nail tried to recall his master's last words. "He did say something about precious things hidden beneath the ground, buried weapons that ancient kings had forged, and those who search the deep finding their salvation."

"Exactly." Val-Draekin nodded. "And that alone, combined with what seeds Roguemoore and Godwyn planted about your heritage, would imply there was something special about that ax and its connection to you."

"Is there not?"

"'Twas merely the power of suggestion made you think that ax was magic. I doubt you felt or saw a thing. Or if you did, it could be easily explained as something else."

"Like what?"

"Mere coincidence."

Nail did not like the Vallè questioning what he had seen with his own eyes, felt with his own heart; what he *knew* to be true. "I saw it, the magic. Tendrils of blue light snaking up the hilt of the ax as I wielded it. Right before I struck Jenko. *He* saw it too."

"Do you even know what it was you both saw?"

"I know what I saw," he answered defensively. "I cannot deny it."

"I'm only saying, perhaps another explanation exists for those tendrils of misty blue light. Some science behind the mystery?"

"What is *science*, some Vallè word?"

"Science." Val-Draekin let the word flow like music off his tongue. "'Tis a gift from the stars, that which in time explains all things mysterious."

The answer was nonsense. Bottom line, Nail did not want his memories, much less his beliefs about himself, being thrown into question. Wielding that ax had made him feel special like nothing or no one ever had, made him feel important, connected to greater things, divine things. He hated to see that memory besmirched with the cynicism and skepticism of someone who hadn't even been there.

Val-Draekin said, "As we discussed in the glacier, there are many secrets that have been kept from you, Nail. Roguemoore imagined you to be one of great import. And he hinted of it numerous times. But all he ever offered were hints. Did you not find that odd?"

"Of course I found that odd." Nail could feel the frustration boiling up within him again. "I know he was hiding something. That he knew more than he let on."

"He planted seeds and dangled hints in front of you for a purpose, Nail."

"Why?"

"Because those most devious know the power of suggestion is more powerful than reality. Reality can be brutally disappointing, whereas there resides limitless possibility in mere suggestion. It is the driving force behind belief and faith."

"Are you saying that Roguemoore and Godwyn and Culpa and Hawkwood are all wrong? Are you saying I am just a nobody?"

"It is what we do with our own selves that defines us. Not where we came from. Or who gave us birth."

"According to holy writ, a bastard is nothing in the eyes of Laijon."

"Those are no more than old words likely written by addled old men. You needn't pay *The Way and Truth of Laijon* any mind."

"How can I ignore it?" He felt Ava Shay's turtle carving against his chest and thought of her. He even remembered things she had said to him. *It must be sad, always belonging to people.*

He met Val-Draekin's hard gaze. "They may likely just be old words written by addled old men as you say, but they are still words read to every child in Gul Kana. And every child grows to be a man or woman who is more than happy to enforce the rules behind those words. Which leaves little place for a bastard. So even if I do not subscribe to those words, as one who is fatherless, how can I just ignore them? They affect me daily. In the eyes of Laijon, I do not matter. Slaves do not matter. Believe me, as someone who has lived it, because of what is written in *The Way and Truth of Laijon*, the father-less feel like they do not really even exist." He looked up into the trees. "It *is* sad, always belonging to people."

Val-Draekin shifted his position against the aspen, rewrapping his splint as he spoke. "Just so you don't think you are alone in this, Roguemoore imagined me to be one of great import too, both of us linked to his cause. Or so he cleverly suggested."

Nail was so tired, every muscle and bone in his body spent and weary and sore. He remembered what Hawkwood had told him about his parentage in Ravenker, wondered now if any of it was real. *Only the youngest Raijael can be the Angel Prince.* Under the glacier, he had already told Val-Draekin what Hawkwood had said about that.

"Why would the White Prince hunt me?" He voiced the question out loud. "If I am of such scant importance as you say, why did Aeros Raijael attack Gallows Haven? Liz Hen claimed Aeros asked about Shawcroft, asked about me. I heard Baron Bruk say things with my own ears. He said I bore great resemblance to someone important. I even found the note Shawcroft wrote, the note that talked of my scars and tattoos." He stared hard at the dark-eyed Vallè sitting in front of him, willing him to answer with the truth. "What do you know of it all?"

"And how did the scars and tattoos come about?"

Nail explained how he'd gotten the mark of the cross on the back of his right hand when Dokie was struck by lightning, how the mer-maid had raked his arm underwater, how Stefan had tattooed him, how the red-haired warrior woman from Sør Sevier had branded him a slave. He reiterated how Shawcroft thought the marks of great significance.

Just talking of the markings made them flare with a strange heated soreness, uncomfortable even here in this cold place.

"And what do you think of the scars and tattoos?" Val-Draekin asked.

He had never considered his own thoughts on the subject. "They are unique to me, these scars and marks; I suppose I wear them with pride. They are important, if you must know. I feel they were also destined for me. Omens of a sort, for good or for ill I do not know."

"I say they are naught but random coincidence," the Vallè countered with a certain measure of cruel indifference. "And you only attach significance to the marks and scars and tattoos because of the power of suggestion."

"You seem quick to belittle everything about me at all times." Nail hung his head.

"I only want you to accept the *truth*," Val-Draekin said. "Fact is, there could be any number of folks currently bearing a slave brand, a crosslike scar, and injuries from a mermaid, or a combination of two or three, or none."

"How can you be so certain?"

"I'm not. But you asked what I thought of your scars and tattoos. I say they are meaningless. Naught but misty blue light on a battle-ax."

"Really? I don't know what that means."

"The power of suggestion is a trick, a trick as simple as making fire appear using a pinch of white powder and a snap of the fingers."

Nail was stung by the brutal frankness of the Vallè's opinion. *Maybe it's better to just have people lie to you and spare your feelings.*

He couldn't help but stare with trepidation at the dark-haired fellow before him, wondering just who his traveling companion was, what secrets he hid. For all his honesty, Val-Draekin seemed the most mysterious of anyone he had ever met.

"The power of suggestion." Val-Draekin met his gaze coolly. "If what Hawkwood suggested is correct, and let's say certain people really believe that you are the youngest son of Aevrett Raijael, particularly if Aeros believes this, then of course the White Prince would want you dead. You are Aeros' greatest threat. You, Nail, may very well be the reason he marched across the breadth of Adin Wyte and Wyn Darrè, destroying and killing all in his path. Aeros may have attacked and destroyed two kingdoms based solely on the mere suggestion that you are in reality the Angel Prince and he is not."

Every word the Vallè spoke haunted Nail.

Val-Draekin met his gaze with firm resolve, saying, "So, as it turns out, you really are important . . . but merely through the power of suggestion. The question is, who planted that suggestion in Aeros' mind and why?"

The Vallè's assertion chased away Nail's previous sense of fatigue, replacing it with anger and a deep-rooted guilt. *Lives lost because of me. Hundreds of thousands. Perhaps millions.*

With sharpened senses, he looked around the small aspen grove. The wind had died, and a light cloud of dust hung for a time in the still air above their ravine. "But is it all real?" he murmured to himself, almost inaudibly.

Val-Draekin heard his soft pronouncement. "Aeros believes he is Raijael reincarnated, the second coming of Laijon's son in the flesh. And if you are who people *suggest* you are, he wants you dead. According to the prophecy in *The Chivalric Illuminations of Raijael*, in the last days before Fiery Absolution, the Angel Prince and his armies will converge upon Amadon and reap great slaughter. *The Moon Scrolls of Mia* talk of the Five Warrior Angels returning to the Five Isles and staving off the Angel Prince's crusade. Aeros Raijael does not want to see the return of the Five Warrior Angels. And you represent the return of the Five Warrior Angels, and the destruction of all his plans."

"And that's what this is all about, our quest?" He thought of the dwarf lost in the glacier. "Roguemoore's quest was to retrieve the weapons of the Five Warrior Angels, so we can stave off Aeros' attack?"

"Or so Roguemoore and the Brethren of Mia believe," Val-Draekin answered.

"It's all so messy," Nail said. "Naught but madness. *The Way and Truth of Laijon*. The Brethren of Mia. *The Chivalric Illuminations of Raijael*. None of it adds up. Like you said before, all likely just the mad ramblings and writings of old men."

"Yes, and as you so perfectly stated before, Nail, people believe those mad ramblings and writings. People like Roguemoore and Godwyn and even your friends Liz Hen and Dokie. They all of them believe in a version of this madness. Even you believe to a certain extent, especially regarding those things that have been suggested in your mind. Things cleverly planted there over time." Val-Draekin paused but a moment before ending with, "Roguemoore and Godwyn believed you to be one of the Five Warrior Angels returned, Nail."

A thrill crawled up Nail's spine. *One of the Five Warrior Angels returned?*

Was the Vallè just toying with him now?

*The power of suggestion . . .*

Val-Draekin went on, undaunted. "They also believed I am one of the Five Warrior Angels returned. And Hawkwood too, and Jondralyn Bronachell, and a fellow named Squireck Van Hester. Together the five of us were the Slave, Thief, Assassin, Princess, and Gladiator. The Brethren of Mia's plan was to gather us together along with the weapons of the Five Warrior Angels before Fiery Absolution." The Vallè's cold glance continued to cut into the night. "But it is all madness."

"What makes you think it's all madness?" Nail challenged. "Did Hawkwood also believe in the gathering of the Five Warrior Angels?"

Val-Draekin sharpened his gaze, now focusing on Nail. "Close to Hawkwood, were you?"

*Hawkwood saved my life,* Nail thought. *Hawkwood told me at least something about my parentage. Whether it was true or not . . . it was at least something.* But he didn't put voice to any of that.

It appeared he didn't need to, for the Vallè seemed almost to read his mind. "You felt Hawkwood was the first one to speak truth to you, truth of your destiny. A destiny you have been seeking your entire life. A destiny not even you or Roguemoore or any of the rest of them can fully fathom."

*How could he know what Hawkwood said that day in Ravenker?* It seemed everyone insisted on speaking to him in riddles. And Nail was weary of it. In many ways, conversing with Val-Draekin was the most maddening of all.

"What is prophecy?" the Vallè asked. "Your *Way and Truth of Laijon* is rife with it. As is Sør Sevier's *Chivalric Illuminations*, and the Brethren's *Moon Scrolls of Mia*. Even the oghuls have their Hragna'Ar prophecies of rape and pillage and the awakening of the nameless beasts of the underworld and skull-faced monsters. And all these numerous prophecies have their similarities. Yet they all contradict too. A convoluted mess. Legend and prophecy are so common as to be cheap. They all cause division, confusion, hatred. They all talk of war and glory and conquest and revenge in the name of Laijon, in the name of the Five Warrior Angels. 'Warrior' is even in their celebrated name. You're right, Nail, it is messy. It is madness. *The Way and Truth of Laijon* is full of naught but contradictions. At the time of Fiery Absolution, *The Way and Truth of Laijon* clearly states that those of the Church of Laijon must fight to stave off invasion, but at the same time, according to the same book, the White Prince must reach Amadon to fulfill Fiery Absolution. Two opposing commands. And in the end, many will die so that Fiery Absolution may take place at the appointed time in the appointed place, and the lands of Gul

Kana will be destroyed to the point that it will be in no more need of saving than Wyn Darrè or Adin Wyte. And the really twisted thing is, if you *don't* believe that there is to be a Fiery Absolution, that there is going to be a return of the Five Warrior Angels, then you are not *really* a true believer and damned in the eyes of your kin. *The Way and Truth of Laijon* and its myriad prophecies of doom and war and Absolution quite clearly want us all to perish. The book itself seeks the end of the Five Isles with a deep yearning. King Jovan and the grand vicar and five archbishops and all men of that ilk cannot wait for the end; they cannot wait for it all to be over and their prophecies fulfilled. The notion of Fiery Absolution is a hateful idea and a hideous thing. Even Aeros Raijael fights and kills and crusades for his own slightly different version of the same horrid notion."

Pure anger crept into the Vallè's eyes. "To most humans, it seems religious ideologies are easier to fight and die for than even friends and family. . . ."

The Vallè was now giving Nail a hard and merciless stare, as if the entire mess were indeed his fault. "We are only guaranteed this one life, Nail. And this one life is too short and precious to wait for the second comings of Warrior Angels that may or may not exist, or worse, to hasten them to fruition through violence and war. When the truth is, there will likely be no miracles or saviors in the end. . . ."

He trailed off again, face softening some. Then went on. "At least the Vallè educated themselves about all creeds and belief systems rather than blindly following one set of tenets. At least the Vallè can see the absurdity of them all. We have known this secret for centuries. Yesterday's beliefs and legends and prophecies should not be revered nor sought after. Yesterday's wars should not matter today. Yesterday's heroes should be forgotten and not worshipped. Why follow the beliefs of our grandfathers? Because they followed the beliefs of theirs. Who is to say they were ever right?"

Nail stated, "But Roguemoore believed you yourself were one of the Five Warrior Angels returned. Does that not mean anything?"

"Does it mean anything to know that the dwarf believed the same of you?"

Nail had always wanted to believe there was something extraordinary about himself. It was just the way orphans and bastards thought—that there was a great destiny awaiting them somewhere. So of course it was easy to think that he might very well be one of the Five Warrior Angels returned. It was heady, fanciful stuff.

Yet he also knew, the realities of a bastard's life were far removed from fantasy.

"It will not be self-righteous blind faith in Warrior Angels that will save the Five Isles," Val-Draekin continued, "but rather those with humble doubt, those who take it upon themselves to hone the strength of their own will and intellect and fight against the power of suggestion, fight against faith and blind belief . . ."

He paused again, reflective. Then carried on, "But that is unlikely to happen. I know the nature of humankind."

"And what is our nature?"

"That when it comes to faith, what men fear most is the truth they already know in their hearts, yet deny."

"What do you mean?"

"They know it is all false. Their beliefs. The fanciful tales and fables and miracles of the past written down in ancient texts. They know deep down it is all nonsense. Yet still they *believe*. And the cycle of madness and delusion will never cease. It just doesn't matter. Destroy all scripture? I think not. Everything can be redone. Everything is endless. The disfunction and folly will go on until mankind . . . until mankind is no more."

Nail thought about the Vallè's words. "So if you truly feel this way, why did you and Seita go along with Roguemoore's quest to find such ancient and meaningless weapons and angel stones? Why risk your life for such folly?"

"The thrill of it." Val-Draekin's answer was swift and casual. "For the adventure. It is just what we Vallè do." A crooked, mischievous smile spread over his face. "This adventure is just part of the game we have played for generations, the game we Vallè have played for centuries . . . the game we all still play. It is a game against human nature, a game to master the power of suggestion."

"But you've nearly died many times on this adventure, for this *game*. Seems like a risk for nothing. You can never know what will happen."

"Correct." Val-Draekin's answer came more slowly this time, more calculated in its delivery. "You see, illusion surrounds us, Nail. That is part of the game. None of us can know what will happen, not even up until that very last moment of our lives. And then, in the end, what you saw . . . might not even be what you thought you saw."

*Be mindful: the Vallè worship no man; they worship only the power of the witch.*
*They worship their game. They worship at the altar of a human woman they*
*claim changed into a Vallè. A miracle it was. A biological impossibility that the*
*Vallè claim will one day happen again. . . .*
—THE BOOK OF THE BETRAYER

## CHAPTER FORTY-SEVEN

# CRYSTALWOOD

16TH DAY OF THE ANGEL MOON, 999TH YEAR OF LAIJON
ROKENWALDER, SØR SEVIER

The ribbon had been returned! Krista Aulbrek crept through the silence that shrouded the Rokenwalder dungeon, bare feet making not a sound. Gault's blue ribbon was again tied around her ankle. She felt more confident with it there.

The passageway between her cell and Borden Bronachell's was hung with absolute darkness, a suffocating blackness she had grown used to over the last handful of days—she'd lost all comprehension of time. One measured step after the next, her breathing even and precise, Krista moved assuredly, her heart rate only slightly elevated. Despite the total darkness, over the last few days even the smallest movement, gesture, or breath from the bearded man in the cell across from her had become somehow visible. Her awareness of every tick and sound in the dungeon was to the point that she could tell which of Bogg's gaolers walked the corridor just by the rhythm and shuffle of their feet. And she figured that over five years in captivity, Borden had grown even more attuned to the silence.

She had been patient with the gold coin Squateye had slipped her, meticulously rubbing it against the rough corners of her cell for days, soundlessly working it down into the shape she desired, a lock pick sufficient for her two main needs: escaping her cell, and killing Borden Bronachell. Her newly fashioned needlelike weapon driven far enough into the man's eye would do the trick.

She owed it all to Squateye. It had been less suspicious for the dwarf to smuggle a coin for her to shape into her tool, than smuggle an actual lock pick or knife. And once she had fashioned a pick from the coin, it had taken Krista only about fifteen minutes to be free of her collar and to open the lock to her own cell. She took painstaking caution in pushing open the rusty-hinged metal door. Escaping ropes and chains, breaking out of cages and cells, picking locks, these things had never been her strong suit. But she moved with confidence now.

With her own rank and stuffy cell now several steps behind her, the thin, deadly instrument of her long toil clenched in her fist, she drifted ever closer to the man's cell, mind focused on the next task— murder. Silently she crept. The injury she'd suffered from the heavy iron maul of the Knight Chivalric was still a dull ache in her chest and stomach. She had healed some and felt immeasurably better, but her entire midsection was tender to the touch, breathing a chore.

Once at Borden's cell, Krista leaned her right shoulder against two of the vertical bars, settling herself into the perfect position. The leverage against the two bars felt just right. All was soundless, but for the snoring drifting from the back of the cell. With long hours of muscle memory built into her delicate fingers, she painstakingly slipped the lock pick into the mechanism. *Similar lock . . . fifteen minutes should be all . . .*

With each guttural snore from Borden, she eased the shard of coin farther into the lock. When her thin tool passed the first slender metal tine, she stopped, waited for another snore, then eased it farther in, feeling the first tiny click of many.

Borden's rhythmic snoring reverberated from the back of his cell. He slept against the far wall nightly. In the few times the gaolers had walked through the corridor with torches, Krista had studied her own cell, and also the cell across from her. They were identical in size. She knew—once she had Borden's door opened—just how many paces it would take to reach her prey. His snoring continued. So did she, working the lock, the rhythm of the man's heavy breathing relaxing her. She rested the side of her head against the two vertical bars above her shoulder, easing the lock pick ever inward. Slow and smooth. The snoring grew in volume.

*A sound . . .*

*The click of the lock . . .*

Her mind barely registered the movement. But when she felt Borden's skeletal, cold fingers wrap around her neck, she yanked the lock pick straight out of the mechanism and stabbed the back of his hand. His grip only tightened.

And Krista instantly knew she was in trouble.

Borden Bronachell had her head pinned against the bars, strong fingers pressing hard against spots right under both of her ears, the spot her Sacrament of Souls had taught her would close off the carotid arteries and cause a person to black out almost instantly, the spot that if enough pressure was used, could cause instant death.

The thought scarcely had time to flitter through her brain before she felt herself fall into blackness, morbidly intrigued at the speed with which she lost consciousness.

† † † † †

The unspeakable foul putridity that jerked Krista into half wakefulness was beyond unholy. She had taken a whiff of Dugal's smelling salts several times before, a nasty concoction meant to rouse a person from faking unconsciousness or death. It was horrid. But whatever she had just inhaled was ten times worse.

She heard sloshing sounds and grunts. Torchlight flickered from a stained cobbled ceiling—a cobbled ceiling that slid above her in jerky motions. It dripped with water, and brown sludge. *Or just my wicked imaginings to match the stench.* Bile rose up in her throat, and she vomited from the surrounding stink. It was then she realized her mouth was gagged. Vomit shot from her nostrils and seemed to burst straight out the corners of her eyes. Panicking, she retched and then struggled for breath.

"Take the gag off," a familiar voice said from somewhere behind her, or above her, or both. The gag was removed and cool water dumped over her face. The puke-sopping gag was swiftly replaced and cinched tight.

Still feeling like she was suffocating, Krista could barely grab a breath through her clogged nose. She lay on her back in her prison garb, arms pinned to her sides, body wrapped in rope. She couldn't quite orient herself or get a grip on the flickering reality—or unreality—moving jerkily above. *Is it a ceiling?* Then, in a brief moment of lucidity, she realized that someone was gripping her under the armpits, dragging her through a tunnel of sludge, black and brown chunks of filth that lapped up over her bound legs.

"She stuck that poker into my hand enough times before she dropped," a second voice said, also somewhat familiar. *Borden Bronachell!*

"But the needle she made of that coin," the original voice said. "It worked on that lock just like I said it would, no?" It was Squateye speaking.

"Worked on opening the sewer grating too," Borden continued. "Slipping her the coin worked. You are the truest of friends. But your dungeons of Rokenwalder proved easy to break out of, with the right tool. Not like Purgatory under the Hall of the Dayknights in Amadon. Now that's a prison no man can escape."

"I wouldn't be so sure."

"Purgatory is impenetrable."

"Truth is," Squateye said, "most dungeons are a joke. All of them have their weaknesses." A moment of silence as they dragged her along, and then the dwarf continued, "Bogg was growing suspicious. We needed to act fast."

"Just as long as these wounds on my hand don't get infected in this sewer."

The only thing keeping Krista somewhat awake was the murderous odor blanketing her, but she felt herself quickly losing consciousness.

The dwarf said, "We must get her to Wyn Darrè as swiftly as possible. Seabass and what he may have gleaned from *The Angel Stone Codex* await us."

"Does she know the truth?"

"Dugal and Aevrett treated her like a pet, both controlling her for opposing purposes, both keeping her from her real destiny."

"Bogg is not easily duped, Ironcloud."

"Aye, he will know of your escape by now. He knows these sewers as well as I. He and his pet may very well be awaiting us when we spill from them, shit-stained and dirty, into the bay."

"And I hear his pet is even deadlier than her . . . but we need him too."

Krista felt her mind drifting, the two voices continuing their conversation. The reek of the place was so overpowering. The two ethereal and dreamlike voices talked of nothing and everything, not much of it making any logical sense now.

Before she lost all awareness, Krista imagined they were talking of Dugal and Bogg, talking as if her master and the dungeon warden were the same.

† † † † †

Krista woke abruptly, gasping for breath, her entire body plunging into ice-cold water. Clear thought instantly assaulted her brain. She struggled, her arms and legs still bound. Then her head broke the rippling skin of Straits of Sevier. The night sky above was moonless—a velvety, impenetrable black. A stout wooden quay was within arm's reach, tendrils of low mist spilling over it, thick with the bitter stink of the sewers. The buildings of the city rose above the shadowy dock, grim and tall amidst a faint haze of fog. The uppermost window of the stone tower behind the dock glinted a pale yellow, reflecting square patches of light back into the choppy waters around her.

Coarse hands grasped Krista around the waist, brushing at her rough-spun prison garb, scrubbing, washing. She could sense the chunks of shit and sewer filth floating and bobbing in the surrounding waves. In the commotion, the gag around her mouth had come loose. But before she could call out for help, she was hauled from the water and dumped forcefully into the bottom of a wooden skiff among two long oars and an iron anchor. The gag was lashed tightly over her mouth again, and the ropes securing her arms to her body pulled tight.

Krista rolled onto her side in the bottom of the boat, gazed up at her captors with a hard, pointed stare. The gruff visage of the dwarf, Squateye, loomed above, two narrow eyes glinting down on her in the faint light of the moon—his black eye patch was gone.

Borden Bronachell stood just behind the dwarf. He gave her no more than a passing glance, then bent over bulwark, unhooking the skiff from the dock. He gave a powerful shove and the boat drifted from the quay. Krista kept her cold gaze trained on Squateye, wondering at his betrayal, wondering at his game. *Or is his name Ironcloud?* By the look in his squinting eyes, Krista could tell the dwarf knew what she was thinking.

*Does he not know nothing escapes Dugal's awareness, nothing escapes*

*Dugal's grasp. Especially something as majestic as this—an escape from the dungeons of Rokenwalder and the capture of one of his precious Bloodwoods.* One thing was certain: Borden Bronachell would soon be a dead man. And the dwarf would suffer worse.

Behind Squateye, Borden was unfurling the sail.

A streaking shadow launched itself from the dock straight into the boat, crashing into the man. Borden and the shadow landed hard in the bottom of the skiff next to Krista, clawing and fighting.

The shadow was Hans Rake, Bloodwood daggers flashing like lightning in both hands as he struck at the man. To Krista's surprise, Borden blocked the blows as quickly as Hans could strike, and he threw the boy off. Together they stood, Hans backing away from Borden, wary, his glaring eyes meeting the other older man's challenge.

Squateye snatched one of the oars from the bottom of the boat and swung. Hans ducked under the blow. He dove on top of Krista, his black blades suddenly punching into her chest and neck and arms. "Bastard!" Borden yelled.

Krista could do nothing to stop his unexpected assault but roll onto her side, stunned, bleeding, the pain sharp and harsh. *What poisons I cannot tell. Or 'twas just the frosty sting of a naked Bloodwood blade piercing warm flesh over . . .*

There was a loud *thump*. Hans slumped unconscious and slid off her. Borden Bronachell looming over the boy, a second oar clutched in his hands.

"Ain't never seen a man best a Bloodwood like that, much less two Bloodwoods in one day." Squateye dragged Hans' limp body away from Krista, eyes on Borden. "You blocked his blows with naught but your forearms. Had you a blade of your own, I reckon Shadowwood would be dead, rather than knocked out cold." The dwarf hauled Hans up by the armpits, shoving the limp body against the side of the skiff. "Help me throw him over."

"No." Borden tossed the oar down. He jerked a coil of rope from under the sidewall. "I told you we needed him too. He will be of more use to us alive." He began wrapping the rope around Hans' inert form. "We need all of Dugal's pets."

"I'm not sure it wouldn't be best to just kill them both now." The dwarf helped with the rope. "Now that they are both disabled. You continually surprise me, Borden. I only knew one man ever bested a Bloodwood. And that man was Ser Roderic Raybourne."

"Lest you forget," Borden said, "I taught Shawcroft everything he knows."

Borden secured Hans, binding him the same as Krista was bound, arms tight to his body, legs tied together at the ankles. When he was done, his eyes cut through the darkness toward the dock. "It's Bogg," he announced.

"Aye." Squateye looked toward the wooden quay. "You mean Dugal."

"One and the same," Borden whispered. "Like Squateye and Ironcloud. Two people at once."

Krista levered herself into a sitting position, blood pooling under her. Hans had poked her good. She could barely see over the bulwark. The dock was now fifty feet away, shrouded in shadowy mist. But she could clearly see the blocky form of Bogg. His vile dog, Café Colza, circled at his feet. She breathed deep. A stab of pain arched through her and she swooned, clenching her eyes shut.

And when she opened her eyes, the scene on the dock had changed. Bogg was gone. She spied the unmistakable silhouette of her master standing there in the gloomy shadow where Bogg had been. Black Dugal stood tall. He stood in a position of both coiled restraint and looming threat, eyes like faint red slits. His Bloodeye stallion was there with him, its breath a white pluming mist, eyes like blazing coals biting through the night. But neither Dugal nor his mount stirred as the boat drifted away from the wooden quay. Still, Squateye and Borden looked on, concerned.

But something was in the water, splashing its way toward the boat.

Krista couldn't see what it was. Her strength failed and she slumped back down, head cracking against the hard bottom of the boat. The pain in her chest and arms was almost too much to bear. She could feel warm blood seep from the many holes Hans had created.

"We must tend to her." Squateye pressed thick hands to her wounds, attempting to stanch the flow of blood. Krista barely registered what was happening. She felt grim sleep creeping over her. *How must Dread be doing without me?* A deep sleep from which she feared she would never awake. *Has the Bloodeye missed my nuzzles against her neck?*

Her eyes fogged over. She breathed, a panicked breath, blood gurgling up her throat. Her foggy eyes were trained on Borden Bronachell, wondering if he would help Squateye. "Help me tend to her, Borden," the dwarf said. "It's more than a ten-day journey to Wynix. Maybe longer if the winds are light. And I doubt Tyus Barra will have many medicines with him."

"'Tis Culpa's young cousin will be meeting us?" Borden asked. "The one you say is mute?"

"Aye, the mute."

"That damned dog is swimming out toward us," Borden's voice rolled over the boat as if from a great distance.

"Café Colza Bouledogue?" The dwarf's concerned voice questioned from somewhere deep in Krista's head. "Bloody Mother Mia, we don't need that slobbering horror anywhere near this boat."

"Even the dog can be of use...."

... And that was all she heard as the blessed blackness of sleep swept her away.

*And to bring about the end of all things, a false bishop of Laijon will sacrifice himself for one who drinks the Blood of the Dragon. 'Twill be a simple act of hanging, gone unnoticed. And only then shall the demons arise from the underworld, following what meager light glows from crooked streams of silver, liquid silver that carves glinting paths through furious hard stone, silver that legend tells shall lead all demonkind to the great above, the sun, the dawn, the rain, and the stars. Up from the underworld they shall arise, walking on the bones of the human dead.*
—THE ANGEL STONE CODEX

# CHAPTER FORTY-EIGHT
# BISHOP HUGH GODWYN

### 17TH DAY OF THE ANGEL MOON, 999TH YEAR OF LAIJON
### STANCLYFFE, GUL KANA

Beer Mug padded along the gritty streets of Stanclyffe just ahead of Godwyn and Liz Hen and the mules. The shepherd dog seemed to suffer no ill effects from the poison darts, looking as healthy as the day Godwyn had first met him.

Dokie Liddle was a different story. The Gallows Haven boy, secured atop one of the mules, intermittently in and out of consciousness, was barely clinging to life. It had been seven days since they'd left the glacier, six since they had fought off the oghuls in the cabin. Liz Hen had tended to the boy nightly, making sure he was well hydrated, mashing portions of food into the water, forcing him to drink in his few moments of coherency. He had survived for this long only because of her.

As Godwyn guided the two mounts past the Cloven Hoof Tavern, the ten-thousand-foot cliff rose into the gray clouds above the town like an irrepressible weight over him. He wore his cloak tight around his neck. And he could still feel the dull ache where the oghul's fangs had sunk into his flesh. Though she tried to hide it, every time Liz Hen caught sight of the purple bruising on his neck, her face would twist in disgust.

He'd heard of bloodletters' addiction to the bite of an oghul, but had never realized how real the pull of the toxin could be. *Some pleasing chemical in their fangs.* Since the incident in the cabin, the intimate desire for the euphoric feeling of the oghul's bite had smothered him—an entity more powerful than the wraiths. Both dread and anticipation filled his heart. Especially when he saw the oghul street vendor step from the door of the corner building at the end of the lane. The beast stooped over the large brick oven under a tan awning. The same woman from their previous visit was with him, a kind-looking lady, but for the gruesome bruise blossoming along the left side of her face and neck.

She spied Godwyn's group approaching and tapped her burly companion on the shoulder. The oghul's scowling brown eyes instantly found Liz Hen, focusing on the Sør Sevier longsword strapped to her hip. He stood straight. Imposing. Arms and legs like tree trunks, the brute wore a stained leather apron and a belt lined with a brace of cooking knives. As Godwyn and Liz Hen stepped under the awning, the bishop again spotted the red dot tattooed on the oghul's face just below his left eye—like a tear of blood—a sign to those who knew what foul drugs the oghul dealt in. Certain bishops of Gul Kana had a similar such secret sign, a way to tell which bishops had been anointed by the grand vicar himself in Amadon. Any holy man who did the three-fingered sign of the Laijon Cross over his heart, ending with his thumb pointed toward his navel, was one such chosen bishop to be especially revered. Godwyn himself had been anointed by the grand vicar, though he had not yet found occasion to use the signal. But such sacred signs were different from what he was dealing with now. *Bloodletting.* Before him, the oghul's grotesque purple lips were lined with deep cracks. Wiry hair burst from his scarred head in one odd clump, brows thick and unruly. Two scum-crusted fangs shot from swollen gums upward out of his mouth and up past his nose. Godwyn could almost imagine what they would feel like sinking into his flesh. *The pain . . . and then the pleasure . . .*

The oghul spat a small gray rock from his mouth onto the roadway. "Fat juicy girl come back to finally let me fhuck her?" His eyes never once left Liz Hen, his voice deep and husky. Liz Hen glared.

"Or she ghonna shtick me with that shword?" He grinned. Beer Mug growled.

The lady with the bruised neck eyed the big shepherd dog warily. "S'ist Runk don't coddle to dogs. Or cats, for that matter."

"We've brought no cats." Liz Hen's brow furrowed.

"Good." The woman turned and awkwardly curtsied to Godwyn. "Name's Mardgot." The bishop acknowledged her with a slight bow of his own.

Liz Hen's hungry eyes were fixed on the large brick oven against the outside wall of the building. It was smoking with several large hocks of ham. Godwyn was also hungry, but could scarcely break his gaze from the oghul's jutting teeth and swollen gums. *He's ready to feast.* Godwyn shuddered.

"Dokie is sick." It was a struggle just to talk; the wound on his neck was swollen and sore. Godwyn motioned to the boy tied to the swayed back of the mule.

"Sick?" the oghul asked, a curious tilt to his thick brow. "How?"

Godwyn reached into the front of his cloak and brought forth a thin silver dart—one of the poisoned needles he'd pulled from Dokie. "Have you seen its like before?"

The oghul leaned over, inspecting the silver dart. "The boy hash gone playshes he shouldn't have."

"He was struck by many such darts," Godwyn said. "He requires special medicines. You know of which medicine I speak, S'ist Runk." He touched the top of his own cheekbone, just below the corner of his eye. "Your tattoo. I know what it means. I know who you are. I know you have the medicines the boy needs."

S'ist Runk grunted, and Mardgot's face was suddenly not so kind as her gaze fell on the open neckline of Godwyn's cloak. She could clearly see the purple traces of his own bruising. Jealousy filled her eyes. S'ist Runk's brown orbs were also focused intently on the bruising on Godwyn's neck. "What potions you sheek is most precious, most exphenshive. Will take much gold coin."

"We haven't coin of any kind," Godwyn said, then swallowed hard. "But I can pay in other ways."

S'ist Runk looked at Liz Hen, grinning madly. "So you gonna let me fhuck the girl's juicy ripe twat?" A string of drool dripped from his bulbous lips.

"You know what I'm offering," Godwyn answered. "More precious than sex."

"Mardgot wont like whaht you offerhing," the oghul said.

The dark pall of jealousy that had fallen over the once kind-faced woman had turned to glaring anger.

"I offer two days' worth of my blood." Godwyn regarded the oghul with a long, meaningful stare. His sore neck was in need of relief, and the oghul's gums looked swollen, inviting. He felt one part fear, one part elation, one part anticipation. *Offering myself up like some common whore . . . more precious than sex . . .*

"The boy does loohk sick," S'ist Runk observed. "I do not think I have enough potion that you seek, though."

"We will take whatever you have."

"I only have what I have. For the rhest you must sail to Lhord's Point. I have enough to keehp him alive till then . . . maybhe."

Godwyn nodded. S'ist Runk nodded in return, looking at the woman next to him. "Prehpare the bashement." Mardgot scurried off into the building. The oghul moved toward Dokie. Beer Mug gave a low warning growl. S'ist Runk ignored the dog and pulled a long, curved knife from his belt. He cut the ropes securing Dokie to the mule, sheathed the blade, and scooped the boy up in his thick, gnarled arms. "Follow me." He brushed past Beer Mug, carrying Dokie into the building.

"Beer Mug will guard the mules," Godwyn said to Liz Hen. His heart fluttered with nerves as he hitched their two dun-colored mounts to the post just under the awning. He then grabbed the girl by the shoulders. "What you are about to see will be hard to watch, Liz Hen, but I'll need you to come with me. I will need you to stay by my side."

"I've already seen it," Liz Hen said. "Lest you forget, I was in the cabin with you that first time."

"Yes." Godwyn met her eyes. "Yes, you were."

Together they followed the oghul into the building. S'ist Runk led them across a warped wooden floor to another door at the back of the dark room. He nudged the door open with his booted foot, revealing a dimly lit hallway and a narrow set of stairs descending. The oghul took the stairs carefully, Dokie cradled in his arms. Godwyn and Liz Hen followed. The basement room they entered was damp and cold and smelled of water-rotted timber. The roof was hung low and made of long, drooping beams of dark wood. Mardgot was already there, two lit sconces in either hand, their flames aflicker.

A stone slab sat in the center of the murky room, a thick woolen blanket hastily thrown over it. S'ist Runk set the boy on the blanket. Mardgot hung the sconces on the wall. In the soft yellow light Dokie's face was sunken and white as bone, his breathing shallow. Mardgot gathered two vials of liquid from a nearby cupboard, one dark red, the other filled with what looked like water. She handed both to S'ist Runk.

"Rauthouin bane," Godwyn said aloud as the oghul uncorked the clear vial and set it on the stone slab next to the boy.

"And Blhood of the Draghon." S'ist Runk picked up the wine-colored mixture next. "Together, these potions help heahl your friend." He picked Dokie's head up in one large hand, tilted it forward, and lifted the vial to the boy's lips.

"What if it's just more poison?" Liz Hen said, frantic, her eyes boring into Godwyn. "Didn't we fight against this kind of madness in the mines? The poison he just put in Dokie is made of something named after the nameless beasts of the under—"

"Leave now!" The oghul let Dokie's head fall back down to the stone slab. "Red-head'd bitch not trust Blhood of the Draghon? This is great insult! Must leave now!"

Liz Hen's eyes were wide as dinner plates. "But—"

The beast snarled, "Only the bravehst oghul pirates shneak into the Blhoodwood Foresht to harvest Blhood of the Draghon! You will not insult them!"

Liz Hen backed away. Godwyn motioned for her to remain silent. Perhaps it had been oghul pirates who had harvested this batch, but he knew of another man who snuck into the Bloodwood Forest to collect Blood of the Dragon. A man named Praed and a band of four thieves named the Untamed. Praed was also known to deal in Blood of the Dragon.

"This bitch leaves now!" S'ist Runk snarled again, eyes fixed on Godwyn.

"Let me take a sip," Liz Hen said quickly, moving toward the table. "Let me test this stuff you are pouring into Dokie." The oghul growled.

"You do not know what Blood of the Dragon is." Godwyn stepped between her and the table. "You must not drink it."

"And Dokie should?"

"Blood of the Dragon can heal near anything, Liz Hen. But it is rare and it is dangerous. One sip can give almost anyone unnatural good health. But it comes with a heavy price."

"Let her drink." S'ist Runk thrust the vial toward Liz Hen. "Let it paint your eyes red, girl, red just like your hair."

Liz Hen snatched the vial from his gnarled fingers and put it to her lips, eyes bouncing from the oghul to Godwyn to Mardgot and back. She tilted her head back and took a quick sip, then swallowed. Then waited. Everyone stared at her as if she might burst into flame. Then her eyes widened in pleasure; Godwyn's heart sank.

*How many must the Brethren of Mia corrupt before this madness is over . . . ?*

S'ist Runk laughed. Deep and loud. "Now you won't stop whanting it, girl." He grinned wildly. "Drink more, and you will be someday become indeshtructable. That is Blhood of the Draghon." Then the oghul snatched the vial of red liquid back from her.

Liz Hen's eyes followed the vial greedily as S'ist Runk propped Dokie's head up again. The beast slapped the boy's face to rouse him into semi-wakefulness, then dumped the remainder of the wine-colored draught into his mouth. Dokie choked, but swallowed it down in several gulps, delirious and unaware of what was even happening.

The oghul removed the stopper from the second vial and poured all the clear rauthouin bane down the boy's throat too. "Enough to keep him alive for a week, maybe more." He held up both empty vials. "You musht go to Brown R'elk manor house in Lhord's Point for more Blhood of the Draghon. Brown R'elk a very rich and inflhuhential oghul tradher and alchemhist with the same tattoo under hish eye." He pointed to the red dot tattooed under his own eye.

Godwyn nodded. The oghul stared at him hungrily now, gums seemingly twice as swollen as before, swollen in anticipation of the coming feast. Godwyn loosened his cloak, revealing his swollen purple neck for S'ist Runk. *What person can face this horrid yearning torment daily and not succumb to the wraiths?* He swallowed hard, the pain in his neck nearly unbearable now, the anticipation great. "Just me," he said. "Two days' worth. Leave the girl alone. That was the deal."

S'ist Runk was on him before he could even give voice to his last request, gnarled hands seizing the back of his head, dirty fangs sinking deep into his flesh. The initial force of the beast's crushing bite struck Godwyn with breathtaking agony, what he imagined the strangle of the hangman's noose might feel like. Foamy blood trickled from the corners of his own mouth as he struggled in the oghul's grip. Then the toxins from the beast's savage teeth took effect, and Godwyn could feel the throbbing pain loosen its hold, replaced with the ecstasy and blissful darkness he had yearned for.

*The flares of the sun burnt the tops of the mountains to silver cinders. 'Twas those silver flares and whips that the beast of the underworld didst fear. And whoso controlleth the Blood of the Dragon commandeth the beasts. Thus I named that silver sun Dragon Claw and deemed it the source of all life, the supplier of all death.*
—THE WAY AND TRUTH OF LAIJON

# CHAPTER FORTY-NINE

# STEFAN WAYLAND

17TH DAY OF THE ANGEL MOON, 999TH YEAR OF LAIJON

DEADWOOD GATE, GUL KANA

T he unbearable blackness of the accursed mine was suffocating. It bled into the air and into every fiber of Stefan's being. He feared he would become a wicked, desperate ghost, a wraith, wandering the underworld's caverns, crying, wailing, gnashing his teeth forever. *Or just a blundering fool in the dark!*

The bow strapped to his back was his only comfort. *Gisela.* He had been crawling in the blackness for what felt like days; the unrelenting worry that oghuls still chased him was a torture to his already stressed body. The upward gradient he had been following was so gentle as to be almost imperceptible. But he followed it, crawling in the dark, blind, feeling his way with his hands, dragging his injured leg behind him.

He tried to ignore the debilitating effect his maimed ankle was having on the rest of his body. Shock from the injury and everything else was tightening around his mind. Now and then he would stop and check his injured ankle with prodding fingers. It was swollen to nearly twice its normal size within the boot. There was naught to do but ignore the pain and keep crawling.

At every fork in the road, he chose the route that seemed to go up and out. If a staircase or tunnel didn't go up, he doubled back until he found one that did. All in complete blackness. He wondered if he shouldn't be like Dokie or Liz Hen and give thanks to Laijon for keeping him alive. But speaking to a god he didn't really believe in seemed a silly notion. Yet he couldn't help but wonder if something of the divine hadn't intervened with that oghul.

*But there was no oghul . . .*

*No dragon . . .*

*No skull-faced man . . .*

He did not want to think of himself as mad.

*But have the wraiths completely possessed me?*

Both knees and the palms of his hands had become raw from the crawling. He could feel the dirt and rocks embedded in his skin, imagining them burrowing into his bloodstream. Even if he escaped this place, he would take part of it with him.

He crawled as if in a dream, ignoring all pain, so lulled by the monotony of one hand in front of the other, left, right, left, right, shuffle, drag . . .

. . . so consumed with the journey, he almost fell into the abyss.

Exactly as before, his hands dropped out from under him, and his chin smacked against the stone floor. Like in a horrendous repetitive dream, his heart hammered as he scrambled back.

His left shoulder bumped into something, knocking it, rattling along the floor. He froze in place. Whatever he'd just made contact with was man-made and sounded tinlike in the hollow silence. He reached for the object. Found it. It was cold, metallic. Familiar.

It was a tin bucket with a stout wire handle, rusty and well used. He hugged it to his belly, his hands lovingly caressing its surface. *Human made. Not oghul made. Somehow, somewhere, sometime, somebody else like me was in this place, this demon-spawned underworld. Maybe I am not alone.*

He set the bucket aside and cautiously felt for the edge of the drop-off again, not wanting to fall into it. Perhaps it was just a small ledge, merely a flight of stairs. *I've no more rope left!* He found the ledge, lay flat on his stomach, and reached his hand downward as far as he could. But there was nothing.

He snatched the bucket and dropped it over the rim and listened...
...and never heard it strike bottom.

Keeping one hand on the lip of the chasm, he dragged himself a few feet to the left and came to another bucket. He dropped that one into the pit too. It never made a sound. He scooted a little farther, found a small nail, then a rake. He dropped them over. Nothing. He moved on, finding several more buckets, a small spade, a shovel, and lastly, what felt like a pickax. None made a sound when he tossed them over the edge.

He eventually came to a wall that blocked his way. So he scooted in the opposite direction, back toward the right, past where he'd begun, finding more buckets, more nails, more mining tools, throwing them all into the gaping pit.

Last he found one very long flat piece of lumber before he reached the opposite wall. He did not throw the lumber over the edge. He judged the cavern to be about thirty paces across, from wall to wall, dead-ending at the edge of a bottomless abyss.

This was where he would die. He slumped against the wall, the battle lost.

Alone he sat, accompanied by nothing more than a great yawning black silence and dwindling hope. He sensed oghuls were now hunting him. Wraiths, too. Possibly even dragons and silver-skull-faced knights. All of them searching the deep, dark places for him, tracking him through the mines by the trail of blood he knew his knees and ankles and hands had left smeared along the floors.

And now they would find him alone with no arrows and a useless bow in this enchanted little dead-end tunnel. Every sound his agonized lungs made was exaggerated by the cold silence. He was so thirsty. He coughed, chest-plate armor constricting his lungs. He coughed again, a guttural, scratchy sound that blasted from deep in his chest, the sound resonating in the air, echoing back and forth down the tunnel from which he'd just come, alerting any oghuls or fiery beasts of the underworld to where he was.

Deep aches had settled into his bones. His muscles brimmed with cramps and pains. His head threatened to burst with the clamor of surging blood and pain. And with his foot—naught but a throbbing agony that assaulted him like never before.

*Ignore it! Store the hurt in that hollow place in your mind.*
*Think, Stefan, think.*

He didn't want to turn around. Didn't want to backtrack. Yet the fact was, the deep and bottomless hole before him gave him no choice. *But I've come so far. . . .*

Frustration mounted. Rage swelled. A boiling, seething, painful rage.

He reached out and snatched the bow from off his back. He hurled it angrily as far as he could out over the pit, expecting to hear the hum of its twirling flight down, down, down, into the nothingness of the abyss, never to reach bottom.

*Gisela. Gone.*

But instead he heard the bow strike ground. It clanked and clattered across a hard stone floor not more than ten or fifteen paces away.

He unstrapped the empty quiver from his back next. Tossed it out over the abyss. He heard a *twang, twang, clatter, twiiiing* as it skipped over hard stone some thirty or forty feet away. He grabbed a pebble from the floor and tossed it. It too lit on solid ground.

*Idiot! Stefan! Idiot!* The tunnel he'd been following ended at the edge of a bottomless pit, that was for sure, but the tunnel itself picked up again not more than thirty or forty paces away. *But I'm no Cotton Stansfield at a Mourning Moon Feast athletic competition. I can't jump that.*

He tossed another pebble. Not quite as far. It lit against the far corridor. He tossed a dozen more, gauging that the opposite rim of the tunnel was likely only fifteen feet away.

He felt the length of lumber at his side. It was easily fifteen paces long. It was a foot wide, at least two inches thick, and solid. *But can I stretch it over the pit?* He took three deep breaths, collected his thoughts, and formulated a plan.

He placed one end of the lumber flush with the lip of the drop-off, then rolled onto his back, the stone floor cold under him. He scooted forward until his legs were over the edge of the chasm, both feet dangling down into the nothingness. He half rolled onto his side, grasped the board with both hands, and lifted, rolling onto his back again at the same time. The wood was heavy, but he placed its length firmly over his stomach, over his forehead, inching it back until he could grip its end with his thighs. Then he sat up, lifting the board as he went, hand over hand, balancing it as he rose up, the end of the board between his legs—like a soldier walking a tall ladder up against a castle wall. He sat up all the way. The length of the lumber was now standing on end, clenched tightly between his legs, towering fifteen feet above him. Luckily, the roof somewhere above was high enough for that. Slowly he let the top of the board continue in its arching path down, dropping, dropping, in an uncertain plummet. He kept hold of it with both hands, falling with it, praying to Laijon it was long enough to catch the opposite ledge.

It was. The board smacked hard against the far rim of the trench.

The reverberation shot up through Stefan's arms, and he lost his grip, face and body smashing down against the lumber with a slap, his chest-plate armor absorbing the blow.

And there he lay, arms and legs a-dangle, suspended on a thin piece of wood over empty air and nothingness. His heart thundered. One breath. Two breaths. Three breaths. After his bones stopped quaking, and his frame solidified from the quivering mess it had become, he melted onto the length of lumber under him.

His bridge.

But he dared not move. Dared not crawl forward. *Is it thick enough? Wide enough?* These whirling thoughts spawned other questions that immediately began to develop into buds of doubt.

Wind washed up the tunnel from behind, racing over his flesh. *I'm no longer alone.* His heart beat faster as he heard the guttural sound of oghul voices in the distance behind him.

He inched forward, the sound of beasts in the tunnel behind him growing, the glow of their torches now a flickering haze of light. The lumber creaked and groaned under him as he crept forward. Ever so slowly he moved, the board dipping farther at its center, bowed inward under his weight . . .

. . . and he could feel it letting go . . . splintering . . .

The oghuls, dozens of them, torches aloft, were suddenly pouring into the cavern behind him, all shouting oghul curses. He scrambled forward, the board bouncing under him, creaking and cracking as he reached the opposite edge and rolled to safety, hugging the surface of the floor, spent, staring out over the chasm at the growling beasts, their gray visages dancing in the light of their torches, burly bodies bristling with heavy rusted armor and weaponry. Fear and tension drained from Stefan's body like some form of otherworldly sweat as he met each one of their hungry gazes.

*I made it!* his mind screamed. *Rotted angels and Bloody Mother Mia, I made it!*

The chasm was behind him. He had conquered it. The oghuls gathered on the other side were snarling, their long and sharp fangs useless to them now. The length of wood had held. It was only inches from his feet, still stretched over the pit, bowed in the middle and a little worse for wear. Several of the torch-bearing oghuls were heading toward it. Stefan kicked the board into the chasm.

He turned and spotted his bow on the ground and snatched it up. *Gisela.* His heart soared when he saw the precious weapon was undamaged. Stefan left the empty quiver where it lay and limped down the corridor away from the abyss and the oghuls, turning for one last look . . .

. . . and seeing nothing.

No oghuls. No cavern. No torchlight. No bottomless pit.

The hairs along the back of his neck sang with warning. Only a smothering blackness stared back at him as if none of it had ever existed.

*It had to be real!* He whirled in frustration, face smashing into a stone wall.

He stumbled back and fell into a puddle of cool mud. He gasped aloud at the feel of it squishing between his fingers. *Water!* His tongue immediately sought the ground, tried to suck the moisture free. *Dirt! Bitter!*

*Is it even real . . .*

He searched the floor with his hands, tracing the source of the mud to the rock wall. Water seeped from the rock. Kneeling, he placed his face to the wall and let the beautiful coolness trickle over his lips and tongue. It tasted like iron, but good.

Then he saw a sliver of light from the corner of his eye.

Light streamed through a cleft in the wall just above and to his left. A beam of hazy white, slanting down through the dust into his space. It was faint, ghostly, and *white*! Not red and fiery and demonic, but *white*! Like it was coming from a place where things like trees and flowers and sunshine might live and breathe. He stretched his hand out into the beam, trying to make out the color of his own worn and bloody flesh.

Stefan stood and peered into the crack from whence the light had sprung. The fissure in the wall was about five paces high, perhaps a foot wide, and extended into the rock wall for what seemed about twenty paces, emptying into another tunnel—a tunnel with light so blinding it hurt his eyes!

Without thinking, he shed his blood-splattered chest-plate armor and tossed it aside, overjoyed to finally have an excuse to be rid of it. With his bow in hand, he shoved his body into the cleft, wiggling his way sideways toward the light, slowly inching his way forward. His back was smashed against the rock behind him, his chest scraping painfully against the wall in front. He could feel his tunic tear and peel away against the rough stone. Still, he pushed onward, the light of the tunnel beyond beckoning, bow held out in front of him, Gisela guiding his way.

Soon the crevasse seemed to constrict inward, and he found it hard to breathe, hard to move at all. Panicked, his heart thumped. A suffocating dread crept over him. His breath quickened. And with every labored gasp for air, it seemed the rock pressed inward. He was so near the end.

*Three deep breaths . . . three deep breaths . . . three deep breaths like Val-Draekin taught us . . . then hold it.* And when he held his breath, he felt the walls loosen around his body. He held his breath again, tried to squirm forward, gripping his bow.

*Guide me, Gisela. Lead me to safety.*

One last push and he spilled out into the tunnel on the other side and collapsed as startled bats clinging to the ceiling took flight, swirling in mad haste toward the light.

And what a light it was . . .

. . . so dazzling he had to clench shut his eyes, the warmth of it melting over him like liquid fire. He scrambled toward the source of the warmth, crawling, dragging his leg, only briefly opening his eyes. Through stinging tears, he squinted into the coruscating brilliance. A fleeting image. *An exit!* His aching gaze drank in the sight.

He crawled, and crawled, almost in ecstasy.

Soon he smelled the mingled fragrances of pine and aspen and saw more clearly the round outline of the opening of the cave, the scent of things familiar spurring him on.

Then he was outside—in the sunlight.

Alive!

His bleeding hands covered his face, as the scintillating brightness of his surroundings was almost too much to bear. Through straining, watery eyes he looked, sensing a faint wash of green here and there, only tenuous images. The sun flashed stark and bright reflections, *trees*, long and tall and towering and creaking in the breeze.

*Aspens! Nothing ever seemed so heavenly and fine!*

His laughter was like wind rippling through the brush. He was stunned by the spaciousness of the outside world around him. He breathed in the aroma of trees and leaves and dirt and sun. The fragrance of grass and pine filled his heaving lungs.

He crawled, the feeling of the brittle twigs against his bloody hands almost too overwhelming to describe. He tore a handful of weeds and grass from the ground and rubbed them over his face, relished the feel, the texture, the life within.

Then he lost hold on the soil beneath him and rolled down a hill toward the sparsely treed floor of a narrow gully, laughing, not caring at all.

At the bottom, he sat up, his wounds forgotten. Nothing could hurt him now. He tilted his head back, singling out the elusive scents of pine, willow, moss. As the mixture of unmistakable smells flooded him, saliva swelled under his tongue, reminding him that he was ravenously hungry. He gazed up. But the brightness of the light stung his eyes, scraped them raw. He shut them tight to stave off the pain.

And that was when he heard the voices.

Not oghul voices but unintelligible human voices that slowly sharpened into a babble of coherent words that eventually took shape.

He forced his eyes open again.

Over the brushy green slope floated two ghostly apparitions, their familiar faces wavering in and out of sight during those initial blinking moments. Dissolving. Reshaping themselves. His eyes struggled to adjust to the confusing brightness of it all. Two gleaming swords sparked shards of sunlight into his eyes, blinding him further, adding to the chaos.

"Stefan," both people called out to him at the same time.

*Help!* he wanted to reply, but was astonished to discover that his voice would not respond when he tried to speak. He swallowed, breathed deep. Tried to speak again. No sound issued forth from his dry throat but a hissing rasp.

"Stefan," the voices called again, and the two people above suddenly became one. *More illusions!* He sat up and shielded his eyes from the sun, squinted, tried to concentrate on the strangeness he spied on the slope above.

*It's Seita!*

The Vallè maiden approached. Her two wavering forms converging again, coming into focus as one. She wore her gray cloak tied at the waist, face mostly concealed within the cowls of her hood, a familiar leather satchel thrown over her left shoulder. She held a tremendously long sword in her right hand, its thin hilt curved and graceful in the shape of a crescent moon. The lethal-looking weapon she carried didn't gleam or sparkle like a normal sword, but merely hung menacingly, suspended in her grip, creating a pitched white void in the tall shadows of the aspens.

"We thought you were dead," she said. "Are you hurt?"

"I don't know," Stefan's voice finally cracked. Her image shimmered, and he wondered again if the Vallè before him was even real. "Where is Culpa?" he asked.

She stopped a few steps away and cast her green-eyed gaze back toward the cliffs above. "Culpa's behind me, up the hill and through the trees some, making his way as best he can along the bottom of the rockfall." Seita pushed the hood of her cloak back, eyes still on the slope of aspens and jagged rock wall rising up behind her. When she turned back toward Stefan, her face was grim. "When I saw you stumble out of that cave, I left Culpa immediately and hurried to you. . . ."

She paused, as if trying to find her next words. With grave concern in her voice, she continued in a hushed whisper, "Culpa was hurt in the mines, Stefan. He is sorely injured. Dying. I can scarcely fathom what stamina must live within him to have kept him alive this long. He carries *Blackest Heart* strapped to his back, insisted on it, refused to let me take it from him. He can barely toddle about in what remaining armor he has. It was all I could do to get him to agree to let me carry his satchel."

"What happened?" he asked.

"Culpa fell into the silver." She no longer whispered.

"Fell into the silver?" Confused, Stefan stood, legs wobbly, ankle flaming with pain. Then, horrified, he remembered the mines above Sky Lochs and the silver streams.

"I'm surprised Culpa made it as far as he has," Seita went on, gulping. "Don't be alarmed when you see his injuries. . . ."

Her eyes searched the surrounding trees as if looking for oghuls or worse. "We must not tarry, Stefan. The Dayknight is a liability to us now. We will have to leave Culpa here. . . ."

She paused again, once more choosing her words carefully. "Something terrible is soon to occur in Amadon. And only I can stop it, Stefan. Only I know of it."

"Your visions?" He gathered his balance, ankle aching.

"Aye." Her green orbs nervously scanned the slope above once again.

"I've had visions too," Stefan muttered. "There is a beast of the underworld deep in the mines. Did you see it too? A knight in red-scaled armor with a silver mask? I thought it was a Skull man, but with the pale face of a Vallè."

"Skull man?" Seita turned back to him, eyes now wide. "That looked like a Vallè?"

It seemed all he could do was stare at her. *Beautiful. She's always so beautiful and fine.* The pale perfection of her face was such a welcome sight after the ugliness of the mines. He looked down at the long white sword in her hand. Then he looked back up.

A mantle of concern had passed over her features. "There are no dragons here." Her eyes were fixed on his, sharp brows furrowed.

"I know what I saw," he said.

She stepped toward him, placing her other hand on his shoulder. "Cast your evil visions away, Stefan. Remember, Culpa said those mines could play with your mind. Many things and creatures can play with your mind. They say even the merfolk give those they capture visions before the slow drowning death overcomes them."

"You're saying I just imagined it all."

"Aye. You were lost in there for some time."

He was angry. "What makes your visions real and mine not?" His ankle hurt, and he fought to keep his balance.

"Because I am pure Vallè." She tightened her grip on his shoulder, steadying him.

Stefan looked up the hill again. *Is Culpa Barra even up there? Am I even out of the mines yet? Is this just some cruel dream?*

The delicate hand on his shoulder felt real.

"Look." Seita raised the marvelous sword into his line of vision again. "We found it. *Afflicted Fire.* The angel stone too. It's in the satchel."

Stefan's eyes took in the full measure of the astonishing weapon the Vallè carried. It was as long as she was tall, a bright round ruby of deep red set within its white pommel. The weapon's curious crescent-moon-shaped hilt and cross-guard looked carved of one solid piece of walrus bone, or the tusklike horns of some beast of the underworld, or something else entirely. Its blade was forged of glorious silver mixed with twisting veins of translucent ivory that seemed to pulse red light from somewhere deep within. It was the largest, most magnificent sword he had ever seen.

And it didn't seem real.

Seita reached into the leather satchel hanging from her shoulder and pulled forth a black swatch of silk, held it toward him. Without thinking, Stefan reached out his hand. The Vallè maiden dumped the silk's contents directly into his palm.

It was a sparkling red stone, the same exact size and shape as the blue stone Gisela had pulled from the cross-shaped altar in the mines above Gallows Haven. The same size and shape as the black stone from Sky Lochs.

The red stone's innards seemed to glint and glimmer with smoky red waves of dancing light. It burned cold as ice against the dirty and ragged flesh of his hand.

It didn't seem right, holding it. He felt the slave brand on the underside of his wrist flare in sudden pain. He stumbled back, leg muscles nearly giving out, shards of agony shooting up his injured ankle next. The stone dropped from his hand into the foliage at his feet. Seita quickly scooped it up into the silk and stuffed it back into her satchel—Culpa Barra's satchel. *Where was the Dayknight?*

Stefan gathered his bearings, taking in the fullness of the surroundings. He and Seita were at the bottom of a grassy slope of brush and aspen. The mine he had stumbled from was naught but a dark hole in the broken cliff wall some fifty feet up the slope behind the Vallè. The rocky cliff above the mine wasn't that high, but extended to both the right and left for about two hundred feet in either direction. Behind him was a boulder-strewn outcrop of scrub oak and low-lying bracken. The outcrop stretched about a hundred feet toward another cliff that dropped away to an uneven landscape consisting of the tops of hundreds of pine trees, all jutting into view just above the cliff's ledge. A great dark forest of pine receded into the distance among rolling hills.

There was something hazy and odd about the landscape. He looked back at Seita.

*None of it seems real.* As if reading his mind, the Vallè reached out and swiped her left hand across his forehead. "You're covered in blood," she said, her palm and fingers smeared with red. "Are you injured?"

*Oghul blood!* He recalled the blood-splashed chest-plate armor he'd abandoned in the mines, looked down at his red-splattered arms and pants covered in blood not his own. *I did kill that oghul in the mines! It wasn't the wraiths warping my mind.*

"I thought you were dead when the roof caved in on us." Seita leaned in and kissed him lightly, her delicate lips brushing against his.

Then she unslung the satchel from her own shoulder, and slung its leather strap over his. "You carry them now. Both the black stone and red stone are in there." She adjusted the strap tight. "It will now be up to you to protect the satchel and the stones, Stefan. I need my arms free to wield this sword if oghuls draw near."

Stefan wanted her to kiss him again. Her lips were his only link to reality, his only link to something real and warm and alive. Their eyes met briefly.

There was movement above. Then Culpa Barra broke through the trees midway up the hill, hobbling down toward them, using his Dayknight sword as a crutch.

Stefan stared in horror.

The man on the hill above still wore his black-lacquered Dayknight armor. Most of it, anyway. The right side of the armor, from mid-thigh up to the neckline, was completely melted away. His entire left arm was *gone*, as was a good portion of the right side of his torso. The right half of his battle helm was melted away too, from the chin guard up to where his ear *should* have been.

Under the helm, half of Culpa's face was naught but a blackened mass of charred flesh and bone. The jagged, bloody wreckage of his jaw and eye socket was streaked with rivulets of hardened silver, as was the entire gaping right side of his body. It appeared the searing silver alloy had melted it all away, flesh, bone, armor, then hardened, cauterizing the wounds and melding both flesh and iron together into one solid mess of simmering black armor, silver, and flesh.

Thick webs of blood seeped and bubbled from the destroyed half of Culpa's face. With every husky breath he took, blood bubbled and ran in livid red streams from his charred scalp clear to his feet.

*Now I know I am in a dream!* Stefan wondered if he himself wasn't still just wandering the Deadwood Gate mines in a never-ending nightmare.

"They are coming." The Dayknight slurred his words, leaning heavily on the hilt of his sword, his remaining eye foggy with pain, gaze bouncing uncertainly between Stefan and the Vallè. "Do not let the oghuls capture me, Seita." Despite the gruesome injuries to his face, Culpa's rough speech was clear.

Stefan could not tear his gaze from the man's melted face and exposed jawbone, or the pink tender tongue underneath forming words against half-destroyed teeth.

"Don't let the oghuls get me," the Dayknight repeated.

*Blackest Heart* was still secured to the baldric over his left shoulder as Seita had claimed, undamaged by any silver liquid.

Stefan had only a moment to take it all in before several dozen oghuls burst from the cave above. Suddenly the air was filled with throaty shouts and vile curses as the marauding beasts surged out of the mine and down the hill toward them, rusted arms and armor a-clatter, all of them brandishing stout longbows and rusted oghul weapons of various make.

"Don't let them take me for their Hragna'Ar," Culpa said again, his lone eye on the long white sword the Vallè maiden carried. "Get *Afflicted Fire* and *Blackest Heart* to Jondralyn, get them back to Amadon."

Seita bowed. Suddenly in her other hand was a dagger, black as polished coal.

She stabbed the blade hilt-deep into the silver and blood-streaked mush of the Dayknight's melted face, then pulled it straight back out.

Culpa Barra folded at the knees, dropping face-forward against the slope with a thud, sliding down the hill among the leaves and twigs, his body coming to rest against Stefan's feet, dead.

*None of this is real. None of this is real. None of this—*

The oghuls were charging down the hill toward them.

Without hesitation, the Vallè unhooked *Blackest Heart* from Culpa's back and thrust it into Stefan's arms. "Run!" she shouted. Then she was gone, sprinting away from Stefan straight in the direction of the opposite cliff ledge and the forest of pine below, the sword, *Afflicted Fire*, clenched tightly in her fist.

Stefan ran after her, black crossbow in hand, Culpa's satchel bouncing at his shoulder, his own precious bow clinging to his back, injured ankle protesting in agony with every harsh step.

But he couldn't keep pace with the Vallè. And the armored beasts were quickly gaining, rumbling up behind him with thunderous speed.

A flock of thick-hafted arrows hummed through the air like angry wasps to his left, one clipping the back of his shoulder and spinning off into the air.

Seita, still racing for the cliff ledge fifty paces ahead of Stefan, did not dodge or duck or even seem aware of the arrows that whooshed by. She continued to run at a full sprint, cloak billowing out behind her, gaining speed with each graceful, loping stride.

And when she reached the top of the cliff, she launched herself over the edge.

Stefan watched the Vallè girl soar out into the air, *Afflicted Fire* secured in her fist as she struck the topmost reaches of the nearest tree. Pine needles and dust billowed in the wind as the weight of her body set the thin pinnacle of the tree swaying and bending back. She clung tight to the top of the pine with her free hand, swinging herself around, legs clutching for purchase on the tossing boughs.

Stefan still ran. Almost upon him now, the pursuing oghuls breathed foul at his neck, their heavy footfalls shaking the ground. His legs churned, injured ankle threatening to give out with each throbbing step.

"Jump!" the Vallè called out, her precarious perch over thirty feet from the cliff's edge—a craggy drop that now presented itself directly under Stefan's bounding feet.

Momentum carrying him forward, he launched himself over the ledge and into the air toward Seita with every last speck of strength he had.

He sailed above the landscape but a moment, flailing all the way, cloak dragging against the wind as he dropped. The floor of the forest awaited. A hundred feet down. Thick with rock and scrub oak and scattered patches of white heather, red butterflies fluttering in the breeze.

Stefan smashed into the outer boughs of the pine twenty feet below Seita's roost. Like a rag doll he fell, crashing and tumbling out of control, unforgiving branches clawing at his cloak, his clothes, his face, ripping and thrashing. Pain tore through his entire body, and he lost his grip on *Blackest Heart.* The crossbow spun away as he felt the sting of a thousand spiky pine needles biting into his flesh at once. Downward he plunged, head over heels. Every rigid branch he crashed into brought pain, sharp and severe. With a weighty torturous thud, he struck the ground feetfirst. Agony lanced through his legs as both of his knees were driven up into his face. The rest of his body hit the heather-studded turf, and the breath was punched from his lungs. Curtains of red butterflies burst up from the bracken and peat and flapped madly above.

As his body slowly unfolded itself in the grass and white heather, it seemed every joint and piece of him was twisted at an awkward angle. Stefan rolled onto his back, staring straight up at the swooping boughs of the pine. And then he rolled over onto his side again, crying out, tears of frustration and pain streaming down his face as he took in the full measure of his injuries.

The whole front of his body was drenched in blood, red like fire and hot against his skin. His two mangled legs gave him a shock. One leg was shorter than the other by half, as if the leg had been compressed together within his dark leather leggings from foot to knee socket. His other leg was twisted and bent at an awkward angle, the paleness of the six-inch shard of bone shockingly jutting from his pant leg white against the dark stains of blood on leather.

*Blackest Heart* was gone. His own bow was gone too. *Gisela!* Both had been ripped violently from his back. Lost.

*Where's Seita?*

Crying in both fear and pain, Stefan began crawling from under the pine tree as if trying to escape his own torn and battered extremities, forearms and elbows chewing into the twigs and grass and dirt under him, tender exposed bone dragging in the leaves.

Still, he scrambled desperately forward, searching for some safe space he somehow knew he would never find. *I'm dreaming and this is not real!*

But the dream he was having was naught but a hollow and haunted space in his mind, bursting with horror and strife.

After just a few paces he found his own bow in the heather,

bowstring snapped in twain, but otherwise unharmed. *Gisela!* Feeling his trembling fingers wrap around its familiar wood stock, he breathed a faint sigh of relief, his one and only joy in this nightmare. He caressed Gisela's name with bloody hands.

*Blackest Heart* was suspended in the bracken before him, hanging just an arm's length away in a pile of soft brush, its landing perfectly cushioned. Stefan reached up and ripped the weapon from the brush angrily, wanting to fling it away as if it were the cause of all his agony. But he hadn't the strength left in him for that.

He rolled onto his back again and hugged both weapons to his chest, the longbow named Gisela and the crossbow *Blackest Heart*, his entire being overcome by the pain pounding through his legs. He propped his head up on a tuft of grass, clutching the bows tight. The mottled-gray cliff rose jagged and craggy behind him. A thin line of blue sky was visible between the cliff and the row of tall pines before him. The red butterflies were lazily settling all around him like thick bloody snowflakes.

Oghuls were howling above, their grunts and growls echoing off the cliff wall, seemingly right on top of him.

*Have they shot their arrows into you, Seita?*

He stared at the sky, brain unfocused. There was no way out of the mess he was in. Then he felt an unnatural warmth against the palms of his hands and his chest. It was *Blackest Heart.* The wood of the crossbow appeared to shimmer at the edges, and a ghostly black mist seemed to coil around the weapon's stock.

He remembered what Nail had told him of *Forgetting Moon.* Nail had felt some form of magic within the battle-ax when he'd confronted Jenko Bruk in Ravenker. Nail had seen a blue light radiate from the ax. But Nail also had a blue angel stone. . . .

He could hear more oghul voices now, distinct and clear, accompanied by the clatter and clamor of their armor. *They will be here soon!*

His heart pounded. *Culpa Barra's satchel!* By some miracle it was still draped over his shoulder. He hurriedly shrugged it off. Clutching both bows to his chest with one hand, he used his other hand to open the bag's flap and dig inside. He felt both swaths of silk, the twin lumps of both angel stones still within. One of the stones came unwrapped in his searching fingers, and he pulled it forth—the black one, the stone that belonged to *Blackest Heart*. It fit perfectly in his hand.

There was a commotion in the pine tree above. Seita dropped from the canopy of branches, landing lightly in the shrubbery and grass near the trunk of the tree, the long, shiny white sword with the crescent moon hilt in hand. The Vallè maiden looked glorious, as lithe and agile and clean as ever, gray cloak and leather armor spotless, as if the entire disastrous journey hadn't caused her a moment of stress or pain. She moved toward him with an unobtrusive ease, seeping through the foliage like a glorious pale mist, red butterflies scattering in her wake.

At her approach, Stefan found himself clenching the black angel stone tightly in hand, pressing *Blackest Heart* and his own bow to his chest with what little strength was left in him. *I saved them!*

Seita grabbed Culpa's satchel from the ground with her free hand, flinging the leather strap over her own shoulder, calm eyes roaming the length of the ragged cliff face above. The sound of charging oghuls was growing louder in the distance.

"Let me help you." Seita grasped Stefan by the nape of his cloak and began dragging him through the undergrowth, his shattered legs howling in agony. He clenched the stone in his hand and the two bows against his chest, not wanting to lose them, nausea overtaking him, the pain unbearable. He resisted his mind's best efforts to black out from the all-consuming terror he felt. Seita dragged him about ten paces, propping his back against a tall white aspen so he was sitting upright, facing her.

She jabbed the sword *Afflicted Fire* into the ground next to the aspen, then knelt motionless before him, white hair glinting in the sunlight. Her pale skin and fey ears looked very foreign to him now—as if he had never known her at all.

*Did I once love her?* It felt as if love poured out of his soul like a pure river of light toward her. *Can she not see it?* He felt so disoriented.

He remembered their kiss. "I must be dreaming," he said, the ground beneath him trembling to the drum of guttural oghul shouts. He drank in Seita's aquiline appearance and splendorous round eyes that stood out so strongly, so overwhelmingly against the landscape beyond. Even here in this grove of trees, Seita's strong Vallè features dominated all beauty. "Am I dreaming . . . ?"

"I am not a dream." A sad smile touched Seita's lips as her delicate hand latched on to the crossbow clinging to his chest. Stefan reacted, clutching *Blackest Heart* to his body, resisting her pull.

But she yanked the crossbow from him, standing quickly. "'Tis only Vallè quarrels that fit it anyway." She set *Blackest Heart* on the ground next to *Afflicted Fire*, both just out of his reach.

Then she knelt back down before him again, her severe green eyes like chips of glacial ice, impassive and sharp. Stefan's fist tightened around his own bow. *Gisela!* He would not let her have it. The black angel stone hidden within the grip of his other hand grew warm. He slid his arm to his side, stuffed his curled fist under his thigh, hiding all traces of the stone from the Vallè.

His heart raced and his eyes widened when he spied the dull glimmer of oghul armor in the far copse of trees beyond her.

"This is our parting," Seita said, following his gaze. "The ending I saw. Oghuls chasing us, you propped against an aspen, an arrow buried in your chest, pinning you to the tree."

"What arrow?" His own vision was going in and out of focus, dry mouth gulping for air. In the distance, hundreds of oghuls burst from the forest, their savage cries piercing the air. "You can't leave me."

Seita turned back to him. "So heavily besieged, I dare not tarry," she said. "With *Afflicted Fire* I could possibly kill them all. But I haven't the time. I've got to get back to Amadon. This quest has gone on far too long already."

A thin black dagger appeared in her hand. "It's Hragna'Ar, and you do not want to be taken alive by these bloodsucking fiends. The poison on this blade is exact, two minutes at most, then the darkness will take you."

Stefan's heart beat faster, his breathing quickened. He had never felt so wretchedly alone and helpless.

*Gisela!* He held his own bow close to him.

"Farewell, Stefan Wayland." In one fluid motion Seita thrust the black blade between his ribs clear to the hilt, then pulled it straight back out. He clenched the black angel stone tighter in his fist in an effort to stave off the pain that never came.

Seita left the dagger in his lap, took *Blackest Heart* and *Afflicted Fire* in either hand, and then bounded around the aspen tree and disappeared behind him, and he saw her no more.

Stefan's entire body felt numb. Blissfully comfortable.

A thick-hafted arrow streaked from the throng of charging oghuls and punched deep into his chest, its iron tip piercing clear through his body, the arrow's brown-feathered fletching quivering below his chin.

Oghuls by the hundreds came streaming toward him. More thick arrows whizzed by, all of them now aimed at the fleeing Vallè escaping somewhere behind him. The oghuls charged straight at Stefan like ravaging thunder, their spiked and spined armor jouncing with an unholy racket that echoed hollowly in the trees, all of them brandishing rusted cruel weapons, all of them shouting foul oghul curses.

Stefan couldn't move if he wanted to, nailed to the aspen tree as he was.

He held his bow tight to his body, clutching the black angel stone, feeling some warm power flowing from it.

When the first of the monsters reached his position, he knew not what to expect, perhaps a sword in the stomach, or an ax to the face. But the beastly mass paid him scant heed. They flowed around him in two delirious waves, all of them after Seita. As quickly as they had appeared, they were gone.

And there was naught but silence.

*This is our parting,* she'd said. *The ending I saw.* The thick arrow jutting from his chest had not yet registered pain in him. But as he felt his heavy breathing slow, a blurred disorientation along with the return of immense loneliness seemed to fill his entire being. He felt his eyes fluttering closed, but fought with all he had to stay awake.

He lifted the angel stone. It was a struggle, fingers trembling as he uncurled them. The palm of his hand and pads of his fingers were burned and blistered where he'd gripped the stone. But he felt no pain. But the magic had *burned* him.

He gripped the stone tight in his fingers once again and placed his clenched fist against his chest just above the arrow, feeling the slowing beats of his own heart.

*Blackest Heart.*

He couldn't catch his breath.

And then the wavering vision of one last oghul in dark leathers stepping cautiously from the woods came into focus. Thick sheets of iron plate armor were buckled to the straggler's thighs and forearms, rusted and worn. A square war hammer of immense size was hooked to the baldric slung over his shoulder. A brace of bone-handled knives was tied to a crudely fashioned buckler at his hip. Other than that, the beast wore no helm and carried no weapons but for two meaty hands, both balled into a large fists. Tiny sparkling jewels were embedded in the claws that burst from his knuckles. This gray-faced oghul was a brute, larger than the others, flat-nosed and keen of eye, his lower lip swollen.

A second figure slipped from the woods just behind the oghul, a copper-haired girl in a forest green cloak, the dull hilt of a short-sword just visible at her leather belt. The girl wore black pants and leather boots with dark leather thongs twining around each foot clear to the knee.

The two newcomers slunk through the trees toward Stefan in a manner suggesting they did not want to be seen. As they drew near, Stefan saw the oghul's eyes were as black and piercing as the angel stone warming in his own hand. The teeth protruding from both the top and bottom of the beast's thick dry lips were shockingly long and sharp.

The girl's blue eyes were crisp and cold beneath the two dark smears of black ash covering her face. The inky smudges stretched from underneath each brow, down over her eyelids and over her cheekbones on either side of her stark face. Two feathers were tied into her hair just below her left ear, shockingly white against the dark green of her cloak and surrounding pines.

Stefan felt his whole body go slack; the only thing holding him upright was the arrow pinning him to the tree. His vision again began to waver and fade as the black-eyed giant stood over him. Then the oghul bent down, stiff armor creaking as he seized hold of the bow clenched to Stefan's chest. Stefan struggled to hold on to the weapon.

*Gisela!*

But his limp hand was no match for the oghul, who wrestled the bow away. With the weapon in one clawed hand, the oghul snatched Seita's black dagger from Stefan's lap with the other. He examined both for a moment, then stood and handed the bow to the copper-haired girl, slipping the dagger into his belt.

The oghul crouched again and stripped the black angel stone from Stefan's clenched fist. Stefan hadn't the strength to fight him off.

*Does my mind play tricks on me?*

The oghul stuffed the black stone under his swollen lower lip between two jutting fangs, then sucked on the gemstone hungrily.

*Much like Father would suck on a pinch of tobacco.* But his father was dead. He couldn't even picture the man's face anymore. Or Liz Hen's. Or Nail's. Or Seita's . . .

His vision blurred as both strangers turned and vanished into the density of the forest from whence they'd come. *The bow is gone!* And Stefan's fading memory of Gisela with it.

This was not how he wanted things to be before death could lay its cold claim. "Bring it back." His body was so numb, he couldn't even feel his own voice crack. "Bring Gisela back." He couldn't even feel the tears he knew were welling in his eyes.

One red butterfly landed on the arrow jutting from his chest. Stefan watched as both butterfly and arrow rose and fell to the slow rhythm of his own rough breathing.

Then, with a rapid flutter of its wings, the red butterfly flew away.

And the final thing Stefan saw before all things grew dark . . .

. . . the arrow lodged in his chest had stopped moving.

*For even the vanity, frailties, and foolishness of dishonest men can fulfill prophecy and make cursed things blessed.*
—THE WAY AND TRUTH OF LAIJON

# CHAPTER FIFTY
# TALA BRONACHELL

### 19TH DAY OF THE ANGEL MOON, 999TH YEAR OF LAIJON
### AMADON, GUL KANA

When Grand Vicar Denarius finished his priesthood blessing over Lawri, Jovan favored both of his sisters with a dismal smile and continued his back-and-forth pacing.

Today Tala's brother was doing his utmost to look official, kingly: silver crown atop his head, decorative silver chain-mail tunic over black leather pants, and a long, black, fur-trimmed coat. Sky Reaver, the blue sword of Aeros Raijael, hung low on his belt.

But despite his regal bearing, Jovan would not stop his tense pacing at the back of the room. His every irritable movement and grim look was putting all those gathered in the infirmary, including the Vallè doctor, Val-Gianni, on edge. It didn't help that just behind him was an array of medical tools, saws and knives and scalpels and other horrid-looking items, hanging on the wall. To Tala, the whole room seemed harsh and jagged and sharp and seething with hidden pain.

Lawri Le Graven was the focus of everyone's attention. Tala's blond cousin was sitting on a four-legged wooden stool directly behind an old stone oven in the center of the room. She wore a golden-colored dress that almost matched the ashen, pasty yellow of her face. The whites of her drooping, bloodshot eyes were streaked with sickly green behind black, milky pupils. Her breathing was forced and heavy. Sweat beaded on her forehead and exposed left arm—an infected arm that was the ghastly shade of a rotted plum. The arm was stretched out, palm up, atop the examination table before her. It was a thick wooden table that, to Tala, looked more like a butcher block than anything.

Denarius placed the stopper back on his bull-horn flask of priesthood holy oil and stepped back from Lawri. He bowed to Val-Gianni. "By Laijon's will, both her arm and her life are in now in your care, sawbones."

"Save her arm," Mona Le Graven pleaded, her own worried face nearly as pasty and pale as her daughter's. "The sickness hasn't completely taken it yet. It looked healthy enough to me."

"Healthy enough?" Jovan scoffed, still pacing heavily behind them all. "Foul-smelling thing needs to come off."

It did smell. Like a dead dog bloating in the gutter on a hot summer day. The stench permeated the room even over the sterilizing ointment Val-Gianni had spread over her swollen wounds—raw distended wounds that crisscrossed the length of her forearm from wrist to elbow, puffed and sallow with infection. Herbs and spices and scented flowers were piled on a table next to a stone basin of water, their strong fragrance not even enough to mask the smell. The fact was, Tala's cousin was sick, and the cause of that sickness was her own infected arm, an arm that she had let go rotten all herself.

"Just chop the damn thing off already." Jovan scowled. Tala glared at him, knowing this was all his fault.

"Let the Vallè do his job," Jondralyn said, hand resting against the small of Mona's back reassuringly. Half of Jondralyn's head and neck was still covered in cloth bandages, though Val-Gianni had earlier mentioned they should come off in a few days. The stitches would remain for a time. But her eye was a loss, and she would soon be fitted with an eye patch. And she would bear a terrible long scar across her face until the end of her days.

"Just chop her arm off," Jovan repeated, still pacing.

"You're only scaring your aunt with such talk, Jovan," Jondralyn said.

"So what?"

"Lord Lott is not here for her," Jondralyn went on. "He is not here to comfort his wife. Lest you forget, he's off preparing for battle with the rest of your *men* of the court."

The king, still pacing like a caged saber-toothed lion, glared at his sister. "And lest you forget, if you were worth a tinker's shit in battle, I would have sent you too, *Ser* Jondralyn."

Tala could hear the tightness in Jovan's voice. *He wants an argument. He wants a fight.* Jondralyn ignored her brother's jibe and held on to Mona's arm, comforting the woman. The young Le Graven twins, Lorhand and Lilith, were there too, eyes wide with fear as they trembled behind their mother.

Squireck Van Hester stood directly behind Jondralyn, scowling at the king. The Prince of Saint Only had been favoring Tala's sister with his company daily, hourly, hovering protectively over Jondralyn continually. And Tala could tell her sister did not appreciate his constant presence.

Val-Korin was here too. He lingered near Val-Gianni, ready to render advice or aid. Denarius also stood near the Vallè sawbones, as did the five archbishops: Vandivor, Donalbain, Spencerville, Leaford, and Rhys-Duncan—all of them dressed in their finest robes and gold necklaces. Glade Chaparral leaned against the windowsill at the far end of the room; light streamed through, illuminating his bright Silver Guard armor. His three henchmen, Tolz, Alain, and Boppard, stood at attention next to him. Dame Mairgrid was there, hovering over Tala's younger brother, Ansel, who looked on in mute fascination. Others present were Lars Castlegrail, commander of the Silver Guard, and Tomas Vorkink, Landon Galloway, and Terrell Wickham, the steward, chamberlain, and stable marshal of the castle. Everyone of note was stuffed into the small room.

Tala's eyes couldn't help but stray to the limbless Jubal Bruk, who sat propped up on a cot in the far corner. The baron was watching the proceedings with great concern. As Tala stared at Jubal Bruk, all she could think about was how the Bloodwood's game had spiraled so far out of control—Lawri's well-being was continually in the balance.

Val-Gianni began poking and prodding at Lawri's arm. The girl squirmed under his touch, bearing the pain in silence.

"You won't cut off her arm like Jovan ordered, will you?" Mona reached for her daughter. Jondralyn pulled her back. Jovan met the woman's concerned gaze with naught but contempt, a hard light growing in his eyes. He continued his pacing.

"Please don't cut off her arm," Mona said again.

Val-Gianni looked up from his work. "If she is willing to follow my instructions, allows us to drain her arm of infection daily, and takes the medicines I give, we might be able to buy her arm a few more days. Might even be able to save it." He positioned himself behind Lawri, reaching for a ceramic vial. Val-Korin propped the girl's head back and Val-Gianni forced the herbal draught down her throat.

To Tala it didn't seem right. *She's swallowed enough potions.* As she watched Val-Gianni and Val-Korin work, her mind again drifted to the Bloodwood. The situation had fallen into madness. *And poor Mona.* Tala looked from Val-Gianni to her distraught aunt—her son framed for murder, her husband off preparing for war, her daughter . . .

... her daughter's infected arm spread out on a wooden table, head tilted back whilst two Vallè practically forced more potions down her throat. Tala wondered when all the hurt and insanity would end.

Tala's stomach twisted noticeably when she heard the slither of steel drawn from a scabbard. "Enough!" a deep-timbred shout boomed through the room. And Jovan took one long stride toward the examination table, fur-trimmed coat billowing behind like a black storm cloud, Sky Reaver suspended in both hands above his head.

And the blue sword came slashing down like lightning, blade striking the wooden examination table like a heavy clap of thunder.

Val-Korin and Val-Gianni jumped back from Lawri with startled faces, the ceramic vial clattering to the floor. Mona screamed, one sharp screech of horror. Lorhand and Lilith cried out in terror.

Then breathless silence.

Jovan wrenched the blue blade from the inch-deep groove sliced into the length of the table. Lawri's arm was severed just below the elbow. One clean and bloodless thin line. Lawri didn't move. She just stared.

"Lawri likes blood so much"—Jovan wiped the blade on his coat, looking right at Tala—"I figured I'd give her a cut to remember." He slammed the blade home in its scabbard. Jovan looked at Val-Gianni coldly. "Just dip her arm in boiling tar and be done with it. Seemed to work just fine for Baron Bruk."

Lawri looked up, emotionless, green-streaked eyes meeting Tala's. A heartbeat passed. It was as if shards of ice ripped open Tala's spine when Lawri slowly lifted the remaining stump of her arm from the table, saying, "What handsome court boy will want me now?"

Dark red suddenly flooded from the grisly wound.

Val-Gianni and Val-Korin leaped to Lawri's side, rags pressing down on her arm to stanch the pluming gouts of blood ...

... blood that was streaked with green.

✝ ✝ ✝ ✝

Tala stood before the cross-shaped altar, her back to the large stained-glass window above. Each deep red pane cast a scarlet, dust-filled haze over the tapestry hanging across the room. The tapestry was a likeness of Mother Mia. The Raijael worshippers of Sør Sevier referred to Mia as Lady Death. And the armies of the White Prince brought *death* to Gul Kana. Just thinking of her besieged kingdom brought an enormous weight of sadness that filled the whole of Tala's body. That combined with all the trouble the Bloodwood had wrought within her own life was nearly too much to bear. For several moons now the sheer power and presence of the Bloodwood had haunted her every thought. But now the Bloodwood was silent.

"Show yourself!" she screamed into the hollowness of the chamber. But there came no answer. Not even an echo of her own voice could be heard in the daunting spaciousness of the high-ceilinged chamber. The room's ruby-tinted, smoke-streaked walls just stared back at her silently.

"I'm right here, right now in your secret ways!" she roared. "Violating your precious haunts!" Nothing answered, as if the very room swallowed up her shouts in smothering oblivion.

"Show yourself!" Her voice strained under the power of her scream. "Explain yourself! You foul monster! Talk to me if you dare! Come slay me if you dare! I'm here waiting if you dare! You rat-fucking Bloodwood!"

Nothing.

She'd come here straight from the infirmary. Lawri's arm was gone. She hadn't even brought a weapon. It didn't matter anyway. There was nothing.

Nobody.

Her eyes roamed the unbearably quiet room, her tortured mind traveling back to the gladiator arena more than a moon ago. *I don't want him touching me,* Lawri had shouted, *or touching Tala.* Then she'd tossed the severed head of the dead gladiator at the grand vicar. Tala thought she would never see a more horrid sight than that.

Until today in the infirmary. The image of Jovan striking off Lawri's arm was now a dark blot forever seared into her mind—her stunned mind. As she stood here in this grim room awaiting the Bloodwood, her heart was caught between beats in a silent cry, her mind naught but utter vacancy of thought, unable to comprehend what she had witnessed. *Is Lindholf even aware of his sister's plight?* In the slave quarry, her cousin probably wasn't aware of much beyond his own torment. *I've betrayed so many!*

She stared at the altar in the center of the room. *Even Lawri dreams of this cursed crypt.* Streaking the stone were dried rivulets of blood—Sterling Prentiss' blood. At the base of the altar, mingled with ashes and dirt and fragments of bone, were strange little carvings that curdled her blood with their unholy blasphemy. She had not seen them in her previous visits to this cursed place. Beasts of the underworld!

Curved jagged teeth and horns, scaled flesh and hooked wings, forked tails of bone and claw. *Dragons! How did I not see them before?* If this horrific stale place where Sterling Prentiss had been murdered could get any worse, Tala couldn't imagine how. As if her life could get any worse.

"Show yourself!" she shouted one last time. She wanted to cry. Yet no sound issued forth. Her lungs strained with pain as tears of unfathomable sorrow streamed over her face. "Just show yourself, stupid Bloodwood," she mumbled.

"Call for a Bloodwood," a familiar voice said from behind her, "and a Bloodwood will come."

Heart jumping in her chest, Tala whirled.

Hawkwood stood in the doorway, black cloak wrapped around his body from head to toe. Strapped to his back were two cutlasslike swords, their familiar spiked hilt-guards staring back at Tala accusingly. *But I threw them in the underground river!*

With a graceful gesture the man drew the hood back from his angular face with both hands. His gaze sliced through the red-hazed air, lingering on her as he stepped into the room.

"Are you a Bloodwood?" she asked him. "Are you *the* Bloodwood?"

"That is a long story." As he drifted toward her, his smile was wry, introspective, *captivating*. And she did not like it.

Tala remembered asking Roguemoore if Hawkwood had once been a Bloodwood assassin. The dwarf had never answered. Nonetheless, here the man was in the secret ways, almost admitting to his true nature. He *was* from Sør Sevier. A smidgen of fright infused her soul, and she stepped around the altar, keeping it between them.

He stopped, noticing her fright. "You've gotten yourself involved with a Bloodwood and don't know what to do, correct?"

She remained silent. Wary.

"You needn't fear me, Tala."

"What are you doing here?" she finally asked. "Shouldn't you be in Purgatory?" Immediately she realized the stupidity of the question. He'd been locked in Purgatory before, after the duel with the Dayknights, and he'd escaped. Of course he could escape a second time. *Blessed Mother Mia, even Glade and I wandered around in Purgatory virtually unmolested!*

Of course if Hawkwood had escaped a second time, Jovan had to know it. But he had not admitted to any such thing. Nor had Leif Chaparral. But that didn't surprise her. Individually they were both incompetent. Together, doubly so.

"What are you doing here?" she repeated.

"The secret ways are a dangerous place for a princess." He pulled one of the swords from over his back, set it on the altar between them. His gaze met hers coldly. "You've clearly ventured other places under the city that few have been, Tala."

"I go where I choose. What of it?" She would reveal nothing. "Again, answer my question. What are you doing here?"

"Perhaps I watch over you."

"I don't need watching over."

"I've no doubt." The corners of his mouth curled in a wry smile again. "But this game you play with the Bloodwood, you cannot win, Tala."

"Are you the Bloodwood who plays games with me?"

"You know in both head and heart that I am not."

*Head and heart?* She looked down at the sword he'd placed on the altar—the cross-shaped altar upon which Glade had murdered Sterling Prentiss. *What is he trying to tell me by showing me the sword?* Truth was, she didn't know what she knew anymore. Or what she herself even wanted. She looked up at him.

But his eyes were fixed on the sword, or more on the cross-shaped altar under it. His hand reached out and caressed the stone. "I wonder who else knows this altar is here?" he murmured almost to himself. Tala watched him, utterly vexed. His hands drifted over the altar, over his sword. Then he looked up at her. "I know you are frustrated," he said. "I've followed you here to help you, Tala."

"I need no help." *Lawri needs help!* All she could think of was her armless cousin in the infirmary. She felt the tears spring up in her eyes. She just wanted it all to end. Just wanted this seemingly impossible-to-win game with the Bloodwood to be over.

"Jovan cut Lawri's arm off," she mumbled. "Where will she ever get another?" Tala choked back the sobs she felt coming, ignored the tear she felt crawling down her cheek. "You wish to help?" she asked. "Can you regrow Lawri's arm?"

His eyes softened. "Not even a million faithful prayers to Laijon could regrow Lawri's arm. In that regard, the gods of each of the Five Isles are useless. As am I."

She met his gaze unwaveringly, demanding a better answer,

willing him to say something that might actually be helpful. Perhaps he had been a Bloodwood once. And perhaps he was not the current Bloodwood who plagued her. Still, she knew enough about Bloodwoods to know that he acted like one, vague and cryptic. And she'd had enough. Tala placed both her hands on the altar and leaned over it, leaned toward him. "State what you want plainly"—she swallowed hard—"or stay the fuck away from me."

His eyes narrowed. "You are smart, Tala. Smarter even than Jondralyn." He drew his cloak tighter around himself. "I am here to offer you the same as I offered your sister. Though I've no Sacrament of Souls to help teach you my craft."

There was a moment of silence between them. The implication of what he offered was clear. *His craft?* But it had only been an implication. And her patience had worn thin. "I said speak plainly. You did not. Now leave me alone."

Two languid hands rose up and pulled the hood back over his head, concealing his face again in shadow. "You will think on my offer, though?"

She stood straight, stoic. Folded her arms. Her indifference had reached a peak. "I will make my own way," she said.

"As I thought." He bowed to her. "But if you change your mind, just return my sword to me." He turned to go.

"And how will I find you?"

"The Val-Sadè," he said, and then took his leave, vanishing through the dark opening of the distant door, leaving his sword on the altar.

She breathed deep, relieved that he was gone. *How can I be so inconsistently weak and strong and afraid at the same time?* Emotions overwhelmed her in a warm flood. The lump in her throat grew. Tears welled up. Everything had just become more complex. *Does he really want to teach me his assassin skills? Train me as a Bloodwood? Does he really think I am smart? And what is Val-Sadè? Where is Val-Sadè? Who is Val-Sadè? Blessed Mother, he couldn't just answer me plainly!*

She snatched up his sword, knowing for a fact that it was one of the ones she had taken from Glade and tossed into the river. *How did he get it back?*

A flash of silver light cut through the scarlet shadows and drew her attention. Her tear-streaked gaze fell upon the horrid cross-shaped altar again, and she wondered if her eyes were playing tricks on her. In the center of the altar stone was a curious splash of silver—a coin-sized splatter that hadn't been there when she'd picked up the sword. Tala wiped her eyes with the back of one hand and stepped to the altar, Hawkwood's sword still gripped tight in her other hand.

Another drip of silver splashed down atop the first. She looked to the shadows of the arched ceiling to see a third droplet fall from the darkness, landing atop the first two, splashing, little pinprick splatters radiating out from the bigger puddle. She leaned over the altar. It was liquid—a curious silver liquid.

She reached forth her right hand, dabbed the tip of her pinky finger in the small puddle. There was a sizzle and smoke. She yanked her hand back, stunned. And when she looked at her tingling finger, the very tip of it was entirely gone.

---

*The King of Slaves could banish evil with naught but a look.*
—The Way and Truth of Laijon

---

## CHAPTER FIFTY-ONE

# NAIL

23ND DAY OF THE ANGEL MOON, 999TH YEAR OF LAIJON
West of Tevlydog, Gul Kana

The two mares were tethered in front of a deserted tavern in the middle of the abandoned town, dining on naught but stale water and moss. It appeared the neglected horses had been standing in front of the same trough for weeks.

Val-Draekin wanted to see if the two raggedy beasts were tame enough to ride. One was dapple gray, the other near black. Both were still saddled and bridled, the mangy tail of the dapple gray swatting at a swarm of gnats. With his leg still splinted, the Vallè's limp was pronounced as he stepped gingerly across the tavern's wood-plank porch toward the scraggly, lean horses. Their gaunt eyes widened as the Vallè drew near. Nail padded silently behind.

This was the first hamlet of any significance Nail and Val-Draekin had come across since leaving the glacier behind twelve days ago. It lay in the bottom of a twisting, boulder-studded valley of harsh pine and jagged cliffs. From the safety of the trees, they had observed it most of the morning before venturing down a rocky hillside dotted with gray thistle and blue flowers and entering the town. The place was hauntingly empty, a random cluster of thatched-roof cottages with darkened windows, a two-story wooden tavern in the center. The tavern's porch was naught but a set of rickety stairs under leaning eaves, one deadened lantern hanging useless in the lifeless air. The sky above the valley was white, roofed over by a thin layer of clouds.

Before entering the tavern, they'd searched the vacant cottages for food, finding nothing but cold stone hearths and bareness. The tavern had yielded even less, just empty cupboards and dust. Not even one piece of broken-down furniture remained in the entire town. "Likely used for burning," Val-Draekin had surmised.

"I reckon these hills were once teeming with humans," the Vallè remarked as they'd conducted their search. "Miners, farmers, loggers, hunters, trappers, all used to call these woods home. Until recently. Now looks like they've all fled their cabins and undefended villages for the protection of the bigger towns like Deadwood Gate or Tevlydog. Hragna'Ar seems to have everyone in the north spooked. And rightly so."

Val-Draekin surmised they were north of Deadwood Gate, possibly even closer to Tevlydog. In the twelve days since leaving the glacier, injured and tired as they were, they had not journeyed far in the Vallè's estimation. Nail had carried his companion a good portion of the way. Val-Draekin had only started walking by himself the last two days. More of a slow, ponderous limp, really. Still, they had plodded along through the forests and hills, catching fish if they could, which would be their only nourishment beyond a few wild blueberries. The streams and lakes were sparse. They slept cold under the stars, no gear, just the same travel-worn clothes on their backs they'd come out of the glacier with, not a single weapon for defense between them. There had been days where Nail had grown so hungry, it seemed that someone was constantly squeezing down on his stomach with a tight fist. Finally having horses to ride would be a fair boon indeed.

Val-Draekin stroked the snout of the dapple gray. The mare eyed him nervously. "I haven't any food for you, girl," he said, his soothing voice seeming to calm the horse. "I wish I did. But I don't. Perhaps together we can find something down the road." The Vallè beckoned Nail with a soft wave. "Come round slow; see if she'll let you mount up."

Nail flicked a strand of blond hair from his eyes and stepped off the porch, drifting cautiously around the dapple gray, the palm of his hand caressing her flank tenderly. He took hold of the saddle horn and pulled to see if the saddle was secure, and to see if the horse would jump. Both stayed steady. So he heaved himself up, the horse nervously shuffling a few steps sideways. But Nail settled into the saddle and steadied the mare with a squeeze of his legs. Val-Draekin untethered the horse from the hitching post. She nickered and snorted and tossed her head almost joyfully.

The Vallè was in the midst of untethering the second mare when Nail heard the *wwhhhppt!* of air and the wet smack of an arrow striking horseflesh. The dapple gray under him bucked and bellowed and let loose a ghoulish scream that pierced the silence of the abandoned village. Nail was tossed out of the saddle, landing hard in the dirt with a thud that knocked the breath from his lungs.

Another *wwhhhppt!* and the mare jumped again as a second arrow sank into her flanks next to the first, quivering. Val-Draekin snatched hold of her tether by the bit and tried to rein her in. But the frightened arrow-shot mare bolted away, yanking the Vallè into the dirt next to Nail.

Oghuls thundered from the forest surrounding the town, dozens of them, iron-booted feet echoing off canyon cliffs, crude armor a-clatter, spears and axes gripped in large gray fists. Nail lurched to his feet as they came charging from every direction. He scrambled to help Val-Draekin stand. But they were too late to run and were instantly surrounded, rusted and ragged spearheads bristling in their faces, pointing threateningly.

"Down on your knees!" the lead oghul rumbled, a helmetless blunt-faced fellow with a large, crooked nose and tapered forehead. Thick ringlets of filthy chain mail draped his chest and shoulders and dangled down past his thick thighs. He carried no weapon but for two mighty gauntlets of iron.

"On your knees!" he barked again. The clarity of his words was startling to Nail, who had only ever heard oghuls grunt and snarl. A spear was thrust within an inch of his face. Nail dropped to his knees as ordered. Val-Draekin did likewise.

"Tie them up!" the lead oghul ordered. Rough hands grabbed Nail's wrists, yanking them behind him, forcing his hands together palm to palm as leather cords were wrapped tight around the wrists.

Val-Draekin, also now bound, met Nail's gaze. "If it comes to Hragna'Ar," he said, "rest assured, Nail, I will slay you myself. You needn't suffer that."

"Shut up, Vallè scum!" The lead oghul clubbed Val-Draekin in the side of the head with a ponderous gauntleted backhand. Val-Draekin sagged to the dirt, unconscious, blood welling from a gash between his left eye and ear.

Strong hands hauled Nail to his feet, tearing the right side of his tattered shirtsleeve almost clean off. White-hot pain flared the length of his arm. *The mark of the cross, the mark of the slave, the mark of the beast!*

All the oghuls stopped and stared. The entirety of his arm was bare. The mermaid scar on his right arm and the slave brand on the underside of his wrist were red and raw, as was the cross-shaped scar on the back of his right hand. The black tattoo Stefan had given him aboard the *Lady Kindly* was also exposed.

"What's this?" the lead oghul snarled, motioning to the markings. "Who are you?"

"Nobody," Nail sputtered, wincing at the sudden stinging soreness engulfing his bare arm.

"Take him away!" the oghul growled.

"Ragn'R!" another oghul shouted.

"Ragn'R!" the throng of oghuls blared in unison.

† † † † †

The steep, winding trail led the horde of oghuls through thick pines slathered with moss and aspens and boulders roped with leafy vines. The thin sheet of clouds had vanished. Still, the chill of the evening air bit deep. Nail's lungs were hurting from the climb. As he trudged up the path, thongs of leather binding his hands behind his back, it was hard to keep his balance. Aspen branches reached over the trail like whispering claws, knocking into him.

Nail was so hungry, he found both his mind and body could scarcely function. But onward he plodded, afraid to rest, having already felt the sting of the lead oghul's barbed whip once. The gangly oghul clomping up the trail just ahead of him led the scraggly black mare by the bit. Val-Draekin was tied, stomach down, on the horse's swaying back, his hands bound behind him, legs dangling from the left flank, head from the right, dark hair matted with dripping blood. Nail didn't know the fate of the arrow-shot dapple gray. The sad fact was, out of sheer weariness and hunger, he and Val-Draekin had fallen into the oghuls' trap: the two mares had been merely bait.

They were high above the abandoned town now. Between gaps in the trees, Nail saw grim canyon walls rising above, peaks tinged with purple and red from the sunset. He stared up at the rough cliffs through the breaks in the trees, thinking he saw something hanging up there among the cruel gray rock. He grew light-headed looking up, so he focused back down on the trail at his feet.

They eventually entered a narrow draw, craggy columns of rock rising up on either side. The oghul leading the black mare stopped, untied the unconscious Vallè, and threw him over his own shoulder like a sack of potatoes. He continued on up the path, leaving the horse behind. The trail was rugged, a ruthless set of uneven stairs chiseled straight up the rock face. The stout oghul in front of Nail seemed to manage the ponderous climb just fine, even with Val-Draekin draped over his back.

After about a half hour of tedious hiking, the bleak path emptied them atop the cliff overlooking the valley. Near the edge of the cliff were two woolly musk oxen, twelve feet tall and scraggly, one with an oghul rider. Liz Hen had been right: the dirty beasts did look like upside-down mops, clumps of hair falling from the crown of their backs clear to the ground, massive tusks sprouting from their heads.

Beyond the two musk oxen, at the edge of the cliff, were five thick wooden posts pounded deep into the ground. The three heavy iron chains trailing from the three nearest posts over the rim of the cliff were rusted and scarred. The two farthest posts were also linked to similar iron chains. But those chains were coiled in the middle and connected to the top of cages constructed of iron poles lashed together with smaller chains, rope, and leather thongs. The square iron doors of both cages were swung open.

Nail was shoved toward the nearest of the cages. It couldn't have been more than three feet high, its crude iron poles and small door caked with filth. The cage's round underside looked exactly like the lid of one of the heavy iron cauldrons Baron Jubal Bruk used to boil his grayken oil. It was also stained from long use. The cage's circular roof was similar in shape and design to its bottom.

As the lead oghul began untying Nail's hands, the oghul carrying Val-Draekin dumped the Vallè, his leather armor caked with dirt and blood, before the farthest cage. The beast crammed Val-Draekin's limp body through the door of the crude pen.

Nail's hands were untied, yet he dared not move. He could only watch as the door of his unconscious travel companion's cage was pushed shut and then locked with a large iron lock. Val-Draekin leaned awkwardly against the iron bars of the makeshift pen, unaware of what was happening, his bleeding head listing, both arms lifeless at his side, both legs sticking straight out between the bars.

There seemed to be short whispered arguments between several of the oghuls about the scars visible on Nail's exposed arm, then the lead oghul grasped him by the back of the head and forced his face toward the opening of his cage, trying to shove him in. Nail struggled briefly, but the oghul was too strong. He soon found himself locked in the pen just like Val-Draekin, both legs sticking between the gaps in the bars. The scum-covered contraption reeked of rot and ruin. Had there been food in his stomach, Nail would have purged it from the stink.

He watched as five oghuls grabbed the heavy chain attached to Val-Draekin's cage, whilst five others lifted it. The Vallè's legs dragged in the dirt as they carried the pen toward the cliff. They set it down and slid it carefully over the rim. The five oghuls guiding the chain slowly lowered Val-Draekin's cage down the side of the cliff and out of view.

Then the oghuls marched toward Nail. He clutched the bars of his own pen tight as they lifted him toward the cliff and lowered him over the edge. The cage twisted and clattered against the lichen-covered rock face as it descended jerkily. His heart hammered against his ribs when he looked down. Two hundred feet beneath his dangling legs lay the unforgiving boulder-strewn base of the cliff. He spied the thatched-roof huts of the abandoned town hunkered in the trees far below.

The wind kicked up and groaned over the valley as his cage swayed to a stop some twenty feet below the precipice of the ridge. Val-Draekin's cage hung ten feet to Nail's left, slightly higher than his. The Vallè was still unconscious. To Nail's right were three other cages similar to theirs, arms and legs dangling from each. Crows pecked at the stiff, blackened limbs jutting from the two farthest cages.

But the man in the cage nearest his was alive. One curled hand reached between the bars toward Nail. Two widened white eyes stared from a blackened face, unblinking, dark pupils fixed on him. *Unblinking.*

The man had no eyelids. No brows. No hair on his head at all. Nor skin on his face. His whole body had been stripped of its skin. He was naught but pale sinew and red muscle and scraps of clinging flesh.

Nail knew this was not the work of the crows. The man had been flayed alive. Recently. By the oghuls above. *Hragna'Ar!*

Nail's mind flew back to the Sky Loch mines, back to the blood-filled cauldron and the trapper atop the altar. *Hragna'Ar!* He couldn't believe there was such savagery in Gul Kana. *Oghuls! How could such monsters even exist? How could the world be full of such savagery?*

The fleshless man tried to speak, pink tongue curling from his lipless, gurgling mouth. The noise was naught but a sickly wheezing hiss. He thrust his skinless arm out farther, stretching his clawlike fingers toward Nail. But the poor man's tender butt and thighs were stuck to the iron floor, his back to the iron bars behind him.

Nail looked away, doing his feeble best to ignore the eerie sounds issuing forth from the man. He tried uncurling his own clenched fingers from the bars of his prison. But they too were stuck to whatever foul filth stained the iron.

Horror-stricken, he realized . . .

. . . he was sitting in the torn and rotten remains of similarly flayed men.

*The Last Warrior Angels will lay false claim that it was I, your Blessed Mother Mia, who brought about the fall of Laijon. My own son, Raijael, will lay false claim that 'twas I who stole Dragon Claw, that handless hand he thought his birthright, that fell weapon I alone stripped from the corpse of the Last Demon Lord, that vile silver abomination that hath shredded the flesh of Laijon.*
—THE MOON SCROLLS OF MIA

# CHAPTER FIFTY-TWO
# JONDRALYN BRONACHELL

### 24TH DAY OF THE ANGEL MOON, 999TH YEAR OF LAIJON
### AMADON, GUL KANA

Squireck walked silently beside Jondralyn, steel-toed boots clicking against the marble tile floor, Dayknight sword girt at his hip. His polished black armor glittered with the sharp yellow reflections of the vast chamber's thousand candles.

They had the Temple of the Laijon Statue entirely to themselves. It was near midnight of the last day of the Angel Moon, and the temple, normally sunlit from the tall stained-glass windows above the gallery, was dark but for the dancing flames of the many candelabra. Jondralyn was always overwhelmed by the vast hollowness of the place and the majestic chamber's splendorous height and domed ceiling three hundred feet above. Her own heavy boots echoed through the temple as she circled the gray-veined pale stone dais of the Laijon statue. She wore Silver Guard armor. Her sword was strapped to her belt under a thick black cloak, the cowl of which was pulled over her head, concealing her in shadow. She hid her face, ashamed.

It had been a little over two moons since Gault Aulbrek's sword had slashed her. Less than two weeks since she had reopened the wound whilst in the Rooms of Sorrow. And two days since Val-Gianni had removed her bandages and fitted her with the eye patch. She had purposely sequestered herself in her own bedchamber, doing naught but staring at her own grotesqueness in the mirror. She stared at the one long scar that now defined her. It was red and ragged and fierce, stretching from the top of her face to the bottom. A scar that was only partially covered by a black eye patch for an eye that was gone. It seemed so unreal. And she couldn't accept it. She couldn't face the world.

At least the bandages had hidden what was underneath. Now she felt so vulnerable. She wished to fashion a helm or mask to cover her hideousness. She did not want to be seen in public, ever.

But she had promised Squireck that she would accompany him to the Temple of the Laijon Statue prior to his fight in the arena with Gault Aulbrek. He desired to pray before the great likeness of Laijon, and he'd wanted her by his side. He wanted it to be on the eve of the Eighth Day before his bout.

Now she hid behind the cowl of a cloak, not even wanting Squireck to see her, unless it was through the shadows cast by a thick, dark hood.

The Prince of Saint Only stopped and stared up at the statue.

Jondralyn dared not look up. She could not bear it, for fear the hood would fall from her face, exposing her. That, and she could not bear to look upon the spectacularly carved face of Laijon with its perfectly squared chin, smooth lips, nose, jaw, eyes, and brows, all so precise and elegant and peerless in beauty. No, she could not look up at all that perfection without having to acknowledge her own lack.

"This statue of Laijon," Squireck began, "has been my ideal, the reason I trained so hard in the dungeons under the arena with sword and ax and maul, to hone my own physique, to build my own muscles. I dreamed of this statue whilst I knelt in prayer for hours, begging Laijon to deliver me from mine enemies. Now, my body is naught but a vessel to honor the great One and Only."

"You should pray," she said, focusing on the tiles of the floor. His hero worship of the statue's unbearable beauty was like pointed daggers scraping across her soul.

"We've the place to ourselves," he said. "'Tis an honor to gaze upon such magnificence, do you not think?"

"I'd rather just go."

Squireck noticed she was not looking up, or at him, but straight at the floor.

"You needn't worry, Jon. I've seen the scar. I know you wear an eye patch. I do not judge you." His gaze traveled back up to the statue.

*But he does judge me.* He had been revolted by her face when the bandages had come off in the Rooms of Sorrow. She'd borne the brunt of his reaction. He could never take back that initial look of horror that had spread across his face. She would remember it always. And now that he continued to feign devotion toward her, continued to somehow always be near her, always be willing to help her—it was just too much. She just wanted space away from him to breathe. She did not trust the attachment and devotion she saw now in him.

She stared at the base of the raised dais before her. Stared at the statue's carved booted feet, stared at the five black-and-silver cauldrons and the tendrils of incense swirling from each, stared at the five life-size marble oxen that bore the burden of the smoking cauldrons, each boulderlike head facing outward as if on watch. Each cauldron's surface was gilded with symbols inlaid in white, black, green, blue, and red. This was the first time she'd noticed the symbolic detail. The colors were representations of the magical angel stones and weapons of the Five Warrior Angels: *Blackest Heart, Ethic Shroud, Forgetting*

*Moon, Lonesome Crown,* and *Afflicted Fire,* the Five Pillars of Laijon.

*Ethic Shroud.* She pictured the glorious white shield in her mind as a coldness settled over her skin. She recalled what Lawri Le Graven had said in Sunbird Hall. *The weird dreams are full of weird things buried in cross-shaped altars. . . .*

"The wreath of white heather atop Laijon's head," Squireck was saying, "represents the purity of his cause. It was sheer brilliance that Tala twined a similar wreath for me. I always figured 'twas you who put her up to it."

She answered, "The wreath of heather was Tala's gift and Tala's alone."

"As you wish," he said curtly. He was growing impatient with her. "The symbolism of me wearing the wreath in the arena was surely ordained in heaven," he said. "I will wear it again when I face Gault."

She wished she had not come with him tonight.

"Did I not look the spitting image of the statue, Jon? In the arena, fighting with the wreath atop my head, did I not look exactly like this statue?"

Jondralyn didn't need to look up to remember the wreath circling the statue's head, or what the Prince of Saint Only had looked like in the arena. She'd seen both Squireck and the statue plenty before. Squireck had been all hardened muscles and magnificence. And at more than five stories tall, the likeness of Laijon was carved of Riven Rock marble, one arm held aloft and a great sword in that hand pointing skyward. The great statue of Laijon—the focal point of worship, pilgrimage, and faith in all the Five Isles—was all hardened muscle and magnificence. And yes, in the arena, Squireck had looked exactly like the statue.

"He is my cousin, you know," Squireck said.

"Who?" Jondralyn asked, distracted by her own thoughts.

"Ser Gault Aulbrek."

"Yes, I did know."

"His mother, Evalyn, was my father's eldest sister," Squireck said. "She wed a Sør Sevier nobleman, a lord of the Nordland Highlands named Agus Aulbrek. 'Twas a controversial marriage at the time. They were both assassinated. Gault was their only surviving child. I'd never laid eyes on him until I saw him chained in Sunbird Hall."

"I said I know who he is." She really wanted to go.

"I wonder what he knows of the Brethren of Mia, of the lost angel stones and weapons of the Five Warrior Angels."

"Why would he be privy to any of the workings of the Brethren of Mia?"

"Gault's mother, along with my father's other two sisters, Elynor and Elyse, held secret allegiance to the Brethren of Mia. It is why they defied Edmon. How my mother and two aunts came to know of the *Moon Scrolls* is unclear. But my own mother also paid secret homage to the Brethren. Was she who got me involved."

She had never before heard him speak of Beatriz Van Hester. "How is your mother now?" she asked.

"How would I know?" Squireck's answer came quickly. "Adin Wyte is long conquered, my father the forgotten king of a ruined kingdom, the fate of his queen a mystery, especially to one such as I, one who has been locked away for murder."

He turned, facing her squarely, his black armor creaking as he straightened his stance before her. "Did you not keep up with the goings-on in Saint Only whilst I was imprisoned? Did you hear no word or rumor of her fate? Do you not know if she still lives? Did you show any concern at all?"

Jondralyn felt immediately ashamed that she had not. She had failed her once betrothed in many ways. Even now she was impatient with him for nothing, for her own insecurities. *I have been so selfish my entire life—*

"Why did you agree to come here with me, Jon?" he asked, the quiet fear in his eyes all too evident.

"Because you asked. And I did not want to disappoint you."

"You did not wish to come at all."

"That is not what I'm saying."

"It is exactly what you're saying."

He was right. And she was growing frustrated with him.

"I love you, Jon," he said. "I always have."

"Squireck, please," she sighed. "You are my friend. That is all I want. Friendship. Cannot that be enough?"

The fear in his eyes quickly changed to bitterness, then annoyance. "If you are not interested in me as more than friends, why come to watch me pray before Laijon tonight? Why spend any time with me?"

"I wish to support you, to share in your triumphs. And I hope you will be there for me, too, when I need you. But as friends."

"I can't accept that," he answered. "To be just friends is a mistake. It is wrong. I can't be near you without *wanting* you, Jon."

"And I cannot give you what you want."

"Why not?"

"I can't explain." She put as much reassurance in her voice as she could. "I just don't see you as any more than a friend." She felt nothing for him. Harsh fact was, she scarcely thought of him at all. Hawkwood consumed her every thought.

Sometimes it was enough just to be near Hawkwood and hear him speak—it didn't even matter about what: Bloodwoods, assassins, anything he said could arouse her passion for him. She finally looked up and met Squireck's gaze sternly, not caring if he saw her scar. "Romance. Desire. It will never happen for us. I wish it could, but it won't. It's just a feeling I have about these things, an instinct."

Hurt and confusion melted over his face. She wished this conversation had never started. "Besides," she said, "relationships are difficult, full of resentments. We would make each other miserable in the end."

"Have I not treated you well?"

"You treat me wonderfully." *But I can never forget that look on your face when you first saw my scars in the Rooms of Sorrow.* It was going so wrong, this conversation. She needed to guide it in a new direction. Make him feel like there was some hope. "You have taught me so much of the Brethren of Mia. Led me down paths to knowledge that I would never have found on my own. That is what is important to me. To our relationship. Our common goals in stopping war and suffering. We've much to accomplish together, you and I. But when it comes to love . . . the truth is, you can do better than me, Squireck."

"And you presume to know what is best for me? It is your love I want. Not mere friendship. I cannot accept less than I give. I will not be *just* your friend."

"Please don't end our lifetime of friendship over my choice. Such a thing would do great insult to me as a person. It would make me feel that . . . that I have only ever been a potential lover to you, and not a real person with my own hopes and desires." Her voice was growing harsh. "Is that all I have ever meant? Is that all I have ever been worth in your eyes, Squireck? Love? Romance? Sex?"

"And where is the crime in desiring such things? Lest you forget, we were betrothed once."

"But that is over. And you must listen to me now, hear what I am saying *now*. I cannot give you what you want. I've my own issues to deal with. I would make you so miserable. So unhappy." She repeated, "I cannot give you what you want."

"But you can give Hawkwood what he wants?" he snapped. "That is the type of man you desire. A traitor. A killer. A loser who killed your very own mother—"

She slapped his face. Her blow hardly moved him from his spot. Her hand stung. "You do not know Hawkwood like I do," she snarled.

She knew of the rumors—that her mother had not died in childbirth, but rather by the poison of assassins. Roguemoore had mentioned as much. That her father believed it. That her father had gone to war against Aeros because of his belief in those rumors. She'd also heard the rumors that Hawkwood had been the assassin. But she did not believe that rumor. Would not.

"You do not know Hawkwood like I do," she repeated.

"I know him well enough," Squireck said coldly. "He uses you, Jon. Uses you for his own ends. He is lecherous and most foul—"

"It is you who is lecherous," she shot back.

"I am no lech." He scowled, lips pursed in anger. "I am better than Hawkwood in every way. Born of royal blood. Blessed by Laijon in the arena. Can you not see?"

"He has done naught but fight for our cause, same as you."

"Right. Exactly. He has read the *Moon Scrolls*. He's plumbed the secrets of Mia. He knows the history of the Five Warrior Angels. He knows history is bound to repeat itself. He knows the prophecies. Your beloved Hawkwood knows that the destiny of the Princess lies with the Gladiator. He connives to thwart the will of Laijon. He is a lech."

"*That* is in the *Moon Scrolls*?" she asked, suddenly horrified at the prospect. "That the Princess and Gladiator are to be together?"

"Hawkwood is using you, Jon. And you don't even know it. I've seen his leering looks. I see his lusts. He wants to take your maidenhood, not out of love, but to thwart the will of Laijon."

Nothing he said was helping. It just confused her and made him seem more weak in her eyes, made her want to withdraw more, to lash out at him.

"It is you who stares at me with lust, who leers at me uncontrollably." Jondralyn knew her words were cruel and meant to humiliate. She also knew they were not completely true, but still they spilled forth in a rush. "It is you who treats me as if I'm naught but a potential sex partner. That is the one thing Hawkwood has never done, stare at me as you do."

"How can you say that if he's the one you rut with?"

"How dare you accuse me—"

"So he has not *stared* at you in the throes of passion?"

"How dare you presume the manner of my relationship with him?"

"The point is, I am no lech. And still you accuse me of such. And I enter the arena on the morrow to fight for you, Jon, to kill Gault Aulbrek, my own blood kin, the man who maimed you. It is I who seek to avenge you. All whilst Hawkwood does nothing."

"I do not need anyone to *avenge* me."

"Yet that is the type of man I am," he continued on, as if he hadn't even heard her. "Honorable and true. Hawkwood was on that oxcart with you and Gault for days and did not kill the man. Did not avenge you as he should have."

"He was injured, as was I."

"You make excuses for him."

"He saved my life. He stitched me together."

"Stitched you together?" Squireck scoffed. He took a step back, throwing up his arms in exasperation. "And you believe that? Everything he says is a lie. How can you love such a liar? It is unacceptable."

*He sounds so much like Jovan in his fervor. Irrational. Unpredictable.* She found that she was actually scared of this man standing before her. This imposing *stranger* in Dayknight armor. *He hasn't listened to a thing I've said.* It was the most maddening conversation she'd ever been in. Ever heard. She did not feel safe. She never had.

"I can love who I want." She let the words hang between them. His eyelids tightened as he glared down at her. *I am not answerable to him.* "It is I who decides where my heart falls, Squireck. Not you."

Hurt. Bitterness. Anger. Betrayal. Humiliation. Resentment. Every one of those emotions was evident in his face, every one of those emotions had slithered right through his defenses and set up camp behind his eyes. But it was the helplessness she saw in his slackening face that made the final decision for her. *He is all talk.* Everything he had previously said was naught but feigned bravado. And it was his utter lack of confidence that she despised most.

"It's best I go." She bowed to him. "I will leave you to pray by yourself."

"Go then," he said, straightening his posture, that feigned poise and confidence creeping back into his tone. "Run from your problems, Jon. Do not face them."

*My only problem is you.* She was already walking away from him, boots clacking against the marble tile. *Yes, my only problem is you, Squireck Van Hester, and you've made me feel like I should be running, not walking.*

"Love is not full of resentments as you say, Jon," he called out, his voice growing in conviction. "It does not make everyone miserable. I am not skeptical and cynical like you. I am not afraid to take a chance and open my heart. I won't give up. I did not give up in prison. I did not give up in the arena. I fought. No matter how difficult things were, I fought. I triumphed."

She had moved around the Laijon statue, almost out of earshot now.

"I will win you in the end!" he shouted. "You will choose me!"

*A true soldier never steals anything; he merely takes it. A true soldier shall always keep his sword loose in its scabbard, ready for slaughter.*
—THE CHIVALRIC ILLUMINATIONS OF RAIJAEL

# CHAPTER FIFTY-THREE
# GAULT AULBREK

1ST DAY OF THE FIRE MOON, 999TH YEAR OF LAIJON

AMADON, GUL KANA

An unseen orchestra above Gault Aulbrek played a somber melody. Squireck Van Hester, Prince of Saint Only, son of King Edmon Guy Van Hester and Queen Beatriz Van Hester, famed murderer of one of the five archbishops of Amadon and renowned gladiator of the Amadon Arena, stared at Gault from across the sand-covered iron platform. Along with the resonance of the orchestra somewhere above, sunlight streamed down on Squireck from the rectangular hole in the ceiling. Gault remained in shadow.

The sand-covered platform they stood upon was five feet wide, twelve across, and several feet thick. It boasted four stiff chains, one rising from each corner up to four stout iron hoists and pulleys. The platform hung a few inches above the cobbled floor of the arena's underground catacombs, suspended from the four chains some twenty feet below the arena's sandy surface above. Ten Dayknight guards in black armor stood in the shadows circling the platform, spear tips glinting in what faint yellow light reached them.

Squireck was taller than Gault by a good four inches. But he was not lanky. And he was not awkward. He was all bulging muscles and might, long hair flowing in blond waves over broad shoulders. He wore naught but a white loincloth tied at the waist and a wreath of white flowers about his head. A black longsword was gripped in his right hand, its black-opal pommel marking it as a Dayknight blade. His left shoulder bore a square brand—a gladiator brand.

Gault bore the twin RR of the Riven Rock slave quarry, red and raw upon his own neck. He once again carried the Sør Sevier sword he'd brought with him from Ravenker at his belt, the sword that had struck Jondralyn Bronachell's face. He reckoned it was a symbolic gesture that they had returned it to him. They wanted him to fight with it. They wanted him to be defeated with that exact same sword in hand. They had also given back his Knight of the Blue Sword armor. He wore the armor now and held the helm in the crook of his left arm.

"Cousin," the Prince of Saint Only acknowledged him from across the platform, bowing his head slightly. Gault did not return his cousin's bow.

He glanced into the darkness to his right and met the frightened gazes of Lindholf Le Graven and the girl Delia. Both stood about ten feet to the left of the platform; both still wore their dusty Riven Rock slave garb of simple make. All three of them had been pulled from the quarry not three hours ago and marched through the streets of Amadon to the arena. Ten days in the quarry, but it had seemed like a lifetime. Every muscle in Gault's body felt abused and useless. Aches blanketed his body, and both hands were worn raw from working the rock. His stomach burned with hunger from the pitiful rations. Upon entering the arena, he'd been allowed a few requests: one was water for himself, Lindholf, and Delia; the other was a razor to shave his head bald. Both had been granted. And the simple act of shaving the dirty stubble from his head had made him feel slightly more like himself after the painful drudgery of the quarry. His request for food had been denied. Lindholf and Delia had been told that they would be hung for their crimes in the center of the arena after the fight between Squireck and Gault.

The platform shook; the four chains creaked and groaned. The sound of the orchestra above dwindled to a cheerless, dull hum.

"Make no mistake, Ser Gault." Squireck's voice again broke over the dying tide of music. Gault turned his silent attention from Lindholf and Delia to the tall man on the platform before him. "I am not Jondralyn Bronachell." Squireck's eyes tightened as he went on, "I am no *mere* woman. I am a true knight of Gul Kana. I can fight, furious and savage. And you, cousin, will die here today."

Gault remained silent.

"You can also thank me for that armor you wear," Squireck prattled on. "'Twas me who insisted it be returned to you. Not that it will do you any good. Amadon will see you die in the colors of the enemy."

"And you with no armor," Gault finally spoke. "What foolishness is that?"

"I am the *Gladiator*." Squireck's posture straightened even more, if that were possible. "Laijon is with me. He will see me victorious. Blessed Mother Mia guides my sword."

"Your surety implies I am naught but a dead man in the eyes of Laijon," Gault said. "What makes you more special than I?"

"I am one of the Brethren of Mia." Squireck held his head high. "I have the truth."

"The truth?" Gault scoffed.

"Laijon has already shown me his mercy and favor, in this very arena."

"Or perhaps you were merely better than the other fighters," Gault said, a droll lilt in his tone. "However *few* there were."

"Several dozen," Squireck boasted. "'Twas only by Laijon's will they were slain."

"You give the gods too much credit."

"I humbly give Laijon all credit."

Gault spoke softly, succinctly. "Then I will make this as simple as I can, cousin, so we can both be assured whose side the gods are on. You say you've killed several dozen men? Well, I have seen ten years of war. Killed *thousands* in the name of the gods. I *spit* on both Laijon and his son Raijael." Gault spat on the sand-covered platform between them, his voice rising. "And I would fuck your precious Mother Mia in the ass."

Squireck blanched. "You've truly *no* honor."

"I fuck honor in the ass too."

The music's swell and crescendo above had stopped. The chains of their platform rattled again. Squireck looked up. Gault, too.

A loud voice shouted, "History will know it as the Great Battle of the Fire Moon!" The voice boomed from above, reverberating down through the rectangular hole in the arena floor, loud and succinct. "The enemy of Amadon and all Gul Kana, Knight Archaic of Sør Sevier and personal guard of the White Prince, Aeros Raijael, Ser Gault Aulbrek, against our own arena champion and Dayknight, the Prince of Saint Only, Ser Squireck Van Hester!"

The throng above roared.

The platform the two fighters stood upon began to rise toward the arena floor with a grinding of gears. Gault hated to admit it, but as the platform hauled him up, he was awed by the immensity of the crowd's deafening, swelling sound. Soon his head was above ground and still rising, the arena finally revealed around him in all its glory. The light of the sun illuminated flowery stonework palisades, tan awnings, and tall columns. Crenulated balconies rose up in majesty, circling the grandstands brimming with spectators.

As the platform drew even with the arena's sand-covered floor and settled to a stop, Gault's gaze fell upon the king's suite above the orchestra pit. Two spear-wielding Dayknights stood on either side of Jovan Bronachell. The grand vicar and the Quorum of Five Archbishops of Amadon were seated on a riser behind the king. Other nobles and Gul Kana royalty were gathered in the suite. Gault noticed Jondralyn Bronachell, cloaked and hooded. He could only imagine what the injuries hidden under the cowl must look like now. Injuries he himself had gifted her.

With a jerk, the platform settled into place, flush with the arena floor.

The herald above the king's suite leaned into the copper tubes that magnified his voice and bellowed, "Let the fight begin!"

The crowd erupted in a thunderous wave of noise that punched Gault right in the gut. *Do they come to watch the beauty of battle?* he asked himself, gaze soaking in the scene, the massive roar nearly drowning out his own thoughts. *Or do they just come out of a curiosity to watch violent death?* If the throng were as inured to the horrors of war as he, battle-tested even a little, they would not rush to watch men bleed for sport. Or so Gault figured.

The din eventually quieted. And Gault drew his sword.

Squireck faced the throng, shouting, "A true soldier and honorable man would strip off his armor and fight as I do!" There was a challenge in his eyes, which raked the crowd. Then he lifted both arms as he faced the king's suite, Dayknight sword gripped in one hand, showing everyone in attendance how exposed and vulnerable he was, his back to his enemy. "A true soldier and honorable man would fight on equal terms!" Then he turned and pointed his sword at Gault. "Are you, Ser, an honorable man?"

Gault didn't speak any louder than was necessary for Squireck to hear. "You want to act a fool and fight in your underwear with flowers atop your head, then that is between you and Laijon." He let the helm slide from the crook of his arm into his gauntleted hand, then placed it over his head and waited.

The vast horde jeered and mocked and booed.

Squireck smiled triumphantly as the crowd's disapproval rained down. Through the eye slit of his helm, Gault studied his foe, measuring the man's weaknesses, uncaring that the people of Amadon did not like him or his armor or his honor. Their boos turned to cheers as Squireck set his stance. *I can best him easily sword-on-sword.* Gault didn't move. He just stood there, sword held loosely in hand, blade dangling casually at his side. *But I mustn't let him get hold of me in hand-to-hand combat. Weight and strength will work to his advantage then.*

The Prince of Saint Only launched his attack, charging, magnificent Dayknight sword swinging at Gault's head, a great arching stroke that made the very air hum.

Gault merely stepped back and slightly to the side.

Squireck's blade missed him by a foot. The momentum of the attack carried the prince forward, and he was thrown off balance, stumbling easily within Gault's reach as the wreath of white heather tumbled from his head to the sand.

Gault didn't move to counter. Again, he just stood there, sword held loosely in hand.

Squireck righted himself quickly, scowling, long blond hair tousled, black blade wavering menacingly between them. He launched his second attack, a powerful swing from the opposite angle. Gault merely stepped back again, this time checking the blow with a rapid backhanded counter, deflecting the Dayknight blade over his head.

Then he brought his own blade swiftly back around, the very tip carving a thin line in Squireck's upper torso from shoulder to shoulder. A long sliver of red welled from the Prince of Saint Only's bare chest as he tottered back, surprised. The wound dribbled dark blood down his front.

Squireck glanced at the wound, roared, and attacked again.

Gault killed his cousin with the same move he'd used on Jondralyn

Bronachell in Ravenker, only this time he didn't pull his final blow.

His Sør Sevier blade clove the Prince of Saint Only's skull straight down the center to mid-nose. Jerking the sword free of bone and brains, Gault swept his weapon up and around and struck the man's head from his neck.

The Prince of Saint Only's knees folded as he toppled sideways to the arena floor, cloven head landing in a puff of sand at his feet.

Silence filled the arena.

Wind rippled the tan awnings above.

Gault's sword was stained red, gripped in one gauntleted hand. He tossed the weapon to the ground, then reached up and pulled off his Sør Sevier helmet. The breeze bit into his skin as he threw the helm in the sand too.

His eyes lanced through the crowd, locating King Jovan Bronachell.

There was a heavy rattle of chains as the wrought-iron gates on either end of the arena rose up with a deep rattle and grind. An armored knight rode out from the southern gate on a sorrel charger, a rope and meat hook fixed to his saddle horn. Behind the horseman came twenty armed Dayknights, all fully armored, all charging toward Gault. Twenty similar Dayknights also ran at him from the northern gate.

Gault bent and picked up his cousin's severed head by a matted clump of bloody blond hair and walked casually with it across the sand in the direction of the king's suite.

Twenty long strides of measured purpose, and he hurled the Prince of Saint Only's cloven head as high and far as he could. Over the throng of musicians the head spun wildly toward the king of Amadon, long hair whipping thick, ropy trails of blood and brains as it soared.

But Gault didn't see where Squireck's head landed. Instead he ate a face full of sand, tackled from behind by the rushing Dayknights.

*The grace of the great One and Only be with the people of his church in those final fiery hours of Absolution. For the sword of Laijon is bathed in blood.*
—THE WAY AND TRUTH OF LAIJON

# CHAPTER FIFTY-FOUR
# TALA BRONACHELL
### 1ST DAY OF THE FIRE MOON, 999TH YEAR OF LAIJON
### AMADON, GUL KANA

Tala sat in the king's suite with the young Le Graven twins, Lorhand and Lilith, at her side. Jondralyn was slumped in her chair on the other side of Tala, the hood of her cloak pulled over her face. The twins' mother, Mona Le Graven, sat behind Tala with Mona's eldest daughter, Lawri—all of them awaiting the hanging of Lindholf.

Lawri's face was pale, and weariness and defeat veiled her eyes—sickly orbs streaked with green. Her arm, or what was left of it, was wrapped in white bandages and concealed under a thick cloak on her lap, hidden from curious eyes. Val-Gianni had plied her with rare Vallè medicines to help ease the pain and lend speed to her healing. And she seemed to be doing well, despite all. The Vallè sawbones and Val-Korin sat near Lawri too, their eyes ever watchful.

In the six days since Jovan had chopped off Lawri's arm, Tala hadn't found the right words to express her heartache to her cousin. They had remained apart, Tala feeling guilty, knowing that the entire horror was her fault. And now here they were, finally together again, in this most horrific of places.

The wind howled and sobbed as it broke over the towering columns of the arena. Within the king's suite lived an ailing silence broken only by the awning snapping in the swirling air. Squireck Van Hester's headless body had been hooked and then dragged back to the iron platform, then lowered into the bowels of the arena, sand raked over the bloody trail. The rectangular hole where the platform had disappeared was still visible, like a haunted dark cave punched into the floor of the vast fighting pit. It pulled at Tala's gaze. *A place of ghouls and wraiths.*

All in the king's suite had seen the Prince of Saint Only's severed head sail through the air toward them, split from crown to nose, blood and brains raining over the orchestra below as it landed with a wet thump at Grand Vicar Denarius' feet. The Dayknights guarding the vicar had simply scooped up the head and placed it in a leather sack.

Tala couldn't wrap her brain around the fact that the gruesome bloody orb had belonged to a man she once knew. She couldn't push the terrible images of the day's events from her tortured mind. She hated the arena, loathed the pointless slaughter. In the past, she had kept her eyes closed during the gladiator bouts.

But she'd watched this time, wanting to see the Prince of Saint Only slay the enemy. Wanting to witness the death of the Sør Sevier knight who had participated in the slaughter of innocent citizens of her kingdom. She'd wanted to see the knight who had injured her sister suffer equal amounts of pain.

*But what was proven today? Gault Aulbrek still lives.*
*What holy laws did Laijon uphold with today's result? None.*

Squireck's grisly death had been met with gasps from those in the king's suite, followed by sniffles and weeping moans of distress that continued still.

"Oh, recover yourselves, people!" Jovan's admonition burst forth in a rush of breath, the first words from his mouth since Squireck's murder. "Can you not see? It is a good thing the Prince of Saint Only is now killed and dead. It is only what he had coming. Laijon's will toward that traitor is now finally known! God hath spoken! And now we get the further honor of watching Gault Aulbrek hang for his crimes!"

Jondralyn rose at her brother's words. "You have just sealed the fate of all Gul Kana and the entire Five Isles today with your selfishness and folly." The hood fell back slightly, her face no longer hidden in shadow. "Do you not know who Squireck is? Do you not know how important—"

"Do I not know how important he was to you?" Jovan raged. "No! I do not know! For it seems you had forsaken him long before I!"

Under the fringe of the hood, Jondralyn's face stiffened into a mask of hate. With the scar and eye patch, there was a fierceness to her that was almost captivating. In Tala's opinion, there was no reason for her sister to hide behind the cowl of the cloak. She was still the most beautiful woman in all Amadon.

Jondralyn slumped back down into her seat, the fight taken out of her too easily this time. Tala had never seen her sister give up so quickly.

*But who can blame her? We are all of us lost and alone.*

The tip of Tala's finger was missing, just a sliver of it, eaten away by some dripping silver she'd touched in the secret ways. But the sight of it made her feel alone. *So many mysteries. So many lies.* She'd taken Hawkwood's sword, hid it inside the hearth in her bedchamber.

A low drumroll sounded from the orchestra pit underneath the king's suite. The attention of all was once again drawn to the floor of the arena and the dark rectangular hole there. With the distant grind of gears, the iron platform rose a second time to the sand-covered deck of the arena. Three thick wooden gallows poles shaped like inverted *L*s appeared from the hole, growing taller as the platform ascended, a hangman's noose dangling from ring bolts on the underside of each braced tail of the *L*.

Three prisoners—Gault Aulbrek, Lindholf Le Graven, and Delia—rose up from the hole too. Each prisoner stood under one of the gallows poles, a wooden stool at their feet, each stool tied to a rope of its own. Gault was still in his Sør Sevier armor, which glinted dull and lusterless. The two others were dressed in naught but dirty prison raiment. Ten Dayknights were lined up behind the three prisoners and the three poles.

Dressed all in black, the cloaked and masked executioner stood directly in front of Lindholf, the centermost prisoner on the platform. The barmaid stood under the pole to Lindholf's right, the Sør Sevier knight to his left, all three with hands bound behind their backs, RR slave brands burned into their necks.

The crowd was silent. The drumroll swelled.

Tala's eyes clung to the three waiting nooses. Judging from the height of the stools, and the length of the ropes, she knew what type of execution this would be. A short-drop. No ten-foot drop and quick snap of the neck for any of them. It would be a long, lingering, and painful struggle for breath as they all slowly suffocated. Jovan was truly the cruelest person she knew. Lindholf did not deserve a death like this. Perhaps the other two did. But not Lindholf.

The ten Dayknights stepped off the platform and took up their stations, three in front of the gallows poles, the remaining seven ten paces behind, all facing the gallows poles.

The herald above the king's suite shouted into the copper tubes, voice booming. "We have all come to witness justice! A justice to be long remembered! You have come to the hanging of the two assassins who murdered the Dayknight captain, Ser Sterling Prentiss, the two assassins who conspired to kill our beloved king, Jovan Bronachell!

The two assassins captured by four of our own Silver Guard, including the valiant Glade Chaparral."

Glade and his three Silver Guard cronies, Tolz, Alain, and Boppard, stepped out from behind the king's seat and took their bows. Tala wanted to vomit as a smattering of applause sounded, applause that grew in volume, followed by cheering. Only she knew Lindholf did not deserve any of this! *And Glade Chaparral can rot in the underworld for his part in all of it.*

The applause died and the herald's voice again boomed. "And you have come to witness the hanging of your enemy, Gault Aulbrek, Knight Archaic of Sør Sevier! For the great One and Only will not be mocked in his own house of slaughter! Laijon's justice shall be served!"

The crowd was again feverish, their roar of approval staggering. *Laijon's justice indeed!* Her brother had perfectly woven Squireck's death in the arena and Gault's subsequent hanging into one all-encompassing blanket of truth and fairness and convenience for him. Tala had nurtured a hope that Lindholf would be spared. But there he was, down there in the center of the arena, standing under a gallows pole, frightened and alone. There was scant little justice in any of it. *Where is Laijon now?* her mind cried. *Where is truth and fairness now?*

The cheering eventually died down.

"Has Lord Lott Le Graven come to accept his son's treason?" she heard Jovan ask their aunt Mona.

"My husband has come to accept that Lindholf was never any son of his," Mona answered. "As have I."

Anger flared in Tala's heart. All of Mona's children were present. Jovan had ordered them all to watch the execution of their brother.

And deep down Tala knew it was all her own fault. Her own failure. *Lawri's arm. Lindholf's fate at the end of the hangman's noose.* It was all because of her and the game with the Bloodwood. *I was so out of my depth! Whatever did I hope to win?*

Now all she could do was watch the destruction she had wrought.

The drums of the orchestra rolled as each of the condemned was helped up onto a stool by the three Dayknights positioned in front of them. The masked executioner tightened the nooses around the necks of each of one by one. Soon the low wail of bagpipes joined the drums, and the crowd fell into silence.

The executioner picked up the rope tied to the barmaid's stool. He took a step back from his work, his masked face turning toward the king's suite, awaiting the signal from the king. The orchestra's dawdling melody spread its low, captivating tendrils as all in the arena awaited Jovan's go-ahead.

Tala's gaze fell on her cousin. *Lindholf.* Even from so far away, she could see that his deformed face was frozen in pale terror. Her heart went out to him. He had no idea why he was even down there with a noose around his neck. She'd told Glade some semblance of lies. She had told Lindholf nothing.

The drumroll raced to its zenith and crashed to silence.

And Jovan gave his signal.

The executioner yanked the stool from under Delia. The barmaid dropped naught but a foot, rope snapping taut. Her legs kicked as she thrashed at the end of the swaying rope, face straining and red.

As Delia struggled, the executioner walked to the opposite end of the platform and took hold of the rope hooked to Gault Aulbrek's stool, his masked face again looking up at the king's suite, awaiting the signal. And Jovan gave it.

The Sør Sevier knight dropped, rope snapping tight, gallows creaking as he swung and twisted, Sør Sevier armor glinting shards of flickering light. Gault did not struggle. He merely closed his eyes, as if in comfortable acceptance of his fate.

*Gault Aulbrek finally dead!* She wanted to cheer the sight, but there was still one person left to hang.

The executioner moved to the middle and grasped the rope

attached to Lindholf's stool, again turning to the king's suite, await-ing the signal . . .

And Jovan gave it.

Lindholf dropped.

Silence followed.

There was a crack and *whoosh* of air somewhere above the arena, and a crossbow bolt punched into the executioner's masked face right between the eyes.

He toppled forward, face slamming into the platform, steel tip of the crossbow bolt jutting bloody and sharp from the back of his cloaked head.

One of the three Dayknights in front rushed to his aid.

Another loud snap and *whoosh* of air from somewhere above Tala, and a second quarrel slammed into the wooden gallows directly above Lindholf, a thin black cord tied to the haft. There was a gasp from the crowd as every eye followed the thin black line—a line that stretched from the gallows pole to high above the king's suite.

Tala whirled in time to see what looked like a giant man-sized bat launch itself from the highest crenulated stone balcony above. It flew, its black hooded wings flapping in the wind as it dove straight down toward the center of the arena.

"May the wraiths take us all!" one of the archbishops screamed.

"Blessed Mother Mia!" someone else shouted.

And then Tala realized it wasn't a bat at all. *It's the Bloodwood!*

Her mind reeled as she watched the hooded assassin sail straight toward Lindholf. Black cloak aswirl, one leather-gloved hand gripping the taut cable, the other grasping a black crossbow. The Bloodwood fired a third quarrel into the Dayknight kneeling over the executioner. The bolt sank into the knight's back plate armor and dropped him.

The assassin sailed over Tala's head, sliding down the rope with increasing speed. It was then that she noticed the brilliant white sword with a crescent-moon-shaped hilt strapped to the Bloodwood's back, partially concealed by the fluttering black cloak. As long as the assassin was tall, the sword was total gleaming majesty, shooting shards of bright light in every direction.

The crowd gasped and shrieked.

The Bloodwood slowed its descent and let go of the line, landing gracefully on the platform in front of Lindholf's dangling form. The hooded mantle kept the assassin's face shrouded in shadow. The Bloodwood set the crossbow down on the platform as the remaining nine Dayknights drew their swords and rushed forward.

The Bloodwood clapped, two gloved hands smacking together loudly. And the air around the three gallows poles was a sudden haze of misty white chalk. Then from over his back, the assassin smoothly drew forth the long glittering sword with both hands.

In one sweeping downward arc, the assassin struck the iron platform with the glorious white blade.

Sparks flew.

And the entire platform exploded in a fifty-foot flourish of billowing fire and smoke. The charging Dayknights reeled back. The crowd shrieked and panicked and began scattering for the exits en masse.

The flames licked the sky but a moment, dwindling fast.

And when the smoke finally drifted away, the platform was gone. The Bloodwood, the gallows poles, the three captives, everything *gone*.

All that remained was a black rectangular hole in the sandy arena floor.

"What in the bloody fiery fuck was that?" Jovan shouted. "Where did they go?" His eyes blazed with righteous anger. "Where did my captives go?"

*Humans, beware the Dragon, the most sly of all deceivers. Has that largest of all Vallè secrets a purpose and a name? It has. But I will reveal that purpose and name only at the end of all things, but only after the demons of the underworld are done meandering where the dark reigns eternal, only when Viper has finally spoken.*
—THE ANGEL STONE CODEX

## CHAPTER FIFTY-FIVE

# LINDHOLF LE GRAVEN

1ST DAY OF THE FIRE MOON, 999TH YEAR OF LAIJON

AMADON, GUL KANA

**T**hey hung me! Despite the noose being gone for at least a half hour now, Lindholf Le Graven kept gulping for breath, lungs heaving as he stumbled along behind his rescuer. *They enslaved me! Hung me!* The pain in his neck. Tightness in his throat. He just couldn't seem to suck in enough air. *How am I still alive?*

Dark was the underground stone chamber where they finally took rest, lit only by a few scattered torches.

Lindholf, Delia, and Gault had followed the mysterious figure from the catacombs under the arena to this lonely, cold place, hands still bound behind their backs. The cloaked stranger who had led them here gripped a tremendously long white sword in one leather-gloved hand, a black crossbow in the other.

Once they entered the room, the figure set both weapons carefully against the wall, then quickly moved behind Lindholf, a black dagger in hand, slicing through the bonds that bound him.

"Careful!" Lindholf tore both hands from behind his back.

"Such ingratitude," the cloaked one said. "Launching such needless complaint to the one who's rescued you."

Lindholf *knew* the voice. His back stiffened and his already thumping heart beat faster. *It couldn't be!* "Seita?" he asked quizzically.

"Aye." Seita pocketed the black dagger and pulled back her hood, revealing the sharp, pale face that he was all too familiar with. Her brilliant white hair danced with yellow light under the torches. "A grand rescue, would you not say?"

The rescue *had* been dramatic. One moment Lindholf had been dangling at the end of a hangman's noose, rope tearing into his neck, legs kicking. Then all was chaos and fire, the noose cut from his neck. The platform had dropped into the floor of the arena, and the Dayknights in the catacombs were swiftly killed by Seita's flashing white sword.

And several dozen dark passageways later . . . here they were.

"You saved me," Lindholf said in a rush, casting a nervous flick of his dark-pupiled eyes toward Delia and Gault. "Saved us all, I mean."

Gault was just visible in the faint light, hands bound behind his armored back. His bearing was that of a skeptical man long punished by war, eyes deep and cold, biting into the Vallè princess. "Cut my bonds," he ordered.

"Ser Gault Aulbrek, *gladiator* of the arena." Seita dipped her head to him. "An honor to meet one of Aeros Raijael's renowned Knights Archaic. Fate has kissed you today in ways you cannot even fathom."

"I only wish to be free." His voice was gravelly and strained.

"Well." The Vallè princess shrugged. "I don't really know you. Other than seeing you in my visions, that is. And therefore . . ." She paused. "I know for a fact I should not trust you." Her thin lips curled into a sharp little smile. "But your daughter, Krista, we were once the truest of friends, she and I."

Gault's eyes narrowed.

"Kill her, Gault." Delia's eyes raked into the Vallè princess with fury. "Kill the pointy-eared bitch." It looked as if the barmaid was about to reach out and strangle Seita herself. "This damnable Vallè tried to slay King Jovan. I saw it with my own eyes. She is the cause of my father's illness, the cause of every single painful moment of my life."

"And now I am your savior," Seita said calmly. "Your part in all this is not yet over, girl, so hush."

"Fuck you," Delia shot back.

"Maybe someday," the Vallè said. Then her demeanor brightened, attention again on Lindholf. "I have many visions. I rode swift and hard to get here in time to save you all. The trouble you've caused me, Lindholf Le Graven."

"Was it Shroud of the Vallè you used to create that fire?" Lindholf asked, feeling himself blush with shame.

"Shroud of the Vallè, yes." She met his hungry gaze. "I can get more soon, if that is your wish. But you must do all I ask in the coming days, Lindholf."

"Of course," he agreed eagerly, eyes darting about. "Where's Val-Draekin?"

"Dead." Her answer was frank and quick in the coming.

"Dead?" he repeated, heart crawling up into his throat.

"Aye, lost in a glacier." She picked up the crossbow. "But we have this, Lindholf, *Blackest Heart*." She handed the crossbow to him. He held it warily. It was made of some sort of pitch-black wood and black string, scary-looking and deadly.

He couldn't help but notice that Gault's piercing eyes were fixed on the weapon too.

"It seems fitted for some manner of bolts unlike any I've ever seen," the man said.

"It takes Vallè-crafted quarrels," Seita said. "After all, it is a Vallè weapon."

She grabbed the white sword next, held it up before Lindholf. "We also have *Afflicted Fire*. The sword and the crossbow, they are what is most important to us now."

Lindholf marveled at the sword gleaming in the torchlight. It was as long as the Vallè princess was tall, a bright red ruby set in its pommel. The weapon's crescent-moon-shaped hilt and cross-guard seemed carved of some odd substance like bone, something *unrecognizable*. And its sleek blade was fashioned of shiny silver and pulsing, twisting veins of glassy white. The swirling, luminous steel itself seemed somehow *alive*. It reminded him of the shield he had found in the Rooms of Sorrow, *Ethic Shroud*.

"That is not all." The Vallè princess leaned the long sword against the wall and produced a leather satchel from the folds of her cloak. She unstrapped the flap and pulled forth two small oval stones. They nestled together in her leather-gloved hand; one glowing red, the other so black it seemed to swallow the torchlight. "Angel stones," she announced.

They were the same shape and size of the white stone Lindholf had found. Delia leaned in for a better look. Gault Aulbrek drifted forward too, staring hard at the remarkable little gems, a latent craving in his gaze.

The red stone sparkled and danced like shimmering fire, smoky waves of inner light glinting back up into the bald man's haunted eyes.

But to Lindholf, on closer inspection, the black stone, though peculiar in its own way, seemed naught but a small hunk of coal, lusterless and dull.

"Are you ready for your first task?" Seita's keen eyes pierced into his. He nodded. "Splendid," she said. "Your first task will be to show me where you and Delia hid *Ethic Shroud* and the white angel stone."

His heart lurched in his chest as he shared a quick glance with Delia. "We hid them in a cellar behind the Filthy Horse Saloon."

"Hidden is good," she said. "We must be wary of the white stone. For some say a curse may very well lie heavy on it still. You did not touch it, did you?"

"I dared not touch the stone." He had always kept it within the black silk.

"We must retrieve them with great haste," Seita said. "For that saloon is the very place the Silver Guard will search for the barmaid first."

"Then what?" Gault snarled. "We will forever be hunted now."

Seita met his glance coolly. "I wouldn't be so sure, Ser Gault, for I know the perfect little island of rock to hide the three of you upon."

Lindholf's gaze fell back down to the stones in the Vallè's hand. "The black one doesn't seem real." He felt the cross-shaped scar on the back of his hand begin to burn, same with where the mermaid had raked him. Same with the slave brand on his neck.

As if she could sense his pain, Seita reached up with her free hand and caressed the deformities on the side of his face. "The stones are real enough," she said.

Lindholf's face almost melted into her soft touch. Her hand drifted up, caressing the top of his scarred and mangled ear. "It's all real enough, my dear Lindholf, all of it."

---

*Think not of those who are slain in the name of Laijon as dead, but rather raised up to live among the loftiest and brightest of stars. For every soldier shall have a taste of death, and only in that day of Fiery Absolution be fully saved.*
—THE WAY AND TRUTH OF LAIJON

---

# CHAPTER FIFTY-SIX

# NAIL

1ST DAY OF THE FIRE MOON, 999TH YEAR OF LAIJON

WEST OF TEVLYDOG, GUL KANA

They'll be skinnin' you next," rasped the flayed man in the cage hanging next to Nail. The man's stark white eyes stared back at him from a raw-skinned face, unblinking, two unnerving lidless orbs continuously agape.

Human rot filled the air as Nail's mind crawled out of a most uncomfortable half sleep. A harsh thirst clawed at his throat. His eyes creaked open to the cold light of dawn, squinting into the thin air. Dread settled over him like a heavy blanket.

The sun had barely crested the tree line. Tendrils of pearly mist flowed amidst the pine and aspen two hundred feet below. From his precarious perch, the scatter of grim cabins and abandoned stone huts at the bottom of the valley seemed naught but a cruel deception. *Bloody rotted angels!* He cursed inwardly. His own cage hung near the top of the cliff, some twenty feet under the precipice of the ridge. The gray stone wall behind him was speckled with lichen and streaked with green moss adrip with water he could not reach.

A mournful wind kicked up and moaned over the fog-shrouded foliage below. Nail's cage rattled and swayed. He clutched the bars tight. Dust trickled down. His shirt was naught but tatters, right arm bare to the elements, flaring in pain. The tattoo and mermaid scars stood out like beacons, as did the cross-shaped scar on the back of his hand and slave brand on the underside of his wrist.

Some ten feet to his left, Val-Draekin hung in a similar cage, alive and alert. The Vallè seemed to suffer no ill effects from yesterday's blow to the head. To Nail's right were three other cages, crows perched atop each, bony arms and legs of men long dead drooping like crooked sticks from between the bars of the farthest two. The flayed man in the clattering cage closest to Nail was still alive, blackened legs a-dangle, curled and blackened hands clutching the bars of the swinging enclosure.

"They're comin' for you." The man's tortured voice choked forth, scouring Nail's nerves like the rasp of a dull saw blade. "Hragna'Ar oghuls on that cliff, skin you alive they will. You and the Vallè both."

From somewhere above, guttural oghul shouts shattered forth, echoing over the valley. Nail recalled the Sky Loch mines and the blood-filled cauldron, the helpless trapper atop the altar. *Hragna'Ar!* His eyes shot up the rock wall behind him. Rough clefts and crags gleamed orange and red from the first bright rays of dawn.

With a rattle of chains, Val-Draekin's cage was suddenly rising up the cliff in uneven, jerky motions. Nail glanced up. Several oghuls were pulling from above. Val-Draekin struggled within the confines of his pen, fingers frantically tearing at the leather thongs holding the cage together. Nail had tried to free himself last night, only to discover the web of ropes, leather, and chains holding his iron cage together had been coated with some form of resin, a substance that looked to have hardened over time. The thick iron lock securing the door was solid, unmovable. Still, the Vallè strained against his cage, a long shard of pale bone now in his hand. A human bone he had likely found in his cage and sharpened to a razor point.

"They're taking him up for Hragna'Ar," the flayed man cackled.

Nail uncurled his fingers from the bars of his cage. They were stuck to the rotted flesh caked to the iron's cold surface. Bile rose up in his throat knowing he had been sitting in the torn and decayed remains of previously flayed men all night.

Suddenly Val-Draekin busted the door of his cage open. He swiftly clambered atop the round pen, grasping the heavy chain.

A thick-hafted arrow hissed over his head and down into the misty trees below.

Wary now, the Vallè slid from the roof, clinging to the swinging door of the cage, feet propped against the bottom of the enclosure. Two more arrows rained down in rapid succession, one clipping Val-Draekin's tattered leather armor. The cage continued to rise, clattering as it jostled against solid rock.

The top of the pen was level with the edge of the cliff now, the burly hands of several oghuls grasping hold, their broad visages grim and flinty eyes resolute as they hauled the cage up.

Val-Draekin launched himself into the air toward Nail. There was a fluency of ease within the Vallè's every move. Arms outstretched, he plummeted, deft hands catching the bottom rungs of Nail's cage. The force of the Vallè's landing was a jolt to Nail's pen, tilting and spinning it severely on its chain. Nail again clung tight to the iron bars.

Val-Draekin scrambled up the cage to eye-level. "Let's get you out of here." Congealed blood was still matted in the Vallè's hair from yesterday's skirmish.

Wincing in pain, his previous injury from falling into the glacier slowing him, Val-Draekin wedged his feet on the floor of the pen between Nail's dangling legs. He gripped one of the iron bars with one hand, the other producing the sharpened bone from the folds of his leather tunic.

Another oghul arrow clattered off the roof of Nail's pen with a thump, spinning away into the air. He watched it plummet the two hundred feet to the trees below. With a rattle of chains, he felt his own cage begin to rise.

Val-Draekin slipped the shard of bone into the heavy iron lock. There was a loud *click* and the locking mechanism was open. The Vallè moved aside and the door swung wide. Another oghul arrow zoomed by. Nail struggled forward, the seat of his breeches momentarily sticking to the rotted flesh under him. Fear took hold as he stared straight down at the mist-laced forest far below.

"We mustn't tarry." Val-Draekin braced his feet against two of the iron bars, one hand clutching the open door of the pen. He leaned out as far as he could over the abyss. "I'll swing the cage around." He nodded to the pen holding the flayed man. "There's a ledge just under that overhang right above that other cage. We can take safety there."

Nail spied the ledge the Vallè was talking about, a cleft in the rock above the flayed man's cage, maybe a foot wide and three feet long at most.

"I'll jump first!" Val-Draekin, pain etched on his ashen face, shoved against the mossy stone wall with one hand, causing the cage to stop spinning. Another arrow clanked off the iron bar just above his straining grip.

Val-Draekin leaped toward the flayed man. He sailed through the air, landing lightly against the bars of the other pen. The skinned man cackled and immediately began clawing at the Vallè.

Nail's confines rattled and scraped against the cliff, still rising in jerks and starts as the oghuls pulled on the chain from above. His heart thudded heavy in his chest as he shoved his way through the tiny door, his entire body now suspended over nothing but air.

Another arrow whizzed by and down into the tree-studded gorge far below.

Nail jumped.

His body felt leaden as he dropped. *I won't make it!*

Val-Draekin, crouching low, one hand holding fast to one iron bar of the flayed man's pen, feet braced against the floor, stretching his other hand toward Nail, catching him by the left wrist. With his right hand, Nail frantically grasped for the bottom of the cage, stiff fingers clinging to the iron. Gaining purchase, he scrambled up the side of the cage until he was level with Val-Draekin and the skinned man.

Up close, the man was a horror; no eyelids, no brows, no hair, no lips, no skin, naught but ragged pale sinew and blackened muscle, gnats crawling in the crevasses, raw body stuck to the floor of his prison. Nail gagged on the stink. Aeros Raijael had destroyed Gallows Haven and murdered villagers. But what had been done to this man was a savagery that existed separately from war. This was a type of butchery that should have been stamped out by the armies of Amadon long ago. It made Nail angry.

"Keep climbing," Val-Draekin urged.

Nail pulled himself atop the pen, both hands grasping the heavy chain. Another arrow clipped his shoulder and bounced away, drawing blood. He lurched to his knees, clinging to the chain with all his might, wincing in pain.

The Vallè climbed up beside him. "When they pull us level with the cleft, we just slip over onto it."

But the cage had stopped rising.

Several blunt-faced oghuls gazed down at them from above. The one with the bow leaned precariously out over the ledge, readying an arrow. Another was hammering at the chain holding their cage with a huge rusted cudgel, trying to smash the heavy links trailing over the ledge. Nail felt the terror consume him; a few more blows with that hammer and the links would snap, sending the entire cage complete with Nail, Val-Draekin, and the flayed man down into the gorge.

The oghul with the cudgel suddenly dropped to his knees and slid off the ledge, rusted cudgel tumbling with him. The beast's heavy-armored body plummeted past Nail's perch, a black arrow with black fletching jutting from his burly gray neck.

*Someone above shot the oghul!* Nail's surprised gaze met Val-Draekin's. The crash of iron on iron could be heard above, the clamor and shouts of fighting.

Val-Draekin wasted no time in climbing up the chain, reaching the cliff top above with a swiftness of ease, disappearing over the rim.

With a loud clap, the chain snapped, and the cage dropped.

Nail flung himself toward the cliff, catching the rim of the hidden cleft with both hands, dangling, the panic-stricken squeal of the flayed man plunging to his death sounding from behind. A moment later came the distant crash of the cage as it struck the rocks two hundred feet below.

Nail tried to pull himself to safety, but his strength was quickly giving way. Another oghul dropped from the cliff above, heavily armored body spinning past, its terrified cry pealed through the air.

"Nail!" Val-Draekin shouted.

"I can't hang on!" Nail called out, frightened eyes gaping up into a cool breeze, blond strands of hair kicking across his vision, the wind almost wanting to pluck him from the surface of the rock. The Vallè's pale face was suddenly visible, steady eyes staring down at him.

"We'll throw down a rope!" Val-Draekin shouted, face vanishing. Suddenly a length of chain clattered sharply against the gray stone nearby. "Grab it!" the Vallè hollered. "We'll pull you up."

*We'll?* Eager to be free of the barren expanse of air pulling at him from behind, Nail grasped the rusted links and clung tight with both hands, not even daring to breathe. Slowly he rose, feet braced against the mossy cliff as he ascended.

Once on level ground, Nail scrambled on hands and knees straight away from the cliff and toward the two dead musk oxen lying in heaps in the distance.

Once he felt safe, he let himself take three huge gasps for air.

"Gather yourself," a strange voice said, a female voice. "You're safe now."

Still on hands and knees, Nail cast fearful eyes on the stranger standing next to Val-Draekin, the savior who had helped the Vallè lift him to safety.

It was a copper-haired girl about his own age. A fleece-lined cloak of lush forest green billowed out behind her as she stalked toward him. Hood tossed back, the dull hilt of a plain shortsword just visible at her belt, the girl wore black breeches and dark leather boots with black leather thongs wrapped around each boot clear to the knee. A black quiver full of black-shafted arrows with black fletching was strapped to her back. She gripped a longbow in one hand, a bow similar in shape to the ash-wood Dayknight longbows both Godwyn and Stefan had carried, yet hers was painted black as midnight.

But most noticeably, the girl's blue eyes were cold pricks of light underneath the two dark smudges of black ash smeared over her face. The black greasy smears stretched from underneath each brow, down over her eyelids and over her cheekbones, coming to a point almost at the base of her jaw on either side of her sharp face. Two long white feathers were tied into her hair just below her left ear, fluttering bright in the sun that had just crested the rise.

The girl's gaze was harsh as it met Nail's. "You're one sorry sack of useless-looking sod. Hardly worth saving in my opinion." She turned in the direction of the two musk oxen and yelled, "Cromm, looks like he survived."

A gray-faced oghul in dark leathers rose up from behind one of the dead musk oxen. A savage-looking brute with a low forehead and blunt nose, larger than any oghul Nail had ever seen, thicker and taller in every way, broad sheets of heavily used iron plate armor buckled to chest, thighs, and forearms. A brace of knives was hooked to a buckler at the grim fellow's hip and a huge war hammer with a square head strapped to the baldric over his shoulder. Four long teeth protruded from both the top and bottom of the monster's thick lips like daggers.

Nail stood, wary, legs still shaking from the ordeal on the cliff.

The oghul seemed to be sucking on something as he stared at Nail with black eyes, steady and calm, eyes that drifted to the back of Nail's hand and the cross-shaped scar there. "Cromm is glad the marked one did not fall," the beast grunted, the timbre of his voice deep but clear.

Nail slid his hand behind the back of his pant leg, glancing at Val-Draekin.

"The marked one is shy." The oghul looked at the girl. But the girl seemed not to care as she began picking through the belongings of the dead oghuls at her feet.

"We killed them all to save the marked one." The oghul bowed to him slightly. *Marked one?* Nail glanced down at his own hand and the scars that now seemed to burn. The oghul continued, "This mark's very interesting to Cromm."

Nail was surprised at how coherent the oghul's speech was, despite the fact that the beast seemed to be sucking on something like tobacco as he spoke. Nail had only ever known oghuls to grunt and growl.

He took the measure of their surroundings. *They had killed them all!* Two oghuls lay dead at his feet, one with an iron-spiked mace in his grip, the other with a broad double-bitted battle-ax, both with black-hafted arrows jutting from their gnarled faces. Another two oghuls lay in crumpled heaps near the girl, their skulls crushed, resting in dirty pools of blood. A fifth oghul was sprawled out on his back dead, not ten paces in front of Nail, two more ink-black arrows jutting from its neck.

The two musk oxen were sprawled in the dirt in pools of blood, ivory tusks caked in dirt, both their woolly brown backs still laden with unwieldy-looking saddles and thick canvas bundles, contents a-scatter. The musk oxen were in roughly the same spot as yesterday, directly in front of the five wooden posts pounded deep into the ground, heavy iron chains trailing from the posts over the rim of the cliff.

Two dun-colored stallions cropped the grass just beyond the dead musk oxen, saddles and bedrolls strapped to their backs for long riding. Both horses appeared at ease amidst all the carnage.

"Cromm, stop staring at the boy. Let's gather our stuff." The copper-haired girl wrestled the remaining two arrows from the neck of one of the corpses lying in front of her. The oghul's body jerked as the arrows tore free, accompanied by half of the creature's throat. The girl flipped gore from the two arrows, pulled a dark rag from the folds of her cloak, and began wiping them down, cold gaze again on Nail. He nervously flipped a lock of stray hair from his eyes, suddenly self-conscious.

She looked away from him just as casually as she had studied him, as if he mattered not at all. "Gather what supplies we need from the dead," she ordered no one in particular, or all of them, then stuffed the black arrows into her quiver. "I'll cut a few hanks of meat off these musk oxen. We mustn't tarry. There's bound to be more of these Hragna'Ar savages about. More than Cromm and I dare fight anyway." She tossed the bloody rag to the ground and pulled a long carving knife from her belt.

"Who are you?" Nail asked.

"Not even so much as a thanks before this one starts demanding answers?" The girl cast her dark gaze at the Vallè.

"My pardon," Val-Draekin bowed to her. "Nail is clearly a bit shaken up still. I'm Val-Draekin." He bowed at the waist slightly.

"Val-Draygin?" the oghul named Cromm grunted questioningly, grim eyes tightly focused on the Vallè.

"Not Val-Draygin," the Vallè corrected. "Val-Draekin."

"I don't recall asking for your names," the girl said sharply, gripping her curved knife. "I merely wanted a thank-you now that you are safe. And that is that. It was Cromm's idea, after seeing your friend hanging in that cage. For my part, by the Blessed Mother Mia, I'd sooner slice both your faces off as look at you, considering you're both clearly the destitute sort, unable to offer any payment for services rendered. Now help loot these brutes like I asked, if you're to earn your keep as we take you back to Amadon."

"Amadon?" Val-Draekin exchanged a quick glance with Nail. "What makes you think we are going to Amadon?"

"Where else would you be going?" she asked with a somewhat roguish air. "We could stuff you back in the cages if you'd like."

Val-Draekin circled around the oghul named Cromm with caution, limping again as he searched the nearest oghul corpse. "You needn't worry about us earning our keep. I shall gladly pay you both handsomely upon our safe passage to Amadon. I've friends there with much coin."

"Now you're speaking the language a pirate might understand." The girl again looked up at her oghul companion, smiling now. Cromm's bushy brows raised as he sucked more vigorously at whatever was in his lip.

"Yes, you shall be paid handsomely," Val-Draekin repeated.

"As you say." The girl's face was again emotionless. "But you'll be walking behind us. We do not share our horses. And if we don't get paid as you say . . ." She held the curved knife up between them. Val-Draekin nodded.

The girl looked to the dead musk oxen. "We shouldn't have slaughtered those foul beasts so swiftly. They're slow mounts, but better than walking."

"Cromm wanted the meat," the oghul said. "It's good they died." Then he canted his thick neck to the side, eyes again on Nail. "My name is Cromm Cru'x. But you can call me Cromm. And you shall eat musk ox with me tonight."

"Thank you." Nail dipped his head toward the black-eyed giant. "Cromm Cru'x."

A surprised look came over the oghul's husky face. He reached up and dug into his lower lip with one big finger, pulling a small black stone from his mouth. "You spoke it right," he said, pointing with the rock pinched between index finger and thumb, looking at the copper-haired girl almost proudly. "The marked one knows Cromm's name and can speak it." The rows of teeth within the beast's smiling mouth were sharp and jagged as splintered bone. Nail noticed the tiny gemstones that were embedded in those teeth and shuddered, finally coming to realize it was an actual oghul he was talking to.

"Cromm likes it when folks pronounce his name correct," the girl said.

Cromm jammed the black rock behind his lip again and struck a somewhat relaxed pose, hooking thick thumbs through his belt. The oghul also had jewel-encrusted claws jutting from more than a few of his curled knuckles, gleaming and sparkling with color. *Everything about him is disconcertingly odd. . . .*

The oghul just stared at him, expectant.

"Nail is my name," Nail said. The oghul's smile widened further.

"Since everyone insists upon making introductions, my name is Bronwyn Allen." The girl swept copper locks up into the cowl of her hood and pulled the hood over her head, black-stained eyes mostly hidden in shadow. She turned to Val-Draekin. "Consider yourselves lucky Cromm has the silver-wolf's eye. And consider yourself lucky that he hates this particular group of Hragna'Ar oghuls more than he hates the Vallè. He recognized those scars on your friend even from afar. The marks on Nail's hand and arm are why he insisted on saving you two. He claims there is an oghul legend, a Hragna'Ar prophecy from generation to generation that makes mention of one such human with similar marks on his flesh."

"Prophecy?" Nail's gaze shot to Val-Draekin.

"Yes, prophecy," the girl continued. "Prophecy that the oghul who befriends such a marked man and escorts him to Fiery Absolution shall become legend. I think it's nonsense. But whatever. Cromm is my friend, and one indulges their friends."

"Cromm will become legend." The oghul was smiling still, large gleaming eyes on Bronwyn. "Told you we would find more than just revenge and treasure at Deadwood Gate."

*A slain enemy is a peaceful enemy, and the world oft cries for peace.*
—THE BOOK OF THE BETRAYER

## CHAPTER FIFTY-SEVEN

# CRYSTALWOOD

1ST DAY OF THE FIRE MOON, 999TH YEAR OF LAIJON

WESTERN SEA SOUTH OF KAYDE, SØR SEVIER

Krista Aulbrek woke to the sound of shrieking gulls. The birds circled above, stark white against the clear azure sky. She lay on her back in the bottom of a smelly wooden boat beside two long oars and a mud-coated iron anchor, hands and feet bound with rope, filth clinging to her prison garb. The stench of fish and stale salt water was pungent. And the dirty confines of the boat were less than luxurious. Greased wool and black tar caulking filled every crack and joist between every wood plank beneath her.

She sensed the forms of Borden Bronachell and the dwarf Squateye behind her. *Or is his name Ironcloud?* He no longer wore an eye patch. When she raised her weary head, she had to squint against the brightness of the sun-hammered sea. A warm breeze washed smoothly across the open expanse of water.

Before her, a vast seascape of tranquil blue stretched off to the west, a thin dark line of land cresting the horizon to the east. Were she not so ill, the scene would have likely stolen her breath. Instead it merely frightened her. Up until these last few days of half wakefulness, she never knew the ocean could be such a desolate place, so staggeringly immeasurable and infinite. Perhaps it was the poisons still in her bloodstream that caused her such anxiety. Sure, she'd seen the sea from afar before, stood on the stony shores of Rokenwalder and gazed out upon the endless waters. But she'd never been floating in a small sailboat smack in the middle of the ocean, swallowed up by it on all sides. She felt nauseous.

A dog barked.

Her eyes flew to the tiny white boat trailing hers some thirty paces distant, a length of chain connecting the two vessels. Café Colza Bouledogue, stumpy front legs braced on the prow, stared back at her with deranged beady eyes. He barked again, rusted-spiked collar tight around his neck a dull glint in the sun.

Hans Rake, sitting just behind the dog, stared across the distance at Krista, his fiery green eyes graced with conceit, annoyance, calculation, and rage all at once. With but a glance, even at a distance, Krista could discern Hans' every peevish, complicated look and mood. The blond strip of hair atop his head was awash with sunlight, bright in contrast to the garish blue Suk Skard clan tattoos covering either side of his skull. He still wore the black leather greaves and armor that marked him as one of Black Dugal's caste.

"Like being cast adrift with a saber-toothed lion," Borden said from behind her. The former prisoner sat on the center bench of the skiff, directly under the billowing white sail. Borden was fuller of face now, in clothes and boots that fit, not the tattered pants and shirt and bare feet of the Rokenwalder dungeon. He still had thin legs and arms, but his overall skeletal look was gone. His beard was trimmed, no longer a natty mess. "Had to stop in Suk Skard the first day, get another boat just to haul him and that dog. Raging lunatics both."

"And just when we think he's run out of little black daggers," Squateye followed, "another comes spinning toward us. Sometimes I think we ought to just drown the both of them." The dwarf handed her a hunk of stale bread. Hands bound in front of her, Krista took it and lifted it to her mouth.

"We kept your Bloodwood friend tied down in this boat for a time," Borden said. "But even tied up he is liable to be causing all manner of havoc. It's why he's in a separate boat now. The dog too is a handful. And those ropes would not have held him long."

To her best estimation, they had been afloat a week, with her unconscious at the bottom of the sailboat for most of the journey, bound and tied with all the worth and dignity of a sack of potatoes. She swallowed the bread and looked to the dwarf for more.

"It's not easy keeping someone as sick as you alive for near ten days," the dwarf said, handing her more bread. "Liquefy the food; force it past your lips. It's about all we could do. You need to regain your strength now that the worst is over." *Ten days!* Her mind reeled. "And the bobbing of the boat," the dwarf continued. "The seas have not always been as kind as they are now. But you did not vomit once. A miracle, that."

The sea was calm now, but she recalled the motion of the sail-boat during the storms, could feel it in her bones, the seasickness and torment. But the dwarf was right; she had not vomited. She would choke back whatever illness assailed her even if it killed her. She remembered the very last time she had puked. Seven years old. At the dinner table of King Aevrett Raijael, fine porcelain dishes, silver goblets, and Rokenwalder royalty all around, she spewed her dinner of roast chicken and honey-butter scones. Aevrett's son, the young prince, Aeros, had scooted from the table horrified. Aevrett's horrid wife, Natalia, had ordered Krista and her father from the dining hall.

"Sorry I spilled." She recalled her embarrassed apology as Gault escorted her from Jö Reviens. Then later, on hands and knees, her father holding up her hair, she'd spewed again into a Rokenwalder gutter. "I keep spilling, Papa," she said over and over. But Gault had patiently cleaned the puke from the front of her dress, offering what comfort he could. She knew she had ruined his evening; it wasn't often he was invited to dine with Prince Aeros and the king.

Of course Gault had gone off to war with Aeros soon after, leaving her with those two monsters, Aevrett and Natalia.

She could still feel her dagger sinking into Aevrett's chest. *But Natalia was still alive.* She swallowed the last hunk of bread, shifted her position in the boat, the ropes about her ankles biting into the skin, her hair, light upon her head, rippling at the wind's soft caress. *Like a father's touch . . .*

She looked out toward Café Colza and Hans, noticed that the chain that connected the two boats was slack, dipping low into the water.

"We best be wary again, Borden." The dwarf rose, his eyes darting across the water toward the other boat too.

Hans stood, foot propped upon the sidewall of his small vessel. His voice carried a throaty, indignant lilt as it cut across the water. "Now that Crystalwood is again awake, I will see her slain. I will see that she is naught but a pretty little corpse before you turn her from Black Dugal's caste." He produced a black dagger from his leather armor.

"And here I thought we searched him," the dwarf said sardonically. "Best we duck down behind the bulwark lest he throw it, as he's thrown the last ten or so. Blessed Mother Mia, do the daggers hidden in his leathers have no end?"

"I will not throw this one at you, dwarf." Hans held the Bloodwood blade up, dull and black. "'Tis my last, and I will not waste it on you." He stepped up onto the sidewall of the small skiff, the bulldog barking as the boat wobbled. "I aim to slay you by my own hand." He eyed the shrinking expanse of water between the two boats.

"I wouldn't risk it were I you," Borden called out. "The seas south of Kayde are known to be thick with sharks and other such devilry. You won't make it far."

Krista knew Hans, knew her fellow assassin would pay the man's warning scant heed. Sure enough, Hans bent at the knees and dove headfirst into the sea, slim leather-clad body knifing beneath the crust of the blue water with hardly a splash.

Borden and the dwarf each grabbed an oar, readying themselves for the fight.

When Hans' head broke above the sea, Café Colza barked again. With a furious wag of the tail, the dog jumped into the water too, ungainly body landing with a clap.

Hans pulled himself along the length of the chain with grim determination, tattooed head streaked with water, Café Colza furiously paddling along behind.

"Rotted angels." Borden slapped the skin of the sea with the flat of the long oar. The dwarf followed suit. Over and over they smacked their oars into the water, creating a frothy ruckus.

Krista thought she was seeing things as there was suddenly a woman's head gliding in the water next to Hans. The abrupt sight of her beautiful pale face and long red hair startled even Borden and Ironcloud, their oars now suspended over the ocean.

Hans stopped pulling himself along the chain, head barely above water, cold eyes staring at the woman before him.

She had a fragile-looking chin, delicate lips, and a thin nose. Her wide round eyes were like two crystal green shards of light. She smiled, revealing a row of thin pointed teeth. The bulldog reversed its course, heading straight back toward the boat it had just abandoned, water churning in its wake.

*Is this creature just some cruel vision?* Krista's mind was awhirl, wondering if the wraiths ate at her soul or if the Bloodwood poisons still worked their dread magic somewhere. Café Colza was soon scratching at the side of the small skiff, trying in vain to claw his way back aboard, rusted-spiked collar clattering against the wood.

Hans gripped the chain tight in one hand, the other hand brandishing his black dagger before the strange woman's face. Inches from the dagger's tip, the woman's ghostly visage floated above the deep, a serrated row of slender gills fluttering along her pale neck. *Mermaid!* The creature was like something thrust up from the underworld. Krista's father, Gault, had called them mers, sometimes nixies.

"Get away from me!" Hans stabbed at the mermaid, missing as she ducked under the water. Hans' fright-filled eyes scanned the now-empty sea before him. She reappeared behind him, mouth agape, screeching, harsh and vivid. Hans whirled in the water. As the shriek faded, the woman's thin lips peeled back into a wide grin. Two rows of pointed white fangs gleamed as she brandished her own weapon in her webbed, clawlike hand. It was a needle-thin weapon made of bone.

Hans lashed out with his own dagger. The mermaid drifted back, casually avoiding his lumbering blow. Her wide green eyes blinked slowly, gills on her neck rippling with each slow breath. Hans struck again, slow in the water. Then he simply disappeared—as if something beneath had reached up and forcefully yanked him below.

The red-haired mermaid still floated there, her round eyes climbing up the side of the sailboat, locating Krista's startled gaze.

There was a shared silence between them. In fact, all was silent. Borden. The dwarf. The entirety of the ocean. Even Café Colza had stopped his mad scratching at the distant boat. Then the mermaid dove forward, pale back and bony spine curling up and slithering under the water, glistening tail arching above the skin of the sea like polished glass, shimmering scales like glistening little gems. Her silvery splayed tail slipped beneath the blue, and she was gone.

"We can't lose the boy." Borden breathed deep. "Or the dog."

"He's already gone." The dwarf met his worried gaze. "And there's no telling how many more of these demons are under us."

A plume of dark red water bubbled up around the chain near where Hans had clung. Horror washed over Krista. A purple swirl of entrails and red viscera coiled up out of the deep next, spreading around the chain in an ever-growing pool, like so many eels trying claim some grim ocean territory.

"Foolish fool." Borden scowled. "He shouldn't have gone into the water."

*He can't be gone!* Krista could scarcely breathe.

Then Hans' head broke through the circle of guts, mouth spewing water as his lungs heaved for air. He floundered. Coughed. Then he shouted, "Gutted the bitch!" and began pulling himself along the length of the chain toward Krista's boat.

Two more merfolk spun up from the water, males this time, screeching and shrill, the fullness of their bodies exposed, all sinewy muscle and glimmering scale. Bonelike weapons in hand, they dipped back below with a splash. When they resurfaced, they slashed at the chain right in front of Hans. The Bloodwood reversed course and headed for his own skiff, pushing the bulldog aside, scrambling back aboard swiftly. Once he was safe, he leaned over the sidewall and grasped Café Colza by the iron-spiked collar and hauled the dog to safety too.

The mermen reappeared, tried pulling themselves aboard Hans' boat, screaming, gruesome fangs gnashing. Hans' black dagger flashed out, raking the webbed hands of the nearest one. Café Colza tore at the other with slavering jaws. The two mermen dropped back down into the sea, leaving broad trails of blood along the side of the skiff. The two merfolk slithered about just under the surface of the sea now, naught but rippling silhouettes circling Hans' boat.

And then they were gone, vanishing into the deep as if they had never existed.

The sea was once again calm.

"You bloody fool!" Borden called out toward Hans. "I warned you of these waters."

Hans met Borden's gaze with an impaling glint. With that look, Krista knew, Hans would not rest until his captors were dead. Not even the fiendish horrors of the vast Western Sea would stop him.

Krista sucked in a deep breath as a singular white fin broke the surface of the blue ocean some hundred paces behind Hans' boat.

"A great white," the dwarf muttered. "It could swamp us if it has a mind to."

The huge fin plied the sea in a lazy path, wending its way between the two skiffs, a great swell of water piling up before it. Suddenly the fin took aim and darted toward Krista's sailboat in a straight line. "Brace yourself!" Borden cried out, dropping his oar, grasping the sidewall. The dwarf did the same.

Krista's heart lurched as the ominous shark bore down, nearly as big as the sailboat she was on. The thud of the beast striking the side of the skiff was loud and jarring, and the boat lurched violently to the side. All three aboard were jerked from their feet, tumbling into the bottom of the boat.

As the sailboat righted itself, Krista scrambled to her knees and saw the shark's fin surface on the other side, heading for some spot between the two skiffs again.

"If it gets hold of that chain, it'll be the end of us." The dwarf grabbed his oar and readied himself against the sidewall of the skiff, as if he meant to fight the beast with it. "He'll pull us both down."

The shark moved slowly and silently toward the chain connecting the boats, grim eyes now peering above the water, ominous and full of death. The monster tipped on its side, massive mouth agape as it swallowed the entire spool of mermaid guts in one great gulp, then slid below the blue skin of the ocean and was gone.

It took a moment before anyone dared breathe.

On the opposite boat, Hans Rake started laughing. Whether he laughed out of sheer joy of seeing Borden and the dwarf nearly drowned, or out of pure relief at having survived his dip in the sea, Krista couldn't guess.

Borden eyed the dwarf. "I am gathering more strength with each day out of that cell, but when we reach Wynix, that boy will be hell to contain. If he can take on a mermaid whilst treading in the sea, no telling what he's capable of."

"Indeed," the dwarf agreed. "His training with Black Dugal is complete. I say the sooner we kill him the better."

"We still need him," Borden said.

"Dugal's black kestrels will always be able to find Hans Rake."

"And will Dugal find him too? We are not done with Black Dugal yet, Ironcloud. The Brethren of Mia still has use of him."

"Dugal might not follow Hans or the girl, but he will follow that dog. He will follow us all the way to Amadon, for if *The Moon Scrolls of Mia* are right, his bloodline is essential for Fiery Absolution."

Borden's eyes were fixed toward the north, as if he believed Black Dugal was truly following them. "And when he does find us, I will be myself again. I will again be Borden Bronachell, Dayknight, King of Gul Kana. And I will be ready."

*And Laijon returned shall set fire upon the Atonement Tree upon which he was hung, which shall devour the ethic Vallè shroud.*
—THE WAY AND TRUTH OF LAIJON

## CHAPTER FIFTY-EIGHT
# TALA BRONACHELL

2ND DAY OF THE FIRE MOON, 999TH YEAR OF LAIJON

AMADON, GUL KANA

Seita had returned to court. She reclined on the divan near Tala's bedchamber door, thin legs crossed, feet propped on a green velvet footstool. The Vallè princess wore black leather breeches with a red felt stripe down each leg and a black jerkin studded with silver at the collar, a thin white silk shirt underneath.

Mornings in Tala's room were always peaceful and cool, even in the middle of summer. Tala sat at the edge of her bed wrapped in a plush quilt of thick maroon-colored yarn, a quilt her mother had knitted. One of the few things that reminded her of Alana Bronachell. Tala stroked the fabric with distracted fingers as she listened to her cousin.

"I sometimes dream I'm reaching out for you, Tala." Lawri wore a soft yellow nightgown. She was propped against the bed's dark umber headboard just to the right of Tala, her legs tucked under a rich woolen blanket of deep blue. The heavy curtains were thrown open behind her, letting the gray morning light of dawn spread over the room's rich wood furniture and huge stone hearth, where Hawkwood's sword was hidden. "I'm reaching out my hand to pull you to safety. You're lost and injured and in a dark tunnel somewhere with no floor, clinging to the walls, blood covering your chest. I am flying on the Silver Throne, and I have to save you before you fall." She dropped her eyes to the stump of her arm atop her lap; it was wrapped in white sackcloth bandages. "But then I realize I have no hand." Then she looked up, hopeful. "I truly believe Laijon has a plan for me and all shall be well."

Tala remembered the very moment seven days ago when Lawri's missing hand had been wrapped in sackcloth smelling of vinegar and poppy seeds and taken from the infirmary with the rest of her arm. The severed appendage was tossed into Ser Osten Northanger's oven in the small blacksmith shop under the castle's east end rookery.

*So many have been hurt.* She thought back on the stab wounds Jovan had suffered in the assassination attempt, the facial injuries Jondralyn had suffered at the hands of Gault Aulbrek. Her brother had been laid up for days; her sister had remained in the infirmary for some time, injured face wrapped for over a moon.

Yet Tala's cousin had gone from delirious and close to death, to almost perfect in mind and body after Jovan had cut off her infected arm. *Could it have been the green balls of medicine I fed her?* The Bloodwood had claimed it was Vallè medicine in those marble-sized balls. The Vallè healed thrice as fast as a human. Plus Val-Gianni had been plying her cousin with enough Vallè healing draughts to sedate an ox, which perhaps explained Lawri's overall comfort these last few days. But with each question seemingly answered, another ten arose.

She looked at the missing tip of her own finger, burned away by some silver acid dripping from the ceiling in the red-hazed room where Glade had murdered Ser Sterling Prentiss. *Lawri's arm is severed and there she sits as comfortable as you please, and this tiny wound still stings like an Avlonian wasp.*

In fact, Lawri seemed in fine spirits today. *I truly believe Laijon has a plan for me and all shall be well,* she'd said. But Tala knew nothing would ever be *well* again. *How can anyone feel so relaxed and comfortable after what happened to Squireck Van Hester?* Her heart grew instantly leaden thinking of him again. A lump formed in her throat, and she almost wanted to cry; the weight of her grief could be so heavy.

"Your optimism and dreams are fascinating, Lawri," Seita said.

Tala had not seen the Vallè princess in over a moon. Seita claimed she had gone back to the Isle of Val Vallè with Val-Draekin, who had stayed there. She had arrived back to Jovan's court just this morning and come straight to Tala's room, asking of Lawri's injuries, fretting over the girl nonstop. Tala recalled how Seita had wished to be friends not long before she had left. Tala wondered if they still were.

"Do you think my dreams will come true?" Lawri asked Seita, gaily fussing with the folds of her nightgown with her good hand, as if her every arrangement of the fabric was a new joy to behold.

"I cannot say for a certainty," the Vallè answered. "But there are a few dreams I myself have hoped to come true, and others . . . not so much. Some dreams, I fear, may be the workings of the wraiths."

At the mention of the wraiths, Lawri's pale face seemed to darken. Then it brightened again almost as fast. "I should tell you, Tala, my Ember Gathering has been scheduled for the morrow." She was still stroking her nightgown. "The grand vicar granted me quick dispensation. In light of all that has happened to my family, you know, all that has happened as of late, Lindholf's crimes and imprisonment, my infected arm. Denarius will perform the ceremony himself."

"I thought you didn't want the grand vicar touching you." Tala felt a hint of anger creep into her tone, the image of Lawri, naked, being blessed with the holy oils of Grand Vicar Denarius flashing into her mind. "I don't understand."

"Don't make such a terrible fuss," Lawri said. "You always get so cross about things you don't understand."

"But we all heard what you said in the arena." Tala was mystified. How could someone go from such abject horror to eager delight in so short a span? *Vallè sorcery? Glowing green pills?* Or likely the deceptive, honeyed tongue of the grand vicar at work. Lawri had been so adamant in the arena when she'd voiced her displeasure. "You did not want Denarius touching you. Remember?"

"I was wrong." Lawri shrugged. "It's simple as that. According to my mother, I was sinful and I was wrong. Since Jovan rid me of my arm, Denarius has been anointing me with priesthood oils and blessing me daily. It was a mistake not to trust him. A mistake to avoid him. Only through the power of His Grace's faith and prayers have I healed so fast."

Tala couldn't bring herself to admit aloud that she'd seen Lawri naked with the grand vicar. *What would Lawri say if she knew?* Tala couldn't think of anything worse than being so exposed before anyone, much less that toad, Denarius.

Lawri straightened up in the bed. "The grand vicar says my Ember Gathering on the morrow should rid me of all unpleasant dreams and fill my tender soul with naught but good thoughts."

"Have you been discussing your dreams with the vicar?" Seita inquired.

"I've confessed many things to Denarius in preparation for my Ember Gathering. One must be pure of all sin, pure before Laijon to enter into the ash and flame."

*What inappropriate and pointed questions might the vicar ask of you, my dear Lawri?* Tala could no longer see the grand vicar as anything but the lech he was.

Seita spoke up. "Pray tell, what horrible dreams does the vicar claim your Ember Gathering will wash away?"

"It's mostly when I dream of my brother that I feel despair." Grief tightened about Lawri's green-flecked eyes. "He's done such grievous things, Lindholf has. All but destroyed the Le Graven name. Mother thinks I have become all but unmarriageable because of what disgrace he has brought us."

"That's just not true," Tala said.

"Which part?" Lawri asked. "That Lindholf has not done grievous things, or that the nobles are lining up to marry me?" She held up the stub of her arm.

"Your brother is innocent," Tala countered. "I know he is. Lindholf did not conspire to assassinate my brother. He did not kill Sterling Prentiss."

"They hung him in the arena, Tala," Lawri snapped. "I watched. You watched. How much more proof do you need of his guilt? They *hung* him."

"He was not hung; he . . . he *disappeared*." Tala still couldn't wrap her mind around all that had happened where Lindholf was concerned. "He vanished. You saw it as well as I. A poof of smoke and they were all of them gone."

"I hate him." Lawri threw the covers off her legs. "Wherever he is, I *hate* him."

"Don't speak like that," Tala said. "You don't hate him. He is your brother."

Lawri stewed, sitting at the edge of the bed now, frail fingers listlessly toying with the bandages around her stump, her once wistful eyes clouded with suspicion.

Tala carried on, "Don't you recall when your brother could send us all into merry peals of laughter with just a word or a goofy look?"

"He wasn't even really all that funny, as I recall." Lawri abruptly stood, slipping her feet into the two soft leather slippers under the bed. Her eyes darted about the room, falling on the chest of drawers nearby. She grabbed one of Tala's brushes off the chest.

"Forgive Lindholf, please," Tala pleaded, feeling that everything was her fault.

"I'm afraid I must take my leave of your chamber, Tala," Lawri announced waspishly, running the copper-handled brush through her hair with brusque purpose. "I must ready myself for my Ember Gathering. I must study my prayers. I must be fully ready." She dropped the brush and threw a shawl over her yellow nightgown, attempted to tie it at the neckline with her one hand. Seita stood and helped her. Once the shawl was secure, Lawri headed straight for the chamber door, grasping the brass knob. She turned and looked back at Tala. "You of all people should be happy for me and my Ember Gathering, but I sense only jealousy in you, Tala." She unlatched the door and walked out into the gray corridor, slamming the door hard behind her.

Discouraged, Tala's eyes fell on the great hearth against the wall and her access to the secret ways. *I must escape this prison too!* The clue to Lindholf's disappearance and Lawri's misery was out there somewhere, and she meant to find it. She meant to escape this confining castle and find Lindholf. Every single conflict within her was tied to the Bloodwood and the secret ways.

"Lawri is not the awkward, coltish girl we think she is," Seita said. "Still, I worry for her and her Ember Gathering with the grand vicar."

"Why?" Tala's spine froze, her eyes glued to the black depths of the hearth as her mind churned, wondering if the Vallè princess also knew of Denarius' lecherous ways.

"I fear the Ember Gathering will change her in ways that we both will not like," Seita said.

"How so?"

"You do not know what goes on during an Ember Gathering?"

Tala felt a trifle annoyed by the question. She turned from the fireplace to find Seita was again sitting on the divan, feet propped on the footstool before her.

Tala answered, "I know nothing of the Ember Gathering. You know as well as I that it is a secret ceremony, a coming-of-age ritual only to be administered once during a girl's lifetime, never to be spoken of again by the participants. Nobody knows what goes on during an Ember Gathering. Until they go through it."

"And don't you find that the least bit odd?"

"It's just the way things are, have always been."

"I find it odd that most humans do not even know the most basic doctrines and sacraments of their own church."

"Well, the Ember Gathering is a sacred ceremony; of course they keep it secret. Keeping the secret is part of womanhood."

"What of the Ember Lighting?" Seita asked. "The coming-of-age ceremony for the boys is a public celebration for all to see. Yet the girl's Ember Gathering is kept secretive. Why is that?"

"It is sacred, I guess."

"That is your reasoning?"

"Other than what I've already said, I don't know why it's never talked about."

"And you've never cared to find out?"

"It's not important. Seems the least of my troubles."

"'Tis disappointing to hear such apathy coming from you." Seita sighed. "For it appears the Ember Gathering is indeed but one more confirmation of the severe feeblemindedness of the women of Gul Kana."

*Feeblemindedness?* Tala's annoyance had shifted to offense. "What do you mean?"

"Do you not even wish to know what goes on in an Ember Gathering?" Seita asked. "So that you may have the choice whether to participate in the ritual or not when your time comes? Do you not wish to at least become educated on the subject, to at least be prepared for the entirety of all it entails?"

"Who would tell me anyway when, as you said, no woman is allowed to speak of it?"

"But they could, if they so chose to. Would you listen?"

"And help them betray an oath, help them go against the will of Laijon?"

"What is the will of Laijon but a silly fantasy?" Seita shrugged, a light giggle in her voice. "What are the wraiths and the beasts of the underworld but make-believe monsters to scare children into obedience?"

Tala's spine was once again a frozen block of ice. *We tread on blasphemous ground.* "And I suppose *you* know what goes on in an Ember Gathering?"

"Of course. Why wouldn't I? The Ember Gathering is based on a simple Vallè fertility ritual, but over the centuries it has been perverted and twisted into something almost unrecognizable by the grand vicar and Quorum of Five Archbishops, perverted into nothing more than a secret orgy for them to slake their lusts on. The Ember Gathering and the guilt that comes with it gives the church men control over your body and mind."

The blood coursing through Tala's spine and veins was now so icy, it burned. She could feel her face flush. "You lie" was the only response she could formulate.

"If you are to become a ruler of this kingdom, Tala Bronachell, you must learn all you can about your church and its deep well of secrets."

*Ruler?* Her mind reeled. She hated vague conversations and strange insinuation. She had walked out on just such a conversation with Hawkwood not long ago.

"Let me speak plainly to you now," Seita went on, "so for once in your life you will be fully aware. The Ember Gathering is a sustained and ritualistic cleansing of your body. You are first stripped of all raiment. Naked, you stand before the vicar and archbishops as they cover your body with consecrated oils and gray ash, their probing hands blessing you; health in your bones, strength in your sinews, fertility in your womb. You in turn make many promises, one of which is that no matter who you wed in mortal life, you willingly consecrate your immortal soul to those servants of Laijon who were not allowed to marry in mortality."

Tala's mind spun with the implications. She wondered if Lawri's previous dream was but a metaphor of her marriage to Denarius in the afterlife. *Or is it all nonsense?*

Seita continued, "Every servant of Laijon has been promised many heavenly sessions. They are each of them promised wives as numerous as the sands of the sea when they die."

Tala was stunned and sickened. "You lie," she muttered.

Seita appeared to ignore the accusation. "At the end of your Ember Gathering, you will swear an oath to never speak of the sacred blessings given you nor the promises you made, lest your heart be torn from your chest and buried in a dung-filled grave. The Ember Gathering has been thus for centuries."

"You are just trying to scare me," Tala muttered. "Just trying to play with my mind." The way the Vallè princess talked to her now reminded her of the Bloodwood assassin who stalked the secret ways and tormented her so. "Why lie to me?" she asked. "You are purposefully misleading me. If what you say is the truth, someone would have said something about it by now and exposed the truth of it all. A disturbing secret like that would never last for centuries. You are full of lies."

"It is you who has been lied to," Seita said. "You and everyone else who believes in *The Way and Truth of Laijon.*" The Vallè princess rose from the divan. "There is more you must know, Tala. More you must contemplate. And it will be hard to hear."

"Yes, tell me more lies, please I implore you." She tried to sound sarcastic.

"What if I were to tell you that the dragons are but a myth, that they never existed, that the beasts of the underworld were but an ancient rumor, a mere fiction created to scare the children and keep people in line?"

"I would say the nameless beasts of the underworld were real," Tala countered. "And you should not speak their name in my chamber."

"Dragons. Dragons. *Dragons.*" The Vallè princess mockingly repeated. "I can say the name as much as I desire, Tala Bronachell, for nothing will happen if I do. The ridiculous fear of dragons and the fiery pits of the underworld has become a religion unto itself. But it is all completely false. Everything you believe is but a fraud. Those things supposedly banished to the underworld are not to be feared."

"Why did you even come back from Val Vallè?" Tala asked. "You should have just stayed there with Val-Draekin. I thought you wanted to be my friend. A friend would never say such things."

"A friend will always share the truth, Tala. For the truth is all that matters."

† † † † †

That night King Jovan summoned his entire court to Sunbird Hall. Tala, still in a horrible mood, was one of the last to arrive. When she entered the chamber, the Silver Guard were already in place along with dozens of Dayknights, all stoically lining the walls and alcoves and both staircases at the eastern end of the hall, spears at their shoulders. The crowded chamber was thick with the smell of smoke, baked bread, and other foods prepared by the new kitchen matron, Dame Nels Doughty, and her staff. Torchlight threw a warm glow over the chamber, and the arena orchestra was set up at the hall's far end playing a soft melody.

*Are we here to mourn or celebrate Squireck Van Hester's death?*

Tala felt immediately stifled by the place. There were too many people. Her heavy velvet dress didn't help. She wanted to seek the balcony and breathe in the fresh air. Her mind had been on Squireck all day, heart in her throat. She'd been thinking of Lawri, too, worrying. Thinking of the cruel things Seita had said about the Ember

Gathering, growing angrier by the moment. *Yes, the entire castle is naught but a stuffy, inescapable prison full of confusion and pain.*

Lawri Le Graven entered the chamber from one of the side doors. She wore a peach-colored gown, white lace at the neckline. Seita was with her in a slim black dress. Tala wasn't sure if she wanted to talk to her cousin or the Vallè again tonight at all.

Tala made her way in the opposite direction through the stuffy room toward Lawri's mother, Mona Le Graven. Mona stood near Jondralyn and young Ansel. Tala's sister was dressed in full Silver Guard armor, shined and polished, eye patch covering her eye, long scar from Gault Aulbrek's blade trailing angrily across her face. Ansel clung to her armored leg.

King Jovan sat just behind Mona and Jondralyn at the long table on the raised dais next to the always shrouded Silver Throne. Jovan wore black pants and a black tunic trimmed with silver secured at the waist with a belt of shiny silver looplets. The royal crown rested upon his head.

*"Attention!"* There was an official-sounding shout from a Dayknight just outside Sunbird Hall's open entry doors. Every royal who was sitting stood, including the king.

Glade Chaparral's entrance into the hall was met with the rolling of the orchestra's drums, heavy and deep, followed by the tremendous, gut-punching gong of the orchestra's centerpiece, a large iron bell. Glade was dressed in full Dayknight black-lacquered armor, a black war helm in the crook of his arm, as were the three men marching just behind him with the confidence of newly knighted Dayknights: Tolz, Alain, and Boppard. To most in Sunbird Hall, they looked like the most dashing heroic men in all Amadon.

But Tala was not fooled by their looks, for she knew them all to be naught but thugs, wretches, and utter lackwits in every way. In days past, Tala herself had felt that mysterious cloud of heavenly air engulf her every time those bold eyes of Glade's met hers. But when the four young Dayknights stepped up before the king, a smug smile was on Glade's face, and Tala could do naught but shudder in revulsion.

Grand Vicar Denarius and the Quorum of Five Archbishops of Amadon entered the chamber next, the orchestra swelling with a sweeping sound.

The four new Dayknights turned to face the vicar as Denarius beckoned for silence from the orchestra. When the music died, Denarius bowed to Jovan, then made a sweeping motion with his hand, including all four Dayknights in the gesture. "If it please your Excellency, may I present Ser Glade Chaparral of Rivermeade, Ser Tolz Trento of Avlonia, Ser Alain Gratzer of Knightliegh, and Ser Boppard Stockach of Reinhold. Gul Kana's newest Dayknights. Blessed and knighted by my hand in the Hall of the Dayknights earlier today as you bade me do. From this moment henceforth, all four are now beholden to Laijon and the Silver Throne."

Tala detected a few disapproving looks among some of the older Silver Guard present and even a few of the Dayknights. Mutters and low murmurs spread throughout the hall. At the unfavorable reaction of the crowd, Glade grew abruptly full of fidgety impatience. Tala felt a hollow sort of melancholy, for she understood the unfairness of what the king and vicar had done in knighting these four so early. Most had come here expecting to mourn the death of Squireck Van Hester, not celebrate the promotion of four undeserving Silver Guard. The murmurs continued to grow around her.

"Hush!" Jovan shouted, sweeping the assemblage with an unforgiving glare, the timbre of his voice strong and commanding. "As His Grace clearly stated, he merely did as I bade him do!" His gaze darkened. "These four valiant young men brought the ones responsible for the murder of Ser Sterling Prentiss to justice. 'Twas these four who rooted out the foul assassins who sought my own death. Never before have any four knights done so much for the Silver Throne. They have earned their place as Dayknights!"

The king's eyes narrowed to calculating slits. "And if any of you take issue with their advancement, feel free to work it out with me in the arena!" His voice had almost turned into a low growl as he unsheathed the blue sword, Sky Reaver, with a hiss of leather on steel. "Lest any of you forget, I have seen war! I have fought in battles! I fought and bled at my father's side in Wyn Darrè!" He stabbed the sword into the table before him, plates, mugs, and crockery jumping. "With Aeros Raijael's sword I shall take the head of the next man who utters his disagreement!"

A stunned silence followed his words. Every face in the crowd looked upon the king with as dignified and grave deference as they could.

A desperate wretchedness filled Tala's heart, for she knew Jovan walked a razor's edge. Her brother was going against custom in granting Dayknight status to one so young as Glade, denying the grandest of knightly accolades to those more seasoned and worthy, those who had served and worked their entire lives for such honor.

And again, Tala felt as if it were all her fault, as if it had all come about through the Bloodwood's machinations, all through her own meddling in the affairs of the realm. Indeed, an unspeakable desperate wretchedness filled her. *I'm so alone! No mother. No father. A brother and sister so close yet so far removed from me, I'll never again reach them.* A suddenness of terror unlike anything she had ever before felt seemed to assault her entire body. *The sad thing is, the Bloodwood's games have been my only company, my only sustenance.* The Bloodwood's machinations were nothing more than a weak thread to sew shut the wounds her parents' absence left, a salve for the pain of her fractured family and heart.

Jovan wrenched the blue sword from the table, stabbing it back home into the sheath at his belt with authority. "My four new Dayknights are heretofore charged with hunting down the criminals, Lindholf Le Graven, Gault Aulbrek, and the wench Delia, and whatever traitor to the Silver Throne helped the three escape the hangman's noose. Glade Chaparral and his fellow knights have the full backing of the Silver Throne and will be given full authority and access to every quarter of Amadon, full authority to investigate, interrogate, and execute anyone involved in this treachery."

Jovan glared down at Mona Le Graven then, as if her son's many alleged crimes against the Silver Throne were all her doing. He smiled wickedly then, knowing that he had just thrown Glade's advancement in her face. Then he yelled, "Now let us celebrate the knighting of these four Dayknights with food and wine and dance!"

The fickle crowd's mood instantly changed, sensing a grand party was about to begin. The orchestra again swelled to life, and trays of food were carried in.

Her brother had not even mentioned the death of Squireck in the arena yesterday. *How can the royals so callously have forgotten him so soon?* Tala asked herself, disgusted. *Can a man truly be a hero one day, nothing the next?* The last few years of Squireck's life had been unconventional and heartbreaking. Tala wished for at least just a candle to light in his memory, or better yet, a wreath of white heather to place upon her own head. Swiping the tears from her eyes, she found Denarius was staring right at her, leering with a gross lust, his gaze sliding over her body from head to toe and then back again, lingering on her lips, then her eyes.

Tala whirled in disgust, only to find Lawri standing behind her. Seita, too. Seita's father, Val-Korin, approached. The Val Vallè ambassador wore a long black robe, the red brass pendant of his rank hung casually about his neck from a slender gem-studded silver chain. "A shame about your arm," he said to Lawri upon arrival. "The loss of a limb is tragic indeed, more so to one so young and of such divine health. 'Tis a shame Seita did not return to court earlier. Perhaps she could have helped stave off the horror of you losing that arm."

Lawri looked at the Vallè princess. "Whatever could Seita have done?"

"Well," Val-Korin said, also looking at his daughter. "I suppose we shall never know. I have not had much of a chance to speak with my daughter since her return." Seita's face was impassive. Val-Korin continued, "But before she went east with Val-Draekin, my daughter mentioned that she'd a dreamed a dream, and in that dream you, young Lawri, were minus one arm. I find that curious."

"'Tis true." Seita bowed to Tala's cousin. "I had just such a dream."

Lawri's eyes grew wide with astonishment. "Really?"

"I only blame myself," Val-Korin continued. "I should have paid more attention to my daughter and perhaps Val-Gianni could have gotten you the right medicines for your infection sooner. I've forgotten how awfully accurate Seita's dreams can be."

Seita added, "I also dreamed you had green eyes, but everyone knows both you and Lindholf have the most beautiful of dark eyes. Like ink they are."

Tala's own vision swam as she tried to focus on her flaxen-haired cousin. *They play with you, Lawri. The Vallè play with us all!*

"I've similar dreams as Seita," Lawri mumbled, her dark Le Graven eyes on the bandaged stump of her arm. "Dreams that my eyes have turned to green gemstones."

Val-Korin's gaze narrowed as he seemed to study her. "Look at me, girl."

Lawri looked up.

"Well," Val-Korin said. "I must say, you and my daughter are right, for you've the most alluring green flecks dancing in your eyes, Lawri Le Graven. Just like gemstones, most alluring and mysterious indeed."

† † † † †

The newly made Dayknights—Glade, Tolz, Alain, and Boppard— were the center of attention in the midst of Sunbird Hall, smoke and food and music and dancing aswirl around them. But Tala had turned her back to the festivities hours ago. Jovan and Jondralyn sat at one end of the king's table. Tala sat at the other end of the long table with Ansel, the ruins of their dinner spread before them, the stone dais underfoot strewn with thick white rugs, soft to her bare feet. She had kicked her shoes off earlier.

"I've begged aid from every corner of Gul Kana." Jovan's tone was brusque, making scant effort to conceal his impatience. "Fighters and warriors have flooded into Amadon from afar. Leif Chaparral should have already arrived in Lord's Point. The defense of our borders against Aeros Raijael is the priority of my armies, not Hragna'Ar oghuls in the north."

Jondralyn sat back, Silver Guard armor creaking against the chair, a look of exasperation dropping over her. "But rumors grow in the north that entire towns are being overrun by oghuls. Cities as large as Tevlydog and Wroclaw are coming under threat."

"The threat from Sør Sevier is a thousand times greater. And that is where I shall send my resources, not some piddly outposts in the north."

"I warned you moons ago that Hragna'Ar was getting out of control. Why don't you send Glade Chaparral north with a legion of knights to stave off the problem? It's a fool's errand sending him off hunting Gault and Lindholf and the barmaid. Those three are long gone. Send *me* north if you must."

"Ha." Jovan snorted. "I doubt I'll send you anywhere ever again." Then a bored, almost lazy smile spread over his countenance. He didn't even look up from the table, almost as if he found it tedious to meet Jondralyn's eyes. "But I imagine, if Squireck still lived, I could send him north to fight oghuls for you, and all would be well."

Jondralyn fell silent at her brother's cruel derision. To Tala, the whole tenor of the discussion was now growing unfavorable to say the least. And it was clear Jovan was thoroughly bored with the conversation, which was never a good sign. He glanced back at the row of Dayknights standing at attention behind him, their backs to the velvet-draped wall, arms folded over black breastplates and mail, longswords in silver-studded baldrics slung over their silver surcoats.

Then he finally looked at Jondralyn. "I will not have you question the decisions of the Silver Throne any further. And that is an order."

Jondralyn straightened in her chair, gathering courage. "I merely wished to beg favor of you—"

"Enough!" Jovan slapped the table, his voice strident. "Enough begging of favor already! You've completely ruined my dinner with your ceaseless prattle about all the numerous things you think I should be doing better! There is nothing more pathetic than a woman trying to gain the king's favor—"

"I seldom seek the king's favor," Jondralyn sneered. "I only try and offer counsel as any good sister would offer her brother. It's all I've ever done since father died. I thought I had gained some trust in your eyes. 'Twas you who knighted me, lest you forget. As one of your knights, what would you rather have me do?"

"What would I rather have you do?" Jovan, both elbows planted on the table before him, pointed at her sharply, silver bracelets around his wrist ajingle. "I desire you renounce your vows as a Silver Guard and again become agreeable and genteel and mannerly and such, you know, as any good sister would for her brother the king."

Jondralyn said nothing in retort, her face red.

Her silence seemed to placate him as he continued more softly, "See. I daresay you know me to be quite amiable when you merely do my bidding and shut the fuck up."

Nobody spoke for a moment after that.

"They are fighting," Ansel said, concerned little eyes focused on his older siblings at the end of the table. "They fight and argue and be cross with each other."

"Yes," Tala said, grabbing Ansel by the arm and standing him up.

"Let us go, we needn't listen to them bicker."

Jovan abruptly stood, pointing at Tala. "Don't think this doesn't concern you either." Tala blanched as he made his way toward her. *Seems we are both always condemned in his eyes, Jondralyn and me, Jovan's two sisters, his chattel.* Every bit of her body and soul shrank as he approached, towering over her. She was suddenly deeply upset by the sheer unease he inspired in her.

"You are the most vexing of all, Tala," he grumbled. "A secret keeper. Slinking about like a thief in the night. You've become naught but a sullen, sneaky, cumbersome burden to the Silver Throne."

She scarcely dared speak. Sneaky, yes, she could agree to that. But cumbersome? That she vexed him so thrilled her somewhat. A defiant flame of pride sparked in her chest. "So what? Perhaps I like to sneak."

His face reddened.

"Leave her be," Jondralyn pleaded. "Don't drag Tala into this."

"Yes, you two sisters of mine are *sneaky,*" Jovan said, eyes bouncing between Tala and Jondralyn. "But I fancy I am trickier than you both. Your constant stubbornness and betrayals avail you nothing, the both of you."

"We only want what is best for our family and kingdom," Jondralyn said.

"No!" came Jovan's swift retort. "I don't believe any of that. You are still my sisters, are you not? It is your *duty* to make yourself humble and pleasant before me. Your chances to prove your value to the Silver Throne are becoming few. And once those chances run out . . ." Jovan left the threat hanging as he whirled and strode from Sunbird Hall, the line of Dayknights marching at his heels.

A moment passed.

Jondralyn stood and moved down the length of the table, grasping Tala by the forearm. "Heed me now, Tala. The castle may soon become too dangerous for either one of us. We must think of what alternatives are left. It is clear, our only worth to our brother is what marriage value we bring to the Silver Throne. Whatever plans he has, though advantageous to him, shall be less than promising for either of us. One day"—her voice dropped to almost less than a whisper as her eyes roamed the hall—"I fear we must conspire to either kill him or flee."

*When the innocent are found guilty, how art thou cut to the ground. One of Laijon's anointed can always pay penance and satisfy the law. But death of the anointed is the price.*
—THE WAY AND TRUTH OF LAIJON

## CHAPTER FIFTY-NINE

# AVA SHAY

2ND DAY OF THE FIRE MOON, 999TH YEAR OF LAIJON
MONT SAINT ONLY, ADIN WYTE

As Ava Shay hiked the cobbled footpath with Mancellor Allen, Enna Spades, and the Spider, she took in the spectacular vista. The cloistered trail that wound up the side of the Mont to the fortress above was lined with garlanded trellises of arched wood resting upon slim columns of stone, weeds and thorny briar growing about their base. It was also lined with apple trees that swayed gently in the wind, their white summer blossoms pungent. Through the vaulted arches of the cloister's outer wall, she had a grand view of the stable and cathedral two hundred feet below and the half-destroyed city of Saint Only even farther down the mountainside.

Several hundred of Aeros' warships were anchored in the western bay. The Adin Wyte peninsula stretched green and hazy to the north beyond the city. The canvas tents of two hundred thousand

Sør Sevier soldiers peppered the peninsula's landscape, little white specks receding into the distance as far as the eyes could see, every fighter down there awaiting the siege of Lord's Point that was soon to come.

The lofty castle of gray stone, jagged battlements, and narrow towers rose up magnificently before Ava. The beacon atop the tallest tower burned bright. It was the grandest structure she had ever seen, a marvel that swept her breath away. It was called the Fortress of Saint Only. And for good or ill, it was her new home.

Upon their arrival days ago, Aeros had gifted her with many fine gowns, insisting she wear them at all times, as she did now, a pale green affair that clung to her bodice and hung to her feet. Beside her, Enna Spades wore her traditional Knight Archaic blue cloak and armor. Her fire-red hair almost glowed in sunlight. Mancellor Allen wore the livery of a Knight of the Blue Sword, and Spiderwood wore his black leathers.

Mancellor led the group up the Mont and under the spiked portcullis of the outer gate and into a cramped warren consisting of many squalid alleys and winding staircases. Ava's gown billowed dust at her feet. Up they ascended through narrow streets toward Bruce Hall, the bulky structure that dominated the grand fortress, Ava realized this would only be her second time inside the hall since Aeros' arrival in Adin Wyte.

They reached the wide outer staircase that led to Bruce Hall's main entrance and marched up. She prepared herself for the foul odors she knew were to come. Sweat clung to her brow and collected moist and uncomfortable under her arms. It had been a rigorous hike from the stables below, and she didn't know how armored knights such as Mancellor and Spades could manage such exertion in such heavy plate.

The massive wooden double doors to the grand hall were already swung wide, and Ava, Mancellor, Spades, and the Spider entered the stench and gloom. Bruce Hall was a lofty and vulgar chamber, massive in both width and breadth. Ava reckoned she would never grow used to the filth and ruin and musty stink. The floor was fashioned of large flat stones laid in squares, battered, scuffed, stained, and worn, and all of them covered in a layer of scum and dried feces.

Most of the hall's sculptures and other furnishings were tipped over and scattered about. Soot-stained banners, red with white crossed spears, hung haphazardly from the rafters and arches. Tapestries, tattered and hanging ascant, lined the eastern and western walls, great strips torn and detached, revealing the mildewed stone beneath. Blotched mosaics were interspersed between the wormy tapestries, spears and lances too, but again, most of those had fallen from the walls, littering the floor like matchsticks. Even Ava could tell that this was not the mold and worn usage of noble antiquity, but rather plain purposeful neglect. Every square inch of the place looked seldom, if ever, cleaned. But what made the place so utterly horrid—mangy-looking dogs were everywhere, most lounging in puddles of their own piss, some of them maimed, all with ears alert, eyes glowing in anticipation, as if each and every one of them expected some scrap of food to be tossed from all who passed by. Ava nearly gagged at the pungent smell.

Mancellor led the group in a twining path around many dusty chairs, bronze tripods, inlaid braziers, and dog shit, eventually bringing them to the Throne of Spears at the southern end of the squalid hall. Aeros Raijael, Jenko Bruk, Hammerfiss, and a dozen other knights were gathered near the throne.

A large white stallion stood there in the center of the group. It was Ser Gault Aulbrek's warhorse, Spirit. The steed looked royal and stoic, like a gleaming crystal shard in the filth and gloom. There was a longsword and a Knight Archaic helm hooked to the beast's saddle horn, both also Gault's.

A tall and extremely fair-haired man with squared and handsome features lingered near the horse. Ava had never seen him before. He wore Knight of the Blue Sword armor and livery. He immediately bent his knee when he saw her. But Ava ignored the man's bow, looking beyond him to the fireplace and balconies. A hearth large enough to double as a bedchamber sat smack in the center of the western wall, its once showy stone-carved mantelpiece coated in melted wax and grime, its innards jammed with the torn-up remains of chairs, beds, tables, and any other unwanted thing. Higher up, above the hearth and tapestries, a stone-railed gallery rimmed the entire hall on all four sides, accessible by only one set of stairs along the northern end. Ava wondered if the gallery led to any secluded alcoves or terraces that overlooked the sea. If so, she wished to go up there for some fresh air. Far above the gallery rose stained-glass windows. The glass so soot-covered, what light shown through was grim and uncertain, casting a shimmering, dull-colored tinge over everything, lending the chamber a spooky glow.

"She cares little for my fealty," the fair-haired man who had bent his knee to her commented. "I must say I am hurt, Lord Aeros."

"Perhaps she prefers King Edmon," the White Prince said. His skin appeared so ashen in the dim light, it seemed to bleed into the white of his tunic and cloak. His dark eyes, black as spilled ink, were fixed on the Throne of Spears.

Ava followed his gaze. The throne itself was a large but simple wood-carved chair upholstered in red velvet. A large drooling sheep hound the color of mud lounged on the seat of the throne. The dog was asleep, slobber draining from its floppy jowls and dripping down the front of the chair. On either side of the spiked throne stood men-at-arms, four total, two per side, all in the red-and-white livery of Adin Wyte. They stood as rigid as statues, halberds with gilded spearheads at their shoulders.

King Edmon Guy Van Hester sat in the shadows on the scum-covered floor at the foot of the throne looking up at Aeros. "Pray sit down upon my throne, Your Grace," his croaking voice sounded. He held up one grubby hand imploringly. "Oblige and favor me so. Or at the very least have your lady sit here to please me."

The dog on the throne woke with a snort and licked the old man's hand. Ava grimaced in disgust.

"I thought I ordered you to have this chamber cleaned," Aeros said, reaching up, gripping the reins of the white stallion in one white-leather-gloved hand. "I gave you enough servants for the task, the very same servants who've been scrubbing my own bedchamber, which I hope to be ready soon." He stroked the horse's muzzle.

Edmon's sagging eyes roamed over the entire group, the stallion included. "I entreat you all, excuse me my laziness. But my wife is gone, disappeared, mayhap dead. Was Beatriz who kept up with the cleaning. I've dismissed all her servants but one, the lovely Miss Leisel. She will bring your esteemed lady friend refreshments soon, my lord Aeros, if it please you."

To Ava's ear, Edmon had a strange way of speaking, and of moving. He wobbled to his feet drowsily, almost like a pure invalid. He wore a tattered cloak of a sort that, like his breeches, seemed to be cut for a much smaller person when he stood.

He stepped toward Aeros cautiously, moving with a curling stoop, bandy-legged and haggard, as if he would soon crumble to dust. He beckoned toward the fair-haired knight next to Aeros. "Leisel will have cool drink for you too, good Ser."

"You're an embarrassment, Edmon," the fair-haired knight said. "Your throne room is an embarrassment. Has your son's murder charge in Amadon disgraced you to the point of complete uselessness?"

Rumor was Edmon's only son, Ser Squireck Van Hester, had murdered one of the Five Archbishops in Amadon, bringing crippling shame upon the once-noble king of Adin Wyte. Despite Aeros having destroyed his kingdom, the White Prince had let Edmon rule in the fortress anyway. Though all knew it was Aeros Raijael who was in charge. Edmon Guy Van Hester was now naught but a sad-looking old man reduced to eking out his days in the impoverished reek of a once-grand hall.

"I live by thine own mercy, fair Lord Aeros." Edmon now made an odd sniffling sound as he talked. "As I said, I seem to have misplaced my wife. Was she who kept things tidy." His cloak fell aside at the hip, revealing the worn pommel of a sword and scabbard hooked at his drooping belt. Skeletal fingers curled around the weapon's hilt as Edmon drew the sword slowly from its hardened leather sheath.

"Yes, I live in disgrace." He held the sword's hilt forth for Aeros. No light gleamed on the blade—it was naught but dull metal. "Take it and slay me now if you must; execute me for my gross incompetence before you."

"Nonsense," Aeros said. "I've come to introduce you to the new Lord of Saint Only, your new master, Ser Ivor Jace." He beckoned to the fair-haired knight who had earlier bowed to Ava.

"You would replace me?" Edmon straightened some, resheathing his sword. With that one gesture, Ava thought she could see the once-noble and imposing man somewhere inside this lamentable creature named Edmon Guy Van Hester. "Ivor's been here for a while now, and you would replace me with him now?"

"You've always known I would replace you with him," Aeros said.

"I implore you, say it is not so." Edmon's posture wilted again. "That such gentry as yourselves hath visited such horrid and detestable barbarity upon us, upon our entire kingdom, yet let me keep my throne room and castle and entire fortress only speaks to your divine kindness, no? Why change things now, at this late hour?"

"Had you acted like a man and not treated this place so unspeakably disagreeable, perhaps I would let you continue your pathetic little reign, but alas, things being as they are, Ser Ivor Jace is now the new ruler of Saint Only and the new King of Adin Wyte."

Ava looked again at the blond knight who bowed to low Aeros.

The first noticeable thing about Ser Ivor Jace was his height. He was tall, not nearly as towering as Hammerfiss, but almost. He had a sculpted yet doggedly handsome face complete with a row of scars across his jaw and neck that gave him a slightly unnatural, mocking air. A natural self-assurance pervaded his already noble physique.

"Ser Ivor is a bold knight." The White Prince's voice now carried across the broad expanse of Bruce Hall. "He would fight all Gul Kana with naught but his bare hands if I so ordered." Aeros' gaze found Jenko Bruk, then lingered on Mancellor Allen. He then turned to Edmon Guy Van Hester once again, unforgiving eyes now piercing and black as a demon's curse. "Listen well, Ser Edmon, for you will now learn some few things about your own realm. Or perhaps I remind you of things you already knew. Ser Ivor was once a gallant knight under your own command. Ser Ivor was once an Adin Wyte soldier, raised in the far north at Storm's Watch. Ser Ivor survived my attack on Storm's Watch. I gave him rank in my armies. And he proved his quality in war. He is a man now beholden to the covenant of Raijael. In fact, he was the hero of the Battle of Kragg Keep. Now I make him Lord of Saint Only. What think you of that, Ser Edmon?"

"As you deem it, so shall it be done," Edmon sank back into the shadows at the foot of the Throne of Spears, stroking the leg of the velvet-covered chair with long bony fingers, the slobbering sheep hound atop the throne looking down at him lazily.

Aeros handed the reins of the white stallion to Ivor. "I honor you with Ser Gault Aulbrek's steed." Ivor bent his knee to Aeros, then reached out and grasped the reins with his left hand. "The warhorse is named Spirit," Aeros said, "and may he bear you well."

"I am honored," Ivor said, bowing again.

To Ava, the man certainly seemed fond of bowing, but it also seemed all a grand act to her.

"Spirit is one of only five such white stallions," Aeros went on, "grand mounts meant for my Knights Archaic, of which you are now one."

Ivor again bent his knee. Spades and the Spider exchanged glances as Aeros bowed to Ivor in return, then continued, "Gault's sword and helm are hooked to the saddle horn. We shall fit you with the proper armor later." His gaze circled the gloom of the hall, falling on a slip of a blond girl who approached. "Ah, yes, now let us drink."

The tawny-haired girl of about fifteen came bearing a huge hollowed-out oxhorn brimming with dark mead. She stepped demurely into the circle of knights and bowed to Aeros. And Aeros bowed back to her.

Ava was taken aback, for the fetching young girl had such soft eyes and such a bright trusting countenance. Her delicate ivory face was freckled about the nose and bridge of her cheekbones.

"Young Leisel." Aeros' lips curled into something that was not quite a grin. "Bringing cool refreshment for our newest Knight Archaic right on time." He turned to Ivor. "The honor is yours."

Ivor Jace snatched up the massive oxhorn with his right hand and drank lustily, then offered the mead to Spirit. The stallion snorted and stepped back, ironshod hooves clacking hollow against the stone floor. The horse eyed the oxhorn under its nose with a look of utter contempt.

"Well, never you mind ,then, finicky nag." Ivor furrowed his brow, then bent his knee to the horse. "All the more for me." He smiled, glittering eyes on Aeros. "I've always found a stout warhorse makes for the best of drinking partners, but alas, the steed you've bequeathed to me seems preposterously disinterested in the notion."

"Ser Gault was not the type to drink with the equine." Hammerfiss smiled—a wide spreading of his already wide mouth. The blue Suk Skard clan tattoos spanning his face stretched in merriment. The small fetishes tied in the tangled mass of his beard jingled. "I'm afraid Gault's stallion never developed a taste for grog of any kind."

"A shame that," Ivor said. "Nothing like a drunken horse to liven a gathering."

"Ha! I always did like your flair for the absurd, Ser Ivor." Hammerfiss laughed heartily. "I for one say it is good to have you with us again." The red-haired giant then snatched the oxhorn from Ivor, drinking the mead down in one gulp, laughing riotously.

Ivor laughed too. "Since you're the next biggest thing to a war charger, drink up, my new equine companion, drink up."

Hammerfiss' smile widened. "You're lucky I don't mind being called a horse." He clapped the man on the shoulder. "I do miss fighting by your side, Ser Ivor."

Ivor grinned. "Well, we shall soon be fighting side by side, Ser Hammerfiss. Within days I reckon."

"Splendid." Hammerfiss tipped his head in admiration. "For that, I cannot wait."

"I would surely like a swig of that mead." Edmon Guy Van Hester's voice croaked to life again. He glared at Leisel. "Would you at least oblige and favor me with some more dog food?"

The girl dug into the cloth pouch at her belt and tossed a handful of dried pellets of jerked beef on the floor under Edmon. The old king scrambled to gather the dog food. The slobbering sheep hound on the chair above him bounded down too, lapping the jerked beef from the floor before Edmon could reach it. Several other dogs rumbled over, growling as they jostled and squabbled.

"Spades and Hammerfiss and Mancellor you already know," Aeros said to Ivor, ignoring the dogs. "But allow me to introduce Ser Jenko Bruk."

Jenko, also in Knight of the Blue Sword armor, stepped forward. Ivor shook his hand vigorously. Jenko was big and strong, but he was nowhere near as tall as Ivor was.

"And my lovely *princess*, Ava Shay," Aeros said, emphasis on the title *princess*.

Not knowing what else to do, Ava bowed before the new Knight Archaic.

"Most beautiful to be sure." Ivor spoke with an arrogant, honeyed voice.

He reached forth and took her hand into his own, brought her fingers to his lips and kissed the back of them. Ava felt her flesh crawl at the gesture. Ivor's eyes bore into hers. "What glorious children you will create, my lord Aeros. What glorious children with such a divine princess such as Ava Shay."

As Ivor released Ava's hand, dread slithered through her every vein like creeping serpents. She glanced at Jenko. His face burned red with jealousy. *Am I already pregnant?* The thought struck her hard. The fear of it nearly strangled her then and there. Her one consolation; she recognized these feelings of sudden pernicious dread as her own conjurations, not some foul delusion induced by the wraiths. The wraiths had left her alone for nearly a moon now.

There was a cacophony of barks and yelps from near the Throne of Spears, and the area was a chaos of whirling bodies and flashing fur as more dogs joined in the fight over the last morsels of jerked beef. Old king Edmon was right there in the tussle, snarling and fighting along with the dogs.

Hammerfiss loosed a loud guffaw. "I place two coppers on the old man!"

"And I say the sheepdog takes the prize!" Ivor shouted.

Ava's nerves and stomach could scarcely tolerate the horrendous noise and chaos caused by the quarreling dogs. "May I take some air on the balcony?" she asked Aeros in a gust of words.

"Of course, my princess." Aeros bowed to her. "Dog fighting is a sport for warriors, and you are no warrior yet." One languid hand gripped her shoulder, the palm of the other on her stomach, gentle. "We shall both be looking after your health from now on. You needn't sully yourself with the hounds, nor the shit, nor Ser Edmon's stink."

✝ ✝ ✝ ✝ ✝

Much to Ava's chagrin, Spades accompanied her to the balcony. They passed under the frowning arch of the gallery onto the terrace, leaving the floor of Bruce Hall below, stepping into the fresh air. Colorful butterflies fluttered up from the balcony's chest-high stone railing. Ava gripped the banister with trembling hands, light-headedness taking hold. Spades leaned into the railing by her side, taking in the view.

They were high up face of the Mont, naught but jagged cliffs and a rocky shore of billow and spray below. The sandy channel to the east gave way to Lord's Point some ten miles distant, beyond that farms and wooded glades stretched to Lokkenfell. The peaks of the Autumn Range faded into the farthest horizons.

Lord's Point Cathedral stood out in stark splendor against the vast maze of streets and buildings of the city. The walled castle stood out too. Ava had never seen such a huge place. And she now had the bird's-eye view of it. She wondered how Aeros' army could take such a populous. Some fifty thousand Sør Sevier soldiers were already camped south of Lord's Point, awaiting the siege. She had traveled north with that vast contingent as they'd slaughtered their way up the Gul Kana coastline. Near two hundred thousand more Sør Sevier warriors awaited on the peninsula north of Saint Only.

To the west she could see the cliffs of Wyn Darrè and the five Laijon Towers jutting heavenward. From this one vantage point Ava could see both Gul Kana and Wyn Darrè, all while standing at the tip of Adin Wyte. Many said the view from the fortress of Saint Only was the grandest view of all in the Five Isles.

A veil of puffy clouds drifted in directly overhead, lazily pushing toward Lord's Point. The billowing clouds were moving on Gul Kana, just as she knew Aeros' armies would soon do. The White Prince planned on striking Lord's Point soon. He had divulged some of his plans to her. The ten-mile channel of ocean that separated Saint Only from Lord's Point was shallow. The fickle tide, he had explained, would retreat for some four to six hours every afternoon, so low one could actually walk from Mont Saint Only to Lord's Point across the muddy sands. During that span of low tide, his army of two hundred thousand waiting on the peninsula north of Saint Only would cross the expanse and attack Lord's Point from the west, whilst the fifty thousand he'd left south of Lord's Point would advance on the city from there. Aeros had also told her he had one more special surprise in store for the poor hapless souls of Lord's Point.

"Aeros means to wield the great ax in battle," Ava said out loud, suddenly wanting to spill her secrets to the woman standing next to her.

Spades slipped her hand into the silver buckler at her belt, pulling forth the copper coin she always carried—the Gul Kana copper with Princess Jondralyn Bronachell's image. With a wistful look she flicked the coin in the air, catching it lithely, doing it again and again.

"Did you not hear me?" Ava inquired, somewhat annoyed.

"Aeros means to wield *Forgetting Moon*?" Spades repeated.

"And wear *Lonesome Crown*." Ava watched the flickering coin in the woman's hand. "He will also carry the two angel stones. He fashioned a special leather pouch just for them, a pouch to wear at his belt. He believes the stones hold magic powers that will make him indestructible."

"Is that what brought you to the balcony, to betray Aeros, to divulge your lord's secrets to me?"

"No." She gulped nervously. "I came out here because . . ." She straightened her back with resolve. "Because . . . though I couldn't help but admire the general splendor of Bruce Hall, I prefer the out-of-doors."

"Ha." Spades' lips curled into a wry little smile. "The girl tells a joke. I think."

"Perhaps," Ava muttered, gazing back out across the sandy strait.

"If only Mancellor Allen could hear your wit. He would laugh with you indeed. Jenko, too, maybe. No matter how hard I've tried to work the lust out of that boy, I see how Jenko still looks at you."

Ava's heart lurched at her words. Spades had a knack for keeping her off balance at all times.

"Jenko will never be yours, though, or you his," Spades went on. "Which is for the best, really. Even had you married and settled for the peaceful life in Gallows Haven, Jenko would have ultimately disappointed you. He has too much of the rake and rambler in him." Spades was no longer tossing the coin. "But Mancellor, worse than even Gault, practically fawns over you. And don't think for a moment his innocent little gallantries go unnoticed by Aeros."

"Why do you torture everyone so?"

"Just be careful how you react to those gallantries, or I fear Ser Mancellor will suffer the same fate as Gault."

"Mancellor has nothing to fear from me. Nor ever did Gault."

"Oh, the pleasant torments and bitter sweets of young love."

"I know naught of what you speak."

"Sure you do. It's just a game we girls play, comes natural to we few who are so pretty. 'Tis how we ofttimes get those things we most want out of life, this game of men. And I for one can tell that you are well versed in it."

Ava had learned what warning signs to look for within Spades, learned when the woman was itching to torment and tease. This was clearly one of those times, and Ava wanted no part of it. *Only madness lies down this path.*

"I recall when I was a girl," Spades said, "lying under an apple tree and looking up, imagining all the apples as tiny worlds where the Warrior Angels lived, imagining myself as one of those Warrior Angels, living among the stars, ruling a world of mine own, wondering how I was to accomplish this, knowing it was a man's game and that if I did not play this game of men, I would never sit upon the heights of the stars."

Ava recalled the conversation about stars and Warrior Angels she'd had with Nail. She had accused Nail of goddess worship when he had said similar things.

*But who's to believe anything Spades says?*

Ava turned from the dizzying view, turned back toward Bruce Hall, wondering if the stench-filled room below wasn't better than this pointless banter with Enna Spades.

She was building up the courage, readying to take her leave, when she caught a glimpse of her own face in a dull window just to the left of the stone archway. She was taken aback, gazing at her own image, a face wreathed in shadows of dirt. She rubbed the glass clean with the sleeve of her shirt and stepped back into the sunlight just a smidge.

The image gazing back startled her. She was far prettier than she remembered, actually radiant. It was a frightening beauty she saw.

*Does Aeros truly fill me with his essence?* Her eyes sparked green fire. *I possess you and I purify you,* he'd once said. *Everything I do is holy. When you lie with me, I place into you the healing power of the gods. Our heavenly seasons are blessed by both Raijael and Laijon. In them, I take upon myself your pains, your troubles, and your sins. I even take the wraiths that dwell within you upon myself. I bear your burdens.*

She let her hair tumble into her eyes, trying to cover her face. *Is it his translucence that shines through my own skin?* There was a terrible beauty about his own bearing. *Is that in me too? A beauty seared by madness and trauma?* But she could see hers was a more vulnerable and untamed beauty, his more controlled and cruel.

*And my eyes are green!* Aeros had twin eyes of a blackness so profound, they seemed to split the very midnight skies.

*I belong to him! I am naught but his princess.* And that was the game of men, it seemed. As Aeros' property, her only living purpose was to satisfy the lust and glut of his loins. She looked away from her own image, an image that now seemed to be wavering and warping in the dusky glass.

Spades was staring at her, firm curiosity in her gaze.

In the space between them were five butterflies dancing around each other: one white, one black, a green and a blue, and the fifth one bloodred.

The red butterfly landed on Ava's shoulder but a moment, then fluttered off. . . .

*Humans, you ask, how shall they be best destroyed? By the hollow of their ignorance shall they be destroyed, neath the boiling belly of the storm they didst conjure themselves shall they perish.*
—THE ANGEL STONE CODEX

# CHAPTER SIXTY
# BISHOP HUGH GODWYN

### 4TH DAY OF THE FIRE MOON, 999TH YEAR OF LAIJON
### LORD'S POINT, GUL KANA

I can agree to those terms, feeble as they are." Brown R'elk's voice was smooth as the smoke drifting up from his curling pipe. The oghul lounged on a plush red-velvet couch with his bare feet up on a stool covered in bear-hide leather, the ivory mouthpiece of the pipe he smoked clicking against his teeth. His stylish manor house and leisurely speech combined gave him an air of distinction and sophistication Godwyn could not have imagined ever existed in oghul-kind.

Brown R'elk had a wedge-shaped face of gray-frosted umber and lucent eyes of a rich dark brown. The red teardrop-shaped tattoo on his cheekbone just below his left eye marked him as one who dealt in dark alchemy. He wore a plush violet fur-trimmed coat that reached to his bare heels and an elegantly stitched shirt of fine linen underneath. His pantaloons were fashioned of smooth ox-hide leather and clean.

In fact, everything about Brown R'elk and his residence was clean and fine. He lived in a tall and stately three-story manor near the Lord's Point town square. Lush and trellised gardens of ivy had marked the gated entrance, just as S'ist Runk had described.

"I could ask for more from you, old man, but I wish to help the boy heal fully." Brown R'elk drew on the pipe with one last deep breath and stood, setting the pipe aside. "Such a fine doggy you are." He petted Beer Mug atop the head, then walked across the smoky drawing room to a dark wood cupboard set against the far wall, returning with two copper beakers, one in each hand. He handed Dokie Liddle the first beaker. It was brimming with Blood of the Dragon. Liz Hen Neville eyed the red draught hungrily.

Blood of the Dragon was rare and it was dangerous. But together with rauthouin bane it could heal near anything. One sip could give almost anyone unnatural good health. But its healing powers came with a heavy price for some. Addiction. And Liz Hen was clearly addicted.

Dokie pulled the hood of his gray cloak back. Ashen-faced and ill, he furtively drank down half of the red liquid and handed the beaker to Liz Hen. She shed her cloak and swiftly gulped the remainder down whole, then cradled the copper beaker protectively in both hands, eyes searching the room for more. Her cloak drooped open in the middle, and the Sør Sevier sword she wore at her hip was now clearly visible.

Brown R'elk seemed not to care, offering Dokie the rauthouin bane next. The boy drank it, the clear draught almost instantly adding a healthy pallor to his skin.

"I can feel it," Dokie said. "It gives me strength." He bowed to the oghul. "Thank you, good Sèr." Brown R'elk dipped his thin head in return.

"You're practically healed." Liz Hen hugged Dokie, the copper beaker still in hand. "It's a miracle we got you off that glacier as poisoned as you were. A miracle we got you back to Lord's Point." When she released the boy, her bloodshot eyes cravenly searched her empty beaker and roamed the room again.

*It's already happening to her!* Drinking Blood of the Dragon would eventually change the chemistry of one's body, turning the eyes red. Bishop Godwyn blamed himself for her addiction. *But there is naught to be done about it now. . . .*

He lowered the cowl of his own cloak, preparing himself, heart beating faster now in anticipation.

"You've agreed to the price, old man." Brown R'elk said, eyes narrowing, now focused on the purple telltale signs of bloodletting at Godwyn's neck.

The bishop nodded, his entire body shaking with an expectation of its own. It had been such a long journey to reach this place. They had set sail from Stanclyffe eleven days ago, arriving in Lord's Point yestermorn, again taking up lodging at the Turn Key Inn & Saloon. During the voyage, Dokie had recovered most of his faculties the first few days, and then showed steady improvement each day thereafter. The medicines that S'ist Runk had plied the boy with had worked miracles.

Godwyn's own addiction to bloodletting had occupied his mind for most of the journey. Ever since Stanclyffe, he could scarcely focus on any one thought for long. And now his eyes were but twin points of stinging agony, his stomach knotted in pain. Not to mention the profusion of sweat he could never escape. *Yes, I agreed to the terms, but it is no feeble price to me. . . .*

With swollen gums, Brown R'elk drifted casually toward him, his disconcerting, hungry gaze focused solely on Godwyn. The bishop stood still with an anticipatory meekness; every muscle of his face quivered in nervous anticipation.

As Brown R'elk's teeth sank into his upturned neck, an all-consuming bliss and ecstasy enveloped Godwyn.

† † † † †

"I am Leif Chaparral, Captain of the Dayknights!" Leif's voice rang out over the crowd. The tall knight with black-rimmed eyes and long dark hair stood atop the stone podium in the middle of the Lord's Point Square, the spires of the city's cathedral looming over him. Lord Kelvin Kronnin stood next to the dark-eyed knight along with a mix of blue-clad Ocean Guard and soldiers in the Wolf Guard maroon-and-gray livery of Rivermeade.

"As you all know," Leif continued, "an army of the White Prince camps naught but ten miles south of Lord's Point! Some fifty thousand strong!"

The crowd below him was teeming with a mixture of knights and other Lord's Point denizens, all shoulder-to-shoulder. Many of them shouted, "We shall fight the White Prince! Let us at 'em!"

Leif quieted the crowd with a wave of his arm. "Fifty thousand they have! But fear not, we should soon have twice that gathered in Lord's Point!" Cheers rose up from the crowd. Leif stepped back and soaked in the thunderous sound.

His black-lacquered armor was shined to an obsidian polish, and the silver surcoat draped over his shoulders gleamed. The silver-wolf-on-a-maroon-field crest at his chest marked him as Rivermeade nobility, and the black sword with the black opal-inlaid pommel at his belt confirmed his rank as Dayknight.

Godwyn carried a similar sword hidden under his own gray cloak. Strands of hair clung to his face under the stifling hood. His eyes were stinging nonstop, and his gut was jumping, sweat soaking everywhere from head to toe. He stood with Liz Hen, Dokie, and Beer Mug in the middle of the throng. *It's too crowded here . . . too loud.*

He wished to move on, but what Leif was saying was nothing short of historic.

Once the thunder of voices died down, Leif continued. "Knights from the breadth of Gul Kana have rallied under the colors of Amadon and Lord's Point! Rallied to wage war under the banners of Rivermeade and all points beyond! Thousands more arrive every day!" More cheering followed.

What Leif said was true. Ever since Godwyn had arrived back in Lord's Point, the entire composition and makeup of the city had changed drastically from when he had last been here. It was no longer merely merchants, burghers, and other assorted tradesmen milling about. Knights and mercenaries clogged the cobbled streets now, contingents and small parties of every stripe, complete with horse and tent and squire and all the bristling accoutrements of war.

"He's such a handsome knight." Liz Hen's eyes were wide and red as she gazed up at Leif Chaparral. *Blood of the Dragon, still changing her, working its foul magic inside her head . . .*

"Last night I received ill tidings from my spy in Saint Only!" Leif Chaparral shouted. "Aeros Raijael has amassed near two hundred thousand soldiers on the peninsula north of Saint Only, just across the waters from here!"

Godwyn figured most gathered here had already heard the rumors and expected Leif to confirm as much. But Leif was a fool for being so forthcoming about what spies he may or may not have in Saint Only.

Leif went on, "The White Prince plans on launching an attack on Lord's Point with the full might of his army from across the Saint Only Channel! I do not yet know the day of the attack, but it will be soon! It will begin at low tide, two hundred thousand knights charging across that tenuous stretch of sand that separates Lord's Point from Saint Only! And we shall let him come!"

The crowd was once again in an uproar, swords drawn and thrust heavenward, angry shouts for war issuing forth. Leif again silenced the throng with another crisp wave of his hand. "Fear not! We of Gul Kana will muster all arms! Knights! Soldiers! Mercenaries! Gaolers! Every *man* in this city able to wield a weapon will be ready! I shall know the hour of the attack! And when Aeros Raijael marches his army out onto that precarious stretch of sand, he will not expect us to charge out meet him in battle! We only need engage him in battle long enough for the flooding tide to rise up and sweep his army away!" Cheers thundered forth.

"Many of us will perish!" Leif continued and things quieted again. "But we shall be more prepared than they, for every available boat in Lord's Point will be dragged across the sand behind us! Only we shall have a means of escape when the tide rises up! True, many of us will die, but most will escape alive! The entire army of Sør Sevier will founder in the strait! Two hundred thousand dead at the hands of a few!"

Beer Mug rubbed against Godwyn's leg. He petted the top of the dog's head. *Leif is a fool!* A smart carrier pigeon swift of flight could have this news back to Aeros in but hours. *It will not be long before the White Prince is made privy to Leif's plan.*

"The war for Gul Kana starts now!" Leif shouted. "Jovan Bronachell and Grand Vicar Denarius will rejoice that we fighting men of Gul Kana have done our part, that we have defended our kingdom before the great day of Fiery Absolution! Know that you men gathered here today will soon be ushering Fiery Absolution and the return of Laijon himself! For it will be by the sum of this battle that Laijon will judge us! It will be by the tally of each of our beating hearts! For it is not us brave men who will make this slaughter against our foe, but the almighty One and Only himself shall guide our weapons. Laijon will use the strength of our arms as an instrument to protect the tender women and children of this city!"

"Tender women?" Liz Hen muttered with disgust. "I think not." Her red-hazed eyes met those of Godwyn's. "If there is to be a battle, I mean to join it. I've a sword of my own and know how to use it, by God."

† † † † †

The Turn Key Inn & Saloon was empty when they returned. They found Otto the serving boy sitting in the back courtyard under the porch awning, reading a book. The inn's courtyard of gray stone and weathered gables was empty but for a stout covered wagon sitting smack in its dusty center. Two piebald ponies were hitched to the wagon's tongue and neck yoke, their hooves padding restlessly at the dirt.

"Saloon's empty, Otto," Liz Hen said as she stepped onto the porch behind Godwyn, Dokie, and Beer Mug. She was picking her teeth with a thin boning knife she'd pulled from the kitchen. "I helped myself to the ribs stewing at the boil."

Otto looked up from his book, glaring at the girl, irritation gathering on his scrawny mug. "What'd you go and do that for; them ribs were meant—"

"Why's there a wagon and team of ponies parked plum center of the yard?" Liz Hen pointed with the tip of the knife.

Otto answered, "I was sitting here reading when Derry stumbled out of the stables drunk, passed out in the dirt over by the weapons racks." The stone beyond the wagon was lined with several weapon racks bristling with swords, spears, batons, clubs, chains, leg irons, large iron keys, and several scuffed and dull suites of gaoler armor gathering dust underneath. The courtyard was set up with enough weaponry and armament for the gaolers to practice their various gaoling techniques. Derry Richrath was the owner of the Inn; a stout old cob himself, he was also a former prison guard.

"Derry bein' drunk don't explain nothin' about that wagon," Liz Hen commented, annoyed.

"Does too." Otto shrugged, looking down at his book again, flipping a page.

"Are you daft or just dumb?" Liz Hen asked, her agitation growing.

Otto marked his page with a finger. "Well, I couldn't very well enjoy my book whilst constantly noticing Derry Richrath out of the corner of my eye just layin' there face-first in the dirt as he was." He gazed up at Liz Hen expectantly.

The girl merely glared down at him, brow wrinkling in further annoyance. As long as Godwyn had known Liz Hen Neville, the girl had never been one for gentility of manners, and now that she was hooked on Blood of the Dragon, she was becoming even more pushy and rude. "You still ain't explained nothin'," she said.

Otto sighed, "So I went to the stable, hitched Colin and Poor Boy up to the wagon and parked it just so, blocking my view of Derry layin' in the dirt, then went back to enjoying my book."

"You mean Derry is passed out on the other side of that wagon?" Dokie piped in. He stepped off the porch and into the courtyard, hustling around the wagon. Beer Mug followed. "He's here!" Dokie did the three-fingered sign of the Laijon Cross over his heart. "He's snoring."

"Bloody Mother Mia." Liz Hen cuffed Otto in the side of the head with a swift swat of her hand. "You don't just let folks pass out in the dirt and drag a wagon in front of them so you can enjoy a book."

"Says who?"

"Says me! I should know! I worked a tavern before!" She gave Otto another backhanded swat to the side of the head. "You clodpole! May the wraiths take you. I wager you're not even trained as an ostler either."

A look of peevish displeasure came over Otto. "I'll do what I want around here."

"When the sky rains carrots and potatoes, you'll do what you want."

"I don't have to listen to you."

"Only a clodpole would take the time to hitch up a wagon and park it in front of a drunk you didn't wanna look at rather than just help the drunk inside, you stupid."

"I got my own way of sorting things out."

Liz Hen smacked him again. Godwyn grabbed her wrist. "Just help Dokie lift Derry into the saloon, would you?" Liz Hen wrenched her hand from his, gave him a cold stare, then clomped down the stairs of the porch.

Halfway to the wagon she kicked off her boot. "Stupid pebble in my shoe!" She turned over the boot and shook it. Nothing came out. She grunted in disgust throwing the boot aside. Foot now bare, she hopped toward the weapons' rack and hoisted up her leg, propping it against a squat wooden keg. She began whittling away at her toenails with the boning knife she'd previously used to pick her teeth.

Godwyn's gaze roamed past the courtyard's horse stable toward the ten-mile strip of ocean that separated Saint Only from Lord's Point, thinking of Leif's plan to stave off Aeros Raijael's coming attack. The ebbing tide, for four to six hours each afternoon, was so low one with a quick stride could actually walk to Mont Saint Only. But when the unpredictable tide rose again, it rose brisk and rapid, up to fifteen feet deep in less than half an hour. Many ill-fated travelers had been swept out to sea having misjudged those tides.

"Useless knife." Liz Hen gave up trimming her toenails and jammed the knife into the dirt at her feet. She began gathering up a pile of heavy gaoler armor, buckling the stout iron vambraces over her forearms.

"What you doing?" Dokie asked. "I thought you were gonna help me haul Derry inside."

"You heard that Dayknight in the square," Liz Hen said, fixing the greaves over her legs. "He said even turn keys and gaolers should fight Aeros' army when they attempt to cross yonder strait." She unhooked the Sør Sevier sword at her belt, set it aside.

"You don that armor, Liz Hen, and some Sør Sevier fighter is liable to mistake you for a real knight and run a spear though your gut," Dokie said.

Otto added, "Or someone is apt to hang you when they find out you're but a girl. You oughtn't be found inside a man's armor like that."

"I've reasoned it out." Liz Hen dropped the cuirass over her shoulders. "Once I'm fully geared up, ain't nobody gonna mistake me for no girl, specially when I chop my hair off."

"But Seita won't be able to braid it if it's chopped," Dokie said.

A deep welling of sadness filled Liz Hen's eyes. "Be that as it may, I see no other alternative, Dokie." Beer Mug sniffed at her armor and barked. "Ain't no armor here fit for a dog," she said. "I'm afraid this is one battle you'll have to sit out, Beer Mug." The shepherd dog whimpered as she struggled with the straps of the cuirass.

Godwyn stepped forward and helped the girl fasten the cuirass around her back. Then he set the gaoler helm over her head. It was a close helm with a moveable visor that she pulled down covering her face. She picked up her sword. Though the strain of travel and adventure had shrunk the girl's heavy limbs and flabby cheeks by some, she still looked like an imposing fighter in the gaoler armor and helm. And with that Sør Sevier sword in hand, she looked tall and broad and deadly as the stoutest of men.

"Are you sure you want to do this?" he asked her.

"The White Prince destroyed my town and slaughtered my family." Liz Hen's voice rang strangely hollow from under the helm. But her determination was evident. She brandished the sword before her, crouching, as if to launch an attack on some unseen foe. "I will not stand around whilst Aeros' armies again invade my homeland." She stood straight and flipped the visor away from her face—a face that was now a red mask of rage. "I will kill Aeros Raijael myself if I can!"

"You're crazy if you join in the fight." Dokie looked at her askance. "Such thinking will only get you killed."

Godwyn said, "No, Dokie, she is doing just what she ought." The words seemed to tumble from his mouth of their own volition. "And I will follow her into battle."

He was surprised at his own admission. *Is the bloodletting causing me to not think clearly . . . ?*

"Then I will fight too." Dokie headed for one of the piles of dusty armor.

"You needn't help, Dokie." Liz Hen snatched off her helm. "On account of your delicate health, you needn't fight."

"If you fight, then I fight too." Dokie hefted one of the close helms, studying it, as if he wasn't so sure of his convictions just yet.

"Well, bloody rotted angels!" Liz Hen exclaimed. "We shall fight side by side, Dokie—you and me together; Godwyn, too."

The shepherd dog barked.

"And Beer Mug with us." Dokie's face brightened.

"Yes!" Liz Hen nodded vigorously, scooping up the boning knife she had used to pick her teeth and cut her toenails with. Gripping a lock of her own fiery-red hair in hand, she began sawing through it as close to her skull as she could.

*Women, be ye seeker, sufferer, or postulant, if thou abhorest life, change it, purify*
*yourself, deliver yourself from your own free will, bridle your passions, and*
*submit with utmost forbearance to discretion, obedience, and the oaths of your*
*Ember Gathering. Submit to the love of Laijon.*
—THE WAY AND TRUTH OF LAIJON

# CHAPTER SIXTY-ONE
# TALA BRONACHELL

### 4TH DAY OF THE FIRE MOON, 999TH YEAR OF LAIJON
### AMADON, GUL KANA

The sleek black cat with moon-shaped eyes stepped hesitantly across the grass of Swensong Courtyard, one tentative foot before the next, drifting silently toward an old stone sculpture of a small girl clutching a jug of water to her chest. The cat immediately grabbed Lawri Le Graven's attention. Kneeling, hand outstretched, Tala's cousin beckoned. "Here, spooky cat, closer now." The cat padded forward, sniffing the girl's fingers. "See, you needn't be scared."

Lawri looked better in the full light of the courtyard than she had in days. The color of good health infused her cheeks and face, the wrap about the stump of her arm the only clue anything was wrong.

"Don't be afraid, spooky cat," Lawri repeated. The cat pushed itself up against her hand. "I shall name you Spooky," she said happily.

"You're a sweet boy, and you shall stay in my chamber. I will feed you as many biscuits as you like and feed you little bites of mother's rhubarb pie. My kittens in Eskander love to get into mother's rhubarb pie."

A soft breeze brushed Tala's cheek, and with it came the gentle fragrance of the garden's lush flora. Her gaze wandered over the courtyard's myriad cobblestone paths and summer flowers of lavender and white. The grounds were rife with sculpture and weather-beaten statues, many of Laijon, some of long-dead grand vicars and heralded knights. They were everywhere, interspersed among the gardens and green bushes.

Trees heavy with summer leaf lined the ivy-draped stone walls of the yard, gray crenulated battlements rose up beyond that. Swensong Spire at the southern end of the yard stood like an elegant needle piercing the blue skies above. Swensong Courtyard had always been one of Tala's favorite places, a place of serenity in comparison to the castle's grim corridors, her preferred place to seek reprieve.

But of late, it seemed there was no solace found in Amadon anywhere.

"Will you lift the cat into my lap?" Lawri asked, sitting on one of the garden's carved stone benches. Tala picked up the cat and set it in her cousin's lap. The feline purred and curled up, quickly becoming an inklike void against the girl's billowy white gown, purring in gentle reassurance.

Tala adjusted her own velvet cape, fastening it at the neckline with a delicate silver brooch, then brushed cat hair off her sleeves.

"This sweet cat is a bright omen." Lawri stroked the feline. "Now that I have rededicated myself to Laijon and Denarius, blessings have begun to rain down upon me and my family."

"Blessings?" Tala asked, somewhat aghast. "A sweet cat that will sit in your lap hardly makes up for all that has happened to you and your family."

"Don't be so gloomy," Lawri said. "My Ember Gathering has

taught me how to look for the good things in life. Denarius is wise and thoughtful in his teachings."

*Ember Gathering!* Lawri's had been yesterday. Tala thought back on all the horrid things Seita had said about the Ember Gathering. She thought she had banished those lies from her mind, yet here the lies were, returned to the forefront of her thoughts, gathering again like a lump in her gut.

"The Ember Gathering has changed me in ways you shall never know, Tala. It has made me see the bright things in this world, not the dark. I am grateful for my blessings, and those of my family."

"Blessings?" Tala repeated again, feeling her brow crinkle in annoyance. "Lindholf was hanged in the arena. Or are you talking of his escape? Is that a blessing? Nobody knows where your brother is, or if he even yet lives. No matter, because alive or dead he is a hunted man! What blessings do you speak of, pray tell?"

Lawri looked up, angry. "The grand vicar promised that the great One and Only will again grant favor upon me and my family. It was promised in my Ember Gathering."

"Again with your Ember Gathering?" The phrase almost passed like poison through Tala's lips. She was sick of hearing about it. "I've been told what goes on in those Ember Gatherings, Lawri. I hear they strip you naked and bless your body. That you stand before the grand vicar and archbishops as they cover you in ash, blessing your stomach and loins so that you will bear lots of babies, that they have you promise yourself to a servant of Laijon after death—"

"Why are you full of such hate?" Lawri asked. "Why say such awful things?"

"Am I wrong?"

"I am not at liberty to speak of it."

"Because you are afraid they will cut out your heart and bury it in a dung field if they discover you broke your oath and spoke of things you are not supposed—"

"You have it all wrong," Lawri growled. "You do not understand how sacred and special it is."

Tala reined in her anger. She was more upset with herself, really. She didn't know why she had just badgered her cousin so heartlessly. *It's Seita!* Tala felt nothing but hatred for the Vallè princess. *She seeks to divide us.*

"Don't you get it, Tala?" Lawri continued, petting the cat on her lap rapidly. "The Ember Gathering gets me one step closer to finding a suitable knight or lord for marriage. It is what my family most wants for me. What I most desire."

Tala recalled the moment Jovan chopped off Lawri's arm, the first words Lawri spoke then. *What handsome court boy will want me now?* Marrying a gallant knight or lord had always been Lawri's main ambition.

The cat suddenly squirmed in Lawri's lap. She struggled to hold on to it with one arm, but the cat dropped to the ground. She reached with both arms to pick it up, then jerked back quickly, a look of clumsy disbelief on her face, realizing her one hand was no longer there. The whole episode made Tala feel guilty and sad.

Lawri sat a moment, looking down. "Will you carry Spooky to my chamber?" she finally asked. "I wish to keep him."

An apple struck the flanks of the cat, exploding over the grass in pulpy chunks. The cat dashed behind the stone sculpture of the girl carrying the water jug.

Another apple splattered against the statue followed by the loud guffaws of Glade Chaparral and his three Dayknight companions: Sers Tolz, Alain, and Boppard. The four Dayknights came sauntering up the stone path toward Tala and Lawri, black-lacquered armor agleam in the sun, long black swords dangling at their belts.

With a shout, Glade drew his weapon and broke away from the others, spying the cat slinking through the garden, giving chase. "No!" Lawri screamed.

Glade swung wildly with his wicked blade, chunks of sod spinning into the air as the cat dodged the blow. The tip of his sword sliced repeatedly into the grass just behind the darting cat. "You'll kill him!" Lawri ran after Glade. "Leave Spooky alone!"

The cat skittered under a row of thornbushes, the foliage too thick for Glade to follow. He sheathed his sword, turning to Lawri. "What? Did I just chase your lone prospective husband away?" he laughed. "Deformed as you are, I wager you'll grow into an old cat lady just nicely." Tolz, Alain, and Boppard laughed too. At the sound of their mirth, what earlier joy and optimism lit Lawri's face quickly melted away.

She whirled and confronted Tala, shouting, "Why does everyone hate me? Why!"

Then she dashed away, white gown billowing behind her. She ran down the path and disappeared into one of the arched stone doorways leading into the castle.

"You ass!" Tala stormed toward Glade, slapping him hard across the face. Tolz, Alain, and Boppard laughed hard at that, too. Glade, surprised by the slap, tried to strike her right back, but she blocked his blow and whirled around and stormed off, having no desire to prolong the confrontation with Glade, hating him more than ever now.

She hated Amadon Castle. She hated everything about it and everyone who lived within it. She wished for nothing more than to escape the only home she had ever known, the prison that kept her daily. . . .

She thought of her meeting with Hawkwood in the secret ways not long ago. The man had offered to train her in his dark arts. *I will make my own way,* she'd answered.

*If you change your mind, just return my sword to me.*

*And how will I find you?*

*The Val-Sadè.*

Tala didn't know what the Val-Sadè was, but she still had his sword—it was hidden deep within the hearth in her bedchamber. Her every thought was now bent on escaping the castle. *And why shouldn't I?* Lawri was mad at her. Lindholf had disappeared. Squireck Van Hester was dead. Jovan was evil. And Jondralyn paid her scant little mind.

As Tala made her way under the dark archway and into the castle, she wondered if anyone even loved her at all.

*Feeble indeed is the conniving of Laijon, Mia, Raijael, and those who deem*
*themselves the Five Warrior Angels. For only Blood of the Dragon can again take*
*up Dragon Claw and join with the Skulls.*
—THE BOOK OF THE BETRAYER

## CHAPTER SIXTY-TWO
# CRYSTALWOOD

5TH DAY OF THE FIRE MOON, 999TH YEAR OF LAIJON

WYNIX, WYN DARRÈ

Krista Aulbrek, bound hand and foot, sat against the sidewall of the sailboat with Borden Bronachell and the dwarf, all three of them gazing through the white morning mist at Hans Rake. They watched as the Bloodwood stuffed a slip of paper into a tiny copper tube tied to the leg of a black kestrel. The patient bird, perched on the prow of Hans' small boat, launched itself into the air with a swift flutter. Café Colza barked as the bird disappeared into the fog.

Krista couldn't tell north from south in the murk, but she knew the kestrel would fly straight back to Black Dugal.

Hans looked across the stretch of water separating the two boats and smiled at her. The harrowing dip in the sea with the merfolk seemed to have calmed the Bloodwood. He had lounged against the sidewall of his boat ever since. He'd even stopped digging at the wood around the iron brackets securing the chain to his boat.

They had been adrift nearly two weeks now. It seemed like a life-time. The small boat was almost a worse prison than her cell in the dungeons of Rokenwalder. According to the dwarf, they were near-ing Wynix along the far southwestern coast of Wyn Darrè. Calm and windless weather had slowed their journey or they would have already arrived. The dwarf had assured Borden that some fellow named Tyus Barra would be awaiting them in Wynix with horses and weapons.

Krista could feel her body recovering from her myriad injuries. She tried to extend her sleep whenever she could. When she had to relieve herself over the side of the boat, Borden would untie her, then he and the dwarf would graciously look away. They would always tie her back up when she was done. She didn't feel up to fighting them anyway. Besides, where would she go? And perhaps that is why Hans had given up his fight too.

Stored under the canvas in their sailboat was a cache of food and about two dozen water skins full of fresh water. The food was mostly jerked stag and dried salmon, a few soft apples and hard onions and turnips. Once a day, Borden would grab the chain connecting the boats, pull Hans' skiff halfway toward them, and toss the Bloodwood food and a water skin. It seemed they were going to great pains to keep the boy and dog alive.

The conversations between Krista and her travel companions had been sparse. The dwarf no longer answered to the name Squateye, insisting his name was Ironcloud. But Krista would always know him as Squateye, and a traitor.

Borden and the dwarf conversed aplenty, though, but it was all talk of the Brethren of Mia, *Moon Scrolls*, and something called *The Angel Stone Codex*. It was this codex Ironcloud was most eager to show the other man. Borden would mostly just talk about his children,

Jovan, Jondralyn, Tala, and Ansel. In fact, he talked about them so much, Krista could recite their names and ages and details of each.

In fact, he talked of them now, casually sitting on the bench in the center of the skiff. "What I wouldn't have given to communicate with my children these last five years. Alas, there were no kestrels to whisk my messages to Amadon."

His statement sent a pang of anger through Krista. "Perhaps Squateye could have helped you with those messages." Sarcasm laced her voice, eyeing the dwarf she once knew as Squateye. "Seems *Squateye* had ample opportunity to lend a hand."

"She finally graces us with a comment," the dwarf said from his place near the prow.

Krista ignored him. "From what I gather, you let the man rot in the dungeons of Rokenwalder for five years knowing exactly who he was, knowing that his family likely thought he was dead."

"I needn't explain myself to you," the dwarf said.

Ironcloud was vastly different than Squateye in temperament. Where Squateye had been full of openness and jovial advice, Ironcloud was an asshole. Krista wondered which personality was the true one. Over the years she had taken comfort in Squateye's honesty. *How could he have fooled Dugal so thoroughly? Or had he? Dugal must have known. But if so, why did he do nothing?* There were layers of conspiracy behind everything Dugal did.

"No, you needn't explain yourself to me, *Ironcloud*," she said. The dwarf just stared at her, emotionless. "It just seems no child should go without hearing from their father."

"I know you miss your father," Borden said, "as I miss my children. Seems sorrow is our common lot, Krista Aulbrek. But everything has a purpose."

That the man had read her so easily filled her with unease. She remained silent under his gaze, trepidation growing in her heart. And as always, there was nowhere to turn for comfort. There never had been. Not in five years. Not in ten. Not even when her father was around. The memories of him were so dim—yet she was a prisoner to them, a prisoner to her father's memory.

She so desperately wanted to nuzzle the neck of her Bloodeye mare, Dread. The warmth of her horse was one thing that could truly calm her. She could feel herself getting both worked up and sad about a great many things. Killing would make the pain go away, would make her mind numb again. *Would Gault be ashamed of the daughter I am? Would he be proud that I am an assassin?*

"I know you think Gault Aulbrek is a perfect man," Borden went on. "But there may come a day when you shall find out things about him that will upset you greatly."

Real fear coiled around her spine at his words. *Can he read my thoughts?* "What do you know of my father?" Her mind flew back to Ser Aulmut Klingande and the things King Aevrett had uttered in the gardens of Jö Reviens before she had stuffed her dagger into his heart. Solvia Klingande had no reason to lie, not in that moment. *Why would the woman claim such things about Aulmut and my mother if it wasn't true?* Deep down she knew it was all just a twisted game set up by Dugal. *But what am I to learn from it?*

"The perfect king," Borden began, "the perfect soldier, the perfect *father* is only without flaw because he is off fighting for his kingdom. The man who is constantly present will never be as perfect as the one who is away, the one who is gone. Any young girl is bound to romanticize her father, especially if he is nobly absent because of a war. That is all I am saying. That is all I know of your father. I imagine my own daughters feel the same about me, for I too have been gone long."

She could feel the ropes that bound her wrists cutting into her flesh. It was as if her hands, of their own volition, wanted to reach out and wrap around Borden's neck and silence him for implying that Gault was less than he was.

"Wake me when we reach dry land." Krista settled down into the canvas rolls at the bottom of the boat, done with the conversation, wishing she had never started it. She turned her back to Borden and Ironcloud, forcing her eyes closed, hoping sleep would somehow sweep her confusion and emotions straight into oblivion.

She couldn't block Borden's voice. "I know that both you and your friend Hans are now fatherless."

"He's not my friend," she muttered. *He stabbed me. That I remember.* "Hans Rake was never my friend."

"What do you mean, he's not your friend?" Borden asked. "You're both Bloodwoods. Assassins. Cold-blooded murderers. To be frank, the worst kind of human there is. You share that honor with him."

Krista rolled back over and sat up, noting some form of deep observation lurking behind Borden's eyes, as if he knew all about her, more than she knew about herself. His words bothered her greatly. And he wasn't done. "You are both *murderers*." He hissed the word *murderers*.

"I am no murderer," she said, her gaze straying to the dwarf. If the real Squateye were truly there, he would defend her against this slander. He knew her, and her purpose. But the dwarf met her gaze with a blank stare, both eyes dark and mysterious. Gone was the filthy leather eye patch, gone was almost everything she remembered about the one-eyed dwarf who had helped Dugal train her all those years. There was no help within him. *You are both* murderers, Borden had said with such conviction.

She recalled her Sacrament of Souls. Black trees. Grass as green and lush as the carpets of royalty. She thought of all the dead prisoners, all the dead rapists and thieves, all the dead *murderers*. Real true *murderers*. All dead at her hand. Now, in her current plight and confusion, she wondered if she had ever done Dashiel, the patron god of all Bloodwoods, any honor. Her eyes strayed toward Hans and Café Colza in the other boat. They had drifted closer now, the chain connecting the boats drooping heavy in the water. Hans' frigid stare lanced back at her, intense and full of purpose. *He stabbed me! Poisoned me!* She would have no problem slaying him. *But I am no murderer!*

The contradiction ate at her. And Black Dugal had easily seen that confusion and conflict within her. Now it all festered under the bruise of so many betrayals. Hans. Squateye. Dugal. Even Gault. They were all full of betrayal in their own way. *Trust is fleeting, while betrayal is timeless.* She had read that in *The Book of the Betrayer*. Truth be told, Borden Bronachell was the one person she knew who had not yet betrayed her. "I am no murderer," she repeated, trying to garner favor somehow.

"You are the very definition of a murderer." Borden sat forward on the bench.

She met his stern gaze, did not break away from it. "I am a good person."

"No." He stood, towering over her. "You are not." There was a singular threatening rigidness about his bearing. One thing was for sure: Borden was clearly the type of man not so casually turned from his purpose or opinion.

"I am good," she said, wondering if just by saying the words, it would make it so.

"Good people kill in self-defense," Borden said. "Or they kill because they're hungry, or afraid. *Good* people do not kill for the art and pleasure of the act. By Mother Mia's precious light, I know what foul deeds are involved in your Sacrament of Souls. You have been brainwashed by Black Dugal. You are young and you are naive and you have been misled, Krista Aulbrek. You have let yourself be taken advantage of through and through."

His assertion hurt. It also filled her with a black ire, an even greater need to prove him wrong, to show him she was not the monster he described, nor was she the naive, manipulated girl he claimed she was. "What few I killed deserved to die. They had justice coming to them. And I was merely the vessel that meted out their punishment."

"What *few* you killed." His voice was almost a snarl now. "I know how many prisoners Bogg pulled from the dungeons, and it was no mere *few*."

Krista wondered if her soul wouldn't just seep out and away into the watery emptiness that surrounded her right then and there. "They were in the dungeons. Naught but criminals. They deserved to die."

"You've used that defense before," Borden shot back. "And as I said, *we* were in the dungeons. Both you and I. Naught but criminals, right? Do I deserve to die in some Sacrament of Souls? Do you? Does being imprisoned make one man worse than another? Does the prisoner not have hope, or dreams, or potential to change? Or are those imprisoned naught but forgotten souls, condemned to be used in some cruel sacrament."

"I am not their judge. I leave that to the gods."

"No, you were just their executioner."

"I shall kill you."

"A tough little girl you are." Borden sat back down. "You forget who is tied up and who is not."

Krista looked down at her own bound hands. *Had there truly been cruelty in the hands that wielded her daggers during her Sacrament of Souls?* The inner chasm in her soul widened, threatening to swallow her up, just like the irrepressible force of the giant ocean surrounding her. *Perhaps I should just throw myself in . . .*

The dwarf cleared his throat. "Seems every person's toil, when pursued steadily and faithfully enough, even be it murder, is apt to effect them. Even in cruelty. Krista is who she is, Borden. As is Hans Rake."

"You helped train me." Her gaze cut into the dwarf. "Or did you forget, *Squateye*?"

"I taught you how to create disguises and escape dungeons, and that was all. 'Twas Bogg who taught you all those *other* things."

"And Bogg was Dugal all along," Borden added. "Like I said, you are a misled little girl. You cannot even see truths right in front of you."

Her eyes remained fixed on the dwarf. "And who were you all along? Ironcloud? Squateye? Who?"

"My real name is Ironcloud. That I have told you. And you can refer to me as such."

"I will call you Squateye."

"You are a stubborn one," Borden said. "But I aim to show you a better way, Krista. I know who you are. I know what destiny awaits you. For I, too, am as cruel and guilty as you. I, too, have done things that weigh heavy on my soul. I, too, know what it is like to commit terrible crimes and strip people wholly of their lives."

"And I suppose you now aim to tell me what lives you have destroyed," Krista said with as much sarcasm as she could muster.

"Yes," Borden answered, a hollow look flushing over his face. "Yes, to you I will confess my sins, Krista Aulbrek. What think you of that?"

"Suppose I've no choice." She shrugged.

He swallowed hard. "Seventeen years ago I stole two babes from their mother. Remember when I told you of the woman you resemble? She trusted me. Two blond twins. *Special* children who many in the Five Isles would seek to kill. A boy and a girl. And for their safety I disguised them both, and then hid them where they would *never* be found. . . ." He trailed off, haunted eyes cast to the sea.

"That does not sound so awful," Krista said, though at the same time pure dread spiraled up into her gut, twisting and churning. "And here I thought you were going to confess something serious."

"You are right," Borden continued. "What I did for those twins, stealing them away as I did, that was not my great sin, for I knew many evil forces sought to slay them. No, hiding those two children was a good thing, for they are still alive today. . . ."

He paused as if to collect his thoughts, then looked straight at her, eyes now emotionless. "My first sin came when I dropped hints that the stolen twins were under the care of Ser Torrence Raybourne, King of Wyn Darrè, and his younger brother, Ser Roderic, both of them the truest of friends."

Krista could feel her heart slowly tightening within her chest. "And what was your second sin?"

Borden's eyes darkened to pits of black. "My second sin came when I asked Ser Torrence and Ser Roderic to go along with the ruse. Yes, Krista, my second sin was when I asked them to steal two similar-looking babes, a boy and a girl, babes for the forces of evil to hunt and kill, two children to act as bait whilst my *special* twins remained safe in anonymity and comfort."

Krista found that her heart had almost stopped its beating.

She could not tear her gaze from his cold, pitiless gaze as he continued. "I stole the life from two innocent children. And their lives have been naught but loneliness and hardship ever since. For seventeen years they have been living a lie."

*True heroism consists of conquering the pitfalls of the soul, whatever manner they may wage the battle. For anything can be accomplished, if you but set your mind to it and persevere.*
— The Way and Truth of Laijon

# CHAPTER SIXTY-THREE

# NAIL

### 4TH DAY OF THE FIRE MOON, 999TH YEAR OF LAIJON

### TEVLYDOG, GUL KANA

s they entered Tevlydog, the sunset horizon was glowing as red as coals in a forge. Nail trudged just ahead of Val-Draekin. They were both still shoeless, clothes raggedy. The Vallè limped along as best he could. In front of Nail, Bronwyn Allen led the two dun-colored stallions by the reins, the white feathers tied in her hair fluttering in the breeze. Her muscular oghul companion, Cromm Cru'x, walked at her side. They were both dressed in better raiment, and they carried a myriad of weapons. The oghul was again sucking on the small black stone. When he wasn't sucking on it, he kept it in a leather pouch at his belt. Nail recalled the street vendor in Stanclyffe saying some oghuls would suck on rocks to stave their thirst for blood.

It had been almost three days of hard travel since Cromm and the girl had rescued Nail and Val-Draekin from the cliff and Hragna'Ar cages. Nail had learned early on that the dark-eyed girl tolerated no slacking from her companions. Even though they were both shoeless, Bronwyn expected Nail and the Vallè to keep up with the horses, even when Val-Draekin's limp became a hindrance and slowed them down. Nights consisted of sleeping under the stars in the cold air, thin blankets thrown over them. For weapons, Nail carried an old rusty hatchet he'd pulled from one of the Hragna'Ar oghuls, Val-Draekin a worse-looking dagger with an even duller edge.

Bronwyn exuded a confidence unlike any he had encountered before, especially in a girl so near his own age. She was eighteen. And the dark stains of black ash smeared around her eyes and cheeks reminded him of the war paint on the Sør Sevier warhorses of Aeros Raijael's army. It wasn't until almost half a day of traveling with the girl that he finally realized the black smudges were permanent tattoos. And under those tattoos, her eyes always bore a somewhat indifferent, faraway expression. But she wasn't the only one with a questionable look, for Cromm was constantly eying Val-Draekin with something akin to suspicion.

Though their conversations had been sparse, there were a few details of his travel companion's lives Nail had pieced together. Bronwyn's father had been a Wyn Darrè trader who labored out of a small port north of Ikaboa. He dealt in rare goods, the type of rare goods gathered mainly by oghul pirates. Cromm had been one of those oghul pirates. He bought, sold, pillaged, and stole a lot of things, but his specialty was an extremely scarce and hard-to-get drug the oghul had called Blood of the Draygin.

Their first night together, Bronwyn had mentioned the death of her father. He was killed when the armies of Sør Sevier stormed the shores of Wyn Darrè just north of Ikaboa five years ago. Bronwyn had nearly been killed herself, and her older brother had been taken captive by Aeros Raijael. "Never was there a more determined or smarter fighter than Mancellor," she'd said. "My brother was not the type to die quick. He is the type to make the best of any situation, a survivor." She pointed to the ink around her own eyes. "I blackened my own eyes in his honor." She looked at her oghul companion then. "Cromm found me near death in the carnage left by Aeros' armies. He owed my father a debt, and so nursed me back to health aboard his ship, the *Ja Tr'all*. I joined his pirate crew and have been raiding the Bloodwood Forest for Blood of the Dragon ever since."

"And where is the the *Ja Tr'all* now?" Val-Draekin asked.

"Sunk," Cromm answered with a grunt. "And all my crew dead with it."

"It was sunk off the east coast of Gul Kana not five miles south of Wroclaw," Bronwyn confirmed. "We chased the oghuls who done it clear to Deadwood Gate. Took our revenge on the last of them when we rescued you."

Neither Nail nor Val-Draekin had offered much if any information on why they had been near Deadwood Gate themselves. And neither Bronwyn nor Cromm had asked, which was good, because Nail found it hard to think of all the friends he had lost. He often wondered where Stefan was. Dokie and Liz Hen, too. It had been so long since he had seen Stefan. Roguemoore was dead. Val-Draekin had been his sole companion for so long now.

And now, together, they had finally reached Tevlydog.

It was a large town, thousands of gray buildings thatched with shadow. The place was naught but dingy streets and dreary alleyways and other such sordid dwellings. Not nearly as big as Lord's Point. But Nail had never seen a town so trashy and grim. Troops of dogs rooted in crooked alleys. And what passersby he saw were a mixed lot. About half were oghuls; the other half were timid-looking humans.

"These bastards need to learn to stand up for themselves," Bronwyn growled. "Hragna'Ar is spreading, and nobody here has the balls to stop it."

"The streets seem mostly empty to me," Val-Draekin mentioned.

Bronwyn looked back at the Vallè. "Rumor is, King Jovan has summoned all fighters to Amadon in preparation for the coming battle with the White Prince. The summons has emptied most every town in Gul Kana of able-bodied fighters, left towns like Tevlydog susceptible to being overrun by Hragna'Ar oghuls and thieves, outlaws and beggars."

"We don't look like much more than poor beggars ourselves." Val-Draekin hustled his step, drawing up beside the girl, injured foot dragging in the dust. One of the horses whinnied and stepped aside for him.

"Easy, boy." Bronwyn gripped the reins, soothing the horse with a soft whistle. "With no coin or anything to trade, how do you expect to purchase mounts?"

"It'll be dark soon," the Vallè answered. "We can sneak about, steal some mounts, better weapons too, more suitable clothes for Nail and me."

"Oh, let's do," Bronwyn said gleefully. "A bit of thievery and we shall fit right in with the locals, no?"

Her oghul companion turned his thick neck. "Cromm will help in this theft." His passive eyes were on Nail. "It will be good to get the marked one a horse."

Bronwyn said, "Cromm is greatly looking forward to being added into the oral history of his kind for his accomplishment. Escorting the marked one to Amadon for Fiery Absolution is a big deal for an oghul like him." She cast a wry grin at Nail. "He shall be a legend."

"I can't tell if you are being serious," Val-Draekin commented.

"A *Vallè* who cannot tell if he is being played a fool?" Bronwyn laughed. "Now that's a first."

"What's not to understand?" The oghul grinned too, thick gray tongue licking out over swollen gums before slipping back in. "Cromm said he will help in the theft, and so he will help. And then he will take the marked one to Amadon."

"Cromm's an honest pirate and an even honester oghul," Bronwyn added. "He can always be taken at his word. But if you're gonna go a-thieving with the likes of us, we must get one thing straight, Ser Vallè."

"And what is that?" Val-Draekin asked.

"You will be letting me pick the mark." Her shaded eyes narrowed. "You see, Cromm and I have the Pirate's Honor. A fair fight and Blood Price are the pirate's way. We don't *sneak* about like thieves in the dark. We choose a mark equal to us in numbers, and we will always meet a man face-to-face when appropriating items against his will."

"But why place yourself at even the slightest disadvantage?" the Vallè asked.

"Who says we place ourselves at a disadvantage?" Bronwyn's eyes were dark slits, never wavering from the Vallè. "Luck is always on the side of those willing to look into the eyes of those they take from."

✝ ✝ ✝ ✝ ✝

They finally came upon a stable, a low gabled barn crisscrossed with dark ribs of timber at the end of a half-cobbled street. A squat, derelict cottage of stone and thatch hunkered just behind it. Horses could be seen within stable, dark shadows in the gaps between the wood slats. There was a sign over the barn's double-wide door that read, HORSES FOR SALE. PONIES AND PACK MULES WANTD FOR TRADE. MUSK OX NEITHER BOUGHT NOR SOLD NOR TRADED NOR EVEN WANTED.

There were three burly men lounging on a bench against the barn's outer wall, mercenaries from the look of it, rough leather armor and shortswords at their hips. All three were shaggy-haired and bearded. A fourth man, bald and bare of shirt and very muscular, stood directly under the barn's sign with his back to them. He was pounding a hunk of metal over a waist-high anvil with a giant iron sledge.

"We're requisitioning a few of your mounts," Bronwyn said upon their approach.

The bald man turned, sledge now in one hand. He was wearing an apron tied at the neck, the front of it charred and filthy. His pants and boots were also a good deal soiled. He had a barrel-like chest and a heavy-looking head, face round and fleshy. His flat eyes appraised the oghul first before falling on Nail and then the girl. His eyes lingered on the Vallè last, large fingers curling around the thick haft of his sledge. He swiped beads of sweat from his brow with a rag. "We're closed for the day," he said abruptly, and went back to work.

"We'd be obliged if you opened back up," Bronwyn said. "Sun ain't down yet anyway. No horse stable I ever heard of closed before dark. Place like this ought to stay open till sundown at the very least, no?"

The mercenaries lounging against the barn exchanged amused looks. The bald man grunted. "I don't take business advice from little girls with feathers in their hair."

The girl plowed on, undaunted. "If you're not going to answer King Jovan's summons to war, then you've no need for any of the horses in that barn. As for my friends and I, we're heading to Amadon to fight for our country. We need more mounts than just the two we already got."

"A *girl* fighter?" The bald man sneered. "You think you're gonna be a knight?" He eyed them one by one. "A Vallè knight? An oghul, too? I think not, lassie."

"We will need two mounts," Bronwyn repeated with a casualness of ease that surprised Nail.

The man's face flushed. "Bloody rotted angels, I said we're closed for the day, leastwise for any oghul purchases. Now all of you git."

"I reckon you don't understand," Bronwyn said. "We aim to take two of your horses. Best you order one of your mates to amble on into the barn and get a few ready."

"Two mounts exact." Cromm grumbled, the timbre of his voice

getting the attention of everyone. Nail and Val-Draekin exchanged a concerned glance as they saw the men's hands all go to their sword hilts.

The bald man canted his head to the side as he gave Cromm a most unmannerly look. "Can't you read the sign? I ain't got no musk ox for oghul purchase."

"Cromm prefers a horse anyhow," Bronwyn interjected.

The bald man shook his head. "Had I even a mule or a some half-dead nag, I wouldn't sell to no bloodsucking oghul." He eyed the dun-colored stallions behind Bronwyn and Cromm. "Perhaps it's me that should be *requisitioning* your horses."

"Two mounts." Cromm let go the reins of his horse, holding up two fingers, lips peeling back to expose a row of sharp teeth and inflamed gums. "A horse for the marked one. A horse for the Vallè. Cromm will take something else from you." The oghul covered the distance between himself and the bald man in two long strides, suddenly face-to-face with the man.

"I said they ain't for sale." The bald man stood his ground, gruff with impatience, hand straining at the haft of his huge hammer. "And I ain't no bloodletter neither so—"

Cromm slapped him across the face. It was a backhanded blow that staggered the man sideways against the barn. The three men on the bench jumped to their feet, hands on the hilts of their swords, eyes agleam and ready for a fight. Nail could feel his heart pounding against the inner walls of his chest. He had no real weapon to speak of if it came to a fight, nor did Val-Draekin, just rusted oghul garbage.

The bald man whirled back toward Cromm, eyes blazing, cheek red and welling. "You son of a bitch. You just slapped me in the midst of a civil conversation."

"Cromm's a blunt-spoken fellow," Bronwyn added. "I imagine he just felt the conversation was done."

One of the three mercenaries drew his sword, held it out, ready.

In one fluid motion, the black longbow was off Bronwyn's back, a black arrow nocked and aimed at the man who had drawn his blade. "Cromm ain't one for too much jabber," she said, pulling back on the bowstring deliberately, the creaking of the bow ominous, dark eyes sighting down the shaft. "Cromm ain't got time to lavish lengthy conversation on the stubbornness of fools. And this here conversation run itself off the trail some while back. Best you put that poker away and run into that barn and get two horses saddled and ready, else I'm liable to get real testy. Cromm, too."

"Fuck you, bitch!" the man snarled, and spit directly in her face.

"Shouldn'ta done that." Bronwyn let the bowstring go.

The black arrow punched straight into the man's eye socket, knocking him back forcefully, pinning his head against the barn.

As he hung there, the sword slipped from his limp hand.

*She just murdered him!* Nail's mind reeled as his heart thundered.

Cromm lunged forward and snatched the bald man in two meaty hands, twisting the man's head to the side, sinking his fangs into the exposed flesh of his neck.

The man's body seemed to wilt in the oghul's arms, all limbs sagging, sledgehammer thudding to the ground in a puff of dust, eyes rolling back into his skull.

*Madness!* Horrified, Nail nearly vomited.

Bronwyn had another black arrow nocked and pointed at the closest of the two remaining mercenaries. But they were no threat now, both gaping openmouthed at their limp friend and the brute-faced oghul feeding at his neck.

"Cromm was never one to stave his passions." Bronwyn directed her comment toward Nail. "You'll have to excuse him this one indulgence."

*Bloodsucking oghul.* It was a common enough insult, it held scant meaning. He'd used the slur many times himself. But Cromm was an actual bloodsucking oghul. *And Bronwyn murdered that other fellow over a horse!*

When Cromm was done feasting, he released the bald man, who folded to the ground in a pitiful heap, pale-faced and clutching at his bleeding neck, wheezing as hard as a horse after a long gallop.

Blood dripped from Cromm's bulging lips down the front of his armor.

"I suggest you boys go saddle up two horses," Bronwyn said to the two remaining men. They dropped their swords and bolted down the street, nearly tripping over each other as they went.

"They run away," Cromm grumbled.

"Reckon we can take what we want, then." Bronwyn hooked the black longbow to the baldric slung over her back. "We should be fast about it, though. No telling how many ruffians those two are liable to return with."

Two large strides and the oghul shoved open the barn door, entering.

Bronwyn stooped and picked up two of the swords left by the mercenaries, holding one out for Nail. "Don't look so squeamish."

"I've seen worse than this." Nail snatched the sword from her, trying to keep a look of indifference on his face, knowing he did a poor job of it. He looked away, watched the last sliver of the sun ease its way down behind the buildings to the west.

Bronwyn handed the other blade to the Vallè. Val-Draekin took the sword. "You really don't believe in thieving on the sly, do you?"

"This, you mean?" She motioned to the arrow-stuck mercenary pinned to the barn and the bald-headed fellow still gulping for air at their feet. "This is nothing really. 'Tis all about confidence and looking capable. Besides, when Cromm starts feeding, that'll startle the will to fight plum out of everyone."

She tossed a sooty wink at Nail. "Even the most seasoned of combatants blanch at an unscheduled bloodletting."

THE BLACKEST HEART

---

*There is a pleasant equality in death, for the king is as dead as the foot soldier
or slave. Ye honor the slain by regaling each and all with tales of their glorious
deaths. But Raijael shall never be slain, nor shall a drop of his blood be drawn by
the hand of man, for he shall remain spotless before all war.*
—THE CHIVALRIC ILLUMINATIONS OF RAIJAEL

---

## CHAPTER SIXTY-FOUR

# MANCELLOR ALLEN

### 5TH DAY OF THE FIRE MOON, 999TH YEAR OF LAIJON
#### SAINT ONLY CHANNEL

For the last five years there was a desire burning in Mancellor Allen's soul—a simple yet secret desire. He wished to pray. He wished to drop to his knees and call upon the great One and Only to save him. As the army of Sør Sevier had advanced across the sand—a sunbaked sheet of ocean floor void of all water—he wanted so desperately to do the simple three-fingered sign of the Laijon Cross over his heart.

*But I can't be seen blaspheming in the eyes of Raijael.*

So in lieu of the real thing, he preformed the ritual in his head—just as he had done a thousand times before. And for what it was, the prayer gave him some measure of comfort, calming his mind, readying him for another battle he did not wish to fight.

He seldom wanted to fight. But it looked like he must, for the army of Gul Kana was lined up before them in the sand before Aeros Raijael, some two hundred thousand men, not even half of them ahorse.

*It is a cursed day.* He felt the cursedness of it deep down in his bones. Mancellor was a patient soul who trusted in intuition and believed deeply in symbols and omens. And something felt wrong about the coming battle. But what can a lone man do? Besides, despite his current rank, he knew he was really naught but a Sør Sevier slave; the brand on the underside of his wrist marked him as such.

Sør Sevier soldiers receded into the distance behind him, teeming legions of mounted knights stretched to the left and to the right for miles. Squires. Hounds. Rowdies. Knights of the Blue Sword. Across the vast expanse of crusted sand the warriors of Aeros Raijael were a glittering wave of looming death near a quarter million strong, a sparkling iron-tipped forest of spears and plumed helms, alive and moving. Banners and battle standards fluttered above. Every knight rode straight and tall atop a huge warhorse, face obscured behind the blackened eye slits of a glistening helm. Gleaming plates of armor sheltered their mounts' foreheads whilst iron-studded armor flapped against lathered flanks and legs. War paint streaked each steed's sweaty hide in random patterns, spirals around their eyes, ears dyed white and rimmed in blue.

Like thunder, they advanced over the sand at a heavy gait, churning the seabed up behind them. Bagpipers, trumpeters, and drummers brought up the rear whilst archers comprised the front ranks with the Angel Prince and his Knights Archaic; Mancellor, Hammerfiss, Enna Spades, and Ivor Jace, all on white stallions. Mancellor's own steed, Shine, was a mountain of solid muscle under him, his only reassurance, perhaps his only friend. The Gallows Haven boy, Jenko Bruk, rode beside Aeros, a bulky canvas sack strapped to the flanks of his dun-colored charger. The black-clad Spiderwood on his Bloodeye beast rode beside Jenko.

As Mancellor well knew, this was an army accustomed to war, a veteran and merciless crusading force of both men and women that reveled in naught but destruction and slaughter. And though he would fight beside them today, and though he had fought beside them for the past five years, Mancellor considered every one of them his enemy. For to him, they had always appeared and acted more like demons from the underworld than honorable men and women of flesh and blood. The glistening horde surrounding him was what pure death looked like, a grim reminder of the lessons of *arduous truths* inscribed within *The Way and Truth of Laijon*, that *the wraiths of death stalk every life, everywhere.*

The precarious strip of ocean that separated Saint Only from Lord's Point was naught but dried sand now, patchy with matted seaweed and puddles of seawater, the ebbing tide having receded to both the north and the south—as it had each afternoon for a handful of hours every day since the dawn of time. The Angel Prince's Army would have to cross the ten-mile stretch of land quickly, for the return tide could be unpredictable in its swift arrival, surging to fifteen feet deep or more in less than half an hour.

When they had first started across the sands, the coastline around the city of Lord's Point had been a distant, undulating haze, bereft of human activity of any kind, a haphazard patchwork of gray stone buildings interspersed with hundreds of wharfs and boardwalks and quays and thousands of small boats of every kind. There were no large ships docked in Lord's Point, for even at high tide the water was too shallow.

With about a mile left to go before reaching Lord's Point, Aeros slowed his gait, his army reining up behind him.

"Ah, splendid!" Mancellor heard Hammerfiss shout with gruff enthusiasm. "The bastards mean to fight us after all!"

Judging from the size and makeup of the Gul Kana host spilling forth from Lord's Point, Mancellor hoped it would be a swift battle.

Aeros had more than two hundred thousand soldiers behind him, whereas the fighting force that poured from Lord's Point looked to be less than a third of that, perhaps a quarter. And as the distance closed between the two armies, Mancellor could tell, most of the opposition was afoot, only several thousand were ahorse or even wearing full armor fit for a knight at all. Despite their lack, they presented a bristling hedge, and Mancellor still felt ill at ease, for they were stalled in the middle of the strait.

Still, Aeros awaited them. And the Gul Kana army eventually came to a stop some two-thousand paces away, just out of arrow range.

"A bloody fight indeed," Hammerfiss gleefully announced.

"And I imagine not a woman fighter among them," Spades muttered with disdain.

Two horsemen broke from the opposing throng and rode straight for Aeros and his Knights Archaic, one in black armor, one in blue livery. The knight in blue carried a banner of truce, white fabric flapping above his silvery helm.

"We shall ride out to meet them! Knights Archaic, follow me!" Aeros spurred his horse to a trot, the rattle of harness and armor sounding in his wake, wondrous hair flowing out behind him, billowing white and splendorous in the wind. He wore a light tunic of chain mail under a cloak of white and a sword at his hip. Mancellor spurred his horse forward, following Hammerfiss, Spades, and Ivor Jace.

Ivor, the newest member of Aeros' Knights Archaic, carried a shield and a longsword hooked to the baldric stretched over his back. Hammerfiss carried a huge ball mace wrapped with spikes in one hand, and in the other a massive silver shield with a heavy iron boss painted blue. Enna Spades, longsword buckled to her hip, carried a crossbow and quiver of thick quarrels strapped to her back.

When Aeros' contingent reined their mounts before the two knights from Gul Kana, both men removed their helms. Mancellor recognized one of the knights as Leif Chaparral, his black-lacquered armor and silver surcoat dusted with sand, the silver-wolf-on-a-maroon-field crest marked him as Rivermeade nobility. A sword with a black opal-inlaid pommel hung at his side. Mancellor had met the Prince of Rivermeade twice before, once during a parley in Aeros' tent, then again in Ravenker with Jondralyn Bronachell. That was also the last time Mancellor had seen Gault Aulbrek or Aeros' blue sword, Sky Reaver.

"You are outmatched," Aeros said matter-of-factly. He spurred his stallion nose-to-nose with Leif's black steed. Both horses snorted brusquely at each other. The Angel Prince continued, "I've two hundred thousand battle-tested warriors behind me, and fifty thousand more already on Gul Kana soil just south of Lord's Point waiting to join us."

"This I already know," Leif acknowledged, then he beckoned to the knight next to him. "Lord Kelvin Kronnin of Lord's Point."

Lord Kronnin, in the silver armor and blue livery of the Lord's Point Ocean Guard, held his battle helm stiffly under the crook of his right arm. His head was shaved. He had angular features. An old scar traced a path from the bridge of his nose down his jaw. Kronnin dipped his head to the Angel Prince, though his hard-edged face remained stoic, seemingly unimpressed with Aeros or the Knights Archaic or the two hundred thousand fighters behind them.

Aeros ignored Lord Kronnin's bow of deference, cold gaze still on Leif. "Why have you brought so many souls out here to be slaughtered?"

Leif's black-rimmed eyes were just as piercing in their intent, dark hair rippling in the breeze. He spoke with a cool nonchalance. "I bring unto you sorrowful tidings in regards to your man, Gault Aulbrek. King Jovan Bronachell did unto Gault what you foul swine did unto Baron Jubal Bruk. Gault's limbless and cockless body was impaled on a stake and placed atop an oxcart and then paraded through the streets of Amadon for all to see. Spit and piss and shit were all hurled at his pathetic corpse."

Aeros paled at the news. Mancellor heard a grumble rise from somewhere deep within Hammerfiss' lungs. The large man's fists were bunching in anger. Spades' face tightened in rage as she drew her sword and spurred her stallion forward, facing Leif, her eyes like shards of ice. "'Twill be you I seek to slay first on this fucking miserable seabed battle." The tip of her blade was instantly at Leif's armored chest. "I will ride straight for you, and you shall die slowly at my hand."

"And what makes you think there will be a battle, you stupid bitch?" Leif snickered, at the same time wisely backing his mount away from her.

Leif then dipped his head to Aeros. "I thought it the honorable thing, to let you know of Gault."

"And you have done so," Aeros replied. "Why should I not order Spades to just slay you now?"

"I shall get straight to the point of why I rode out to treat with you," Leif went on, making sure each of his words was aimed straight at Aeros. "We both desire the same thing. We both of us seek Fiery Absolution. We both of us wish to hasten the return of Laijon. We both of us seek our own glory. As does my own lord, his Excellency, King Jovan Bronachell—"

"What are you saying?" Lord Kronnin interrupted, his face a mask of red, a hint of betrayal forming behind his startled gaze.

Leif barely glanced at him. "I'm saying King Jovan has sent me here to offer up the armies of Gul Kana in final surrender."

"Are you out of your fucking skull?" Kronnin snarled. "Bloody rotted angels, this is not the plan we agreed upon."

Leif met the angry gaze of his partner. "Look about you, man. We are outmatched in every way. The army of the White Prince cannot be vanquished by force of arms."

"This was not the plan," Kronnin repeated heatedly.

Leif's black-rimmed eyes returned to the Angel Prince. "I declare our forces shall be joined together. We shall both march toward Amadon, toward Fiery Absolution. And you, Lord Aeros Raijael, shall reign as Laijon returned."

"May the wraiths take you, Leif Chaparral!" Kronnin growled. "Prophecy states the armies of Gul Kana shall fight! Fight even unto the death! We are to fight before Fiery Absolution. Nowhere does it say we should just give up in surrender to our enemy and declare him Lord. I have read the words in *The Way and Truth of Laijon* myself."

"This is not up to you, Kronnin," Leif answered with dry indifference. "It has already been decided by Jovan and the archbishops in Amadon. 'Tis not our task to fight Aeros' army, merely to show Laijon we are willing to fight to do so. We are here to prove unto the great One and Only that we are men of faith, that we believe in his words and promises in *The Way and Truth of Laijon*. And yes, I have read the holy book too. In fact, I have had the words of prophecy read to me by His Grace, Grand Vicar Denarius himself. It was none other than the vicar who let me know the truths within scripture. We are here on this battlefield to hasten Fiery Absolution, not destroy each other and prevent it from ever happening."

"This is madness!" Kronnin spouted.

"I am sanctioned by Laijon's holy vicar," Leif's dark-rimmed eyes lanced into Kronnin. "I pay no allegiance to the blasphemous *Moon Scrolls* I know you and Ser Culpa Barra are so beholden to."

Kronnin growled. "This interpretation of scripture you and the vicar follow is naught but bewildering madness and suicide!"

"With all due respect, Ser Kronnin, you are wrong."

Kelvin Kronnin whirled his destrier, set spurs hard to the beast's sweaty flanks, and raced back toward his army at full gallop, leaving Leif behind, alone.

"Let Lady Death take him, then." Leif spit into the sand. "Kronnin has always been a secret goddess worshipper. His days are numbered."

"Each time we meet, your behavior bewilders me." Aeros' eyes cut into Leif's with a poorly veiled distaste.

"I only wish to spare lives by averting a needless slaughter."

"A great disappointment, that," Aeros said. "For today I brought special weapons to lay waste your army. Weapons most desirous to all."

Leif unhooked the Dayknight sword at his belt and tossed it, sheath and all, onto the dry seabed before the Angel Prince. "I've no wish for war."

Aeros' eyes narrowed to cold pricks of darkness. "I already know that you are the type of man who schemes and betrays. Why betray Kronnin and your own armies with surrender?"

"I see no point to this war," Leif answered, bowing slightly in the saddle. "But clearly Lord Kronnin wishes to fight. Give me but a moment with him, and I promise that he too shall throw down his arms and you shall ride freely into Lord's Point."

Before the Angel Prince could agree or disagree, Leif Chaparral spun his mount and raced after Lord Kronnin.

There followed a moment of silence, then a rush of comments.

"It's bullshit." Spades glowered, hard eyes following Leif's retreating form.

"She's right." Hammerfiss shot Aeros a frank stare. "They are wasting our time."

"I say attack them now," Ivor Jace added. "Ride them down even as they retreat."

Mancellor said nothing. He didn't feel it his place to offer an opinion, nor did the Angel Prince look to him for one. That ominous cloud that had hung over him, that ill-fated dreadfulness he could not escape, seemed to strangle his every thought.

Aeros' dark eyes remained fixed on the enemy host. "Let us prepare our advance," he said, spurring his mount back toward his own army.

† † † † †

Conflict raged within Mancellor. As he awaited Aeros' command, he felt the bulging muscles and power of the stallion under him. Shine was bequeathed to him upon Beau Stabler's death. *When one is in the midst of doubt and the collapse of creeds, what makes a man join his enemy?* he wondered. *Instinct? Self-preservation or selfishness? What can be more ill-omened that that?* He did not want to draw his sword and fight today. Though he clung to his faith in Laijon, honorable words like *gallantry* and *chivalry* seemed long dead to him, replaced by *cowardice* and *betrayal* and *murder*. His heart had been naught but a hole in his chest for the last five years, a windy cold chasm. And he feared his choices had made him an unfeeling monster in the eyes of the great One and Only. He could only pray Laijon would forgive him.

*Or is it naught but betrayal I've found myself involved in?* He did not know the answer. But through it all, he knew what lived within his heart. Trust. Trust in Laijon's path for him. Trust that the great One and Only would eventually show him the way. But the onslaught of blood and gore and mangled bodies of these last five years had blunted his senses. He had grown inured to war's horror and devastation. Each callous death at his own hand was as effortless, painless, and soulless as the last. *All I do is but an act until Laijon delivers me up into his glory.* Leastwise that is what he had told himself nightly, hourly. In the midst of combat, he stepped out of his body, waged war in the name of the Angel Prince as though the battleground were a theater to him. He took upon himself the mummer's role as Aeros' devout fighting man out of sheer want to survive. He played the role out of a need to feel as if Laijon had chosen this path for him and would eventually show him the *why* of it.

*These last five years of captivity have been naught but a trial of survival and faith.* Until Laijon revealed unto him that sign he so desperately sought, he did what he could to survive. He knew within the deepest parts of his soul that he had been spared for some grand reason. He felt he had a purpose to serve before Fiery Absolution, felt it in his heart, felt he'd been given a spiritual witness that he himself would play a role in bringing about the return of Laijon. He trusted that Laijon had a plan, and he trusted that plan included him.

Mancellor had fought beside the Angel Prince for five years, seen Aeros' keen savagery, watched him slay with a brilliance and heartlessness that never ceased to amaze. And not once had Aeros been injured. Not once had he shed a drop of blood. A feat so miraculous it had even given Mancellor pause from time to time made him question if indeed there wasn't something divine about the man. But he had also witnessed the unfairness and brutal bullying, the myriad bloody, cruel horrors done in the name of Raijael. He had seen the rape and murder Aeros had personally committed under the banner of this crusade. *And there must be a purpose to my witnessing it all!*

Everything in life was symbolic. And Mancellor clung to the symbolism his own Wyn Darrè fighting tattoos represented—the dark streaks of blue ink his sister, Bronwyn, had tattooed under each of his eyes the day before he had gone off to war in defense of his country. Though he had told Aeros that the tattoos were meant to deflect the harsh light of the sun from his eyes, in reality, to a Wyn Darrè soldier, the twin tattoos under the eyes represented a balance between war and harmony, ferocity and guidance, and most of all family. And that is why his sister had been the one to tattoo him.

He carried Bronwyn's memory with him every day, wondering if she still lived. One thing he recalled, his younger sister always had a white feather or two tied in her coppery hair. She should be about eighteen now, that's if she had survived the attack on Ikaboa so long ago. Mancellor had seen his father killed by a Sør Sevier sword. Niklos Allen had been his name. Mancellor's heart ached over his death every day, for other than Bronwyn, Niklos was all the family had. Mancellor's mother had died when he was but eight. He remembered little of her. A lump forming in his throat, he pushed all thought of his family from his mind, not wanting to feel sad as well as ashamed.

He was brought back to the present as Aeros' stallion began snorting and stomping heatedly in the sand. The Angel Prince calmed his mount. "Bring me my weapon." He beckoned to Jenko. The Gallows Haven boy spurred his mount forward, a look of almost pained nervousness on his face.

The Angel Prince untied the bulky canvas sack hooked to the saddle behind Jenko and pulled forth the huge battle-ax Mancellor and Jenko had taken from the boy named Nail in Ravenker. Mancellor's heart lurched at the sight. It was the most finely honed weapon he had ever laid eyes upon, a gigantic double-bladed battle-ax with curved and gleaming edges and sharp pointed horns. It was a huge weapon, but looked to fit perfect and light in Aeros Raijael's grip. Murmurs of amazement and awe began to drift through the ranks behind the Angel Prince.

Jenko eyed the weapon hungrily, a creeping obsession in his gaze. Mancellor wondered if the same look could be found in his own eyes, for he too wanted to possess the ax, suddenly wondering if the weapon would fit as comfortable and light in his own hands.

"Now the helm." Aeros beckoned.

Jenko twisted in his saddle, reaching into the sack with both hands, pulling forth a large battle helm. More murmurs of astonishment sounded through the ranks.

Mancellor found himself staring even harder. The helm was crafted of burnished bronze with gold and silver inlays, two glorious oxhorns jutting from each side, curved and pointed and striking and marvelous, each one hewn of some shimmering ivory unlike anything he had ever seen. Ava Shay had been right. She had described just such a wondrous helmet as they'd sailed to Mont Saint Only aboard the *Eagle Rose*.

*Ava Shay . . .*

He did not want to think of her. She had hinted they could take Aeros' two treasures and run away. He suddenly realized it was not bad omens and dread he had been feeling all day, but rather something else.

*This helm is my sign! The ax and the helm both!*

Aeros donned the helm, and Mancellor's heart sank, for when the Angel Prince placed the horned helm on his head, he seemed to instantly transform into something straight out of legend, some heavenly creature. It seemed both ax and helm were designed just for him. Astride his glorious white stallion, battle-ax in hand, the Angel Prince looked like a marble sculpture of a warrior angel crafted of the most brilliant white stone.

With skin the pallor of moonlight, helm aglitter in the sun, Aeros Raijael illumed the already sunlit surroundings like the eastern star ashine.

He left all amazed who gazed in wide wonder. All bowing in deference to the glorious God before them.

"Today will be a day long remembered!" Aeros raised the battle-ax high in one hand as if it weighed nothing, his voice commanding the seabed. "Today will be a day marked in *The Chivalric Illuminations* as the first day of the coming of Laijon returned! For today your Angel Prince goes into battle wielding the *Forgetting Moon* whilst wearing the *Lonesome Crown*, two angel stones in the pouch at his belt!"

*Angel stones!*

Mancellor recalled the brilliant blue stone he had previously seen in Aeros' tent. Flat and oval with polished round edges, its translucent innards had shimmered blue shards of brilliant smoky light and stolen his breath.

Heart racing, Mancellor made note of the small leather pouch tied to Aeros' belt.

The Angel Prince continued, his voice rising, "I, Aeros Raijael, the supreme spirit, the Lord of both heaven and the underworld, the Lord of all worlds, the preexistent world, of this world, and the next, and the ones beyond that, have finally come to fulfill destiny! For I am the long-awaited return of the great One and Only, whose arrival was foretold by the Warrior Angels long ago! I am the giver of life and the bringer of death, created before the very foundations of the world! I am known by many names, the Angel Prince, the true and living Heir of Laijon, the great One and Only! And as the prophecies in *The Chivalric Illuminations* have foretold, I, Aeros Raijael, the heir of Laijon, Mia, and their one and only son, Raijael, have now returned to reclaim what is rightfully mine! Let this be an announcement to all that the time has come when all the weapons and stones of the Five Warrior Angels shall soon be mine and all will call me God!"

As if all two hundred thousand of Aeros' warriors had heard the words—*and perhaps they had*—a thunderous cheer rose up that shook the very ground. The immensity of the roar startled Mancellor to his very core.

The Angel Prince shouted, "Prepare to attack!"

Hammerfiss trotted his stallion out before the armies and raised one balled fist into the air—the signal for all to draw their weapons and ready for battle. The signal was mimicked down the line by every Knight of the Blue Sword. Soon the rasp of two hundred thousand swords unsheathed sounded across the seabed.

Shine's hooves padded apprehensively under Mancellor. He heard the wet sucking sounds of his mount's shod hooves in the now muddy sand. He looked down and saw that the once sunbaked seabed was snaking with rivulets of advancing tide, black beetles scampering everywhere, some afloat on the thin layers of rising water.

He tightened his grip on the reins, tried to calm his mount, tried to calm his own beating heart. *The tide rises fast.*

Mancellor expected to see the armies of Gul Kana, flags of

surrender flying as Leif had promised. But instead, Leif Chaparral and the army of Gul Kana was charging toward him, the bristle and glitter of weapons held aloft.

*They fight!*

And all Mancellor could think of was a shiny helm and battle-ax and two angel stones. *Send me a sign, oh Laijon!* He had searched his dreams for that sign nightly, searched every landscape he traversed, searched the eyes of every man he killed.

And today his path was finally laid out before him, his deliverance. The *Forgetting Moon* and *Lonesome Crown*. The long wait had all been a test of his faith.

Yes, today the weapons and stones of the Five Warrior Angels had finally come within his reach.

And when Laijon provided the moment, they would be his.

> *Facing the truth shall be your only haven from the gallows.*
> —THE ANGEL STONE CODEX

# CHAPTER SIXTY-FIVE
# BISHOP HUGH GODWYN

5TH DAY OF THE FIRE MOON, 999TH YEAR OF LAIJON

SAINT ONLY CHANNEL

Leif Chaparral and Lord Kelvin Kronnin led the attack, their banners fluttering over the helms and spear tips of the thousands who followed.

The two armies thundered toward each other, creating a fearsome sound. The very seabed shuddered. Hugh Godwyn, near the middle of the Gul Kana army, could feel the fear welling up all around, sheer and all-embracing. Still they ran. Godwyn too, Dayknight sword clenched tight in hand, blinking against the shards of sunlight bouncing off the shined armor of the knights in front of him. His own labored wheezing echoed under the suffocating gaoler helm jouncing on his head. Sweat trickled down the sides of his face. The heavy iron armor was sweltering and ill-fitting. The cool rippling seawater at his ankles offered scant relief; black beetles tossed in the froth underfoot.

Liz Hen Neville and Dokie Liddle ran beside him, faceless under similar gaoler helms, both encased in similar iron plate. The girl gripped an unwieldy iron shield in one hand, the Sør Sevier longsword she had stolen so long ago in the other. Tall and heavyset, she looked every bit the formidable fighter she wished to be. Dokie seemed horribly out of place, wispy and slight, armor rattling about his thin frame. He, too, carried a shield and sword, dwarfed by both. Beer Mug bounded along just behind the boy, gray fur already soaked. Godwyn had to forcefully swallow his own fear and impulse to turn and flee. It seemed a lifetime ago that he had been a simple bishop watching over a small mountain abbey. Now he was charging into war in the middle of an ocean. He followed the teeming mass through a dip in the seabed, water up to his knees briefly. Then the army was soon again running on a flatter surface. Onward they loped, mud-splattered, sand and mire kicked up all around.

There was a whistle and crack of air.

One of the fighters running near Godwyn was suddenly sprouting an arrow from his mouth just under the rim of his half-helm. The man fell forward into the ankle-deep water with a splash, dead. More arrows rained down, clacking against armor and shield. There were screams. Some fighters fell. Others peeled away from the charge.

Godwyn waded through the rising water again, almost knee-deep now. Liz Hen, Dokie, and Beer Mug were still with him. Ahead in the distance they all heard the clash and shouts of war as the two armies finally met. Sword crashed against shield. Men roared and bellowed. Horses neighed in terror, bloodcurdling and loud, horror instantly raging from the throats of the injured and dying. As this chaos swarmed toward them, Dokie came to a standstill, shaking and petrified, sword and shield wavering in hand. Beer Mug, ears alert, moved in front of the boy protectively, gray eyes darting nervously.

"We've got to keep going." Liz Hen's voice echoed from under her helm, urging the boy on. "We've got to help with the fight!"

Godwyn risked a glance backward and saw the line of draught horses, thousands of them, pulling fishing boats, skiffs, and small sailboats over the seabed and soupy sand. Leif's plan was contingent upon the boats reaching the battlefield in time. The battle was but a delay to drown Aeros' army in the rising tides, the trailing boats an escape route for Leif and what Gul Kana fighters might survive. Derry Richrath and his young ward, Otto, were somewhere in the throng of boats, helping; their entire team of Turn Key Saloon ponies and draught mares had been drafted into the fray.

"They're dragging the boats out now!" he called out to Liz Hen and Dokie.

Liz Hen tore off her helm and bellowed, "I didn't march all the way into this fucking channel to just hike back to the boats!" She brandished her sword above her head, bloodshot eyes ablaze, red hair cropped clear to her skull. "Today I fight for my freedom!"

"I gotta fly in my helm!" Dokie tossed his shield down—it was immediately swallowed underwater. With one gauntleted hand he swatted at his armored face. "I can't take it!" He pushed the gaoler helm up over his head—it also plopped unceremoniously into the water. Flies buzzed about the boy's face. He swung his sword at the flies with wild abandon. Liz Hen ducked out of the way.

"You're gonna hurt someone!" Godwyn tossed his own shield aside, snatched hold of the boy's wrists with one hand. "Stop!" He gripped the boy tight. "Stop!"

"Beetles and flies everywhere!" Dokie was panicked. "The gnats will come a-swarming next! I know, I was on the beach in Gallows Haven, I seen it!"

Beer Mug was barking up a riot now, bounding around Liz Hen with a mighty splash, frantic. Suddenly the bishop found himself in a swirl of pounding hooves, his startled gaze scarcely registering the sudden tumult all around: the blur of Sør Sevier armor, slashing weapons, Gul Kana men screeching in retreat, some falling hacked and bloody. Sør Sevier blades appeared to leap and slash from every direction. He swung his own sword at a passing rider, blade glancing off the charger's armored neck. The blow shot pain up the bishop's arm, staggering him. Something smashed heavily into his back, forcing him to his knees, bloody water splashing up under his helm. Sputtering, he scrambled to his feet, then another blow slammed him back to the ground, Dayknight sword spinning from his hand. On hands and knees, cold water lapping up into chest and face, gulping down seawater, he frantically clawed through the thrashing channel for his lost weapon. *A mad pursuit.*

He lurched to his feet empty-handed, gazing upon an ocean suddenly littered with the dead and injured. Men fought. Men fell. Hooves stirred and splashed the blue waters, the sea now rife with smears of deep scarlet. Heaps of hacked and tortured flesh, both horse and man, piled one onto the other, hollow eyes staring up from the knee-deep waters like a nightmare. All semblance of strategy from either side was gone.

*It's been so long since I've seen real war!*

"Liz Hen! Dokie!" he called out. "Liz Hen! Dokie!" But it was as if his young companions had simply ceased to exist. The shock and panic swarming around him was almost paralyzing to behold. The swirling bloody tumult was everywhere, in every direction, as far as his eyes could see. His mouth was parched.

Yet it was not water he sought. He'd already swallowed a mouthful of it to no avail. He'd always thought the brine of the sea smelled like dog vomit; add blood and horse guts and Laijon knew what else, and it was almost unbearable. Still, his aching thirst was unrelenting in its torture; it clawed at his every thought and soul. *Bloodletting.* Even in the midst of this chaos it was all he could think of. *Today is my time to die.* He knew it with a quavering certainty. He braced himself for it, waited for the killing stroke to crush his skull.

A Sør Sevier knight fell in the water at his feet, helmetless. A woman, her gray face a mask of pain as the crimson-streaked water swallowed her up, blood bubbling from her mouth, gauntleted hands clutching at the spear in her chest. Godwyn tried to yank it from her body to no avail. He gave up and searched for another weapon. Black beetles were everywhere, greedily feasting on the gore and red viscera. He found the water swirling around his thighs was no longer cool, but warm with blood.

"Beer Mug!" Dokie's wild scream called from behind him.

Godwyn spun about. A massive bull-necked knight with a wild beard and blue-tattooed face bore down on the boy and the dog, his huge white stallion charging hard. Godwyn recognized the gleaming armor and blue livery that marked this knight as one of Aeros Raijael's Knights Archaic. The five knights were legendary. All who followed the wars in Adin Wyte and Wyn Darrè knew their names. This broad-faced brute was Hammerfiss. His flying mane of red hair flamed in the sun as his massive ball mace swung low in a crushing arc, skimming the water as it swiped upward toward Dokie's exposed face.

Liz Hen lunged forward to block Hammerfiss' blow, heavy gaoler shield upraised, bloodshot eyes wide with fear. In a spray of water and twisted iron, the shield exploded upward, flinging the girl backward into the sea. Liz Hen disappeared underwater as Hammerfiss' ball mace crushed the next Gul Kana fighter in his path, armor and bone crunching.

Liz Hen rose up from the ocean, paunchy face streaked with blood and seawater, cropped hair matted to her scalp. Hammerfiss whirled, stern-faced, his stallion bearing down on the girl once again, corded muscles under spiked armor bunching as the beast charged. Liz Hen again dropped to her knees, sludge and grit splashing up into her mouth as Hammerfiss' spiked mace sailed over her head, decapitating the Gul Kana fighter behind her. His body crumpled into the blossoming red waves. Hammerfiss swung again, the spikes of his mace tearing open a third fighter's midsection. The surprised fellow tipped into the sea, floating momentarily, a string of steaming entrails unraveling from his stomach, slithering and coiling down into the water.

Liz Hen clambered back to her feet as Hammerfiss rode on, war charger kicking up frothy water in its wake, the chaos of the battle swallowing them up. Beer Mug lapped at Liz Hen's face, the dog's head and gray haunches all that remained above water now. Dokie stumbled toward the girl and dog, horror etched on his face.

*We'll all soon be dead.* Everywhere Godwyn looked, the once-blue sea was streaked with scarlet, sunlight glimmering off blossoming pools of red, man and horse thrashing. He considered shedding his armor right then and there, for he knew once the water reached a certain level, its weight would drag him down. "Let's get back to the boats!" he hollered at Liz Hen and Dokie.

A riderless horse fell sideways into him, its lathered neck spouting blood high into the air from a deep gash. Godwyn was pushed down into the sea as the horse rolled over on top of him. Water enveloped them both. Gagging on the sour taste of salt and blood, Godwyn untangled himself from the beast's jerking legs. Frantic, he squirmed free, regaining his feet as the horse continued its death throes, a dark pool bleeding out around it.

The rising tide was waist-deep now. Heart hammering, Godwyn heard a chorus of horrendous pain-filled screams like no other, thousands of voices sounding at once in the distance. He could only see one fin at first, a boil and swell of water rolling toward him, smooth white triangle jutting from the channel pale as bone.

The great white shark rose up from the water, mouth agape, biting a fully armored Sør Sevier knight in half, swallowing the top half whole. Then, in a teeming mass, the rest of the sharks swarmed, the larger ones plying the deeper parts of the channel, sharks in the hundreds, fins and tails whipping as they forced their way through the battlefield, following the dark rivers of blood. Knight and steed alike fled before them.

"Is that sharks?" Dokie muttered from behind Godwyn. He turned just in time to see the boy faint, small armored body folding face-first into the sea, red silt and sand and black beetles swirling up over him.

Beer Mug paddled toward the spot where the boy had vanished.

"Dokie!" Liz Hen plowed through the waist-deep waves toward the spot where Dokie had disappeared, her sword held high above the water. She knelt in the bloody sea in search of her friend, hauling the boy to his feet with her free hand. He was unconscious, but breathing, red bubbles forming around his nostrils.

"Wake up!" Liz Hen screamed into his face. Holding her sword out in defense, she propped the boy up with her hip. Beer Mug, treading water now, licked his face.

Godwyn waded toward them, shoving abandoned armor and dead bodies aside, grabbing Dokie under the armpits from behind, hoisting his limp form up out of the water. "We've got to retreat!" he shouted at Liz Hen. "We've got to head for the boats!"

Liz Hen seemed to wholeheartedly agree this time. She slapped away a floating helm and a purple coil of guts and started toward Lord's Point. Godwyn followed her, Dokie's unconscious form pressed to his chest, while Beer Mug paddled along at his side.

Another white stallion reared up in their path, the beast and rider turning in the water to face them. *Another Knight Archaic!* Godwyn's weary mind cried out in dismay.

*Enna Spades!* The most foul and vile of all Aeros' Knights Archaic, notorious throughout the Five Isles. The warrior woman bore a sword nearly as long as her body, silver armor and dark blue surcoat bloodstained red. Her hair flowed out behind her like a ragged red flag, hair that almost glowed like firelight when touched by the sun. There was a feral, animal-like bearing about her freckled face, and her squinting eyes were fierce and cold, twin orbs that bred naught but evil as they cut toward Liz Hen.

"That's a Sør Sevier sword you carry!" Spades pointed her long blade at the girl. "You dare befoul the weapon with your cursed hands!" Then she set spurs to flanks, and in loping strides her powerful white stallion splashed forward.

Liz Hen met the woman's charge with a wild swing of her sword. In one sweeping blow, Spades knocked the blade from Liz Hen's grip. And just like that, the Sør Sevier sword that had accompanied Liz Hen on so many adventures spun off into the water and disappeared. Beer Mug barked and snarled, biting at the flanks of Spades' horse as a spear-wielding Gul Kana knight drove headlong into Spades with his dun-colored destrier, knocking the red-haired warrior from her steed. Both horses toppled into the sea on top of Beer Mug with a foaming red splash.

A twisted pile of legs and hoofs thrashed as both Spades and the Gul Kana knight scrambled to get above water. Spades stood first, ramming her sword down into the neck of the screaming destrier of her foe. The dun-colored horse righted itself, spewing blood high from the slick arterial wound. Spades ducked under the spray as the destrier reared up, then dropped down on top of her, sinking them both under bloody froth and scarlet.

Two white sharks shoved their great bulk straight into the fray. Spades' stallion, blood-streaked and bleating, retreated and stumbled away, eyes wide and frenzied. Spades did not resurface as the sharks tore into the dun-colored destrier on top of her. Godwyn stumbled away too, Dokie Liddle squirming away from his grasp, awake now. The boy stood nearly chest-deep in the water, young face a mask of terror at the sheer amount of noise and watery carnage surrounding them. "Are those sharks?" he mumbled, voice barely audible over the bedlam and madness.

"Godwyn!" Liz Hen cried out. Weaponless, she was facing two swaggering Sør Sevier knights. Together they bore down, longswords glossy with blood. One was a Knight Archaic, glimmering helm covering his face. The other wore the livery of a Knight of the Blue Sword, a great helm upon his head, eye slits dark and deadly.

Beer Mug, paddling for all he was worth, was the only thing between the girl and the two knights. "No!" Dokie screamed.

Then the Knight of the Blue Sword pulled the helm from over his head and glared at the girl. "Liz Hen?" he muttered.

"Jenko Bruk!" she roared, rage as red as the bloody sea flooding over her face, confusion creeping into her bloodshot eyes. "You wear the armor of the enemy!"

The knight named Jenko Bruk lifted his sword, eyes tightening at the corners. He was a good-looking young man with wild dark hair, a puzzled look of his own growing on his handsome face.

"Nail was right!" Liz Hen bellowed. "You are a traitor!" She waded through the gore and pandemonium straight toward Jenko, hands balled into fists.

"I don't want to kill you!" The tip of Jenko's sword was poised between them.

"Fuck you and the legless bearded fucking cunt of a baron who sired you!" Liz Hen plowed forward, water and red viscera swelling up around her armored body. Jenko and the Knight Archaic with him advanced on the girl, mere paces away from her now.

"Mancellor!" Came a shout of sharp intensity to Godwyn's right. "To me, Mancellor Allen, to me!" The shout was frantic. "You and Jenko rally to me!"

A soft breath of fresh air grazed Godwyn's face as he whirled and beheld the most marvelous sight rising up in the center of the ocean's lashing wet butchery and gore.

Sitting regal atop a magnificent white stallion of sheer majesty—without a spot of red or ruin upon him—rode the White Prince himself, Lord Aeros Raijael. The glamour and fine white brilliance of his bearing was unmistakable amid the floating black beetles and sodden dark slaughter. A horned helm of peculiar make crowned his head—the ghost-white coloring of the helm's curved horns perfectly matching his ghost-white skin. Reins of his stallion in one hand, Aeros effortlessly wielded a glimmering double-bladed battle-ax in the other. The splendid ax shone in the sunlight with a dazzling bravura that nearly blinded Godwyn. *Forgetting Moon!* Godwyn's mind reeled. *Aeros Raijael wears* Lonesome Crown *and carries* Forgetting Moon!

"Ivor has Leif Chaparral and Lord Kronnin trapped!" Aeros yelled. "Rally to me! We shall finish them off!"

The white bulk of a massive shark shoved its way out of the water right under Aeros. Mouth yawning open, the shark rolled onto its side, clamping down on the White Prince's stallion, engulfing the horse's front quarters in its tremendous gaping maw, twisting. With a throaty gurgle the horse was pulled below the rose-colored skin of the sea, caught in the beast's powerful jaws. Aeros fell tumbling into the gore-lathered water, horned helm and battle-ax flying.

*Forgetting Moon!*
*Lonesome Crown!*

Godwyn watched as both shiny artifacts disappeared beneath the tossing and churning channel. There was a maelstrom of swelling and frothing of water where Aeros and his horse had vanished as the shark squirmed and thrashed and feasted.

Jenko Bruk, the closest to Aeros, unhooked his breastplate and tossed it away. Undaunted, he lunged headfirst into the red soupy water, muscular body arrowing straight for the place where *Lonesome Crown* and the *Forgetting Moon* had disappeared.

More sharks pushed past Godwyn on every side, dozens of them, slithering along the surface of the seabed, half submerged, their barrel-like bodies boldly shoving through the armies, sweeping aside everything in their path, swallowing armored knights from both armies whole. Horse and man fled in terror.

It was clear who was winning the battle now. It was no longer

Gul Kana versus Sør Sevier, but rather panicked knights on both sides seeking to save themselves from the sharks, spearing and stabbing at the water. Only a scant few sharks floated belly-up amidst the human limbs and horse entrails. And more came, white fins and bubbling bloody swells announcing their approach.

Godwyn's attention was drawn to the Knight Archaic nearest him, the one who had arrived with Jenko. The Sør Sevier knight had lost his helm and was stabbing at a shark under him. What set this particular knight apart from the hacking and slashing shark-infested slaughter swirling around him was his calmness. He stared down at the shark beneath him with a seemingly detached and cool resolve, stabbing it over and over. The knight had eyes that were bold and fierce and determined, and he bore what appeared to be thick smears of dark war paint under each—a Wyn Darrè trait. He also had carefully pressed braids of a strong russet color that draped down his back, wet braids, sodden with bloody water and chunks of torn flesh.

Something blunt and hard struck Godwyn in the back of the head.

Clutching his skull, gulping in the squalid, blood-soaked air, vision swiftly blurring, Godwyn tottered forward to his knees. Filthy water and black beetles and Laijon knew what else forced their way down his throat. Head barely above water now, Godwyn tried to stand, every muscle in his body raging in protest. Mind swimming with fractured thoughts and delirium, he felt himself droop face-forward into the swirling, bubbling red, letting the sea swallow him whole. *And I welcome death. . . .*

Godwyn found himself cowering, hugging the seabed, willing himself to just die, and die quick, sifting his fingers through the sand beneath him, knowing that his life would soon be blessedly over.

Hooves of heavy horses stomped all around him, none striking that crushing blow that would end it, though. Sharks slithered over his back, pressing him farther into the sand, face-first, none of them taking off his head as he so desired.

Weariness had drained him, and his lungs burned for air . . .

. . . and he welcomed the death that closed in over him.

And then he heard a voice.

*I ask for no man's pity.* The voice was muffled, as if from a distance. But it was the unmistakable voice of his father. *Every day is a gift, son. We Godwyns push on. As would any man who values his honor. Today is not the day you die. Your great sacrifice has not yet come.*

The words of his father bolstering him, and with every ounce of strength he could muster, Godwyn shoved himself up from the floor of the sea, arms straining, silt and sand embedded in every crevice of his armor.

Head now above water, chaos churning around, he hauled himself to his feet, searching the swirling tumult for a Sør Sevier knight to kill.

And his eyes fell upon Aeros Raijael.

The White Prince was still alive.

Helmetless, weaponless, Aeros was again standing chest-deep in the center of bloody turmoil. Yet it was no shark or Gul Kana soldier the Angel Prince fought.

It was Beer Mug.

The dog was attached to the White Prince's left forearm, jaw clamped tight. The dog dangled and thrashed, teeth sunk deep into Aeros' shiny vambrace. Blood, red and livid, welled from under the armor. Beer Mug's hind paws clawed at Aeros' legs and torso, front paws raking deep furrows in the man's gleaming chest plate. The White Prince struggled to stay upright in the stomach-deep water, struggled to shake the dog from his arm. But Beer Mug clung tight, fighting.

"Kill him, Beer Mug!" Liz Hen yelled, pushing her way toward the fight. "Kill him! Drag him down into the sea, and I'll help you drown the son of a bitch!"

*Your great sacrifice has not yet come.* Godwyn heard his father's voice again. Without hesitation he charged toward Aeros Raijael.

*I saw a myriad of battlefields, the pale white flesh of the young dead that slept*
*and suffered no more. 'Twas I, Raijael, most gracious, most merciful, who yet*
*suffers. 'Twas I who remained alive to sleep no more.*
—CHIVALRIC ILLUMINATIONS OF RAIJAEL

# CHAPTER SIXTY-SIX
# MANCELLOR ALLEN
### 5TH DAY OF THE FIRE MOON, 999TH YEAR OF LAIJON
#### SAINT ONLY CHANNEL

Lonesome Crown and *Forgetting Moon* are lost to the sea!
Ripe with fear, Mancellor Allen pulled with all his might, trying to wrest his sword free of the great white shark that had just killed his stallion. Up to his chest in bloody seawater, it was a desperate struggle. Horse entrails, gray, pink, and violet were afloat all around, sleek and glimmering wet in the sun. They swirled and snaked and bobbed in the choppy waves as if in merry celebration of Shine's dramatic demise.

He couldn't believe his trusted steed was dead, but so too was the monstrous beast that had bit the horse in half. His sword was still buried hilt-deep in the shark's tough flesh, and the dead monster was rolling over in the choppy red waves now, his weapon slowly disappearing beneath it. His straining hands abandoned the sword.

It was then that he saw the blood welling from the wide slash in his right arm bracer just below his shoulder armor, a slash so deep he marveled his arm was still functional at all. He rolled his shoulder, almost fainted from the agony. But such was the slash and chaos of war. Ofttimes injuries went unnoticed until the end. But he felt it now—a near-crippling pain. His knees almost buckled. *Grit your teeth and bear it! Pain is only temporary, Mancellor Allen; you cannot let it knock you out of battle.* That was the Wyn Darrè way. For *The Way and Truth of Laijon* commanded all to shrug away the cloak of unrighteous doubt and carry on unwavering in battle. *You were born to fight on! And Laijon hath set you on a path toward destiny!*

*Lonesome Crown! Forgetting Moon! Where are they now?* The question struck Mancellor again like a cold ice pick in his spine. Determined, his gaze scanned the horizon. The rising tide had put everything at almost eye level now. And as far as he could see, it was all the same—a sunlit scarlet mayhem of staggering immensity. The once-cold waters were warm with blood. The entire Saint Only Channel appeared like a boiling fire of splashing red flame, a thunderstorm of screams and shouts that tore at his ears and scoured them raw. Bodies floated all around, sharks tearing at their flesh.

And then he sensed something else in the water at his feet. Something sleek and sinuous slithered by, some fishy creature that pulled at his mind, wanted to latch on to his legs and drag him down into the pooling red depths and drown him.

The pain in his arm was intense. He felt the light-headedness steal over him as the scorching agony pulsed through him. *You cannot let it knock you out of the fight!* He had to keep telling himself. In Wyn Darrè, you fought on, no matter how gravely injured, you kept in the fight until you either conquered your foe or were killed. *Pain is only temporary. A second. A minute. An hour or a day. It will eventually subside!*

He spotted Hammerfiss and Ivor Jace in the distance, both still ahorse, their white stallions bucking and braying in the rioting sea.

Ivor's sword flashed in the sun as he hacked at both man and shark. Hammerfiss' round mace was a spiked ball of gore and blood, thunderously crushing heads. Spiderwood was there too, black daggers slashing. His Bloodeye steed was tearing and kicking at man and shark with a savagery Mancellor never knew could exist in a horse. *But where are Enna Spades and Jenko Bruk?*

Aeros Raijael was the closest to him, not twenty paces away, his skin now the pallor of a glowing full moon against the dark scarlet sea. He was helmetless, blond hair whipping about as he fought with—of all things—a big gray shepherd dog. The dog's jaws were clamped tight around Aeros' arm, teeth cutting into the silver vambrace. Blood poured from the armor.

"Kill him, Beer Mug!" shouted a plump Gul Kana knight with short-cropped red hair and a puffy round face full of freckles. "Kill him! Drag him down into the sea, and I'll help you drown the son of a bitch!"

The red-haired Gul Kana soldier wore ill-fitting iron armor of a strange make, no gauntlets, no weapon. Still, the soldier was charging toward Aeros, bloody water welling up before him. Another Gul Kana knight in similar armor followed, a much smaller fellow, mousy in comparison, head barely above water. An old man with a soppy gray mustache trailed after the two, wearing the same strange armor as the others. All three were sloshing toward Aeros Raijael as fast as the thick red slurry would allow.

Mancellor pulled a dagger from his belt. It was only then that he noticed his own helm was gone. *Everything lost in the confusion and horror.* But the helm was of scant concern now, for he knew he would have to shed the rest of his armor soon lest it sink him. The tidewaters had risen so fast.

The red-haired Gul Kana knight reached the Angel Prince first, large body crashing headlong into both Aeros and the shepherd dog, all three sprawling under thick red water. Aeros rose from the sea quickly, scarlet seawater streaming from his stark white hair. He clutched his injured arm to his chest, the silver vambrace shredded, blood flowed viscous and dark. The gray dog resurfaced next, paddling straight toward the Angel Prince. The red-haired knight burst back up from the ocean too, following the dog.

But the mousy Gul Kana knight was on Aeros before either could get there, tearing and clawing at the Angel Prince with small hands. "Smash his face, Dokie!" the red-haired fellow yelled. The old man with the drooping gray mustache joined the mousy one, and the two of them easily dragged Aeros underwater again.

Mancellor had never seen the Angel Prince injured before, and the raw fear in Aeros' eyes had been real. He had to face it; everyone on this battlefield was going to die today. Mont Saint Only was nine miles behind him, its ever-burning beacon likely still visible to anyone who took the time to look. Lord's Point was at least a mile in front of him, a dark line of buildings barely discernable in the distance.

And then he saw boats. Between himself and Lord's Point, there were hundreds of them, all afloat, men scrambling from the blood-soaked sea to safety.

Aeros' head burst from the sea again, mouth agape, gasping for air. The dog and redheaded knight swarmed over him, pulling him down swiftly with the help of the boy and old man, the four of them holding the Angel Prince under. Sharks circled the thrashing swarm of bodies.

Mancellor had never read *The Chivalric Illuminations of Raijael*, but had heard every one of Hammerfiss' recountings of the scripture to the point he had most of it memorized. Within the *Illuminations* the sentiment was the same for warriors of Sør Sevier—you do not let the pain knock you out of the fight. *Especially if you are the Angel Prince and indestructible!* And Aeros was down there somewhere fighting for his life.

Almost neck-deep in water, dagger still in hand, Mancellor pushed his way through the sharks toward the pile of squirming bodies, one thing on his mind—*I must get to the angel stones in the pouch at Aeros' belt.*

Mancellor pulled the old man off Aeros, dragging the fellow back and away, thick bloody water making his every move sluggish and slow. The Angel Prince's head shot up from the channel again, open mouth sucking in air.

"Leave Godwyn be!" the red-haired knight swung a large balled fist at Mancellor. In water so deep, it was an awkward punch. Mancellor dodged the blow and shoved the big fellow away. The shepherd dog snapped at him. He shoved the dog away too. The red-haired knight drifted back toward him, rage blazing in round, bloodshot eyes.

"Liz Hen!" the mousy knight yelled, his own head bobbing below the ocean and then back up. "Watch out!"

The one named Liz Hen was swallowed up by froth and bloody spray as a charging white stallion chest-deep in the water bulled him over. It was Ivor Jace, atop Spirit, blond hair like a banner rippling in the wind, sword awhirl as he struck at the knight named Godwyn. The old man ducked beneath the sea, Ivor's sword whistling over his head. Mancellor pushed the mousy knight named Dokie away from Aeros. He grabbed the Angel Prince by the waist, pulling him toward Ivor's white stallion.

And that's when he made his move.

With one swift stroke of his dagger, Mancellor sliced away the leather pouch at Aeros' belt. *Angel stones!* His heart pounded as he stuffed the pouch with the two precious gems into the pocket of his leather breeches—a deep pocket. The deed was done quickly, unseen under so much bloody water, undetected in the raging storm of war.

"Climb onto the horse behind Ivor!" he shouted, shoving the Angel Prince up. "We've got to get you out of here. We're all doomed to drown!" With all the strength he could muster, pain lancing through his shoulder and arm, Mancellor helped lift Aeros Raijael up onto Spirit.

"Even the seas dare not drown our Angel Prince!" Ivor declared, vigorously hauling Aeros up into the saddle behind him with one strong arm.

Liz Hen rose from the sea, clawing at Aeros' leg. Spirit kicked the girl in the chest plate, sending her sprawling back. The stallion whirled in the water, kicking at sharks next. "The ax and the helm!" Aeros cried, gripping the blond Knight Archaic tight with his one good arm as the horse spun about. "We must find them!"

"They are lost to the sea!" Ivor shouted, gaining control of the animal, aiming Spirit toward Mont Saint Only. He set spurs to flanks and the muscular stallion bounded off, bloody water splashing up as it pushed through the frothing chaos toward Adin Wyte.

Mancellor was still floundering in the thick of war, a frenzied white shark thrashing before him. Liz Hen, Dokie, and Godwyn were lost in the battering torrent. The shepherd dog too. Mancellor's heart failed a beat as he tried to move away from the gnawing, crazed shark. Up to his chin in the sea now, every move he made was a sluggish exertion, swathes of bloody spume rolling over him.

He lost his footing, felt his armor pulling him down. Fear raked his soul as he ducked below the surface, unhooking bucklers and leather straps as fast as he could in the slosh. He pulled off his cuirasses one at a time then came up for air, tearing at his vambraces next. He could scarcely see through the thick red seawater coating his eyes. Agony bit into him once his injured arm was wholly exposed to the salt water. It hurt, cold and dreadful, like a dagger constantly plying under his skin, driving stinging bolts of pain through his every muscle. Waves crashed into his face over and over, and then calm.

When his eyes cleared, he beheld a terrible yet captivating sight and wondered if he were hallucinating. Not ten paces away, a silvery-haired woman of striking pale elegance rose up out of the violet sea before him. She faced a stricken, wide-eyed Gul Kana knight, naught but his head and shoulders above water. The woman was young and naked, pale breasts streaked with bloody seawater as her slender body seemed to hover above the Gul Kana fighter.

She wielded long sharpened bones in both of her webbed, clawed hands. She struck swift and sure, sinking both crude weapons into the knight's throat, then yanking them out just as quickly. The surprised fighter grabbed at his neck and drifted back.

The naked woman curled forward and dipped below the sea, her scaled fishlike tail glimmering like polished armor as it slapped against the bloody channel.

"Merfolk!" someone shouted.

Two more of the creatures spun up from the crimson waters, half human, half fish, both males, chests and arms corded with muscle, the lower halves of their scaly bodies aglitter in the sun, shining like jewels of diamond, copper, and emerald.

"Watch out for those gill-fucking monsters, Lord Kronnin!" Leif Chaparral yelled as he pushed passed Mancellor, neck-deep in swirling scarlet, black shoulder plate armor cutting through the sea. Leif was headed in the direction of Lord Kelvin Kronnin. The Lord's Point knight was struggling with the mermaid now, her clawed hands raking his face. Hammerfiss was there all of a sudden, still on his stallion, massive spiked mace crushing both Kronnin and the mermaid straight into the sea. Water spouted pink and violet over the neck of his white stallion.

Hammerfiss was manic, grinning and laughing. Mancellor had seen his fellow Knight Archaic get like this before. Berserk. The large bearded knight was now alive and thriving in the only place he had ever considered home. War. And this was a bloody war beyond description. Hammerfiss gleefully spurred his mount straight for Leif Chaparral, his stallion half swimming, half galloping, in its ponderous charge.

Leif raised his sword to meet the mountain charging toward him.

Mancellor lost sight of the fight as a bloody wave lapped up into face and over his head. Then something brushed against his leg. He spun, kicking out, legs near useless in the water. Something snatched him around the hips, clawing at him from below.

And he was yanked beneath the sea.

Water folded over him, pressed inward with all-consuming stark red oblivion. He swung out madly, a desperate attempt to free himself from the hands that pulled at him, hands that found purchase and climbed up his body. Slithery arms encircled his chest, pinning his hands up around his own neck, clutching, squeezing the breath from him.

And then he saw her slender ghostly visage.

Inches away she stared with stony, glaring eyes, lids blinking, slow and delicate. Her thin-boned face was pale and fine, her chin, lips, nose, and brows seemingly cut of glamorous white marble. As she breathed, a serrated row of gills fluttered along her sleek neck. She squeezed him, naked breasts pressing against his chest, fishy tail coiling around his legs. One webbed hand reaching into his pocket for the angel stones, stones that were growing warm in his pocket.

Mancellor struggled in her bitter grasp, mustering what strength he could, trying to wriggle free, trying to shake off her searching hand, surprised to find such strength in the mermaid's dreary touch. Pain burned through his heaving chest. His lungs called for air. The wound on his arm ached so sharply that all other senses were pinched and frozen into immobility. A soul-shattering terror engulfed him as the mermaid opened her mouth with a muffled hiss, bloody and wet. Fangs, fearsome and sharp, hovered in the deep just a hairsbreadth from Mancellor's face.

He felt himself losing consciousness as her tail constricted.

And everything changed before him. He found himself awash in a flame of crimson light. Bright pockets of fire pulsed in waves around him whilst runnels of bloody red seawater flashed and burned against his skin. It felt as if the entire Saint Only Channel were folding over onto itself. Sparkling water throbbed with ruby light, like gemstones, like *angel stones*. The mermaid's webbed hands now curled around the two gemstones hidden in his own pocket. . . .

Crimson light blossomed brilliantly, a bloody bright redness that illuminated everything: the swarming sharks, the slithering mermaids, the churning legs of fighting knights, the dead bodies encased in armor littering the floor of the channel, and most strange of all, symbols. Flickering and wavering pockets of flame in every direction: squares, circles within circles, crosses, all of them a-twinkle, all of them aglitter and blooming with red-flowing fire.

. . . And the mermaid began pulling the angel stones free of his pocket. The entire ocean was suddenly pitched in black.

Yet somewhere deep down below in the blackness, Mancellor saw them, fluttering in the water. Half-formed images, multiplied. Hard to capture, like light refracting through prisms and gemstones and then slanting though stained-glass again and spreading out over a polished cobbled floor like a giant puzzle, a puzzle sounding against the darkest fathoms of his soul, a puzzle that slowly solidified.

He saw *himself*—fighting in a gladiator arena, Jenko Bruk at his side. A green dragon. A skull-faced knight in green armor. A city boiling in silver and blood. A crumbled stone abbey full of thieves. A tower. Falling. A young dark-haired queen . . . a girl he so desperately loved, but could never have—

Something crashed into him, and he was torn from the mermaid's grasp.

With a sudden surge of energy, he launched himself toward the surface of the sea, clawing his way upward, crimson bubbles churning. When his head broke the skin of the ocean, sunlight engulfed him, bright and raw. It felt as if he'd been underwater for a harsh eternity. Pain-scorched lungs near to bursting. He choked. The taste and smell of so much death and blood gagging him.

His hand went immediately to the pocket of his leather breeches, finding the two angel stones still there, safe and sound. Both now hot against the palm of his hand.

The shrill shrieking of the merfolk all around sliced into his ears and scraped along his every nerve ending. But it was that very starkness of their screams that woke him. He took the measure of his surroundings, as grim as they were, everything still a hopeless bloody wet havoc.

Spiderwood fought beside Hammerfiss now, the red-haired giant still astride his white stallion, the Bloodwood atop his Bloodeye steed. Naught but the neck of each horse was above water now. Both men were engaged in battle with Leif Chaparral and a small contingent of a dozen mounted Gul Kana knights. Every horse with a rider struggled in the gruesome cruddy filth of the channel, armored knights weighing them down. Sharks and merfolk still slithered among the combatants too.

Mancellor was swimming, feet no longer touching the bottom of the channel. A swell of the tide lifted him high, tossing him straight into the flanks of Spiderwood's Bloodeye horse. The Spider kicked him away. He was hemmed in on almost every side now, merfolk, sharks. He saw a boat, a small white skiff, bobbing and twisting in the waves almost drunkenly. Without thinking, he swam toward it, his injured arm all but useless. Dark water lapped against the boat, bloody streaks of flesh and viscera washing down its side in fresh twining rivulets. He ignored the pain, ignored everything between himself and the boat and paddled straight for it with all the strength he could muster, knowing it was his only escape.

Enna Spades stared down at him from the sidewall of the boat when he finally reached it, hair matted red and stringy to her pale face. "Aboard!" she shouted. Most of her armor was gone. She held a long wooden oar in one hand, angling it toward him, urging him to grasp hold. Jenko Bruk stood in the boat just behind her, also armorless, a long spear held firm and ready in his grip.

"Grab it!" Spades shouted, the oar still extended as the boat nosed into another wave, lifting the prow. The bloody wash almost sucked Mancellor under the boat. The currents of the channel were gathering strength, lazily pushing and pulling him in the rolling swells. Spades nearly pitched face-first into the bloody channel as a second furious wave lifted the skiff's aft end high. Jenko lost his balance and fell to his knees.

It was then—as the boat listed forward on the foaming wave—Mancellor caught a glimpse of the ax and the helm.

Both *Forgetting Moon* and *Lonesome Crown* were jammed under a white wooden bench near the rear of the white skiff. From the angle of the boat rising in the water, Mancellor caught just the merest glimpse of both treasures. He felt the angel stones grow instantly warm in his pocket. Hot. Burning. *The moment Laijon hath promised me.* Then the skiff rolled back away from him, and they were gone from sight.

Sputtering for air, Mancellor swam toward the boat as it swung out of the trough of the wave. Spades was once again at the sidewall, oar reaching out. In the rising surf, the stern of the boat slewed to the right. Bloody waves buffeted and hurled Mancellor against the side of the skiff. He felt the oar slap against his shoulder. Another wave tossed him high, and strong hands seized the neckline of his shirt. It was Jenko. Mancellor scrambled up the side of the skiff, Jenko helping to haul him up by his tattered and sodden shirt. He slid over the wooden sidewall and flopped to the bottom of the boat, choking for air. The skiff had about a foot of crimson water sloshing along the white floorboards.

"Lucky bastard!" Jenko lifted him to his feet. The Gallows Haven boy wore naught but leather breeches and a ragged, bloody shirt clinging to his back. Spades also wore little: leather breeches and thin leather belt, sheathed dagger at her side. Her sopping black undershirt clung to her flesh, torn in many places.

The boat was about twenty paces long by ten wide. Not big, but safe. But other men were attempting to climb aboard on every side. Knights, fighters, all of them panicked and bloody, armorless and wet, some even naked as the day they were born.

"They'll swamp us!" Spades shouted, oar cracking the head of the first man into the boat, sending him toppling over the bulwark back into the sea. Jenko stabbed his spear at the first face he saw, splitting it wide, the dead man sliding back into the water.

"Help us, you fool!" Spades screamed at him. "Row us away from here!"

There were so many men clinging to the sidewalls trying to lift themselves aboard, Mancellor knew the boat would soon overturn. He scanned the vessel for a weapon, finding the shiny ax and helm lying in the rippling red water, both artifacts jammed under the white bench.

Spades clubbed men with her oar. "We've got to get out of here!" she yelled again. "Untie the long oars and hook them into the rowing frame." Mancellor saw the oars strapped to the sidewall. "Row us away from this madness!" Spades screamed.

Mancellor lurched forward, seizing *Forgetting Moon* by the haft, tearing it from under the bench. Despite its great weight, the double-bladed battle-ax fit perfectly in his two straining fists. He lifted it high, gripping it tight, injured shoulder howling in pain as he brought it crashing down onto the exposed back of the nearest man crawling aboard.

The ax's curved blade sliced the hapless fellow in half as if he were made of thin wisps of air, burying itself deep into the sidewall of the boat, wood splintering. The bottom half of the dead man's torso dropped into the sea, the top half spilling into the skiff, bruise-colored guts slithering over the white floorboards.

"You fool!" Spades yelled, throwing away her oar. "You'll tear the boat apart with that thing!" She leaped forward and shoved Mancellor aside. He slipped in the slop of guts and went down hard, clutching his injured arm.

Spades grabbed the ax haft and ripped the weapon free of the wooden sidewall. She jammed the weapon back under the bench. "Lady Death take you, leave it be!" She drew the dagger from her belt. "Get the long oars into the rowing frame like I ordered!" She whirled, dagger slicing into the throat of the next man to climb aboard, blade gleaming with blood.

Jenko, balanced against the aft sidewall, stabbed down with his spear into the next man who clawed at the white walls of the skiff, yanking it free.

Something heavy hit the boat. It lurched roughly to the left. Mancellor was tossed to the gut-strewn floorboards again. He crawled through the sloshing blood and slime toward the long oars, unhooking them from the portside bulwark, standing, struggling to fit each into the rowing frame. The boat lurched again. A shark thrashing near the stern, Jenko's spear hitting it over and over.

Mancellor shoved the oars into the frame and pulled, muscles straining against the press of the sea, pain shooting from his injured arm through his entire body. The drift of the tidewater was too strong. It didn't seem to matter how hard he rowed toward Saint Only; the boat was at the mercy of the current.

A flash of silver spun over the sidewall of the boat, landing with a thud, wriggling at his feet, squirming. He kicked at the flopping creature. The beast unfolded gangly little arms and screeched a horrific sound. It was one of the merfolk, a male. Sharp bone weapons were clutched in his clawing webbed fingers. Mancellor's heart failed a beat as the monster slithered along the bottom of the boat straight toward *Forgetting Moon* and *Lonesome Crown*.

"Kill that gill-fucking fiend!" Spades kicked at the creature with her bare feet, knocking the slimy half man onto its back. Heaving gills along the beast's neck splayed wide, hissing for air. Jenko whirled and stabbed the tip of his spear rapidly down into its slithering fellow's chest twice. Blood welled from each wound. The merman grimaced in pain, thin purple lips curling back to expose gruesome rows of sharp pointed teeth. Jenko stabbed it in the chest again, then whirled, stabbing at another man attempting to board.

Then he stopped fighting and stared out over the ocean.

Spades stared too, eyes wide in horror.

Slicing and coiling through the churning mass of drowning men, sharks, and merfolk, cleaving the entire battlefield right in half, came a sea serpent. Its flat head, the size of an ale keg and color of polished bronze, came gliding above the water within twenty paces of Mancellor's boat, tongue flickering out slippery and fast, large round eyes on either side of its head keen and watchful.

As long as the tallest of pine trees, the serpent moved smooth through the channel, pushing up scarlet swells of floating battlefield carnage before it. The bulk of its tan-and-umber-striped body was submerged underwater. But judging from what was exposed above, the beast's girth was as big and round as two full-grown men. It confidently plied the red channel, sending even the sharks and merfolk scurrying for deeper haunts. At least a hundred more serpents slithered right behind the first, a slithering line of dark death stretching off into the northern horizon.

"Bloody Mother Mia!" Jenko swore, gore-coated spear still in hand, legs braced against the sidewalls of the boat. The skiff rose up in the swirling eddy created by the passing serpents. And the drift of the ocean seemed to be taking them south.

"We're pointed the wrong direction!" Spades shouted. "Mancellor, turn us about!"

"The current is too strong!" Jenko hollered back. "And there's thousands of men in the water between us and Adin Wyte! We can't go that way without them swamping us! We're cut off from Saint Only!"

Spades struck with her dagger at a half-dressed man who'd managed to scramble aboard during the distraction. The stunned fellow reeled back, neck sliced open from ear to ear, grinning wound gaping wide as he fell over the side. The skiff was tipping and yawing alarmingly, one of the sea serpents jostling it from beneath.

Spades fell against the sidewall, dagger tumbling from her grip. "Then row for Lord's Point, Mancellor!" she roared. "Row for Lord's Point before these damnable serpents swamp us!"

Mancellor rowed, wide eyes fixed on *Forgetting Moon* and *Lonesome Crown,* the two ancient artifacts sliding along the bloody floorboards of the boat, his mind caught by the grip of the two angel stones in his pocket.

> *In time, the squalor of war, all the entrails and stench and lakes of blood and screams of the dead, seeps into the dirt. In time, the torture and terror and agony fade. In time, war takes upon itself a rousing and romantic shape, a pleasing nostalgia bathed in naught but beautiful glory. In time, all things sanctioned of the gods become righteous.*
> —THE ANGEL STONE CODEX

## CHAPTER SIXTY-SEVEN

# BISHOP HUGH GODWYN

### 5TH DAY OF THE FIRE MOON, 999TH YEAR OF LAIJON
### SAINT ONLY CHANNEL

The sea serpent plowed through the battle, its slithery body slicing through the red water, bloody filth unfurling in its wake. Bishop Godwyn treads water with Liz Hen and Dokie, the channel's swift-flowing undertow pulling at his legs. Luckily, his gaoler armor was long since discarded, now somewhere at the bottom of the channel.

Liz Hen had removed most of her armor too, naught but her breastplate strapped around her chest. She was sluggishly swimming toward a rider-less horse, the beast neck-deep in the rolling waves. Reaching the horse, she threw her leg over its back and pulled herself up into the saddle. She punched the first man who tried to pull her from the saddle right in the face, snatching the man's sword from his hand as he fell back. She stabbed at another knight nearby. It didn't matter anymore who was who, whether one was from Gul Kana or Sør Sevier; it was every fighter for himself, and Liz Hen was attacking everyone. Beer Mug paddled in the water at her side, panting long heavy breaths, head barely above water.

Leif Chaparral struggled with a shrieking mermaid. He was in a desperate fight, head constantly sinking below the surface. Hammerfiss, atop his white stallion, the beast sturdy in the gathering waves, pushed his way toward Leif. Another fighter, a Bloodwood assassin on a demon-eyed steed of pure midnight, with wide flaring orbs as red as the bloody sea, was right behind Hammerfiss. *Spiderwood!* The dark-haired newcomer in black leather armor was the very image of Hawkwood, only his hair was cropped short.

Hammerfiss ended the mermaid's life quickly, crushing her head with one heavy blow of his spiked ball mace. A scarlet spray of blood and brains sprinkled the already scarlet sea. At the same time, Spiderwood swiftly had Leif around the neck with a black leather cord, strangling him. Leif's dark-rimmed eyes bulged as he struggled to escape.

Liz Hen shoved her newly acquired mount into the fray, her horse thudding straight into the Bloodeye, knocking Spiderwood from the saddle. Leif slipped away and dipped under the scarlet skin of the channel. Hammerfiss swung his mace at Liz Hen. The girl parried, but the heavy mace snapped her sword and plunged straight down onto the forehead of her mount, crushing it. The horse disappeared under Liz Hen into the swirling water and vanished. Liz Hen sank with it. Beer Mug dove down after her.

"We've got to save her!" Dokie drifted in the water near Godwyn, panic on his face. "She'll die down there! Beer Mug can't pull her up from the bottom of the ocean!"

Two burly hands grasped Dokie by the nape of his jerkin, hauling him up out of the water. The boy's legs kicked as he was pulled straight up the barnacled side of a wooden sailboat and over the portside bulwarks. The boat rose up in the swell, the bloody wave breaking over Godwyn's head. His vision was suddenly awash in red oblivion as the filth-ridden salt water raked his face, then sunlight again.

"Grab the rope!" A coil of rope slapped the water near Godwyn's head. He seized hold and held fast as the men in the boat pulled him up and over the sidewall, sodden body landing with a wet thud against the floorboards. Weary, he looked up at his rescuers. It was Derry Richrath, the proprietor of the Turn Key Saloon, and the serving boy, Otto. Both Derry and Otto were encased in gaoler armor. A dozen wide-eyed soldiers cowered against the sides of the boat, all armorless and sopping, all recently rescued from the horrors of the channel, trauma etched in their faces.

Dokie gripped the sidewall, frantic eyes scanning the ocean. "Liz Hen! Beer Mug!" Godwyn scrambled to his feet, joining Dokie at the prow. "We have to find them!" the boy screamed.

"They're gone!" As the chaos of battle swirled around the sailboat, Godwyn's straining eyes scanned the red-churning horizon. Sharks plied the waters, great jaws ripping and tearing and feasting. Mermaids pulled any fighter they could get their webbed hands on into the deep. Serpents coiled around both horse and man. It was bedlam. A macabre dance of frenzied destruction and pure vicious slaughter.

*And Liz Hen is gone!*

Godwyn whirled, focusing on the unfurled sails of the thousands of sailboats in the distance, skiffs and fishing boats that had been dragged out for just such a rescue—the current and drift of the tidewaters scattering them in all directions. The nearest one was overturned, men scrambling up its barnacled hull as sharks and merfolk tore at their legs. Lord's Point was in the distance, rolling breakers still white with foam and unbloodied. "Someone help me unfurl the sail!" Derry shouted at the men cowering in the boat. "Gather oars and row! Do something, you bloody fools!"

A black dagger spun passed Derry's head and buried itself into the chest of the first knight to stand. The stunned man fell forward clutching at the blade, moaning, blood pooling under him. Godwyn whirled again. Spiderwood was balanced on the starboard bulwarks, a second black knife in hand, slicing open the neck of the serving boy, Otto, with a wicked flash. The boy slid silently over the side of the sailboat and disappeared into the sea, leaving a wide streak of blood in his wake.

With a shout of rage, Derry Richrath snatched up a long wooden oar and swung it at the assassin. But the Bloodwood ducked the blow, kicking the staff away, his blade slicing into Derry's neck next, brutal and savage. Derry toppled overboard and was gone.

Spiderwood was now perched on the sidewall of the skiff like a raptor about to swoop down upon its prey, with Dokie Liddle cowering just under him. Like lightning the Bloodwood struck. And just as quickly he was gone, wrapped in the thick coppery coils of a sea serpent and yanked roughly backward. The assassin stabbed at the beast as he was pulled under the crimson depths of the channel, water thrashing as both Bloodwood and beast disappeared. "Bloody Mother Mia!" Godwyn exhaled. Then he turned and yelled at the men behind him. "Do as Derry said! Gather oars! Row!" Every man lurched to his feet in search of an oar, some untying the sail.

Dokie stood on shaking legs and leaned against the prow, pointing. "It's a miracle!" he exclaimed. "Look, Godwyn, Leif Chaparral approaches as if by magic!"

Godwyn looked. It was Leif Chaparral. The top half of the Dayknight's body seemed to float above water, as if a horse was underwater, buoying him up and carrying him toward them.

Beer Mug paddled madly just in front of Leif.

"Come on, Beer Mug!" Dokie shouted. "Come to me!"

Leif drifted stomach-deep through the bloody swells and waves, Beer Mug leading him straight to the sailboat. When he reached the vessel, Godwyn and Dokie could tell it was not on some horse's back he rode, but rather on some unseen knight's shoulders. They pulled Leif aboard and he wasted no time in turning back toward the scarlet waves, leaning against the bulwark, reaching down. "I must save the knight who carried me here!"

Liz Hen's florid round face and cropped red hair broke the skin of the foaming sea just under Leif's outstretched hand. Her eyes shot open as she sucked down a huge gulp of air before her head bobbed back below the rippling surface.

*She couldn't have carried him all this way?* Godwyn's mind reeled.

Hammerfiss was just beyond the girl, still ahorse, still fully armored, white stallion struggling to swim under his weight as he aimed the beast in their direction. The Knight Archaic's cruel eyes met those of Leif. "That boat is mine!" he bellowed.

"Help me, you bloody fools!" Leif screamed. "Help me lift him aboard before that killer gets here!" Leif's eyes were on Hammerfiss pushing through the water toward him.

Liz Hen surfaced again, huffing for air. Leif latched on to her gaoler breastplate, lifting with all his might, straining. Godwyn reached down to help. Dokie, too. Together the three of them hauled the big girl aboard. She flopped to the bottom of the sailboat with a thud just as Hammerfiss reached them. Leif ducked aside as the huge knight's mace came arching down, the spiked weapon splintering the sidewall of the sailboat with a thunderous crash. Hammerfiss snarled, yanking the weapon free.

Then a shark thrust its huge bulk between the burly knight and the boat, sending both Hammerfiss and his white stallion reeling back in the frothing water.

"Beer Mug!" Liz Hen cried, scrambling to her feet. "We have to get him!"

"Row away!" Leif shouted. "Row away now! That insane knight is not done with us yet!" Indeed, Hammerfiss was still miraculously atop his horse, heading toward them again, mace upraised. "Row!" Leif screamed.

And the dozen frightened men behind Godwyn rowed.

† † † † †

"I couldn't see under the water," Liz Hen muttered, her back against the portside bulwark, sitting next to Godwyn, tears streaming down her face. "I held on to Beer Mug's tail! He dragged me to the boat! Leif on my shoulders. The dog saved us! And we couldn't save him."

"That dog was a brave fellow," Leif said, crisp white sail flapping in the wind above his head. "I too wish we could have saved him."

They had sailed almost to Lord's Point now. Thousands of rescue boats, all brimming with bleak-faced Gul Kana knights, surrounded them in the ocean. A lump had formed in Godwyn's throat at the thought of the dog's demise. His gaze roamed the channel, hoping the dog would somehow reappear. But so many had been lost to the mercy of the sea. The sun now hung blighted and raw over the blood-colored waters. Crabs scuttled among the heaps of floating bodies, and the seagulls cried above, their shadows weaving over the red-stained waves rolling ashore. White fins of sharks, slithering up from the depths, still plied the battle's ghastly harvest.

In the distance rose Mont Saint Only, ten miles away, its beacon still afire. Squinting at the fortress in the sunlight, Godwyn was numb to it all, the scars on his swollen neck calling to him. *How utterly pathetic am I, wanting a Bloodletting so soon. . . .*

He tried to regain some sense of sanity, but he could still hear the distant chorus of screams. *This does not feel like a dream. Yet, it doesn't seem quite real, either.* The frothing sea still heaved through the channel, violent and bloody, tossing and boiling as if another war raged beneath its churning scarlet surface. *People are still dying out there. . . .*

"How many of the enemy I have slain today," Leif Chaparral

muttered. The Dayknight leaned against the mast now, dark-rimmed gaze fixed on the still teeming channel. "A hundred thousand? Two hundred thousand. Has Absolution been forever staved?" A great darkness fell over his face, as if he had done something wrong. Then his countenance immediately brightened. "A great victory will be recorded. Even in *The Chivalric Illuminations of Raijael* will this day be recorded. Aeros and all his Knights dead. The great Leif Chaparral the victor." Leif's dark eyes cut into Godwyn's. "Nobody can survive out there, right? Aeros is dead, no?"

"I can't possibly see how anyone could have survived without a boat," Godwyn murmured. It was almost too difficult even to speak. Fatigue hung like a mantle over his weary shoulders. Somehow he had survived the boiling scarlet maelstrom of war.

*And all I had yearned for was death. . . .*

Leif's victory was an accident. Godwyn knew many battles could be lost because of overconfidence and dumb miscalculation. And it seemed the White Prince had succumbed to both today.

Dokie rested in the bottom of the boat on the other side of Liz Hen, all three of them squished together among the few dozen other traumatized Lord's Point fighters.

"Tell me we can go back to Brown R'elk's fine manor house, Godwyn." Liz Hen looked up to him, pleading. "All I can think about is that red draught he serves. Drinking it makes my head swim with golden light and all things pleasurable. And Laijon knows, I'm in desperate need of that now."

*I am not the only one.* Godwyn wished he had never allowed the girl to become addicted to Blood of the Dragon. *Two of a kind, we are. . . .*

He studied the pained faces of Liz Hen and Dokie. Though they had been a meddlesome duo in the past, he felt a great love and kinship for them now. Dokie seemed to suffer no ill effects from either the rauthouin bane or Blood of the Dragon. Perhaps whatever addictive properties residing within the drugs had been rendered dormant by the poisonous darts. Godwyn knew the downward path he and Liz Hen were on would be a slow and torturous death, likely driving them both insane at the end.

"Beer Mug can survive out there," Liz Hen said, hope growing on her freckled face. "Beer Mug will not give up. He will find us again."

"I do like your spunk and optimism, boy," Leif's eyes fell on her, admiration in his tone.

"She ain't no boy." Dokie sat up straighter. "She's Liz Hen."

Leif's face twisted in puzzlement. "What's Lishen?"

"Her." Dokie nodded toward the big girl next to him. "*She* is Liz Hen."

"Leyshon?" Leif couldn't quite wrap his tongue around the girl's name. Something cold gripped Godwyn's heart as he saw the dark look that crept over the Dayknight's face. Every man in the sailboat was paying attention to the conversation now. Leif again asked pointedly, "Who is Leyshon?"

"It's pronounced Liz Hen," Dokie said. "Not Leyshon. She's a girl."

"A girl?" Leif's brow furrowed. He was no longer leaning against the mast. "A *girl* . . . saved me?" Then his face blossomed with anger. "A *girl* fought in my army, as a knight of Gul Kana? A *girl* fought in my *war*?" He shouted the last word. Murmurs and groans of disapproval traveled through the boat as all eyes fell on Liz Hen.

"And what's wrong with a girl fighting in *your* war?" Liz Hen climbed to her feet, facing the Dayknight, rage billowing outward from her like a storm cloud. "I've killed men and Sør Sevier knights and even oghuls before!"

"But you are a girl?"

"That's right!" She smacked one balled fist into the gaoler breastplate she still wore. "Me! Liz Hen Neville! I *am* a girl, what of it?"

"What of it?" He moved swiftly, carefully keeping his balance as he stepped over injured men and oars. "You deceive us with your short hair."

"I deceive no one." She stood her ground.

"*The Way and Truth of Laijon* strictly forbids a woman to take up arms in combat, unless it be sanctioned by the grand vicar himself!" Leif was inches from her, finger pointing in her face. "And I do not recall Denarius *or* Jovan sanctioning anything of the sort."

"I don't give a gob fart what they sanctioned." Liz Hen straightened her back and leaned into his pointed finger, letting its tip rest against her forehead. "I *saved* you."

"You will *hang* for this *deception!*" Leif whipped his finger away from her haughtily. "*I* will hang you!"

"*Hang* me?" Liz Hen's face twisted with incredulity.

"Yes, *hang!*"

"Fuck you and the slimy slaggy stoat who fathered you!"

Leif backed away from her, head cocked to the side, dark-rimmed eyes narrowing to thin black slits. "What did you call my father?"

"And fuck your little eye sockets and pretty black eyeliner too—"

Leif's fist crashed into her jaw. Stunned, she tried to fight him off. But Leif's continued blows rained down swift and hard, one after the next. Dokie leaped to his feet, lunging to her defense, slipping on the watery floorboards, going down in a heap.

"Please stop striking her!" Godwyn stood, grabbing the Dayknight from behind, pinning the man's arms to his side. Liz Hen dropped face-forward onto the floorboards of the sailboat with a crash, unconscious.

Leif shrugged the bishop off. "I swore an oath!" he shouted, his long finger now pointed in Godwyn's face. "An oath to never see another woman fight in battle lest I hang her and burn her myself!"

"But you've likely already killed her." Dokie knelt, holding Liz Hen's battered face in his arms.

"She'll live," Leif spat, grim eyes still fixed on Godwyn. "But when we dock, she's to be bound both hand and foot and thrown into the castle dungeon. The deceitful bitch *shall* be hung in Lord's Point Square as soon as we reach shore!"

✝ ✝ ✝ ✝ ✝

Lord's Point Square was empty but for a handful of confused onlookers come to witness the hanging. Godwyn stood in front of the stone podium in the middle of the square. Dokie was at his side, tears streaming down his face. Leif Chaparral was on the platform just above, lofty spires of the city's cathedral rising up behind him. He was once again dressed in the full Dayknight regalia—black-lacquered armor shined to an obsidian polish, silver surcoat thrown over his shoulder, silver-wolf-on-a-maroon-field crest over his chest plate, black sword with the black opal-inlaid pommel at his belt. Godwyn knew the man had lost his armor and sword in the battle with everyone else. Yet here he was, dressed anew, as if a second set of polished armor and sword had been awaiting him.

Next to Leif was a stooped, bearded man wearing the dark umber robes of the clergy, a bishop the Dayknight had dragged from the cathedral to oversee the hanging. A bedraggled mix of blue liveried Ocean Guard stood at attention to Leif's left, all battle-weary and worn. A tall wooden scaffolding and gallows pole loomed at Leif's right.

Liz Hen Neville stood before the gallows in naught but a thin tan coverlet thrown over her tattered underclothes, hands tied with rope before her, short-cropped red hair gleaming like fire in the harsh sun, bruised face a mask of grim bitterness.

"Though we have achieved great victory over our enemy, our triumph has not been without stain!" Leif's voice boomed over the emptiness of the square. "This girl bears witness to what few acts of unrighteous cowardice tarnished our victory!"

He beckoned the Lord's Point bishop forward. The stooped man handed Leif a thick scroll-worked-leather-bound copy of *The Way and Truth of Laijon*. As the Dayknight leafed through the pages, Liz Hen's frightened eyes found Dokie. Her lips quivered. "Do not weep, for I shall soon be with Laijon; I shall be with Zane and Beer Mug and those I love."

But to Godwyn it felt as if the girl didn't believe her own words. *War changes everyone. War has knocked the belief in Laijon straight out of us all.* Beset with doubts that harried his every thought, Godwyn knew what he must do to save her. *But dare I? Can I?* There was only one thing he could think of—another bloodletting at the hands of Brown R'elk. That all-consuming desire had created a horrible hole in him, a poverty of mind and soul. He was surprised by the want and clarity of his own dark cravings.

On the stone platform above, Leif found the page he desired. "From the Acts of the Second Warrior Angel, I quote. 'Unless such deed is both sanctified and consecrated by the grand vicar himself, Laijon shall smite unto death any such woman who takes up arms against her fellow man, be it in war or in defense of her own self. In the name of the great One and Only, a swift hanging shall be her end!'" He slammed the book closed with authority, handing it back to the Lord's Point bishop. "What say you to that? It is against *The Way and Truth of Laijon* for a woman to fight in battle without the blessings of the vicar!"

The Lord's Point bishop bowed to Leif in confirmation, placing the holy book in the crook of his arm, speaking loudly. "There are many such similar verses to guide us in war's endeavor! If this girl has fought in war without proper blessings, then I therefore deem this hanging blessed of Laijon, and so it shall be recorded."

"So it shall be recorded!" Leif grasped Liz Hen by the back of the neck and forced her to a kneeling position at the edge of the podium, her grimacing face just above Dokie now, frantic eyes scanning the empty square. *Beer Mug is not here to save you today, my dear Liz Hen.* Godwyn's mind raced. No savior to swoop in from the skies and bear you away. Weariness clung to him like a sodden cloak, heavy with guilt and regret. There is only me, and I know what I must do for her—

"The girl before you has defied Laijon by taking up arms against her fellow man!" Leif's shout echoed. "I myself found her today amidst all the chaos. She was dressed as a man, in full battle armor, a bloody sword in hand!"

Those gathered in the town's square stared blank-faced at both Leif and Liz Hen.

"'Tis by the will of Laijon she shall hang!" Leif bellowed, voice now hoarse.

A morning wind that smelled of salt dragged over the plaza, carrying with it the cries of the gulls circling overhead. The warm breeze lifted a lock of Godwyn's shaggy gray hair from his sweat-dampened forehead. *Yes.* He breathed in deep. *I know what I must do.*

"You cannot hang her!" he yelled.

Several of the blue-liveried knights behind Leif ran to the edge of the podium and thrust their spears down at him threateningly.

"You cannot hang her!" Godwyn repeated. "She did not know the fullness of the law! She merely wished to fight for her homeland! She is innocent!"

"Innocent," Leif scoffed. "I saw her myself, a *girl*, fighting in war without so much as a by-your-leave from King Jovan or any servant of Laijon, much less the grand vicar. You saw her too, old man. You were there. You were witness to her treachery. Ignorance of the law is no excuse!"

"I saved your life." Liz Hen's voice was a stark hiss of anger.

"You went against the will of Laijon!" Leif yanked the girl to her feet by the scruff of her coverlet and makeshift smock. "The debate is over. You will hang."

"She is innocent!" Godwyn pointed to the leather-bound holy book in the Lord's Point bishop's hands. "I, too, can quote from *The Way and Truth of Laijon*. 'To satisfy the law, a bishop anointed of Laijon can stand in proxy for the one being executed, if he believes that person to be innocent, and justice shall be served.'"

Leif seemed taken aback by his pronouncement. "Is this true?" he asked the bishop of Lord's Point.

"Aye, it is true." The bearded man dipped his brow to Leif in a dutiful if not resigned response. "But I will not hang in her stead."

"You may be right." Leif turned back to Godwyn. "But as you can see, the bishop of Lord's Point is not willing to atone for this girl's sins."

"I am Bishop Hugh Godwyn, a servant of Laijon anointed by the grand vicar himself," Godwyn announced proudly. "I served Laijon within the Swithen Wells Trail Abbey for five years. And I say the girl is innocent, and I shall stand in proxy for her!"

"No!" Liz Hen wailed, tears rolling down her cheeks. "You mustn't!"

Godwyn went on. "You are now honor bound by scripture to hang me in her stead, Ser Leif."

"How do I know you are not just some imposter set on thwarting my will?" Leif snarled.

Godwyn looked straight at the other bishop on the podium and did the three-fingered sign of the Laijon Cross over his heart, ending with his thumb pointed down at his navel—a sure sign only those who had been anointed by the grand vicar in the Royal Cathedral in Amadon would recognize.

"He gives the sign of one duly anointed of Laijon," the Lord's Point bishop intervened. "It is his right to stand in proxy for the girl, if he so chooses, and the girl shall be set free."

"Set free?" Leif's face was a mask of incredulity.

"As Laijon as my witness, she shall be set free," the Lord's Point bishop confirmed pointedly. "Not even a Dayknight such as you can go against the words of *The Way and Truth of Laijon*."

Anger festered in Leif's gaze as his dark-rimmed eyes cut into Godwyn. Then just as swiftly the anger disappeared. "Cut her bonds," he ordered his knights. "Let the old man hang in her stead if he so wishes! Bring him forth!"

Gauntleted hands stretched down and hauled Godwyn roughly onto the podium, cold fear finally taking root in his gut.

"You mustn't do this, Godwyn," Liz Hen pleaded as the rope around her wrists was cut. "You must look after Dokie, look after yourself."

Godwyn shook off the gauntlets gripping him, bowing to the girl. "Just find Roguemoore and the others and let them know of my fate."

"Enough talk." Leif shoved Liz Hen off the podium. She lit hard in the cobbles at Dokie's feet. Leif yanked Godwyn roughly toward the wooden scaffolding, dragging him up the makeshift staircase behind the gallows pole.

Once atop the wooden platform, standing in the center of the trapdoor, Godwyn had a grand view of the courtyard. A thin-faced oghul watched from the distance. Brown R'elk. The well-dressed oghul's rich brown eyes stared up at him hungrily. The teardrop-shaped tattoo on his gray-frosted cheekbone stood out stark and red. The oghul's lips curled back, revealing white teeth sharp and long, gums engorged.

Seeing those fangs, the slavering mouth, Godwyn knew he had done the right thing, ending it like this. He tore his gaze away from the oghul, looked down at Liz Hen and Dokie. They stared up at him, horrified. But there was nothing he could do to give them comfort. Leif cinched the noose tight under his chin. The slack in the hangman's rope would make for a long hard drop. A quick snap of the neck. An instant death.

*'Twas a life well-lived. Few make it to my age. . . .*

With that thought, Bishop Hugh Godwyn looked up. How beautiful the sky appeared. How blue. How calm. How vast and deep.

With a creak and a clank the trapdoor under his feet was released, and the breath was sucked from his lungs. He dropped.

There was a loud snap. No pain. Just darkness. Peace.

And then nothing. . . .

*Love of god is not always equal to the love of good.*
—THE ANGEL STONE CODEX

# CHAPTER SIXTY-EIGHT
# LINDHOLF LE GRAVEN

5TH DAY OF THE FIRE MOON, 999TH YEAR OF LAIJON

AMADON, GUL KANA

I f it please m'lady"—Delia's voice echoed against the chipped stone walls of the decrepit old abbey—"could you give me word of my father?"

"Your father is dead," Seita answered sharply. The Vallè princess wore leather breeches laced up the sides, black boiled-leather armor under a pale-gray sleeveless tunic, and a black belt studded with links of mail. As Lindholf watched her move about the abbey, he admired how fine her silken hair was, her skin pale in the wan light, luminous and beautiful. "He is no longer at the saloon. The Silver Guard told him you were hung in the arena. He died a few days ago," she said with finality.

"He died?" The color drained from Delia's face. The girl was still dressed in her prison garb, as was Lindholf. "He died believing I was a traitor? How can he be dead?"

Gault Aulbrek rose from the stone bench; his armor creaked and groaned as he placed a hand on Delia's shoulder, glaring at Seita. At all times, the Sør Sevier knight strode hale and straight, and today was no different, but now there was also danger in his eyes. A singular sensation of sickening anxiety shot up Lindholf's spine. They had been left on Rockliegh Isle for some time now, and Seita had just returned by boat with scant provisions. He sensed Gault's impatience was at a boil.

Seita had rowed them ashore five days ago after their escape from the arena and after a quick journey to the Filthy Horse Saloon where they had picked up *Ethic Shroud* and the white angel stone Lindholf and Delia had hidden there. The Vallè princess had claimed Rockliegh Isle was the very place Hawkwood had disappeared to when he'd first escaped Purgatory. She claimed it was safe and secure from searching eyes. The three weapons of the Warrior Angels were all hidden within a large canvas potato sack under the stone bench behind Gault in the corner of the abbey's entry room. The crescent-moon-shaped hilt of *Afflicted Fire* was visible, the sack not quite long enough to fit the weapon entirely. The abbey itself was a crumbled-down relic of moss and cobwebs situated in the middle of a stand of weather-torn trees. Brush and bramble guarded the doorless entrance. Rockliegh Isle was situated in Memory Bay a half mile east of Amadon, a small outcrop of jagged rocks and boulders, a tall, thin lighthouse at its northern end, an old wooden dock at the southern, a grassy slope and an old abbey in between.

"You're shocked, I daresay." Seita looked at the barmaid. "Remember, your father was a very ill man."

"But I did all you said." Tears crawled down Delia's face. "You promised if I completed all of your tasks, he would be spared."

"Well, unfortunate things often happen at the least opportune times."

"Why don't you tell the girl who you really are?" Gault's voice was harsh. "Tell her that you are a Bloodwood assassin from Sør Sevier and that you merely used her and her father in your twisted Bloodwood games."

"Strong accusations, Ser gladiator," Seita commented. "What makes you so sure you know who I am? What makes you so sure of yourself?"

"I know a Bloodwood when I see one."

"Very well." Seita faced Delia. "I am a Bloodwood assassin from Sør Sevier."

Lindholf's spine froze. *A Sør Sevier assassin? The Vallè princess? Is this who Tala warned me about, the cloaked figure in the secret ways?*

"We've been five days on this Laijon-forsaken island," Gault said. "And it's time I took my leave of it."

It seemed Seita was bracing for a challenge. "And pray tell, where will you go from here, Ser gladiator?" she asked, her green eyes now aglow in the dim light.

"I shall go anyplace I please, any place but here."

"Best get rid of that armor you wear, then, for it clearly marks you as Ser Gault Aulbrek of Sør Sevier, the man who chopped Jondralyn Bronachell's face and the Prince of Saint Only's head."

"I'm scarcely worried about my armor," Gault growled. "I'm more concerned that you've marooned us on this dreary island with scant amounts of food and nothing to do but watch over strange weapons and stones. I already know how Lindholf found the shield. But you've yet to tell us anything of how you came to possess the sword and crossbow? And now you row back to the isle full of advice about how I'm dressed. I want your boat. And I aim to have it. I aim to leave this place today."

"Impatience does not suit you."

"Make no mistake, I also aim to take the weapons and stones with me."

"You do not want to make such threats." Seita's eyes were now shards of ice, unforgiving. "The weapons are not for you, Ser gladiator. Not all of them. Not yet anyway."

"Why do you keep calling me *gladiator*?"

"It is who you are."

"Well then, this *gladiator* is taking his spoils." Two quick strides and Gault was at the stone bench. He reached underneath and snatched up the large potato sack, the hilt of *Afflicted Fire* jutting from it.

"No." Delia rushed to him. "You mustn't go." She grabbed the sack with one hand, the hilt of the white sword with the other, tugging on both. "Who will protect me if not you?"

*She really loves him?* Lindholf's heart quailed at her words.

Delia tried to wrestle the potato sack from Gault. The sword's icy-sharp blade sliced open the canvas, spilling the contents at her feet; *Blackest Heart*, *Ethic Shroud*, the small leather pouch containing the three angel stones, all clattered against the stone bench and floor.

The barmaid stumbled back, *Afflicted Fire* still in her grip. In the pallid gloom of the abbey, the sword appeared like a pure stream of light, as if made of stardust and fire. Her eyes widened, marveling at the weapon in her hands. *Afflicted Fire!*

"You're behaving like spoiled children." Seita picked up the shield. "Hand me the sword, girl."

"No, Delia." Gault tossed the ruined canvas against the paint-chipped wall. "Give it to me."

Hands trembling, Delia looked from the Vallè to Gault and back, not knowing who to obey. There was a moment of strained silence. The knight's eyes tightened.

"I wouldn't do it, gladiator," Seita said casually.

"Why?" Gault's reply was just as casual. "Because you're a Bloodwood?"

And in one fluid motion he snatched the sword from Delia, swinging it at the Vallè princess, long white blade cutting through the air swift and merciless.

Seita ducked the arcing blow, shield upraised. *Afflicted Fire* rang against *Ethic Shroud*, lightning and thunder, deafening and bright, sparks illuminating the room. Seita was flung to the ground, shield tumbling from her grasp. Gault staggered back against the stone bench, sword reverberating with a keening hum in his hands.

The scar on the back of Lindholf's hand flared in sudden pain. The slave brand too. The marks of the mermaid. They all burned as sparks showered down around him.

The bald knight gathered himself and charged. Seita rose to meet him, two black daggers drawn. The bulk of Gault's heavy shoulder crashed hard into the Vallè's chest, knocking her reeling into the wall. The knight was on her quick, strong hands and iron grip clamping around each of her thin wrists, the crown of his head smashing into her forehead with a sickening thud. Both daggers dropped from the Vallè's limp hands.

Gault head-butted her a second time, hard.

Lindholf watched the light radiating from the Vallè's luminous eyes fade. She slid down the wall, blood welling down her face.

"She may be a Bloodwood," Gault said, his cold hard eyes roaming the abbey's brush-clogged entry, "but bulk and strength always prevail in a hand-to-hand." Blood trickled from his own forehead too.

*Blessed Mother Mia.* Lindholf did the three-fingered sign of the Laijon Cross over his heart. He knew Gault was no slouch when it came to bravery and combat. He had seen the man stab a slave in the neck with the bone from a severed arm in Riven Rock Quarry. But the cruel efficiency with which he dispatched Seita had been brutal and gruesome and hard to stomach.

The Vallè princess folded over onto her side against the abbey's stone wall, lifeless. "Is she dead?" Delia held one hand over her own mouth in shock.

Lindholf's heart thumped in his chest as he dropped to his knees over Seita. Shallow breaths emanated from somewhere deep within her chest, coarse breaths that grew ponderous in their frequency. *She lives....*

Gault grabbed *Afflicted Fire* from the floor. He snatched up the small leather pouch containing the three angel stones next. He jammed the crossbow *Blackest Heart* under the crook of his arm, then hefted the shield *Ethic Shroud* by the leather strap attached to its back, and marched from the abbey without a word.

"He means to leave us," Delia gasped. "I actually think he means to go." She rushed to the door, watching as the Sør Sevier knight made his way down the grassy slope toward the wooden quay and the small rowboat left there by the Vallè princess.

Seita moaned. Lindholf looked down. The Vallè was facedown on the stone floor now, trying to prop herself up on two elbows, blood dripping from her chin and the white locks of hair dangling over her groggy eyes.

"He just can't leave us like this!" Delia stood at the door, looking out with an ardent, passionate gaze. She turned to Lindholf. "I'm going with him." She dashed out the door.

Never before had Lindholf felt so suddenly crestfallen and alone, unable to move a muscle to follow her. *Only heartache lies there. For her, I might as well not exist. For everyone, I may as well not exist. Not Delia. Nor Tala. Nor even Seita.* Even his own mother had chosen to abandon him in the end. *No. I cannot follow Delia.*

Seita managed to roll back onto her side. She was propped on one elbow now, trying to position herself against the wall. Blood covered her face in thick wild streaks.

"Help me sit," she muttered. Lindholf steadied her. "I cannot think straight. How long has Gault been gone? Did he take the weapons? The stones?"

"He's heading for your boat now," Lindholf answered.

"You must go with him." She placed a small black dagger into the palm of his hand. "You must go with Gault. Bring the weapons and angel stones back to me."

"I cannot steal from Gault. He is too strong." Lindholf's mind was a ball of confusion as he stared down at the dagger in his hand. Black as polished coal, it felt unnatural, wicked. Tala had carried just such a weapon. She had dropped it in the secret ways when Glade had slain Sterling Prentiss.

"This blade thirsts," Seita said, her voice frail. "It is poisoned. Stick Gault with it, and he will die within moments. It's a rare gift. So keep it safe. For a Bloodwood rarely parts with a blade. You needn't kill him right away. Bide your time. But when you do, bring the weapons and stones back to me, Lindholf. You can do it. I've trained you. Val-Draekin has trained you. We have prepared you for this. You are the Thief, and this task has fallen to you." She seemed to be losing consciousness again. "Now go." She shoved him weakly away, eyes drooping closed.

He looked toward the door; the sunlight and freedom beyond the opening seemed so hollow, so full of hurt. Still, he stood on wobbly legs, rolling the dagger's blade in a strip of potato sack. He tucked the weapon into the waistline of his prison garb, covering the hilt with his shirt, then exited the abbey, leaving Seita's shallow breathing behind.

Gault and Delia where already situated in the small rowboat, the Sør Sevier knight pushing the tiny vessel away from the dock with the length of a long paddle.

Lindholf's nervous pace carried him swiftly over the grass. He reached the wooden dock at a full sprint. Two long strides over the quay and he jumped. He landed on his chest in the center of the rowboat, right between the knight and the barmaid, *Afflicted Fire* and *Ethic Shroud* piled on the floorboards under him.

*Blackest Heart* rested on the surface of the shield, just inches from his startled gaze.

*Oh worthy day, you too shall pass into night long and drear. Oh glorious song,*
*how the ancient minstrels did strain. Oh beautiful lover, hear with delight these*
*tales of blood and war so fondly revealed. The beggar begs. The soldier is bold.*
*And dark angels of silver only live by nightmare. And oh, the glorious Pillars*
*of Laijon. Five in all. But only one, unmovable and shrouded, holds the key and*
*buried secrets to Absolution.*
—THE WAY AND TRUTH OF LAIJON

# CHAPTER SIXTY-NINE

# NAIL

### 6TH DAY OF THE FIRE MOON, 999TH YEAR OF LAIJON
### WROCLAW, GUL KANA

**B**ronwyn Allen claimed she would secure them a boat somewhere south of Wroclaw. Nail believed her. The girl seemed
born of a fierce, unshakable determination, a grit and resolve
bred purely for theft and piracy and cold-blooded murder. And Cromm
Cru'x was devoted to her, deferring to her judgment in all things.

"I don't like them," Nail said, his voice nearly a whisper above the
clomping hooves of his bay gelding. "She is unpredictable. The oghul,
too. We should leave them both. Make our own way back to Amadon."

"That oghul practically worships you," Val-Draekin said, eyeing
the backs of Bronwyn Allen and Cromm Cru'x riding the trail about
thirty paces ahead, the tails of their dun-colored stallions swatting at
flies. "Cromm believes his destiny is tied to yours. Easiest and safest
way back to Amadon is with them."

"But Bronwyn murdered that man in Tevlydog. I do not trust her. What if she turns on us?"

"She will not." The Vallè patted the neck of his own steed. "We are clothed now because of that girl, we ride good mounts because of that girl, we've food because of her. I am not complaining." He clicked his tongue, urging the horse forward at a trot.

As Nail watched Val-Draekin ride ahead to join Bronwyn and Cromm, he knew what the Vallè said was true. *I am in fresh clothes.* The patchwork leather armor he wore was not the best, but better than nothing. And he sat astride a spry bay gelding, a sword tied to the saddle.

With all four of them mounted, they had made good time since Tevlydog. They followed the roadway along the southern outskirts of Wroclaw now, Bronwyn leading them toward the ocean that lay just beyond the town's keep. Nail cast his gaze north toward the gray shape of the city—Wroclaw sat proud atop a slanting ridgeline of green elm, limbs bent and stretched from years in the wind.

Like most villages and cities in Gul Kana, Wroclaw had a decrepit old castle clinging to its outer edge. The road they followed led them up to the keep, then veered around it. Though the bulky stone fortress was a gaunt shadow of its former splendor, it was still ten times the size of the keep in Gallows Haven. The ungainly wreck was surrounded by a shallow mossy moat of sinewy dark water, a reeking wallow of sludge and weeds. Clumps of sodden grass and lily pads lay flat and lifeless around the moat's rippling edges, whilst dandelions reluctantly poked their yellow heads between briar and nettle. Several dead trees, bare of leaf, stood spindly and crooked in the keep's sparse entry ground along with five cloaked knights, dark hoods obscuring their faces. But each of the five knights wore a different and distinct color of armor under their open cloaks: red, blue, green, white, and black. It was not plate armor per se, but rather scaled, and of an odd, curious make.

Nail's heart twisted with ice at the sudden sight of these strange knights in the courtyard, for under their shadowy cowls they looked like five faceless Bloodwood assassins. One of the knights—the white-armored one—lifted his head briefly to the sun, and Nail thought he saw a flash of bright silver under the fellow's hood. And then a saber-toothed lion stepped from behind the knight in white armor. The beast was black of mane, majestic, head large and shoulders heavy. It had two long silver teeth like daggers and glowing silver eyes.

The road carried him onward, and the lion and five cloaked knights were lost from sight behind the courtyard's stone columns and heavy walls. Nail set heels to flanks and trotted his bay gelding forward, drawing even with Val-Draekin, Bronwyn, and Cromm. "What did you make of those strange men in the castle yard?" he asked.

"What strange men?" Val-Draekin asked.

"I saw no one," Bronwyn added.

"Cromm saw them." The oghul dug the charcoal-black rock he'd been sucking on from his lower lip, held between his burly thumb and forefinger, saliva dripping. "The silver-faced knights in bright colors are an omen."

Nail waited, but the oghul didn't explain himself any further than that. He looked at Bronwyn; her face was typically obscured under the hood of her own forest green cloak, and she certainly hid behind her tattoos.

He cast his gaze again toward the ocean in the distance. From under the hooves of his horse clear to where the southern horizon met the blue sea were fields softly asway, golden motes of rye swimming in the lazy breeze.

It was a pristine view, and Nail soaked it in.

They crested a gentle rise, and he spotted a slender black-haired girl in a white dress with a white handkerchief tied about her head skipping merrily through the rye. Why she was so carefree and joyful,

Nail couldn't guess. Perhaps she too was just enjoying the beauty of nature. The scene reminded him of the charcoal sketch he had made of a bright-haired girl in a simple dress carrying a pail of water through a meadow of flowers. He'd always imagined the girl in the sketch to be Ava Shay and the flowers to be daisies. But Jenko Bruk had crumpled the drawing in his fist and tossed it to the floor of the Grayken Spear Inn.

It seemed that moment had been the beginning of all Nail's heartache.

*Where are they now, Ava Shay and Jenko Bruk? Do they still even live?* Nail felt guilty for whatever fate they now suffered. *I could have saved them.* That one betrayal would forever haunt him.

The breeze gathered strength as Bronwyn led them down a desolate boulder-studded bluff toward a small fishing port nestled within a windy inlet of water-worn rock ledges. The port was no more than a half-dozen rickety white huts and a frail dock that stretched out into the choppy ocean.

It was growing hot, and being so near the sea again, Nail desired to bathe, deeply desired it, just wanted to jump straight from his horse right into the sea and scrub himself clean. As his mount wended its way down the rocky slope, Nail watched a group of fishing boats all a-sail, struggling toward the quay.

Bronwyn reached the head of the wooden dock first, water lapping against the shore beneath. She dismounted. Cromm slid from his mount too, his wide feet landing heavy on the ground. Nail's legs were sore from long riding, yet he remained in his saddle. Val-Draekin too.

One vessel was already tied to the far end of the wavering dock, a good-sized fishing boat with a tall mast and furled sail. There were six fishermen climbing from it, gathering their gear. Soon all six were trudging up the wharf toward Bronwyn and Cromm. The fishermen were a ragged lot, rough-spun breeches and white shirts worn and stained, four carried coils of rope over their shoulders, one dragged a net behind him. The gray-haired man in front carried a thin bow in one hand and a quiver full of arrows with gray goose quills in the other. All six had sheathed boning knives at their belts.

They slowed their gait when they saw Bronwyn and the oghul, steady on their feet as the dock shifted with the rolling waters underneath. When Bronwyn pulled the black bow from over her shoulder, the six fishermen stopped altogether. Nail did not want her to shoot them. The oghul stepped up onto the dock, gums swollen and inflamed.

Nail's heart shuddered.

"We are here to requisition your boat," Bronwyn announced loudly.

"Our fishing boat?" the grizzled man with the bow and quiver of arrows said. He was a skinny fellow with yellow, nervous eyes and a swooping mustache. He reminded Nail of Bishop Hugh Godwyn. "Our boat ain't for sale. And we don't want any trouble."

"Don't want any trouble?" Bronwyn repeated. "I'm actually impressed with your steady thinking, Ser." She gripped the black bow tighter in her fist, her other hand pulling an arrow from her quiver. "Does gloomy weather or sunny weather make you more fearful, Ser?"

"Pardon?" The man looked at her askance.

"There is an old oghul saying," Bronwyn went on, "that bad things only happen on sunny days."

"So." The man's brow furrowed as he looked back at his fishing partners.

"So." Bronwyn shrugged. "Hot weather makes everyone mean and bitter."

"Cromm is mean and bitter even in thunderstorms and blizzards," the oghul said.

"What my companion is trying to say," Bronwyn continued, "is that the heat is about to set him off into a rage. And patience is not one of his virtues."

The oghul grinned at the man, thick lips pulling back, exposing flesh-tearing fangs. Horror fell over the faces of all six fishermen.

"'Tis rare Cromm is even this polite," Bronwyn said. "But he can be very useful in the requisitioning of things, if he has a mind to." She nocked the arrow to her bow, aimed it at the fisherman's chest. The man stepped back, eyes wide with fear, not even bothering to ready his own bow.

"Do not kill him." Nail spurred his mount forward, placing it between Bronwyn and the gray-haired man, her arrow pointed steady at his chest now.

"Bloody Mother Mia." Bronwyn spat the curse like venom. Her eyes were like cold pools of moonlight under her black tattoos. "We need the boat. What's one man to you?" Her brows furrowed to sharp points. "Even if I slay all six of them, what of it?"

"It's murder," Nail said. "They are just fishermen."

"Murder?" she hissed. "Lest you forget, you ungrateful little shit, we killed plenty of oghuls when we rescued your sorry hide. You didn't seem to mind *murder* then. Or is an oghul life worth less than that of a human?"

The bay gelding shifted under him, feeling his nervousness.

"Perhaps we can trade our horses for the boat." Val-Draekin dismounted and walked his horse up to the old fisherman, handing the fellow his reins.

Bronwyn let the tip of her arrow waver, her gaze meeting Cromm's. The oghul nodded. She put away her arrow, eyes still on Nail. "You will learn Cromm and I are not an unprincipled pair if someone offers but a simple solution." She peered around Nail's horse at the gray-haired fisherman. "A trade then, four horses for the boat?"

"It is a bad trade," the man said.

"Or Cromm can suck on your neck whilst I place an arrow into the heart of every man with you."

"We'll take the horses," the man said.

† † † † †

Val-Draekin untied the sailboat from the dock whilst Bronwyn and Cromm situated their saddlebags and supplies under the bulwarks, the oghul once again sucking on his black rock as he worked. Nail settled himself in the prow, watching as the six fishermen led their newly acquired horses up the boulder-strewn slope.

The black-haired girl in the white dress Nail had previously seen running in the fields of rye came bounding down the slope toward the fishermen. She threw her arms around one of the men, hugging him tight, fear on her face as she pointed back up the slope. Above them, atop the desolate rocky bluff, the five cloaked knights from the old keep appeared like flat black silhouettes against the sun-baked horizon, bleak spears of multicolored light sparking off their scaled armor in every direction. The black saber-toothed lion was with them.

"Rotted angels and the bloody Mother Mia too," Bronwyn muttered. The whites of her eyes had turned to narrow slits as she looked up at the five knights in the distance.

Val-Draekin seemed utterly spellbound by the sudden appearance of the lion and the cloaked knights. Cromm was similarly transfixed. "The silver-faced knights," the oghul muttered as their boat drifted free of the quay. "More oghul legend coming true."

As subtle as flowing mist, the five knights made their way down the slope toward the girl and the group of fishermen, the black saber-tooth on their heels. No longer backlit by the harsh sun and shards of light, what grabbed Nail's attention most about the five striking knights—beyond their brilliant suits of glimmering armor—was that they each indeed wore silver masks under their hoods, but these masks were in the shape of human skulls. They also had silver whips lined with sparkling silver barbs coiled in their gauntleted hands.

The six wary fishermen were now rooted in place as the lion and the five knights descended toward them. The girl cowered behind one of the horses. One of the skull-faced knights—the one in white armor—let his whip slowly unspool. The shimmering whip dripped quills of hissing silver into the rock and grass. The two groups faced each other without a word.

There was a wet-sounding snap as the knight struck. The whip's silvery tip arced high into the sunlight, exploding back down, tearing almost halfway through both the fisherman and the haunches of the bay gelding behind him.

Icy fingers clawed straight into Nail's guts as he watched the man fold in half and the horse topple over dead, sliding to the ground almost in two separate pieces. Blood and a thick sludge of guts drained from both corpses and down the hillside.

Two horrifying deaths in one crack of a whip.

Suddenly the whip flashed again, like lightning, and the rocky bluff filled with the terrified cries of the fishermen and the baying of the dying horses. It took every ounce of effort for Nail to bite back his own outcry of horror. For nothing could be so savagely efficient in creating instant gouts of blood and death as the sizzle and slash of the knight's silver whip. It sliced through man and horse alike as if flesh and bones were made of naught but air.

It had to be a dream, this new hideousness. *The silver in the tombs!* Nail could see the stuff now, dripping from the walls, melting the wooden stool in the Sky Loch mines.

Anger coursed though Nail at the vile injustice. *The men had merely traded their boat for horses in an effort to remain safe from us, safe from Bronwyn . . . from me.*

*And they will all die anyway.*

Nail looked away when the sabor-toothed lion went for the girl. A moment passed. And when he looked back, she was dead. All the fishermen were dead. The horses too. The whip-wielding knight turned his silver face toward Nail's group at the end of the quay, one white-gauntleted hand sweeping the hood back from his skull-faced mask. Then he slowly drew the silver mask up over his head.

The pale face of the creature beneath was both unsettling and exquisite at once, almost Vallè-like in aspect, but unlike any Vallè Nail had ever seen, ears more pointed and thin, face almost feminine. The pure white pallor of the knight's skin was both arresting and frightful.

The knight's two silver eyes bore into Nail with both fire and malice, cutting into his soul, stark and merciless. And with that one commanding gaze, Nail's will seemed to crumble, as if not only his soul was being sucked from his body, but also every bone and sinew was coming apart, trying to claw and tear its way out of his skin.

"That one is staring right at me," Nail said loudly, touching the hilt of his sword to make sure it was still at his belt. The scars on his skin burned.

"Skulls," Val-Draekin said, the look in his eyes as bleak as a winter's gale cutting across a Sky Lochs glacier. "That is what they were called before all history of them was wiped clean. Seita dreamed they had returned to the Five Isles. I refused to believe her."

"Skulls?" Nail met the Vallè's anxious gaze. "In the Sky Loch mines, Culpa Barra mentioned something about the Skulls."

"Aye, he did," Val Draekin acknowledged. "*The Moon Scrolls of Mia* mention the Skulls but a handful of times. But that is not their only name." The Vallè's eyes remained fixed on the slope of bloody carnage above them and the black lion and cloaked knights who'd caused it. "They were presumably made extinct when Laijon banished all demons into the underworld during the Great War of Cleansing. Despite Seita's dreams to the contrary, I did not believe they would ever return."

"Who would return?" Bronwyn's voice was laced with impatience as she shoved the boat farther from the dock with a long oar. "What would return?"

"An ancient race of Vallè," Val-Draekin said, his voice grave. "The Aalavarrè Solas. Those who helped the oghuls tame the beasts of the underworld. Those who rode the Dragons in days long past. *The Moon Scrolls of Mia* referred to them as the Skulls. *The Way and Truth of Laijon* names them the Last Demon Lords."

---

*Between truth and lie and legend shall be a veil, and only on the heights of the stars shall dwell those who know the Slave by his marks. And in that final day their eyes shall be turned to the tree of fire and that Dragon Claw we've sought since the beginning of all things. That fell gauntlet that didst slay Laijon, that silver-clawed hand I didst steal from my son and place over the tomb of my beloved . . .*
—THE MOON SCROLLS OF MIA

---

## CHAPTER SEVENTY

# JONDRALYN BRONACHELL

6TH DAY OF THE FIRE MOON, 999TH YEAR OF LAIJON

AMADON, GUL KANA

**T**his place is no good. Jondralyn gripped Hawkwood's hand, her cloak suddenly hot, constricting. It was like she was back in the Rooms of Sorrow, only this spacious chamber Hawkwood had led her to was an ominous haze of ruby light, a grim and gritty room of white-plastered walls and wood benches smeared black with smoke residue. Dirty rags and furs were crammed into the cracks in the walls in front of her; two wood-plank doors stood behind her. Shadows drenched the corners of the room and vaulted ceiling above. High on the wall to the left was a lofty stained-glass window, each sunlit pane so fiery red, it almost hurt her eye. To the right hung an intricately stitched tapestry of Mia. The Blessed Mother's gaze was drawn to the cross-shaped altar in the room's center. Dried rivulets of blackness ran down the altar's sides, as if someone had poured buckets of tar over it. There were ashes, bones, pigeon shit, and rat droppings strewn about its base, plus numerous carvings of the nameless beasts of the underworld—vile images that burned themselves into Jondralyn's mind with their unholiness. Worst of all, the surface of the altar was stained with a dark substance. *Fresh blood!*

Jondralyn shuddered, fingers tightening around Hawkwood's hand, wondering what foul sacrifice had recently taken place in this hidden crypt. Splatters of some liquid were sprinkled over the blood on the altar, shiny and silver in hue.

The curious gleam of the silver drew her farther into the room.

Hawkwood pulled her back. "We must be careful."

There was genuine concern in his eyes, fear almost. She had never seen him afraid before. Together Mount Albion and Amadon Castle were a honeycomb of passages, hidden galleries, staircases, and secret ways. It made her uneasy knowing there were rooms like this that even she had not yet discovered.

"Why have you brought me here?" She voiced her concern.

"'Twas Tala who first led me to this place." He let go of her hand and stepped to the center of the room, pulling the hood of his cloak back from his face. He leaned over the altar, studying its blood-crusted surface with crisp, dark eyes. "Your sister knows more about the Bloodwood lurking in the castle than she lets on."

"Are you certain?"

"I followed Tala here not long after Lawri lost her arm. Your sister seemed distraught. No, more like *deranged*, shouting for the Bloodwood to appear, demanding a conversation from the empty darkness."

Jondralyn felt her face twist in horror. "Was she taken with the wraiths?"

"No. She was lucid enough. I revealed myself and spoke with her briefly, gave her one of my swords, offered to teach her my craft."

"Teach her?" Jondralyn questioned. "As you promised to teach me?"

"Aye."

She did not like the thought of Tala learning to be an assassin.

But more important, there was one thing Hawkwood had said earlier that still needled her. "You mentioned Tala shouted for the Bloodwood. Did the Bloodwood come?"

It seemed Hawkwood hadn't heard her, as his gaze lingered on the scarlet surface of the altar, his eyes narrowing to cold slits. "I can't help but think that some secret lies in this room, Jon. The answer to all of our questions."

He turned from the altar, his piercing eyes roaming the room, searching.

Despite her unease, she felt her every sense was heightened just being in his presence. The last time she had seen Hawkwood, they had made love, and also the time before that. Those occasional couplings were nearly all she could think of. What few times he'd dared venture into her chamber had been risky and brief. But she needed him more than just occasionally. Standing so close to him now, soaking in the familiar scent of cloves and leather that clung to him always, rekindled that desire in her.

"I wish to come with you after we leave this place," she said, reaching up to his face, placing her hand gently over the faint wounds caused by Squireck Van Hester in the Rooms of Sorrow. His scars were nearly healed, unlike her own. "I cannot stand to be in the castle with my brother much longer."

He leaned into her touch. "You must keep abreast of the goings-on in the king's court, not hide in the shadows with me."

"Jovan taunts me. Threatens both Tala and me at all hours. I fear I will do something rash if I am forced to remain near him much longer."

"I promise, we shall begin your training soon." The burning passion in his own eyes caught her by surprise. "And with that training you will learn patience. For to learn the skills of a Bloodwood is to learn the art of death." Again, the smoldering heat of his twin dark orbs seared through her soul. She could see the scars of his face tighten.

*What are you thinking, Hawkwood?*

It was this question that always plagued her. No matter how much she loved him, there would always be part of him she could not fathom. She saw that part lingering in the back corner of his eyes, always there, always just out of reach.

"We *are* destined for each other?" she asked, not able to shake the words of Squireck. *The destiny of the Princess lies with the Gladiator.* "We are meant for each other, are we not, Hawkwood?"

He leaned away from her touch just slightly, a look of chilly self-reproach momentarily crossing his face. *What does he know that I do not?*

Jondralyn wanted so desperately to reach forth and touch him again, but let her hand fall to her side. *Does he finally see my face for what it truly is, horrid and scarred and mangled?* It was an insecurity she knew she would always live with. In the wake of Squireck's death she had felt naught but self-pity.

Sudden shame washed over her. Around Hawkwood, she'd almost entirely forgotten about Squireck. Initially she'd felt tremendous grief at the Prince of Saint Only's death, but at the same time breathed deep and free. Before his death in the arena, her former betrothed's faithful presence had become a burden, suffocating in its devotion. The moment Squireck died, she never imagined the horror of seeing his brutal beheading would abate, though within a few short days it had. Guilt swarmed her conscience at the thought. She blamed herself for his demise. She had been so cruel to him. *And the prophecy of the Five Warrior Angels now a ruin with the death of the Gladiator.*

"All is not lost," Hawkwood said, as if reading her mind. "Roguemoore had a theory. To succeed as one of the Five Warrior

Angels returned, you, Jondralyn Bronachell, would need to secure within yourself the traits of all Five Warrior Angels: Thief, Slave, Princess, Gladiator, Assassin. And I mean to train you in all."

"How do you train one to be a slave?"

"Indeed, how?" His gaze again fell upon the altar, brow furrowing. "A verse from *The Way and Truth of Laijon* has vexed me ever since I met with Tala in this room."

Eyes cutting into the altar, he recited the passage. "Oh, that King of Slaves, that great One and Only! Oh, that day of his fall! Oh, that we could go back to that day when Mia placed the five of Final Atonement into the flesh of his wound. Oh, that we could accompany his body as it was borne into the tomb. For when we ventured into that veiled place days later, that great Cross Archaic we found empty. For Laijon had been translated into heaven, the weapons and stones with him.'"

"Aye, a passage from the Acts of the Second Warrior Angel," Jondralyn said.

"But there is also a verse in *The Moon Scrolls of Mia*." Hawkwood leaned over the altar again, fingers hovering above the silvery splatters in the middle of the dried blood. "I can't recall the exact wording, but the *Moon Scrolls* speak of dragons and silver. Silver claws or some such . . . and Laijon's tomb."

"You think this is Laijon's tomb?"

"I do not know." Hawkwood placed both hands against the blood-crusted edge of the altar's capstone. "Whatever silver stuff was dripping over this altar stopped some time ago." He looked straight up into the shadows above, then back down. "I've a feeling this altar jealously protects something deep within."

He pushed against the slab, budging it only a mere few inches, the sound of rock grinding against rock echoing through the red-hazed chamber.

"Help me," he said, straining at the slab. Jondralyn leaned all her weight into the altar stone and pushed. It tumbled to the floor with a thunderous *boom!*

Together they glanced at each other, then peered down into the hole, Jondralyn's heart thudding against her ribs. There was no rotted god down in the darkness, no corpse of Laijon, no stark white skeleton.

In fact, the cross-shaped hollow was empty but for one simple thing.

A silver gauntlet.

It rested palm up at the bottom of the altar—a simple hunk of weaponry, really, yet exquisite too. It had an extended cuff and polished arm bracers that would reach clear up to a man's elbow if needed. Red light seemed to ebb and flow like rippling waves over its intricate leaf-shaped scales of armor. There were small holes in each of the gauntlet's curled fingertips, as if something was meant to be fastened or screwed into them . . .

. . . *or as if something were meant to grow out of them.*

"What did you find?" Lawri Le Graven's unmistakable voice sounded from behind them, gentle and lilting. Jondralyn whirled. Hawkwood already had his sword out, curved blade glimmering like fire in the red-lit room.

Lawri stood just to the left of the tapestry of Mia, a wicker basket clutched in her good hand, the stump of her arm wrapped in bandages. The long black dress she wore made her ashen face and tawny hair appear almost ghostlike in the shadowy corner.

"What are you doing here?" Jondralyn asked in a breathless rush.

"Don't you know?" Lawri canted her head to the side. "I came to gather harps and baubles and bracelets and other shiny oddments for Tala's wedding."

*Harps and baubles.* Jondralyn's mind recoiled. *She's gone insane!*

Hawkwood sheathed his sword with a rasp of steel on leather. "What do you mean, Tala's wedding?"

Lawri stepped softly into the room, gazing at the open altar, round green orbs almost catlike in their curiosity. *Since when are her eyes so green?* The wicker basket slipped from the girl's grip to the floor—it was empty.

"I've dreamed of this place ever since Tala was stabbed by the Bloodwood." Lawri approached the altar and looked in.

Then she looked directly at Jondralyn and began unwrapping the bandages from around her arm.

Jondralyn sucked in a breath. "No, Lawri, do not." She reached out, but Hawkwood stayed her hand with his own.

The bruised and fleshy stump of Lawri's arm was soon uncovered, bare and raw in the red light. Without hesitation, the girl reached down into the altar with her good hand and brought forth the silver gauntlet, a look of pure awe on her face as she held it up in the scarlet glow of the room.

Then she carefully placed the open end of the gauntlet against the stump of her arm, the scaled arm bracers seeming to mold themselves instantly to the flesh just below her elbow.

Cold dread coiled like a serpent around Jondralyn's spine as Lawri looked straight at her again, panic rising fierce and bold in her bright green eyes. "Get it off me!"

Hawkwood lurched forward, grasping the gauntlet with one hand, her shoulder with the other, pulling on the armor with all his might, but to no avail. He released his hold on the girl, a grave look falling over his face. "I can't remove it."

Lawri's horror-stricken eyes shone green and bright in the myriad reflections cast over her silver-scaled arm.

And then the curled fingers of the gauntlet began to move.

† † † † †

## TO BE CONTINUED IN
## *THE LONESOME CROWN*,
## VOLUME THREE OF
## FIVE WARRIOR ANGELS

## Seasonal Moons of the Five Isles

A year is 360 days.
There are fifteen moons (months) per year.
A moon (month) is twenty-four days long.
A week is eight days long. There are three weeks per moon (month).

Afflicted Moon................Winter
Blackest Moon
Shrouded Moon
Mourning Moon
Ethic Moon.....................Spring
Angel Moon
Fire Moon
Blood Moon...................Summer
Heart Moon
Crown Moon
Thunder Moon.................Fall
Archaic Moon
Lonesome Moon
Forgetting Moon
Winter Moon..................Winter

## Five Tomes of Ancient Writings

*The Way and Truth of Laijon*
*The Chivalric Illuminations of Raijael*
*The Moon Scrolls of Mia*
*The Book of the Betrayer*
*The Angel Stone Codex*

## Five Weapons of Laijon

*Forgetting Moon*: battle-ax. Angel stone: blue for the Slave.
*Blackest Heart*: crossbow. Angel stone: black for the Assassin.
*Lonesome Crown*: helm. Angel stone: green for the Gladiator.
*Ethic Shroud*: shield. Angel stone: white for the Thief.
*Afflicted Fire*: sword. Angel stone: red for the Princess.

# Timeline of Events Leading up to *The Forgetting Moon*

*5000–6000 Years Before*—Humans arrive on the shores of Gul Kana.

*1000 Years Before*—Thousand Years' War of the humans, dwarves, oghuls, and Vallè begins.

*Year Zero*—Laijon is born.

*18th Year of Laijon*—Laijon is thrown into the slave pits.

*19th Year of Laijon*—Rise of the Five Warrior Angels and rise of the Demon Lords.

*20th Year of Laijon*—Laijon unites all races against the Fiery Demons and Demon Lords (some call this the War of Cleansing, some call it the Vicious War of the Demons).

*21st Year of Laijon*—Death of Laijon and banishment of all demons to the underworld.

*21st Year of Laijon*—Raijael, son of Laijon, is born to the Blessed Mother Mia.

*22nd Year of Laijon*—Church of Laijon formed by the last three Warrior Angels in Amadon.

*40th Year of Laijon*—Raijael banished from the church and flees Amadon to Sør Sevier.

*40th Year of Laijon*—Raijael begins his twenty-year war to reclaim his crown as Laijon's heir.

*60th Year of Laijon*—Death of Raijael in war, after having conquered Adin Wyte and Wyn Darrè.

*200th Year of Laijon*—The Church of Laijon retakes Adin Wyte in war from Sør Sevier

*220th Year of Laijon*—The Church of Laijon retakes Wyn Darrè in war from Sør Sevier.

*300th–400th Years of Laijon*—Sør Sevier slowly retakes Adin Wyte and Wyn Darrè in war

*500th–900th Years of Laijon*—The Church of Laijon reclaims Adin Wyte and Wyn Darrè.

*900th Year of Laijon*—The Brethren of Mia formed by a secret group of scholars.

*900th–985th Years of Laijon*—Battles continue between Sør Sevier, Adin Wyte, and Wyn Darrè.

*985th Year of Laijon*—Shawcroft fights two Bloodwood assassins atop a Sky Lochs glacier.

*986th Year of Laijon*—Shawcroft and the boy, Nail, arrive in Deadwood Gate.

*989th Year of Laijon*—Sør Sevier launches its final crusade against Adin Wyte.

*994th Year of Laijon*—Adin Wyte conquered by Sør Sevier.

*994th Year of Laijon*—Shawcroft and the boy, Nail, arrive in Gallows Haven.

*994th Year of Laijon*—Sør Sevier launches its final crusade against Wyn Darrè.

*997th Year of Laijon*—Squireck Van Hester slays Archbishop Lucas in Amadon.

*999th Year of Laijon*—Wyn Darrè conquered by Sør Sevier.

*999th Year of Laijon*—Sør Sevier prepares for the Final Battle of Absolution against Gul Kana.

# CHARACTERS IN
## *THE BLACKEST HEART*

## ROKENWALDER, SØR SEVIER

*Crest*: the Blue Sword of Laijon

*Colors*: blue sword on a white field

KING AEVRETT RAIJAEL: King of Rokenwalder and Sør Sevier.

QUEEN NATALIA RAIJAEL: Wed to Aevrett, from Kayde, Sør Sevier.

AEROS RAIJAEL: 28, the Angel Prince. Son of Aevrett.

SPIDERWOOD: Aeros' Knight Archaic bodyguard. A Bloodwood
   Assassin.

HAMMERFISS: Aeros' Knight Archaic bodyguard.

BEAU STABLER: Aeros' Knight Archaic bodyguard.

ENNA SPADES: 27, Aeros' Knight Archaic bodyguard.

GAULT AULBREK: 38, Aeros' Knight Archaic bodyguard.

AVRIL AULBREK: Wed to Gault. Mother of Krista.

KRISTA AULBREK: 17, Crystalwood. A Bloodwood assassin.
   Gault's stepdaughter.

AGUS AULBREK: Gault's father. Lord of the Sør Sevier Nordland
   Highlands.

EVALYN AULBREK: Gault's mother. Sister to Edmon Guy Van
   Hester of Saint Only.

MARCUS GYLL: a Rowdie.

PATRYK LAURENTS: a Rowdie.

BLODEVED WYNSTONE: a Rowdie.

RUFUC BRADULF: Hound Guard captain.

KARLOS: a Hound Guard.

ALVIN: a Hound Guard.

BLACK DUGAL: Head of the Bloodwood assassins.

MANCELLOR ALLEN: 22, Knight of the Blue Sword. From Wyn
    Darrè.

HANS RAKE: Shadowwood. A Bloodwood assassin.

AULMUT KLINGANDE: a Rokenwalder noble.

SOLVIA KLINGANDE: Wed to Aulmut.

DAME PORTEA: head laundress in Aevrett's palace.

BOGG: warden of the dungeons of Rokenwalder.

SQUATEYE: dwarf gaoler and cohort of Bogg.

# GALLOWS HAVEN, GUL KANA

BARON JUBAL BRUK: Baron of Gallows Haven and owner of the
    *Lady Kindly.*

JENKO BRUK: 18, Baron Jubal Bruk's son.

BRUTUS GROVE: works for Baron Jubal Bruk.

OL' MAN LEDDINGHAM: owner of the Grayken Spear Inn.

AVA SHAY: 17, works at the Grayken Spear Inn.

TYLDA EGBERT: 16, works at the Grayken Spear Inn.

POLLY MOTT: 16, works at the Grayken Spear Inn.

GISELA BARNWELL: 15, Maiden Blue of the Mourning Moon Feast.

SHAWCROFT: also known as Ser Roderic Raybourne.

NAIL: 17, a bastard boy under the care of Shawcroft.

STEFAN WAYLAND: 17, friend of Nail.

DOKIE LIDDLE: 17, friend of Nail.

ZANE NEVILLE: 17, Liz Hen's brother.

LIZ HEN NEVILLE: 18, Zane's sister.

BISHOP TOLBRET: Bishop of Gallows Haven chapel.

BISHOP HUGH GODWYN: Bishop of the Swithen Wells Trail Abbey.

## AMADON, GUL KANA

*Crest*: the Atonement Tree

*Colors*: the silver Atonement Tree on a black field.

Silver Guard. Silver Throne.

KING BORDEN BRONACHELL: Former King of Amadon and Gul Kana.

QUEEN ALANA BRONACHELL: Wed to Borden. Sister of Mona Le Graven.

JOVAN BRONACHELL: 28, Borden's son. King of Amadon and Gul Kana.

JONDRALYN BRONACHELL: 25, Borden's daughter.

TALA BRONACHELL: 16, Borden's daughter.

ANSEL BRONACHELL: 5, Borden's son.

DAME MAIRGRID: Tutor to Tala and Ansel.

SER STERLING PRENTISS: Dayknight captain.

SER LARS CASTLEGRAIL: Commander of the Silver Guard.

SER TOMAS VORKINK: Steward of Amadon Castle.

SER LANDON GALLOWAY: Chamberlain of Amadon Castle.

SER TERRELL WICKHAM: Stable marshal of Amadon Castle.

SER OSTEN NORTHANGER: Blacksmith of Amadon Castle.

DAME VILAMINA: Old kitchen matron of Amadon Castle.

DAME NELS DOUGHTY: New kitchen matron of Amadon Castle.

GRAND VICAR DENARIUS: Grand vicar in Amadon. Holy Prophet of Laijon.

ARCHBISHOP VANDIVOR: Quorum of the Five Archbishops in Amadon.

ARCHBISHOP DONALBAIN: Quorum of the Five Archbishops in Amadon.

ARCHBISHOP SPENCERVILLE: Quorum of the Five Archbishops in Amadon.

ARCHBISHOP LEAFORD: Quorum of the Five Archbishops in Amadon.

ARCHBISHOP RHYS-DUNCAN: Quorum of the Five Archbishops in Amadon.

SER CULPA BARRA: 28, a young Dayknight.

TATUM BARRA: Ser Culpa Barra's father.

DELIA: Barmaid at the Filthy Horse Saloon.

GEOFF: Patron of the Filthy Horse Saloon.

SHKILL GHA: an oghul. Gladiator.

ANJK BOURBON: an oghul. Gladiator trainer.

G'MELKI: an oghul.

ROGUEMOORE: Dwarf ambassador from Ankar.

HAWKWOOD: from Sør Sevier.

TOLZ TRENTO: a young Silver Guard.

ALAIN GRATZER: a young Silver Guard.

BOPPARD STOCKACH: a young Silver Guard.

HIGGEN: slave at Riven Rock Quarry.

WOADSON: slave at Riven Rock Quarry.

MAIZY: a nobody.

## ESKANDER, GUL KANA

*Crest*: the Saber-Toothed Lion
*Colors*: black lion on a yellow field
Lion Guard. Lion Throne.

LORD LOTT LE GRAVEN: Lord of Eskander, Lion Throne.

MONA LE GRAVEN: Wed to Lott. From Reinhold. Sister of Alana Bronachell.

LINDHOLF LE GRAVEN: 17, Lott's son, twin to Lawri.

LAWRI LE GRAVEN: 17, Lott's daughter, twin to Lindholf.

LORHAND LE GRAVEN: 12, Lott's son, twin to Lilith.

LILITH LE GRAVEN: 12, Lott's daughter, twin to Lorhand.

## RIVERMEADE, GUL KANA

*Crest*: the Wolf

*Colors*: gray wolf on a maroon field

Wolf Guard. Wolf Throne.

LORD CLAYBOR CHAPARRAL: Lord of Rivermeade. Wolf Throne.

LESIA CHAPARRAL: Wed to Claybor. Sister of Nolan Darkliegh.

LEIF CHAPARRAL: 28, Claybor's son.

SHARLA CHAPARRAL: 23, Claybor's daughter.

JACLYN CHAPARRAL: 21, Claybor's daughter.

GLADE CHAPARRAL: 17, Claybor's son.

## AVLONIA, GUL KANA

*Crest*: white with silver overlay

*Colors*: silver overlay on a white field

Marble Guard. Marble Throne.

LORD NOLAN DARKLIEGH: Lord of Avlonia.

ELYNOR DARKLIEGH: Wed to Nolan. Edmon Guy Van Hester's sister.

LESIA CHAPARRAL: Nolan's sister. Wed to Claybor Chaparral.

## STANCLYFFE, GUL KANA

MARDGOT: Stanclyffe street merchant.
S'IST RUNK: an oghul. Stanclyffe street merchant.

## LORD'S POINT, GUL KANA

*Crest*: Blue of the Ocean
*Colors*: blue
Ocean Guard. Ocean Throne.
LORD KELVIN KRONNIN: Lord of Lord's Point.
EMOGEN KRONNIN: Wed to Kelvin.
BEATRIZ VAN HESTER: Kronnin's sister. Wed to King Edmon
    Guy Van Hester.
RAYE KRONNIN: Kronnin's baby daughter.
SER REVALARD AVOCET: one of the Ocean Guard.
PRAED: leader of the Untamed—a small gang of roaming thieves.
LLEWELLYN: part of the Untamed.
CLIVE: part of the Untamed.
JUDI: part of the Untamed.
DERRY RICHRATH: owner of the Turn Key Inn & Saloon.
OTTO: worker in the Turn Key Inn & Saloon.
BROWN R'ELK: an oghul merchant.

## BAINBRIDGE, GUL KANA

*Crest*: Purple Stag
*Colors*: purple stag on a black field
BARON BRENDER WAYLAND: Uncle of Stefan Wayland.

## SAINT ONLY, ADIN WYTE

*Crest*: two Crossed Spears
*Colors*: two white crossed spears on a field of red
Spear Guard. Throne of Spears.
KING EDMON GUY VAN HESTER: King of Saint Only and Adin
    Wyte.
QUEEN BEATRIZ VAN HESTER: Wed to Edmon. From Lord's
    Point.
SQUIRECK VAN HESTER: 28, Edmon's son. Prince of Saint Only.
    Gladiator.
EVALYN AULBREK: Edmon's sister. Wed to Lord Agus Aulbrek of
    Sør Sevier.
ELYNOR DARKLIEGH: Edmon's sister. Wed to Lord Nolan
    Darkliegh of Avlonia.
ELYSE KOHN-AGAR: Edmon's sister. Wed to Lord Nigel Kohn-
    Agar of Agonmoore.
SER IVOR JACE: warden of Mont Saint Only.
LEISEL: a servant girl.

## WYN DARRÈ

*Crest*: the Black Serpent
*Colors*: black serpent on a yellow field
Serpent Guard. Serpent Throne.
KING TORRENCE RAYBOURNE: King of Wyn Darrè.
QUEEN BIANKA RAYBOURNE: Wed to Torrence. From
    Morgandy, Wyn Darrè.
KAROWYN RAYBOURNE: 19, Torrence's daughter.

SER RODERIC RAYBOURNE: Torrence's brother. Known as Shawcroft.

CASSIETTA RAYBOURNE: Torrence's sister.

MANCELLOR ALLEN: 22, Knight of the Blue Sword in Aeros Raijael's army.

BRONWYN ALLEN: Mancellor's younger sister.

IRONCLOUD: Dwarf from Ankar. Brother of Roguemoore.

SEABASS: Dwarf from Sigard Lake.

TYUS BARRA: Ser Culpa Barra's younger cousin, mute.

CROMM CRU'X: Oghul pirate.

# VAL VALLÈ

VAL-KORIN: Val Vallè ambassador.

SEITA: Val-Korin's younger daughter.

BREITA: Val-Korin's older daughter.

VAL-DRAEKIN: boyfriend of Breita.

VAL-SO-VREIGN: bodyguard of Val-Korin.

VAL-GIANNI: Vallè healer (sawbones).

VAL-CE-LAVEROC: gladiator.

VAL-RIEVAUX: gladiator.